# A Soul to Embrace

## Duskwalker Brides
### Book Eight

## Opal Reyne

# <u>Author's note on language</u>

I'm from AUSTRALIA.

My English is not the same as American English.
I love my American English spoken readers to bits. You're
cute, you all make me giggle, and I just wanna give you a big
ol' hug. However, there are many of you who don't seem to
realise that your English was born from British English,
which is what I use (although a bastardised version since
Australians like to take all language and strangle it until it's a
ruined carcass of slang, missing letters, and randomly added
o's).

We don't seem to like the letter z.

We write colour instead of color. Recognise instead of
recognize. Travelling instead of traveling. Skilful instead of
skillful. Mum instead of mom. Smelt is a past participle of
smell. We omit the full-stop in Mr. Name, so it's Mr Name.
Aussies cradle the word cunt like it's a sweet little puppy,
rather than an insult to be launched at your face.

Anyway, happy reading!

# <u>Pronunciation guide</u>

*People:*
Jabez – Ja-bez
Zylah – Zai-luh
Weldir – Wel-dur
Lindiwe – Lind-i-wey(updated for better clarity)
Merikh – Merr-ick
Raewyn – Ray-wen
Daefaren – Day-far-in
Lehnenia – Luh-knee-na
Mericato – Merry-cato
Zerik – Zeh-reek
Laele – Lay-le
Silveria – Sil-very-a
Ulair – Ul-lair

*Races:*
Elysian – E-lee-see-an
Delysian – Dee-lee-see-an
Anzúli – An-zoo-li

*Places:*
Nyl'theria – Nyl-ther-ria
Lezekos – Lee-zee-key-os
Otholla – Ou-thol-la

*Other:*
Synedrus – Sa-ni-dri-us
Draflium – Dra-flume
Rankae – Ran-kay
Ookmanik – Ook-man-ick
Jabeziryth – Ja-bez-ah-ry-eth
Nyl'kira – Nly-keer-ah

To all the villain-loving MonsterFuckers out there,

this book is for you.

We all know who he is and what he's done. We know he's a devious bastard who may not deserve a redemption arc, but it won't come easy and we'll get to grin through it as he suffers.
To fall for your enemy, and a female monster at that... well, sometimes the naughtiest of boys get the best rewards.

I would like to give a big shoutout to the wonderful **sensitivity readers** who helped to make this book a safe place for those I am trying to positively represent. As you all know, representation is a big part of what I want to do, but I want to do so in a way that isn't harmful.

Thank you to Diamond, Erin, Nicole, Anica, and Trev for your contribution towards BIPOC sensitivity.

I would also like to give a special thank you to Crystal for your contribution towards BIPOC and overall sensitivity.

I appreciate all the time and effort you put into helping me with this book. You will forever have a place in my heart.

# ONE

*I tried to fuck with a god, and this is what I get.*

Coughing up another light spray of blood, Jabez fluttered his eyelashes against falling particles of debris. With his hands pushing upwards and his knees bent, he used his quaking legs and arms to hold back the weight bearing down on him. Cold sweat trickled down his temple, his neck, his chest. Darkness surrounded him, making it impossible to see through the thick shadows.

How long he'd been buried beneath the dirt, the rubble of his castle, and his own ego, he had no fucking clue. Hours, surely. Days, perhaps.

The last tendrils of his magic were draining from his body and threatened to weave out of him permanently. The pain prickling beneath his flesh was excruciating. It sparked through his veins like lava slowly trying to harden into crystals, and he felt it in the marrow of his bones, in the snapping fibres of his muscles, in every cold drop that expelled from him.

It couldn't compare to the suffocating fear of his strength waning.

With all his might, he held onto the magic currently saving his life. The thick golden chain around his neck began to melt against his skin as he used up the last of its borrowed magic, and he let out a grunt through his clenched fangs. His skin blistered, but he fought against the need to scream.

The purple glow above flickered, his protective dome

faltering. Every attempt at trying to teleport moved his dwindling mana in a different direction, and the rubble would creak and almost crush him – forcing him to reinforce the dome rather than escape.

Hissing through his fangs, the intense burns covering half his body, if not more, continued to ache. His melted skin felt tight, and his exposed bones drying was excruciating, but there was a numbness due to damaged nerves. Trying to heal his own body while keeping himself alive was proving futile – he couldn't do both.

His mana flickered in its last ethereal embers.

The weight of his failures came crashing down upon him. The blood-curdling roar that escaped him was accompanied by pain no living creature could stay conscious for. Jabez instantly blacked out.

The first time he woke, claustrophobia choked at his burned throat.

The rubble above had created a pocket of room that allowed him to breathe, to thankfully keep *living*.

A numbness rode his body, his mind. A sluggish hand slapped his own face as he palmed it of dust, so he wasn't breathing it in. He attempted to move his other arm to assess the grainy ache in it, and felt his fingers twitch, the tug of his elbow bending at the command to bring it forward.

Nothing happened.

Jabez glanced down towards the unresponsive limb. Heat bled from his face before he tilted his head back. *No,* his mind whispered, as he bashed the back of his skull and tapered horns against the cracked floor of his throne room.

*No,* he thought, bashing it once more, his eyes narrowing up at nothingness with utter spite.

"No!" he roared, tugging on his crushed arm until the fibres of his muscles, his tendons, his very skin began to rip. "I refuse! I didn't do all that I have done just to die here!"

With his right arm, he reached above his head to clasp a piece of jutting stonework. He pulled with what strength he had left, and agony radiated around his knee. The pain informed him that his right leg from the knee down was also crushed beneath rubble.

No amount of pulling was going to free him.

"I have ripped myself from jaws," he told himself, his eyes narrowing further into a tight glare. "Survive. I must survive."

It's what he'd always been doing.

With a snarl, he shoved the claws on his right hand into his left biceps, and sliced through skin, through muscles, through pain. He cracked his own bone, severed the few remaining tendons, and freed his arm from the wretched stone that kept him pinned.

Dizziness vibrated his sight when blood coursed from his severed arm, but he quickly placed his right hand over the stump. A red-and-black glow came from his palm, but it was weak and flickered.

A whimper of agony slipped from his blood-covered lips.

The use of his magic when it was already so drained was more painful than the removal of his own arm. Once he managed to stem the bleeding, he laid back against the ground to pant in short, shallow breaths. His vision blurred, but his eyelids flickered to combat it.

*Don't. Don't fall asleep.* Bile rose in his throat, his stomach wanting to punish him for going beyond the borders of his wretched Elvish abilities.

The thick, coppery smell of his own blood was sickening, but the repercussions of it being in the air were more gut twisting. He wasted what little magic he had left to boil it until it was dry, and a fever broke out across his cooling skin. He shivered.

But now that one limb was free, he reached above to grab the ledge of stonework once more. His arm shook, yet he pulled, and pulled, and tore at his own body until a high-pitched scream belted out of him. He didn't stop, absolutely refusing to, until he tore away his leg from the knee down.

In the limited space, he couldn't reach down to stem the bleeding. He bent his intact leg until he could place his left foot against the gushing stump, and concentrated. He saw no light this time, not with his eyes shutting against his will, but the wound thankfully closed.

*I just need a corpse and to feed.* He needed meat. *Then I can regrow them.* Or rather, transplant them.

The magic was forbidden to the rest of his Elvish kind, but he'd long ago thrown the morals of a prudish, uptight species to the wind.

*I can survive this...*

He had to.

The second time he opened his eyes, he knew it had been too long.

The smell of his blood perfumed the air, and he utilised his ability to boil it. Nothing happened except for an intense wave of sickness and wrongness overcoming him. Light-headed, sweat-slicked, and weak, the reality of what he'd done was slow to digest in the fuzziness of his mind.

The heat that engulfed him fought against the intense cold shivers that trickled through his nervous system.

*So I'm down to a choice, am I?* He chuckled into the darkness, while his eyes rolled in delirium.

He clicked his fingers and the tiniest spark came from the motion. Not of flame, but of essence. The very last tendril of it.

A magical spark which could reignite, or there was a chance he could snuff it out with potentially ever-lasting consequences. The outcome was uncertain, but it was a risk he was willing to take.

The scrape of stone against stone above reverberated through the layers crushing down on him. The sound sent goosebumps along what little of his flesh remained unscorched, but he swallowed down the fear.

Jabez closed his eyes in disquiet. *So be it.*

He focused on any remaining traces of his spilled blood and boiled them until the scent dispersed. In doing so, he pushed out the last of his magic until he completely emptied the well within his body. A rush of coldness bled through his veins and behind it came more lava.

Tears of agony dotted his eyelashes, but he clenched his fangs through the pain when another shift of stone came from above. His throat clamped up, his body quaked, but he refused to let the sickness of magic depletion be the reason he passed out again. *Ookmanik,* the Elvish called it.

*Stay awake,* his mind whispered.

He would greet whatever was digging for him amicably, rather than deliriously. He would fight, even if his attempt would be pitiful, and utilise every ounce of life force he had left. Even with two limbs missing, he would show them how formidable he was.

He was no victim, and nothing to be pitied.

No Demon was a match for him, and he would make sure they knew that. *I must use their fear of me.* Just as he used it to make sure he was kept on a useless, self-proclaimed throne.

When dim light peeked through cracks, he swiped his face constantly of falling dust. A scent came to him, but he only distinguished one thing from it: a stranger.

He didn't know this Demon. It wasn't one of his direct minions, which could either be a blessing or a curse.

When the worst of the weight was removed, he was able to slide the slab of stone above him just enough to wedge himself into a seated position. The more rubble the stranger removed, the more he was able to shove out of the way until he could manoeuvre what was left of his injured body towards freedom. He chose his movements carefully, ensuring that nothing shifted suddenly and crushed him further.

Then a single hand gained freedom.

Someone sniffed at his clawed fingers, spreading hot breath over them, and he grimaced. He said nothing, despite the urge to shout callous commands in disgust. He wasn't a piece of meat to be smelt, and he made sure to kill all those who considered him food.

He and his potential rescuer shoved a large slab to the side, and Jabez was able to squeeze his shoulders free of the rubble.

*Freedom,* he thought with relief. But at what cost?

Who had come to free him? Friend or foe? These days, everyone had been considered foe. His minions placated him out of fear, while many others did so because of the hope he promised: the chance for a true life beyond the borders of this barbaric forest.

Blinking against the bright light after being in the dark for so long, he was thankful for the setting sun. He didn't have the magic to cast a skintight barrier against it.

A moving shadow drifted above him, just as a black clawed

hand came into view when it pressed down next to his head.

His wavering, dizzy gaze drifted up. He struggled to focus through the fuzziness and blinking dots to see who had come to be either his rescuer or his demise.

All the fight he had left in him gusted out in the wake of the being before him.

He couldn't defeat it. Not in the current state he was in, and perhaps not even before that.

"Fuck," he whispered as his arm fell and his head craned back in exhaustion.

Despite the cloudiness of his vision, the white blur and the dark-yellow glow were unmistakable.

The chuckle that came through his cracked lips was from someone who understood that they were staring their reaper in the face and lacked the will to fight it.

"Come to finish the job, have you, Mavka?" he slurred, unable to even muster up a sneer before his eyes rolled back.

For a moment, he swam in blissful nothingness. Unfortunately, it was taken from him when the Mavka grabbed his hair and tore him from the rubble.

He winced back to alertness when something hard raked down his back. *Ow...* The back of his skull thunked against a jutting rock before his entire body rolled over it.

"Ow!" he belted out when his shoulder butted into an obvious tree root. "Watch where you're going!"

He received a strange chitter in response.

He hissed out a sharp breath when his shoulder wedged against something hard, and he felt a stretch up his neck. A few strands of his firmly gripped hair were yanked out, and he reached up with both hands to try and take the worst of his own body weight.

Only one hand came up, and he opened his eyes to assess the stump of his left arm. Shit. He'd forgotten.

Unable to tilt his head to the Mavka dragging his limp body down the mound of his castle rubble, like they were some kind of barbarian and he was a club, he shifted his focus to the eight-foot hedges that came into view. They appeared to have been shoved on an angle due to some force, likely from the power that wretched redheaded human had thrown upon the ground.

The Mavka yanked him over a small ledge of earth carelessly. He crashed to the ground, almost kneeing himself in the damn face with his only remaining leg.

Fighting against his waning consciousness and the black dots swirling in his low vision, he tried to think about who was manhandling him like an ogre.

He hoped it was Merikh finally collecting on Jabez's promise that he'd leave his kin be, so long as that bear-skulled, bull-horned Mavka joined him, but he doubted it.

Jabez was too delirious to think any further. Until they finally released his hair, which pulled his head upright, he was unable to assess them.

It likely wouldn't matter anyway.

His fevers were worsening, and before long, without healing, he was likely to... die. Without blood, he'd have nothing to sustain himself through the ookmanik sickness.

Soon, the crystallisation happening within his body would reach his chest, and his heart would stop.

# TWO

After what could only have been days of intense torture, Jabez eventually opened his eyes peacefully, and in his own time.

Darkness greeted him, but that wasn't a sight he was unaccustomed to. He'd been living, like most Demons, out of the sun's rays. However, unlike a normal awakening, gnarly and twisted tree roots dangled from the dirt ceiling. They forked across it like a net to keep whatever large tree they belonged to from crashing down on top of him.

Most of his vision was grainy and muted, his sensitive sight allowing him to only see so much in such deep shadows. Although his vision was far superior than a human's, not even a full-fledged Demon had the sharpness of a Mavka's sight.

A Mavka he could hear whimpering just beyond his feet.

Jabez lifted his upper lip in a twisted sneer before smoothing his features.

*How long have I been out?* By the pungency of his own scent, the dryness in his mouth, and the hunger that pervaded him, he figured days.

He tried to count what he could remember. He'd spent most of a night and possibly a day holding up his damn castle from crushing him. Then he'd spent an unknown amount of time trapped beneath it. With this Mavka having dug him out during the last rays of sun and then running with him, another rising and setting of the moon had passed.

*Then they fucking tortured me.*

For days, all he'd felt was agony. So much so that had he

been a weaker being, he would have *begged* for them to end him. Even swimming in the waves of death's ocean, he hadn't been that pitiful.

The question was: why was he still alive? If they didn't kill him, the ookmanik sickness should have.

He should be a rotten corpse or, sickeningly, *food*.

Yet... he somehow felt better.

He lifted his hands to his head at the migraine that shot across his skull from the dehydration. *Hands,* plural. He threw them away from his face, twisting his palms one way and then the other. He wiggled the fingers of his left hand that had not long ago been missing.

*They... healed me.* Without lifting his head, Jabez finally looked down through his bottom lashes at the Mavka he could scent there. *Were they not actually torturing me, but aiding me?*

Wiggling the toes of his right foot, surprised to not only feel them but also see them, he vaguely remembered the suffering. At each interval, the pain had drifted further and further from his torso as it *crawled* down his limbs.

He touched his face once more. Jabez noted the burns from whatever magical explosion the redheaded human had detonated were gone. Actually, all of his extensive and near-fatal injuries were gone.

The only pain that remained was from the residual effects of ookmanik. That was unlikely to fade, although the worst of it had receded.

*Shit. Despite the Mavka giving me back most of my strength, I have no magic with which to defend myself.*

Only a fucking idiot would fight against a Mavka, and Jabez wasn't an idiot.

Unfortunately, no matter how long he stared at them, he couldn't fully discern who they were through the lack of light. He saw the white bone of their skull, their antlers, and general body shape, but it wasn't enough to recognise them.

They were also shuddering as they curled up against some form of exit, with a set of white orbs seeing into him. They chittered, and Jabez noted the fretful hint in it. They shuffled back against the exit, blocking it further like a skittish animal.

Once more, an irritated sneer curled his upper lip, but the moment his fangs were bared, they let out a warning growl. He cooled his features as he slowly pushed up with his elbows to sit.

He eyed the unpredictable creature before him.

*He's guarding the exit to ensure I can't leave.*

The moment those words formed in his mind, two things became apparent.

Firstly, he saw his own body properly, and noted he was naked – likely due to soiling his clothes while unconscious. He'd no doubt also sweated an unholy amount, considering he was over the worst of the ookmanik.

Secondly, and curiously, Jabez realised this Mavka was actually a *female*. Despite never coming into contact with a female Mavka before, he'd know the difference in scent anywhere – and she'd left it everywhere in this dark hole.

The chuckle that fell from him was rather snide. "Have fun curiously poking around while I was naked?" he asked, refusing to cover himself.

She chittered in return, but her glowing orbs, the only colour and thing he could properly see, morphed from white to teal. He tilted his head at that. *I've never seen a Mavka have teal orbs before.*

He noted it, but ignored it. He'd been expecting orange in reaction to guilt, or for her to shine a reddish pink in shame at his accusation.

He didn't actually mind, nor care. He was thankful to not wake up in disgusting clothing, somehow semi-clean, and she could poke and prod considering she healed him. He also doubted she knew what any part of his body meant. His ass felt fine, so at least she hadn't gone sinking her fingers where she shouldn't.

He was concerned that his body glamours had faded now that he'd completely lost his magic; mainly the fake Demon streaks that'd marked his skin, and those that physically changed him. His 'seam' had altered, returning him to his more Elvish species nature. It meant his dick and balls now hung freely and, unfortunately, dangerously between his thighs. They weren't tender, but she'd no doubt wiggled them in curiosity, unbeknownst to an unconscious Jabez.

*Ah, the things I have done to protect myself.*

At least the white patch of hair at his groin partially concealed them.

As he'd first surmised while delirious, this wasn't a fully formed Mavka. Adult, yes. But her intelligence was low; therefore, he assumed she'd also lack physical development. She would be nothing but skin and bone, and even now, in the darkness, he could tell she was grossly underweight.

Despite all his observations, they did nothing to explain why he was here. Nor did they enlighten him as to what he should do to free himself from this female, who obviously had little intention of letting him go amicably.

He needed to escape.

*My friendship with Merikh should aid me.*

His time with his friend had been short, but it had been enough for him to develop a deep understanding of the bloodthirsty skull-headed species. Jabez would use all he'd learned in the last few hundred years to escape.

*This isn't the worst situation I've been in.* Nor the strangest in his long life. *I've also had worse captors.* Just the reminder caused a shudder to race down his spine.

*I must be patient and remain as non-aggressive as I can.* He was in the presence of, essentially, the brain capacity of a moving tree with fangs and claws.

She would be faster than him, stronger than him, and quicker to annoy than him.

He also knew a staring contest with her would get him nowhere.

Bringing his knees up, he placed his right elbow on his thigh.

"Alright, Mavka. Let's figure out what your stage of development is. Can you understand the words I'm speaking?"

He received chitters, a tilting skull that rattled loudly like dried bones were stuck inside it, and dark-yellow orbs. The sound was telling. *Doubtful, then.*

Just to double check, he stated in the sweetest and friendliest voice he could muster, "Your mother, the Witch Owl, is a slug, and I hope she burns."

He obtained the same response. *She doesn't understand.* She was reacting to the tone of his voice, not the meaning of his words.

He covered his mouth and looked off to the side in thought. *This isn't ideal.* He tapped his forefinger against his lips.

"Okay, female," he stated with his gaze slipping back to her. "I'm going to have to play a rather nasty trick on you. However, if you don't let me out of this hole within the next few minutes, I, the great Jabez, will be forced to relieve myself in this hovel you call home."

How long he'd been unconscious, he didn't truly know. If he counted the initial few days, and then the days she'd likely healed him over, he knew it'd been at least a week. He'd had no food, nor water within that time. As an Elysian Elf, his body clock still rotated with Nyl'theria's triple sun cycle, despite being on Earth for over three centuries.

He couldn't change his biology, but it did aid him in this situation. He needed to pee, to eat, and to drink water, before the third Nyl'theria day of dehydration began to wither him.

Jabez reached his hand out to the female Mavka. Her blunt snout dipped to his reaching palm before she tilted her head once more. Jabez wiggled his fingers, and his long nails – which *almost* appeared claw-like – clicked between them.

"Come on. Take my hand. I won't bite." Yeah, because hers would be far more devastating.

He didn't even offer a grin, which would have flashed his fangs, in case it came across as threatening. He kept his expression neutral.

When she didn't take the bait, he held his own hands together to demonstrate, before reaching out to her once more. He positioned his feet in preparation, just as she tentatively placed her palm in his.

He simply held it for a long while, letting her get used to it. Hers was warm and rough from walking on all fours, but the texture wasn't unpleasant.

Although awkward at first, her unsure muscles eventually loosened, and her orbs turned a bright yellow in joy.

*Sucker.* Jabez yanked her arm as hard as he could, making the Mavka crash face first into the dirt wall behind him as he shot for the hole she'd been guarding. Within seconds, dirt shifted and distressed squeals came from behind as she scurried to give chase when he left what he realised was a burrow. Her growl was loud, menacing, and a warning to Jabez that running was futile.

Which was fine, as he had no intention of doing so – yet.

Turning around, he held his hands up in surrender, and waited for her to exit. With orbs bright red, she halted, lowered her four-legged stance, and snapped her maw at him. She slammed a humanoid hand upon the ground, claws raking into the dirt, before tossing clumps of it as she pointed towards the opening behind her.

Jabez slowly, and cautiously, stepped to the side. She followed, but wasn't incited to hunt due to his snail speed. Then, once he was out of eyesight, he gripped the base of his dick and answered the call of nature. The scent alone had to be off-putting to her, and hopefully it made her leave him alone.

In the dim moonlight, he spotted his torn pants on the ground.

A spectator appeared, huffing over him, and he tilted his head back with his eyes half-cast in annoyance. *I guess she doesn't care.* Placing one hand on the closest tree for balance and to 'trap' him there, she released chitters at him while pointing back at the entrance of her burrow.

It showed that she understood the concept of language, but just simply didn't know his or vice versa.

"Get it now?" He eyed his pants once more. "Yeah. You didn't want the scent in your home, so hopefully you'll understand from now on that I'm like most creatures and need out of your imprisonment. Demons, humans, and even the Elvish are not like you, Mavka. What we consume, we must expel."

He received no audible answer.

*Why am I bothering to talk to her?* he thought with a sigh. *It'll be like talking to a tree.*

Once done, he stepped back. As if that was her call to action, she attempted to grab his arm so she could drag him back into her burrow. Predicting it, Jabez dodged it by ducking and turning, then he held his hand out.

"Wait. I need food." He mimed eating while patting his stomach.

Not understanding, she reached for him again, and he snapped out a quiet growl before miming the same motion. The Mavka paused and observed him silently.

She did the same action, and a gurgle came from her stomach — hungry and then persistent. Her yellowed orbs turned red, and she licked at her maw.

Now that they were no longer in her burrow, his eyesight improved immensely. He examined the shape of her skull further.

It was Jabez's turn to tilt his head. "I feel as though I've... met you."

Yet, without a doubt, he didn't know this adult Mavka. He'd memorised all their skull and horn variations. *She has a rabbit skull, but antlers like the fox Mavka.* Although her antlers were smaller in comparison.

His gaze slipped down her body while she crouched before him on all fours. He noted how almost every bone in her body was visible, and how gaunt and hollow her stomach was. Jabez guessed he could wrap both his hands around her waist and his fingertips would touch.

By the length of her foot arches, she had predominantly rabbit features, and even had a fluffy bunny tail to go with it.

The hollows of her cheekbones lacked skin, which meant the inside of her mouth was exposed. He figured when she grew, that would alter, as would much of her body. He saw no breasts currently on her humanoid torso, but he figured that, too, would change.

*I believe I met Merikh not long after this stage.* He palmed his face. *Fuck. Reasoning with her to let me leave will be impossible.* He dragged his hand down his face in irritation and covered his mouth. *Until then, I guess I'm at her mercy.*

Killing her would only be suicide, as she'd dominate him in strength within seconds. He could attempt it by crushing her skull, but without the aid of his magic, he was barely any stronger than a full-blooded Elf.

Running would only excite her hunger and desire to chase prey until she ripped it in half and consumed it.

He noted the mud stuffed into her nose hole and cocked an eyebrow at that. *She's smart enough to know how to hide from the scent of fear and blood, though.* That was surprising, all things considered.

Jabez rolled his eyes before waving for her to follow.

"Alright, Mavka, let's go eat. I'll hunt, take what I need, and you can have the rest."

Every scrap of meat he tossed at her would strengthen her, but he'd have to share if he wanted food.

When she tried to grab him, Jabez evaded and grabbed her forearm instead. She let out a distressed chitter when *he* pulled *her* along, her steps sluggish and mismatched as if she kept stumbling.

*I must be smart if I want to live.* Because Jabez had one ultimate goal in life, and it was to *survive*.

As he moved in search of prey to hunt, he swiped up his pants with his free hand, then temporarily let her go. Despite the disgusting, although dried, state of them, he donned them with the intention of finding the closest river in which to bathe them and himself.

The mauve pants were baggy around his thighs, with a flap of material that could be tied to reveal his clothed legs or left loose to give the impression he was wearing a skirt. One side loosely fluttered around his knee from being torn when he severed his own leg, while the other side hugged his calf.

He wasn't pleased that this was all he had to wear. Having a curious Mavka nearby was alarming, and his trust in her non-existent.

*It's also cold.*

Although his body *had* adjusted, somewhat, to the seasons of Earth, it was late autumn. Already it was too cool, and that would only worsen as winter came.

*I'll have to discover if we're in the north or south of Austrális, as the north becomes a winter wonderland.* He'd also need to know where he was in the world to plan an exit strategy.

Or just a plan in general.

As Jabez walked, while dragging the Mavka along so she followed his will and not the other way around, he looked up at the canopy of gold, yellow, and orange leaves above. Stars glittered, while a waxing moon brightened everything in its near fullness.

A sense of disquiet fell over him. *A plan, huh? What the fuck do I do now?*

Everything he'd been scheming, all his wants, desires, and actions, had come crashing down upon him. Violently. *Everyone will think I'm dead.* His options were limited.

Sure, he could come back with a flare of arrogant over-confidence, flaunting his survival, but what for? *I knew this was a losing battle the day I approached Merikh.* That had been almost six months ago.

Jabez had known, for quite some time, that everything he'd been doing was pointless. However, he had his reasons for continuing the charade of war. There were vile things he couldn't undo, stances he couldn't back out of without repercussions. Then, there were promises that, if broken, would cause a revolt – against him.

He chuckled up at the leaves. *You were all following the spiteful desires of a young boy.* A teenager who had been wronged by everyone – by the Elves, the humans, the Anzúli, and even the Demons.

The desires and schemes he'd unwittingly trapped himself in all throughout adulthood.

*Ah, the things I have done just to live are rather sickening.*

He looked over his shoulder, and his eyes crinkled in humour. *If she were to learn of them, she would resent saving me.* A foolish decision, really.

He wondered why this female Mavka had even been at the rubble of his castle, but he figured it was a fairly simple answer. She probably saw something bright, shining, and pretty in the distance, and chased after it in awe.

Only to discover a dying Jabez.

*A stone that can wield the power of the sun, huh?* He wondered where or how the Witch Owl came upon such magic. *Has she made contact with the Elysians?*

That made little sense to him, though. He was aware Lindiwe had every right to fear them learning of her, and what Weldir was up to. Not to mention all their miscreant children.

*People do stupid things when afraid.*

The scientist in control of such a destructive power must have been quite the intelligent and unhinged individual. To agree to give it to Lindiwe was, in his opinion, insanity. *Weldir in control of such magic is dangerous.*

No one knew what that demigod was truly up to, not even Jabez. He could turn on the Elysians just as much as he could be their saviour. Jabez had even offered to work with him, and he'd been staunchly denied.

Weldir's answer? *"Why would I help a child incite chaos when I'm perfectly capable of doing so myself?"*

See? Not particularly a knight in shining armour. A selfish god, doing selfish deeds, with no reason given to any. A darkness so strong, and yet so undeniably weak, he sought the power of a human woman wearing a flock of fucking feathers.

He was a conundrum, and a pest.

*If he hadn't shielded Demons from going back through the portal, my war wouldn't have been in vain.*

Oh well.

That was now the past, and he only allowed things from the past to bother him if they fuelled the flames of survival. Hate, grief, sorrow, and loss were things that pushed him forward. His failures were unnecessary thoughts, and he wouldn't allow them to plague him, only revisiting them to learn from his mistakes.

*I could choose to let it all go.*

Now that he was dead in the eyes of all, he had the opportunity to rebuild his life.

He could go back and be a self-proclaimed king of nothing. But that would only put him back in the position he'd been in for the last three centuries.

A man who watched his back as if he'd grown a third eye on the nape of his neck. A man who allowed no one to touch him, except for a defenceless human woman who was now dead – and even she knew not to approach him from behind.

A man who had given promises to change the lives of all Demons, and had been trying his hardest to adhere to that vow, while failing consistently. A man who had been so afraid of those around him that he wore nothing but a simple pair of pants as a bluff. It was his attempt to prove he was completely unconcerned with the fangs and claws around him, so he didn't need a shirt, let alone armour.

He was someone who flaunted his magic, his power, his strength, in order to incite fear.

As a self-made ruler who placed himself in constant danger, who was he to complain about the choices he'd made?

He wasn't forgivable, nor would he apologise. No one would apologise to him for the cruelty he'd suffered at the hands of many, so why should he?

Another deadened chuckle fell from him as he caught the scent of an animal in the distance. *I'm a villain, and an idiot of the highest intelligence.*

Jabez crouched and softened his footsteps, thankful the rabbit Mavka behind him was already just as quiet. They approached a lone deer, and he froze when it looked in their direction. She paused as well and even seemed to hold her very breath. Grass fell from their target's maw as it waited for a sign of movement, and when there was none, the animal lowered its head to keep grazing.

Jabez turned to the Mavka behind him.

He pointed to her, and then the ground, before pushing his hands out. He hoped she understood he wanted her to stay. When he backed up, she attempted to follow, so he did it multiple times until she figured it out.

Then he crept closer, his pointed ears flicking in alertness.

The deer lifted its head up, and Jabez noted the tiny antlers. A male with no herd. The moment it pivoted in the opposite direction of Jabez, he sprinted forward.

It let out a distressed bawl and started to run, but didn't make it far. He grabbed one of its rear legs, yanked it back with his inhuman strength until it slipped to its belly, and sliced his claws against its neck. A low snort came from it as it died.

Just as he began to slice away a leg, the loud, galloping pawsteps that approached had him rushing to finish his task.

He had just enough time to leap away to the closest branch with his prize before the Mavka attempted to tackle the space he'd just been occupying. She immediately descended upon the carcass as Jabez climbed to get out of sight and away from the wind brushing his scent towards her.

Despite the mud in her nose, either the copious amount of blood or perhaps the sight was too much for her weak mind. She roared, releasing a puff of white condensation from her incisor-toothed maw before the air filled with disgusting wet snarls as she ate. The Mavka in a full rage worked on consuming the meat below him as he skinned and consumed the leg he'd obtained.

He had no issue eating raw meat, although he was much more civilised and preferred cooked food. But a meal was a meal.

Once he was finished, he dropped the bone down to her so she could consume it. It would strengthen her bones, and whatever meat was left would surely do her some good. It wasn't like he had a use for it.

Then he leaned back against the tree trunk, partially reclining with his legs crossed. He brought his hands up behind his head and patiently waited for her to come out of it.

He only peeked over intermittently to see how far she was into her meal. When she was merely licking the blood from her hands for the last tasty drops, he knew it wouldn't be much longer.

*Hopefully she runs off into the forest in search of more.*

Then he could sprint away and put as much space between them as possible, with minimal repercussions.

# THREE

For a long while, all Jabez heard was a creature intensely sniffing at the ground. She walked around, searching while scratching at grass, leaves, or whatever.

When whimpering drifted up to him from below the branch he lay upon, he glanced over it to see the Mavka kneeling in the grass. *Damnit, she stayed.* And now she was regaining lucidity. Her orbs were bright blue with little droplets floating around her empty eye sockets – ethereal tears.

His brows narrowed at how quick she was to cry.

Figuring that meant it was safe, Jabez rotated until his legs dangled over the edge, and then he slid off. He landed gracefully, although not particularly softly due to the length of the fall, bending his knees to take the worst of the impact.

The Mavka squealed as she leapt to the side, her hand raised to threaten with claws at his sudden landing. She quickly lowered it, and her orbs turned bright yellow as she darted towards him.

She chittered as she cupped the side of his face, his neck, obviously checking for some kind of wound. He rolled his eyes as he pushed her hands away, surprised she had enough humanity to check his wellbeing.

"Yes, yes. I am perfectly fine. You did not eat your new pet," he stated as he stepped to the side.

The Mavka grabbed his wrist and dragged him in the direction of her burrow. He skilfully twisted his arm out of her hold while evading her claws.

"That way. There is water, and I'm in desperate need of a drink and a bath. We can go to your burrow when day breaks. Until then, we will explore the night as our kinds were intended to."

He may have been the captured pet, but she was no master of him.

Convincing her would be easy enough, considering she had no capabilities to argue. The more he did things, the more she'd learn that everything he did had a reason – most of which would benefit her.

She would eventually grow angered by his constant refusal to do as she demanded, and she'd no doubt force his hand to obey. Until then, he would do what he wanted.

He made her follow by evading every time she attempted to grab his arm. When she went for an ankle, he rolled forward to break her hold and continued on without missing a step. He ducked from her grasp with practised skill – luckily she attempted to be gentle even as she gave warning snarls.

When they came upon a small lake, Jabez knelt beside it. He kept her in the safety of his periphery as he leaned forward, noting how she stood there awkwardly with her claws clicking together.

He didn't check if it was safe. It was clear, and his gut biome was used to swallowing strange water. The Demon part of him had rather good health benefits when it came to parasites, diseases, and worms from water or meat; it kept him healthy from such contaminants.

With a scoop of water nestled in both palms, he raised his hands to gesture to it before drinking, so she could see and understand he needed this to survive. Jabez drank until he quenched his thirst, occasionally looking sideways at the Mavka twisting her skull with distinct rattles coming from her.

*Yes, Mavka. I need food and water.*

Once he was done, he stood and walked around the lake's edge in search of specific herbs or flowers. Since it was the autumn, he had few options, but he took what he found back towards the lake. Jabez removed his pants and placed the herbs on top of them, stepped over the edge, and plunged into the water.

The shivers that assaulted his skin were abhorrent, but he wiped his body as best as he could so he could be truly clean. He scrubbed harder in areas that had a light dusting of hair such as his legs, chest, and arms, as well as his groin.

He spun when he heard whining at the water's edge. The Mavka stood dangerously close as she reached out to him with glistening claws. She swiped at the water, breaking the surface and causing ripples, as if she was trying to manipulate it into getting him to float or drift closer.

"Calm down," Jabez stated with an exasperated sigh. "I can swim. You don't need to wor–" Before he could finish, a heavy splash sprayed over him as she fell in.

He closed his eyes, and with a dull expression, waited for the spray to end. *You're fucking joking.*

The Mavka, unable to float, bounced up and down as she fretted. The water was deep enough that his toes barely scraped the muddy floor, and he watched as she instantly sunk before clawing at the surface. She let out screams, clearly afraid of the water, and was too panicked to get to the edge. Water sprayed in all directions, and she constantly spat it out with orbs bright white as she searched for an escape.

Jabez tilted his head. *If I let her drown, it will give me time to escape.* She wouldn't be able to stop him, and he'd have a clear conscience, as she would eventually heal herself to breathe once more and find her way out of the water on her own.

She was already afraid of it, which meant she knew she couldn't swim – proving she'd be fine if he were to abandon her. *She's done this before.*

Yet his lips flattened as he narrowed his eyes at her. His ears darted back with vexation as his mind spat, *Oh, fuck it.*

Jabez swam closer to the Mavka throwing water in every direction and grabbed one of her small antlers. He dragged her to the edge of the lake while making sure her skull remained above the surface.

He released a bellowing roar when she latched herself to him, and he was forced to bear her weight as she scratched at his flesh. Her hand claws dug into his shoulders and back, while those on her feet gouged at his calves. With his own head beneath the water, he shoved her towards the edge and then forced her over onto land.

Hissing in a breath of pain, he sunk beneath the surface to hide the nasty wounds she'd just scored down his back and legs.

"Fuck. There. Now we're even," he bit out, squinting his eyes in a foul glare. "You saved me, and I saved you."

He looked over his shoulder while pulling on the skin. They were deep wounds, flaring open to reveal muscle, and he bit out a curse.

He drifted his gaze up due to her whimpering. She knelt on the edge and grasped his shoulder, her whining doubling in its volume. Teal magic radiated a glow in the water. His injuries began to heal, stitching shut on their own, and he watched them form on her own body instead.

He gave a sigh of relief. *Without my magic, I would've needed to let them heal naturally.*

Once done, she backed up and sat in a crouch position away from the water. She clamped her hands against her exposed sternum bone with blue orbs and offered him a bunch of fast, incoherent chitters.

*She's sorry.* Jabez just shook his head. *Had she not tried to retrieve me, she wouldn't have needed to bear the wounds she gave me.*

Tsking, he swam towards his tattered mauve pants. Jabez dragged them into the water with the herbs and weed flowers and set about cleaning them.

He eyed her as he did. *She's trying to communicate.* That's what those chitters meant. *Perhaps she's not as low in humanity as I thought.* The fact she was even attempting to meant she could string her thoughts together in some form to know *what* she wanted to say – just not *how*.

It was likely all a garbled mess of emotions and not real intelligence.

After a good sniff test once he was done scrubbing, he donned his pants before he exited the lake and then sat down beside it.

Clean, hydrated, and fed, he felt remarkably better.

He no longer felt like a filthy animal, and the headache that had been pounding in his temples subsided. Which left him with the constant sickness that rolled in his gut due to the magic depletion that continued to plague him – and would only be exacerbated if he attempted to use it.

He had nothing to give.

*I wish she hadn't saved me,* he thought, as he sat a small distance from her.

Had she not been shuffling the rubble above him, he could have laid there buried and waited for his magical essence to reignite. Sure, he still would have faced the sickness regardless, as he'd used too much of it, but it wouldn't have been as bad. He could survive hunger and blood loss, but this was far worse than any injury or missing limb.

He would have eventually climbed out of the rubble and found a creature to feast upon before he went hunting for a human to steal their limbs. Then he would have used forbidden magic to regrow his own severed arm and leg. He would have used vines as phantom limbs to obtain movement until he did these things.

It wasn't the first time he'd regrown an arm; Orpheus had bitten one off in the battle they'd fought almost two years ago.

*Had she just let me be...*

Jabez sighed in acceptance and defeat, then brushed the long white strands of hair from his face. He paused when he felt a large bald patch on the scalp around his right ear.

Crawling to the lake, he peered into his reflection. An angry glare filled his features as his lips curled back.

A curved line from his temple to the nape of his neck had all been burned away. He vaguely remembered the severe burns that had covered most of his upper body. He could only imagine the state he'd truly been in when this Mavka found him, and the loss of his hair was evidence of how numb he'd been to it.

He touched the point of his long ear before fingering the lack of hair around it. *It took me centuries to grow it to this length.* He was annoyed he'd need to restart.

Once more, it had been a show of confidence.

The colour of an Elysian's hair was destroyed in the excess magic they had within their body. It was actually transparent, despite looking white, and showed just how mutated their hair had become after hundreds of generations. Magic was stored in it, and it could be used for many different things.

For Jabez, who had been able to teleport, it had been a weakness. One he flaunted, as he did with the skin on his back.

He searched his body and noticed the 'Demon' markings upon his sides, arms, and shoulders had disappeared. In their place, proper markings had taken their true shape in the form of tiny Elvish runes that swirled around his body in patterned lines. They were so small they were barely legible, and appeared mostly like swirls, knots, and circles.

Along with his loss of power, his glamour had completely faded.

He also took note that he'd lost the golden bangles that were once present on the ankle and biceps of his severed limbs. Although he hated the Elysians for what they'd done to him, he'd worn them as a show of his achievements, so when he finally faced them, they would see his strengths. They would realise how formidable and wise he'd become.

The thick chain around his neck had disintegrated, but it had held unfathomable power and had been the only reason he'd been able to create portals. Such a necklace had also been the sign of a leader. Now it was gone, along with his position as king.

*Fitting.* He would have tossed it into the water regardless.

*The fact that the redheaded woman knew to grab my hair to teleport with me...* His white brows narrowed when he tried to decipher *how* she knew. *That woman bonded to the antler Mavka likely learned of it during our skirmish.*

He remembered that day well, and it wasn't with fondness.

His musings were cut short when he grunted in sudden realisation. He turned his gaze to the Mavka a few feet to the side of him.

He squinted his eyes as he looked upon her before lifting a hand to block the view of her small antlers.

He threw his head back and laughed. "That's where I know you from!" He covered his gut when his laughter made the ball of sickness worsen, and he produced a pained groan. "You're not the Witch Owl's child. You're the child of that idiot

Mavka."

Obviously overjoyed he was cheerful, the Mavka snickered along with him. She came a little closer, and only paused when he shook his head.

"Ah, that was quite the day. You were just a baby. You were a nasty thing, biting at my ankle."

He hadn't even known she'd existed until then, since he'd been too busy threatening and taunting her parents.

"It's remarkable how your entire species can grow in such a short period of time. You're also rather intelligent for a Mavka that I can see hasn't eaten much." He hooked his index finger around the length of a pointed ear in thought. "Is it because your mother was human, and your father half human? Perhaps your kind obtain more humanity the further your parentage is from Weldir."

Although he could tell it meant little in terms of physique and other physical aspects, as she looked fully like an adult Mavka. However, it did answer why she was so good with her magic to heal at her stage of development, as well as knowing to block her nose from scents with mud, make a home, *and* be able to understand instructions so readily.

It was the only thing that made sense.

"I guess not all hope is lost for your kind then." He placed his elbow on his thigh and rested his cheek against the knuckles of his fist. "Your mother truly thought I was going to kill you that day." Jabez tsked as he rolled his eyes. "I may be cruel, but not even I would harm a defenceless child. I knew scaring her would force her hand. Humans are rather predictable like that."

This time, Jabez looked off to the side as he cupped his jaw. He tapped across his lips.

"Although... the idea of keeping you did cross my mind. I could have just trained you to be as formidable as Merikh and a loyal companion. The ever-night knows I'm all out of companions."

He didn't have a single friend of his own. Then again, it was hard to trust anyone in this fucked-up realm. He'd rather have none if it meant he lived another day.

*I barely even trusted Katerina.* He'd chosen her as his

concubine because she was weak, defenceless, and cute when she wanted to be. But her manipulative actions and hatred towards his old friend, Merikh, had shown him she was untrustworthy.

She was toxic, as was he, which meant they worked. Two self-destructing pieces that had a mutual agreement. He promised he wouldn't abuse her, which he hadn't, and she wouldn't drive a knife through his heart.

Perhaps he'd once cared for her deeper than he was willing to admit, but he couldn't bring her back to life. He'd also grown thankful for her absence, as the removal of her persistence in getting him to kill all Mavka allowed him to see the truth: killing them would do nothing.

It would weaken Weldir if he removed his soul-ferrying children, but he would just make more.

Jabez needed to leave Earth and start over in Nyl'theria. He'd need a companion to do that – someone who was his strength and speed, and he their magic and shield.

Jabez needed someone he could trust.

*Perhaps I could try with this female Mavka.* Now that was an idea. *But she's a long way from being able to reason with.* He needed someone intelligent enough to understand instructions.

Or even... what he was saying without a head tilt.

"Alright, female. I've decided," he stated, while cocking a brow. A rather malicious smile pulled at the right corner of his lips.

He would aid this Mavka's growth and see what happened.

*Maybe I can train her to be a loyal guard.*

# FOUR

After a few days of rest and scouting the area around her burrow, leading the Mavka towards Jabez's intended destination had taken a lot of patience on his part. He'd needed to convince his captor, who couldn't understand, that he wasn't fleeing but trying to lead her somewhere. He'd waved his hands beckoningly, offering her smiles while trying to minimise how much of his fangs he revealed.

She kept trying to drag him back towards her burrow at first, but he'd managed to get it into her thick, silly skull that they were to travel together.

Once she realised he wanted her to come with, her little bunny tail wiggled as she followed.

Jabez avoided the sunlight as best he could. He made sure they travelled around it, walking through shade or minimal dappled streaks. He could bear the direct sunlight for a few minutes – unlike Demons that began to disintegrate instantly, no matter how far into their evolution they were.

His bare feet crushed damp, decaying autumn leaves, and the inability to feel the earth on a spiritual level was hollowing. An Elf's intrinsic need to touch the ground with the soles of their feet was vital to their life.

*Whatever.* There was little he could do to change it right now.

Despite knowing where he was in the world, as the Veil's canyon wasn't too far and he'd discovered they were southwest of it, that feeling of loss came from his extinguished magic. It was like another limb had been severed. The emptiness in his stomach had nothing to do with hunger, and everything to do with the lack of natural magic buzzing beneath his flesh.

He missed it and hoped its disappearance wasn't permanent.

For now, he'd abandoned all plans for revenge or returning to the life he once knew. He had a different scheme; one that would take months before he could even begin to enact it.

Jabez was about to cut out a chunk of his life for this Mavka.

Even if it was all worthless in the end, he wasn't the kind of being to give up an opportunity when it presented itself. Either this Mavka would allow him to willingly use her to empower and free himself, or he would aid her by increasing her humanity, then dust his hands of her, forget about their time together, and move on to try something else.

Jabez never placed hope in others, he only saw them as potentials that could be replaced. Such was the life of a lone king on an insecure throne, and the vow of a pubescent teenager.

He let her hold his forearm as though he was a pet on a leash, knowing it made her more at ease.

They journeyed west, seeking a town he knew of well. A town that, every couple of decades, would obtain a protective blue dome belonging to Orpheus – this female Mavka's uncle.

A half day's travel brought them to it just as dusk was settling in. The town was well fortified due to its capabilities to expand itself with Orpheus' ward in place. It was large, and able to hold the capacity of humans living within it with ease. It wasn't as dirty and over-populated as most other towns.

His features brightened in malice at its wooden stake walls, and the lack of a blue dome in place. The one just north of here, perhaps a few hours' walk away, was the one currently being protected – and would be for another seven or so years.

This one was penetrable.

He was about to doom it.

He didn't give a shit.

To Jabez, humans were nothing but cattle for his whims.

He'd led teams of Demons to human fortifications, only to destroy them and let his army feed. He protected his army, ensuring minimal casualties, and watched with abject boredom while protecting the truly innocent behind a ward.

He glanced at the female beside him. *This town will survive.*

She was one creature, and he didn't see her needing to consume every being within this pitiful town.

He could feed her any creature to grow her strength and plump up her lean form, but the only way to increase her humanity was to consume higher intelligence beings. Which is why he brought her here.

However, when the light of dusk was gone, and it was safe for Jabez to cross the clearing, she refused to go with him. No amount of tugging on his part could make her heavy body budge from her spot.

The Mavka chittered, pointed at the town, and shook her head with her orbs turning white before backing up. She covered her muddy snout, which he'd attempted to have her clean out before they even made it here. She'd refused.

"Come on," Jabez stated, grasping her forearm and tugging until his bare heels gouged into the grass. She held his forearm in return, but did nothing. "If you want to grow strong and smart, you need to eat."

He offered another false smile, growing annoyed at having to present them so readily when he could be a rather sour individual. Jabez had very little reason to smile, and only did so condescendingly, maliciously, or threateningly.

When she didn't budge, he sighed.

*Screw this. I have other ways to make her do what I want.*

He twisted his arm from her hold, as she wasn't expecting him to do so, and headed towards the town on his own. She chased him with a soft warning growl. When she attempted to grab him, Jabez put all his combat training into use to dodge her numerous times.

She didn't like that.

Her growl worsened, but at this point, he didn't quite care if he enraged her. He'd just lead her to the slaughter she was about to create, in which a blood-lust would rack her mind like a violent plea. She wouldn't even be able to stop herself at that point.

Just as she managed to grab ahold of his wrist, an alarm bell rang from the town. Shouts wailed through the coming night as a wave of collective fear flittered into the air.

"It's a Duskwalker!" one shouted.

"It's not Orpheus," another yelled from above the wall.

"Everyone, ready yourselves for a potential fight! Hurry!"

The sounds of boots hitting the ground and metal-plated armour grinding against itself caused a clamour through the area. More shouts echoed over the distance, and the chilling wind did little to hide the growing scent of their fear.

She released him to cover her nose hole and once more backed up a step, then shook her rabbit skull, emitting the sound of rattling bones – like her head was brainless. She whimpered as her glowing orbs turned bright red.

Jabez tsked at the nuisance she was being. *I'd much rather not do this, but so be it.* To get things started, he sliced his palm with the opposing thumb claw, grabbed one of her hands to shove it down, and smeared his blood across her snout.

The reaction was instant, and her roar was so loud it blasted his eardrums and left them ringing.

With a deep chuckle in the face of danger, Jabez lowered himself into a crouch as she bared her claws at him. She leapt forward, and he jumped, only to land straight on top of her. She crumbled chest first into the ground, then he flipped backwards and sprinted towards the town.

Wind whistled past his ears and chilled his nose, while his long hair streamed behind him. Pumping his arms as he moved at high speed, his heart barely accelerated, his body formidable and well-trained.

The Mavka was quick to chase him, and almost managed to get her claws into him, but he skilfully sidestepped to avoid her lunges. Just as she was turning to greet him with a snarl, he leapt halfway up the outside of the town's protective wall. Hooking himself to it with the use of his finger and toe claws, he yanked himself higher until he was at the top of the barrier.

He noticed movement and grabbed the head of an arrow to stop it from shooting him in the face, surprising the man who'd nocked it.

He tackled the armoured soldier off the top of the wall and used him as a pillow for his landing on the other side.

The poor fellow was still alive when Jabez heard multiple bones crack before he belted out a scream. He gave the male a quick, merciful death – one that selfishly aided him. He sliced the male's throat open, making his own mouth water at the delicious scent, while ensuring he would become the new target for the now enraged Mavka who landed next to them with a thud.

He leapt away, and within seconds, she descended upon the dying soldier.

Her attention was quickly diverted when an arrow lanced the back of her shoulder. Jabez fled, since being anywhere near the fray would likely see him injured.

Without his magic, he was of little help to her, as he couldn't aid her strength or protect her. He would only be a liability, and all this bloodshed would be for naught if he bit the dust.

He slowed to a nonchalant walk once he was far enough away from the clattering of weapons, armour, and dying yells, then checked his palm to see the small cut was already clotting.

His presence was ignored as soldiers ran past him, all of them racing for the biggest threat. He doubted the humans could see his Demon features – such as his claws and horns – all that well in the dark. He had brown human-like skin, since the grey Elvish undertone was far subtler than most, and he didn't have the void-black, inhuman glistening exterior of other Demons. It wasn't truly flesh, but a magical barrier that held in their insides until they could become complete and grow skin.

At most, they might question the colour of his white, waist-length hair. Unless they glimpsed his backwards-pointing, segmented horns in random torchlight.

At a loud whine coming from behind, he paused briefly, then shrugged and continued on.

As much as Jabez felt for the pain she was in due to the multiple soldiers that charged the 'monster,' he wouldn't waste his guilt on something that couldn't be changed. Even though he'd caused her suffering by bringing her here, this was an inevitable part of her speedy growth. She needed humanity, he required she did so fast, and it would only benefit her in the long run.

*She will be fine,* he thought, reminding himself that she'd heal within a day. *No humans know how to kill her kind.*

She would thank him later. Merikh had when Jabez had done a similar thing to aid his growth when he realised eating humans benefited Mavka. This wasn't the first time he'd done this.

Stopping a discreet distance from the chaos and danger, Jabez turned, folded his arms, and leaned against the side of a building. No one approached him as he watched the Mavka tear into soldiers like their metal armour was nothing but paper.

She scratched off a man's helmet while biting into his shoulder, then tossed her skull side to side until his neck snapped. Once dead, she bit his head off and began to eat from the bleeding hole she'd made. The shape of her maw made her rather grotesquely violent when it came to eating, and she smeared blood all over her skull as she buried it into the gaping wound.

Only a few seconds later, barely halfway down his torso, she threw his body to the side so she could slash across the gut of a soldier who rammed a short sword into her thigh. Her claws caught in the metal breastplate of his armour, and she sent his body flying. He crashed into the side of a house with such force it cracked. The Mavka then proceeded to charge on all fours until her small antlers lanced his gut, and she shoved them both into the centre of the house.

Along with the creaks and groans of timber and the shatter of furniture, multiple high-pitched wails rang out. They momentarily hid the snarls of the Mavka inside.

A woman with three children sprinted from the house. She carried a little boy, likely no older than two, in her arms, while a pair of slightly older girls in pale nightgowns sprinted behind her. They headed towards the bell ringing deep within the village, likely a place where people congregated for safety.

The mother looked back, checking to make sure her young

children followed before shifting the screaming boy in her arms. The moment she looked away, the youngest of her daughters tripped and was separated from her fleeing parent.

The little girl was slow to rise to her feet, and her crying was overshadowed by the Mavka causing unseen mayhem in their home. A fire blasted to life, setting the house ablaze within seconds.

With a quiet, nose crinkling snarl, Jabez pushed off the wall and leapt into a sprint. The closer he got, the more he scented the child's blood from scrapes on her knees and hands, and the power of her fear. Both tingled in his nose, enough to make his mouth salivate, but Jabez's hunger wasn't an uncontrollable beast.

Just as he was about to make it to her, the Mavka burst through the wall of the house with a roar, throwing clay and stone rubble all around. Jabez slid across the dirt and shielded the child from the falling house debris with his body.

Just as he'd predicted, the Mavka turned towards the little girl creating a delicious scent. *Shit, we have to move.* Jabez somersaulted to the side when the Mavka's large hand came down to squash them, and then he hooked his right arm around the little girl's midsection. He lifted her by her side until her legs and arms dangled.

The Mavka dived for them both, but Jabez jumped into the air and grabbed ahold of the straw roofing of the house next to them. The child screamed as her dangling limbs swayed towards the ground, while he held her waist firm. He grunted when the straw began to break, and he looked down to find the Mavka moments from jumping for them.

Just as she did, Jabez booted her skull between her antlers, forcing her back down, and she hit the dirt with a *thump*. He hissed in a breath against the pain that shot up his leg from the power of their collective impact.

More soldiers came to take her attention by shoving their weapons at her, and it gave Jabez the opportunity to let go of the roof. Broken straw cascaded on top of him when he landed, forcing him to close his eyes momentarily against the debris, but he didn't bother to shake it off as he sprinted away with the small child.

Using his increased agility due to his mixed heritage, Jabez headed straight for where the bell was coming from. When too many stupid humans were on the street and heading in the same direction, causing a dangerous and foolish stampede, he jumped to a balcony. He climbed higher still so he could run across rooftops.

When he had a moment, he checked on the wellbeing of the girl. She reeked of fear, and her face was snotty from crying. She was a little shaken up, but he noted there were no other injuries besides her scraped hands and knees.

What mattered was that neither he nor the Mavka had damaged her.

Jabez knew himself to be an evil presence in this world, but he'd never harmed a child in it – at least not by his own hand. He'd also never stood back and allowed his minions to do so either. His reasoning to them had always been that a grown human gave more humanity and bred more for them to eat, but the truth was... he just couldn't stomach the idea.

He'd instigated raids on human towns to feed his minions, but he'd always chosen places containing few young ones. He scouted and then protected where the young were hidden away with their mothers by casting a protective dome over that location. Then his Demons slaughtered the rest, mostly soldiers, and he moved them on before daybreak.

From then on, it was up to the humans to relocate while the sun was shining. Most fleeing their towns survived as they escaped the burning ruins and ventured to other settlements nearby.

He gave the truly innocent a chance, and he thought that may be because he'd never been given one. His innocence had been stolen from him as a young boy, and he'd been at the mercy of dangerous beings for much of his life. He despised humans just as much as he did the Elves, but he knew what it felt like to be small, weak, and defenceless.

He knew what it felt like when no one had given him mercy.

*Alright, this should be close enough.*

When he reached the tallest building in the town that had the bell chiming, he skilfully landed between the narrow gap of two houses with a quiet thud. He propped the child on her feet, refusing to get too close to the exit in case he was spotted. Passing by the alleyway they were in, women and men fled to the towering building. He pushed the girl towards the entrance of the alleyway, onto what appeared to be a main street, then turned and walked in the opposite direction.

He didn't care about nor want a thanks, and the soldiers guarding the assembly point would only attempt to fight him if he lingered.

Allowing himself a brief glance back, he saw the girl had turned as well, and she waved at him with one hand as the other wiped snot from her nose.

*Gross. Don't wave at me, you vile little thing.* He gave a disgusted, disgruntled lip curl before facing away.

When he peeked out of the opposite exit of the alleyway, there were barely any humans on this narrow street. He followed the shadows to keep out of sight as he headed back towards the chaos he could hear at the entry point of the village.

With the child instantly forgotten, his walk was leisurely.

They'd been in this village for less than an hour, and he planned for the Mavka to eat many humans while they were here. They had hours until sunrise would come, and she wouldn't tire. Her wounds would be meaningless to her capabilities, no matter how debilitating they'd be for someone mortal like himself. The humans wouldn't be able to trap her, as he doubted they had Anzúli-enchanted rope or chains, like those Demonslayers wielded.

Jabez peeked up at the glowing moon, and momentarily basked in its rays as it chased away the chill. He opened his red eyes once more to inspect the buildings he passed.

At a shop window that had the word 'seamstress' painted across it, he paused. Something silver resting on the storekeeper's counter grasped his attention, and a grin lifted the corners of his lips.

Jabez shoved the point of his elbow through one of the large glass windowpanes, then shattered his way inside. Being careful to avoid stabbing the bottoms of his bare feet with glass, he ducked his six-foot-nine height within the low-ceiling room, and had to crouch even further when he passed under a door frame to the back.

He found a decently sized satchel bag and shoved sewing supplies into it, including scissors, needles, and thread spools of random colours. He even cut off a few metres of black silky material.

From there, he left to hunt for anything else that could be of use. He found a leatherworker's shop and stole an empty water sack, a pair of black leather breeches, and an expensive-looking hooded cloak that had wolf or bear fur on the shoulders as padding. At a clothing store, he took the largest tunic he could find, disapproving of its cream colouring.

Everything he found, he stuffed into his satchel or threw over his shoulder if it was too large. He even obtained fruit and vegetables from a store for easy eating, rather than having to constantly hunt with a bloodthirsty predator at his back.

Just as he was about to reach where the fighting was still in action – the skirmish loud, and the smell of smoke from multiple homes burning strong – he passed a library. He almost disregarded going inside until an idea flittered through his thoughts.

*If she's to learn, it's better if I have materials to teach.*

With that in mind, he broke in and spent a decent amount of time flicking through the different reading materials available. He grabbed a child's storybook, then singled out two other reading materials he wouldn't find too boring to read repeatedly. He refused to take anything containing romance, as he didn't wish to put silly thoughts into the *female* Mavka's mind.

Pleased with his spoils, he left when he knew he'd been gone too long.

Finally, the Mavka came into view. She was deeper within the village now, and at an intersection that gave her just enough room to move and attack.

Her physique had changed in the hour or so they'd been parted. Although all her bones were still exposed, she was no longer thin enough for him to wrap his hands around her waist with ease. It was hard to see in detail just how much she'd changed, but she would evolve even more as the night went on.

Once more, he leaned against a wall to watch, only to grunt when something sharp was pressed between his shoulder blades. He'd been expecting everyone to pass him, since he was shrouded in the shadow of an awning.

"I wouldn't do that if I were you," Jabez warned, as he peeked over his shoulder.

An armoured soldier wielding a spear had stark, frightened eyes as he looked up at Jabez's daunting height.

"S-shut up, you filthy Demon," he snapped out, before shoving harder and forcing Jabez to step forward so he wasn't lanced. "I watched you lead that monster in here, and-and steal that little girl."

"Well, I *had* no intention of intervening," Jabez stated with a small smirk. "But I guess I am a little hungry."

He stepped forward and swiftly ducked to the side as the soldier thrust his spear, stumbling straight into Jabez's reach. He grabbed the male's helmet so he could pull him closer, then with one hand on his head, the other on his shoulder, Jabez shoved his jagged fangs into the side of the human's neck.

He drank from the man, and the soldier's blood rejuvenated his senses against the exhaustion that had been weighing on him since the defeat at his castle.

Jabez had long despised eating the flesh of sentient beings like a disgusting cannibal, but draining them dry like a vampire had its uses – more so when he had his magic. He didn't need humanity, as he was fully intelligent and fully formed, but he drank from this human as he would have a mindless animal.

He considered draining him dry, but decided not to. The Mavka may come across him, and he left the remains for her – if not, the male was lucky he'd live another day.

Now in a rather grand mood, Jabez leapt to a rooftop to be a spectator, completely out of the way. He pulled a stolen orange from his new satchel and threw its peels on the heads of the soldiers below him. With one leg swinging off the ledge of the house, he watched over the Mavka with the intention of intervening should she truly need aid.

She never did.

*Formidable thing, isn't she?* he thought with a rather prideful sneer. *Even with those teeth of hers.* Actually, he thought that made her bite just as dangerous as any predator-skulled Mavka.

"Hurry up!" someone whisper-shouted below him. "We must kill the Duskwalker before it kills any more men. Go that way. We may be able to get behind it."

*Hmm, I forgot that's what the humans call Mavka.* He thought it to be a rather simplistic name, but merely shrugged.

Those who just spoke were slaughtered within minutes.

After many hours had passed, Jabez noted the amount of corpses in the wake of her destruction. He figured this should be enough food.

Long before the sunrise even began to crest over the horizon, he slipped from the roof and headed straight for the commander of this feeble army. The commander shouted orders until those around her backed up at Jabez's approach from behind.

She turned to face him. She lacked a helmet, and he took in the surprisingly gentle and soft features of her sun-damaged, tanned face. Her hair was a shining blonde, her nose small, and her lips thin.

Just as she went to draw her sword, he cocked his head.

"If you wish to cease this bloodshed, I suggest you call back your men," Jabez explained, looking past the now armed woman to the Mavka eating a corpse.

"Why should we do anything you say, Demon?" she jeered, before pointing her sword up at his straight, pointed nose.

Those around them followed suit, and many sword or spear tips were pointed at his bored face. They glinted in the dim moonlight, and a grin curled his lips back to flash his fangs.

"Because I've purposefully not joined this fray." A malicious glint lifted into his features as he eyed their useless weapons. "I'm not here to feast, only the Duskwalker is. Either lower your weapons and back away, or I'll make sure this entire village burns to the ground."

Such a threat would have been more powerful had he been able to use his magic, but his strong, muscular appearance should have been alarming enough. Especially as he towered over even the tallest man by over half a foot, and this woman by an entire one.

When the commander looked as though she planned to argue, Jabez sighed exaggeratedly and shook his head.

"I lured the *Duskwalker* here, and I can lure it away. Without me, that creature won't leave until it's decimated this entire village and consumed every moving thing it sees. Unless someone else is willing to be bait, and fast enough to get away, you have no other option." Then, he raised his right arm to shrug with it, while also purposefully making his claw-like nails glint in the torchlight a soldier was carrying. "Choose, human, or let your death come. I need to evade the sunlight, but the Duskwalker does not."

"Commander," a man from the side said while lowering his sword. He eyed Jabez warily. "We've lost over thirty men."

"It doesn't attack while it's eating, so long as we give it space and don't move," another stated, stepping back without lowering his spear.

"Are you all so stupid to believe a *monster* is willing to aid us?" she bit at them.

Jabez didn't bat an eye at being called a monster. He found it to be rather endearing, considering he'd been called far worse in his long life.

"Stupid or not, you have no other option." Jabez lifted his hand and gently pushed away a spear tip near his left ear with disdain. "I approached you with the offer to spare more of your people. I'm just as formidable as the Duskwalker. Either do as I say or I'll no longer offer you salvation, and I will aid in your demise." He gave the woman another grin, this time allowing humour to light in his eyes. "Choose."

With a rather adorable little growl, she stepped back with a nod. "Fine. Call back everyone."

"I suggest you all do so slowly and quietly," Jabez stated. "Any sudden noises or movement will gain her attention."

She nodded upwards once more as a silent command, and a few of her soldiers moved away. She refused to take her eyes off his, so he tilted his head eerily, and his ears flicked as he listened carefully to the movement around him.

"Once we're gone, do you promise to lead the Duskwalker away?" the commander asked.

"No," he answered warmly, making her eyes narrow into a

steely glare. "Once she finishes feeding from your fallen soldiers, I'll lead her away before day breaks."

"Bastard," she bit out, but otherwise left with the rest of her soldiers.

The area grew quiet, and all that remained was Jabez and the Mavka as she ate, evolved, and grew. He found it rather serene and peaceful, especially with the hot flames of a nearby building flickering light over her body. He eyed the multiple arrows lining most of her body, her wounds, and the blood that dripped from her.

A dark sense of pride engulfed his chest as he watched her grow stronger with each bite. She'd been swift, agile, and deadly tonight. He needed a companion such as this.

*And just imagine how dangerous she'll be once she's smart.*

He could already conceptualise the possibilities.

*I just hope she isn't as ill-tempered as that red-orbed bear.*

# FIVE

Not long before daybreak, Jabez easily gained the attention of the Mavka by simply throwing a large rock at the side of her body. Since he stood on top of the protective wooden spikes, she was quick to snarl up at him and the severed arm he waved to taunt her with. She chased after him the moment he jumped off and landed on the other side.

When she got too close, he threw the bloodied limb to gain more distance while she gobbled it up.

*We should be fine once we're a safe distance from the village.*

When the smell of blood no longer perfumed the air, he climbed a tree to hide from her. Staying above the lowest branches, the heavy gusts of wind aided him, and she lost his scent. He silently watched her sprint throughout the forest, backtracking to where his smell last lingered before running off in a new direction.

The deep navy of the sky began to lighten as the new day encroached, and Jabez watched it with a sense of detachment.

Only when the huffing, snarling Mavka didn't return did Jabez drop down and wander after her. He brushed his hands of this night.

*So long as I follow her freshest scent, she'll lead me back to her burrow.*

During his travel, he avoided the growing sunlight as best as he could. He checked on his new supplies, rather proud of himself that he'd thought to collect them. The bag was overfull and impossible to close, and the cloak he'd taken swayed back and forth over his shoulder.

Since he lacked the speed of a Mavka, nor did he care to hurry, the daylight hours passed until the gloaming wasn't far from darkening the skies as he reached her territory. Her lingering scent made it difficult to track which way to go, so he searched for other means.

When he found traces of her purple Mavka blood, which was lighter in its colouring than the inkiness of Demon blood, he crouched down next to the droplets. He examined her tracks around them, noting which way she was heading, before following both.

Long before he heard whines and whimpers reverberating through the forest, his pointed ears twitched in alertness. He softened his steps so as to not startle her and approached slowly.

He found her limping as she headed to what he figured was her filthy home. One back leg was lifted, while each press on her left forelimb caused her to let out a higher cry of pain.

He could see just how much she'd changed.

Her torso was thicker to the point he thought hugging her midsection would feel normal. In her monstrous form, the flesh between her ribs didn't appear so sunken or like her skin was about to rot off. Instead, it was full and bulging, nearly consuming most of her skeletal torso. He even thought two, albeit small, mounds had formed over some of her rib bones, but they only hid a few of them from view completely and still left a portion of her sternum exposed.

Her hipbones and collarbones had sunken in and disappeared, as had the bones of her arms and legs. Only those across her knuckles remained.

She no longer appeared ghastly, nor starved. Actually, her figure looked rather curved – almost hourglass – despite the Mavka being hunched forward in her four-legged monstrous form.

She'd eaten many humans, and now she'd only need to eat meat of any kind to thicken her body. Wolves, bears, fish, or birds – it wouldn't matter the creature.

Removing the satchel so it wouldn't clunk around and

spook her, he placed it on the ground as he lowered himself. He held up his hands submissively and crawled towards the wounded female with caution.

Hearing his approach, her white orbs flared bright red as she snapped her skull to the side and snarled in warning. She stumbled as she backed up while turning, then lowered herself into a defensive stance.

Jabez lowered himself further to appear smaller and non-threatening.

"Hey there," he gently cooed. "I mean you no harm."

He scraped at the ground to catch her attention and distract her, further showing he meant no danger. She was littered with injuries and had many arrows sticking from her. Although bloodied and matted, her fluffy fur was lifted in a highly agitated state.

He'd offer to remove those shafts, but he'd only do her more harm. She'd heal them soon enough, and once the night fell, her injuries would mend one by one. His lack of intervention would ensure he didn't needlessly heighten her pain.

"I know it hurts," he offered, shifting his weight to his hands in a crouched position to inch closer. "But you'll feel better soon. You will be smarter, more understanding, and I can teach you."

He could teach her how to speak, how to think, how to *survive*. Jabez could mentor her and hopefully make her compassionate to his goals. She would come to thank him.

He paused his approach when she parted her maw to threaten him more loudly, and he raised one of his brows.

*The inside of her mouth has formed flesh around where her cheeks would be.* There was no longer a gap between her jaws; jagged teeth made of flesh lined either side and filled in the hollow spaces, particularly behind her cheekbones. The appearance was similar to the teeth and mouth of a baby Mavka, and was a sign that she'd fully matured to fill in the crevices and gaps of her skull properly. Her maw now appeared more seamless and fully enclosed, so the inside of it would no longer drool or dry out.

He also noticed her antlers appeared... *smaller,* and had lost their fuzziness. He'd never seen a Mavka's horns change before.

*Most female creatures don't have horns or antlers.*

He'd been wondering why she had them, considering she was female, but he figured all Mavka needed some version of them. However, as she was the first female he'd seen, he hypothesised that the females of her kind went through an additional head evolution to compensate for the change.

Instead of being large and imposing, with four forks on each branch, her antlers had reshaped to only have one main stem and a fork just over the sides of her skull. They appeared daintier, blunter, and their shade of brown had even lightened.

Once she realised who he was, her head tilted and her orbs flashed dark yellow in curiosity. Then they turned a deep blue as she pulled out of her defensive stance. She sat on the ground and chittered at him while patting her body. She visibly tensed and hissed out pained breaths.

His ears flicked when he registered that her chitters weren't as high-pitched as they were before, like her voice had evolved into a more human tone.

She pointed at him as she released more.

"Yes, yes," he stated with a nod, placing his hand on his chest. "I know it's my fault."

She bashed at the ground as her orbs went bright red before pointing at him more sternly — from what he could tell. She was blaming him, justifiably, but Jabez had zero regrets. A few hours of pain against what she had surely gained was minor in the overall scheme of her life.

He'd also suffered very similar wounds, and in the same quantity, and they, too, had made him stronger. Life was cruel, merciless even, but each fight, each adversity he'd faced had strengthened him, as it would her. Nothing was gifted without sacrifice, and he'd saved her *days* of pain over the course of what would be decades, if not centuries, by shoving it all into one night.

He was the embodiment of her reflection, just with healed wounds, both inside and out.

And if his theory about her already increased humanity due to her parentage was correct, then he doubted she'd need to do something like this ever again. He'd like to witness the difference between her and Merikh's development.

Jabez cocked his brow again when she pointed back the way she came and her orbs turned blue once more. Then she patted at herself, rubbing her muzzle and stomach, before pointing that way.

"Are you... *upset* you hurt those humans?" he wondered out loud.

*"Hhhurt? Up-set?"* she asked, her head tilting. *"Hhhumans?"*

He nodded. "Hurt," he answered, gesturing to her wounds before showing the one he'd given himself on his palm. "Human." He pointed towards the human village miles away.

*"No hurt humans!"* she shouted while wobbling forward on all fours with loud, agitated chitters.

A growl slipped from him at her sudden aggressive approach, and he backed up. He narrowed his eyes into a glare, and curled his lips back to flash his fangs in warning.

"There was no other way," he told her sternly. "You needed to hurt humans to grow."

*"No hurt!"* She reared back onto her hind legs like a rabbit, and Jabez stood as well, so he could quickly defend himself. *"No hurt!"*

Before he could put distance between them, her quick approach had him on the back foot – especially as he tripped backwards, refusing to take his eyes off her in case she darted for him. Then, for a single moment, life blacked out when she backhanded him hard across the face. Sent twirling through the air, he jolted back to reality when he crashed into a nearby tree trunk.

White dots and black lightning streaked across his swimming vision. "Fuck," he spat.

He attempted to get to his hands and knees as dizziness threatened to overcome him, but his legs refused to move. With his jaw dislocated from the power of her smack, he tried to reset it as he struggled to rise.

The *crack* that had sounded midway through his back when he'd slammed against the tree, coupled with the pain and immobility, meant she'd broken his fucking spine. He had the use of his arms, but his legs were unresponsive.

*Wretched Mavka and their fucking strength.* No creature should be this strong, and he'd always hated that they were more formidable than him.

A groan rolled out of him when she grabbed one of his horns, and as she lifted him off the ground by it, his body dragged across the rough dirt. She held him far enough away that he could do little more than hang there, his numb legs uselessly swaying.

She roared at him, and he answered her with his own enraged one, causing the veins and muscles in his neck to bulge.

Then she patted her chest while uselessly chittering at him like he had any idea about what she was saying! With his jaw still out of its socket, he could do little more than belt out his anger and clench his fists with quaking arms.

That was until glittering teal magic swirled around them and his wounds mended. She whimpered as she took on his injuries, as if she was trying to prove something to him.

She pointed back towards the human village, then him, then her wounds. Her knees shook, but her spine appeared to be mostly intact, unlike his had been.

"You want to be a healer of the world? Of humans?" A deadened laugh broke out of him. "You're a fucking Mavka! You're a monster, just like me!"

He kicked his now working legs to separate from her. His attempt only angered her, and she swung her arm to slam his body against the ground.

Some things snapped, perhaps a rib and his collar bone, but Jabez merely chuckled despite the pain. He twisted until his legs wound up her arm, and he turned her onto her back. She squealed when he bit into her forearm to make her release his horn.

The moment he freed himself, he lowered to a crouched stance, ready to sprint as he backed up from her. He wheezed against the agony in his torso, yet spat her blood to the side with a feral grin.

She slammed her clawed hands against the ground as she rose into a four-legged position and parted her maw menacingly. Jabez curled his lips back to reveal his fangs and gave her a monstrous, hissing roar. He bellowed it from deep in his chest, engaging his diaphragm and putting all his might into it until it sounded beastly and utterly inhuman.

Her head reared back in surprise, before she sunk lower with another growl coming from her. He stood with a stomp forward and roared again, and she backed up even more.

She was being surprisingly submissive.

"Not everyone is worth saving," he snarled out. "Not humans, nor I. We are *not* worth your fucking pity." He bashed his arm against the trunk next to him before raking his claws over it to show her he had his own to defend himself with. "So fight me, or fuck off if you don't want my damn help."

If she wanted to be a benevolent spirit upon the world, then she wasn't the companion for him. He'd long ago lost the innocence and ignorance to be kind. Nothing deserved saving. Everything and everyone could burn for all he cared! Not in retribution for the wrongdoings done against him, but as penance for their vileness, for the hate and malice in their hearts.

For their greed and selfishness.

When the Mavka did nothing but step to the side to circle him, forcing him to mirror her actions, he dared to step closer with a menacing growl bubbling up his throat. She might be bigger than him, stronger than him, faster than him, but he had *centuries* of intelligence on her.

Jabez was cunning, and the only way he'd survive this was if she made the first move. He would flee, as he'd already proven he was slippery to keep ahold of.

At his wordless threat, she snapped her jaws at him, making a sharp clipping sound, before thumping one of her hind legs. She was backing down, so he towered his height above her lowered stance while keeping a safe distance.

He warded her back like he might a bear.

She thumped a back leg while snapping her jaws again, but otherwise continued to retreat.

Apparently she didn't wish to fight, and she appeared to have better control over her anger than most Mavka. He refused to let his eyes off her reddened orbs and continued to release his own rumbling growl. Even when she faded from sight, he refused to stop his warning, but he did retreat slowly from the area so as to not stir the desire to hunt in her.

Only when everything grew silent did he quieten.

Letting out an annoyed, rolling huff, he looked up at the moonlight glittering through the canopy of leaves. A small chuckle fell from him as his accelerated heart slowed its adrenaline-filled sprint.

*Well, that could have ended badly.*

After going back to find his belongings he'd placed down, he rubbed at his injured chest. Jabez noticed the bruises already blotting around his right collarbone and side. Hissing in a breath of pain, he wheezed and grunted, as he swiped up his satchel and headed towards the lake.

As annoyed as he was about his plan to manipulate this Mavka failing so soon, and how he'd wasted an entire night essentially assisting her, he let it go. There was little he could do to change it, as she likely hated him now, and he wouldn't waste energy on being angered over such a loss. He'd merely come up with a new plan.

He also considered it payment for saving his life.

*Perhaps I can head to the village of Demons.* He cupped his jaw as he thought about what he could do there. *I left a mana stone beneath the village. I can probably use it to my advantage.* It was better than wandering the forest with no direction until he figured out what he truly wanted to do.

*Without my magic, I can't face the Demons.* Not on Earth and definitely not in Nyl'theria – the Elven realm. If they knew he was weak, they wouldn't waste any time before tearing him apart to gain from eating his corpse. It was part of the reason he'd stolen the cloak to hide his identity, although warmth was the main purpose. *I'll have to ensure I remain unnoticed until I reach the outskirts of the village.*

At the lake, Jabez drank from the water before removing his pants and slipping in to bathe. Then, soaking wet and sitting on the grass, he pulled out all his stolen supplies and assessed what he'd gathered as he let himself air dry.

Once he was no longer dripping water, he donned the large tunic designed for an overweight man, finding it loose around his narrow waist. It fit across his wide, muscled shoulders, and the extra room meant it covered his entire torso past his waistline. It was a little short for his arms, so he rolled up the sleeves to just before where his forearm muscles started to bulge.

Already he felt warmer, and sitting in the heat of the moonlight felt sublime. Unlike most Demons, Jabez could not only withstand the light, but it gave him warmth. Basking in it as it shone upon his back, he pulled his ruined mauve pants closer and used the scissors he'd taken to cut the fabric off both legs just below the knees, so they were even.

He also grabbed the breeches he'd stolen and stood so he could see where he'd need to cut them. The waist of the breeches barely came halfway up his muscular thighs. Jabez cut the sections that he needed, which were just below the knee joints to below his calves, and removed the tops and bottoms from them.

Then, he got to work sewing those leather sections to the bottoms of his loose pants so the calves were snug but would keep him warm during the cold winter months that were approaching.

He took no shoes; no human would have feet his size. Plus, as an Elf, despite lacking the ability to utilise his magic right now, anything that covered the soles of his feet was abhorrent to him. It would only make him clumsy, incapable of climbing trees, and he liked to feel the earth beneath him.

Fully dressed, he tested the cloak he'd stolen. It largely fit, as most cloaks were made to cover the human body like a blanket whilst travelling. The length only came to the top of his calves, whereas it likely would have been close to skimming the ground for a human.

The hood was plain, but it was large enough to cover his head even with his horns being in the way.

He fixed the black material he'd stolen to the bottom of the cloak so it would fall to his ankles and shield his feet from the sun during his travels. Once he was done, he fitted the cloak around his body and glanced at the panel of fur now covering his shoulders, noting that it made him remarkably warmer.

Lastly, he donned a leather holster he'd stolen and shoved

the dagger he'd taken from a deceased soldier into it. As much as he preferred to use his hands and claws, a dagger would be useful for activities outside of combat.

Crouching, he selected an apple he'd taken from a produce store and bit into it. He wiggled his nose at the sweet taste, but it was otherwise suitable to curb the worst of his hunger. As he ate, he checked on the remaining items: a water sack he'd already filled, a razor and hairbrush to groom himself, and the three books he'd taken.

He considered tossing the books into the water, as he no longer needed learning material for the Mavka, but decided against it. *Should I be bored in my travels, something to read may be entertaining.*

Tsking at himself, he shoved everything back into his satchel and strapped it across his torso for safekeeping. Then he manoeuvred to lie in the concave of a tree trunk and wrapped himself in the cloak until not a bit of his skin was revealed.

Intending to sleep before he walked to the Demons' village, he didn't wish to awake prematurely due to the sunlight burning him. The cloak and shade of this very tree would protect him.

The moment he closed his eyes against the lightening night sky, a branch snapping in the distance had him flinging them open. He glared at nothingness as he listened.

The female Mavka, now mostly healed, stamped her way into the area on all fours. Jabez pulled back his hood to properly inspect her approach, noting her orbs were a soft red – annoyed, but not enraged. Which meant safe-*ish*.

She came right to his huddled form, and he cocked a brow.

"Come to apologise, have you?" he sneered mockingly. He shooed her by waving a single hand dismissively. "I have no interest in pointlessness. I'm no longer willing to be your little pet."

With a gentle growl, she reached out quicker than he could dodge her. Gripping one of his horns, she yanked him across the ground on his back as she walked away from the clearing.

Rolling his eyes as he was dragged away, Jabez sighed. *Guess I don't have a say in the matter.*

A malicious grin lifted into his features seconds later.
*A pet I'll be, then.*

With a glow of teal flaming at the edges of her clear vision, NoName blocked the entrance to her home with her back.

The area was small, but she didn't mind. She only ever came in here to hide and sleep. Although her antlers occasionally became tangled with the roots in the ceiling, she'd carved herself out enough room to be comfortable some time ago.

It was her home, and a place where she felt safest.

She often travelled among the forest of her territory, unsure and not ready to further explore. Beyond her territory were *humans*, as she'd learned what the furless creatures were called, and she preferred to avoid them.

Despite already learning that some humans were unkind, most had smelt of fear and ran from her presence. Even though her intelligence had been low, she'd already summarised she was a frightening and horrible being who made *all* creatures wary, even those with sharp fangs.

She was unwelcome.

NoName lacked the words to articulate what she wanted. Her mind was empty except for flashes of images, the echoes of scents, and the emotional changes she experienced – like her chest aching, or her stomach twisting.

And, up until the night before, her mind had felt spacious and grainy. Now, it swirled with an overload of information she couldn't fathom, and yet was strengthened by it. It felt right, like she'd merely been sleeping all this time and had fully awoken from a distant haze.

NoName chittered grumbles to herself, upset that the sleeping male before her showed her this. The edges of her sight flickered with orange due to this gross, yucky emotion in her chest, one that radiated with a burning sensation. She didn't like the way her actions had caused so much death, and she wished she could take it back. She also hated how she was thankful for these changes, as she felt more in tune with herself physically, mentally, emotionally, and even spiritually.

NoName didn't want to be a malicious being. From the moment she found an injured animal and healed it because she had this desire to *save* it, her anger and hunger gave way to compassion. She'd heard its cries, understood its pain, and wanted to take that away – not knowing she would be forced to bear the creature's wounds.

Since she had this power, she thought this might have been her purpose: to heal.

She had no idea who she was, what she was, where she was, or what she was meant to be doing. She grasped onto the first thing that gave her meaning other than being a destroyer and clung to it fervently.

She wanted to protect. She also didn't want to be... alone.

Confused, she constantly sought guidance. Yet, she'd been rejected by the humans, other furry creatures, by prey and predator alike. No one wanted her.

Having met someone she thought may be of her own kind over a moon cycle ago, it deepened her desire to learn and understand. How did that male come to be in her territory or how did he even come to *exist?* Why was his *human* companion willing to go to him, but refused to remain with NoName? Why was she not better and safer when she had healing hands?

So many questions, and no answers to be found in the dirt she often scratched at.

She wondered if this strange male creature may be of help.

Despite her anger towards him, and how she wished to bash his head in with a single slam for inciting violence within her, he had been calm.

He hadn't run away from her at the first chance he'd gotten, nor had he smelt of fear. Already he guided her into understanding a few needs, such as producing a foul-scented liquid from some kind of strange, dangling thing between his legs. He also showed her that he needed to consume liquid, whereas she did not, and that he required sustenance, which meant at times he hunted and killed creatures, even if she didn't like that.

She'd try to change that about him.

If she did not need to eat, and could, mostly, withstand her hunger, then he could do so as well.

As much as NoName wanted to chase him off her territory for making her harm others, his cruel actions in that large human dwelling place had showed her one thing: he knew her kind.

He knew eating humans increased her weight and intelligence when she hadn't. At least once she'd calmed down, she assumed he did. Why else would he have led her there to cause destruction? From what she could tell, he hadn't partaken in bloodshed.

Then again, it was hard to truly remember what had happened.

Her gaze swept over him as he lay before her. Even though he faced her, the large brown cloth he was wrapped in covered him from head to ankle. The hood of it rested over his face to hide it, and she could barely peek at the corner of his mouth and his chin.

He smelt and looked different from the humans.

His eyes were a deep red, similar to the bright red of the void-like creatures who were mean and violent to her. He'd shown he had fangs and claws like them, and horns on his head like a few of them. Yet his skin was a deep brown, and he appeared to be tall and fully formed. His ears were pointed, which was another difference to every humanoid creature she'd seen, but it did make her wonder if perhaps he was like the graceful creatures she'd seen in the forest, since they, too, had horns and pointy ears.

He did have fur on his body like an animal, although it was minimal. She often noted the oddly long amount of it on top of his head. It was short everywhere else, and mostly focused between his legs and under his arms.

Then again, the humans had these fur patterns as well.

These were confusing questions she didn't know the answer to. Would he give them to her? She hoped he would. She would force him to.

NoName thought back to a week ago, although those memories were murky now.

She'd seen a bright, shiny light in the distance, and had

instantly been drawn to it. The mean creatures in the misty forest of a canyon had seemingly run from the light, whereas NoName felt the desire to hunt it, keep it, and treasure it. She wanted to put that light in her home, hoping it would be soothing and warm.

Once she started her path, she kept running towards it, upset when it disappeared, but excited to find it. She never would have guessed she'd meet this male in her search for it.

When she scented the trickles of blood, she'd blocked her nose and tried to find the source. Her healing hands could aid the creature, and since it didn't smell the same as the void-like ones, she wanted to show it kindness in a place it may not have experienced any.

When she saw the male's condition, she knew she would be unable to save him within the centre of the misty forest. He'd been missing limbs, barely conscious, and had burns on him like she once had from humans shoving flames against her flesh. Her healing hands would render her incapable of protecting him while she aided him, so she brought him home, hoping he'd stay.

From the very beginning, she'd been able to see a strange coldness in his eyes. He had a stare that came across as unfeeling, uncaring, and nonchalant.

What mattered was that he hadn't looked at her with fear or disdain, even when he'd been naughty.

She lifted her wrist to check on the *bite* wound he'd given her. Yes, naughty creature. She would make sure he didn't do that again, otherwise she could incidentally bite back.

Her sight slipped back to him.

She never would've known he could be so vicious had he not hurt her. Nor would she have known he was a rather strong being. He was obviously very fast, as he'd evaded her many times thus far.

*No hurt,* she thought, with the very limited words she now knew. *No hurt human. No hurt...* she didn't know what to call him.

She understood that their genders were different, as the scent and pheromones he gave off were somewhat similar to the humans with dangly things between their legs. She knew she was female, although she didn't have the names or words for any of this.

She was also smart enough to understand they were different creatures. He didn't smell like her kind, a void-like creature, a human, or an animal. He was a weird thing, who was rather large in height and mass – he constantly towered over her four-legged form.

Perhaps he was one of the few beings who could survive with her. Smart enough to remain indifferent to her moods and be obedient, fast enough to evade her, and strong enough to defend himself when she was angry or enraged.

NoName cupped her bony forehead as blue entered her sight.

She worried she would fail and hurt this male like everything she'd met in the past and accidentally killed.

She was selfish enough to not let him go.

Was that wrong? She didn't want it to be, but trapping him didn't feel good. The human female with bright-orange hair, who had longed to be with the other of NoName's kind, had wanted freedom.

Why did everything want to leave her?

If he tried to escape, she already mourned the loss, knowing his disappearance would hurt her chest with a burning ache. Killing him would make her feel horrible inside. She didn't want to be alone, and she wished she knew how to make the pangs of sadness evaporate.

Her blue sight transformed to its usual teal but darker – possessiveness and sadness all rolled into one. She wanted to keep him, but it felt wrong to do so. She was lonely and scared in a world she didn't know how to navigate or even communicate with.

The male shifted, which made her lower her palm from her bony snout to watch him.

He raised the arm he wasn't lying on, used two clawed fingers to lift the flap of his hood, and red eyes greeted her teal orbs. His gaze was lax and came across as unfeeling, like usual.

NoName shifted under the callous weight of it.

"Thought I might wake to you staring at me," he grumbled,

despite her not understanding a word of what he said.

She tilted her head at him for his incomprehensible words, taking in that his tone was at least calm and quiet. His voice was deeper than normal and had a groggy hint to it.

And although she didn't know his words for any of the body parts in his language, she keenly observed the male creature as he moved around inside her burrow.

He sat up and crossed his legs, positioned his back straight, and stretched by lifting his shoulders up and back, which arched his torso forward. His face twitched as though he found it uncomfortable before leaning his head one way and then the next until cracks sounded.

Then he pushed back the material covering his head, revealing the long flowing fur upon it. On the left side, a bald patch formed a semi-circle around his pointed ear. It started from the ridge above his temple and followed it to the nape of his neck.

From memory, it hadn't been so rounded or smooth before, as if he'd somehow reshaped it in their time apart. She also noticed earlier that he'd clothed his torso, and changed his leg coverings so they no longer looked like dirty, torn rags.

NoName chittered at him, wanting to compliment these changes since he obviously preferred them.

Was he a pretty male? She'd like to think so, not that she truly had anything to compare him to. She also thought little creatures were cute.

The male pulled his bag from where he'd been laying his head upon it and obtained some kind of sack. He drank from it, and the familiar smell of the same wet substance she fell into tingled in her nose hole.

Easily impressed by the existence of such an item, she chittered again at the ingeniousness of ferrying one's own liquid.

Once he was done, he laid the sack down and placed his hands on his legs. He raised the strip of face fur above his eye, and she tightened her back against his only possible way out, with her orbs reddening in annoyance. She wouldn't let him leave, and she had no intention of being tricked again due to him being naughty.

"Alright, Mavka. Let us start your lessons," he stated calmly. Then he pointed to his chest. "Me." He pointed to her. "You."

He only needed to repeat it once before she got the idea, and her small tail tuft swayed in joy. He was teaching her more words! Did that mean he didn't intend to leave? She sincerely hoped so.

She pointed at him. "Me," she repeated, before pointing at herself. "You."

Her tail swayed faster when he let out a small chuffing noise, as the sound was so light and warm that she wanted it to mean something good.

"No," he answered with a shake of his head, instantly making her shoulders drop.

She knew what *no* meant: a denial.

He leaned closer to grab her wrist. NoName instantly let out a growl, her orbs reddening, and evaded his touch. She refused to be tricked again.

Yet, despite her warning, he grabbed her! He curled her fingers, no matter how loudly she warned him back, and tugged her arm, forcing her to point at her own chest.

"Me," he stated, before turning her hand to point at him. "You."

Her growls softened, and she tilted her head, puzzled.

He made her point at herself, while he did so to his own chest. He repeated the word 'me' before making them point at each other with the word 'you' echoing from his lips.

Understanding dawned. When he released her, she repeated what he'd shown her, and this time he nodded.

"Yes. That's correct." He pointed to his chest once more. "Me, Jabez." He pointed to her, then both white fur strips over his eyes drew inwards in obvious displeasure. "Well, shit. I forgot I don't know your name. I doubt you know it either."

He folded his arms and tapped against his thick biceps with his mouth flattened in thought. He mumbled to himself, "I named Merikh, but I had a pretty deep understanding of who he was before I did. He was an angry fucker, always looking to destroy something."

He continued to tap his arm as his two lines of face fur drew together further and his hard eyes narrowed.

"How about... Zylah? Although on Earth it means shadow or shade, there's an Elvish flower in Nyl'theria spelt similarly that glows black in the sun and white at night, but its pollen stem changes colour depending on the season." Then he cupped his jaw and tapped the side of his mouth. "It's quite toxic and exotic. You're a female Mavka, so I think that is rather fitting."

All of his useless chattering was completely misunderstood as nothing but him flapping his mouth open and shut while letting out noisy air. NoName twisted her head constantly, but she couldn't make out his tone amongst all his grumbles and displeased expressions.

"Fuck it." The male then pointed to himself once more. "Me, Jabez – or Jabeziryth, if we wish to get technical and use my full Elvish name." Then he pointed to her. "You, Zylah. *Zai-luh.*"

Then, thinking better of it, he gingerly grabbed her wrist and made her point to herself. He repeated four words constantly – me, you, Jabez, and Zylah – until they were solidified within her mind.

She pointed to herself, and repeated in a grainy, hissy voice, *"Zylah."*

"Yes. Name. Your name is now Zylah." The corners of his lips quirked, before he let out a soft chuckle. "See? I knew giving you all that humanity would benefit you. If you don't end up liking the name, we can always change it later."

Staring down at her finger, she kept it pointed at the long white bone in the middle of her chest as she repeated the *name* he'd given her. Her orbs turned bright yellow in joy, and her tail swayed along with them. She didn't even know something like this existed and was utterly thrilled.

"Alright, Zylah," Jabez stated, instantly making her gaze lift to him in recognition, finding that his red eyes appeared softer than they did moments ago.

Bouncing forward in excitement, understanding that he was calling to her, she exclaimed, *"Me Zylah!"*

Her anger in him subsided completely, and she was pleased that she not only saved him but also went back to get him after their argument. She was given a true sense of self-identity, one which she could use to interact with the world.

She released chitters of thanks, her tummy feeling all fluffy and warm, and they only grew stronger when he made that pleasant chuffing sound at her for it.

"Yes. You, Zylah. Now, let's learn what body parts are. Should we start with toes or face?"

She tried to decipher what his gaze meant. How it crinkled the corners of his eyes and tops of his cheeks, as the sides of his mouth curled upwards. Even though the motion bared his fangs at her a little through a small gap, she didn't find it threatening when it was accompanied by the softness in the rest of his expression.

Her heart even sped up a little, and she found herself wanting to get closer to him. It looked positive, like a good thing, and the fact he was shining it at her felt nice.

*Yes. Zylah no hurt Jabez.*

# SIX

Walking around in the shade of dawn, Zylah followed behind the male quite closely.

In the past two days, she'd been learning all sorts of things from him. What he was, although she didn't quite understand what an Elf was, but now understood he was different from a human. She also learned he was half of one of those void-like, cruel creatures called *Demons*.

She'd been a little put off discovering that, as she didn't really like those ugly monsters. They were mean, and they'd bitten and scratched at Zylah unprovoked in the past. She'd had many fights with them.

Her feelings were quickly put at ease as he moved onto other subjects, buried by the knowledge he shared with her. Every minute of every hour, he taught her a new word. Whether it be *root*, like what dangled from the ceiling of her home, or *burrow*, which was the style of home she had.

In the dark of night, Jabez had managed to convince her to let him leave – supervised, of course. Zylah didn't plan to let him out of her sight, as he'd proven he was a naughty Elf-Demon male who played tricks.

Once they were outside, he taught her about the sky, the world, and gave basic names for everything. Tree, grass, moss, moon, stars, lake, water, and so much more.

Today, now that she was letting him venture further – her trust in him had grown – he was teaching her specifics.

As he crouched down low into a patch of grass, she

inspected the clothing he wore. She now knew the names of the various items, as well as their *colours*.

The black material attached to the bottom of his brown cloak crimped around the backs of his heels, while the plain hood rested between his shoulder blades. Since he'd begun to wear it, and the cream tunic underneath, he stopped shivering as much. He appeared to be a cold creature, which made sense since he lacked *hair* on most of his body, unlike Zylah, who was covered in sleek black fur.

His mauve pants were tight around his knees as he parted grass stalks to better reveal a yellow plant in the ground. The black leather around his calves creaked with a strain over his taut, bulky muscles. Wayward strands of his long, straight white hair slipped forward to hang down his broad chest, while his ears twitched, making the golden earrings dangling from them glimmer. A streak of moonlight glinted and sparkled off the singular bangle around his left biceps and right ankle.

Zylah was happy to know what most of these things were, and momentarily looked down at her claws as she subtly wiggled her fingers. To understand her own body had been utterly enlightening, and she was growing more beholden to the male.

"Dandelion," Jabez stated quietly, plucking the small yellow flower. Still crouched, he turned and lifted his dark-red eyes up when showing it to her.

*"Dandelion flower?"* Zylah asked, crouching next to him, and she purposefully brushed her shoulder against his.

"Yes, correct. This flower's name is dandelion."

Even though she didn't understand the structure of his sentence, the fact he continued to speak to her as though she did meant she was piecing it together in her mind. The language was complex. She often made mistakes, but he *gently* interrupted her responses to correct her.

Although that crushed her confidence, she knew he had good intentions behind making her feel this way. This was a step in her development of *talking*, as he put it. She liked the clarity it brought to her mind, although much of what remained was a jumble of pictures rather than words. With Jabez's help, that would fade and her abilities would grow, and she was appreciative of that.

Still low to the ground, he leaned on one hand and shuffled forward to obtain a stick of leaves. She came closer to inspect it along with him.

*"Leaf branch,"* Zylah stated confidently.

For some reason, he quietly chuckled at that – which instantly had her shoulders turning inwards self-consciously. She'd learned what chuckling was by asking him when he produced such a pleasant sound. She did this often, pointing at him and making him explain until she understood something he said or did.

"Branch," he stated, before gesturing to the small, bushy deep-red leaves. "Leaves." Then he raised his hand towards the tree beside them. "Claret Ash tree."

Just as he went to place the branch back on the ground, no doubt to show her something new or further explain something in better detail, she picked it up. It appeared so tiny and delicate between her thick fingers and sharp, curved black claws.

*"Red,"* she stated, before she cupped the side of her head in deep thought.

He paused and waited for her to attempt to state what she wanted, which she couldn't always do. She appreciated that he never rushed her.

*"How red?"*

*"Why* red?" he asked, raising a singular white brow.

Her orbs flickered a reddish pink, and she chittered quietly.

"Embarrassment," he stated, pointing to the corner of his eye. "This colour means embarrassment or shame. Well, that's what I'm assuming, at least – if all you Mavka have the same orb colour shifts."

*Embarrassment? Shame?* That's what this tight emotion constricting her chest was called? She hated this feeling. It always made her want to squirm.

The colour deepened until he placed a warm hand on her shoulder. Her gaze had dropped to the ground, but she lifted it upon his touch. He didn't do so often, but she liked how big and warm his palm was.

"Don't worry, you'll get it."

His eyes bore into her orbs. There was a cold sharpness to them, as though they reflected a hard pain he couldn't seem to shed, but she noted it was softer than when they first met. Although she didn't know the word yet, to her his eyes screamed patience. She didn't think he'd be helping her otherwise.

Then, as if to demonstrate this, he gingerly took the stick from her. "Why is this red?"

*"Green,"* she stated, looking up at the rest of the tree that was predominantly red with a mixture of yellow, orange, and a touch of green.

"Yes, usually it's green," he stated. Then he cupped his jaw as he plonked himself on his arse and crossed his legs. "Fuck. How the hell am I supposed to explain something as complex as seasons? It's not like I can just change them to show you each one."

Zylah sat down as well. When Jabez rambled like this, he always attempted to explain something – even if it wasn't certain she would ever understand. But she liked his deep, honeyed voice, and the way it lulled her mind and had her insides fluttering – she could listen to him endlessly.

Jabez obtained a new stick, one barren of leaves, and drew into a patch of dew-wetted dirt. He carved four lines before quickly getting up. He inspected the *Claret Ash* tree and then climbed it to obtain a branch that still had green leaves.

He laid it next to the first line and placed the yellow-leafed one next to the second line, then removed the leaves from another branch and placed it next to the third. Lastly, he obtained some flowers and put them on the last line.

He started with the barren stick and showed it to her. "White," he said, before making his hands trickle through the air. He'd shown her this motion when referencing rain. He hugged himself and purposefully shivered. "White. Cold."

Zylah understood, and she perked up, lifting her skull higher. *"White rain?"*

He chuckled. "You got that fast. Snow. White rain is called snow." In response, Zylah nodded as if she understood – which she did, surprisingly. He placed the stick on the ground. "Winter. Snow happens in winter."

He moved onto the next branch.

"Flowers bloom." He picked up the flower and fisted his other hand to show a bulb. He opened it. "Bloom." To make sure she comprehended, he placed the flower in his fist and pushed it out as if it was growing. Then he referenced all around them. "Flowers bloom everywhere." He picked up the barren stick and then the green-leafed one. "Leaves bloom, green. Spring."

She quickly learned that summer was when the trees all turned green again. She also learned what fire was called, and that it was hot, as he used colours and the term "ouch" when touching it. She'd had a lot of experience with that.

Then finally, he showed her the last branch with the yellow leaves. "Autumn. Leaves fall." He plucked them one by one while showing her what fall meant.

Although this had been a rather slow and lengthy conversation, it showed her the world rotated on a cycle. She'd seen these things and had witnessed the changes. She somehow felt closer to the land around her, and even more at peace within her place among it.

*"Seasons?"* she asked, peeking at him before pointing at each one. *"Summer, autumn, winter, spring?"*

His sharp, fanged teeth flashed at her when the corners of his lips curled. "Excellent. Good, Zylah. Yes."

A small part of her melted under the compliments and his smile, and her chest stung in a wondrous way. For a male who had such dangerous features, and often looked at the world coldly, he'd been rather kind to Zylah.

Slyly and hoping to be unnoticed, she leaned a little closer to steal a sniff of his cheek, before shuddering as she pulled back. She didn't know the name of his scents, but with the way they filled up her home, she knew she enjoyed them. They were masculine, but light and earthy, like the surrounding forest.

He smelt different, like he'd come from a faraway world to bless them with his scent and presence.

Whether he ignored what she'd done or hadn't noticed it, Jabez continued his explanation and circled all the seasons with a stick.

"A year." He did so again, repeating the action. "One year." He put up a single finger before doing it one last time.

He explained that these seasons happened repeatedly, which she, of course, knew. Zylah just didn't know why. She figured 'a year' was what it was called.

She looked forward to the day they could have a proper conversation and she would understand him better.

She'd like to learn who he really was, where he'd come from, and why she'd found him beneath a bunch of stone. Who was Jabez, and why had she never met another creature like him?

Zylah studied the sharp clip of his smooth jaw, his high cheeks, his stern brow, and deep-brown skin. Her gaze followed the strong line of his nose, and then his full lips that hid sharp razors behind them. Her focus flicked up to his long, pointed ears – a feature she'd only seen on animals and not humans – before looking over his black horns.

She liked his horns a lot, as well as his *nails* that appeared like small claws. These were features they shared, and it somehow made her feel closer to him.

What she adored most was that he seemed to... *understand* her, like he'd met another of her kind before. Had he befriended them? If he'd been this attentive in the past, she wondered why they'd left his side at all.

He'd been rather patient in her learning, and so informative that she had hope they would soon be true companions. She wanted to voice how she felt, what she needed, and see if perhaps he knew what her true purpose was.

Why was she here? Why had she only ever met one other *Mavka*, as he called her? The humans called her Duskwalker. She wanted to know why she had so many names, and what their meanings were.

Her orbs shifted to bright yellow when he lifted his eyes, tipped with white lashes, to her skull. He didn't grin, didn't smile, but he had a dark intensity to his gaze that always made her feel uncomfortable in the strangest, but oddly remarkable, way.

Zylah liked having his eyes on her, like he was capable of seeing past the borders of her flesh and her inability to communicate, and truly *see* her. They pierced so deep.

She chittered happily at him, and a white brow raised back. She came a little closer, wanting to feel his heat she'd only ever felt briefly or get a stronger draw of his scent. To just be near his presence even more.

He looked away too soon, sighing as he did.

"You'll figure it out eventually," he stated, disappointing her when he stood and moved away. He looked towards the forest. "I'll take us to the lake again. I also want to teach you how to transform into your more humanoid form like other Mavka."

He continued their lesson along the way, showing her different plants while giving her their proper names. He even managed to have them sneak up on a small creature and capture it.

He called it a rabbit.

He directed her to block her nose with earth to hide its scent before he grossly pulled it apart. Although she didn't like the needless death, and instantly grew sour at him for it, she accepted it. Zylah grumbled the entire time, as he showed her its bones, its blood, and its different insides while explaining it all to her.

She learned in that lesson what an animal was, what kind it was, and...

That her skull matched this creature's.

It felt wrong to kill it.

With his eyes closed, his body relaxed, and his mind dozy, Jabez wrinkled and wiggled his nose against the musk surrounding him.

For quite a number of days, the mixture of Zylah's surprisingly pleasant scent – a rather gentle tangle of jasmine and violets – had tamped down the wet dirt, clay, tree roots, and mould.

Once he identified what her particular scent was made up of, his mind put it to the side, leaving the rest strong in his senses.

His sense of smell wasn't as good as a Mavka, and he thought it may even be weaker than most Demons, but it was still heightened in comparison to humans.

And he was covered in the grime of her home. It clung to his cloak he constantly wrapped around his body protectively. He felt like a burrowing animal, cowering in some pathetic hole in the ground like a mouse.

But it was more than that. Deeper, even.

Once more, his nose wrinkled, and he cringed at the choking memories that rose up from the depths of his mind. Memories of a time he'd much rather forget and always struggled to do so.

A time and place that had greatly shaped who he had become, and it had been hundreds of Earth years since he'd experienced it.

Yet, in the span of an Elf's life, it was only twenty-one years ago, almost twenty-two. Then again, to an eleven-year-old, who had been trapped for almost six Elvish years, the passage of time had felt both vast and constricting.

Although his *prison* hadn't been as dark as this burrow, the shadows had been deep. A green light in the centre of a round room ensured he'd been given plenty of light, *protecting* him from the sun.

He hadn't appreciated that false light then, and never grew fond of it. As much as he understood the Elysians – the Elvish – had thought he'd prefer it, considering he burned within minutes under the three suns in Nyl'theria, he'd missed their warmth while he rested in the shade. He'd missed the way they twinkled into a room and cast mesmerising fractals from every reflection.

The bars shielding him had been made of mere silver, gold, and bronze, but they weren't what truly kept him from bending them to escape. No, the magical reinforcements kept him caged and seething in his confinements.

At first, all he'd smelt was the rock that surrounded him and his own scent, as he was alone for the first three years. But, as he grew older, and his senses sharpened, the more he'd been able to smell beyond his cell.

The scent of dirt that lay just beyond the metres-thick rock.

The roots of the gigantic central tree he'd once called home. The smell of mould in the earth, the decay as insects followed the cycle of life.

These things would one day become his salvation, but for many years, they were choking. They'd suffocated him, reminding him that he was deep beneath the ground. Hidden away from everyone, to protect everyone else from *him*.

Forgotten by all.

And lost within himself.

He'd been dying on the inside the longer he lingered alone, except for the daily distraction of food. They also supplied him with various materials over time that they'd one day *regret* giving him.

As much as Jabez understood *why* they'd imprisoned him, he couldn't deny how cruel it had been. They hadn't denied it either and took no action to change his situation. Then again, had he really given them the chance?

A young Jabez had been angry after so long. He'd been filling with spite, the craze of his lonely thoughts, and the depression and anguish after being confined in such a small space. When their stupid, lame gazes turned sympathetic, his vengeance only grew. His mind deepened into chaos, and his desire to listen to their voices waned.

Until other Demons were placed in cells by his side. Jabez had, in some way, reverted to a more Demon-like temperament. Come near, and he'd bite. If they weren't close, he'd claw the air through his bars to tear at their skin for a speck of blood they continued to starve him of. Speak to him, and they'd receive obscenities in return.

That was only when he was coherent, but he often wasn't. The starvation of nutrients he lacked turned him rabid, and the Elves could only speak with him after they muzzled him and tied him down to give him blood infusions. Otherwise, the scent of their bodies, their blood and meat, sent him into a frenzy.

He always felt pitiful afterwards.

All the while, they gifted him books, let him learn, *thinking* his magic was tame. That he, as a half-blooded Elf, didn't have strong capabilities. That the rock and re-enforcements around him kept him pinned as much as his broken will.

The first thing he'd done with his magic was erase the smell of dirt, to hide and shield from it so he didn't have to feel like a filthy creature. He suppressed the anguish and betrayal that stung at his entire being from when he'd first been placed in his prison, his cell, his glorified *cage*.

The scent of wet dirt somehow always brought him back to those first few years. He'd hated the smell when he first escaped and would rather step into the heat of burning ash than scent it. But as he grew older, and his mind dulled the sharpness of the memories from his youth, the smell of dirt eventually just became a mundane odour. Until it bothered him no more.

Only to drown him tenfold when he'd been buried alive by a rather devious bitch covered in a cloak of feathers, who he'd been spending decades trying to strangle.

Then, once more, he'd learned to erase his emotional attachment.

But, as he lay beneath the ground in Zylah's burrow, night after night, with the smell of fresh roots dangling above him, it became harder to ignore.

Half asleep, he attempted to shift one way, before realising that made him face directly against an earthen wall. His stomach knotted, his chest tightened, and his lungs stung. The scent clung to him even when he rolled over towards the small central space of Zylah's home.

The more the memories resurfaced, the colder his features became, while sweat slicked his skin. His flesh tightened over his bones, like he was trapped and confined, and his throat threatened to close.

*Fuck!* Jabez roared in his mind as he shot to his hands and knees. He turned his face towards the exit, to Zylah fucking blocking it like she did every day. Sunlight peeked around her, and he shuddered and shooed her to the side.

"M-move, Zylah," he demanded, weakly turning to her. He moved into a crouched position so he could walk closer, and growled when she didn't get out of the way. "Jabez outside!"

At the booming depth of his voice, and the command he put in it, her orbs flashed white. She chittered nervously as she slipped out of the way, and Jabez tried to hide the panicked way he dived for the exit.

He hissed the moment sunlight cascaded onto his skin, and it continued to bathe him as he crawled through the tree roots shielding her burrow entrance. The autumn sunlight was hot against his flesh, threatening to sear him if he remained in it for too long. Had he been a full-blooded Demon, he'd have been burned to a crisp within seconds.

To get out of its heat, he skulked to the side and shoved his back against the trunk of a tree. The leaves shaded him just enough, with his cloak hiding him from dappled light, and he huffed through anxious breaths to steel himself.

*I thought I could do it... but I can't.* He couldn't handle being in her burrow any longer. *Even now, all I can smell is dirt.* It clung to him like a second skin, just to ruin his usually calm, sane mind. Well, he wasn't sure if he was truly sane.

He cupped the shaved side of his head and groaned at himself.

The deep, long scar there reminded him there was a distinct hole in his mind, one that blurred two worlds together. A journey he'd forgotten, and the actions of cruel people that only further twisted his heart with hate. But he could no longer decipher if they were... Elves... or humans.

*Fuck. It's been too long. I can barely remember shit.* Like most adults who were thirty-seven years old, his memories of his youth were... muddled. Accompanied by the fact that it was worsened for those who lived fifteen times the lifespan of a human, and that he had obtained a deep wound not long after escaping his confines, he... he no longer truly knew if his memories were clear.

And he hated being questioned about it.

*I don't remember anyone.* Not his wretched mother's face. Not his stepfather, or his surname. He didn't even remember if he had family beyond that, although, somewhere in the back of his mind, he thought he *might.*

What he did remember was the conference chamber filled with snobby, blurred faces belonging to the councilmembers who put him away. He remembered *why* they put him in his little cage.

Shifting nearby drew his attention, and he watched as Zylah exited her burrow. She struggled to leave, as her antlers, despite being much smaller than when he first met her, often tangled in the roots.

Palming his face and lifting a knee to rest his elbow on it, he waved at her to show he hadn't run off.

*We have to leave here.* He'd been hoping to hold out on his mind cracking so he could properly explain to her why they would be vacating her burrow. Even if he despised it, it was her home, and he already knew she had a deep attachment to it.

*I will have to trick her.* He'd take them on their daily walk, and she wouldn't know they just wouldn't return. However, he didn't wish to upset the Mavka, as he was trying to gain her trust despite their lack of communication.

*She's fucking smart, though.* Smarter than he ever could have given her credit for. *I was right. The further the lineage from Weldir, the quicker the Mavka can gain humanity.* Although her physical characteristics continued to be like every other Mavka.

In half the amount of humans it'd taken to feed Merikh, Zylah was shredding him in the learning battlefield. She learned words within the blink of an eye and was already trying to figure out how to string sentences together. Yesterday, when he'd realised just how quickly she was able to soak in information, he even taught her how to count to one hundred, and he hadn't needed to repeat himself.

He'd thought anything like counting or math would be out of the question for weeks, or until she ate more humans. At every turn, Jabez underestimated her wit.

*When I first met Merikh, he could talk, but it was like talking to an idiot.* Someone had been slowly teaching him, whether that be the Witch Owl, or perhaps even Weldir somehow sharing his voice. Regardless, *someone* had been guiding Merikh.

*But he'd eaten at least fifteen humans by that point, by my estimations, and then however many dozens after we met.*

Zylah had eaten around thirty humans due to him, and maybe two before that, but she just needed to know the words.

She needed knowledge, not more humanity. Once she understood something, it registered almost immediately.

*I had to go hunt down humans for him, and it still took forever for him to truly become intelligent.*

Already, Zylah knew how to utilise her magic to some degree, such as healing a wounded Jabez.

He chuckled behind his hand. *Merikh would hate being beaten by her.* He hated being beaten by anyone, just like Jabez.

Zylah slowly crawled her way closer, and he lowered his hand so he could watch her. She fidgeted nervously, scratching at herself in uncertainty, and he figured it was from how he'd left her home in a regretful panic.

*She figured out how to transform within seconds.* All he'd needed to do was show her she could retract her claws, and then she'd curiously wondered what else she could do.

*I think she's met another of her kind.* She must have in order to know she could stand on two legs, rather than just walk on her hands. *It takes others of her kind* years *to figure that out.*

Merikh may have been the first he'd truly ever come across, but he'd been watching and observing their kind for hundreds of years. He inspected his enemy to figure out their weaknesses – of which there were very few – and their strengths, which evolved constantly and varied between each animalistic feature.

Zylah had a mean jump and was shockingly fast – but not as fast as Orpheus. The feline-skulled Mavka was the best at climbing, whereas Merikh was the strongest, like a bear. The bat-skulled Mavka would have one day learned how to fly, had he not died. Each new characteristic shaped them to be different, yet all were remarkably strong beings.

Which made killing them difficult, despite him now knowing *how* to end the life of a Mavka.

He took in Zylah once more, noting that she'd changed to her more monstrous form for ease of moving around her small burrow. She refused to close the distance between them, and the white colour of her orbs revealed she was wary of him.

He was only just managing to settle his panted, anxious breaths. The gentle, cool wind chilled the sweat on his forehead and neck, while also drying him.

"Sorry to tell you this, but it's time to move on from here," he stated, momentarily lowering his gaze to the bright sunlight sparkling against the dewy grass just beyond his feet.

She tilted her head with her orbs returning to their natural teal.

*If the other Mavka don't watch out, Zylah will surpass them all in no time.*

# SEVEN

Walking in the sun, Jabez carefully adjusted the hood of his cloak to avoid the light. He peeked down at his bare feet and noted they were mostly shielded from the burning rays by the attached black hem of his cloak. A minor quick sting occasionally assaulted his toes when he stepped too far out of the shade.

The tall grass helped to hide the lower half of his body, and he lifted his gaze when they came to the top of a short hill. For a few hours, they'd been crossing meadows by following the shade. When they couldn't avoid the light as the sun reached its peak, he decided to just brave it.

Now that it was around midafternoon, he found the travel easier. He also basked in the heat, letting it soothe him – only because his cloak protected him.

They followed the top of the hill until a village within the distance became visible. Jabez pointed to it with his cloak covering his hand and explained what he could about everything. He wasn't familiar with the farming lands beside it, but he thought by the long stalks that a great deal of it was corn.

Zylah listened, taking in the new information readily, as she always did.

His eyes flicked to her walking on two legs beside him, before quickly averting his gaze when it landed on her naked breasts. His cheeks warmed – not that he truly understood why. She was covered in fur, although it did little to hide her dark-grey nipples since the fur between her hips and breasts was sparse.

*Perhaps we should find a place to reside somewhere close by.*

Having access to human materials, all of which he'd steal within the cover of darkness, would greatly improve their lessons. She still needed to learn how to read, although he *had* taught her the alphabet by scribbling it in the dirt. Her burrow had been too small and inadequate for him to instruct her comfortably.

It would also be good for Jabez to have a food source that didn't upset the soft-hearted Mavka. She didn't like it when he hunted for meat, nor that she kept being the one who would finish his meal. It disturbed her for some reason, which he thought was ridiculous. She was one hundred percent a carnivore – a predator.

Denying this part of herself would be denying a large part of who she was. *If I hadn't come along, I don't know how fast she would have evolved.* He'd forced her hand and made her gain humanity.

His gaze came to her once more and lifted to her rabbit skull. He noted the black flesh that had formed between her upper and lower jaws, her more feminine antler structure, then he observed the grace of her stride.

Without him, he pondered if Zylah ever would have reached full maturity as a Mavka.

And speaking of maturity... Jabez flicked his eyes away once more when they'd absentmindedly fallen upon her breasts again. This time, his ears heated.

*I need to clothe her*, he thought, which was a strange notion to a creature such as him.

Not only did most Demons not wear clothing unless they were in the final stages of their evolution, but the Elvish people weren't prudes. They didn't frolic around half naked, but they also didn't deny their true naked form. Even Jabez, for most of his life, had worn very little – although he'd had a multitude of reasons for this.

However, ever since he'd taught her how to transform into her humanoid form, her nudity had been making him...

uncomfortable. Perhaps it was because most developed Demons and Elves didn't flash their naked breasts or pubic mound confidently.

Zylah had no idea about the concept of nudity or modesty. *She is covered in fur.* That seemed to make little difference to Jabez.

She was naked, everything somewhat exposed, and her feminine humanoid body was a little too sensual for his liking.

Although her breasts were small, they were perky and jiggled with each of her footfalls. He hadn't realised her rib bones had sunken so much with each new creature he fed her that they were now mostly hidden behind the mounds.

He attempted to stay in her shadow, but her transformation offered him less than he'd anticipated. *When she first stood in her monstrous form before I took her to feed, she'd been over eight feet tall.* Now, she was barely seven feet, and only a mere three inches taller than him – which was nothing.

He cast his gaze to her feet, noticing how human they appeared. *When she's in her monstrous form, she walks on her toes like a bunny.* Now, her feet were short and flat, and almost... dainty like a woman's. The only thing keeping them from being truly humanoid was her puffy rabbit toes.

The difference between her two forms was rather vast. Her black fur grew shorter except for the collar around her throat and chest, which almost hid her sternum and attempted to make the top of her breasts look fuller. He wished that fur would cover her dark-grey nipples, breasts, and abdomen.

Her legs stopped bowing, and had thinned into two feminine, muscular limbs. Her thighs were dense, which accentuated her wide hips and, annoyingly, supported a rather large and round rump. Her rabbit tail sat above it and somehow made her arse look... cute?

Which, of course, alarmed Jabez.

He chalked it up to the fact that rabbits were cute creatures, and his... appreciation was due to that.

It didn't help that her waist was narrow, giving her an hourglass figure. Except he disliked this feature, as it showed she required more food to stabilise her body – more meat, which she cried about consuming.

He was also dreading forcing the issue if it made her curves more pronounced. Even now, her thighs and backside were thick and plump, making them womanly and strong.

*Once more, she proves me wrong.*

He'd been thinking that she would lack overly feminine features, especially breasts, considering what she was. Their smallness reflected this, as if they'd never function how a human woman's would, but the fact that she had them *at all* was what puzzled him.

*Then again, her antlers became smaller.* And he'd never seen nor heard of a Mavka's skull and horns changing... ever. *I'm guessing each gender goes through a different pathway of evolution.*

Musing about it wouldn't answer his questions, but he did like pondering it.

He looked at the village one last time before making his decision. *I'll figure out how to come back here and find suitable clothing for her.*

Not just because his gaze had more of an appreciative leer to it than even *he* was comfortable with, but also because it just felt... right to do so. He couldn't have her walking around like a naked animal when he was treating her like an adult woman. That's what his lessons were about; he was making her understand the world and language so they could finally converse.

So he could proposition her.

*I'll also pinch a few more books, and perhaps some parchment for us to write on.* Now that she understood the concept of speech, he was fine-tuning sentence structure – something that was complex. He couldn't just point to words and say, "This is what *when*, or *how*, or *who* means." They were intangible concepts, and they required more repetition because even *he* struggled with how to explain them.

"Jabez," Zylah called, her voice no longer monstrous due to her being in her humanoid form. She whacked him on the shoulder a few times. "Come."

Desiring to stay in her shadow for protection, and seeing no issue with deviating from their listless path, he followed Zylah's direction. He was curious to see what she'd scented, and why, for the first time in their travels, she wanted to go a certain way.

She took them to a flattened area of grass and pointed to it. Jabez knelt down on one knee in the middle of the squished stalks, his ears flicking as he touched the tracks and disturbances in the dirt that indicated something large had lain there.

"Mavka," she stated, crouching next to him. "Like lizard?"

He eyed her as she spoke before inspecting the grass once more. He picked up a singular loose scale and sniffed it.

*She's right, this has the scent of a Mavka. Only a few hours old too.* He scanned the area to see that its path came directly from the north, then headed east – the direction they'd been going.

"A lizard Mavka?" Jabez asked, cupping his jaw and furrowing his brows in thought. When recognition flashed within his mind, he waved behind his backside. "With a tail and a raven skull?"

Zylah nodded. "Yes. I have–" She chittered the words she was missing, waving her hands around. "Him."

"You have met him before?"

She nodded, patting the end of her snout. "Human female. Orange hair."

"He was travelling with a human woman with orange hair?" he asked, trying to fill in the gaps of her speech for assistance.

Zylah chittered appreciatively, her orbs flaring bright yellow. Out of the corner of his eye, he caught her little bunny tail wiggling happily.

His humour in her tail's reaction was short-lived, as something became apparent.

"You're fucking joking," he bit out, just as he picked up a stray hair. He sniffed it, but he wasn't totally sure of the semi-familiar scent. "That little bitch... she *survived?*"

How had a measly human survived whatever catastrophic magic had nearly disintegrated Jabez? Because if his assumptions were right, and he had a big feeling they were, this was the same redheaded woman who had almost killed him. It had to be, considering she had battled against him with two other Mavka brides – Reia and Zylah's mother. He couldn't remember her name. Even the Witch Owl had faced him that day.

Just to make sure, he turned to Zylah. "Did she have a burn scar on her face?" He ran his hand down the left side of his face.

"Scar?" She mimicked him before nodding. "Yes. This."

The growl that escaped him was beastly. *How?* How had she survived? *She died in my arms.* Or rather, his meat shield had disintegrated in his hands until even he started to burn from the false yet very real-feeling sun bomb that struck the centre of his castle. Not even his skintight sun barrier spell had been able to survive it, although it likely had aided in him not being destroyed instantly.

*At least I now understand why that woman assisted them.* Somehow, the raven skull had gotten her on their side after his twin, the bat-skulled Mavka, had died. *She was skilled in battle, so she'd either been a soldier or a Demonslayer.*

With a snarl, Jabez fisted the Mavka scale that would disappear from the world in a day, leaving behind no trace of him.

*It doesn't matter.* How she survived was pointless and inconsequential to him. Hopefully their paths never crossed again.

When Zylah quietly chittered in unease and fidgeted by scratching at her forearm, his anger waned. His aggressive sounds were making her uncomfortable.

He eventually sighed and dropped the scale. Jabez looked up just as a subtle breeze fluttered his clothing around his torso and whisked his hair forward.

*Screw it. It's mere retaliation.* That's what happened in war. He made many moves, and he knew they – especially the Witch Owl – would eventually make their own. He could allow his annoyance to fester, or just accept it as part of the callousness of war and hate.

His lips did curl in the strangest form of pride. *You were close, Lindiwe.*

Had Zylah not saved him, he doubted he would have lived much longer. He would have bled out, his magic sickness would have killed him without healing assistance, or a Demon would have eaten his unconscious body.

*Your own grandchild thwarted your plans.* When she discovered this, he could only imagine the unbridled rage she'd feel.

He'd been fighting against that woman for centuries, and they'd gone toe-to-toe so many times he could no longer count them. She thought him cruel because of what he'd done to her children, but he often wondered if she ever realised he retaliated just the same.

*I did what was done to me, and then more.*

Whether it be Lindiwe's actions, or the repercussions of leaving him bleeding to death to retreat herself, he'd faced many adversities due to her and Weldir's interference.

The sacrifice had been noble, whether he wanted to admit that or not.

Resigning to let go of his anger of the past, Jabez stood to assess the easterly direction the redhead and her Mavka had been travelling. He checked the raven skull's tracks to see which way his claws pointed.

*If we continue on our path, we may run into them.*

He'd much rather avoid anyone who may be hateful of him while he was so powerless. He also refused to be cornered like prey, having to rely on the power of his companion for assistance.

They couldn't go back, as he didn't want to return to Zylah's burrow. North was towards the Veil, which meant more chances of running into a Demon – who would likely know his face or scent. That was fine, so long as they couldn't escape into a dense and Demon-filled forest to inform others.

He turned towards the village. *I guess we'll go deeper south.*

There may be a few caves, and mountain Demons had a tendency to live in solitude. They were harsh creatures, but less territorial except for their specific nest areas. They almost lived like a hive, keeping to themselves in their caves but understanding that those residing above them needed to cross their dwelling entrances to get higher.

With Zylah by his side, he doubted those Demons would

come within sniffing range of them.

Zylah grumbled to herself as she sat inside a shallow cave that had formed halfway up a small mountain covered in forest. Much bigger than her burrow, she moved around with ease and picked up a rock to scratch at the ground in annoyance. She considered throwing it at the back of his head, but decided against it, knowing it would only make him growl at her.

She peeked over her shoulder at Jabez, noting he'd removed his cloak for the first time in days.

She'd already summarised that he wore it to protect his skin from the sun, as she'd seen him wince a few times when the light touched him. She'd never understood why he'd worn it in her home.

A home he was refusing to return to.

He kept saying no. That they would be staying here from now on. Zylah was disgruntled about this, as she longed to go back already.

She watched his arms move as he did some task all by himself. He held dark-grey fabric that shimmered in the smallest amount of light. She didn't know what he was doing.

And she couldn't approach him either.

Jabez didn't like being snuck up on from behind, and he could be quite snappy when she did so. He would snarl and turn his head to her before quickly quietening, as if he hadn't meant to have a small outburst. It was enough to warn her that he didn't like people behind him.

Yet, he often gave her his back, as if he trusted her despite his misgivings – so long as she kept her distance.

If she approached from the side or front, he didn't show a shred of irritation. She often wondered if he'd been attacked.

*Jabez has scars,* she mused, eyeing the way his white hair was brushed over his left shoulder.

It'd taken her a long time to notice them. They were so small, so thin, so weak in appearance, that she kept thinking she was mistaken. From afar, even to her, his skin looked mostly flawless except in a few spots.

Those spots with deeper, larger scarring made her realise what all the hairline marks were in his skin. He had a large scar that partially revealed itself throughout his hair and where it was now shaved. She'd seen a deep one on his lower back and then obvious claw marks on the back of his right thigh. She only saw these places when he bathed, which she watched since he didn't seem to care.

She'd also inspected them when she first brought him to her home, and knew they were different to the black, magical markings he'd somewhat explained to her.

However, there were these barely noticeable, hairline scars all over his body. She'd even touched one and it felt like nothing. His skin was smooth, but there was a slightly darker discolouration like the rest of his bigger scars.

He had them everywhere. The worst was his throat and his back between his shoulder blades, as if... creatures kept trying to target his vital points. Even his poor ears appeared mangled, as if they'd regrown many times.

Or perhaps she was wrong, and these lines in his skin were normal.

Like he could feel her gaze on him, Jabez looked over his shoulder at her. Her sight turned a reddish pink, and she quickly looked up to the rocky ceiling to avoid his stare.

"Still upset with me?" he asked in the tone he often gave her when he'd cocked a brow.

"Yes," she grumbled in response, wiggling her head to show her annoyance. "I want home."

"I told you, we can't return home." He gave her a sigh, as if she was being bothersome. "It's dirty, smells rotten, and it's small. This is better." He lifted his hands, one holding grey fabric while the other held a silver sewing needle – something he'd explained to her. "Most Mavka first live in a cave. The fact you dug a hole like a rabbit doesn't surprise me, all things considered with your anatomy, but a cave is better. I can... deal with a cave."

Zylah chittered in argument, despite understanding a large majority of what he'd said.

She hated that she couldn't bend him to her will when he

truly didn't wish to do something. She'd learned that Jabez was remaining with her of his own volition, and not because she demanded it. He'd shown that he was truly in control of his actions, where he was, and where they went.

Zylah was faster than him, but he was more agile and had a better ability at reading what she'd do. It was like he saw her next five steps before she did.

So, if she handled him by grabbing his arm or horn, and he let her drag him around, then he didn't care. He was fine with her direction when she didn't know how to voice her wants. He accepted it.

When he refused, she was unable to grasp him, no matter how she tried.

She didn't know why he remained with her, and she also didn't care. He was staying because *he* wanted to; it alleviated the weight of her guilt.

So, when he put forth his demand about their relocation that he sprung on an unsuspecting Zylah, who happily followed him, she conceded. She wanted to keep him pleased in hopes that he would continue to stay at her side willingly.

She enjoyed his scent, his mostly calm presence, his deep, rumbly voice. She'd even begun to appreciate his appearance, especially his ears – she was learning they were rather expressive. They were more honest than his voice and face.

They seemed to reflect an uncertainty she couldn't see in his constant bone-chilling stare.

He appeared cold and cruel, like winter. Yet he also came across as warm when he was patient with her, occasionally chuckling until even the ice in his gaze thawed into something much nicer.

They were rare, those moments, but she didn't mind either side of him. Now that she was beginning to understand his words, his growls had softened, as if he'd only been doing them to speak in *her* language.

Since she hadn't responded beyond making wordless noises, Jabez once more sighed. After using his fangs to cut the black string attached to the needle, he spun to face her.

"I know this is hard, Zylah. Change is never easy, but we can't go back to your burrow."

"Okay," Zylah conceded, as her shoulders dropped. "We stay."

His red eyes narrowed before gentling. "Alright. I have something for you." He stood and presented the material in his hands to her. "Time for you to wear clothing."

She took it from him without a shred of understanding as to the significance of the material. But she was happy he'd gifted her something, and she sniffed it when she noted his luscious scent all over it.

When they'd passed the village much earlier in the day, Jabez had disappeared inside it. Zylah had been thankful he hadn't intended on making her cause destruction within it. He'd returned shortly with a second bag filled with varying scents, and the dark-grey cloth folded over the top of it.

He'd already started eating from the contents of the satchel.

When they'd found this cave, and evicted its occupants in the dark of night, he'd shown her what else he'd obtained. An empty notebook for her to use for further studying. A reading book, which he'd added to the two he'd apparently already had – not that she'd seen them before. Then, he'd shown her a dictionary, a small pile of food and, lastly, the material.

Since then, until long after the sun rose once more, he'd been busy with the cloth. Zylah believed their time together would have been different if she hadn't been sulking for hours. They'd argued about her wanting to go home.

Her displeasure dissipated with the light weight of her gift.

As if he could tell she didn't know what to do with it, he gestured for her to come closer and give it back. He knelt while directing her to stand in the middle of the loop of fabric, and he pulled it up her body.

"It's a dress," he stated, as he threaded her arms through the thin shoulder straps.

Then he stepped back as always, putting space between them.

Zylah touched the silky material and chittered happily. She liked it, and seeing as he also wore clothing, it meant she didn't feel uneasy about it. Now that she thought deeper on it, she preferred this; everyone else was clothed, so she should be as well.

"Shit," he rasped out, lifting a hand to cover his mouth and dart his eyes to the side. "I think it may be too short."

The length of it came to the tops of her thighs. When she turned her head, she noticed that her tail was barely covered. The moment she twisted her body or lifted her arms, the bottom of the dress slipped between her back and upward-pointing tail tuft.

"I like it," Zylah stated, more comfortable with her tail exposed. Covering it felt odd on her fur, and she itched at her torso when she realised there, too, felt odd. "It is... good? What is better than good?"

"I don't know," he answered. "Pretty, I guess? I doubt you mean something strong, like beautiful or majestic." Then he shook his head while scratching at the side of his neck. "But even that's a stretch. I don't know how to sew, so everything I'm doing is shitty in comparison to a proper seamstress. If I took you to our village..."

He paused, as if his rambling reminded him of something harsh. His features turned ashen, like they did when he was unwell, before they hardened into something deeper.

She wished she understood enough to ask him what was wrong. Why had his face suddenly looked so strained that even his lips thinned? There was obviously a darkness within his mind, and Zylah didn't lack the heart to delve into it, just the words to express that to him.

"I think that's out of the question for now," he said, before sitting down once more. He shuffled his bag closer and yanked out the notebook with an annoyed roughness to his movements. "Alright. I think it's time you finally learn how to read and write."

Zylah tilted her head at his disgruntled appearance. She hoped that wasn't due to her.

"Thank you, Jabez," she stated, and his gaze flicked up to her in surprise. She chittered nervously, then soothed her heart by patting her chest. "Thank you for the *dress*. Thank you for... teaching me."

Her sight shifted to a bright reddish pink in embarrassment, and she squirmed under his regard. Even more so when he cast her an odd smile, which only lifted one side of his lips. The tips of his ears drooped a little, which made his features soften somehow.

"You're welcome," he answered warmly.

Zylah melted under the power of that warmth when it touched beneath her sternum and radiated.

# EIGHT

*I keep remembering this girl*, Jabez thought, as his eyes slowly cracked open to muted light. Midday had arrived, and he was safely protected from its rays.

Lying on his side with his back against the wall for protection, he took in the curled-up lump next to him. His chuckle was quiet so as to not disturb his companion of nearly two months now.

Jabez didn't know if she thought she was being sneaky, but each dawn that they lay down to sleep, Zylah kept inching towards him. Any closer now, and she'd be touching him.

He preferred her to not lie so closely, as he didn't wish to incite any affection on her side. However, he was also deeply aware that this was likely a Mavka longing. Merikh, the bear-skulled Mavka, had also chosen to sleep within reaching distance when they'd once been friends.

Which, at first, annoyed Jabez, as he was a deeply untrusting individual. It'd taken him a long time to learn that Merikh had two reasons for doing this. He'd claimed it was for Jabez's ultimate protection, as, at the time, he'd needed someone to watch his back in his own castle. But deep down inside, the male Mavka had just longed to be near his only companion.

As much as Jabez had growled at Zylah for doing it at first, he eventually accepted it as he did many, many decades ago. She sought warmth in order to erase her loneliness... like a kitten with its littermates, or a pack of wolves hunkering down for the night.

That was just his assumption, though.

*At least she doesn't have quills to stab me with,* he thought fondly, as he quietly shuffled to his back.

Staring up at the rocky ceiling of the cave, he let his mind wander. Every time he blinked, he was met with images of someone from the past.

The face of a small child; a little Elven girl. Someone he'd forgotten and was only beginning to piece together why she was returning to him. It'd been centuries since he'd seen her, after all.

Her face had been round, cute, freckled, and always smiling in his direction. Her big brown eyes looked at him with adoring awe, while white corkscrew hair fluttered around her head. If her long hair wasn't neatly braided into protective styles, it was often messy from play, while regularly sporting a purple leaf or two.

Jabez remembered delicately pulling leaves from her hair before patting over the top of it gingerly.

Her face came to him in different memories. Sometimes she was sitting across a table from him, pretending he was a guest at some fancy restaurant as she fed him different sweets. Other times, she was next to him as he tutored her in classes she was failing in.

Then there were the occasional times where she'd be hovering a mere inch from his nose to wake him in the morning. Or she'd be behind him as he sat on a hospital bed, brushing his long hair with as much care as he took in removing leaves from hers.

*Did... I have a sister?* It was a question he'd begun asking himself only recently.

His time as a child had grown fuzzy after he fled to Earth. The scar on the back of his head throbbed in answer, and he'd long ago realised his memories may be missing pieces.

But he did know the truth; his anger had been real. It had been justified. His hatred had bred from his time in captivity, and from the way his own people had turned their backs on him.

His mother had been a crazed scientist, nosediving into

chaotic experiments under the guise of progress. She'd wanted to help her people, even if it was against the order of the council. A radical woman willing to do anything and everything to get to a solution, even if it put her own life in danger.

Even if it meant... his father had no say in his creation, no consent. Jabez had always hated that. He'd despised that he'd never met his father, and neither had his mother because he'd been nothing but a corpse his mother had poked and prodded... and stolen from.

Just as Jabez was poked and prodded.

It was only in the reminder of this little girl's face that he remembered it hadn't *always* been done to experiment on him. No, he was beginning to remember being rather sickly as a child. He remembered being hungry, despite always having food. He remembered feeling malnourished and weak, even though he was a healthy weight and taller than his classmates.

What he didn't understand was why his last encounter with Merikh was the reason for these memories resurfacing. Merikh had nothing to do with that part of his past. Actually, it was long before the Witch Owl had ever been born, and Weldir had still been trapped within his own domain.

But there had been a light scent clinging to Merikh's fur. It'd smelt so familiar, and yet so distant. He still couldn't place who it belonged to, and it nagged at the back of his mind like a constant ache.

His musings darkened. At every turn, he tried to delve deeper into the fog of his memories.

To why he was here, and how he got himself here. Not just in this cave with Zylah, but into this very realm.

A maelstrom of chaotic events shaped his life path. Many were his own fault, and most of those were shadowed by the fact that he couldn't help it.

At a mere eleven years old, he'd been... *suffering*. He'd done many things he'd regretted then, and even now.

As much as his mother had tried to pamper him, the truth of his birthing was revealed to him at a young age. He was different, he'd always known he was different, and it was impossible to hide the truth. He'd been the only one with claws, fangs, horns, and red eyes. It hadn't mattered that everything else about him appeared the same as his fellow Elysians.

He was part Demon.

The people had accepted him, but his mother couldn't shelter him from their untrusting gazes. A select few had even looked upon him with disdain, as if he was an unwelcomed sight.

In the end, it was his fellow classmates who had broken him.

Jabez had been the only one of his kind. Not just within his school, but any school. In no corner of the city had anyone looked like him, acted like him, or shared his Demon traits. He'd been living as an outcast, even if his home had been warm and loving.

His eyes narrowed at the ceiling, both as a glare and a way to see deeper into the haze of a memory that had always been a blur. The day where he'd snapped.

A day he regretted, as it was what initiated the horrible life he'd thrust upon himself.

He'd killed an Elysian child, although he himself had been the same age. He'd never been able to forgive himself. No matter that it had been a bully who hated Jabez because he'd been born a half-Demon and looked and appeared different. No matter that the bully and his friends had tied him up by his horns at lunch while they attempted to rip out a few of Jabez's newly growing fangs. The death had been undeserved.

He and them... they'd all been young, foolish.

Jabez had been dying on the inside.

Something had come over him when he bit at the child's hand to defend himself and the taste of something delectable slipped down his throat. The bloodbath he'd carried out had been utterly forgotten in a traumatic episode. He only knew he'd done something wrong as he walked the halls covered in blood, unsure of *what* he'd done, but he knew his stomach finally felt *sated* for the first time.

Everything else was a blur, but... he now distinctly remembered patting that little girl's head as he cried into the cloud of her hair. How she'd wailed in his arms while hugging him tightly in return. How he'd hidden them so they couldn't be found, afraid of what he'd done, and how much trouble he'd be in.

He refused to face that same regret all his life, which is why he'd saved that human girl in the village. It was why he never allowed his Demon army to feed off the truly innocent under his watchful gaze, even if he helped to break down the walls of a village.

Lifting a single hand, he stared at the lines on his palm, unable to hide from his own claw-like nails tipping his fingers. The pathway of his life had been smothered in the blood of many, and he'd tried, with all his might, to prevent it despite constantly failing.

*The dream of a petulant teenager.* Oh, how those fateful events forced him into a life he'd much rather have not led.

A life he kept needing to dig deeper into for self-preservation. He yearned for the day he could finally let go of it by ending this war which had never met a battlefield. He'd much rather have fought against the Elvish people who'd turned their backs on the very creature they sought to create — especially as they were the reason for his existence.

But even then... his heart had long been giving up in this endeavour. The opposing pieces of his playing board had been stuck in another realm, and he was unable to gouge his claws into their throats. Each year he'd grown, he'd become more spiteful, until one day... he'd fully matured. In that maturity, having governed thousands of Demons who were their own beings, he understood that controlling a large group of individuals was truly impossible.

He long ago learned that what his past entailed wouldn't have happened if it wasn't for the mistakes of a few young boys. Moreover, the Elvish government wasn't entirely at fault, even when, through fear, it had condemned him to be buried beneath the ground in a prison.

A fear he now fully comprehended. A fear that lingered in his shadow; it was always with him. It'd been in every corner of his castle, between every stone gap, and within each of his breaths.

A fear he'd been controlling, so it didn't tear into him and swallow him alive.

His hand finally fell to rest against his abdomen, and once more, he stared up at the cave's ceiling.

*What a pointless endeavour,* he thought, as he let his gaze slip to the sleeping creature beside him. *Well, perhaps not.*

Zylah's lessons had gone exceedingly well over the past nearly two months since he'd met her. She was quick to pick up reading and writing over the last few weeks since they'd settled in this cave. Now that she was able to read mostly on her own, he'd obtained a few books that were more advanced.

She was currently able to have somewhat proper conversations and utilised the dictionary he'd acquired on her own. His lips cracked a grin at the numerous times he'd seen her reading the dictionary without his direction. When she read the novels, she would occasionally bend the book to him, point to a sentence, and ask him to explain a word she couldn't understand the definition of.

Jabez tried his best to explain, even when the concept was complex. He often sat quietly by her side and watched in case she needed assistance. It allowed him to recede peacefully into his thoughts like he had for most of his life.

Before long, she'd no longer need his assistance. Which meant he'd soon be able to proposition her.

He'd extend the same invitation to her as he had to Merikh the last time he'd seen him. *If she joins me in Nyl'theria, then we can rally the Demons living there.*

Then, finally, he could fight his way into the Elven city of Lezekos. He could finally step out of the shadows and live the life he'd been missing.

He didn't even wish to govern it. He didn't truly desire to be a king. He wanted peace, and the only way to achieve that was within the protective dome the Elysians lived under. Then he'd invite all the Demons who were close to the completion of their evolution to join him, of which there were many thousands.

Over time, the lesser Demons would consume each other and evolve, and they, too, could join them. Then, when there were only a few lesser Demons left, they would eradicate them and live like real people. Their children would go to schools, their people would craft and have jobs. They could discover Nyl'theria and hunt for lost artefacts and ruined civilisations.

By the time they understood the technology of the Elysians, they could then take over those advancements. By that point, Jabez assumed he'd be rather old and ready to pass. He'd like that, to one day close his eyes in old age and die peacefully, and not fear his death might come from the jaws of a Demon.

It's what he'd always *longed* for. To live out the rest of his life like a normal being and be nestled in comforts.

He hadn't been given a day of that since the moment he'd been locked away in his youth.

Jabez licked at the inside of a tooth that had grown back after the other children's cruel yanking. Like any other Demon, his fangs grew back when they went missing – a rather charming trait that not the humans, or even Elves, had.

Growing restless with his thoughts, he sat up. Placing his elbow upon a singular bent knee so he could cover his eyes, his ears twitched with irritation at himself and the dreams of the little girl who haunted him.

*I'm tired.* He'd been thinking that for years.

His movements disturbed his companion, and Zylah shifted with alertness. She quickly sat up and put space between them by shuffling away nervously.

Jabez waved his free hand when he figured she was only doing it because she'd been caught sleeping so close to him. "Don't worry, Zylah. I don't mind anymore."

"Really?" she asked, her tone full of hope.

"I'm aware you've been sleeping beside me for the better part of a fortnight."

She chittered, which had started to become less of a way to communicate and more of an infrequent, albeit cute, sound that reflected her emotions. It caused him to lift his hand away to peek at her, and he found her teal orbs had shifted to a reddish pink in embarrassment. She was too easy to make uncomfortable, which often had him wanting to playfully needle her – despite never doing so.

She scratched at the ground. "I did not think you knew."

He chuckled mildly at the ridiculousness of that.

"You know I have sharp senses. I sleep lightly so I can hear and smell people approaching me." When she didn't calm, he rolled his shoulders back to stretch them. "Like I said, it's fine. If it makes you feel better, you're welcome to sleep next to me. Your warmth is pleasant, especially as we're deep in winter now."

His gaze landed on the dead campfire. He lit it every night in order to take away the bite of cold his Elvish body just couldn't handle. That was something he deeply missed about his lack of powers – he couldn't shield himself from the cold or the sun anymore.

His nose scrunched at the loss, and the weakness he experienced without it. He'd never realised just how deeply he'd relied upon his magic until it was completely gone. He tsked at his stupidity and complacency.

Learning to be without it had been quite the adjustment, like a limb was missing. He wished to breathe and know that each breath drew in strength and mana. He missed the comfort and security of it.

He missed feeling like himself and like he wasn't a weaker being.

His stomach grumbled, and he once more tsked. *I need food.* And not just the food he'd been stealing from the crops and farms of humans, but meat. He was aware of how much his need for meat bothered his companion, but he wasn't willing to grow sickly like he had as a child.

*At least she now understands, since we've spoken about it.*

She'd thought he was just cruelly hunting for sport and didn't understand that his internal organs didn't work like hers. Her hunger was ever present but unending. His, however, was easily soothed and required he did so or he'd wither away.

At least her hunting lessons had been going well, and she rarely succumbed to a bloodthirsty rage.

He'd hunt without her, but she refused to allow him out of her sight. It was as though she worried he'd run away at the first opportunity he had, as if he'd changed his mind about being her companion.

He could have escaped at any time.

She'd soon discover as to why he hadn't.

*So why haven't I asked her yet?* They were able to

communicate quite well now. He was sure if he explained about the Elven realm and about the Elysians, she would comprehend their conversation.

So why hadn't he had that conversation with her? Why was he... putting off asking her to join him in his conquest?

As his eyes landed on her teal orbs and rabbit skull, he still didn't know the answer to his hesitation.

*Could it be... that I'm worried she'll reject it?*

Or was it deeper than that?

# NINE

Zylah walked beside a cloak-covered Jabez more closely than usual. With the sun gone after their earlier hunt and adventuring throughout the day, he'd propped back his hood to reveal his face.

*He smells really nice.*

Zylah kept trying to get closer so she could sniff him while his scent was freshly coming off his skin.

He didn't talk much except for when he was explaining something to her, but she liked the sound of his deep voice and the way it wrapped around her mind. It lulled her. She often squirmed when she realised she'd stopped listening to his words, too distracted by the way listening made her feel all warm inside.

Her heart would quicken at random and odd times whenever she looked at him.

*He is a* beautiful *male,* she thought fondly, as she took in his features.

The silvery tips of his eyelashes framed his red eyes and made them pretty. Zylah wanted to caress the curled strands to discover if they were as soft and delicate as a moth's wings like they appeared. She had an abject fascination with his pointed ears whenever they twitched with alertness or drooped, and with how the bridge of his straight nose would crinkle when annoyed or disgusted about something.

His gaze was always heavy, and she often found herself shying away from its cold weight. Yet, when she took in his sleeping face at dawn, she found it alluring and handsome.

She needed to suppress the desire to pet his strong brow, cheeks, or jaw when they appeared softer in expression.

She liked when he looked at peace, as if his troubled gaze told stories she couldn't fathom. She also preferred to glue her sight upon him when he was looking away from her, so she was free to dwell on the way it made something light and fluffy sprout in her chest.

There was a cunning glint to his eyes as he led her through the dark forest beyond the mountain. The moonlight shone upon his brown skin and the inhuman, grey undertone that was always present in it, highlighting the straight line of his nose, his full lips, and white eyebrows. It glinted upon his black segmented horns that tapered back over his long, straight hair, and the golden jewellery hanging from his earlobes, as well as the hard bangles around one biceps and ankle – the limbs that hadn't been missing when she first met him.

Despite the gentleness he displayed with her, she knew this creature to be ruthless in nature. How he had led her to the humans to devour... How he saw no issue with death... Even how nothing seemed to truly anger him. She knew these things meant there was a dark cavern within him.

There was very little warmth to be found if one only looked at the surface of his expressions, but Zylah was watchful and observant of her companion. She instinctively felt there was more.

She longed to know why he was shielding it.

When his red eyes slipped to her, she subtly brought her snout forward to hide her stare. He was incredibly watchful too, and he was exceptionally wary.

Zylah didn't know if that wariness was due to her, or if this was just how he was with the world. He was difficult to get close to, like he preferred an arm's length of distance from any creature.

*But he said it is okay if I sleep next to him.* Once more, like it did at noon when they woke, her heart squeezed in tenderness.

She'd been so nervous about being discovered that she often slept light. She quickly moved if she sensed he may be waking, especially as his heart rate always seemed to... accelerate from his dreams.

Zylah had taken his approval with giddiness and a boost of confidence. *He likes me near him.* That was how she took it, and it allowed her to shed some of her anxiety.

Zylah had been struggling to let go of her worries around him. Although his little huffs and growls had been constant in the beginning, they'd diminished in the month they'd relocated. She also knew her anxiety was due to her inability to communicate properly, which had waned with every day, every *hour*, that she added to her vocabulary.

Her chitters of unease and bashfulness were also becoming less frequent. It helped that Jabez never belittled Zylah for her faults, although he was direct in correcting her for her benefit. At first, she'd hated it, as he obviously knew what she'd been insinuating, but she was now thankful for the direction.

Which meant she now felt ready.

There was much she longed to know about the world and her place in it. She ached to know what lay beneath the frost of his exterior.

Jabez led them to a decently sized river. He drank from it, as she knew he would, before he blatantly stripped to bathe. Zylah, now knowing that he preferred to be clean, did so as well so she could be more... attractive to him. If she cleaned and neatened her fur, she hoped he would allow her even closer.

She found herself wanting to touch in strange ways. She wanted to caress his cheek or pulsating jugular. She longed to know if his big chest was as soft as it appeared, or if his muscled abdomen was firm. What did his skin feel like? Was it as warm and smooth as she vaguely remembered upon healing him?

Zylah wanted to... hold him. She wanted to sniff him directly on his skin.

She desired to worship this beautiful male creature with gentle touches and hoped he might do so in return.

Seeing she had removed her beloved grey dress, he turned his back to her even more. He often avoided looking at her when she was unclothed, whereas she had little desire to avoid looking at his naked body.

And when her gaze slipped down the deeply arched curve of his back right before his round backside, she wanted to follow that cavernous, muscled spine with her fingertips... or even tongue. Her abdomen tightened in response to her thoughts, although she didn't tear her sight away from him in the darkness.

The scar on his lower back and the claw marks on his thigh were more prominent in the moonlight, as were the strange black symbols across his skin. They looked like letters and shapes, but in a language she didn't comprehend.

Jabez didn't wet his hair. Instead, he wrapped the long, thick length of it around his horns to keep the silky strands above the water as he washed his face. Droplets sluicing off his strong body glittered, and suddenly her tongue dried.

He was quick to leave the water, as if the cool temperature was unbearable for a long duration. Zylah was forced to remain behind in order to scrub at her fur – although it was, thankfully, short in most areas except around her neck and tail.

Once done, she exited the slow-moving river on her hands and feet, the pebbled bank crunching beneath her footsteps. She shook the excess water off while a safe distance from him.

Jabez sat on the grass naked except for part of his cloak covering his groin, waiting to dry before dressing again. Zylah didn't mind the wet, and placed her dress back on simply so he wouldn't avert his gaze from her.

It hadn't taken her long to notice he was uncomfortable with her nudity, although she didn't know why. His eyes constantly flicked away, as if he'd found them drawing back to her without his knowledge and he caught himself.

*He's staring up at the moon again.* He did this quite often. His chin would lift and his brows would furrow in deep thought.

She did the same, wondering what he saw in the brightly lit hovering orb. Was he receiving answers, as if he could hear its whispers when she couldn't? Then again, she found it quite mesmerising. The stars twinkling around it and the blue dust in the sky made it even more hypnotic.

After a little while, he placed his clothing back on and

finally released his hair from his horns. Her fingers itched so badly to touch those white strands to know if they were as soft as they appeared.

To quell that itch, Zylah stroked her damp collar of fur.

When he sat back down, Zylah remained where she was. The distance between them was wide, and she looked up at the sky once more as her questions bubbled up her throat and got stuck.

How should she pose her questions? Which ones should she start with? Would he... even answer them?

The teal in her orbs slowly morphed into blue in sadness. He'd never once spoken about himself, and she feared that was entirely intentional. He may not like her prodding for answers.

She swallowed the lump in her throat and tried anyway.

"Jabez..." she started, before having to quieten her nervous chitters. She refused to look at him, despite knowing he'd lowered his gaze to greet the side of her skull. "Why are you here?"

Silence greeted her. It hollowed out her chest the longer it dragged on. In her peripheral, he raised his hand to cup his chin.

"I don't understand your question," he eventually stated, making a soft whine escape her. She'd asked the wrong thing. "Are you asking how I came to be here with you?"

The hope that filled Zylah had her twisting towards him slightly, and she placed her hand on the ground for balance. "Yes. How did you come to be here? Why did I find you... *hurt?*"

When her sight landed on his eyes, she found herself incapable of drawing away from them. Perhaps if she matched his confidence, it would force him to speak.

He was the one to break away to look up at the moon.

"I've told you that I am part Elf," he started, while touching the tip of his pointed ear, then running his hand along the horn above it. "And that I'm part Demon. I'm not from this world, Zylah."

Her orbs shifted to a dark yellow in curiosity, and she gestured to their surroundings. "But this is the only world."

He huffed, which she took as a short laugh. "There are

many worlds. This is Earth, and it belongs to the sentient humans. Where I'm from belongs to the Elysian Elves. They're a single species of Elves, and all others come from different worlds and look different."

He stood, approached the riverbank to pick up a jagged stone, and then came to kneel in front of her. With the stone, he drew a circle, and in it drew strange, uneven shapes.

"From what the Elvish learned hundreds of years ago, Earth is large and holds many continents. Each one is surrounded by oceans, which are the vast bodies of water you see when you reach the end of land." He pointed to one large mass. "We are currently on Austrális. This landmass is roughly the size of my world. There is only one continent, and our only ocean is freshwater and technically a gigantic lake you can't see across to the other side. It would only take a person an Earth month to walk its entire distance, just like Austrális. A year in Nyl'theria, the Elven realm, equates to fifteen here, although we have quadruple the amount of days in comparison."

Zylah looked down at the new world he was drawing, which only depicted one landmass. He drew a circle near the edge of its shoreline before lifting his face to hers.

"The Demons came from another world and began taking over a very long time ago. They destroyed every village, every city, every Elvish population until only one remained. This one – Lezekos City. It's where I was born, and it's the last stronghold for the Elysians."

As he spoke, he marked an X in different locations before once more drawing a circle around Lezekos City.

"Then how did you get here?" she asked, perplexed by all this. She barely understood the world she currently lived in, and the idea that there were many more was daunting.

"I was born as an experiment. You asked about family and parents after reading your books. My mother took Demon seed and conceived me to discover if there is a way she could help the Demons evolve into fully formed creatures. Before she could learn of that answer, I was labelled an outcast and imprisoned for five years at a young age."

Zylah chittered in unease and cupped her hands on her lap. "They trapped you?"

"Hmm. Trapped isn't the right word. I walked into my cell willingly after I instigated a... fight." He sighed as he sat back on his ankles. "Regardless, I was young. I escaped when I was seventeen with other Demons the Elves had imprisoned for their 'safety' and stole a portal stone as I did. That portal led to here, to Earth, and I have stayed here for over three hundred and fifty years. I built an army, elected myself as a leader and saviour for my own protection, and even built a castle as my home."

A spike of annoyance flittered into Zylah. Despite that he was sharing, she knew there had to be more to this story. She could count to three hundred and fifty, and she knew what years were.

"What else did you do?" she grumbled, refusing to let him skip over so many years.

His features grew dark and cold, like a *glare*. "My companions were Demons. I spent my years surviving, and trying to make bonds and friendships where I could with those around me. I grew a village for the Demons, and I hunted humans to help my people grow just as I did for you. I did what I needed to, especially as I was fighting a war against the Elysians for what they cruelly did to me. I was in my prison for over seventy human years and was, justifiably, angry."

"You had other companions?" she answered, picking from just one aspect to avoid the weight of the rest.

"I had very few, most of whom left my side," he answered without a shred of emotion, making his deep voice dark and foreboding.

Reddish pink entered her sight as she quietly stated, "I will not leave your side."

And Zylah meant that with every bit of confidence. After spending so much time with Jabez, she had no intention of letting him go. He was her only companion, and she'd already proven she wouldn't leave his side no matter where he went — even if it meant abandoning her own home.

She'd been hoping for a rare chuckle, or perhaps a fond smile at her admission. So, when she brought her sight back to him, she hadn't expected his expression to look so empty.

Unsure as to why his brows had narrowed mistrustingly or

why his lips had pressed into a hard line, her chest tightened.

"As charming as your words are, you know very little about me," he stated without a shred of remorse, his eyes meeting hers with a stern heaviness to them. "There is much I've done wrong, all in the name of self-preservation. I am, at heart, an entirely selfish person, Zylah. I have enough self-awareness to know who I am, and that is an inherently Elvish trait. When one lives as long as an Elf, you have the time to reflect quite heavily. My life is not fleeting, although it is as easily ended as a human's."

"Then I will protect you," she answered with the tiniest growl.

His eyes crinkled, finally giving his expression life, as a laugh burst from him. His pointed ears pressed back, and he covered his face to stifle the genial sound.

"Yes. I'm well aware that is how you perceive our dynamic."

"What is that supposed to mean?" she grumbled, her sight once more changing to reddish pink.

"I was a powerful being, Zylah," he stated around chuckles. "The magic you use to heal – I once had such magic. I intend to have it again. Until then, sure, you may be my protector, but even then, I don't need your aid. I'm stronger and faster than any Demon or human, and I have far more experience in battle than anyone living."

Zylah folded her arms with a harrumph. "You're not stronger than me."

"I can't deny that. But once I have my magic back, you'll see the shift in our dynamic. Much will change."

But she didn't want it to change. She liked how they were. She liked that he could rely on her strength, even if he didn't *need* it. It made her feel good. She liked feeling as though she was his protector and was needed, while secretly aching for more. She wanted to hold him so she could shelter him.

She wanted to know what it was like to be held in return.

"You were hurt," she said in irritation to remind him that he wasn't as strong as he stated. "I healed you. Why?"

"I was attacked in retaliation. As you know, like Demons, I'm susceptible to the sun, although not as instantaneously. An enemy of mine managed to harness some kind of sun power in the form of a bomb. You found me just as I used the last of my magic to protect myself. Alone, I held the weight of my collapsed castle off myself, and healed my body enough to survive. No one else could have achieved such a grand feat by themselves."

Zylah wasn't so sure of that. She thought she could do something so grand, as she was stronger than even him. She may not be able to heal herself, but in a full sun cycle, she magically healed on her own.

She wouldn't have needed days of aid, like he did. *He is weaker than me*, she thought with a sulk.

Still, she let it go, her tail twitching with the knowledge that they were finally having a proper conversation. It moved faster when his features relaxed, softened, and even looked... *warm* in her direction, like he felt relieved too.

"Why do you... *know* me?" she asked, wanting to understand a different topic. She peeked at him as her fingers fidgeted on her lap. "You know me better than I do."

"I know Mavka. You're not the first of your kind I've befriended." Jabez cupped his jaw and rubbed it, then tapped the side of it. "Actually, I believe Merikh would be your uncle. I doubt you'd know him, but he has a bear skull and bull horns. I met him when he was a little more advanced than you, but it took me years to bring him to your level of humanity." His voice filled with mirth, his cheeks crinkling along with it, as he said, "If I'm being honest, you are quite remarkable, Zylah. You may be the most intelligent Mavka to walk this world, and I believe it's because you're further away in your relation to your grandfather than the others."

Throwing a hand in his direction, she grumbled, "My grandfather?" What even *was* that? Like a father, but further? "See? You know more than I do about me."

"You're the grandchild of a demigod, whose full godhood is restrained. His name is Weldir, and he's..." Jabez stopped mid-sentence as he looked off into the forest. "It doesn't matter. Weldir is a contradiction. He's powerful, and yet undeniably weak. He requires *others* to do his bidding on Earth, as he's unable to touch it. All Elysians are brought up learning about his history and how it is intertwined with Demons."

"Is he good?"

"Hmm. That is entirely based on perspective. I don't know how to answer that for you, as my opinion is unlikely the one your kind shares."

Ugh! What an entirely cryptic answer!

She hated it when he did that, and it often made her want to smack him – albeit lightly.

A strong breeze pulled her gaze forward when it crested over the water, making it slosh harder against the pebbled shore. Her orbs shifted to a deep blue.

"What... is my purpose?" she muttered quietly.

Could Jabez answer that question for her? She wanted to believe she was here to heal, yet she hadn't truly saved anyone except for this male. Everything else she'd longed to help had been ruined by her claws and fangs in the end.

*My hands are covered in so much blood.*

"Your purpose is whatever you wish it to be," he stated confidently. "Weldir created his children to ferry souls to him, but you have your own free will. You may do what you want."

*I can make my own purpose?* Why did that instil so much hope inside Zylah and instantly make her chest swell? She wanted to be a good force within the world. Someone kind and protective. That's what her heart told her, and she placed her hand over the organ when a strange tenderness caressed it.

Perhaps he misunderstood why she'd dug her claws into her chest, because Jabez stated, "If it helps, I don't know what my purpose is either. None of what I hoped to achieve has been possible, and for a long time, I've wondered if there was even a point to it. I know why I was born, what my purpose was *meant* to be. Despite knowing the answer to what my mother sought, I refused to accept such a future for myself."

Zylah brought her skull back to Jabez and tilted it. "What was it your mother sought?"

Again, his eyes narrowed, and his lips flattened along with them, making him appear disgruntled.

"I can't tell you that," he stated darkly.

Zylah tilted her head the other way with her sight turning

deep yellow. "Why not? If you know the answer..."

"Because that is a secret I've never shared with another. It's something that would put my life at risk should the wrong people hear of it."

"But I would not share your *secret*." She patted at her chest to show him the truth of that. "You can trust me. I would not do something that could hurt you."

His ears drooped as he shook his head. "There are certain things you should never share beyond yourself, no matter what. You don't know who you can trust, and just because someone is your friend now, doesn't mean they always will be."

"But I do not have any secrets," she snapped, her maw chomping at the air in irritation. "There is nothing I would not share with you. I trust you."

Jabez slapped a hand over his face, and a muffled sigh escaped from behind it. "That's because I already know all your secrets. I know your kind, your bloodline, your strengths and weaknesses."

"I do not have any weaknesses." She wiggled her head confidently as she pushed her shoulders back. "I-I'm strong, and I heal within a day."

"That's not true. You just don't know of your own weakness, and now that Demons know of it, your vulnerability is a glaring one. You may be immortal, but you can still be killed."

"But I always heal," she said stubbornly, despite momentarily losing her confidence. Zylah wrung her hands in her lap, then attempted to soothe herself by pushing out the wrinkles in her dress. "Much... much has been done to hurt me. Demons have tried, humans have tried. *I* always win. I always... return."

"If someone was to break your skull, you wouldn't return." His hand darted up to rub at his nape before he lowered it to his own lap. "That isn't a wound a Mavka can heal from. It is permanent."

Zylah chittered in unease as she raked her claws down her bony snout. "My skull? Is that why Demons have tried...?"

Whenever she'd fought against them, they always climbed

onto her back and tried to touch her skull. They'd grip her antlers and try to separate them, as if... to split her face in half, but she'd always thought it was stupid of them, as her skull was one of the strongest parts of her body. Her leg could be broken, but her skull... she'd thought it was indestructible.

*Was I wrong? If so...* She caressed it with a cold pang radiating behind her sternum and her gut tightening.

"That is your weakness, and a secret of your kind that has been shared with Demons."

"Why?" she cried, her sight turning white, before flicking to blue. "Why would someone reveal something so horrible to them?" Her hands shook as she pointed to the forest. "I have tried to befriend the Demons but they always hiss and growl. I have always known they don't like me, but I did not know they..."

A curt whine escaped her at the thought. She didn't know they'd hated her enough to destroy her.

*I have never tried to hurt them.* They didn't always attack. Most were wary of her, like they knew she'd win any battle, but if there were many... they weren't as fearful.

This had stopped only recently. The Demons hadn't attacked Zylah since she found Jabez. Then again, they hadn't come across many. It was like the Demons had been hunting, and no longer were.

When Jabez didn't answer her, and only silence greeted her questions, she whimpered as she met his gaze.

In that moment, there was something about his expression that appeared deeply strained. Two muscles on either side of his jaw had knotted, and his red eyes held a spark in them – an emotion she'd never seen before. Regret? Perhaps pity? She didn't know what to call it, what it was.

"Why would someone share such a secret? What have Mavka done so wrong that we deserve to be hurt like this?" An awful emotion clung to her chest, and it caused her sight to shift to a deep blue until the bottoms of her orbs broke. Little droplets began to sparkle in her vision like floating rain. "Not even the humans have been kind."

Jabez parted his lips, only to close them. His eyes flicked to the forest, and he stared into the shadows with a closed expression for a long while. A gust of damp wind wrapped around them, making her shiver under the sadness of what she'd just discovered.

"Weldir is keeping the Demons trapped in this world, and they can't escape due to his ward. Killing your kind may be the answer to Demons returning to Nyl'theria."

His ears twitched, before drooping further until he hid the one closest to her with his palm. He'd never hidden them before, but she was too hurt to decipher why he would.

Zylah whimpered. "What does that have to do with–"

"That's why it was shared, although that person now realises it doesn't matter. Nothing will bring down that ward, and they shared it stupidly in anger." He regarded her from the corner of his eyes. "If it helps, I know they have come to genuinely regret that decision, and what it took to learn that secret, as it has hurt a friend he deeply cared for in the past... and perhaps the present as well."

Zylah wanted his words to make her feel better, but they only hollowed out her chest more. To do such a terrible thing... and regret it later, just proved how wrong they knew it was to begin with.

"Who... was it?" Zylah asked, needing to know.

His answer was slow to come, and quiet, like he didn't wish to answer her. "The king of Demons."

She didn't even know who that was.

Instead of asking for further clarity or for more information, Zylah lost herself to sadness. She just whimpered with her hands limp in her lap, unsure of how to swallow all this. She wished she hadn't discovered this truth, despite understanding that learning of her own weakness was vital to the longevity of her existence.

"You know... I only discovered recently that your kind can cry ethereal tears. Regardless if it's a sign of deep sorrow, it's rather beautiful."

Zylah chittered in answer, as her *tears* floated from her faster.

Two knuckles gently stroked her cheekbone, startling her in surprise. Jabez had never touched her skull before, and it was the only reason she pulled her distant gaze away from the grass and pebbles.

Concern laced his expression, and she'd never seen it appear so soft and tender before, as though he... *cared* for her wellbeing and sadness. For some strange reason, it only made her whimper more.

"How can I help?" he asked gently, his voice lighter than usual.

She shook her head, producing only a subtle rattle from it now. "I do not know. I feel cold, and... lonely."

Lonely because it was harrowing to know that the only creature who seemed to care for Zylah was the male before her, when she had so much compassion to give to the world. Cold because that loneliness felt harsh and barren, like the winter they were now in.

Her desired purpose was even more hopeless if the world not only despised her, but wanted her taken from it.

Jabez shifted into a crouching position and came closer while unbuttoning his cloak. He flung it around her back and settled it upon her shoulders, and the blanket of it was comforting, but not strong enough to fight the pain stinging in her chest.

The warmth he'd left upon the material tried to bleed into her. But it wasn't enough. It didn't seep into her bones, it didn't warm her heart.

His gentle, pretty scent flittered into her nose hole when he put them barely an inch apart to place it upon her. Despite the small distance, she could almost *feel* his heat caressing her, and she wanted more of it, more of his scent, a touch that wasn't a brief caress.

She lifted her hands and slid them around Jabez to draw him close. He stiffened in her arms, but Zylah didn't care. The moment his heat pressed against her torso, she tightened her hold on him and pressed the side of her skull into the crook of his neck with a high-pitched whimper.

She shuddered against him as she cried, and sheathed her claws when she worried she was digging them too deeply into his tunic-covered back. Her sight deepened in its desolate blue, making the world around her look gloomy and melancholic.

"Fair enough," Jabez stated, as his body softened and he

leaned into her. Then he wrapped his arms around her shoulders to deepen the hold.

The fact that he was returning it bled tenderness into her heart, making it easier to wade through her hurt. He didn't reject Zylah, especially when she needed someone the most, even when she could tell he was... uncomfortable with it. He even began to rub her back, like he wanted to stroke the pain away.

"Does that feel better?"

Zylah nodded in answer, before nuzzling into the side of his neck affectionately. She almost wanted to start licking him to taste his musky aroma, but instead tongued the drool within her mouth.

Just as she made to thank him, he finally pulled away, and she struggled to weakly hold on.

*This may be a pointless endeavour,* Jabez contemplated, as he sat cross-legged within their shared cave. Asleep with her back to him, Zylah lay curled up on her side.

He stared at the back of her white skull and dainty antlers, with one elbow resting on his knee and his cheek planted on the knuckles of his fist. The fingers of his other hand drummed against his opposing knee, while he mused on their conversation by the lake.

*What a way to make a guy feel like a bastard,* he thought, his eyes narrowing in her direction – but not *at* her.

Jabez wasn't angered by her words, her tears, or her feelings. He found them rather justifiable. What he'd done... a part of him had come to regret it.

*I was angry.* Katerina, a companion of his, had just died, and the weight of her death had crushed him. It'd taken Jabez almost a year to shed the worst of his anger, his need for retribution. *I took my pain out on the feline-skulled Mavka, and then immediately shared his kind's weakness with my army.*

In those months, his dislike for Orpheus, and *especially* his blonde-haired female who had delivered Katerina's death blow, had turned into unbridled hatred. He'd wanted them dead – for her. To finally give Katerina what she'd sought. To make up for... failing her.

For not keeping her safe when she was under his sworn protection.

He wasn't just a man in a relationship, which was complicated at best. He was a 'king,' an all-powerful being. A wicked blend between Elf, Demon, and consumed mana stones. A cold-blooded hunter who heartlessly slaughtered people.

A female in his keeping shouldn't have come to harm, let alone died.

He hadn't known how to handle his failures.

But, in the past year of healing, the scorching magma of rage in his chest had cooled into igneous rock. Clarity was produced in the dwindling smoke and steam, and he separated the truth from the lies he'd been telling himself.

He realised his anger hadn't come from a love that had never existed, but from the crutch of vengeance easing the weight of his wounds. Revenge and fury – these were two things Jabez knew how to navigate.

*I shouldn't have done it.* He knew that now, but what did it change? Nothing.

He still wanted Orpheus and Reia eradicated, but at the cost of his friendship with Merikh? *Had I not been so foolish, would that bull-headed Mavka have returned to my side?* He'd thrown away that friendship so many times when it had been the answer all along.

An answer he'd been hoping would now lie with Zylah, but he pondered if his mistake was just too grand.

*Will she grow hateful when she learns it was me?* Obviously his army had attacked her in his broad command to attack and destroy the skulls of all Mavka. *But I tried to undo that command months ago.*

He almost chuckled to himself, but a cold, desolate huff fell from him instead. *Her promises are just as empty as everyone else's.* When she learned of the truth, she would abandon him. Her ethereal tears were proof of that.

Since she'd continued to whimper, produce tears, and shiver despite him doubting she was cold, he'd laid his sleeping blanket over her to comfort her throughout the night. She'd wriggled so much that only the top half of her remained covered, the twisted blankets evidence of a difficult sleep.

*It would be better if I got up and left now.* If he did so sneakily, he could get a far distance between them to escape. Although he couldn't outrun a Mavka, he was fast and cunning enough to mask his scent with the right herbs and tree bark.

Yet, instead of picking his arse up and leaving, he remained seated. He grumbled to himself as he looked off to the side to inspect the early morning sunlight filtering through the entrance.

He'd been unable to sleep.

He'd been unable to leave, not that he fully comprehended why. *I guess in some ways I want to have faith in her.* He also wanted to finish her lessons so that she... stood a chance. The more she learned, the better the likelihood that she'd survive even if he were to disappear.

After meeting her, and learning about her despite their lack of conversation, he'd come to find her rather... charming.

Without turning his face forward, his eyes slipped to the periphery of his vision to look at her.

The first thing he saw was her feet tucked up beneath her plump, round backside to cover it, with her heels against the base of her tail. *Cute,* he thought with mild humour, especially when he noticed her light-grey toe beans.

He didn't often see the bottoms of her feet. Despite them appearing somewhat humanoid, her toes were curled like paws, and the pad of her foot looked like a bunny's.

As he regarded them tucked beneath her rump, her tail caught his attention once more, and he found his cheeks heating. Especially when his groin tingled for reasons unknown.

He'd been trying to ignore it for the better part of the month, but it was growing increasingly harder to deny her sensuality.

Her body was remarkably curvaceous. Her waist tucked in, accentuating wide hips. Her physique was lithe, but filled out more each time she ate, making her look softer, more lush, and more *feminine.* Even her black fur had a pretty shine to it.

The dress he'd made for her barely contained her perky breasts constantly pressing against the low neckline, nor did it hide her rather kneadable-looking backside and thick thighs. Her tail constantly drew his eye, and he didn't particularly like the way his dick jerked again when he stared at it.

Thankfully, it was only her tail that gave him that reaction. *I think...* Or was he ignoring it because that made it easier for him? *Wait... why am I thinking about this right now?*

Worried that his gaze had more of an appreciative leer to it than he truly wanted, his ears were hot when he forced his eyes away from that fluffy appendage. Although he could just see her fully from behind, his gaze drifted up her blanket-covered back and to the way her arms were crossed with her hands cupped at her throat. Curled into a ball, she looked small and delicate, soft and fluffy. She looked at peace.

Peace that he'd been the one to steal from her through his own past deeds.

*She isn't an innocent bystander in all this, though.* All of her kind were part of this war, whether they wanted to be or not, whether they knew they were or not. Their heritage to Weldir, their purpose of bringing him souls, meant they had always been opposing Jabez.

They only had their parents, or grandparents in Zylah's case, to blame.

*But that creed has now likely been abolished.*

With Jabez, the great king of Demons, now presumed dead, his army had no head. Like a beehive without a queen, they had no task, no organisation. They would once more fall into being uncontrolled beasts plaguing the world with their fangs and claws without rhyme or reason.

Unless they governed themselves. *Perhaps the more advanced Demons will find their own leaders.* Some kind of government to enact rules and order – which, behind the scenes, had fallen completely upon Jabez's shoulders.

For now, that was no longer his responsibility, and he found it rather freeing. *I'm tired. I'm too old for this shit now.* Although he still considered himself in his prime, despite being thirty-seven.

*I just want this to be over.* He was tired of it all, of fighting for a better life, of the violence and bloodshed. Just tired.

Zylah wasn't his last chance, but she sure as shit was a good one. *However, she would have to know of the truth.* Not just a little bit of it, but every piece of it. Every deed he'd done, whether it be cruel, selfish, or even good, he would need to reveal to her. His companion in this war needed to be someone he could not only bare his sins to, but if they accepted them, would be his equal.

He needed someone strong. Someone fast. Someone cunning. And most importantly, someone... loyal. Someone who wouldn't dust their hands of this battle simply because they learned of something he withheld.

They needed to understand the pressure he was under, why it was so heavy, and then consent to carry it with him knowingly and willingly.

He couldn't have that if he didn't reveal everything.

*But after earlier...* His hope in Zylah was dwindling. *She's soft natured.* More so than any other Mavka he'd observed, and the majority of the Demons he'd met. *She is caring. She wants to protect and heal.*

He wanted the opposite. To destroy so that he could rebuild everything with a better ideology in mind.

They were two opposing bowls on a scale.

He covered his face in annoyance. *Then why the fuck am I still here if I know that?* Fuck! A growl, solely at himself, slipped up his throat.

It startled the female Mavka, spooking her into waking with a gasp. She quickly sat up, bending her knees and tucking her feet to one side beneath her rump, so she sat on her hip.

"Sorry," Jabez grumbled, rubbing at the nape of his neck in guilt at waking her when she hadn't been asleep long.

White orbs settled into teal at his apology, and he grew annoyed at how soothing he found the natural colour of them.

Now that her orbs were bright, he was reminded of how they'd dripped with floating tears when they were that morose colour of blue. Thankfully they'd returned to their normal, alluring brightness.

He hadn't forgotten how she'd initially tried to cling to him when she first lay down. That clinginess should have rankled him, but he found he just couldn't muster up the annoyance at her.

Rather, he'd placed his blanket over her in hopes of soothing her hurt further – hurt she had no idea he was the reason for. Only then had sleep dragged her under, and he hadn't missed the way she'd snuck the tip of her snout beneath the material and breathed in his scent heavily.

"Is something the matter?" Zylah asked with her bony snout pointed in the direction of the cave opening. "I don't smell anything approaching."

"Everything is fine." He rose to his feet while clutching his cloak, which he had used as a blanket instead, so he could place it around his shoulders. Then, wanting a distraction from his constant thoughts, he said, "The day is still early. I'd like to train for the duration of the sun, and then we can head towards the cornfield village for more supplies once night falls."

Although her lessons were a priority, Jabez ensured he maintained his physique. In doing so, his companion mimicked him when he trained his body; she would do push-ups, sit-ups, and lunges beside him. They'd begun starting their day with a lengthy run side by side, ensuring she didn't start chasing him in an accidental excited rage.

Jabez didn't grow stronger, since this did nothing but maintain his strength. *But it strengthens her.* The more she worked her humanoid form in such strenuous ways, the more in tune she became with it. He doubted she knew that was why he was truly doing it.

Zylah stood, and as she often did, copied him by brushing off her clothing.

"Can... we get more books?" she asked sheepishly, using just the claw of her forefinger to scratch at the side of her snout. "I have already read the ones we have many times."

"It appears I've made a bookworm of you." His lips almost curled into a smile despite the lingering of his disgruntled musings.

Zylah tilted her head at him. "Book... worm?"

"It's a term for someone who enjoys reading."

"I didn't know worms could read, though. Do they burrow

into books like the dirt?"

The hardness of his features cracked, and a warm smile finally lifted into them. Why did he find the silliness of her questions so remarkably adorable?

"No," he said with a light chuckle. "There are many sayings that don't make sense. But yes, Zylah, I'll find more books for you. If there is anything else you can think of before we get to the village, let me know, and I will attempt to obtain it for you."

He mainly wanted to provide Zylah with her own blanket, and perhaps even a pillow despite him not having one himself. *I should also look into getting us proper bedding.* Currently, they both slept on the ground, as Jabez had little interest in softening a space he didn't intend to stay in forever.

But, in the interim of them calling this their home, it would suit them better if he made it more comfortable.

*I'm not like humans.* He also didn't often think like one.

But he currently had a female in his care, no matter her animalistic species, and he should do better to provide comforts. She hadn't needed a blanket, as she didn't grow cold in this chilly season like he did, but seeing how much it'd soothed her during the dawn, he'd like to obtain one for her.

*I'll get her whatever she needs.*

It wasn't like he was paying for any of it anyway.

# TEN

With night shielding where she stood hidden in shadow, Zylah watched as Jabez climbed the side of the cornfield village's walls.

He moved effortlessly, utilising both his hands and feet like a regular Demon to grip at the stakes of logs. His long hair swished and swayed behind him, while his cloak fluttered around his body with each pull up of his strong arms. When he was at the top of the wall, he paused to check the surrounding area within the town before jumping down.

Then Zylah was alone.

Her snout bounced as she took in wafts of strange smoke— some sweet, some musky. Jabez didn't cook any meat he hunted, but he did occasionally boil vegetables and fruits in a pot he placed over his campfire. These smokes smelt similar, but as if their contents were more complex.

Just beyond the wall, muted chatter warbled in her ears – like the humans were speaking softly whilst it was dark.

She stepped closer in curiosity, and her pawed feet crunched in the grass. Her snout pointed one way and then the other, before it lifted to the top of the wooden stakes.

*I want to know what it's like inside.* She'd only ever entered a human dwelling once, and she'd been enraged the entire time. Her memory of it was foggy.

Although she hadn't understood what the swollen, painful ache behind her sternum had meant, she'd come to learn what it was called. How weighing it could feel. Zylah had been…

lonely. Humans lived together, and she'd longed to be part of such a way of life. To not be discarded within the forest like a creature, but someone worth being in the presence of.

That feeling had dissipated with Jabez's companionship. The more they spoke, the warmer her chest radiated. She could no longer imagine not being by the male's side.

Zylah took another step towards the village, her feet itching to explore. She touched the wall, and her claws dug into the rough timber as she hesitated. *He always tells me to wait outside.* She chittered to herself, nervous, excited, and irritated all at once. *I'm smart now. I... I won't get caught if I have a peek.*

Even Jabez complimented Zylah's abilities. Surely if he could go into the village, so could she. She didn't understand why she needed to wait outside anymore.

With her mind made up, she followed the same path as Jabez. Once she climbed to the top, she assessed over the other side of the wall, unsure of what he searched for but observing it was empty. She jumped down, her knees bending to take the worst of her fall, and darted her head in every direction when she noticed how *different* just a simple wall could make the world.

She quickly followed his scent. Stalking low down some kind of path on her hands and feet, she looked at the strange, fabricated environment with wonder.

Buildings lined each side, tall, daunting, and larger than she could have ever imagined. She brushed her fingertips along the nearest wall built with some kind of rectangular stones and dried clay, noting the surrounding roofs were made of straw or tiles.

Zylah sniffed at windows to take in the scents that bled out from the cracks, finding each human smelt different, as did every home. Many windows were covered with cloth, as if they wished for privacy or to hide, while a few were just dark and appeared empty. When she came across ones with firelight and no visual shield, she braved peeking inside to see all sorts of new and interesting things.

Little humans sat down at a dark wooden table with bigger humans speaking to them. *Are they the younglings Jabez told me of?* She didn't know if she found them cute or not, as they looked fairly odd to her. Especially the chubby, tiny thing who could barely even sit upright on their own in some kind of tall seat.

*What a defenceless thing.* She took in the way the adult female wiped at the youngling's overly messy face. The presumed father was busy trying to keep the other two from fighting with hushed but deep commands. *Is this what a... family looks like?*

One of her novels had touched on such subjects, although with much strain. This family appeared healthy and happy, and her orbs shifted into a bright green as she inspected them.

The colour startled her, as she'd never seen it before, nor did she know what it meant, and she shook her head while pushing off from the wall. She'd also been stationary for far too long, so she quickly moved on.

She sniffed at the cool, aroma-filled air to follow Jabez.

Just as she reached the end of the path, she paused when she heard movement, like footsteps and heavy material shifting. She shuffled back, and two male guards wearing silver breastplates on top of leather armour passed her hiding place.

Curious about them, and about human soldiers, she stuck her head out to watch them walk away from behind. Both wore swords at their waists and had some kind of helmet over their heads. Their footsteps were quieter than the clunking of their swords and the creaking of their leather armour.

She scratched at the side of her snout. *They aren't doing a very good job.* They hadn't even managed to sniff Zylah less than a few feet from them! *Perhaps their noses aren't as good as mine.*

Hers was even better than Jabez's.

*Then again... I'm better at everything than Jabez.* She tried not to tell him that, as he was always quite offended whenever she stated such truths. *Well, maybe not everything.* He was better at hunting, sneaking, and speaking English than her, considering he taught her everything she knew, but she thought there was a high possibility she might exceed him in all aspects one day.

She kind of liked the idea of that. *He is very confident.* Currently she could run circles around him, but she'd like to do that metaphorically as much as physically.

Realising she was musing on Jabez rather than exploring the village, Zylah tentatively stepped out onto a much wider path. She instinctually slunk low to crawl on her hands and feet, much like how they hunted to avoid being seen.

Each of the buildings stole her curiosity, as they appeared so unique and yet somehow the same. She didn't understand how Jabez could locate anything when they all had straw or tiled roofing, and similar looking walls. There were no signs to explain what each building contained.

When a different pair of soldiers appeared on the path ahead of her, she snuck down a thinner path like the one before. They patrolled past without ever noticing her presence, and she once more mused on their inability to sense her.

*See?! I am perfectly fine walking through the village.*

Confidence put a spring in her steps, and she walked more self-assured on the wider path. The buildings began to change, as if they were designed to be larger. When the scent of more soldiers approaching drifted to her from beyond, she hid in a narrow gap once more with a quiet giggle.

Just as she was about to leave her hiding spot, the fur on the nape of her neck stood on end when something dropped down behind her.

"Zylah," a body-tingling voice growled in a low and deep tone, causing her head to droop and her shoulders to lift. She froze, as if that would conceal her despite being caught. "I told you to wait outside the village."

With her orbs shifting to white, she chittered nervously as she turned around. Jabez stood before her, and her shoulders lifted higher at the disapproving scowl on his handsome features.

"But I wanted to see," she said, shaking her head around apprehensively.

He darted forward to cover the end of her snout and placed a finger over his lips. His red eyes narrowed at her skull, and the angry glint in them made her stomach knot.

"Quiet," he whispered, making her realise he'd been

speaking in a hushed tone the entire time. "I know you wanted to see, but coming here is dangerous for you."

*Says the male that tricked me into destroying a different village.*

Zylah turned her head away defiantly. "I didn't get hurt or seen."

Surprisingly, he placed his hand on top of her skull and turned her back to him. He'd pulled his hood further down his face, as if to better hide in the darkness. She could no longer see his eyes clearly, but his mouth remained tight.

"It's not about you being seen; I knew you could remain hidden."

Just as he opened his mouth to continue, he placed a single finger over his lips again and she was beginning to realise this meant he wanted her to stay quiet. Two soldiers passed their hiding spot, and Jabez leapt closer to cover her orbs with both his hands to hide their light.

A tremor raced down her spine at the warmth of his large hands on her skull, and the way his strong chest pressed against the tip of her snout. Her mouth instantly watered at his delectable scent as it slipped straight into her nose hole on each inhale. Her breaths deepened to take in larger draws, while her mind grew muddy and momentarily lost the ability to sense around her as joy flittered inside her entire being.

Once they were gone, he removed his hands with a sigh, bringing her back to reality.

Energy continued to buzz around her bloodstream, her lungs tight and her mind dozy as she peered up at his attractive face. *Hehe!* she giggled in her mind. *He touched me!* Okay, maybe only her face, but it was so utterly satisfying that she didn't care it was so meagre.

"Look, we'll speak of this after we leave." He eyed her over before adding, "It'll be best if we stay on the ground, rather than scale the buildings. You may be too heavy to be light-footed."

With that, he waved his hand and directed for her to follow. Her giddiness died at his sternness.

They went back the way Zylah originally came, and she constantly bumped up against his back, trying to look over his shoulder whenever he paused at the end of a narrow pathway. He often looked over his shoulder at her with a disapproving frown when she did so, causing her to back up.

They didn't spot a single soldier or human, and not once were they caught as they crept towards the protective wall. The moment they climbed outside of the village, they walked to where her original hiding spot had been, at the edge of the cornfield.

Before he could scold her, Zylah stated, "See? I knew I could do it."

She put space between them and stood up straight, and only folded her arms because he did. She wouldn't let him bully her into feeling bad when nothing had gone wrong.

He loosened his arms and gave a deep huff of vexation as he pushed back the hood of his cloak. He brushed his fingers through the strands of his hair to neaten it before merely shaking his head.

For some reason, she found the obvious disappointment more harrowing than a scolding.

"Where I first climbed into the village is a housing district. What if you had smelt blood or fear?" he asked with a hissy bite to his tone, waving his hands to the side, then lifting them with tensed fingers to show his ire. "Children, younglings... they often have nightmares, and so do human adults. At night, they fear Demons coming to eat them in their sleep."

Refusing to unfold her arms in petty reluctance, her hands balled into fists when she couldn't deny... that may have been bad.

*If I had smelt blood or fear...* It's true, she may have succumbed to hunger, but it had to be strong and sudden to send her into a craze now.

"I would have just covered my nose hole like I usually do."

His brows narrowed further, and his eyes took on a mean glint. She resisted the urge to chitter in reaction to his darkening gaze.

"You also have to take into consideration that humans are a clumsy species. They often hurt themselves." His hands fell before he shook his head again. "Most women often bleed freely once a month as well. I know you're able to handle small and fleeting whiffs of blood now, but if you were stuck down a tight path of houses with many human women going through such a part of their fertility cycle, you would've been trapped with that scent. What then, Zylah?"

Her arms finally fell, just as the reddish pink of shame lifted into her sight. She scratched at her arm when she realised what she'd done could have led to horrible consequences.

"I'm sorry. I didn't..." she started, her voice small.

Jabez cut her off. "You've asked me to not let you attack humans again if I can help it. Yet you refuse to stay back at the cave where it is safest and demand that you accompany me, despite all these things being present *outside* village walls. The wooden stakes aren't just there for protection; they also form a barrier of scent and sound. But it's not infallible, Zylah."

Unable to respond, her sight fell upon the two bulky satchels strapped to his body. Not only had he managed to sneak inside the village effortlessly, it appeared he'd finished his tasks quickly before he found her.

She'd been hoping to catch up to him and help.

When he said nothing, her sight flicked up to his eyes to find his brows were narrowed at her beseechingly. The expression was strange upon his usually hardened features, as if he truly couldn't understand why she'd allowed such a risk. He looked... deeply *concerned*, and that wasn't something she was used to seeing from him.

"I didn't think of all that," she answered, turning her skull away as she subtly hugged her stomach. "What is a fertility cycle?" She'd never heard of such a thing.

"Don't change the subject," he growled out, his ears darting back in anger.

It made her want to shy away from him. He was rarely angry – only ever calm, collected, and almost... emotionless.

"I'm sorry!" she whined, throwing her hands forward. "I just wanted to see what it was like inside. You have spoken about the humans, their markets, their homes, but I didn't know what it all looked like." She scratched at her arm self-consciously. "I couldn't imagine it, not even when the stories in my books detailed them. I wanted to understand."

"You Mavka and your curiosity," he bit out, before turning.

"Let's head back to the cave."

He was still furious, considering his ears refused to spring back to their normal height and were tight with strain. Even his steps were more like stomps as she followed him, a whimper threatening to crush her chest.

The forest was illuminated purely by her sight, and she longed for the reappearance of the moon to brighten it even further. Jabez stated it changed monthly, explaining this flow of time to her so she could count the year by its twelve full moons.

The fresh, cold powder of winter's snowfall was half a foot thick at first, but became minimal the further to the coast they traversed. Their mountain was small, and it resembled a string of rocky hills.

The walk felt gruelling and lengthy under the weight of her guilt. Minutes passed, and each silent one with a fuming Jabez storming forward only made time seem to drag on.

When he purposefully slowed to force her to his side, he finally broke his silence.

"You asked about fertility cycles," he muttered in a low voice. His ire was still present but had softened in the half an hour, if not more, that had passed.

Her head perked up at the conversation, as she was eager to add to her knowledge. *He is going to tell me?*

"It is something females of many species go through. For humans, they bleed midway through their cycle, and the other half they become fertile. It's how they produce children. For some animals, that can be different; their blood and fertility happen at the same time, or right after each other. It solely depends on the species. It's something you should be conscious about, as you don't like to harm any creature. Knowing this will help prevent you from doing so."

"What about Mavka?" she asked, tilting her head.

He glanced at her from the corner of his eye before stating plainly, "I can't answer that."

She took a few steps forward to be partially in front of him just so she could see his face. "Why not?"

His expression turned dull, his eyelids lowering to show indifference. "Because you are the only female Mavka I've ever heard of. From my knowledge, the rest of your kind are all males."

That was a rather curious thing. She lifted her head enough to view the canopy of bare branches above them in thought.

A giddiness had her tapping a claw against the side of her bony rabbit snout. "So there is something you don't know about us?"

"There are many things I don't know. I've lived a long time, but that doesn't mean I know everything. The world is ever-changing, and tomorrow may be different from a decade from now."

She hummed in answer. At first, she'd thought Jabez to be all knowing because he'd taught her so much, but this wasn't the first time he'd been stumped by one of her questions. She liked that he was willing to admit it.

"Do Demons go through such a thing?" she asked.

Jabez shrugged. "Depends on the Demon and their evolution. Some females go through a 'heat' cycle, but the closer they are to completion, the less likely that will happen. They start to become like the humanoids they eat, whether that be human or Elf. However, that isn't always the case, and some females continue to have one. Demons and Mavka are similar in that they start to become what they eat, although for Mavka, it's mostly limited to their intelligence. I've concluded in my studies that you will never lose your fur and your skull will never grow flesh, nor will it change into anything humanoid."

Zylah took everything in while nodding her head to show she was able to comprehend it all.

"I saw many interesting things in the village," Zylah said coyly, hoping it didn't remind him of his earlier ire.

"I'm sure you did," he answered, shuffling one of the satchels on his shoulder. "Do you want to talk about them so I can explain?"

"No. I understood them. It was nice to see those things in person."

He nodded before wordlessly leading their return home.

The silence wasn't heavy like before.

Just as the sun was rising, dawn coming to touch the world and shower it in light, Zylah's sight shifted to bright yellow in joy as she remembered her rebellious adventure.

*Tonight was fun.*

Still wearing his cloak in case he accidentally knelt in the morning sunlight, Jabez rolled out his newly acquired bedroll. His senses were homed in on the female Mavka sitting in his periphery with her knees propped up and excitedly flicking through pages. Each book he'd acquired for her was of a different genre and choosing had taken up most of his time in the village.

She wasn't very keen on reading stories of war and history, so he'd chosen those with less gory content.

One was of gruesome but heartfelt fairytales, and he was curious to see how she'd question him on unknown and fictitious creatures such as dragons or centaurs. Two others were of adventures throughout fabled kingdoms, apparently part of some kind of unfinished series – the books appeared new, as if someone had chosen to be an author in this dark era. Lastly, he'd taken a more scientific book about herbs and animals, so she had a better understanding of the world she lived in.

Zylah had been rather giddy to receive them. Her claws had twitched with excitement at each one he pulled from his satchel bags.

He eyed her growing pile that had already been six books tall. *She really likes to read,* he thought with humour.

She was already seven pages deep by the time he set up a bedroll for her as well. Then he collected the blanket and pillow he'd taken for her and left them at the head of the roll.

Zylah shifted awkwardly, her shoulders lifting. "Can it be closer?" Her voice was higher pitched than normal.

Jabez looked at the large gap he'd left between their rolls and considered it. The idea left him uncomfortable. Her choosing to lie beside him of her own volition was different to him making accommodations for her to do so.

He didn't wish to blur the lines of their companionship.

His brows furrowed deeply. *If I don't, she'll likely sleep on the ground just to be next to me.* Which would defeat the purpose of him procuring the bedroll in the first place. With a huff and jagged movements to highlight his displeasure, he shifted it much closer but made sure they weren't touching.

"There. Better?" he bit out, only for his forced annoyance to die when her little tail tuft wiggled in delight. He wished it hadn't been noticeable from his view of her side profile, as his cheeks warmed at seeing it.

"Yes. Much better," she chirped happily, before returning to her book.

Defeated by the night, and just by her, he plonked his backside on his own bedroll and pulled a green apple from his bag. His sharp fangs bit through it like butter, and the extra crunch in each bite combined with the sour-sweet taste was satisfying.

He hadn't grabbed as much food as usual since all the items he'd obtained for her had taken up most of the space. He'd considered stealing more material to make her a new dress, so she had something to change into, but just couldn't fit it. He also didn't like leaving her outside of the village by herself for long periods in case a Demon came.

As time went on, Jabez found he was becoming rather... protective of her. Apprehensive as well, which didn't coincide with the fact that her presence was oddly soothing for him.

*I should have known she'd follow me inside one night.* So foolish.

Once she'd been able to fully communicate her wishes to him, she'd asked that Jabez not make her kill humans again. He'd argued with her on that front, considering the more she consumed, the more advanced she'd become, but she didn't care. The idea apparently made her feel 'sick in the heart,' as she put it.

Now that she was able to voice her lack of consent on the matter, he'd thrown the idea out.

So now, even though he disagreed, he would attempt to help her no longer rampage against any humans. Even Demonslayers, should they come upon them. He already expressed he may not be able to help her in that matter, as Demonslayers attacked first without a shred of self-preservation.

*She doesn't wish to harm Demons, either.* He had a feeling that was due to Jabez being a half-Demon himself. *She really is a strange Mavka.* Then again, their entire species was made up of fucking oddballs.

"What's a prost... itute?" Zylah asked, tilting her head one way and then the other as she assessed the new word on the page.

Sucking in a sudden, shocked gasp, Jabez choked on a mouthful of apple when it went down his windpipe. His chest burned as he bashed on it and coughed to dislodge the chunk of fruit, hacking until it flung past his fangs.

"What?" she asked, lifting her skull towards him. "The hero of this story is speaking with one about some special information she may have. A secret."

"I'll explain later," he wheezed, refusing to answer. "Just finish the book first."

She let out a huff through her nose hole and shrugged. She reached for her dictionary, but he doubted the word was in there if she hadn't come across it yet. *Unless she just didn't understand the word and its meaning at the time.*

He reached forward and slapped his hand on top of the dark-green hardbound book. He hated the way his ears darted back and his cheeks heated at the simple thought of her learning about this topic, especially as he couldn't fathom as to *why* it made him uncomfortable.

"I told you there are a few things I won't teach you." Anything of a sexual or romantic notion would be avoided, so as to not put silly ideas in her head. "This is one of those things. I know the definition, and it pertains to words I have refused to explain. Those that require... further depth and demonstrations."

Zylah licked the inside of her mouth, which he took as her way of pouting. "But how will I understand this scene if you do not explain it?"

"It is a woman who prefers the company of men." That was all he'd say on the matter.

"Then how would she gain secrets?" she asked curiously.

"Because her occupation has a tendency to make men

relaxed and stupid. Many prostitutes are often used as a place to lay troubled minds."

"Is this solely a feminine role?"

Jabez sighed when strain flared at his temples, and he pulled back to lean against the cave wall. "No, not always. There are males who do this as well, although I think that is less common within humans. I know Demon males do."

She hummed in thought and accepted his vague answers before burying her face back in the book. Only to lift her head once more.

"Did you ever meet with prostitutes?"

Jabez closed his eyes in mortification and tilted his head back until the ends of his horns prevented him from going further. *Someone strike me down now.* He opened his gaze to the ceiling.

"No. I had other means. Those females would be considered concubines."

"What's a–"

"It's a similar role, except the female only keeps the company of one man." He purposefully left out that they usually tended to someone in a position of power.

Not that he'd had one for nearly two centuries – before Katerina, to be exact. *Jealous little female wouldn't share.* He hadn't particularly minded, as he'd grown disinterested in bedding Demons who had ulterior motives.

"Did you speak with them?"

*Please. Someone strike me.*

"No. I'm not the kind of person to share my thoughts with others." Jabez had always found it hard to lay his heart and sins bare to anyone.

Not even Merikh had been gifted the worst of his dark thoughts. Sharing from the depths of the hollowed-out hole where his heart should be... he was rather uncompromising on the matter.

Satisfied, Zylah returned to the story, only for her head to perk up seconds later. His ears pricked higher in alert when she darted her skull towards the entryway.

"I hear creatures approaching," she stated quietly.

At first, Jabez heard nothing. Then, in the distance,

footsteps crunching within the forest became loud enough for him to detect. He couldn't scent them, but he figured Zylah could by the way she sniffed the air.

He quickly propped himself into a defensive position while eyeing their protective barrier of sun. If it was a Demon, they were safe for many hours. *I doubt they're humans.* If they were, they could only be Demonslayers foolish enough to come to these hills.

The stronghold wasn't that far to the west from here, after all.

Jabez had picked this small mountainous location purposefully, as there were fewer Demons in the area. It was far enough away that Demonslayers approaching would be infrequent, but close enough to the stronghold that it'd give quite a few Demons a spook about choosing this as their home.

Only more advanced Demons chose this area, which meant they were wise enough to leave them the fuck alone.

It was also the only stronghold connected to an Anzúli temple in all of Austrális. Jabez knew it to be the western temple, as each section of this continent had just one: northern, southern, eastern, and western.

"I can't smell them yet," Jabez stated as he flicked his hood over his head, readying himself for any potential confrontation. The bright sun showered this area heavily and left him incapable of walking out without protection. "Can you decipher what species they are?"

Zylah carefully placed her book against the ground and hopped into a crouch to crawl closer. Just as she went to poke her head out, he grabbed the back of her dress to stop her so she didn't give away their position just yet.

"One scent is strange," she stated, twisting her head in a show of puzzlement. "It smells human, but not. The other..." She chittered before sinking back into the cave and darted her skull to him. "The other is Mavka."

Jabez cursed under his breath.

"Does it smell like the ones you've met?" he asked, shoving his hood over his head more to hide his identity, not that it helped.

"No. They smell different."

Her answer didn't particularly matter. No Mavka would be pleased to see he was still alive. *Unless it's Orpheus or the feline Mavka, I doubt they'll recognise my scent.* He just needed to remain hidden, and they'd likely think he was some strange Demon.

"Perhaps now would be the time to tell you I don't have an amazing relationship with your kind," he admitted, causing her orbs to shift to dark yellow. "You will have to speak to them without me and make them leave. Do you think you can do that?"

"Why—"

Before she could finish, a stick breaking close by stole their attention. Those approaching were doing so steadily.

"Are you sure she's this way?" a woman's quiet voice drifted over the distance.

A frown pinched his forehead when he tried to take in their scents, but it was hard to detect them past Zylah's gentle tangle of jasmine and violets. His nostrils were also stained with the smell of humans, cooked food, and straw roofing.

But they were familiar, and he tried to figure out *who* exactly they were.

"Her scent is strong now," a male answered, his voice gruff, deep, and *very* inhuman.

*Are they... searching for Zylah?* They had to be, considering they knew she was a female. His ears twitched as he took in the familiarity of their voices, and in the next instant, he figured out who they were.

*Well... shit.* Jabez covered his lips in thought as he looked off to the side. *It's the fox-skulled Mavka and the dark-haired female.* He couldn't quite remember their names.

His gaze slipped to Zylah, and the antlers on her head. *These are her parents.*

He winced at that. He doubted the fox-skulled Mavka would remember Jabez's scent from their fleeting encounter, but he absolutely would become enraged to know whom she was spending time with.

The whole 'I almost stole your child when she was an infant' would never blow over. He chuckled at that. *I did what I needed to.* Despite that, it failed regardless.

That day was on the very long list of days he'd acted rather villainous and knew it. *But in times of war...* That was always his excuse. *And Katerina had recently died.* Murdered would be more accurate, and by the actions of their kind, no less.

Regardless, his presence here wouldn't bode well.

If they discovered him... well, his intention to tell Zylah the truth would come much sooner than he planned.

The couple were almost upon them when Jabez let out a soft growl. "Zylah..." he warned, hoping to get her to move.

Still frozen in place, she shook her head and shrank downwards.

"I don't know if I can do this on my own," she muttered quietly, laying a hand over her chest. "I have never spoken to anyone but you."

"You'll do great," he reassured, despite not really having much faith in her social capabilities. "I even think you have more humanity than that Mavka."

He knew they'd locked gazes with the way her head turned, then her orbs shifted to a brighter yellow at the compliment. She nodded and faced forward just as her orbs reverted back to their normal teal.

She exited the cave on her own.

Jabez followed to the entrance and pressed his back just within the inside hollow to listen in.

*Please don't fuck this up,* he mentally pleaded.

He needed more time. He'd barely scratched the surface of his past with her and had only laid out different pieces, like a puzzle waiting to be completed once she had everything.

Not until she knew his reasonings could he share his intentions with her.

Intentions he found himself thinking less and less about...

# ELEVEN

Shifting into her monstrous form for additional strength and speed, Zylah hesitantly stepped into bright sunlight.

When she saw the two people disturbing her new territory just within the tree line, she instinctually lowered and placed herself in a defensive stance. With one hand against the ground and her knees bent into a crouch, she raised her fur on end in wariness.

Since they were too busy talking to each other to notice Zylah, she tried to decipher the Mavka and human approaching.

The human appeared to be stout in comparison to her male companion, since she only came to the bottom of his ribcage. Her figure was round and curvy, and she was so plump that her breasts and stomach jiggled with each step she took. Hair so dark it almost appeared black waved around her face and shoulders, while her eyes were a bright brown that changed depths depending on if the light hit them or they were cast in shade.

She was dressed in a cream blouse with a light-brown skirt, and a fluffy, wintry black coat sat around her shoulders. The rounded toe of dark boots pushed up the hem of her dress as she crossed over forest debris.

Once Zylah assessed the little human, her sight moved to the well-dressed Mavka beside her. She knew his skull was that of a fox, thanks to Jabez capturing one to show her. His antlers were unmistakable in their deer-like quality, although much, much larger than her newly evolved, daintier ones.

Despite having no wings, he had a collar of long black feathers around his neck. Other than that, his fur was black with a blue highlight and obviously covered him from neck to toe, much like Zylah. He wore a button-up shirt, black trousers, and even strange boots that left his odd hooflike toes free. She noted the white protruding knuckles on his hands and peeked at her own.

She tilted her head at the orange flame of a curvy woman floating between his antlers. She'd never seen anything strange like that before.

*Why would he carry fire with him?* From her experience, fire was nasty, despite being alluring to stare at and providing warmth.

The little female glanced up from where she was watching her footing before looking down once more. With lips parting on a quiet gasp, she snapped her head up, eyes wide. She smacked her Mavka companion on the arm with bouncing, rushing steps, causing him to dart his arm away with a surprised grunt.

"Oh my god, Magnar!" the female exclaimed. "There she is!"

Zylah chittered nervously. She skittered back at the high pitch of the human's feminine voice, her parted grin, and the way her eyes had homed in on her rabbit skull. Zylah stomped her hand forward to show confidence and that she wouldn't so easily back down.

She had to be brave. *I must protect our home.*

Once they broke through the tree line and walked into the bright sunlight, Zylah turned to them on the small, thin path right next to the mountainside. With her back towards the opening of the cave, and a wall of rock to her left, their scents gently brushed across the dirt to her on the light wind.

There was something familiar about them, but she couldn't place where or how she knew their smells. Despite how comforting she immediately found them, her settling fur rose on end again when the human stumbled over her hasty footsteps with liquid bubbling in her eyes. A soft warning growl left Zylah's parted maw, just as the male Mavka grabbed the female around her centre to prevent her from coming too close.

"Careful, Delora," the Mavka rumbled softly, his voice deep, gruff, and scratchy in comparison to Jabez. It sounded inhuman even to Zylah's ears – which made her wonder how her own voice was interpreted.

"But it's Fyodor," the female, Delora, whined, facing his fox skull. "It's our baby, Magnar."

"She may not remember us," Magnar responded, and his green orbs shifted to a deep blue when his words caused the female's face to appear crestfallen. "Mavka do not remember the beginning of their life. She's now an adult and very dangerous."

Delora brought her gaze to Zylah's rabbit skull with a beseeching furrow to her brows, while her eyes bowed with sadness. "I know, but... I'm hoping she remembers at least *something*." She looked back at him once more. "Our voices, our scents, something."

Zylah tilted her head in curiosity. *They know me?* Could they answer questions she'd been missing, like where she'd come from, and why? Who were her parents, and why had they left Zylah alone all this time?

Why did they... *abandon* her?

Magnar patted Delora's dark hair before brushing down her cheek. "I know you're excited, but slow, my pretty raven. Careful."

The female rolled her eyes while also simultaneously bringing them to Zylah. A soft, caring, and almost welcoming smile curled her lips when she stepped out of her male's arms.

"Hiya there," Delora cooed, holding out her hand and presenting the back of her wrist. "I'm not sure if you understand us, but we mean you no harm. We've been searching for you."

Zylah warily stepped closer to the rock wall to her left, blocking their path forward while also evading the human.

*"I understand you,"* Zylah responded, her voice taking on a monstrous graininess in her more animalistic form.

Delora's doe-brown eyes widened until the whites of them became stark. Her lips parted, and she rasped, "Y-you spoke!"

Zylah tilted her head at that. *"Yes. I can speak."*

Delora turned to Magnar with a frown wrinkling her forehead. "But Emerie and Ingram said she couldn't speak, and that was only two months ago."

*"Emerie? Ingram?"* Zylah asked. She didn't know these names.

Delora brought her gaze forward once more. "Emerie is the human with red hair who you took to your home. Ingram is the Duskwalker with a raven skull who... took her back. They said you lived in a burrow."

It didn't take Zylah long to remember these people.

She hated admitting that her memory of them was... blurry. She remembered the woman's bright-orange hair, light skin marred with redness, and blue eyes, but nothing else about her features. Not the shape of her nose, eyes, chin, or body, nor could she remember what she wore. The male they spoke of... he was a blob of black fur and a white, bony face that lacked shape.

She knew their scents better than their features, and the female more, as Zylah had spent a few hours with her in comparison to the raven Mavka they spoke of.

Zylah sniffed at the air, wondering why this female smelt so familiar. *I... like her scent.* It was gentle but had the strangest coolness to it that she appreciated. *She reminds me of the green apples Jabez eats.* Although she smelt less sour and much sweeter, as if there were different types. *It makes me sleepy.*

When the dark-haired female stepped closer, the back of her wrist still presented, the fur on Zylah's neck rose. Delora's sweet scent may have been oddly comforting, along with her voice as well, and Zylah might have been curious about them, but her protective instincts flared.

She currently had a smaller, weaker being within the home of their shared cave, and his earlier concern hadn't gone unnoticed. At least, she took it as worry and anxiety. Their presence made him uncomfortable, and therefore, Zylah's territorial and possessive aggression was heightened.

*I must protect him.*

She wanted them gone.

She didn't know or trust them.

Zylah stood, making herself taller, and hopefully more threatening. *"I don't know why you've been searching for me, but I want you to leave."*

Delora didn't back down as she expected her to, nor did Zylah sense any unease from her. Magnar, however, quickly gave Zylah a soft and almost... half-hearted warning growl. His orbs remained green as he crept in Delora's shadow protectively.

"Please, Fyodor," Delora pleaded with her eyes bowing beseechingly. "We want you to come with us."

Zylah's head cocked to the side in question. *"Fyodor? What does this mean?"*

Delora's cheeks pinkened as a small smile curled her lips. "It's your name."

*"My name is Zylah,"* she swiftly corrected.

"You have a new name?" Magnar asked while gingerly stepping forward, then sniffing at the air. He snorted out a mild huff. "You also have a companion."

Delora gasped and turned her eyes to him. "She does?!"

"A Demon," he grumbled with mild displeasure. "It smells like they have been living here together for quite some time."

Once more, Delora brought her gaze back to Zylah. Concern glinted in her big brown eyes, made evident by the deep furrow of her brows and the downturn of her lips. Her expression faded, and she tried to smile once more – although it was broken and weak.

"Zylah, then," Delora whispered, before her voice strengthened. "Please come with us. Someone is obviously helping you, and we're so thankful for that, but there's so much we can do for you. We can show you what it's like to be family."

"How to hunt, how to be a Mavka," Magnar added, placing his arm around Delora's shoulders to hold her with tenderness. "We can explain many things you'll need to know that you cannot learn on your own."

Zylah shook her head. *"I don't need your help."*

"Please," Delora begged, stepping forward, only to be dragged back by her Mavka, who was wisely wary of Zylah but remaining unhostile. She could almost feel the tension coming off him, but it didn't heighten her aggression in return. "When we heard from Emerie that you were still so close to the Veil, we thought it might be because you, somewhere inside, longed to be with us again. We searched for you in your burrow, your territory, and it led us here. You don't have to live like this. We can show you a home, and what it's like to not be alone."

*"I'm not alone!"* Zylah barked out with her sight shifting to a deep red. She stamped a singular foot in annoyance and made it thump loudly, wishing they would just understand. *"I have Jabez. I do not need you."*

The words appeared to cut so deep that the female's lips shook as tears flooded her eyes. Then, in the next moment, her tanned features paled.

Yet it was Magnar who asked, "Who did you say?"

A chitter of shame and nervousness exploded from her, and her orbs morphed to a stark white. She cupped her hands near her chest when anxiety flooded her gut. *I should not have said that.* She shouldn't have mentioned his name.

"Fy... Zylah," Delora rasped, and even Zylah could hear how fast her little heart was beating despite the space between them. "Please tell me you didn't just say *Jabez.*"

Stepping back, Zylah almost tripped over her elongated rabbit feet in her monstrous form, just as a small, deep, yet *dark* chuckle rumbled from behind her. Without giving her back to strangers, she looked over her shoulder to see Jabez exiting the cave.

With his hood propped over his head to protect himself from the sun, it cast a rather ominous shade over his features. The red of his eyes became stronger, and the coldness of them even harsher with his silvery eyelashes.

"I guess there is no point in hiding any longer," he stated, his voice void of any emotion.

Zylah chittered as reddish pink entered her sight. She'd told him she wasn't capable of doing this on her own. Instead of removing these strangers from their territory, she'd accidentally spilled the secret of her companionship with him when it had been obvious he wanted to avoid that.

*I failed,* her mind whimpered.

Stepping out from the shade of his hiding spot, Jabez noted the way Zylah had shrunk within herself and even lowered into a crouch. Although he kept the mask of his cruel indifference firmly in place, he understood that he'd just given her too big of a task.

Risking the sun, he reached out to pat the back of her arm and ignored the sting that cut across his knuckles. "It's fine," he stated calmly, before bringing his hand back within the safety of his cloak. "You did your best."

*She's only just learned how to communicate properly.* Hiding one's emotions, thoughts, and secrets was hard for an inexperienced person. Let alone one who had never spoken to strangers.

He wouldn't show any ire towards her, not when he was hoping he could... *mitigate* the problem.

There had also been a nag at the back of his mind and a trickle of guilt sliding down his nape while he'd been eavesdropping.

*My relationship with my parents is non-existent.* Jabez had no desire to ruin that for Zylah, despite knowing his companionship with her may already do that.

Walking to be at her side, he thought, *Let's see just how much she wishes to remain with me.*

Jabez never removed his sight from the human woman before him, nor the Mavka who's orbs had taken on an angry crimson hue. A snarl echoed from him, while his collar of feathers puffed in aggression until they threatened to spike around the back of his fox skull.

*Let's see how much she can learn of my actions before she turns on me.* A rather dangerous thought, considering he could find himself alone against three potential enemies by the end of this conversation.

Yet, in a corner of his untrusting mind, he had... faith in Zylah. Strange – he didn't believe in anyone other than himself.

"Zylah, come away from him," Delora whispered as she beckoned Zylah closer by curling her outreaching fingers. "He's dangerous."

Zylah stepped forward and put her shoulder in front of him protectively. He moved out of her shield to show they were on even footing, despite that he lacked his magic. They didn't know that – they knew him to be a great being of unimaginable power.

A cold-hearted, villainous killer who cackled on his mountain of metaphorical corpses like the psychopath he'd led *all* to believe him to be.

A lie, of course. A mere ruse to incite fear.

*"No,"* Zylah snarled back, her hackles rising.

"Calm," Jabez stated as he stroked her back, never taking his eyes from those before them. He cracked a large grin, flashing his shark-like fangs purposefully. "I'm sure you have questions."

"You're supposed to be dead!" Delora blurted out, stamping her foot forward in outrage. "Y-your castle, it was destroyed!"

"And here I stand," Jabez answered, waving at the ground with both hands. "You have Zylah to thank for that."

"What?" she rasped, her horrified gaze slipping to Zylah.

"That nasty little bomb did quite a lot of damage to me. Without Zylah healing me through it, my chances of survival were exceptionally low. Had she come even a day later, I'd likely be dead." He spared Zylah the briefest glance to show that he lacked any fear of the two people before him. "She's remarkably adept with her healing magic."

"What do you want with her?" Magnar rumbled with a growl, lowering himself into an offensive stance. He pushed his shoulder before Delora, who leaned into his side like it was natural for her.

Jabez tilted his head at him, and his grin grew more malicious. "You know... I never would've guessed that you Mavka could hold such protective instincts towards your children."

*"Children?"* Zylah asked softly, despite the graininess in her voice due to her monstrous form. She turned to him ever

so slightly and tugged on his cloak with an inquisitiveness he found rather cute.

Dropping his malice, as he didn't wish to shine that upon her, he nodded his head towards the pair. "These are your parents."

Her orbs shifted to an unusually bright yellow. *"They are?"*

The tension in her shoulders eased slightly, and he figured it was out of curiosity and awe, rather than truly becoming relaxed in their presence.

"Yes," Delora rasped, her bottom lip shaking as tears welled in her eyes. "I'm your mum, and Magnar is your dad. That's why we've been searching for you."

Zylah placed both her palms against her chest. *"But you don't look like me. You are not Mavka."*

"I told you," Jabez stated without a shred of arrogance in his tone, "your kind are born from a human turned Phantom."

Zylah tilted her head. *"You knew who my parents were this entire time?"*

Jabez offered a benign, false smile. "I always intended to explain this to you, and who they were, where they were."

Delora's brows furrowed in confusion. "Why would you do such a thing?"

"Who do you think gave her more humanity? Taught her how to speak?" Jabez deflected. "To read, write, count? Of course things have been slow, since she needed to learn all that before we could have complex conversations, but I know much about Mavka and the history from the origin of their birthing. All this was planned to be shared in due time. I couldn't explain any of it when the only language she understood was her own chitters."

"But *why* would you help her?" Delora pushed.

"Consider it payment for saving my life." Jabez no longer knew if that was a lie or not.

Sure, in the beginning his intentions had been rather self-serving, but... in the months of learning who Zylah was, he'd begun just simply wanting to aid her.

Much of her future could be filled with violence, and the threat of her life was solely his responsibility. He'd shared the secret to the Mavka's demise with the Demons, and although he couldn't care less about the others, he did feel indebted to Zylah. If he could right that wrong with at least the person who allowed him to take another breath, it was a small atonement for that mistake.

"Okay, you've done that." Delora's features took on a hard edge. "We can take over. We can do the rest."

Jabez chuckled as he folded his arms. "That would be solely up to Zylah."

Delora looked upon Zylah, and her lips parted in disbelief, as if what he said was ridiculous.

"She's just a child! She doesn't know any better!" She fisted the brown skirt of her dress.

His chuckle evolved into full-blown laughter. "She's obviously not a child. She is an adult who can consent to with whom she spends her time."

"She was only born two years ago!"

"And her intelligence already exceeds her parent," Jabez argued, raising a finger at the male Mavka. "You have no idea who she is or what she is capable of. I've seen it, and even I've been amazed."

The fact that Mavka didn't age like a human or even an Elf, but more like a Demon, made this situation strange. Her age was defined by how many humans she ate, not by her length of life. He imagined for some humans that would be difficult to understand, but this woman was pushing human ideologies onto a magical being that could eat her because it suited her, uncaring of their blood relation.

Everything was upside down and skewed, and even he knew little of it made sense – only that this was just how Mavka were. They were odd creatures that existed outside of normality and logic, which had infuriated him for the last few centuries because they had been his enemy.

Her brows drew impossibly tighter. "But..."

"You are the reason for it," Jabez cut in. "You, as her mother, have gifted her evolution the others belonging to Lindiwe can't achieve. It has taken half the number of humans to bring Zylah to this level of humanity, if not less."

"I don't understand," Magnar grumbled as he raised a hand to his snout. Like the idiot he still was, he tapped the point of a claw against the bone.

"Of course *you* don't," Jabez stated with a sigh, rolling his eyes as if that should have been obvious.

"Are you saying that the further they are from the spirit of the void, the quicker their minds develop?" Delora asked with a pensive flattening of her lips.

"From what I've seen in her, yes," he answered. "A Mavka's age has always been irrelevant. Only their level of humanity matters. I've seen Mavka remain mentally younger than those who were born *after* them. An excellent example of this is Orpheus and the feline-skulled Mavka."

With the way Delora's expression turned shy, Jabez gathered she already knew the truth of that. He, however, had known it for a long time.

*Orpheus stopped eating humans when he longed to keep one.* The feline Mavka, on the other hand, didn't give a shit. He'd hunted everyone, humans and Demons, and grew indiscriminately and without care. *And Orpheus has lived decades longer.*

He'd hindered his own development in his pathetic search for a companion.

For a few fleeting moments, Jabez watched as the pair in front of him soaked in the information he willingly offered. Even Zylah had gone pensive.

It gave him time to truly look upon them.

Jabez, admittedly, knew very little about Magnar. He and the twins were the Mavka he'd had little contact with, for various reasons. Magnar had stayed away from the centre of the Veil, and therefore, had been an ignored presence within the forest. He rarely attacked Demons.

The twins, however, were two ruthless creatures and attacked anything out of boredom. Being near them was dangerous, and their intelligence had been so low that having a simple conversation with them resulted in the most humorous example of talking to a pair of moving trees.

From what Jabez could tell of Magnar, he was trying to emulate Orpheus. He stood similarly, spoke similarly, and appeared to even be dressing like him since he wore a nice black dress shirt and pants. There was more of an uncertain stance in his posture in comparison, and it was obvious he let his woman lead in most instances.

His eyes slipped to Delora. She was plump, and it made her appear soft and feminine. Her dark hair waved around her shoulders and framed her delicate, tanned features. She looked healthy, but unlike last time, she lacked any tiredness and instead seemed to shine in a way only a person who had achieved self-worth could.

Like he had the first time he'd met her, he found her beauty rather beguiling.

Then again, Jabez's perspective on beauty was insanely skewed. He found many Demons attractive as well. For Jabez, attractiveness could be born from the most abstract features. He'd found Katerina lovely for the opposite reasons he found the woman in front of him lovely. They were completely different, from their eye colour, body shape, skin tone, and even gaze strength.

Even Mavka were handsome fellows to him, not that he'd ever let one know he appreciated them platonically. But he'd always admired their strength and peculiar exoticness.

Although he'd been struggling to admit it, he found Zylah beautiful as well.

He didn't think his glances upon the female Mavka had been desirous – or, rather, he hoped they weren't – but it was becoming increasingly difficult to deny her sensuality. Sensuality she had no idea she possessed, and something he'd attempted to cover up with a garment that appeared to just make it worse.

It was like it had become a tease of material that was so short he found his eyes following the way it lifted over her furry, thick thighs. Even the way one of the thin straps would slip over her shoulder and lower the material around the top of a breast was eye-catching.

His lips flattened tight. *Why am I thinking about this right now? In this situation, of all times?*

It didn't help that Zylah was currently naked beside him, since her clothing had sunken beneath her flesh. He was finding it hard to look upon her, regardless of her being in her monstrous form.

His thoughts and the silence were broken by Delora.

"It doesn't matter," she eventually whispered, raising her eyes from the ground to him. "I-I, as her mother, can't approve of this. I won't."

Jabez rolled his eyes so hard it pained him. "Like I haven't heard that before." Lindiwe had said something similar once she'd learned of his and Merikh's friendship. "Come now, you can't be that forgetful. I already told you it's solely up to Zylah."

As if on cue, Zylah said, *"I wish to stay with him."*

Before Delora could open that pretty mouth of hers, Jabez spoke over the top of her.

"I'm offering for us to air out some... *differences*." He waved to the ground. "Sit with me, and perhaps I can share some insight into the past. Much of it, Zylah should learn. Then we can allow her to make her choice."

"Why should we do anything you say?" Delora bit out, her gentle features sharpening in hate. He did rather like the defiant glint to her gaze. "I don't trust you, or that you'll *actually* share the truth."

Once more, Jabez allowed a malicious grin to fill his features. "You should take the offer when I'm so willingly gifting it. I can teleport Zylah and I away from here in the blink of an eye, or have you forgotten my abilities, human?"

The emotional woman visibly grew sickened at the reminder of the power he'd once held. He found her terrified expression rather delightful.

*"But you—"* Zylah started.

"Then I can easily take her further and further from your reach," he interrupted before she could share his loss of magic. He made sure his voice held nothing but sickly sweetness, digging into the wound he was creating with feigned kindness when the words were nothing but cruel. "If you found us again, we'd be gone before you even reached the end of our scents. You'd never catch us. What would you prefer? Because, currently, I'm feeling inclined to be benevolent."

*"Is this the magic you told me of?"* Zylah asked, her teal orbs shifting to dark yellow.

He just responded with a smile and a pointed gaze. His eyes

darkened as he brought them back to the pair.

"I'm offering for us to speak on even footing. A temporary truce, if you will, where we all sit in the dirt together." He waved at the ground once more.

Then, to highlight just how little he feared them, and how he expected them to fold to his whims, he smoothly transitioned from standing into a crossed-legged seated position.

After a few moments of mulling, Delora was slow to sit, each of her movements stilted and wary. She eyed Jabez mistrustingly the entire time, even when she pulled on her Mavka's clawed hand to make him sit as well.

Zylah, wanting to mimic them, shifted into her more humanoid form. Her dark-grey dress came to the surface as she sat with her knees together and her feet poking out the opposing side to Jabez. Her shoulder brushed his, and he was certain she sat in a way that touched him in order to silently seek comfort from him.

He didn't mind, and even considered leaning back to help ease her, but refrained due to those before him.

This was one of his favourite positions when having an unpredictable conversation with another. They couldn't stand over him nor he them, giving everyone the illusion that no one was better than anyone else. It also helped to mitigate agitated body language that could be perceived poorly – especially when dealing with Mavka that didn't know how to handle their emotions well.

Lastly, it allowed the others to perceive Jabez as indifferent.

He was sitting in filth with them, his shoulders at ease, as though he was relaxed in their presence. Not a king, not a Demon, but a person who was intelligent enough to have a conversation that wasn't stipulated in cruelty and self-serving gain.

All of it was a lie on his part, of course. At least, before the loss of his magic, that was true. The ability to teleport from one place to another allowed him to also change positions. He could go from sitting in front of them to snapping their neck while standing behind them within a heartbeat.

It was a rather unfair advantage he'd had.

For now, he did this to hopefully reduce their distrust of him by even a little. He lacked magic, and it needed to remain a secret. Acting arrogantly would get him nowhere, although that was his default when faced with any enemy – an enraged being fighting without thought was easier to battle than a cunning and calm one.

Once everyone was as comfortable as they could be in this tense situation, Jabez placed his elbow on his knee and rested his cheek upon the knuckles of his enclosed fist.

"So," he started, stifling the urge to grin manically like a deviant. "Where shall we begin?"

"There's much you have done," Magnar growled, his orbs once more flaring to crimson. "All of it unforgiveable."

"You... you ate me!" Delora exclaimed, throwing her hands forward.

"I did do that, didn't I?" he answered with mirth, humour glinting in his gaze to the point he could feel the heat of it.

"You ate my mother?" Zylah asked, her voice returning to that rather sweet cuteness he preferred. Surprisingly, her tone held curiosity more than disgust.

"In all fairness, I was rather livid at the time," he stated in his own defence. "You're a rather devious woman when you wish to be. It's not often one would defy me, let alone trick me. You played your role rather admirably, and I've always respected you for that moment, despite how much it angered me at the time."

Delora's lips parted in surprise, likely not expecting his response. But it was the truth, and how he'd always felt about it.

"Let's just say I have a rather nasty temper. I'm also a very cunning man. Sure, I ate *a little* bit of you, but I knew my torture would be fleeting and have no lasting repercussions for you. You're a Phantom. Your revival ensured anything I did meant little, except for how it affected your psyche." His brows narrowed as he remembered that day, and it wasn't with fondness. "I also did truly want the Mavka beside you to come to your rescue, which he wisely didn't. I also didn't want to allow the Demons to consume you and grow any additional abilities. It was either me or them, and I guarantee you, their bites would have been nastier."

"W-why didn't you want the Demons to gain abilities?" Delora asked, her lips tightening in uncertainty. "Isn't that what you wanted all along? To strengthen your army?"

"I can't develop Phantom abilities."

Jabez knew it at the time, since he'd consumed Lindiwe a few times, to no avail. But he'd threatened the woman with it to incite fear and make her watch over her shoulder constantly – to haunt her as much as Phantoms could haunt others.

"Sometimes Demons have the ability to gain attributes from those with magic, or even venom from certain creatures – both things I can't do. I'm fully formed and not a full Demon, therefore any additions to my abilities must come from either being taught the magic, the runes, or consuming mana stones."

Her lips pursed, and her eyes darkened in annoyance at him. "That doesn't answer my question."

"Have you ever considered that I allowed my fellow Demons to evolve, but not reach a higher level of power than me?" A rather hollow smile curled his lips. "You forget they eat each other. When they had no need of me, or saw a chance to gain the leadership I held, what would have stopped them from turning on me? A Demon with the ability to turn incorporeal would have been a tough opponent to face, even with my ability to teleport. What would you have done if a Demon had the ability to turn incorporeal and slip inside your ward, your very home, soundless, scentless, and without warning? What then? I couldn't teleport within your ward, but could they have moved through it with an intangible body? What would have stopped them from doing that to me in my very own home?"

It was something that had worried him constantly about Lindiwe, and why he'd put special wards in place to protect himself while he slept. He'd always hated the paranoia – which had the hairs on the back of his neck and on his arms rising – that she could be lurking where he couldn't sense her.

"You could have just let me go," she muttered with a pout present in her voice and her bottom lip sticking forward.

He rolled his eyes at her ridiculous statement.

"Do you know how powerful fear is? It is the biggest tool

in my arsenal. Your fear of me, his rage towards me, made you both predictable."

"Predictable, huh?" She scoffed at him, while averting her gaze. "I bet you didn't see us showing up at your castle."

He smiled at her for that. "No, but that wasn't *your* idea, was it? Lindiwe is as unpredictable as you can get. She has lived over three hundred years and has the experience you lack. Her fear turned into motherly rage, and with the power of a god on her side, she is the only being in this forsaken realm who can best me. Without her, what you did never would have been a possibility."

Delora gave him a rather bored look, her head lifting back superiorly. "It sounds like you admire her."

"Don't you?" he rebuffed, cocking a brow in astonishment. "I may hate that fucking pest of a woman, but underestimating your enemy is foolish. I have never been a fool."

As if she was done with the current conversation, he watched her expression turn spiteful and scheming. Her gaze slipped to Zylah beside him.

"He tried to kill you," she said quietly. "You were nothing but a baby."

"Did I?" Jabez countered. "I'm not in the game of harming children, no matter what they are."

Delora's back went rigid, and she clutched her skirt until the backs of her knuckles paled. "You tried to break her skull!"

"Did I?" he repeated, once more cocking a brow. "Or did I attempt to drive a poor mother who clearly loved her child to take action? How about the father who quickly turned on his own sibling?" Without removing his cheek from his fist, he shifted his gaze to the forest beside them in thought. "You'll be surprised to know just how powerful love can be. I had no intention of truly harming her, otherwise I wouldn't have made a show of it." His eyes slipped back to her. "Or given you the opportunity to prevent it. Devious, no?"

"You're a fucking sicko," Delora rasped.

"I have been called evil so many times over that it gets old. What happens in war is devastation."

"A war we want no part in!" Magnar snapped out.

"And yet... it's a war you have been part of from the

moment you took your first breath."

At Delora's confused face, and Magnar's head rear, he sighed. *Why can they not see it?* Why must he spell this out for every single one of them?

"I actually have very little hate towards Mavka," Jabez admitted, finally lifting his head to sit upright. He wiggled his shoulders back to give a superior air to his aura. "Sure, I have a deep hatred for *one* of your kind and his bride, but the rest of you don't particularly matter to me. But you are the children of Weldir, and he's prevented me from taking action for centuries." He gave a singular, knowing chuckle while shaking his head. "And none of you humans are enraged by it. Then again, you would have to know that the devastation of Demons upon your world solely rests in his untouchable hands."

"He's not the one who brought them here," Delora argued.

"Neither did I. I brought six Demons here. The rest came on their own and then remained stuck here due to Weldir's ward preventing them from going back through the portal I created with a mana stone. Many of them long to return to the Elven world. Without his interference, humanity wouldn't be nearing extinction. Had I been allowed to take them back centuries ago, life here would be vastly different. The history you know is missing vital pieces. Would you continue to side with him, with Lindiwe, had you known that their sole purpose is to keep the Demons here just to spare the Elves? Inherently selfish, isn't it?"

"Life is what it is," Delora whispered as she lowered her gaze. "I've learned to accept it, especially as it brought me here." To give away what she meant, she rested her hand on Magnar's trouser-covered leg. "We can be angry, or just accept that they had their reasons."

"Ugh, such a tender-hearted, meek answer," Jabez bit out with disgust. "I refuse to accept such a notion."

Why were the Elves constantly forgiven for the exact things he was blamed for? What he'd said was true. Without the Elves, humankind and their lives would be vastly different.

Without Weldir, Jabez could have saved hundreds, if not thousands, of human lives by removing the Demons from Austrális. He could have been humankind's saviour as much as the Demons'.

But instead of being thanked for what he'd been attempting to do for hundreds of years, he'd been despised for it.

"You are the most selfish creature I know," she retorted. "Everything you've stated so far has been cruel and selfish. How are you any better?"

"I'm not," he willingly admitted with a deadened expression. "I'm very self-aware that I am a despicable fuck. The only life that matters to me is my own. I'm the product of their carelessness, and then they discarded me like filth. I have spent my whole life wishing to avenge myself for what they did to me as a child."

"And yet you wish to ruin others just to achieve that. I can never see your side, no matter if the truth isn't what I first thought it was. What you did to me, to Magnar, to Zylah... I could never forgive it, nor allow you to make me think better of it." Then her eyes again filled with the tears he knew she'd been holding in. "And what you did to Faunus..."

His head cocked, while his ears twitched. "I have no idea who that is."

"It's the feline-skulled Mavka," Magnar answered.

"Ah." Jabez nodded in understanding. "What I did to Faunus was what was done to me."

"By him, though?" Delora asked, although her tone said she knew the answer to that was already no.

"By Lindiwe. Like I said, I have been locked in battle with her for centuries. Everything she did to me, I did to him. Judge me all you want for it, but I responded to cruelty with more cruelty. Will you pity me now that you know the truth?"

Her lips thinned, and under the weight of his scrutiny, she shied away from his gaze.

"You won't, will you?" He tilted his head and offered a callous grin when he saw she couldn't even muster up a false tear for his sake. "What I did to that Mavka is nothing in comparison to what was done to me by her. And with my inability to hold her due to her Phantom abilities, not once have I *ever* been able to enact such violence upon her. And I'm not a deathless being, unlike her children. My wounds do not heal in a day, and I must go out of my way to fix myself before permanent damage is done to me."

Other than cracking that Mavka's skull, his torture was mediocre in comparison to what Lindiwe had done to him. But no one would cry or pity him, so why should he return the same sentiment?

He also hadn't done it to be needlessly cruel. He hadn't taken that Mavka from the middle of the Veil just to cackle like a villain as he tortured him. He did it to find out how the fuck to kill them, and he was just the unfortunate soul that Jabez had picked. Had Jabez known how they died, none of that Mavka's pain would have existed – Jabez would have just ended him mercifully.

"Why not just teleport away then?"

"I haven't always had the ability. It's actually rather new, in the grand scheme of things." He raised his right hand to look at his palm before turning it over to inspect his wrist. Or, rather, the runic symbols that danced a line around both his wrists – although they had nothing to do with the ability. "I've been able to teleport for a few decades, and it took a buried Elven library to discover such an ancient ability. You'd be surprised what is now locked beneath ruins in dark places not even Demons can infiltrate. I started out weak. Such strength doesn't come from a youngling; it must be taught, earned, or discovered."

"So you can go back to your realm?" Delora asked quietly, obviously losing enthusiasm for their conversation. "Why not just fucking stay there and leave us alone?"

"I have my reasons. But yes, the fact I'm an Elf allows me to cross freely, and only me."

*I've always wondered if that was purposeful.* If, perhaps, the Elves wanted him to return one day in order to seek his forgiveness. *Disgusting.*

He turned his head to the female Mavka beside him and noted that her orbs shone a dark yellow. "You have been quiet."

"I am... listening," Zylah answered softly.

*I doubt she truly understands all of what we've spoken about.* There would've been words she didn't know the definition of, things she didn't understand the true repercussions of. Then again, other than torturing her mother and pretending to want to kill Zylah, nothing else had truly been revealed. Even the depth of his cruelty towards Faunus had been skilfully hidden by Jabez speaking quickly before the human could elaborate.

She'd come to learn of it all eventually, but at least she knew his side before he'd even stated it all.

"I'm not sure if you've noticed, but Zylah hasn't moved from my side," Jabez announced, giving a pause to allow all to digest that fact. He brought his gaze back to her. "So, after learning what you have today, do you still wish to stay?"

Although he remained nonchalant, he had no idea how she would respond. Given that he hadn't denied anything he'd done, much of it rather villainous, her choice could go either way.

"Please, Zylah," Delora implored, reaching out to place her hand against the dirt and leaf debris, when it was obvious she wanted to touch Zylah's knee. "He's not a good person. He's hurt so many people."

"So have I," Zylah answered, her orbs shifting to a deep blue in sorrow. She lifted her palms to stare down at her curved, sharp claws. "How many have I harmed? I've gained much humanity, and whenever I have been attacked, I always wish to defend myself. How am I any different?"

"It's not the same, sweetheart," Delora cooed. "You probably attacked when provoked. *He* attacks because he's a fucking asshole."

"But he cares about me," she said with a whimper. "He teaches me."

"Because he wants to use you!"

That hit a little too close to the truth.

Jabez placed his cheek on his fist once more. "Have none of you ever wondered *why* I know so much about Mavka? A bystander can't learn intricate and secretive knowledge of another species without good reason."

Delora turned a rage-filled, tearful gaze to Jabez. "Because you've pulled them apart like a creep?"

His eyelids drooped in annoyance at her pettiness. "Because I was once friends with a Mavka. For quite a long time, may I add."

"No one would befriend you," she sneered, her nose scrunching up in distaste.

"No? How about Merikh? The bear-skulled Mavka," he answered pointedly. "For decades he was my companion – long before I knew of Orpheus, long before you were ever born, human. I doubt you're aware, since he's a reclusive loner who has a deep dislike of everyone, including his own kind."

"What does this have to do with anything?" Magnar asked, shaking his silly fox skull.

"I cared for him, taught him, just as I'm doing for Zylah. I likely have more knowledge to share with her than you ever could." His gaze tipped to the soul floating between Magnar's antlers. "I even watched the first time your kind bonded with someone."

As if appalled, Magnar hid Delora's soul from him with both his hands. "You can see it?"

"Is it strange that I do?"

"Those who aren't bonded usually can't see it unless they're another Mavka."

Jabez pondered this for a moment. He shrugged.

"It's likely because I'm an Elf. We have the ability to see essences and magic that would usually be hidden to a human." He curled his free hand forward to glance at his claw-like nails with feigned boredom. "My point is: you have no idea of what I want, nor why I'm helping Zylah. Please keep your unsolicited and false assumptions to yourself. You know so little that you're nothing but a tiny blip on the string of history."

Delora's lips parted in disbelief at his sharp rudeness, but he remained indifferent to it. He despised people thinking they knew him and his reasonings when they clearly didn't.

"So, Zylah," Jabez prodded, tilting his face to her rabbit skull. "What decision have you come to?"

Zylah looked between them, before her shoulders turned inwards. It was obvious her gaze fell to the ground with the way her skull dipped forward.

"I'm sorry, but I don't know you."

Tears gathered in Delora's eyes, and a strange whimper fell

from her lips. "But... but we're your parents."

Zylah shifted nervously, then shrugged – which was new. He'd never seen her do that before. "I don't truly understand what that means, nor why it matters. You abandoned me."

"We didn't!"

Zylah clutched her left biceps and turned her head away, in Jabez's direction, as if she needed to see him. Her orbs shifted to deep blue. "But I have been alone."

He took in the solemn colour of her glow, then sighed.

"Because that's the natural evolution of Mavka," Jabez stated in their defence. "You likely grew your antlers and then ran off into the forest like a wild creature. That's not their fault."

He had no intention of manipulating the truth for his own benefit, not when it could have a deeply traumatising impact on Zylah's mental wellbeing in the future. He doubted she'd been abandoned and had just taken the next step in a Mavka's life – one that meant they'd transitioned into adulthood.

Zylah shook her head. "It doesn't matter. I... know *him*. I wish to stay with Jabez."

"There," he stated, uncrossing his legs while simultaneously pushing off the ground to stand. "You have your answer."

Delora and Magnar were quick to rise, so he didn't tower over them, and the Phantom readily took a defensive stance. She'd become rather stupidly brave over the last few years.

"Zylah," she rasped, but immediately quietened when she received a growl in response.

"I have made my choice!" Zylah exclaimed, and Jabez knew by the shaking tone of her yell, and the way her fur puffed, that she was agitated and likely very confused. "I wish for you to leave me... *us*... be!"

Zylah rose to a crouch before quickly leaving – as if to say she'd hear no more on the subject. She didn't enter their shared cave, instead escaping into the forest to put as much space between her and them as possible.

He was surprised she'd abandoned him with strangers nearby, since she could be rather protective and possessive of his presence. *She must be extremely upset.*

His chest tightened in sympathy, causing his forehead to furrow in deep concern for her.

Looking away from where Zylah ran off through the ferns and shrubs, he connected eyes with Delora. Her pain-filled tears did nothing for him. Jabez refused to allow his victory to be worn on his face like a prick, but it sure as shit radiated in his chest cavity.

He had been chosen; it'd been a long time since someone had done that for him.

*And she will be presented with that choice again... and again.*

"You..." Delora sneered in his direction.

Jabez folded his arms across his muscled torso and let his head fall to the side. "Me."

"What you're doing here is wrong."

"How so?" he asked, cocking a brow at her. Confidence widened his stance and straightened his posture, but he couldn't deny his cautiousness at being alone in the presence of enemies – a Mavka, no less.

He hid his wary regard of Magnar by lowering his lids in abject boredom.

"You know what you've done to us!" she screamed, making him wince at the high-pitched, eardrum-vibrating tone. "To them!" She placed her hand over Magnar's wrist, clutching it as if she needed additional support.

*My poor fucking ears.* They twitched as they rang, his sensitive hearing making it far worse.

"I've done many things. It comes with living for centuries." Growing tired of the conversation now that Zylah was no longer present to hear the truth within it, Jabez gave them his side as he shooed them with a wave of his hand. "I'm expecting you to take your leave now, and you best do so to prevent upsetting her further. She will only turn on you should you try to fight me or go after her." Yet, his arms loosened their fold as his lips thinned pensively. "But... you are welcome to return."

Delora's brows twitched as they furrowed, and she rasped out, "Pardon?"

"I have no intention of getting in your way. If you wish to

visit, you are welcome to." He raised the forefinger of his right hand. "However, you must do so alone and without the others, or I will see it as an attack – and Zylah likely will as well. I'll make sure we're gone before you even reach us."

Another lie, but a threat nonetheless.

Magnar tilted his head at Jabez, his orbs taking on a curious yellow glow. It was nice to see something other than red. "Why would you allow this?"

He shrugged as if he didn't know, but he did. Whether it be he was indebted to Zylah, or just felt... *guilt* over what he'd done, something inside told him this was best. With him nearby to control any situation, what harm would there be?

"The likelihood of us being here past winter is low. But if you come searching for her, I won't interfere," Jabez informed them as he straightened once more, before letting a rather vicious glare fill his face. "But know that if the Witch Owl is within sniffing distance of me, remember who it is at my side."

He let that open-ended threat loom over the pair as they eventually – unwillingly – departed. They were slow to retreat, as if their feet were stuck to the earth, but they understood there was little that could be done to change it.

They could fight him, could argue or chase after her, but they had to know it would be a stupid move. It would only enrage Zylah, and it would damage whatever relationship they wished to build with her.

*Perhaps they aren't as idiotic as I first thought.*

Turning his gaze up to the blue sky with his cloak shielding him, he took in a fluffy white cloud and a random pair of birds chasing each other.

Weariness set in, the day late for him, and his lack of sleep from the previous day weighed heavily. *I wonder what you'll do when you hear of this, Lindiwe.*

That woman was no fool. He doubted she would come near him, not with one of her offspring's children in potential danger.

A danger that, funnily enough, didn't exist in his heart.

Something else was beginning to form, and he had no idea why, what it was, or what it meant.

It was only a few minutes before he heard Delora's wailing,

distressed sob coming from partway down the small mountain.

A smile crested his lips.

*Today has given me hope.*

# TWELVE

Sitting underneath a tree, Zylah allowed the winter midday sun to bathe her in muted heat. Her spot was situated a few feet higher up the mountain, the cave mouth just below her, and the dense forest chirped and played its pleasant songs.

She liked hiding here, and hiding she was. For the better part of three days, she'd been avoiding Jabez for a multitude of reasons.

Firstly, she'd struggled to come to terms with the gruesome truth she'd learned. But... leaving with two strangers had been daunting, and her heart told her remaining was in her best interest.

It explained why death seemed to matter so little to him, as well as his indifference to the destruction he'd caused by increasing her humanity. It was because he'd done many horrible things, and she was certain there was... more.

How much more? Just what had Jabez done to make her *parents* so fearful of him? Her mother's wariness had now been deeply ingrained in Zylah's thoughts.

Yet she couldn't deny how much she understood Jabez's side. If he'd truly just been trying to survive... what would she have done in his position? Zylah didn't like pain and could be quick to react negatively to those harming her.

The book about war she'd been reading had shown only the hero's side, but the villain had been so assertive in his schemes – and had believed in his course of action until his fateful death. What if the story had been told from the other perspective? Would she have deemed the hero evil for trying to get in the villain's way?

As much as she wanted to believe it was why Jabez had procured such a novel for her to consume – a way to be manipulative – he'd stated he didn't know its contents when he gave it to her. Reading the summary shared little, so if it was just a coincidence, then it surely was a favourable one.

But something nagged at the back of her mind constantly. The way guilt nipped at her was one of the main reasons she'd been avoiding him.

*I don't care what he did.* Not when it meant he was here with her now. Even if he'd hurt people, potentially those unknowingly close to her, how could she see him as anything but... good? He'd done a lot for her when she'd been insanely lost – and she hadn't known just how much.

He eased her loneliness and gave her someone to care for. He'd always shown immense patience by listening intently to her, even when she'd had little or nothing to say. Jabez didn't make her feel lesser for not knowing something. Instead, he shared knowledge and taught her the correct way to say or do things. He'd been honest, despite the fact that she knew he was hiding things.

He could've denied what they were saying, yet he'd chosen not to. Although she'd been conflicted with her decision, she'd made it because of that fact. She'd sensed no lies from him.

Rather... she felt closer to him, in the strangest sense. If he shared more of his dark past, would she long to embrace it? Or would she wish to flee? How much could she handle before something within her broke?

Was it possible to feel betrayal due to actions that had never affected her? If so, then a part of her didn't want to know. She'd rather live in a fantasy that Jabez was good, that he was as *wonderful* as she thought him to be.

Zylah sighed, her bony maw parting to let it be loud as she lifted her snout away from her book. She couldn't concentrate on it. Something in the story would remind her of him or her parents, and her thoughts would spiral back to reality.

*I wonder... if I can help him.* She didn't know if he needed fixing or not, but if Jabez had done bad things... could Zylah's affection change that in him? She wanted that to be possible.

Her sight turned a reddish pink, and she squirmed a little. It was a silly notion to think she could hold such power over him, but she'd like it to be true. Maybe he just needed someone to be kind to him, to be on *his* side rather than disgusted by his actions.

*So long as he doesn't do those things with me...* So long as he wasn't hateful and violent needlessly while being Zylah's companion, she thought she may be able to forgive all he'd done. *I can teach him to be good. To heal instead of hurt.*

Or was that just foolish?

*He does seem to be rather... forlorn.* Although he'd admitted to doing horrible things, he didn't appear to be excited by them. Then again, he never apologised for any of it – not even when a person he'd hurt had been in front of him.

*Ugh!* She groaned, snapping her book shut. *I do not know what to think!*

It didn't help that Zylah felt out of sorts as of yesterday; she was feverish, her body warm and her mind a little foggier than usual.

She'd felt these things before.

*It's cold.* Winter.

She only remembered one winter, although not well, and a sort of *sickness* had overcome her. At the time, Zylah had curled up in her burrow during the worst of it with her body hot and pulsating – not knowing why or how to fix it.

It happened again in summer, and the dry heat had been dizzying to her heightened senses.

*Does this happen every six months?* From what Jabez had taught her about seasons, years, and time in general, it appeared there was a pattern.

She wanted to ask for help regarding this, but she didn't know how to explain it. Inside felt swollen, but only low in her stomach. Her skin felt hot and itchy, but scratching at her fur did little to help. She'd pant with her blurred gaze searching for something, but she didn't know what.

She was missing information; there had to be something that would explain all this. Would Jabez know?

The idea of asking him was mortifying. Whenever she

looked at him with questions regarding this affliction coming to the forefront of her mind, she'd grow squeamish and silent on the matter. Because it was something obviously internal, it somehow felt... embarrassing?

Perhaps because her nipples hardened and her pelvis pulsed, she found it strange.

All she knew was that she wanted to be left alone.

*It only affects me for a day or so,* from what she could remember. *Would it be strange if I asked him to leave until it's gone?*

She lifted the book to look down at her body. Even now, her breasts looked bigger than they had before, and her nipples were sensitive. They were never sensitive! She often forgot she had them, although lately they'd been frequently hardening whenever she looked at his face, or his smile, and sometimes his back whenever he bathed.

Between her thighs would swell with heat, like it was doing now.

*I feel weird.*

It was like the symptoms of her every-six-months sickness were starting to affect her whenever he was around. Sometimes all he had to do was peer at her and her body fluttered.

It increased her nervousness for what she knew was to come. It was the true reason why she'd longed to be alone. *I hope he doesn't think it's because of what I learned.*

She'd actually had every intention of resuming her lessons until her insides had started to grow warm and her heart pounded heavier. That would only worsen over the next several hours until it peaked and then eventually waned.

Zylah was aware she had some kind of purple slit between her thighs, but it was usually hidden and inconspicuous until the sickness. Then it would swell and puff, and the only thing that could ease this strange ache was rocking on her thighs on her side.

Was it odd to do that? But it was the only thing that stopped the ache, although she didn't know if she found it pleasurable or not. She was always too lost and confused to really register much else but her own fear.

Dropping her book to her lap, she covered her eyeholes and shook her head. *Why do I feel so shy?*

It didn't help that she reacted strangely to Jabez whenever he was near. What had once been a comfortable presence suddenly felt constricting for reasons she couldn't decipher. Her emotions were heightened, and her senses were more acute towards anything regarding him.

The smell of his hair, his skin. The warmth of him, and the way the shadows wrapped around him or dust glittered around his features. How his eyes saw into her, as if they could peer into her very centre.

Her embarrassed glow only brightened when she remembered the way she'd stared at him with longing while he'd slept. She'd left before he could wake when she realised she'd been reaching forward to brush his hood back just a little to better see his handsome features.

*I want to touch him.* She didn't care how or where, just *something*. Her body was itching to do so.

"Zylah," Jabez called out from below, making her squeak in surprise.

Like before, her orbs flared to a reddish pink, as if she'd been caught doing something she shouldn't.

Still, she picked herself up and walked to the ledge of rock before her. She jumped down, falling a few metres to land beside Jabez. She brought herself into a tall crouch, stopping herself from towering a few inches above him, and instead submissively kept herself lower.

Something about seeing his face after so many hours had her pulse fluttering and a bashfulness puffing her fur. She scratched at her neck awkwardly, wishing she wasn't having this intense reaction. Even his earthy scent swelled around her more strongly than usual, making her nipples bud and between her thighs heat.

"Y-yes?" she asked, before noting the bag strapped across his muscled torso. She stood upright as uncertainty shoved its way up her spine. "Are you... *leaving?*" Her sight shifted to a deep blue, and she nervously inched closer in preparation to grab him so he couldn't escape her. "If-if it's about my avoidance..."

His features were expressionless, like a coldness had come over him since the awkward conversation they'd had the other day with her *parents*. He looked down at the bag as if to note it with nonchalance.

"I'm going to head to the village for food."

Unable to help herself, she grabbed his wrist when something lanced her chest. "But you'll be returning?"

Finally, an emotion crossed his features, causing it to tighten and his long ears to twitch. His brows furrowed as he lifted his red eyes to her skull. "I was expecting that you'd ask to come with me, like you usually do."

The relief that swept through her was swift, and her grip on him lost its strength. "Well, yes. I would like to..." Zylah paused.

Isn't this what she wanted? Some time alone?

*But I'm not in the middle of my sickness.* That was when she truly wished to be in private, as she was uncomfortable being gazed upon. It was why she'd chosen to hide in her burrow during it.

"If you promise to return," Zylah stated nervously, her grasp on him tightening once more, "I would like to stay here, if that is okay?"

Like that wasn't the answer he'd been hoping for, his face lost its softness and dulled once more. "If that's what you wish."

Zylah licked at the inside of her mouth warily and decided to push her luck. "Could... could you return tomorrow night?"

His ears shot back like they often did when annoyed, but his face remained the same. They were two conflicting images, making it impossible to understand him in that moment. "Why?"

"I would like some time to... think." She hated that her orbs shifted to orange in guilt at the lie, but she didn't wish to explain it.

Then, to make sure he understood, she lifted his arm so she could cup his hand, and he willingly let her. He dropped his indifferent gaze to where they were touching skin to skin, but Zylah had to stifle the way his warmth bled into her. She couldn't remember if she'd ever held his hand so gently.

Strings wrapped around her heart and grew taut in the strangest ache, radiating tenderness through her.

Distracted by their joined hands, it took her longer than it should have for her to speak. "I wish to talk to you about something, but I don't understand how to right now. I-I think tomorrow will be easier."

Jabez looked to the side before he tugged his hand from hers and turned. "Sure. I see no issue with that. I'll attempt to stay away, but I make no promises."

Zylah chittered nervously when he immediately began to walk away, the bottom of his cloak billowing around his legs. A terrible feeling overcame her, like she'd made the wrong decision by waiting.

What she did know was being in his presence even for a mere few minutes had only made her feel... worse. Her heart rate had accelerated the instant she looked upon his pretty face, and his alluring scent had flooded her mouth with drool. Even her internal temperature had risen, causing a shiver to tear through her at the loss of his warmth. Touching his hand had sent a spark throughout her system, and she'd done everything she could to avoid reacting to it.

The moment he was gone, the urge to sniff where they'd touched *ate* at her like a terrible beast. Unable to resist, she raised her palm to her snout and her orbs flickered purple in reaction. Her body pulsed, and she gave into the desire to lick his taste from her skin and nearly *moaned* when she did.

Now that she was near the cave entry, his lingering scent beckoned her inside. Her avoidance of him in the last few hours made her chest radiate with longing, and she already missed his presence like a horrible ache. The fact that the space was empty, and she was alone, meant everything she'd been holding back finally escaped. She dropped her book carelessly and fell to her bedding, before immediately crawling to his.

She'd never been called to another like this. The beginning of the sickness never nibbled away at her being so intensely before. Zylah shivered as she rubbed her skull over his fresh scent, as if he'd only just been sitting or lying there seconds ago.

*Mmm.* She grabbed his blanket to bring more of it closer.

*He smells so much nicer than usual.* Strong, masculine, divine. It smelt... utterly *soothing.* Her sight flickered with black as she secretly basked in it, her feet kicking while her toes curled in delight. *It would be much better if I had his warmth.* If it was coming right off his skin.

She nuzzled into her palm to relive his silky but brief touch.

This is why she'd been avoiding him. Every time he was near in the last two days, she'd been wanting to rub against him.

Zylah would greedily take his bedding for now.

Given that he'd been asked to refrain from returning to his current place of rest – for an entire night and day, no less – Jabez was feeling rather displeased. Although he'd done what was requested of him, with no objections on the matter, the current heavy downpour only deepened his frustrations.

Soaked from head to muddied toes, he'd given up shielding from the rain under a meagre tree. Dusk was approaching, and he was done being out in the elements like an animal. It didn't help that it was colder than usual, the water having an icy bite to it that was only ever present in winter.

Being closer to the coast stopped snow from forming, and the air was subtly filled with salty brine. He would have been truly pissed off to be caught in a blizzard like the ones that raged just a thousand kilometres north. Thankfully his cloak was mostly weatherproof, and it protected his torso and satchel from getting soaked. It also kept out the worst of the light wind.

*Filthy.* He sneered at himself, watching his footing as he stepped through mud and decaying leaf debris. *I've been reduced to such a pathetic state.*

Then again, he'd once lived off the land like a creature when he'd first arrived on Earth – after escaping his human captors, of course. *I told myself I'd never be subjected to such disgrace again.*

A branch slipped from his grasp when he moved it out of his way, and it recoiled to smack him in the face. It sprayed cold heavy drops inside his hood, and it only soured him further when they slipped down his neck and into his tunic. His feet almost came out from under him in the shock of the hit, and he grabbed that same branch to steady himself before he went arse over head.

*Why am I out in the rain like a bumbling fool?* The answer was simple – Zylah.

As much as he wanted to be annoyed with the female, he lacked the capacity right then to muster any ill-will towards her.

He understood.

*She's avoided me since learning about my past.* He couldn't blame her for that, given her soft-hearted nature. *I had a feeling this would happen.* He'd been prepared for it, and his trip to the village was him further doing so.

He patted his satchel to make sure it had remained dry and protected within his cloak. It held many items, some for himself – mainly food – and some for her.

He had acquired... parting gifts.

*She chose me, but that's because I didn't think to give her another option.* He realised his mistake only once she refused to be in his presence. Then again, it was an option he could only present to her now.

*I told her she could go with her mother, or remain with me, but there was always a third possibility.* She could have chosen herself.

Zylah no longer needed him. He'd taught her how to hunt, about the world, how to read, write, and count. She had enough building blocks to gain knowledge on her own.

If she no longer wished to be by his side, then he had no qualms about handing over his gifts and parting ways. They were useful books, and he was sure she'd understand them after a bit of study.

A book on complicated math, so she could do more than add and subtract. Understanding percentages, multiplication, division, and even algebra were useful tools to have in one's arsenal.

A book on human etiquette would also prove beneficial, especially as it explained complex social cues that she obviously lacked.

And, finally, a book on human biology. This wasn't a book he'd give her in his presence, as it detailed certain aspects about male and female anatomy that he didn't wish to explain. But understanding her own gender, sex, and pregnancy were all important and would save her in the future – should she find a partner.

From there, Zylah could make her own choices, and he could leave with a clear conscience that he'd done all he could. He'd rid himself of this pointless task and move on to...

*Fuck knows what I'll do.*

Now that he'd been away from his false throne, the desire to return to it had dwindled into nothingness. Shirking those responsibilities had been undoubtedly freeing. Having no one watching his every move was relieving.

*I guess I'll return to Spiral Haven.* Also known as the Demon Village to those who never bothered to learn its real name – then again, it wasn't like Demons were truly fond of speaking with Mavka to tell them. *There is magic there I can take.* Hopefully it would rejuvenate his natural mana flow and allow him to heal it.

If not, then Jabez knew one thing with certainty: he was fucked. Without his magic, he was as powerless as a human. He may be strong and fast, but in comparison to many Demons, he'd be considered prey.

*Where else can I go?* No human town would accept him, as they'd see nothing but his inhuman qualities. He couldn't return to Nyl'theria unless he wanted to be eaten.

His only option would be Lezekos, the Elven city, and he'd rather throw himself into the ocean than ever go there as some kind of beggar. *They'd likely just toss me in their fucking prison again.*

There were a few who might take him in, acquaintances with whom he had amicable relations with. He'd be subjected to living like a pauper, or a farm hand, or something equally mundane and boring.

Not really the future of leisure he'd envisioned for himself. A waste of his life, considering what his past entailed.

Everything he'd done would be for naught.

*I'm over this.* This, life, and his meaning and purpose. He'd been reduced to a mundane existence, and the worthlessness that pervaded his thoughts was beginning to take its toll.

At least being Zylah's teacher had offered him *something.*

Then again, her company had been easy. He didn't need to feign interest, as his mind was rather content near her. Instead, he'd just acted as his true self as much as possible, and he couldn't remember when he'd let down the majority of his façade and false arrogance like this.

In the face of others, he'd acted and behaved in certain ways. Conceited, egotistical, immodest. With Zylah, he was nothing but a man – no one of importance – whose every action could be ridiculed.

*Doesn't help I think she's rather cute.* He would have chuckled warmly at that, if the likely departure of their companionship didn't loom.

But he couldn't help finding her bashfulness and awkwardness rather endearing. He always felt awful for chuckling at her for it, since it obviously made her uncomfortable, but it was just too charming. For a creature who lacked skin upon their face, her orbs were revealing of her true thoughts.

And unfortunately for her, Jabez had a rather intimate understanding of what those colours represented. He could almost read her thoughts by which emotion shone alongside her physical tells, like the way her fur would puff or her hands would twist.

She'd even begun to fidget subtly with the hem of her dress when she was nervous, like a feminine, shy woman, and a side lost to Jabez itched beneath the surface. *I thought I was too serious to be playful with another.* Yet the urge to needle and tease her further grew in those moments.

However, he didn't. He refrained from teasing Zylah, as the droplets of his own sensuality could easily leak into the banter. He didn't wish to give her mixed signals, considering the idea of being intimate with her pooled a darkness in the back of his mind.

*Mavka feel too hard.* The line between love and lust to a being who barely understood their own emotions was just too close.

And Jabez had truly lost the capability to love centuries ago. His planned future had always been a lonely one, but that had stopped bothering him when he'd just accepted it. He couldn't even bear to love himself, so another being was completely out of the question.

He was a selfish person. A flaw he flaunted, so all knew to keep themselves protected from his eventual callousness. He cared for no one but himself, which, in turn, protected him from all others.

No one could hurt him if he didn't care.

*So why did I refrain from returning like she asked of me?* He should have just used her request as an opportunity to get as far from her as possible until she lost the ability to track him.

*Ah, yes... the books.* He patted them as a reminder. That's why he was returning instead of just leaving the previous day. There was no other reason. Merely a last duty to ensure he could walk away without a guilty conscience.

Then he'd be off, with the mask of his indifference firmly plastered upon his face.

He'd just pin the last two months to the back of his mind as a time he'd spent with another Mavka. He'd add it to the decades he'd spent with Merikh, which, too, had ended.

A growl escaped him at the pestering resentment that continued to linger, and had since Merikh left. The fact that he'd pushed his closest friend away was irrelevant. Merikh should have seen it as a lapse in Jabez's judgement, rather than taking it to heart.

He paused in his wandering to cover his face in annoyance. *I still regret how I acted upon learning of his blood relation to Weldir.*

He should have seen the signs earlier, considering Lindiwe had been so set on getting between them. But Merikh had hated her, ignored her requests, even laughed at her, and Jabez had been rather content with that – without knowing the truth as to why she was pestering them.

*But I had Katerina in my damn ear.* And she'd figured out exactly how to exploit what they'd learned to get her way, which was getting rid of Merikh, a Mavka. Her hatred of him had been so deep, and he'd been too blindsided by his own feelings of betrayal and anger to turn his ear away from her words.

By the time Jabez had realised what he'd done, it was already too late. And, like the arrogant bastard he was, he refused to apologise to a creature who wouldn't have given a damn about what he said in defence. Once Merikh hated, Jabez knew that feeling wouldn't easily subside.

Especially when the bull-headed jerk presented Jabez with an ultimatum – him or Katerina, which only infuriated Jabez further.

No matter that it'd been a long time ago, he despised admitting he still wasn't over it.

And, in a corner of his fucked-up, absent heart, the idea of leaving Zylah reopened that wound. Or perhaps it was just a new wound. And he didn't fucking understand *why* it would bother him.

Perhaps it was because he wasn't good enough.

His nose wrinkled in anger. *Good enough for what? What do I want from myself? A fucking pity party?* He wouldn't give himself that.

He'd just add it to the pile of shit he refused to acknowledge.

Resuming his trudge through the miserable rain, he headed for the entrance to their shared cave, which lay just down the hill. He'd refrained from returning, but his place of rest hadn't been too far away.

A strong gust of wet wind swept across his body when he came upon the mouth of the cave. The chill of it crept up his spine and hastened his feet inside so he could escape it.

"Zylah, I've returned," he stated, letting her know of his arrival.

He eyed the space within the darkness and found a noticeable lump covered in twisted blankets. Their bedding had been dragged closer until the rolls overlapped.

A small whine met his ears before she stuck her snout out of the blankets to reveal two white orbs. Not quite the welcome he'd been expecting, and he wiped his face of water and shook it from his hand as he stepped further in.

"I've brought you more..." His words cut off when he rent out a choked gasp at the suffocating aroma that slammed into him.

His throat tightened, his ears darted back, and he covered his mouth and nose just as his damn groin tingled. *By the ever-night, what the fuck?!* Heat immediately filled his cheeks and drooping ears at the thick layers of *arousal* pervading the air.

Rain pattered onto his cloak hood when he stepped back while shaking his head. "What's the meaning of this?"

She moved so fast he didn't have time to register it at all, too distracted by the way his cock was lengthening within his pants. One minute he was standing in disbelief, and the next, she leapt forward and grabbed his ankle, tugged him to the ground, then flipped him to his front, dragging him further inside. A yell burst from him, his cloak folding over the top of him and covering his head as he was yanked across the stone floor.

Within seconds, she was above him. Straddling his back, she slammed her hands down next to the sides of his head from behind. Whines flooded his ears as she leaned down and shoved her snout into the crook of his neck underneath the material. Goosebumps rose across his skin at the hot breath that fanned over him from behind.

Fighting with his cloak, he managed to unclip it and shove it away from his head. He panted against the cave floor in surprise, then she *ground* against his backside and fury shot through him. He couldn't believe someone shoved their pelvis against his arse!

*Absolutely fucking not!*

He kicked his right leg to the side, hooked it over her hip, and managed to rotate until she was on her back. Jabez quickly shifted her until she was on her front like he'd been and straddled her waist to keep her down. Despite how she fought him, he grabbed her wrists and pinned them behind her back, needing to use both his hands.

*What in the cursed light is happening?* he wondered, his grip on her arms tightening to stop her from flipping them back over.

He hadn't expected to return to their cave with her like this. Sure... Jabez knew she'd smelt like arousal here and there, but it had always been gentle and never acute like this. He could only wonder *why* it was happening now, considering he'd been gone for over a day!

The snarl that left him was feral, but it snuffed out when she bucked and gyrated in an attempt to get free. She reared her head back, before just laying it upon the ground as she whined.

*"Please,"* she rasped, her orbs flickering between white and... *purple.* He knew the latter meant she was filled with desire, but he just couldn't understand as to what had come over her. "Please help me. You smell so good." Her hips waved as she pressed them against the cave floor before letting out a deep shudder. "It hurts. I ache. Make it stop. You're so *warm.*"

She settled just so she could pant and lick at her snout, and purple shifted permanently into her sight. What drew his brows together was the appearance of ethereal tears, and purple droplets began to float around her skull.

Grappling with the fact that her arousal scent was so strong his cock had managed to harden completely despite their kerfuffle, he tried to figure out what was happening. It didn't help that his heart was racing with adrenaline, flooding his own body with heat under the power of his huffing breaths as they sucked in the tainted, tantalising air.

*Her body is really hot.* She radiated unusual warmth, to the point he could feel it in his groin and where his thighs pressed against her. *Uncontrollable desire.* He turned his head towards the chaotic mess that was their bedding. It looked like a nest, and she'd even dragged one of his shirts closer as if she sought more of his smell.

*She's weak.* The fact she hadn't managed to fight him off was concerning, considering her usual strength.

Realisation trickled down his spine like a cruel fucking joke.

"You're kidding me," he whispered in disbelief as he brought his gaze back to her and her glowing purple orbs. "You have a damn *heat* cycle?"

Any remaining anger fled out of him, and in its place, a

strange flare of desire warmed his cheeks and ears further. So did mortification.

"Jabez," she moaned, as she tugged at her arms before giving up once more. She shivered before whining, "It's so cold."

*Shit. What do I do?* He inspected his placement upon her, and how she was pressed against the freezing stone beneath them.

"I... I can't help you," he admitted. "I can't take this ache away."

He could, but Jabez absolutely refused. She was disorientated, confused, and feverish with need. A female in this state could not consent to any form of intimacy, no matter how much she groped, ground, or begged. He also just refused intimacy with her altogether.

But if he let her go, she'd likely claw at him for aid. For something, anything. Female Demons going through a heat cycle were... vulnerable creatures, and highly sensitive. They sought pleasure, comfort. They nested in scents that soothed them, just as Zylah had.

His gaze turned to the rain.

He could go outside and wait this out, abandoning her on her own, but... *Fuck. I've made it worse for her by coming here.* She'd likely just chase him now, seeking warmth and his scent, and no doubt his touch as well.

*I thought she was drawing away from me because of what she'd learned.* But this clearly explained that he'd been *wrong,* and Jabez wasn't often wrong.

A foul glare squinted his eyes. *She knew this was going to happen.* No wonder she wanted him to leave.

The avoidance was common for a female who was uncertain about her companion, but Jabez also didn't think that was the case here. The fact she'd nestled into his bedding and clothing showed, very blatantly, that she desired him.

*Was she uncertain about... herself?*

Given that he hadn't taught her anything about her own gender, he doubted she had any idea as to what was happening. *The damn human anatomy book will contain only half the information.* It was pointless. He would have needed one that focused on Demon anatomy and the fertility cycles they went through.

*Fuck. What do I do?* He wouldn't be despicable and touch her, no matter that his cock pulsated at the idea. He'd always found her body sensual; she'd never been unattractive to him.

But abandoning her for his own self-preservation would only be unfair.

Closing his eyes when frustration bubbled, Jabez made his decision.

He leaned over her until he was right next to her skull, gentling his tone so it would be taken in softly. "I'm going to let you go. I need you to be good and not turn on me. I will help how I can. Understood?"

She shivered with his voice right in her ear, her neck arching for more, and nodded for him. He tentatively let go of her wrists and backed off her to give them space.

"Go to the bedding," he told her, as he grabbed his shirt and lifted it over his head. He tossed it towards her makeshift nest, then collected his cloak and brought it closer.

When he noticed she was slow to move now, which was so different to how she'd initially leapt for him, pity filled him. Lethargy had set in, which would only be temporary, but it was so different from the aggression she'd just displayed.

He walked over and scooped her into his arms. He grunted as he lifted her hefty weight, setting her down on his bed with her head on the pillow. Just as he made to retrieve his blanket to pull it over her, she grabbed his wrist.

"Please," she whimpered, squeezing his forearm until he winced. "Please don't leave me."

"I'm not," he answered while prying her fingers off.

He grabbed his blanket and pulled it over her before using hers to tuck it behind her like a wall. Then he lifted the material and slid in beside her, although a little higher than her, so he could slip an arm under her neck to support it. He pulled the material over her head to shield her from the cold and then wrapped his arms around her shoulders and forced her face against the centre of his chest.

She squirmed against him but was quick to slide her arms around him in return. She nestled closer, and closer, until every part of their fronts touched. She burrowed into him, under the blanket saturated in his scent, and whimpered.

When she kept rubbing her thighs together, he begrudgingly shoved a knee between them to give her *something*. Wetness spread across it, and his heart pounded deeper, his cock thickening in reaction to a female grinding against him.

With his bare chest providing her with much needed warmth and skin contact – his scent fresh and pressed against her nose, and his heart close to her ears – he hoped this could lull her. He couldn't provide the intimacy she required, but he could soothe her and let her feel safe in his presence while she was suffering.

He ignored how she began to lick at his chest, occasionally flicking one of his hardening nipples and causing him to jerk. His cheeks and ears grew hotter each time it happened, as his own arousal caused his pulse to pound all throughout his body. Her claws stabbed into the flesh of his back, tickling it until he almost bucked at the sensitivity of it with a needy grunt. Her pants cascaded sultry breaths, and his skin prickled as they waved over his bare chest, while his ears twitched each time she let out quiet, sensual moans. Her breasts were surprisingly soft as they pressed into him, and he marvelled at the silkiness of the fur around her shoulders and neck as he stroked her soothingly.

His eyes crinkled in anguish when he was forced to ignore how his cock pressed between them in a tight squeeze and his balls ached in growing need. He was thankful she didn't notice the hardness, nor understand its meaning.

*Fuck me. This is going to be a torturous night.* He foresaw the next hours being long and requiring much restraint on his part.

He'd also have to swallow just how deeply he'd been denying that he'd found Zylah attractive from the first moment she took her humanoid form. How her slip of clothing had been nagging at him, and how her gentle voice had been tingling in his ears. Or how her jasmine-and-violet scent had both soothed him and caused lapses of desire in him when it was lightly spiced from her unhidden arousal in the past.

Hard to deny that when all her feminine curves were not only captured in his arms, but were wriggling in need... for *him*.

And how his body very easily – and readily – responded to it all.

*Shit.*

# THIRTEEN

When Zylah woke, her mind stayed groggy and her body lay limp with lethargy. She struggled to wade through the blur of the last day, and the disorientation was only eased by the warmth and scent surrounding her. She buried her skull into the masculine cushion before her as she tried to bring herself out of her muddled thoughts.

She found it hard to let go, as if the only thing anchoring her in calmness was the male before her. His heartbeat was gentle and steady, his breaths even.

She managed to lift the coverings from her head and look up without disturbing him. With her shoulders nestled between his lax arms, she took in the way he rested against the bedding.

He lacked a pillow, and most of the blanket was resting over her. There were noticeable dark lines under the inner creases of his closed eyes, as if he was exhausted and had only just recently fallen asleep.

The shaved part of his scalp was visible since the long strands of his hair were brushed back and pooled beneath the side of his head. One of his dark, segmented horns was tangled in his hair, while the other was hidden away. She noticed how his long white eyelashes framed his cheeks with spiked shadows, and they looked even more delicate up close.

*He's very pretty,* she thought as her sight dipped to his parted lips. They released quiet breaths that rhythmically pressed his pectoral muscles into her. His jagged, mean fangs were just visible past the soft lips she was moments from reaching up to pet.

It took her too long to notice that his chest was bare, and that waking like this was unusual for them. His back was even towards the entrance of the cave, when usually he slept with it against the wall protectively.

*I like this.* She adored how they were lying together.

Bright yellow flickered into her sight as joy overcame her, and she squirmed a little to get closer. *He's so warm.* His soft, smooth skin tingled her straying fingertips as she touched the hard muscles going to his back.

Then the reality of the last day came to mind.

*I... the sickness!* she recalled with a horrified whine.

White invaded her sight, and she gasped before shoving herself away. She scrambled until her back met the cold wall of the cave, and she flinched in surprise when it felt like the wall struck her; she was still affected by the residual fever from earlier.

Jabez grunted in surprise as her shove pushed him to his back, and he quickly sat up as well. He opened his eyes into tight, tired slits, and the wrinkled creases under them deepened.

With her heart racing in her chest, Zylah cupped her hands to her breasts while shaking her head. *He saw it!* She didn't want to be seen like that! She reached up to grip her antlers as she remembered how she'd acted, how she'd clung to him, squirmed against him, *licked* him.

Reddish pink lifted into her sight in mortification at the same time tears began to float around her vision. *I didn't want him to see it.*

"I'm sorry," she cried, covering her face in disbelief.

Why couldn't he have just stayed away a little longer? Why did it feel like it'd gone on for longer than she was used to? Especially since the sun was bright, as if noon had come and gone.

Silence greeted her apology, and she tried to make herself as small as possible against the wall. With her shoulders turning inwards and her feet overlapping, she refused to look at him.

"I'm sorry," she repeated.

"How often does this happen?" he asked, his voice stern but croaky from sleep.

She whimpered before answering. "Winter and summer. I don't know why."

He let out a loud expire and material shifted. She managed to brave peeking to watch him don his shirt once more. However, she also took in the tangled mess that was their sleeping beds, and how his spare shirt, usually hidden away in a bag, revealed she'd retrieved it like a crazed animal seeking his scent.

*Oh no,* she thought, hiding her face once more. Why did she do that? What else happened that she couldn't remember through the fog of her memories?

"Calm down, Zylah," Jabez stated, his voice surprisingly soft and kind. "It's normal. This isn't the first time I've experienced a female going through this." Then he grumbled to himself, "My first time remaining present, though."

"So... you know?" She was both relieved by that knowledge, and uncomfortable.

"Do you remember how I spoke to you about the differences in fertility cycles for humans and Demons? It appears you have more of a Demon nature regarding this. It's... unpleasant for unmated females." He glanced at her momentarily, but she registered an awkward, uncomfortable glint to his gaze as he averted it. "Your emotions are heightened and I'm sure you're feeling very sensitive right now."

"Did you know...?" she asked, her shoulders turning inwards even more until her back stretched taut.

"No," he answered immediately.

Zylah gasped when he approached and pushed her back up against the wall, but it prevented her from getting away. He merely placed his hand on the crown of her skull, shocking her into lowering her arms.

"You are the first female Mavka I've ever met. I didn't know this would happen."

He appeared tired, and there was noticeable strain in his handsome features. Yet he offered her a warm, and likely sympathetic, smile. It quickly died, and he removed his hand while remaining crouched in front of her.

Despite everything, her tears only floated faster.

She always had this horrible feeling afterwards that something terrible could have happened to her. She hated that feeling usually, and yet it made her entirely beholden to him in that moment.

He'd kept her safe, especially in this wide-open cave. She'd liked her burrow because it'd been small and easy to curl up in when she was like that.

"Thank you." She didn't know what she was thanking him about, but it was all she could muster.

*I still feel so strange.*

"It's fine," he answered. "But I do think it's time we leave."

"L-leave?" She looked around the cave... their *home*. "Why? I don't want to leave."

"I've decided it's time you come to know yourself a little better, but I can't answer those important questions." His head turned to the side as he peered towards the wall. "I know someone who will aid you, and she will be a more fitting person to teach you about what's just happened and why."

"But you said you knew!" she argued. "That you've... seen it before."

He released a sigh as he covered his face with a palm and then dug his fingers into his closed eyes. "I guess the truth is that I *won't* answer these questions for you." Jabez stood and retrieved one of the two bags available, then began to collect his personal items. "Pack light. I know you'll want to bring all your books, but it's best you leave most of them behind."

"Why?" Her books were important to her. Each one had been a gift from him and had helped her gain knowledge. They were so precious to her, she thought she would protect them with her life.

"Because it's unwise to pack heavy when you are travelling through the Veil. I won't even be bringing our bedding. Just food and my shirt."

"We're going to the Veil?" she asked, her voice raspy with surprise.

She'd only ever entered it to follow the bright light that led her to him. She mostly refrained from going in after being attacked by Demons multiple times.

Too much was happening too fast, and Zylah didn't know how to react. Why did they have to leave now? Why couldn't they bring everything? Why must they go into the Veil? It was all so sudden, but she could sense the urgency in him.

He didn't even appear to have slept properly, and she wondered if he had at all the previous day he'd been gone. The fact he was choosing not to rest beforehand was even more alarming.

Her sight flickered with blue. *Why do I feel like I did something wrong?*

"We're going to the inner ring, to be exact," he stated. With his back to her, he reached for one of the blankets and pulled it closer. He whipped out his scissors and cut two holes in it before coming over to her. "It's not the most suitable cloak, but it should hide your skull from a distance and should keep you warm during the night."

He threw it around her shoulders and then tied the ends around her neck.

She fingered the thin brown material. "But I don't feel the cold."

His red eyes bore into her orbs as his lips flattened. "No, not usually, but I'm guessing your temperature is higher than normal. This is just a preventative measure in case the cold suddenly affects you."

Zylah grumbled at that, wishing the cold pang in her heart would settle. *See? He obviously knows about this and refuses to tell me.* Why couldn't he just explain it? She didn't want to go see a...

Her skull jerked back in realisation. "Wait. If we are going to the Veil, does that mean you are taking me to a Demon?"

The corner of his lips quirked, and humour filled his expression. "The fact that you were able to summarise that on your own means you're ready for this kind of journey."

Zylah self-consciously chittered at the compliment. She tried to not be annoyed by the fact it was obviously a *female* Demon, which meant he had companions other than her. It was difficult to hide how she felt about that when her orbs flickered with dark green.

She hated that he saw it, and both his brows raised up, crinkling his forehead – he likely knew what the colour meant when she didn't.

He backed away and handed her an empty bag.

Zylah threw her hands up. "But I don't have anything to bring."

"Pick one book from your current collection. You will be carrying three others I brought back for you last night."

"You obtained more books for me?"

His lips curled higher. "Don't I always when I go to the village?"

That was true. Despite how she currently felt – confused, wary, unsure – she was giddy at the prospect of what she could learn further.

*He always brings me gifts.*

# FOURTEEN

The journey to the edge of the Veil's canyon had been like most of their walks. Zylah listened as Jabez occasionally paused to show her new flora or an animal she hadn't seen in person before. He let her deviate their path if she smelt something unusual in the distance, helping to ease how each step brought them closer to the Veil.

For the longest time, Zylah had avoided that shadowy forest due to the dangers. Jabez had been kind enough to explain that he doubted she'd be targeted, like he had some secret information regarding the Demon attacks and why he thought they'd cease. Knowing that calmed her, but it didn't fully erase her worries.

*What if I cannot protect him?* He was such a weak being in comparison to her. So slow, even when they merely walked. If something went wrong, she worried she wouldn't be able to protect him. *What if I go into a rage?*

What if she ended up being the one to kill him?

He was... smaller than her. Sure, by only three or so inches. Then again, he was much wider and more densely muscled, so perhaps thinking him a smaller creature wasn't particularly true.

*He's also managed to escape me during a rage before.* Bright yellow lifted into her orbs as she thought, *He is a very cunning male.* Even though he wasn't as formidable as her, Jabez was agile and very capable of eluding danger.

He'd obviously been in many dangerous situations, to the

point he could almost predict what would happen in the future. Would that be considered battle hardened, like in the books she read?

He didn't like it when she referenced him as weaker. It tended to make him ramble on about how things between them would be different if he still had his magic. She kind of liked that he had this strange quirk of needing to feel big and strong. She wanted to play with him regarding it, but didn't know if it would be taken poorly.

Her musings came to a halt when the forest cleared away and a massive rip in the earth came into view. Her fur instantly stood on end as a chill crept down her spine. Just being near this place brought on a sense of foreboding and doom, and she itched at her neck in aversion.

They couldn't even see the other side, and nothing but an expanse of forest lay before them at least a kilometre below. Mist flittered all throughout it, some of it white, some black, and Zylah had this urge to scratch across her bony snout at the pungent odour that came from it.

Jabez calmly sat cross-legged near the edge with his hooded back turned towards the west to shield him from the dusking sun. He greedily drank from his water sack before reaching into his satchel once more. Dusting off a washed carrot, he took a bite, and the leafy end of it reminded her of her tail.

"Okay, half our journey is over," he commented as he looked out at the massive crack of earth. "However, it'll now become that much more exhausting."

She took a seat next to him with her feet out in front of her. "Why do you say that?"

"Because it's wise to move fast through the outer and middle rings." His tone was cool and collected, like he was talking about something that mattered little. "How good are you at climbing?"

Zylah cupped her hands to her abdomen and fidgeted with her fingers. "Not very good. My feet slip a lot."

Just as he was about to take another bite, Jabez paused as his gaze slid to her feet. She wiggled her toes self-consciously, and she didn't understand why that caused him to cover his face or why his ears drooped.

He cleared his throat as if something clogged it. "Was that in your more monstrous form? Your feet are more... rabbit-like when you are like that. You may have better dexterity with your humanoid feet."

She tilted her head at that, finding his reassurance calming. "I don't know," she answered honestly. "Maybe?"

"I'll find us the best path and I'll climb below you in case you slip." He finally bit off another chunk of carrot and crushed it between his sharp fangs while squinting his eyes at the horizon with a pensive expression. Then he swallowed and said, "After that, we'll likely have to run for most of the night. Little sunlight touches the ground, and now is when most Demons are waking. They will be hungry, and they will be curious."

"I thought you said we wouldn't be targeted," she grumbled, turning her head away in annoyance.

"No, I said *you* wouldn't be targeted for being a Mavka. But we have to take into consideration the Demon nature when we're passing lesser Demons. They eat everything, including each other, and there's a chance they will hunt for hunting's sake." He pointed what remained of his carrot at her. "Once we get to the middle ring, we can briefly rest, but at the first sign of movement, it's best to get the fuck out of there."

"What is the difference between these... rings?" He'd briefly mentioned them before but hadn't truly explained them.

He circled his carrot in front of them as if referencing the Veil. "The outer ring has more of the lesser Demons, meaning they have less humanoid features, are more savage in their hunting, and are dim-witted. The middle ring is where those who are halfway to completing their evolution reside. Lesser Demons enter through it, but they are wary because a medium-sized Demon can tear them to shreds, especially being more intelligent. The inner ring mainly consists of those who have completely evolved or are close to it, and they are dangerous to the others due to the simple fact that they live in groups for ultimate protection. They are far less violent, but they will quickly drive out other Demons to protect the area. When we are there, we will have little to worry about. I would consider them peaceful.”

“How will we know when we’ve reached each ring?”

“You won’t,” he answered plainly. “But I’ve lived within the Veil for over half my life. I can tell when we’ve entered each section. It’s second nature to me.”

Zylah cupped the end of her snout in thought and kept it there as she spoke. “How long will it take us to get to the inner ring... to this person?”

He tipped his head back, looking up at the sky as he let out a hum. “Not sure. For a Mavka, probably a day, but for me...”

“Because you are so slow.”

He growled out a chagrined huff, his eyes flicking to her with a glare. She chittered, her orbs shifting to a bashful reddish pink, yet her chest radiated with humour and tenderness. Her toes scrunched as she giggled at him.

“Yes, because I’m so slow,” he grumbled, eating the last bit of his carrot with his eyes slitting further. “It’ll likely take me twice as long. If I still had my magic, I could easily teleport us there. It was a rather advantageous ability.”

He propped his elbow on his knee and shoved his chin into his palm. Then he stuck his bottom lip forward.

“What does this mean?” she asked, pointing towards his lips.

“I’m pouting.” He quickly fixed it and they flattened. “Never mind. I would suggest that you turn into your monstrous form once we reach the bottom of the cliff wall. You’ll be able to better protect yourself.”

“What about you?”

His lips curled into what she could only consider a devious grin. “You don’t need to worry about me. With or without my magic, a lesser or medium Demon wouldn’t stand a chance against me. I’ve trained my body my entire adult life, knowing that my magic can easily deplete. Only a fool would solely rest their capabilities on magic alone.”

Jabez then ate a little more food and took a last drink, readying himself to be unable to do either for quite some time. She followed his lead when he stood.

“Alright,” he stated, with his shoulders rolling back. He

tilted his head right and then left until a crack sounded. "Let's get this over with."

Making sure both his hands had a good, steady grip, Jabez carefully leveraged the toes of his left foot onto a lower ledge of stone. He peeked downwards, noting how far he'd climbed down the Veil's canyon wall. They were making good time.

A small rock smacked his left horn, and he turned his gaze towards the night sky. Jabez instantly regretted it. His ears darted back as warmth flooded them and his cheeks, and he quickly averted his gaze to the side.

*Fuck. I shouldn't have chosen to climb beneath her.* But it was safest for her, as he could quickly grab her should she need saving.

The issue was: every time he looked up to check on her, he was gifted with a rather tantalising view – which was a bad fucking thing. He'd never thought about giving her some kind of underwear because it was a foreign concept to him. Currently his cock and balls dangled freely in his pants, as was normal for most Demons and Elves.

With her thighs spread in order to have the best leverage, whatever pussy she had was, thankfully, hidden by a closed slit and fur. But her arse was plump, on show, and her damn fluffy tail kept the back of her short dress up, so the garment was basically fucking pointless.

Disgruntled at the way his groin tingled despite the perilous situation he was in, Jabez softly growled. Then he shifted his left hand to a lower ledge.

Ever since he'd held that female while she smelt like a divine plate of sensuality, and had all her warm curves in his arms, his stupid brain kept zeroing in on her femininity. Her tail, the dip of her hourglass figure, and her thick thighs and round arse cheeks. Even her little grey toe beans kept stealing his attention. He'd even begun staring at her alluring skull a little more deeply, and her orb shifts were starting to affect his thoughts. Her dainty little antlers hadn't gone unnoticed, as they would be good things to tug on since she lacked hair to pull.

*The hell is wrong with me?* He grumbled to himself as he kicked his right foot lower. He tried to think on why he was having such deeply perverse thoughts about this female. *Is it because it's been so long since I came?*

Surely that had to be the cause. *What has it been? Two years?* Something like that. Then again, the idea of fucking his fist, or even another person, after the death of his female companion of nearly two centuries had made him rather disinterested in pleasure.

It was like his body had gone as numb as his heart had already been.

So why the *fuck* did his fucking heart stutter at Zylah out of the damn blue? Sure, she was cute, but that shouldn't be enough.

Yet every time she kicked her feet whenever she read something exciting in one of her books... it always warmed his face – especially as he'd obtained the tomes for her. Whenever she was nervous around him or about herself, he couldn't help finding her fidgeting endearing. She was... soft, both in heart and body, and he was now bothered that he knew about the latter.

*She's a damn Mavka.* Her species wasn't the problem, per se, but the history he shared with them was. *Our relationship can go no further than what it currently is.*

Too much was at risk otherwise.

He also didn't... need a female. He was perfectly fine as he was, being alone and spiteful, like the terrible force he was upon the world. He wouldn't mind some help with his plans, though.

Just as both his feet found a perfect ledge to rest upon for a moment, a loud shift of rock twitched his ears. Then a squeal from above rushed towards him. His nose crinkled in strain as he looked up and readied himself. Just as Zylah was falling, he maintained his grip on the wall with his left hand and managed to grab her elbow with his right.

He caught her drop, and it shunted him downwards. Jabez let out a hiss when it felt like grabbing her had almost torn his arm from his shoulder joint. All the muscles in his arm were on fire, and he grunted at the pull of her weighing him down.

*Damnit. She's so damn heavy.* Mavka were such dense creatures.

He dug his fingers into the rock for better purchase, his fangs bared in pain, while Zylah swung beneath him, emitting squealing chitters. With a quiet roar, he yanked her heavy weight up and pivoted her towards the wall until her feet could get purchase on the same thin ledge of rock he stood upon. Whines echoed from her as she held on with trembling arms, her orbs white with tears floating around them.

"I cannot do this," she whimpered, shifting her feet before gasping when one slipped.

He came closer and placed his right arm around her waist. He steadied her and let her feel secure, like he was a cage for her against the wall. "We're over halfway."

She hugged the rock, but eased a little at his embrace. "I-I'm *scared.*"

Jabez peeked downwards to see they had at least four hundred metres left to descend.

To be fair, she had every right to be frightened. What they were doing was a daunting task, even for him. They both knew a fall from this height wouldn't kill her, although it was questionable as to whether or not he'd survive it. He doubted she'd be able to heal him through such a horrific landing.

He brought his gaze back to her and gave her his best sympathetic smile.

"You've got this. You've done amazing so far."

When she'd managed to calm down enough, he insisted they continue. Once more, he climbed down below her, and she mostly followed his path as she had been before.

A strand of his hair landed in front of his eyes, but he ignored it. He'd been wise enough to tie his hair back into a ponytail before they'd started travelling. The strip of cloth keeping it bound had loosened and currently needed tightening, as it had many times.

Once they were only a few metres from the ground, Jabez jumped, then waved his hands for her to do so as well. She took the opportunity to get away from the wall, and he stepped out of her way so she could land on her feet with ease. He steadied her when she looked unsure, and her knees wobbled before she just gave in and knelt.

She shook her head. "Never again," she cutely whined. "I don't want to do that again."

Feeling pity for her, Jabez knelt on one knee and placed a hand between her antlers. He wasn't used to this – comforting another – but he found it remarkably easy to do it for her.

He gave a singular stroke down her skull. "We shouldn't need to do that again. I know the Veil better than I know the surface. If we ever need to climb up the wall, I'll find a safer path."

It'd just been so long since he'd personally needed to climb the cliff, as he usually teleported whenever he wanted. Next time, he'd make sure it was easier.

When she nodded, Jabez stood and faced the Veil's mist-shrouded forest. He often wondered how others perceived it. *I've always found the mist of the Veil rather tranquil.* It made hiding easier, and the thick dampness of it helped tamp down smells, especially the unpleasant, sickly aroma Weldir's black mist created.

He imagined for humans it was frightening and made it appear haunted.

Since he'd shoved his hood off the moment the sun had faded, he reached back to tighten the strap of cloth tied around the base of his high ponytail. Then he flicked the hood forward to hide his identity from those who might see his face from afar.

Lesser Demons wouldn't likely have come into close contact with his scent, and if they had, they wouldn't remember it.

Noticing Zylah still slumped on the ground, he offered his hand out to her. "Ready? We need to leave."

She jerked at his offered palm, then her orbs shifted to a telling bright yellow. *She likes it when I reach out to her like this.* She willingly took it, and he helped pull her to her feet.

Then, as he'd instructed earlier, she morphed into her more monstrous form.

Once more, he regretted his choices when her clothing sunk beneath her fur and flesh. Suddenly he had a very naked female beside him, and the fact she'd taken on a more rabbit-dog mix in posture didn't diminish his opinion of her.

He metaphorically face-palmed himself, and then leapt into a fast-paced sprint. Zylah quickly caught up and then matched his speed with ease.

The moment they entered the forest, darkness descended upon them. He had no issue seeing through it, and he doubted Zylah did either. The white mist was thickly layered, being winter, but no frost or snow ever stuck within the Veil. It frolicked between the trees, only to be overshadowed by the black mist he knew belonged to Weldir – an annoying reminder that he was always there, touching and feeling, but not truly present.

*Are you watching us? You damn creep.* Had every action or word since Jabez's 'fall' been watched? No, he didn't think so, considering Zylah's parents hadn't known he was alive. What about since then, though? That's if he could see beyond his own mist, which was only present in the Veil.

The nape of his neck prickled in alertness, but he wasn't sure if that was because they were being watched or because he was just paranoid.

At least the environment was warmer, and he would have basked in that if it wasn't for the danger surrounding them.

All around them, tree branches scraped against each other in the intermittent harsh breeze. The area was eerie, although that didn't bother him in the least, but it did make it hard to tell the movement of creatures apart from the gusts of wind. The forest itself was gnarly with many twisted roots, reaching branches, and tight spaces to jump through.

He'd lived in it for so long that these things were normal to him.

The air in the Veil was dewy, and moss lined almost every tree trunk they passed. Despite the darkness of it, it was vibrant with subtle, healthy flora, and he was able to breathe in that life with familiar fondness.

The ground dipped and waved with small hills, short drops, and an occasional river they needed to leap across. The terrain eased the further they ran, and after some hours had passed, the world began to open up as the trees incrementally became larger.

Occasionally a Demon ran near them, its footsteps heavy and fast, but each one backed off. The smell of a Mavka and a Demon travelling together instilled enough doubt in their would-be attackers. That, or they were just too slow and couldn't keep up.

Not all were that wise, and one eventually chased them from behind. Jabez considered ignoring it until he realised it was running on all fours by its double thumps of pawsteps. He also heard the propelling aid of wings flapping, which gave it additional speed that not even he could combat. It would catch up to them eventually.

*Hopefully it'll grow tired or get bored of chasing us.*

It didn't.

When it was close to being on their heels, and Zylah shone reddened orbs at him, he knew he had to intervene before it was too late.

"Keep going," he stated as he slowed his steps. "Stay out of the way."

*"No,"* she replied with a growl, her voice deeper and grainy in her monstrous form. *"I am stronger. I can–"*

"Do as I say!" he snapped, baring his fangs at her with a glare. His senses on high alert like this caused his irritation to strike quicker. "You want to keep me safe? Stay out of the way and don't go into a rage. That's what you can do to help."

She chittered nervously and her orbs flashed white in unease. With a curt whine, she nodded before darting out of the direct vicinity, revealing the speed she'd been holding back.

Frothing pants and cackling came up quickly from behind, and he turned to meet the Demon head-on. Running on all fours with a doggish form, two small bird-like wings flapped behind it. A long tail was stuck up, and it danced behind a semi-humanoid face that was alight with excitement. White foam bubbled from its lips, while sharp fangs gleamed in the intermittent fractures of dappled moonlight. Its entire body was black like a glossy void, proving just how far it was from completion, as it lacked any human flesh.

Even though Jabez had stopped, its mind was so useless

that it didn't even sense the hostility it was sprinting towards. It licked at its maw and cackled as it leapt for him. With claws at the ready, aiming straight for his chest, it flew through the air with its wings flapping to keep its momentum.

Jabez timed his defence perfectly. He stepped to the side and brought his bent leg up at the same time.

With the speed at which it'd been coming for him, and the power of his attack, his knee landing straight into its gut made it fold in on itself. A disgusting choke came from it, as spittle sprayed from its mouth while its wings kinked in agony. Jabez lowered his leg when it crumbled to the ground in an abrupt stop.

Indifferent to the battle he'd foreseen being easy *and* predictable, he came behind its wheezing form and stepped upon its back. Wings flapped on either side of his body as it rent out a strangled hiss from the pressure of his weight, and he reached down to grab either side of its head. He twisted its neck with a satisfying crack, and it became limp and loose.

Just to make sure it was dead, he knelt on it and twisted its head the other way. Its vertebrae sounded like a wet crunch of bones, and he took that as his opportunity to descend. Lips parted, Jabez sunk his fangs into the crook of its neck and drank from it while it was still warm.

He took enough to partially fill his belly and grimaced in disgust when he just couldn't bear to swallow the last mouthful. The taste on his tongue was unwelcome. He spat it to the side before rolling up his sleeve and wiping his forearm across his mouth.

Giving the Demon's blood time to settle in his gut, he walked over to Zylah. He licked at the inside of his mouth as the putrid taste lingered.

"Alright. Let's keep going," he told her, and broke into a run without further warning.

Staying in one spot would only lead more Demons to them.

For a short while, silence lingered between them as he listened to their surroundings. All had gone somewhat quiet. Then again, what made the Veil so eerie, even to him, was the lack of animals and insects present.

There was very little life to be found outside of those with sharp fangs, claws, and murderous tendencies.

*"Why..."* Zylah started, breaking the silence. *"Why did you eat that Demon?"*

"I didn't eat it," he argued, narrowing his gaze at the rushing forest before him. "I just drank some of its blood."

*"But why?"*

Their path became steady enough that he could glance at her from the corner of his eye. Her orbs were teal, revealing nothing. He returned to watching his footing.

"I haven't eaten any meat in a few days. I can only go so long without doing so – it's a curse of my Elven-Demon nature. I prefer not to eat the flesh of humans, Demons, or even Elves anymore, but settling my stomach with blood takes away the worst of the sickness I feel when I go too long without it. Doesn't matter what it comes from, nor how much disgust I feel regarding the taste or action."

Then, as if to prove how much stronger he was from doing so, he increased their pace. Zylah easily kept up with him, and she once more went quiet.

They passed through an invisible threshold and into the middle ring of the Veil's gloomy forest.

*Not much further.* Perhaps another day of running, if not a little less.

# FIFTEEN

When Zylah came upon a big hut in the middle of the dark, early morning forest, her apprehension eroded away due to the scents within the air. Herbs, spices, flowers, and other plants made the area smell pleasant and inviting. There was also a small collection of animals nearby, as if the area was safe.

A garden in the middle of a clearing was fenced off, and the urge to go over and inspect all the new things that lay in the dirt was difficult to resist. From what she could tell, since it was out in the open and fewer trees shrouded it, sunlight would shine upon the growing plants throughout the day. Connected to it and situated in the shade, there was a small enclosure that housed a little wooden building. A handful of round bird-like creatures clucked and cooed from it, while others sporting brown, white, and sandy-coloured feathers wandered around the area.

Between the hut and the garden was a decent-sized open space for one to walk around, and the grass was cut short and well maintained. Some tools with long handles sat up against the side of the home, one with bristles and the other with a spade-shaped head.

The short, wide hut itself had some kind of mixture of hay and clay as a roof. The walls were made of large stones with more clay filling in the cracks, giving it an earthy smell and colour. An oval door led inside it, while the window to its left was round and had some kind of blue glass. All around the home, late-blooming flowers danced on hip-high shrubs, giving a splash of yellow and pink colour against its drearier earthy appearance.

*This wasn't what I was expecting at all.* Then again, Zylah didn't know what she thought she'd find once they arrived.

A shadow shifted into the blue-glass window, like a person had popped their face up from their hiding spot.

No one came outside, but the sounds coming from within made it evident it was occupied.

"She's probably nervous there's a Mavka in her territory," Jabez stated, before pulling back his hood. "I'll make her come out."

Zylah noted his long, straight hair tied back into a high ponytail. She liked the way it revealed all of his sharp masculine features that could often be shielded, especially his wide jaw and high cheekbones. It also allowed his ears to be fully visible, as the right ear could often be hidden away except for its point.

The ends of his hair swayed between his shoulders as he walked towards the door.

Before he even made it a few steps, a loud bang and clash came from within the hut, someone suddenly shuffling around inside it. The door flung open, and a tanned female exited with harsh stomps, waving some kind of wooden apparatus.

She looked human – if it wasn't for the set of pointed, fuzzy ears on top of her head. They were red, as was her short hair, but the tips of her ears had black on the ends of them. A long, fluffy fox-like tail similar in colour to her ears swung behind her, and she hissed a set of feline fangs at him.

"You!" the female shouted, her green, floor-length dress bundled in one of her fists as she hiked it up to storm out. "I should kick your stupid butt!"

Jabez halted. "Hello, Fayren."

"Don't you *hello* me, you devil of a man!" Large glowing red eyes narrowed on him as she wrinkled a small nose. "I thought you were dead!"

Jabez chuckled warmly. "And yet, here I stand."

She stomped her boot-clad feet and showed little fear despite the hostility she obviously wore in her humanoid face. *She doesn't look like a Demon.* At least, not compared to the mean, monstrous versions Zylah had only ever seen – those that had glistening, void-like flesh.

She barely even smelt like one.

*Is this what Jabez meant by the differences between lesser Demons and more developed ones?* She couldn't help being curious about their variations, noting that the completion process reminded her of herself and the vast changes she'd gone through.

Jabez didn't move a muscle, even when she was right before him with her fists on her hips. Barely coming to his chest, the Demon gave a seething glare up at his face. Then she raised her wooden utensil and began whacking him with it.

"Do you understand how upset I was?!" she screeched, jumping up to smack him in the head, and a *thunk* sounded as it connected with his skull. "My whole family mourned. We even held a funeral for you in the village!"

Jabez, surprisingly allowing the abuse, laughed as he attempted to cover his body. With one knee coming up, he curled one way, then the other, before he grunted when she thwacked him in the back.

"By the cursed light, woman, stop it." His demand held no animosity. "Remember who I am."

"Oh, and what is that? Because currently your castle is nothing but a pile of rubbish!"

He skilfully grasped the wooden item and stole it from her. Then he smacked her in the forehead with it.

Aghast, she darted her hand up to cover the spot he struck. "How dare you hit a little old lady!"

"Well, at least you're still honest."

She snatched the wooden item back and pointed it up at his nose with her lips pursed.

"Watch it, grandpa." Then she poked the tip of the utensil towards Zylah. "And you show up, back from the dead, with a Mavka! I thought I was about to be eaten! Couldn't you have removed your damn hood *before* you entered my lands?"

Zylah chittered at the female's slitted glare, her sight shifting to a reddish pink. She backed up a step, uncertain of how to react or how to proceed. For such a little female, she was spritely and vicious!

Jabez stepped behind the female and shoved her in the back to force her to approach.

"Fayren, this is Zylah," he stated, waving his hand towards Zylah standing there awkwardly. "I'm sure you're making her uncomfortable, so I'll ask you to refrain from your usual pestering." Then, when they were right before Zylah, he stepped to the side so they formed a small triangle. "Zylah, this is Fayren, an acquaintance of mine."

Zylah lifted her hand and wiggled her fingers in hello.

"Friendly?" the female asked, casting Jabez a wary glance from the corner of her eye.

"The biggest threat here is me," he answered.

The female's foxy ears perked up, just as her flattened lips smoothed. Her features softened as she offered Zylah a toothy smile.

Now that she was closer, Zylah inspected the wrinkles on her face. Deep, forking lines branched out from the outer edges of her eyes and the corners of her lips. There were lines running from the creases of her small nose to her chin, and her skin appeared to be loose around her cheeks, jaw, and neck.

Zylah had never seen an aged person before. One of her books had detailed such features, and she liked being able to see how the beauty of life had been wonderfully etched into her very face. Her smile was so warm that it managed to calm Zylah's unsteady heart almost immediately.

"I've never met a Mavka in person," Fayren stated, her voice gentling into a sweet coo. Her eyes drifted down to Zylah's feet before coming back up to inspect her small antlers. "Not as big and scary as I was told."

"That's because she's not running at you on all fours with red orbs," Jabez stated, humour lightening his tone.

"You poor thing," Fayren said, her eyes bowed with obvious sympathy. She hiked her thumb at Jabez. "How long have you been stuck with this jerk?"

He folded his arms with a huff. "I find that rude and offensive."

"What?" Fayren's lips parted in disbelief. "You know it's true." Then she covered the side of her mouth, shielding it from him as she whispered, "He has horribly childish tantrums. For a man who is twice my age, you'd think he'd grow up a bit."

Dark yellow lifted into Zylah's sight, and she tilted her head at the little Demon. "You're confusing."

The female threw her head back and cackled. "They've always said I'm a little eccentric." She dusted off the skirt of her dress with her eyes purposefully elsewhere. "I actually think it's one of my best qualities."

Jabez rolled his eyes and huffed. "Yes, yes. You're an annoying little shit. Now, if you don't mind, we actually came here on business."

"I retired from your employment," the female stated, snubbing her nose at him. "I spent all my years fawning over you. Let me age in peace."

"Fayren," Jabez growled, eyes narrowing at her.

She straightened at his warning tone, and all the playfulness in her features dissipated. "Okay, fine. What is it you need?"

"Zylah is looking for some insight into her... gender," he said, turning his gaze upwards coyly. He shook his head side to side like Zylah often did when she was being avoidant. "I thought it would be best if I brought her to another female to explain such things."

"Me?!" Fayren exclaimed, as she placed a hand over her chest. "But I don't know anything about Mavka biology!"

"A female is a female, no matter their species."

"Then get her a book on human anatomy!"

"I did. It will be pointless in this matter." When that didn't seem to placate the little fox Demon, Jabez coughed into his fist before stating, "She's gone through a heat cycle. I figured a Demon would be best to explain this."

Fayren's lips pursed, and her outrage quickly faded. "I see." She gave Jabez another sideways glance. "But you should have been able to explain it."

"Like I said, I thought it best if another female talked to her about it," he answered from behind his hand. He lowered it just so he could raise a brow at her. "Would you really turn away a female in need?"

Jabez appeared to have hit a nerve with the female, and she

grumbled, pouting her bottom lip forward. "You're a conniving man." She sighed, before offering Zylah another smile. "Alright, sweetie. I'll help you."

Seemingly unafraid of Zylah, Fayren grabbed her wrist and dragged her towards the hut. With her other hand, she waved her wooden utensil at Jabez in a threat like she may start hitting him again. "You are to stay outside."

"Yes. I agree that is appropriate." Then, as if he thought it was important to know, he added, "She doesn't produce pheromones."

"No pheromones?" Fayren stumbled in surprise before casting a strange look at Zylah. She quickly steadied her steps and resumed pulling her. "I see."

Zylah looked to Jabez for assistance as she tripped over her own feet, unsure of what was happening or why she was being dragged away. He merely watched while folding his arms, allowing Zylah to be handled in such a way.

*But I don't know this Demon.* She didn't want to be left alone with Fayren, someone who was a stranger to her.

She wasn't given a choice as she was led towards the hut, and the only thing stopping her from pulling away was that this was what Jabez wanted. She chittered nervously, especially when she had to duck beneath the doorway to prevent her skull and antlers from bashing into it.

Zylah was forced to remain hunched forward due to her height.

Once the door was closed with a definitive and heart-clutching thud, her wrist was released.

Fayren entered deeper into her small home, her fluffy red fox tail swaying behind her legs. A small hole had been created within her dress, giving the appendage freedom. Zylah thought that was a brilliant idea.

Before Zylah could take further note of the female, her gaze snagged on the contents of the home. There was little room to move around.

On the left, a small bench of some kind was covered in herbs, spices, and many vegetables and fruit she'd seen Jabez consume. In the middle of the house was a table she knew she'd never be able to fit her tall legs under, with so many items and tools upon it she couldn't name them even if she tried. There were only two chairs, both of which would likely break under her weight.

Then, finally, to the right was a small bed that would require Zylah to bring her knees up to her chest just to fit on it. The blanket was cream on top, but the folded section near the pillows revealed the inside was brown and fluffy.

Lanterns hung from the low ceiling, while more rested on every free surface available – as if to shine as much light as possible.

The home smelt warm, inviting, and well used. Now that she was surrounded by Fayren's flowery scent, the Demon in it became more noticeable. She eyed her shoulder-length red hair, and the way she regarded Zylah warily despite inviting her inside and into an enclosed space.

Fayren looked uncomfortable, as if Jabez had shoved a difficult task onto her that she wanted to be done with as quickly as possible. Hunched forward, Zylah didn't know how to settle her own discomfort in reaction to it.

"Well? Are you going to stand in the doorway or come further inside?" Fayren beckoned her over with harsh hand movements.

It was only then that Zylah realised she'd been too busy admiring and assessing everything and she'd gone motionless. The female placed her hands on her narrow hips, while one of her bushy brows raised. Her fluffy ears were perky, and her red eyes held no animosity.

Fayren's wariness faded and was instead replaced by a confused furrow of her brows. "You seem like a bit of a shy creature. I'm sorry. I didn't mean to spook you." She offered a smile as she stepped to the side and waved at one of the two chairs. "Please, sit. Make yourself comfortable. I won't hit you with my spoon like I did to Jabez."

She even laid it on the table to show she meant no harm with it.

"I don't think I should," Zylah answered, assessing the small seat further. "I'm worried I'll break it."

Its legs were thin and looked like they'd snap as easily as Zylah could rend a thick tree branch in half.

A giggle escaped her. "Don't be. It has survived bigger creatures than you."

Zylah looked down at her body, seeing nothing wrong with it. Still, she trusted the female's confidence and stepped towards the closest chair at the shorter edge of the table and tentatively sat. It creaked under her weight but held.

"Alright. Would you like a cup of tea or some water while we talk? My kitchen can only hold so much, but I have a storage area out the back. I can procure just about anything for you if you have particular tastes." She let out a laugh as she pushed a few strands of her short hair from her forehead. "I've never hosted a Mavka before, so please forgive me if I make a mistake regarding your species."

"No. I don't need anything," Zylah answered, fiddling with the skirt of her dress resting between her spread thighs. "I don't need to eat or drink."

Fayren's thin lips pursed before settling. The other chair's legs scraped against the ground as she dragged it down the longer length of the table to be closer to Zylah. Her movements were slow as she sat down, and she let out a little agonised groan when her joints creaked.

Fayren stared at her for longer than was comfortable, and Zylah grew more anxious. Especially when the Demon's gaze narrowed.

"Sit up, dear child. Slumping like an ogre is unbecoming of a lady."

At her stern tone, Zylah's back straightened and went rigid. "S-sorry."

Fayren smacked the side of her knee. "And close those furry thighs of yours. You don't want people seeing up such a short skirt."

Zylah's knees snapped closed, and she went to roll her shoulders forward self-consciously. She shoved them back and crossed her hands over her lap, unsure of how to sit or how to act. Being scolded by a stranger about the way she sat brought on memories of how she often sat with Jabez, who had never complained about the way she positioned herself.

Her orbs shifted to a shameful reddish pink and the bottoms of them wavered as she wondered if she'd been behaving oddly in front of him.

"Let's start from the beginning," Fayren said, leaning against the backrest of her chair with her hands neatly folded on her lap. "What do you know?"

Zylah figured the Demon meant regarding why they were here. "Well, I'm female," she said, stifling the urge to scratch at her neck awkwardly in case she got in trouble for it. "I have a heat cycle, and-and breasts. I also do not have dangly bits."

"Okay." Fayren gave a noticeably cringing smile. "What else?"

Zylah placed one foot on top of the other in an attempt to make herself smaller. "I'm sorry, but that is all I know."

The female's features visibly dropped and some of her tanned completion greyed. "You're joking," she rasped, her eyes growing wide. "That's... that's nothing at all!"

"Wait! I also have a slit that is hidden away," Zylah added, and her orbs deepened into a more embarrassed glow.

"Yes, but do you know what it is *called*? What it is? What it does?"

Zylah chittered and shook her head. For as long as she'd been alive, she hadn't realised it was so important to know these things. With the way this Demon was responding, it was like she thought Zylah inept.

"I... have only recently gained much humanity." She gave into the urge to scratch at the collar of fur around her neck, while turning her snout away. "Jabez says I'm intelligent, but that I lack knowledge. He has been teaching me."

"By the cursed light," Fayren muttered as she covered her face. "No wonder he brought you to me. I thought he was just wanting me to explain heat cycles and sex, but *this?* No, this indeed requires an in-depth explanation from a female."

Unable to hold back the emotions that were slamming into her – how uncomfortable she felt, how shame seemed to rest on her shoulders – Zylah produced a quiet whine. Her orbs refused to change from their reddish-pink glow, yet the wavering bottoms of them shattered and droplets began to float around her skull. Her heart raced, aching in her chest, and it seemed to make her insides grow hard and strained.

Suddenly her skin felt wrong, and her fur itched.

A warm hand cupped the length of her jawbone, and Zylah flinched at the unfamiliarity of the touch. Fayren steered her face towards her.

"Dear child, it's okay." She offered a tender smile, and her eyes appeared softer and more caring than before. "It's normal to feel shy. You're not the first confused female who has sat in one of my chairs. Many demonlings come to me for knowledge that they can't get, as I'm known for offering assistance regarding this."

"I'm not a youngling, though," Zylah argued, pulling away from her touch.

"Oh yes, I can see that. Just by our conversation I can tell, but if no one has been around to teach you, how else are you to know? That's not your fault."

Supporting herself with a hand on the table, Fayren rose to her feet so she could walk to her bed and kneel beside it. She pulled some kind of box with a latch on it out from underneath and lifted the lid to reveal a large stock of books.

"I have everything we need here. Diagrams of different kinds of Demon anatomy, explanations into the varying kinds of fertility cycles. You'll be surprised by just how different each Demon can be, so hopefully something will be similar to you. We can work this out together."

Zylah watched as she pulled three books from her box, before rising to stand with much effort. She placed them on the table and reassumed her seat.

"Usually I would do a physical examination, but that can be quite uncomfortable for most."

"Physical examination?"

The female gave a small awkward laugh. "I usually would have the Demon lie on the bed and part their thighs for me. It allows me to see what kind of genitalia they have, since there are so many variations. Some of us can lay eggs, or even lack a clit. Some have a spur to inseminate themselves. We really are all amazing, if I'm being honest. It makes the discussion regarding procreating quite unique each time."

Horrified by the idea of a stranger seeing her, and by what she'd just learned, her sight shifted to white. She shook her head. "No. I don't want to do that."

"I didn't think so," she stated with humour curling her lips. She pulled a book closer and began flipping through the pages. "If you can point to what you think is closest, we can go from there. Like I said, please be forgiving, as I'm not very knowledgeable about Mavka. I will do what I can."

The harsh pressure in Zylah's chest eased, as did her tears. She fisted the skirt of her dress before bowing her head. "Thank you. I... really appreciate this."

Fayren nodded before going back to flipping pages. "You're welcome, Zylah. We'll start from the beginning, and then we'll move onto everything else like sex, consent, and how best to protect yourself during heat cycles. The fact you don't produce pheromones is actually a blessing." She lifted her gaze to run it over Zylah's body. "Then again, I already think you'll struggle to keep unruly males away from you. Especially in a dress such as that. Unless that is what you're going for."

Confused about why Fayren would make such a comment about her body, or clothing, Zylah tilted her head and looked down at herself. "Jabez made this for me."

"Pardon?" Fayren wheezed out, before choking and coughing. "He *made* that scrap of clothing for you?"

"I like it. I don't like things covering my tail. I like that he... gave it to me."

Fayren produced a warm laugh. "I think you're mistaking me. The idea of Jabez sewing anything, let alone a female's clothing, is rather humorous to me. I just can't imagine him doing something like that for another."

Zylah grumbled at that. *Why not?* He'd done it for her readily; she'd witnessed him in the act.

# SIXTEEN

With his back towards Fayren's home, Jabez sat on the top beam of the fence surrounding her garden. His eyes scanned over the different fruits and vegetables she had available, although only the winter varieties and hardier herbs were edible due to the colder season.

Night had fallen, so he kept his hood down, but used the rest of his cape as a blanket from the chill. Since this was Fayren's territory, and it was unlikely anyone would come to visit, he didn't feel the need to hide his identity.

She and Zylah had been speaking for hours, which Jabez took as a good sign. The longer they spoke, the more Zylah would learn.

He had no issue being stationary. He welcomed the quiet and solitude, using it to piece together his thoughts.

When he heard the door open, he briefly turned his head to look over his shoulder, only to bring his gaze forward. It wasn't the female he'd been expecting, but part of him was relieved.

She was wise enough to give him a wide berth and to approach from his left, rather than from directly behind. Having spent years within his castle, she knew him well enough to be aware of his quirks.

"You owe me big-time," Fayren muttered, opening the creaky gate to her garden, whereas he'd merely climbed over the beams.

"I owe you nothing," he answered coldly. "This wasn't for

me, but for her."

Seeing she wanted to sit beside him, he offered his hand out to her. She glared at it, then him, before taking it so he could assist her in climbing the fence. She settled her butt next to him, brushed off the skirt of her long green dress, and then laid her hands in her lap.

She stared at him for a long while, and he ignored her as he peered over the garden. She'd speak when she was ready.

A soft breeze rustled his cream tunic, cloak, and horribly sewn pants, and pushed the length of his long ponytail to the side. Her flowery smell was welcome, reminding him of simpler times sheltered within his castle, and her presence a familiar one since his early twenties.

"You shouldn't sit like that," she said, disapproval evident in her tone. "It's unbecoming for someone who was once our *king*."

Just when he'd been enjoying her presence...

"Oh, for fuck's sake," Jabez exclaimed, throwing his hands up. "Can you not nag for five damn minutes?!" He tossed his face to the left. "You better not have nagged at Zylah."

Fayren looked up towards the night sky, then away, while wobbling her head. Her smirk was telling, and it instantly soured him.

"Look, if you wish to sit like someone shoved a pole up your arse, go for it. Leave others alone. It's *unbecoming* to be a nuisance."

Fayren tossed her head back and let out a giggle. "But it's just so much fun. It always gets people riled up."

"It makes people want to toss you into a river. I don't care how old you are, I'll do something to retaliate." A malicious grin filled his features as he eyed the green stalks of the leeks growing in the earth. "I'll start pulling out all your plants. I'm sure that'll teach you a lesson."

He eyed an obvious tomato plant, and the urge was nigh overwhelming.

"Did you bother my chickens?" she asked, bringing her gaze down to his lap.

Pressing his lips together until both puckered forward with the corners turned downwards, Jabez brushed a stray feather off himself. "I merely stole a few eggs. I'm a growing boy. I need all the sustenance I can get."

"You did all your growing up quite some time ago. How old are you now? Five hundred and seventy?"

"I'm not *that* old," he said with a scoff, before he glanced at her from the side. "Five hundred and sixty-seven. I turn thirty-eight in a few years."

"By the ever-night, I always forget just what age you truly are." Her foxy ears darted back, and she shook her head. "It's so hard imagining living for that long."

"Try living it. Then again, you've almost lived a full lifetime for a human-eating Demon. Is this your two hundred and ninth year? I'm sure the passage of time feels longer for such a pest as yourself."

"I feel ancient, if I'm being honest. I left your employment because of the arthritis in my knees. I just couldn't walk up your stairs anymore."

Jabez glanced over at her once more, this time noticing her features. If he was to gauge what age she looked like in comparison to a human, he'd say she was bordering on sixty-five, if not older.

She still had many years left in her, and her youth was undeniably present, even with age. It helped that she still had a rather spritely and playful personality, and her beauty was just as beguiling.

He was sure he'd added to her wrinkles and the sprinkles of grey in her predominately red hair by stressing her when she was under his employment. He was just as eccentric as her, and they'd often butted heads – especially when he'd been younger and much more immature.

"How's your mother?" Jabez felt obliged to ask, even though he really didn't care.

"She's... good. She knows my life is coming to an end, whereas she'll live another few hundred years longer." Her nimble hands, peppered with spots that reflected her advancing years, tightened on each other, but she was skilful in hiding her emotions. "Then again, like you said, that's a human-eating Demon for you."

Jabez knew Fayren's mother well, as she was one of the

few remaining Demons who had survived coming to Earth with him. Lettie, her mother, was only a few years younger than him, and due to her consuming Elves as her first food source, she had a similar lifespan to him. Since their fathers were mostly human-eating Demons, all of Lettie's children were ageing, with Fayren being the eldest. Although, thankfully, some of Lettie's developed Elven blood had allowed her children to live much longer than their fathers.

He'd watched the woman beside him grow up from a demonling and then surpass him in physical age in less than half his life span. It made establishing any form of bond with anyone hard, as he knew he'd likely outlive their demise.

He didn't wish to hold people close to him when they would never live long enough to grow old with him.

Silence descended upon them, heavy and filled with sorrow. He hid it as always, his features adopting a mask of indifference.

His ear twitched when she brushed the backs of her claws over the shaved part of his head. "Look at your beautiful hair. What did they do to you?"

"It matters little. What has happened, happened," he answered with a shrug.

"But I know how much it means to you. My mother told me you shaved your head bald when you arrived here and have grown it as a form of rebirth. To know it's been altered against your will..."

Jabez reached up and snatched her hand before gingerly lowering it. He gave her a look of warning, one that conveyed this wasn't a discussion he would partake in. She wisely lowered her gaze and let it go.

He thought his hair may be as long as it was before he arrived here. He trimmed it to keep it from going past the middle of his back, but that's all he did with it. He rarely styled it and having it in a ponytail was mildly foreign to him.

He just hadn't removed the tie yet.

"Why did you come here, Jabez?" she asked in a small voice. "The others are all out of sorts. If you haven't returned to take back your place, then why risk it?"

"I told you why I'm here. Zylah needed someone to explain

this to her."

"Why couldn't you? You're not unknowledgeable about females." Then she coughed into her hand and muttered, "Quite the opposite, in fact."

He stared at her for a long while, then shook his head and looked out over the garden. He considered not saying anything, but decided she deserved some kind of explanation.

"It felt... wrong. Being the one to explain all this to her, it didn't sit well with me. It's not a male's place. You were the only person I could think of who I trusted enough to reveal I'm still alive."

"Is it because she likes you?"

His face twitched in a subtle flinch, and he darted his gaze to her. "What makes you say that?"

Her lips thinned. "Don't play coy with me, young man. She explained what she can remember from her heat cycle, how you held her. You knew then, didn't you?"

Jabez rolled his eyes away from her. "Young man, old man. Pick one."

She reached up and dared to grab one of his horns, yanking him to look at her. "Do you feel the same?"

His nose wrinkled as his features twisted into a cringe. "Absolutely not."

She narrowed her eyes at him, the red of them much brighter than his own. "Then why did you bring her here? Had you truly been indifferent, you would have boasted your knowledge like a suave fool. You remember, I was *there* when you taught Merikh. You know Mavka better than anyone."

He opened his mouth to refute her, but closed it. He couldn't deny it. He also wouldn't admit to anything possibly damning.

"I have my reasons." At the fucking look she gave him through her lowered eyelids, he palmed his face. "What do you want me to say? That I've seen what happens when a Mavka isn't taught? That withholding the information would only lead her to danger, and being unable to explain it would just be pure negligence on my part?"

"Well, that's a start." She looked down at her lap before lifting her gaze to her garden, then shifted it to the left to scan the trees.

It was obvious she wanted to ask him something but held back because it would upset him.

"Oh, just ask," he sneered. "You have no problem being a nosy little pest, so why start now?"

"Does..." She paused to nibble at her bottom lip. "Does this have anything to do with *Katerina*?" Fayren whispered her name, as if that would make it less impactful.

His mouth flattened into a hard line as he narrowed his eyes into a deep glare. But not at her, at the damn tomato plant.

*Oh, screw it.* It was better he talked about it, and if it had to be someone, at least it was her. She had been a sort of councillor for him, since she was one of the very few he'd shared *some* details with pertaining to his crazed thoughts.

Making sure his tone came across as deadened, he answered, "Yes, it has to do with her."

"Because of what happened to her?"

That was one way to put it, but also entirely inaccurate. "It's more what she did."

"How so? From what I understand, she was rather outspoken about how that Mavka traumatised her."

"What happened between Katerina and Orpheus is far more complicated than that." With his hands between his spread thighs, he tossed his palms up. "There's no denying how she was hurt. What happened was unfair to anyone. She was taken from her home, kept within the Veil, unable to escape, and was essentially stuck with someone she despised. I spent a hundred and eighty-seven years helping her through it, and she truly never healed. Nothing could save her mind from it."

Jabez looked up at the night sky and let a sigh fall from him. He wished the stars held answers, but they'd always been silent and unchanging.

"But she wasn't innocent. She was a victim, while also being a perpetrator who refused to accept her own wrongdoings."

"I don't understand," Fayren said, her brows furrowing. "From what she told everyone—"

"It's only half the truth, and her version of what happened," he said to cut her off, refusing to look away from the stars.

"Like you said, I know Mavka. Merikh taught me all I needed to know about the earlier stages of their life cycle. They're essentially bumbling, uneducated morons who don't know their tail from their damn horns. And it's *worse* when they lack humanity."

He finally turned away from the sky with a frown marring his features.

"Consenting to something when you have no idea what you're doing is no consent at all. If Orpheus was anything like Merikh, he'd likely never seen his own dick before, let alone known where to fucking *stick* it. And I know... I watched them for a long time before I took her away from him, and he was only a little more intelligent than Merikh when I first met him."

Orpheus had obtained far more humanity than when Jabez had met Zylah, enough to talk in somewhat broken and simple English. Someone had been teaching him, and he was sure Katerina had a small hand in that, but his knowledge had been limited.

Maybe Jabez was a little sensitive to this due to being a male himself, but he had his own thoughts regarding what happened – and because of the truth she'd shared with him.

"Whether she wanted to acknowledge it or not, or just simply couldn't accept that she'd done it, Katerina essentially groomed Orpheus by denying him that knowledge, by refusing to educate him. If he was anything like Merikh's earlier stages... then his mind was the equivalent comprehension level of a child, or at the very least, an intelligent dog."

Jabez couldn't help speaking quietly, as if that would make what he said less weighty.

"By thinking him a monster and treating him as one, she abused his naïvety and ignorance. How was that any better than what Orpheus had done to her? Nothing he did was out of malice, which is more than I can say for many other males."

Jabez looked to Fayren, silently asking her if what he thought was wrong. She was a woman – perhaps she would have more insight into a situation he'd struggled to understand for the longest time. He'd completely sided with Katerina at first until she accidentally admitted to certain things that ended up skewing his perception of her.

It painted a very complicated picture of what had truly happened over the many years of him listening to Katerina complain.

"I never thought about that," Fayren stated, then let out a low hum, cupping her chin as she considered his words. "I know Merikh lacked humanity when you first brought him to the castle, but I never even considered Orpheus' mental age with regard to Katerina."

"What's worse, she still refused to communicate or explain anything. She even admitted that to me, stating she just didn't see the point when he was too stupid to understand." Jabez's ears darted back as he shrugged with his hands. "But they truly aren't that idiotic."

He hadn't liked hearing that, nor how she then further manipulated him because she knew sex would make him subservient to her.

Jabez was all for manipulating others, but had he abused a female in such a way, people would consider him truly, *truly* vile and unforgivable. If the roles had been reversed... Jabez shuddered at the thought. *Why are females forgiven for actions they'd condemn a male for doing?* How was that fair?

But he also understood that in the back of her mind, she thought she was doing it to protect herself. She claimed it 'tamped down his aggression,' but Jabez had always been left with one question: How had she lived, for years, with a creature who was walking death if that was true?

If he'd been truly aggressive, she would have ceased breathing long before Jabez had been able to grow infatuated with her from a distance.

Jabez brushed his hands over the top of his head in frustration, expecting to feel loose strands. He flinched, grunted, and finally yanked his ponytail free, annoyed he was having this conversation despite the unexpected relief from finally talking about it.

"I refused to let that be Zylah's future. If no one explained this to her, she would be left open to abuse. Not only would she be like Orpheus, who didn't know his own body, but she could end up like Katerina, who felt taken advantage of. Her pain would have been twofold, and foreseeing that... like I mentioned, leaving her uneducated would make me negligent. It would mean I had a hand in her pain."

Of course things were different, as Zylah, despite her length of life, was physically, emotionally, and mentally more mature than any Mavka he'd come across, other than Merikh. The fact that Mavka didn't age like a human or even an Elf, but more like a Demon, made things complicated. But that didn't take away the fact that ignorance could be abused, and Jabez wasn't the kind of person to do that, nor was he the kind of person to sit by and *watch* it happen.

"Sometimes I forget that even though you still look so young, you have many hundreds of years of experience. To even consider this... you're right. Keeping her uninformed could have had disastrous results for her."

"It doesn't fucking help that Katerina tried to put me in Orpheus' place," he bit out, still rather spiteful over it, even though it had happened nearly two centuries ago.

Once more, Fayren's brows narrowed, and she turned to him. "What do you mean?"

His nose wrinkled in disgust, while guilt, shame, and anger slipped down his spine like hot lava.

"It's no secret that I offered Katerina a new life because I fancied her. She was beautiful, and something about her defiant gaze when she peered at Orpheus humoured me."

"Well, yes. You were rather charming chasing her around your castle." Fayren gave a small laugh, trying to alleviate the heaviness of the conversation. "I suddenly saw the youth on your face, when you always came across so cold and callous."

"I was twenty-six. I was already starting to come into my prime by that point," he admitted. "But I'd bedded enough Demons to have years of experience under my belt."

He'd chosen his sexual companions diligently. Those who he'd been intimate with had all been knowledgeable and nearing completion. Some had more monstrous forms, but that hadn't lessened their appeal to him – actually, sometimes it'd excited him.

"The first time I attempted intimacy with Katerina, she voiced her consent. She helped me remove her dress and even laid on my damn bed."

His face and ears grew hot, both in embarrassment and shame. Knowing he couldn't hide his expression through sheer will, he covered his face with a palm.

He spoke behind it.

"But the moment I touched her, tried to kiss her, she turned as stiff as stone. No matter how much I asked if she wanted me, and she said yes, it didn't take me long to realise that, in her heart, she didn't. I didn't understand why. I tried to do everything right, but I had enough experience to know when a female was ready and wanting. The moment I realised what was happening, I grew so disgusted with myself, and at her, that I just tossed her dress at her and told her to get out."

"Jabez," Fayren cooed, likely due to how his voice dropped an octave in distress, but he pressed on.

"I'll never forget the way she fucking screamed at me for it. It was like she couldn't understand why I was suddenly rejecting her." He dug his fingers into his closed eyes when a growl slipped from him in anger. "It took her some time before she got past her rage and finally admitted the truth. She was only doing it because she thought her body was the price for my protection. That, if she denied me, I'd feed her to the rest of the Demons in my home, even though I *never* said that."

He pulled his hand from his face and turned to Fayren. Her mouth had fallen open in disbelief, yet he could see the anger reflected in her eyes.

She knew he'd never do such a thing. He may have been a cruel prick, but he'd never abuse a female like that.

"In that moment, I felt like Orpheus. I could... *see* how he would have been so confused. She made me a fucking *monster* in her head, before I'd even done something wrong. She didn't see me as a man, but a beast, a Demon, a lesser being. In that moment, I knew she saw me as a monster, just one more tolerable and perhaps more handsome than the one she'd just spent years with. Orpheus was a virgin. At least *I* had the experience to know why she was so cold and could prevent crossing that line with her. But how was that fair on me? On him?"

For the longest time, Jabez had been furious with her.

He couldn't believe someone had dared to manipulate their own mind so deeply. To convince themselves he was a villain when he'd never done anything wrong to begin with.

She came with him willingly when he offered, and he'd tried his best to be patient and woo her properly, only for her to think so poorly of him. Not once had she revealed that she'd felt that way, skilfully hiding it behind false pleasantries and alluring smiles.

Her beauty made it hard to see the truth in her.

And yet, once he realised how she perceived him simply because he was a Demon, he'd still never been cruel to her. He didn't relinquish his vow of protecting her or revoke his help with her own personal vendetta. She remained pampered like a damn princess, just one he kept at arm's length because he could no longer trust her.

While, at the same time, he became a source of healing for her. She spoke to him often, and Jabez had just listened quietly, as advice was never what she sought. She'd get angry at him if he attempted to offer any insight.

She just wanted someone to scream her frustrations at, and he'd willingly taken on that role for her. She had her reasons for everything, and none of this removed the pain she'd gone through. Pain he'd witnessed in her, which sometimes reflected what he felt inside.

Katerina had been hurting for a long time, and he'd felt it wasn't his place to bear any grudges towards her – especially when very little of it had anything to do with him. People who were hurt didn't think clearly. What he'd done in the centuries he'd been alive in comparison to her mere twenty-seven years overshadowed anything she could have done to anyone.

Jabez was a hypocrite in many ways, but not in this instance. He'd done many vile and unforgiveable things.

He shook his head in exasperation, his shoulders loosening as he broke the tension when it was obvious Fayren wouldn't. He also didn't want her to think the worst of Katerina.

"It took me a while to forgive her," he admitted. "But I understood that she was just doing everything she could to protect herself, even if it was wrong. She valued her life more than her body, so long as no one wounded her. I admired her strength in that matter. Her resilience. It's what first drew me to her. Katerina had always been strong."

Jabez lifted his gaze to the sky when he noticed light brightening it into a muted purple. How long had he been sitting here for dawn to be approaching already?

*How quickly time passes in this wretched realm.*

"One thing she didn't seem to understand was the truth made me aware of her thoughts, her behaviour. It's why I rarely sided with her when it came to the accusations she had regarding Merikh. Most of it was lies, but I also knew it was just *her* version of the truth she'd twisted so tightly in her mind that she truly believed it."

Merikh was a whole other battle he'd needed to face with her, and it hadn't helped that he'd been there when Jabez first took Katerina from Orpheus.

"I remember," Fayren stated, rolling her shoulders back. "You could hear them screaming at each other from across the castle. And Merikh had a mean roar to him."

He let his head fall back and groaned loudly. *By the cursed light, that had been such a hard few years.*

Merikh was fucking huge in comparison to Katerina. And he fucking despised her, just as she hated him simply because he was a Mavka. Her prejudices against his kind meant anything he did, even if it was merely to shove her out of the way, had her judging him. If he accidentally touched her breast or her arse because his hand was so big it could hold her entire head like it was a ball, she thought he was assaulting her.

The fact that he got so sick of her drama he left for a few months revealed he didn't want her – he wanted *away* from her.

"My own friend left because of my woman, and I was in the fucking middle of it. Both were angry at me for not intervening, for not shoving the other out of my home. I could see each of their perspectives, and I tried my best to calm them, to educate them on each other. Neither wanted to listen."

There had been no winning.

Jabez eventually gave up and told them to sort it out themselves. Merikh wouldn't hurt her, as he knew it would enrage Jabez, and Katerina had been too weak to harm him in return. They just shared unpleasant words with each other.

Funnily enough, she considered him a stupid brute, yet Merikh had been the one to just avoid her. He turned his anger into mockery in retaliation.

And she'd grown upset with Jabez when he couldn't help scoffing out a laugh because Merikh's insults were so random and weirdly funny.

*Fuck. I miss my damn friend.*

His humour had been as fucked up as Jabez's. His arrogance was born from Jabez's. His sarcasm was a mirror of his own. In some ways, Merikh had formed in Jabez's image simply because he'd been the one to educate him. *It'd felt like I'd... grown up with him.*

Merikh was immortal and undying, which meant he wouldn't age and fade away. There had been relief in that.

They'd been companions for almost eighty years, starting a little over two hundred and fifty years ago and ending barely ten years after he met Katerina. They'd been so close, watching each other's backs, being each other's most trusted confidant, that it was like Merikh was his... brother. For a while, he'd considered that bull-headed Mavka as his only family.

And that had been taken from him by his own stupidity. By Katerina, who kept whispering in his ear, wearing him down, occasionally making him angry at Merikh. Then she'd used Jabez learning of Merikh's blood relation to Weldir – a moment in which his heart and mind had grown weak – and he turned on his only family.

*I lost a lot of affection for Katerina after that.*

He also believed their first sexual encounter was part of the reason he'd never truly loved her – if he'd even been capable of such an emotion. Every little thing she did, anything that was manipulative, or a twisted lie, meant she chopped down his affection bit by bit.

For a long time, Jabez had questioned why he was still keeping her around. It was simple: he'd promised her protection. He'd promised he would get revenge for her, and he was a man of his word. He was also petty and didn't want her to be right that he'd kill her because he had a bad temper, even when she sometimes infuriated him to the point he wanted to bash his head against a wall.

*Because I liked her and still cared about her, even until the end.* He'd been young and infatuated when he first met her, which had made him emotionally immature when it came to her. But over time, and as he'd gotten older and wiser, he'd simply enjoyed her companionship, even if their relationship wasn't fully affectionate.

They'd been... friends, kind of. She was the only person he'd been able to trust to some degree after Merikh's disappearance.

He didn't give two shits about Orpheus. If killing him made her happy, then why should he care? Orpheus would've just been added to the many others he'd ended.

But Jabez had only discovered the truth of how much that vow would ruin his plans.

He sighed as he palmed his face again, tiredness and frustration rolling into him like a drowning wave. He wished he could have explained all this to Fayren, to truly get it off his chest, but he just didn't have the will to share more than what he was currently allowing himself.

His pain from Merikh's absence... the regrets he had... they were just too heavy a burden for him to unload on her – and he was ashamed about them too.

But there was one shame he could share, despite how sour it tasted.

"She made me blind in my war, Fayren," he muttered, filling in the silence they had both fallen into.

"I know..." she muttered. "You let her hatred fuel your own. I did try to tell you that, but you're not really one to listen."

He sneered at her 'I told you so.' Then he glared at her petulance, causing her to lift her eyes away coyly, and he let out an exhausted expire.

"After Merikh permanently left, I was angry at him for leaving me. I thought that if I helped Katerina and rid the world of Mavka, it'd destroy Lindiwe and Weldir's bond enough that she'd break off whatever contract they have. With her gone, and his children fading, it'd weaken him. I just needed a moment, just a day of him being powerless so I could undo his ward. I already knew the code to it, but my magic just couldn't combat his – he's a fucking *god*, after all." He lowered his face so he could turn to her, and softly said, "I wanted to keep my promise to the Demons I boasted to about returning home. I wanted to do right by them too."

"You've always cared about us too much," Fayren stated in a soft, almost motherly voice, as she reached out to squeeze his knee. "You tried to hide it, but many of us could see how much you wanted to help us."

He allowed the intimate touch but was thankful she wisely kept it short and retracted her hand quickly.

Jabez wished he'd known the answer to success was never to be found on Earth.

Had he not been so tied to this realm, to ending Mavka, then he would have seen that going to Nyl'theria and rounding up an army on *that* side of the portal would have achieved much better results. They could have destroyed the Elven city years ago, and then Weldir would no longer need to keep up his ward.

He could have removed the barrier of their return from the other side. He would have been deemed a hero to his people.

"I only had a few years left to keep my promise to her," he continued, before glancing away. "She was dying. She didn't know it, of course, but the magic keeping her young and alive was beginning to diminish. The gilded ore I'd used to make her necklace powered that magic, and I could see it fading."

"I thought you were the one keeping her alive." Her furry ears twitched in interest, the conversation of magic and power items one that stirred passion in her. "Couldn't you just replace it?"

He shook his head. "It doesn't work like that. From the tome I read, it could only be used one time. I could make another if I mined for more gilded ore, but they couldn't be worn at the same time. Didn't matter in the end anyway. Orpheus' bride rammed a fucking sword through Katerina's chest before then."

He still couldn't believe someone under his sworn protection and care was murdered right before his very eyes. *Then again, we both had it coming.* He should have foreseen the failure.

Just as he should have seen the fall of his home. How Lindiwe would eventually bring him so close to death that if it weren't for Zylah, he'd have ceased breathing.

He'd been on a failing path from the beginning. *Had I just gone to Nyl'theria sooner...*

"I'm... tired, Fayren," Jabez admitted with an exasperated huff. "I'm no closer to success than I was two years ago. Two hundred years ago. From the day your mother and I first came here."

She offered him a sympathetic gaze and a head tilt. "Is there nothing you can do?"

"There is – there's actually a few things, but..." He looked over his shoulder to make sure the area was empty before lowering his voice. "The best option would require Zylah venturing with me to Nyl'theria."

She dipped her head forward and came a little closer. "Why are you whispering?" she muttered back.

"Because I considered being the cunning bastard that I am and manipulating her into her complying. However, I'm beginning to feel rather shitty about that."

"Because you like her?" Fayren gave him a cheeky, toothy grin, and he cringed.

"No," he lied. "Because she is so soft-hearted, I just don't see it working. But I need someone strong, fast, and quick of healing to cross that ward with me, and no Demon can cross it. I doubt Weldir would block his children or their descendants from going through it. Why should he?"

He realised he should have tested it with Merikh, but he just hadn't thought of it at the time.

"Have you considered asking her for help? With how highly she spoke of you, I think she might follow you anywhere."

Jabez grimaced at what that could possibly mean.

"That would present me with two choices. I can reveal the truth to her and hope she doesn't grow to hate me for what I have done. Or I can hide the truth and essentially manipulate a female's feelings for me into leading her to bloodshed." He dipped his head towards her and cocked a brow. "Which one makes me less of a villain?"

She opened her mouth and then promptly shut it. Her lips thinned in deep contemplation before pulling to one side.

"Well, when you put it that way... No, I don't think you should do the second option. She's very sweet, and just spending a few hours with her made me want to bring her into my arms for a hug." Then, to break the tension once more, she gave a small laugh, causing the wrinkles around her eyes to crease deeper. "She's quite the creature if she's managed to make you think with a true conscience."

"She is... spectacular. She's so damn smart that she's able to calculate and assess situations on her own. In comparison to the rest of her species, she's pretty special in that way. All I did was feed her a small number of humans, and she has repeatedly exceeded my expectations."

"Sounds like you admire her?" Her question was dripping in coyness.

"How can you not?" he returned, throwing his hands forward. "Had I known, it would have been easier to feed her fewer humans and use her lacking intelligence to convince her."

He probably also wouldn't be attracted to her femineity at all had he done that, which is what he *really* meant. Now she had all these interesting facets to her, while being intelligent and mature, and he found her company pleasant. He *liked* teaching her because she was interested in learning, and it made doing that with her... *fun.*

He'd even begun teaching her shit she didn't really need to know, like what the different stars were and how she could use them to map her way around Austrális. Utterly pointless in aiding her life, but interesting to know – while allowing him to spend more time interacting with her without her realising it was because he *wanted* to, and not because he *needed* to.

"She's now so mentally advanced that she's developing her own personality outside of my control," he continued. "She can already see right from wrong, and her morals are much more benevolent than mine. I doubt any persuading on my part will change them."

"Will you just admit you obviously feel something for her?

You've given it away multiple times from the first moment you brought her to my home."

He folded his arms defiantly. "I won't admit to something that doesn't exist."

He could admire someone without wanting them. Jabez actually hated a lot of people he admired.

"If that was true, you wouldn't have brought her here," she repeated from earlier in a sing-song voice. She kicked her legs back and forth like a cheeky, meddling woman. "I've seen many men deny their feelings, and it never bodes well."

"Why the fuck are we having this damn conversation?" He waved her off while turning his head away. "I shouldn't have started talking to you. You always manage to make me speak of things best left unsaid."

He couldn't believe he'd vented so freely to her! The back of his neck heated in embarrassment, and he suddenly regretted bringing up the matter.

"But–"

"Why does this matter to you? What does this achieve? Why are you trying to push this?"

"Because I want to see you happy," Fayren said, her features crinkling into sorrow – on his damn behalf. "In all my years, I don't think I've ever truly seen you enjoy life." She shrugged a single shoulder. "Sure, I've seen you laugh, but it is only ever in the moment. You always look so pensive and stoic. How many more years will you suffer alone?"

Jabez rolled his eyes at that. "This is the life I was given, much of it deserved. I have no desire for a female of any kind. I have no desire to breed offspring. All I want is to live peacefully, but I must shed Elven blood in order to do so."

"Why could you never be happy with *this* life then? If you just gave up your war..."

"Because I want to laugh in the pool of the blood of my enemies," he said with an added dramatic, eccentric flare. "I want to sit on their corpses, knowing I ended them after what they did to me, to the others, to those who are stuck here. The Elves are vile, and their pretentiousness irks me. Their fanciful city is an eyesore upon the worlds."

"But what if you're missing out on an opportunity for

happiness by continuing to feel this way? How is your blind hatred for the Elvish no better than Katerina's for the Mavka?"

He didn't like how closely that hit to the truth. "Because at least the Elvish would deserve it."

Her ears darted back, and she bit her bottom lip. "You truly are a cold person. It's like there isn't any love left in your heart."

"There isn't." With his icy confirmation, his eyes lowered in callous indifference. "That was taken from me at a mere eleven years old."

She turned a beseeching face to him. "Even us Demons find love and happiness where we can, Jabez."

"I don't need either of those."

"I think you should reconsider that," she stated, lifting her nose to snub him and his lack of feelings. However, her eyes then gleamed with a cheeky, pestering light. "Say you were, hypothetically, to keep a female. What kind would she be?"

He pulled his lips back in an appalled grimace. "The fuck kind of question is that?"

"Oh, just humour me."

"I don't think I particularly want to," he sneered.

She flapped her hand up and down dismissively. "What would you seek in a female?"

"One that doesn't exist?" he answered, and her look of annoyance only made him grin with humour. "Oh, *fine*."

He cupped his jaw as he pondered what would truly please him. The list was exceptionally empty, as he'd never thought about it before.

"I guess... someone smart enough to be self-assessing. Someone who wouldn't be a threat or make me sleep with one eye open in worry they would try to tear my throat out. *That* has happened one too many times."

His words began to die off when he noticed Fayren counting with her fingers each time he said something. He raised a brow, but she cast him a dull glance to continue.

"I don't know. Someone sensual, beautiful, and cute?" He noted that she only extended two fingers, but he ignored it as his gaze narrowed at the garden. "I think... I'd like someone with a tail, oddly enough."

She put another finger forward, and what she was doing became blatantly obvious. It also irked him, and he reached across to unbend the finger she'd refused to extend before.

"What are you...?"

"I don't know which word it was you lack the eye to see, but she has all of those qualities."

Her lips curled up in cunning humour. "Okay, what else?"

Jabez tried to think of what else would please him, but he truly had little idea. Yet one word kept ringing in his mind, loud, and yet so heavy he worried it just wouldn't be possible.

"Someone loyal," he muttered quietly. Not in body, but in mind.

Someone who would choose him over themselves. He was done with being used and having to watch his back around *everyone* he came into contact with. He was tired of those around him trying to manipulate him into getting their way, whether it be with tears, sex, guilt-tripping, or giving him offerings just to gain his favour.

What he wanted was to trust someone beyond himself. And not a single person had given him that – not Katerina, not Merikh, and not even Fayren. He was too wary of their possible ulterior motives.

People wanted and wanted, and he didn't often give any more when he saw it just led to those around him abusing whatever remaining generosity he had. Being a king meant he constantly had people asking him for shit, but *he* had no one to ask for help, no one to lean on.

He'd been alone from the moment he stepped into this horrible realm.

Sure, he had an army, but only because their goal had been the same as his: going the fuck home. They feared him because he made sure everyone knew he was impenetrable, cold, cruel, and heartless just so they wouldn't even *consider* turning on him. Yet so many had done it anyway.

He wanted someone to want his rotten heart. Not because it meant they had power over him, but because it gave him power over them, and they trusted he wouldn't abuse that. *Then again, everyone thinks I'm evil enough to do just that.* So why should he offer his non-existent heart to anyone when they all thought so lowly of him?

Realising he'd gone quiet, and likely made his last statement weigh heavier than he wanted it to appear, he forced a chuckle.

"Someone tall?" he asked, feigning humour. "I must admit, I like the idea of being able to throw them around and I can't do that with most humans or Demons. You're all so fucking short that I'm looking at the tops of your heads."

Her smile grew as she lifted another finger. "Zylah is tall. I even think she's taller than you, Jabez."

"I'm done with speaking to you," Jabez grumbled as he hopped down from his seat. "Dawn is coming, and I'm going to go find a tree to sleep in."

Had she just kept her fucking mouth shut and not said the Mavka's name, Jabez would have continued to play her stupid game.

"Then what am I supposed to do?" she called out as he stalked off.

"I don't know, perhaps go tend to Zylah? She may have questions," he answered, waving his hand in the direction of the cottage.

"You know... it didn't take me long to learn what purple means," she sang at his retreating back.

He halted, his body stiffening, and looked over his shoulder. "Okay?"

She climbed down from her perch slowly and carefully, and her arms and legs trembled as if with strain. "I left her with some rather in-depth books that have quite a few diagrams, many of which show some rather raunchy positions. Of course, for educational purposes."

"What?!" he croaked, his ears flaring with heat.

What kind of deviant did he put in charge of the innocent Zylah? He didn't even think Fayren would have such books! *Educational purposes, my ass.*

"I'm almost certain she's gone exploring, if her scent and orb colour before I left was any indication."

Gone exploring? His damn cock jerked at just the mere suggestion of what that could mean. Exploring *how*? Like... with her own hand beneath the skirt of her dress? Then again, that could mean she was entirely engrossed in the pages like the little bookworm he knew her to be, but that didn't stop his mind from being desirous, nor sharing perverted images with him.

Was she sitting there shaking with need? Was her skin itching to be touched, her fur puffed with the longing to be dived into? Was she panting, her body hot, her thighs tense, and her pussy wet? Worse still, was she picturing *him* as she looked at those diagrams?

If she wanted a physical demonstration, Jabez was sure there wasn't a single position he couldn't show her.

*Fuck. Did I make a mistake in bringing her here?*

He'd only wanted her to learn of her gender and the basics about sex, and what her heat meant, so she could protect herself in the future.

*Fayren... you are a tricky little fox Demon.*

He did not need that Mavka suddenly gaining feminine wiles.

# SEVENTEEN

"Get out of the sun and speak to me properly!" Fayren shouted from outside, jolting Zylah awake beneath the blanket covering her.

The little Demon had been kind enough to offer Zylah her own bed upon discovering she was tired after two days of travel with little rest. Then, after hours of reading all three books from cover to cover, the perverted images leaving her body aching and her mind reeling, she'd almost caved.

Although she knew it wasn't possible, especially after what she'd read, it'd felt like her heat had come back with a vengeance. The only thing stopping her from touching herself was that she was in a stranger's home... and that she didn't wish to be discovered doing it. But the ache wouldn't stop, and it was only upon reading more educational chapters rather than peering at erotic images that she ended up settling.

By the time Fayren returned, a distressed Zylah had tired herself out completely. She blamed it on all the travelling both she and Jabez had done to get there, and how they'd needed to sprint non-stop to the middle ring.

The fox Demon had cooed at her as she directed Zylah to lie down. She even pulled the blanket up to her chin, while checking to make sure Zylah was well, and if she had any questions regarding anything.

The only thing she'd asked was of Jabez's whereabouts. Apparently he'd gone off to rest as well.

Zylah had attempted to deny Fayren's generosity and go

find him, worried due to being apart for so long, but the Demon was stern when she wanted to be. Actually, she was kind of scary when she frowned disapprovingly, causing Zylah to chitter nervously under her glare.

She drew her knees up further, being forced to curl into a ball due to the tiny size of the bed, as she heard Jabez's voice coming from outside. Her orbs sparked to life, turning from black to teal, and she looked around the home she was in.

Despite being in heavy shade from the massive trees nearby, Zylah could tell it was day.

"I'm sorry if I pushed too far," Fayren stated loudly, her voice frantic and filled with worry. "I shouldn't have made you talk about such things."

"You poked and prodded, and now you must wear the consequences of your meddling," Jabez answered calmly, and Zylah could almost picture his dull expression.

"Please reconsider this."

"My decision is final."

At their obvious arguing, Zylah's orbs shifted to dark yellow in curiosity. She pushed back the bedding, brought her feet to the ground, and stood. She made sure her footsteps were light as she walked towards the round window next to Fayren's door.

Standing in bright sunshine right next to the garden's beam fencing, Jabez had his arms folded and his back turned to the light. The familiar cloak covered him from head to toe.

Fayren stood in the shade of a tree, refusing to get too close to the edge for fear of being burned. She waved her hand towards her home. "My house is too small. I had to forgo sleep just to allow her to get some rest."

Zylah flinched when she realised that, for some reason, they were arguing about her. She lowered into a crouch so only her skull would be visible, just so she could watch.

She wished she could see Jabez's expression properly, but she could only make out his nose and the tips of his lips and chin.

"It's only for a day or two," Jabez stated with an exasperated sigh, shaking his head.

"I don't give a shit how long it is, you pompous Elf!"

His response was immediate and held the undertone of a growl. "You know I don't like being referred to as one of *them*."

"What you're asking for is too much," Fayren said. Her red ears were pressed all the way back and had been for the entire conversation.

"You said you like her."

"Oh, don't give me that! Leaving Zylah here with me for even a day is unfair on her and me. My home is just big enough for me, Jabez. The poor girl barely fits on my bed. Where will I sleep? Where will she?"

Zylah's head reared back as white filled her vision. *He is planning to leave... without me?* Her heart clenched in worry.

She'd been concerned when she'd gone to sleep without checking in with him. The last few days had been hard, and there had been a noticeable strain between them. She thought coming here would help lessen that, but now it appeared he didn't even wish to be near her.

She didn't understand why. *What did I do wrong?*

"You'll figure it out."

"I don't know how to take care of a Mavka," she said, shaking her head with her brows furrowing. "What will she even do here?"

"I'm sure she'll be curious about your farm. Show her your garden, your chickens. Mother her like you mother everyone."

"If you weren't standing in the sun, I'd beat you with a stick," the little she-Demon snapped, then gave a hiss through her fangs.

Jabez chuckled. "Which is why I'm standing in the sun."

"Are you even planning to tell her yourself?"

He loosened his folded arms. "Of course. I wouldn't just leave without saying a word, Fayren."

As much as the revelation that he'd been planning to just abandon her here hurt, the fact that he didn't mean to do so without an explanation brought her relief.

Zylah stood and opened the door so she could confront him.

"Jabez?" she asked in a small voice, just as he partially turned his face to her. He regarded her with a dull expression and his arms dropped to his sides. "Where are you going?"

She could have played coy and pretended she hadn't been listening in, but she'd rather face the issue head-on.

Her stomach tightened when he focused his attention on Fayren and the lightest growl came from him. It died out quickly, and he let out a deep exhale as he turned from the fox-eared female. He stepped towards Zylah while skilfully making sure his cloak protected him from the light.

"I plan to go to Spiral Haven," he stated, his gaze meeting hers firmly.

"Spiral Haven?" She'd never heard of this place.

He stopped a few paces from her. "The village belonging to the Demons."

She held one of her wrists over her navel when her stomach twisted with unease. Like before, there was a noticeable strain between her and Jabez, which appeared to have grown since Zylah had entered Fayren's home.

Unable to help it, blue swirled in her sight.

"Why don't you want me to come?"

She didn't know if it was her question, or even her orb colour, but Jabez averted his gaze to the side. "It'll be easier for me to go there alone."

"But I want to come with you."

What if someone hurt him while he was gone? What if he didn't come back? Zylah didn't want to be left behind, not knowing what was happening. This could be a ruse to leave and never return, and the idea made her chest hollow.

"I'm unsure of how the occupants will feel regarding your presence near the village, Zylah. Mavka were recently banned from entering it."

"I can wait outside of it, if need be," she argued. "Just like with the human villages. You do not have to do this... alone."

His features twisted before he smoothed them back to his indifferent mien. "As you once asked of me, I'm now asking for some time to think. Much has happened from before I even met you, and I need time to wade through it. Fayren made me realise this."

Zylah waved towards the little fox Demon, who still stood in the shade. "But Fayren doesn't want me to stay here, and I don't wish to intrude."

"Zylah, that isn't what I meant," Fayren said, her features creasing in a beseeching and regretful manner. She walked through the shade to approach, which gave her a safe path towards Zylah. "It's not that I don't want you here – I just don't have the space to house you."

"You should watch your words in the future," Jabez cut at her, turning his head to give her a small sneer. "Not only have you infuriated me, but now you've upset her with your carelessness."

*He is... infuriated?* He didn't look it.

Zylah assessed Jabez's cooled expression as he brought his gaze back to her, and she realised then just how little she knew about him. It was like he wore a second face; one that didn't reflect the truth in his feelings. For so long, she'd thought this was just who he was, but had he been... hiding from her?

Did that mean the entire time... he'd been discontented, and she'd just been too ignorant to know it?

A small spark of anger ignited in her chest, and she turned her skull from both of them.

"If this is what you want, then okay," Zylah stated with a dark tone, her right hand balling into a fist.

For a moment, relief softened his features, and that only made her angrier to the point her orbs threatened to flicker with crimson. She brought her gaze to Fayren.

"If you give me a moment, I will obtain my satchel from your home."

Zylah spun around and ducked down under the doorway. She snatched her bag from the table in the middle of the tiny home she was forced to hunch inside of and threaded her body through it as she exited.

"What are you doing, Zylah?" Jabez asked, and despite the disbelief in his tone, she refused to look at him.

She was hurt, she was angry, and she didn't know what to do with these feelings. In the past, she would have just chittered, whined, or growled, but she was beyond that now. She had too much humanity to act so animalistic and brash.

She was realising there was a curse to being intelligent. It had almost been... *easier* to be so clueless. Now, she had to learn how to wear her emotions without lashing out like a beast

– despite how her fur had puffed with the desire to do just that.

"If I am unable to stay here, then I won't," she answered, shifting the satchel so it sat more comfortably between her breasts.

A growl slipped from Jabez, and his face dipped so he could glare through his eyelashes. "It's safer if you remain here. We're in the middle of the Veil. It's risky if you go off alone."

For the first time in her life, a bitter laugh slipped up her chest. "Perhaps for *you*," she snapped out, clipping her maw at him as red flickered in her sight. "But I am a *Mavka*."

"Excuse me?" Jabez growled, his eyes narrowing into a glare in her periphery.

"Zylah," Fayren rasped, placing her tiny hand upon Zylah's forearm, and she regarded the little female Demon coldly. "He's right. W-we can figure out a solution so you're more comfortable here. Maybe we can stagger how we sleep, or I'll set up a shade so you can sleep outside. I know that's not the nicest, but–"

She ripped her arm from Fayren's hold.

"I am a Mavka!" Zylah roared at them both, wishing her hands didn't shake with anxiety. "If I'm unwanted, then I have no reason to remain! If it's too dangerous to leave the inner ring, then I will wander it until you're ready to find me."

Or when she was ready to find him. Or perhaps, by then, she may not want to. Right now, she was feeling all sorts of horrible emotions and she, too, wished to be alone.

Usually she'd cling to Jabez, but the last week had been... *hard*. From learning just a taste of his past, to having her heat, to the strain between them, to having to go off on a stupid adventure just so she could be taught a bunch of strange and wildly uncomfortable topics. Zylah had also been hiding how she was feeling, and only now that they were filling her so intensely, did she realise just how hard they were to hold *in*.

Right now, her claws tinged with the desire to lash out. At Fayren, at Jabez, at herself.

It didn't help that she'd gone from being aroused and wanting *him* not even a few hours ago to suddenly feeling crushed. She didn't know what she'd done wrong, but did it even matter?

"You will not go off into the fucking Veil by yourself!" Jabez shouted, stomping forward to finally approach her. "I'll be back in just a few days."

"I'm bigger than you, stronger than you, and faster than you!" Zylah shouted back. "Why is the Veil safe for you but not me?"

"Because I have hundreds of years of *experience* navigating it, fighting in it, *living* in it."

Zylah gave him her shoulder. "You told me other Mavka live within the Veil. That means we are just fine doing so."

"Yes, under wards! They are wary of the Demons, just as you should be. What you're doing is foolish."

Surprised that he was still shouting and truly seemed to be concerned for her wellbeing, some of her anger deflated. She didn't want him furious with her, nor worried; she'd actually thought he'd wear his lying face until she left. She wasn't trying to win anything and had thought this would be a suitable solution.

*I'm used to being by myself.*

Sure, she valued Jabez's company so deeply it ached in her chest, but she could leave him alone for now, if that was what he desired. She understood wanting space, as she'd asked for it herself not even a few days ago. If anything, she'd likely find a tree to sit under and read until she forgot why she was upset in the first place.

Suddenly her bag, filled with only books, felt so comforting.

As much as Fayren had changed her opinion on the matter, overhearing their earlier argument meant Zylah knew the little Demon was only doing so for her sake. Fayren was right. Her home was small, and she hadn't realised taking her bed for a few hours would be such a bad thing – despite the little Demon pushing her to do so.

Zylah lowered her voice while attempting to keep her sadness from her words. "I won't remain somewhere I'm unwanted." She turned to Fayren and wished she had the capabilities to smile at her like she'd often done. "Thank you for welcoming me into your home, and for being kind in teaching me so much. I appreciate it more than you know."

With that, Zylah walked around them and towards the forest. She headed in the opposite direction they'd travelled, summarising that would take her deeper within the Veil to where it would be safer. She didn't wish to head towards the middle ring of the Veil, and absolutely not the outer ring where they'd been chased.

"See what you've fucking done?!" Jabez shouted, his voice so loud it carried over the small distance. "I ask for you to keep her safe here, and now she thinks neither one of us wants her presence!"

Zylah's shoulders hunched self-consciously, but she continued on. She really didn't know why he was so concerned. *I will be fine.* She'd survived for a long while before she met him. *A-a few days is not long.* Not truly.

"I'm not the one who was planning on leaving her with a stranger!"

Ignoring their bickering, Zylah opened her satchel so she could reach into it. She pulled out one of the books Jabez had obtained for her that she hadn't managed to read yet. *Hopefully this does not have difficult words in it.* She'd foolishly left her dictionary behind.

*Maybe I can find somewhere not far from Fayren's.* She could return to visit if he took too long.

Footsteps crunching behind her stopped her from opening the book as a way to distract herself from how she'd been feeling. They approached so quickly she only managed to turn around just in time to greet who was approaching her.

With his features twisted up into a feral snarl – his lips were pulled back to reveal his sharp fangs and his nose was bunched – he grabbed her wrist. Zylah stumbled, her feet hopping, when she was yanked to the right as Jabez took her in another direction – which wasn't Fayren's home.

"What are you–" Zylah started.

"I won't have you wandering the Veil on your own," he growled harshly, cutting her off. "I brought you here, and I won't abandon you in it."

"Then where are you taking me?" she asked, struggling to right her footing and keep ahold of her book.

All she could see was the back of his cloak and the way the

grey fur around its shoulders fluttered. "To Spiral Haven."

"But you said–"

"I know what I fucking said!" he roared, his grip on her tightening. "However, if you won't remain at Fayren's, then I have no other choice but to bring you."

Zylah twisted and yanked her arm from him, then stopped when she was freed. "I will be fine, Jabez. If this is something you need to do on your own, then so be it."

Jabez turned just enough to give her his side profile and stabbed the pads of his fingers into his closed eyes.

"I'm unused to people not heeding my demands, Zylah," he rumbled darkly, and the depth, the quietness, the sheer anger in it, was unnerving. "I'm very, *very* angry right now, and I'm feeling very manipulated by two females."

"I'm not trying to manipulate you," she muttered defensively and clutched her book tightly, disappointed he would think so.

"Whether it be purposeful or an accident, I've been given no other choice but to disregard my own wants for others." He removed his fingers to give her a haunting glare from the corner of his eyes. "To ensure your safety, you will accompany me to Spiral Haven. If you try to force me to follow you through this forest on your whim instead, preventing me from this task, then I will see it as an act of petty defiance. If so, I will take my protection and care as unwanted and rescind it."

With her orbs shifting to deep blue, she brought her hands to her chest anxiously. "What does that mean?"

He pulled his shoulders back and straightened to his full height. "I'll complete this task on my own. Then I will find you and return you to your burrow."

"But you don't like my burrow."

"Exactly. I wouldn't be entering it with you. I'll just be ensuring that you're somewhere safer before I leave... *permanently.*"

Zylah chittered when her heart stung, and the blue in her sight deepened and reflected the depth of her sadness. The bottoms of her orbs wavered, and she tried to stop them from shattering into tears.

Despite her earlier thoughts, suddenly the idea of being

permanently separated from him stung her.

As he stared at her skull, and likely the changes within her, his features twitched with a strange emotion. His expression hardened into stone seconds later.

"Make your decision."

For the first time since he'd lost his magical capabilities, Jabez was thankful for their absence.

The rage, frustration, and hostility that skittered beneath the surface was unremorseful and chaotic. Being forced into a corner like a weak prey animal was not who he was, and he wouldn't react submissively or out of fear. He was known for biting and snarling to get his way, no matter if the opposition was kind and undeserving of his beastly nature.

At least he could do no more than use his words to threaten and, unfortunately, fight manipulation with more manipulation. That, or just walk away without care, which he wasn't inclined to do. Had he retained his ability to teleport... things may have gone differently.

As he'd told Zylah, he'd brought her to the middle of this cesspool of Demons, and he'd safely take her from it. Which meant she had to accompany him, despite that currently being the opposite of what he desired.

*Fayren is right. I care for her more than I thought.* More than he wanted.

Enough to not wash his hands of her the moment she'd walked into the forest like a high-handed female trying to get her way – although he did believe that wasn't a show just to needle him. He knew Zylah enough to understand she truly thought she was capable on her own.

She probably was, but he just couldn't shed this nagging in the back of his mind. He'd taken this female under his protection, and like Katerina, he felt the need to see it through, regardless of the fact that it wouldn't always be in his best interest.

But what he truly needed right now was fucking space. He needed to piece his thoughts together to figure out what the hell he was doing, and why.

*Fayren saw right through me.* Perhaps even better than he usually saw himself.

He'd brought Zylah to a female to teach her of her gender, of sex, and her heat, because he'd been uncomfortable. The question was: why had he been uncomfortable about it?

Like with Merikh, it should have made him chuckle to see her squirm with embarrassment. Understanding this topic was important, and the fact that he had much experience regarding it made him rather desensitised to how awkward it could be.

Watching Merikh fidget with bright reddish-pink orbs had been the highlight of Jabez's life for many years. The big idiot Mavka – because he'd lacked much humanity at the time – could barely look at him afterwards without flaring that colour. And fuck... *teaching* him about a cock and where to stick it, going so far as to give him a physical demonstration with a Demon female, had been humorous to him.

It'd also finally shown Jabez what the colour of desire was.

Poor Merikh. The memory of him, both aroused by what he was seeing and obviously blushing, often made Jabez chuckle. The female had been a naughty one – the idea of having a spectator had aroused her – and Merikh had consented to being shown, so there was no reason to feel guilt regarding it.

However, when it came to teaching this topic to Zylah, it'd left a sour taste in his mouth. The conversation on the fence with Fayren had made it blatantly obvious as to why, and he'd need to dive into his past to figure out what it was that was bothering him about it.

*I'm attracted to her.* He'd just been ignoring it. Although physical attraction was usually enough for him to fuck a female in the past, he could have easily restrained with Zylah due to what she was and what had transpired between him and her kin.

Which meant there was more lurking beneath the surface – tender emotions he hadn't even realised he'd begun harbouring until now.

The more she came out of her shell and became her own person, flashing him hints of her cute nature, or her interest in books, or even kindness, made it harder to deny. He'd made her a freaking dress, for pity's sake, when she had fur that should have been enough coverage for his mind.

But she was innocent, in every sense, and being the one to teach her about life meant he'd been placed in a position of power. Had he turned that platonic knowledge into something much more devious, like sex, then he would have abused that power.

Someone else had to teach her because, in the back of his mind, he knew he was not infallible. Utilising her ignorance to touch with pleasure in mind would have made it no better than what Katerina had done to Orpheus, or vice versa.

And, with each growing day, that worry had been eating him until it exploded during the night he'd spent with Zylah in heat. He hadn't been able to ignore it then, not when his engorged cock had been nestled between them and he'd been quaking with need. The entire evening had required intense restraint on his part, especially as she tried to grind on every part of him she could.

Jabez had almost done so in return when his cock had been throbbing so hard it hurt and had been close to bursting.

The longer it went on, the longer he tried to deny it, the higher the likelihood he'd make a mistake. At some point, all his pent-up lust and confusing feelings would get the better of him if she gave a strong enough indication that she wanted him.

At least with Fayren's help, Zylah would fully comprehend what was happening. She would know where each touch would be leading them and could actually formulate proper consent with complete and utter understanding of what that meant.

Even if it wasn't with him. Even if Jabez and Zylah were never intimate, as he *still* had no plans for such a thing, she could at least walk into that situation with another knowingly.

He'd protected her from himself, *and* from others. He'd shielded her from the potential harm to her mind and heart.

Figuring all this out brought on more questions. Yes, he desired this female Mavka, but was that all? No, obviously not. He'd spent two months with her, and not once had her company bothered him – he couldn't remember feeling that

way before. Everyone usually annoyed him, but he just felt...
*calm* next to her.

Even if he held back many of his emotions, until today, it was usually because they weren't strong enough to surface.

He liked who she was. There was no deviousness, no malice, no ulterior motives, no ploy for manipulation. She merely wanted his company because, apparently to her, it was pleasant.

*My company has never been pleasant to another.*

He was a temperamental person at best, and at worst, he was a complete prick. His indifference regarding other's feelings could cut like a blade, and his anger often made Demons cower.

And in the face of his shouting, Zylah had returned it!

Only Fayren was foolish enough to do so, due to her being a rather spirited female. Then again, Fayren had never attempted to use or manipulate him, and had cared for his wellbeing all her life. She attempted to pamper, placate, and later on in her life, mother him as if she saw who he really was beneath all his different masks.

Those innocent things meant Fayren could scream and assault him with a wooden spoon all she wanted, and it meant she was safe from his ire.

Just as Zylah, apparently, was safe from it.

He cast a glance at her from the corner of his eye as they walked through the forest towards Spiral Haven. His damn chest panged at her state.

No matter that they'd been walking for a good half an hour, the bottom of her orbs still wavered despite the blue in them receding closer to a teal. She was obviously stressed about the prospect of him leaving her and dwelling on it.

Did she think he'd come to such a decision easily?

The truth was: it may have been a lie. A ruse to get that cute fluffy bunny tail of hers to follow him.

The further they walked and his anger cooled, the more uncertain he became.

In his mind, he tried to chalk it up to just wanting to wait to see if she'd accompany him to Nyl'theria. That she would help him, as no one else could, or rather, would. He wasn't ready to let go of that possibility, as it was the best option for giving him a successful outcome in this war he'd started.

A war he still couldn't let go of. He doubted he'd ever be able to. He'd always be thinking of ways to finally get what he wanted.

But was his attachment to her... deeper than that?

He hoped not. He hoped his heart or dick weren't leading him when he needed his mind more than ever. He didn't need to add confusion and complications to their current *friendship*. He didn't want nor need a female companion for the rest of his days.

He also just thought he'd be a horrible mate. He was arrogant, self-centred, and rude. If he did gain a female's affections, he had no doubt it wouldn't take long before he squashed them by just being himself.

Why take such a risk when he foresaw such failure?

Then again, having someone else to lean on did pique his interest, as he'd never truly had that. Someone he could hold as he woke up, hopefully in a comfortable bed and in an Elven city taken over by him and his fellow Demons. Someone warm and soft, but strong enough he didn't have to temper his strength and lust.

*Can't do that with a human.* He'd probably break their hips or bruise their buttery skin. Restraining his strength for the better part of two centuries had taken a toll on his enjoyment of sex. An Elf would hold the same strength as him, but he'd rather launch himself into a fire than bed one of those foul creatures.

And Demons... well, he'd learned it was better not to fully trust them. That, or he'd just had poor judgement regarding those he'd picked in the past.

Once more, he was reminded of Fayren's finger counting as he labelled off things he'd like in a female, knowing she was trying to show him Zylah had those qualities. Apparently he was adding to that list, even without the pesky fox Demon nearby.

Seeing that Zylah was still clutching one of the newest books he'd obtained for her – he couldn't tell which one – he noted that she'd clawed her way through the thick cover. If she clutched it any harder in sorrow, she'd destroy it.

*Fuck. Now I just feel bad.*

Jabez sighed as he turned his narrowed gaze forward before his features softened. Guilt slipped down his nape at the knowledge he'd brought her to this near-teary state.

"Fayren is right," he started, letting his eyes scan the dim forest as a distraction. "I have a horrible temper."

*How did she put it? Horribly childish tantrums?* That was very true, and something he'd never denied.

Zylah chittered and turned her skull away from him.

He stifled the desire to roll his eyes and instead reached out so the back of his knuckles could brush her wrist. "I'm sorry if I upset you, but you shouldn't take it out on one of your books."

He winced when her claws gouged into it deeper, and she turned her shoulder to him and yanked her arm away. He palmed his damn face when her reaction didn't upset him, but instead made his chest swell because he found it adorable. Considering he wasn't particularly fond of the silent treatment, it should have reignited his temper, not made his chest puff with pride that he'd hurt her feelings.

Feelings she obviously harboured... for him.

"It's not that I don't want your presence. Quite the opposite, in fact," he admitted while gentling his tone, hoping to assuage her hurt. "But much has happened to me, and I needed time to sort through it. Spiral Haven is towards the middle of the inner ring, so it's not far, and it wouldn't have taken me long to return."

The bottom of her orbs settled, and her grip on her book softened. She thumbed the damage she'd done to its cover, while he dipped his head to watch his footing over a particularly gnarly set of tree roots.

"From the moment we entered the Veil, my desire to go to Spiral Haven has been sitting at the forefront of my mind. But I've been away from it for quite some time, and I imagine much has changed in my absence."

"What is so special and important about Spiral Haven?" she asked in a rather snarky tone.

The left side of his lips quirked with humour – he was

pleased that she'd finally broken her silence. The tiny smile fell, and he turned his gaze upwards to the thick, dense canopy of leaves. The trees here were much taller than those in the outer ring of the Veil, reaching triple, if not more, of his six feet and nine inches.

"Beneath the city is a mana stone I took from Nyl'theria. I'm hoping it has enough magic left that I can reignite my own." When she turned her skull towards him a little, he shifted his focus to her so his gaze could meet her orbs. "Not having my magic has been weighing on me deeply. It's a natural part of me, one which has been missing, and it's the equivalent of losing a limb to an Elf. We're born with magic, we breathe it, live it, draw nourishment from it, and it feels like breathing through sand without it."

"Why didn't you tell me that? You never share your inner thoughts," she said, her voice growing small as she averted her gaze from his. There was the undertone of hurt and disappointment in her words, and he couldn't deny his constant secrecy. "I would have been more understanding if you'd told me the truth about your reason for leaving."

*Because I could have brought you with me either way.* The fact he wanted time to wade through the mud of his thoughts regarding her was the only reason he'd wanted to leave her behind. In part, he'd been hoping that time would help reduce his desire, and he'd been planning on killing whatever affection he had growing for her.

That seemed wiser. It seemed... better, especially for her.

If he didn't do something stupid, then the likelihood of hurting her with his own flaws would be minimal.

"Fayren has a way of getting under my skin," he admitted, before realising she likely didn't understand that saying. "What I mean to say is that she has a way of breaking through my thoughts when I don't wish her to. Had she kept her opinions to herself, I wouldn't have been so irritated. She did it knowingly, while forgetting her actions and words can have consequences that don't always involve her. She likes to meddle."

By the cursed light, he'd barely slept a wink due to Fayren's pestering. He'd been so restless that he'd almost fallen out of his fucking tree. He'd been frustrated with his thoughts, his chest feeling hollow, while his cock had been so hard he'd considered relieving it just to tamp down his arousal.

He didn't, simply because he didn't wish to be caught stroking his cock by Fayren. He also hadn't wanted her to later discover his sexual scent from wherever he decided to let his release fall, especially as she was cheeky and would have picked on him for it until the day she died.

He could handle pain, but he didn't particularly like the way mortification felt.

"But what does that have to do with me?" Zylah asked, as the bottoms of her orbs wavered for just a moment.

Rather than delving into thoughts that were best left unsaid, he chose to direct the conversation elsewhere. "Was Fayren helpful to you?"

Her skull lowered – she obviously knew he'd deflected her question. "Yes. I appreciated her help."

"Do you now understand why I couldn't explain it all to you?"

Her orbs morphed into a reddish pink, and she lifted a hand to cover the side of her skull to hide them. "Yes."

Jabez couldn't help but release a small chuckle at the bashful way she'd hidden from him. "I hope she didn't tease you too much."

With how Zylah's orbs brightened in her embarrassed hue, he knew Fayren had done exactly that. She gripped her biceps of her right arm.

"She made me realise many things, and I'm grateful for that. She made me understand what I want, how I'm feeling. I feel as though I know myself much better now."

"That's good," he muttered, as his lips thinned. He didn't particularly want Zylah understanding her feelings better if they pertained to him.

Her orbs even flickered with purple, and the glow of it was bright in comparison to the darkness around them. The lightest scent of arousal came from her, and he had to ignore the way his groin tingled in awareness of it.

"We spoke of you," she stated quietly.

*Shit.* This conversation wasn't going how he wanted.

"If things are successful in Spiral Haven, there is a good chance I can allow us to both walk through the village," he said, deflecting from whatever potential topic she was trying to broach. "I'll be able to glamour us both and hide our scents. Perhaps you'll find a Demon who might pique your interests. Many are Elf-eating who have passed over to this realm, and they are all rather tall and strong. Some even have wings and tails, so perhaps something will draw your eye."

There. Hopefully he made her realise there were males other than him.

Her head reared back. "Another... Demon?"

*Yes. Other than me.* Because he wasn't a suitable choice in the grand scheme of things. *If she shows interest in someone else, my attraction to her will diminish.* Not because he was a jealous person, as many Demons were non-monogamous, but due to her attention being elsewhere.

He wouldn't feel the pressure of her constant focus.

Adding more strength to their duo could actually be a gain. *Although, if she chooses a mate, that may complicate things.* She'd be less inclined to leave them behind. *Unless Phantoms of any nature are able to pass through Weldir's ward?*

That presented an unknown. Could a Demon become a Mavka's mate, and therefore turn into a Phantom at all?

*What I could do with the power to turn intangible...* He wouldn't need her, or anyone. His ability to teleport was excellent, but it came with weaknesses. It depleted his magic significantly, and he could be trapped by something as silly as his hair.

He hated how such a simple thing could be used against him. But it was a powered link, like a tether to their essences, and the white in it was a side-effect of the toxicity of magic running rampant throughout their bodies and stealing their natural hair colours. Even the grey in their skin was a byproduct of magic use, as it hardened their veins with a coating that allowed mana flow.

Currently, that coating felt like he had stone just beneath his skin – despite its usual softness.

Due to his deep musings, he hadn't realised Zylah had stopped walking beside him. He turned to find her still clutching her arm, although now her feet appeared stuck and her snout turned towards the ground.

Once more, blue had lifted into her orbs.

"Zylah," he stated with a sigh, hoping to coax her back into walking.

"I don't understand. Why would you say this? Other than Fayren... you have not spoken fondly of other Demons."

"I speak lowly of lesser Demons," he told her. "Those within the inner ring are different. They've either completed their evolution like Fayren or aren't far from doing so. They're no different to me."

"But you are special to me."

Jabez raised his eyes to the sky, calling to no one, as there were no deities who would ever listen to his pleas.

"Let's not speak of this anymore," he said, bringing his gaze back down to her. He turned, giving her his back – something he'd never been truly comfortable doing with anyone until her. "I just wanted to apologise for my earlier behaviour, and how it may have upset you. There's still a lot of distance between us and Spiral Haven."

The fact that he'd even apologised was a foreign concept to him. *What's happening to me?* Saying sorry? What. The. Fuck?

Annoyed with everything right then, Jabez resumed the journey in frustration. Zylah thankfully followed.

# EIGHTEEN

Even before they broke through the thinning border of the forest, the bright-red sunlight before them revealed dusk painted across the sky. Fiery glitters between the swaying treetops cast dappled light across the dirt, and she took in its tranquillity after missing the light within the Veil's shadows.

At her side, Jabez hissed in pain when it got brighter. He squinted as though he found it blinding and almost ran into her to deviate from it.

He forced them to the left to escape its harshness, when she found it rather... mesmerising. Just beyond the tree line, she'd been able to see the reds of dusk casting flaming light against the white clouds and giving their shadows a darker hue as the sky morphed to purple.

Dusk and dawn were Zylah's two favourite times of the day.

The beautiful way colours would splash across the world, each time different to the one before, left her breathless. It felt like the sky was always chasing itself – especially the sun and the moon.

It was a saddening thought that she and Jabez would never be able to share such a serene moment together. Since the sun burned his flesh, he couldn't sit in the last of the day's heat and soak in the colourfulness of the world. Instead, he hid from it like a creature of shadow, a being of darkness.

*Perhaps that is why he can be so... bleak.* He couldn't nibble at the beauty of life in the way she could. Zylah, on the other hand, longed to run to its warmth and revel in the enthralling colours.

Instead, she manoeuvred until her body shielded him from the fiery light. Although it was hard to tell with his hood up, she knew he'd looked at her from the corner of his eye.

Pleasure radiated in her chest at how the red in his eyes seemed to glow, although the feeling was bittersweet.

Their earlier conversation hadn't been forgotten, and it left her heart more confused than ever. She was beginning to feel as though she was alone in her tenderness, which was a rather harrowing thing to discover.

His avoidance was obvious, and she didn't know how to combat it. He deflected, and she submitted because she didn't want to ruin their companionship. *But it's already ruined.*

He was quieter than before, and the space between them felt vast and cold. His apology meant much. She appreciated him informing her that he didn't find her presence bothersome, but she couldn't get to the root of the problem in his weighty silence.

A silence that had never bothered her until now. It didn't help that there was little to teach her in the Veil, as the plants were dreary and lacklustre.

She missed the surface. She missed their cave and the way he sat with her while teaching her how to read. She missed how his features seemed to soften whenever he showed her a simple herb or flower, appearing to enjoy her interest and the way she smelt them or inspected them with abject curiosity.

*I hope he'll feel better once we are done here.*

She hadn't known his lack of magic was so bothersome for him. To Zylah, he was just Jabez – with or without magic. He'd frequently boasted about his prowess regarding it whenever she picked on him for his lack of strength and speed, and she'd merely found it rather endearing. She'd listened like one might listen to another tell a story, humour and tenderness spreading in her chest at his eccentric disquiet.

She didn't care if he was without his powers, and originally thought it frustrated him because it meant he was weaker than her.

She wished he'd told her sooner that it was deeper than that;

it almost seemed to... ache him that he lacked them.

*If he gains his magic again, will he return to the way he was before?* Would he be less cold and perhaps even be more forthcoming, more amicable? She'd thought him kind and gentle before. Would that only grow stronger?

The light dimmed the longer they walked. The sun was falling, but they also appeared to be heading in a large, curved arc through the forest, making it shine elsewhere other than their faces.

"This should be enough," Jabez informed her, as he took them towards the forest's edge.

Zylah didn't expect the scene that would open up before her.

Considering her only experiences with towns and villages were those belonging to humans, she'd been imagining the roofs of houses, and a wall of protective stakes. Instead, a gigantic tree, taller than any she'd ever seen, sat in the middle of a large open meadow.

Only when they stepped into the last of the light, the sun now at their left, did she realise she was mistaken. It wasn't a singular tree, but dozens that were nestled closely together. They hadn't grown upwards, but rather spiralled to the right with their long branches twisting and interlocking with each other.

"It's not a barrier from Demons, but from the sun," she rasped, noting how the canopy of leaves would create a perfect shield.

"That's exactly right," he stated, allowing her just a moment to stand on the top of the hill to absorb the village before descending.

Long stalks of grass brushed against their thighs, and Zylah bent to the side so she could skim her hand over the tops of them, taking in their softness. They danced with the light wind, waving together until they created a pleasant rustling noise.

"During the day, it's impossible for any Demon without a cloak to travel to it. The sun is the real barrier, allowing all those inside a chance to rest before nightfall. Although, any potential of being attacked is very low, so no one inside really worries about night anymore."

"Why do you say that?" Zylah asked, cocking her head in curiosity.

"When it was first created, the three rings of the Veil hadn't existed. Demons of all kinds ran rampant throughout. It's only been in the last century and a half that the inner ring has become safer. They even reduced the number of guards that patrol it."

"Is that how it obtained its name then? Spiral due the way the trees twist, and Haven due to it once being the only safe place here?"

"That's correct," he stated, but she thought she heard the smallest note of pride in his tone.

It didn't take long to cross the meadow. By then, the sun had faded enough and cast the entire area in shadow. It'd be long before day was truly gone, but the forest of the Veil seemed to darken it earlier than it should.

They approached the village, and she saw just how daunting the trees were now that they were up close. Each one spanned metres in diameter, and she couldn't even begin to guess their collective height – a half a kilometre, perhaps more?

If her venture down the Veil's cliff wall was any indicator, she'd hate climbing one of them.

A small gap between each tree was just narrow enough to create a path inside. Already a sickly sweet smell came from within, leaking from every crevice and gap available. Curious about that scent, and the muted sounds of life she could hear within, Zylah's skull jerked one way and the other as she sniffed wildly.

She thought he'd immediately take them inside it, but Jabez led them on a path around its perimeter instead.

At the centre point of each tree, he knelt between large, overarching roots and swiped at the ground. He brushed away dirt and dust before knocking on it, only to shake his head and stand once more.

Night fell by the time a dull thud radiated from the ground when he knocked. Jabez then tore at the dirt with his claws until he revealed some kind of wooden hatch, grasped a ring handle, and yanked on it. It refused to budge at first, and he put in a large amount of force until it cracked and bowed.

A few planks of wood detached where the roots of the tree had grown over them, and only half the door came up. The gap didn't look big enough to fit him through, so he jimmied the stuck pieces sideways until they were freed. He dropped those pieces on the ground nearby and stepped back to reveal a narrow dirt passageway.

He sighed as he brushed his cloak hood back just enough to reveal his face while still shielding his hair. "I know this is less than ideal, but it's better than going into the village from the main entrance." He faced her and then lifted his gaze to her antlers. "I haven't used this route for a few centuries. It's a tight fit, so perhaps it's best if you wait here."

"No," Zylah rejected, shaking her head. "I want to come with you."

"I had a feeling you'd say that." He shrugged as he walked backwards to the opening. "Suit yourself."

Jabez climbed down some kind of ladder made of rocks and roots. The gap was so narrow that his shoulders almost brushed the edges, which, thankfully, meant Zylah was thin enough to squeeze in behind him with ease.

Once they got to the bottom, she realised how little room she had to manoeuvre and struggled with her antlers at first. Something caught around them, and she gave a quiet squeal when she got stuck. Jabez grabbed one, untangled it, and helped her turn without them gouging into rocky dirt and twisted roots.

Facing each other while crouching, her orbs brightened to yellow as she whispered, "Thank you."

He nodded before backing up and turning to walk primarily on his hands and feet, which surprised her, as she didn't think he had the ability to do so. She had to stay a few steps back to avoid his cloak, and it grew so dark that even she had to partially feel where they were going. She often pushed small hanging roots out of the way, and Jabez was kind enough to stop and untangle them from her antlers each time she was caught.

It went on for ages, spanning minutes as distant, muted chatter resonated from above, but all she could smell was dirt and Jabez before her. His breaths were sharp, as if he refused to breathe through his nose in an attempt to escape the smell of wet earth surrounding them.

It took her a moment to notice past his hunched, swaying form that a green glow illuminated the area up ahead. Over the crunch of their footsteps, trickling in the distance tingled her ears. Eventually the smell of water and greenery pervaded the air, and only thickened as the tunnel opened up into a large, spacious cavern.

The first thing Zylah noticed was the deep pool of water, its green glow dimly lighting up the entire area. It was situated in the very middle of an empty pocket of earth, while roots came from the ceiling, the walls, and even the ground to dangle around the edges.

Once they were free, they both stood on a mostly flat piece of land that appeared to be as hard as rock. Even the walls and ceiling looked hard, rather than like loose dirt.

There was nothing else here... yet she could *sense* some kind of power thrumming. It puffed her fur in alertness, pulsating until her nipples hardened in an odd way, but it didn't feel ominous or unnerving. It was coming from the small pool of water that gave constant glittering ripples.

"What is this place?" Zylah asked with awe, looking up at the ceiling. She could barely make out anything other than the vast number of thick roots clinging to every surface available.

"The heart of the village," Jabez answered, unclipping his cloak to let it fall before removing his satchel.

Zylah removed her bag, since he did, and placed it with his.

"Villages have a heart?" Is that why she could feel thrumming?

She turned her head down to him when he gave a small yet warm chuckle.

"No. Most don't." He waved towards the glowing green water. Its light highlighted his brown skin, white hair, and black horns, and even made his red eyes seem to glint, all of it giving him a rich aura. "I grew the trees surrounding this village by the mana stone sitting at the bottom of that pool."

"*You* grew the trees?!" she exclaimed, gasping in surprise.

Once more, he chuckled, but he looked at her from the

corner of his eye this time. Humour brightened his features.

"I told you, Zylah. My power was formidable." Then he drifted his gaze around the large pocket of earth. "It was actually rather weak when I first grew them. Back then, the most I could wield was earth magic – it's what I was best at. I planted the seeds, then spent weeks in the middle of the village trying to grow them. I chose this location because there had been a large lake for them to take nourishment from, and all that remains now is this pool. The roots you see dangling inside it are from each tree reaching for it."

He bent forward so he could grab at the back of his shirt and yank it off. Reddish pink instantly lifted into her sight at his bare torso. His chest was broad and flexed with strength. When he gave her his side, the deep, muscular curve of his spine leading to his round backside was highlighted by the glow of the water.

Mesmerised by the sight of him, Zylah bashfully fidgeted as she looked away. His body was too nice to look upon for her mind right then.

Her heart was still all over the place, and her arousal from the previous night hadn't been forgotten. Now that she understood more about intimacy, the longing to brush her hands over his muscled back and chest tingled her fingers. His body was chiselled yet bulging with muscle, and she wondered if his skin would be as soft as it appeared.

She wished she could remember what he felt like when she'd been hugging him during her heat.

"W-what will happen to the village if you take the stone?" Zylah asked to distract herself from the way her heart picked up at seeing him half clothed.

She hoped what he planned to do wouldn't bring the village harm.

"Nothing," he answered plainly. "The trees are fully mature. All this stone does now is ensure they remain overly lush to give a thick canopy of protection. Removing it should do little more than make a few leaves wilt, but the rest will be sufficient protection." Then he walked towards the water, his mauve pants shifting around his legs. "All stones have a limit unless they are fed additional mana, but even then, they don't last forever. I've poured my own into it for years. All I am doing is taking back what I have given."

Zylah watched as he dropped to sit on the ledge of roots and his pant legs instantly darkened when they grew saturated. He slid in with a splash, and the water came to the centre of his chest while he stood near the edge. It was obvious it deepened swiftly since he swam to the middle, his body gliding through the water with each stroke of his arms.

*I wish I could do that.* She hated that she instantly sunk in any body of water, as if she was just too heavy and dense – like a rock.

Jabez dived beneath the water and disappeared.

Zylah considered coming closer, but decided it was best she stayed out of his way. It gave her time to dwell on what he'd just said.

*It seems like he has sacrificed a lot for the Demons.* He'd grown the Veil for them, this village. *Even if he doesn't really show it, he obviously cares for them.* He hid his true nature and feelings behind indifference, and she was curious as to why.

Why give away power, if he was so power hungry? Why care for these creatures, if he thought lowly of them? *Why help me?*

Her parents had acted as if he was horrible. They spoke of unpleasant things he'd done, things he hadn't denied... but what about the good?

She looked up once more, remembering the scene of the village in the distance highlighted by the beauty of dusk. She wondered if the Demons appreciated him for all he'd done for them as much as she did on their behalf.

Before she could linger on her thoughts, the light snuffed out and shoved her into darkness once more. She brought her gaze down to the pool and flickers of green brightened in moving streaks just as air bubbles breached the surface. With a gasp, Jabez's head popped up, and he immediately headed for the ledge.

He gripped a root before shaking his face of water. He shoved his other arm out, and his enclosed fist glowed with streaks of green before dimming – as if taking it from the water stopped it from radiating magic. Even the thrumming she'd felt earlier disappeared.

He climbed out and sat down with his legs crossed. "I ask that you don't disturb me for a little while," he stated, water sluicing down his naked torso and glittering from the stone in his hands. "What I'm about to do requires the utmost concentration."

"Is it dangerous?" Zylah stated, worry tightening her stomach.

His lips quirked. "This isn't the first time I've consumed a mana stone. I've just never attempted it without any of my own magic before."

That didn't make her feel any better, especially as he didn't *deny* that it wasn't dangerous.

He sighed when she chittered nervously and lowered his hands into his lap. He gave a shrug as he focused his gaze on the stone in his palm and ran the pad of his free hand's thumb over it. It did little more than faintly glow.

"I'll be fine, Zylah. I'll stop if I feel it failing or if it's dangerous." He tilted his head back to give her a smug, raised brow. "I do care for my life, you know."

Although his words did nothing to settle her unease, she nodded and backed up. Nothing she said would stop him from doing this, and Jabez had never truly asked anything of her before now.

The least she could do was try to have faith in him. *He said this is important to him... that it weighs on him.* She didn't want to interfere with his attempt to regain his lost magic.

So, Zylah watched intently as he cupped the stone to his chest, closed his eyes, and bowed his head. Nothing happened as choking darkness descended upon them.

For some reason, that darkness felt heavier than usual, like a cold, foreboding blanket. She didn't know if it was fear that made it weightier, and she fidgeted in the dark as she tried everything in her might to keep herself where she was. To not intervene despite how much her instinct reared its head for her to do so.

Then a charge in the air surrounding him swirled in an engulfing wind, gentle at first but growing stronger by the second. Soft light emanated from the stone and sucked away from it in fluttering, smoky streaks like he was pulling them to his heart, his slightly parted mouth, and even nose and ears. Starting from his heart and spreading up his neck, forks of green glowed from beneath his skin, following his veins and arteries. It made some of the Elvish grey undertone of his complexion shift to green.

Her body tensed and her heart gave a sharp sting when he let out a pained grunt and his features twisted in agony. The stone cracked, glimmering fragments slipping between the gaps of his fingers, while the power in the air grew harsher.

Malicious energy burst into the air, just as the stone shattered.

A bursting growl cut short as complete darkness descended upon them, more suffocating than before. All Zylah could sense was his fast heartbeat, his light breathing, and her own growing frantic. The air calmed, only for it to suddenly grow colder, to rush faster.

A small, dark chuckle echoed through the air, just as that green glow came to life as a set of eyes. It crawled along his limbs like luminous vines, and even seemed to momentarily colour his long white hair to green strands that spread outwards from his scalp. All the symbols, runes, and circles of writing across his body came to life in patches of multiple colours.

His chuckle grew louder as he stood and looked down at the magical lines of light twirling around his fingers, hands, and arms. He threw both arms out to the sides and torches she hadn't noticed before lit up in flashes of fire.

Zylah gasped and stepped back in surprise.

The area got much brighter. It revealed him assessing his body as if he could *see* the magic now running through his entire being. The green faded out as his body began to change.

A red smoky symbol surrounded by a circle of runes on his chest glowed, just as his fangs grew, his nails turned into black claws, his eyes glowed a fiercer red, and the runes... *moved.* They shifted until black, near Demon-like streaks rushed over his sides, his arms, his neck, and even around his hairline.

He looked bigger, fiercer, and somehow... more like a Demon.

Then they changed again, swirling over his body like a ribbon that even covered part of his face, while his hair darkened to black. They shifted once more, just covering him from the neck down to his sternum, and up his fingers and hands like he'd dunked them into an inky liquid.

She wondered if these were the glamours he'd once told her of. She was too mesmerised to look away from his symbols shifting and sliding across his body like water.

They reverted back to what she now knew to be his true self: Elvish runic symbols that either created circles on his body, or left rings and runic ribbons up his limbs. Even a triangular symbol on his side returned, as did the multi-pointed star on his mid-back.

Then he was gone within an instant. Not invisible, as his heart and breaths ceased as well.

Uncertainty crept up her spine, barely believing he'd just disappeared into thin air!

"Oh, how I've missed this," he stated, just as he materialised back into the space, but on the opposite side of the pool.

He was gone again, and she looked up when she heard movement on the ceiling. She'd looked too late, and instead watched him fall to land on his feet and a single hand with ease.

The roots around her shifted as the area rumbled. Loose rocks clicked and clacked against the ground as the pool of water bubbled and dropped in volume. Everything in the air felt charged, like when lightning was about to strike the top of a tree.

With orbs turning white in worry, Zylah stepped back. The back of her right heel caught around a root that had shifted, and she tripped over. She landed on her backside and an elbow with a loud *oomph.*

As if he'd forgotten about her presence, she saw the moment his head *creepily* twisted to the side to face her.

Zylah shrieked when small brown roots began to twine around her arms and legs. She fought them, kicking as she twisted to get away before being yanked right back as more grew over her. She broke them repeatedly, gaining freedom, only to be dragged back down when more and more encircled her limbs.

Just as her strength appeared to be winning, and she managed to tear her right arm free so she could claw at the ones wrapping around her midsection, her wrist was grabbed. Pressure weighed on her waist as Jabez shoved her arm back down against the ground until vines could capture it once more.

Long white hair brushed over her tossing skull, and his earthy scent fluttered all around her. Sitting on top of her and now pinning down both her arms so all she could do was kick her legs, he let out a chuckle that had her heart wanting to burst.

She'd never heard anything more evil and menacing, the depth and bass of his voice thumping through her like an ominous beat. Panting in fear, she managed to glance at his features, and he looked entirely crazed. His irises glowed with the faintest red, while his eyes were narrowed, and yet... somehow filled with utter glee. His grin almost made him look insane and vicious with his sharp fangs bared at her.

"*This* is what power is," he rumbled, his face drawing closer as the press on her wrists grew tighter and stronger. "*This* is what true strength is."

"Let me go!" Zylah roared, her sight flickering red before snuffing back into fearful white.

Her fur puffed in aversion when his face lowered until it was right next to hers. She tried to bash her skull against his, only to whimper in the realisation that even her antlers were trapped. It strained her neck when she tried to get them free, causing a snarly groan to bubble in her chest.

"I told you things would be different between us if I had my magic," he stated, his voice *dripping* with so much malice she could almost taste it in the air.

Zylah didn't know what else to do but struggle against the vines as they continued to grow. Her thighs twitched when they slipped under the skirt of her dress, and her abdomen tightened as more slipped over it. They even swirled around her breasts, cupping them from below as they crossed over her chest.

Every part of her was being captured in order to force her to submit. She twitched when the roots caressed sensitive spots, their roughness tickling her inner thighs, chest, and pounding forearms right behind where his hands were. The strangeness of those sensations had her jerking in surprise at their pleasantness and it cut through her tension.

He wasn't leaning heavily on her, as if he was merely pressing her down but not trying to hurt her. Actually... the longer she remained trapped, the more she realised that nothing hurt. Her body wasn't being strangled except for when she tried to pull away, and the constriction gentled whenever she stopped.

Fighting was obviously pointless – there were too many vines for him to manipulate with the tree roots surrounding them. The energy radiating off him felt... unusual and chaotic.

None of this felt right. Not his laughter, not the feel of the magic, and not what he was doing. This wasn't the Jabez she'd come to know.

"Fuck. Why do you have to smell so damn *nice*?" he growled right next to her ear hole, and she winced when his hold on her wrists tightened painfully.

Zylah froze beneath him. *Wait. Did he... did he just say I smell nice?*

It was only then that she noticed something hard and long resting against her abdomen, and it appeared to be coming from the centre of his groin. It didn't feel like the vines, but she thought she may have originally mistaken it for a big one with the way it'd grown against her.

Fayren had not only shown her diagrams of different Demon female anatomy, but also common ones of male genitalia as well. At the time, she'd wondered what kind Jabez had – if it was more human in nature, or more Demon-like. She'd seen it be small and dangly between his thighs, but she'd never seen it hard like in those diagrams.

Trying to figure out what was happening, Zylah chittered nervously, only to let out a cry when his face buried into the fur of her neck. Nuzzling into her until she shivered, he took in a deep draw of her scent.

With her senses overly alert and her fur disturbed, her skin was sensitive against his deep breath that followed, making an incidental moan escape her.

Fear gave way to a string of other emotions, but none were more powerful than the one that made her *pussy* clench in reaction to him. His body was heavy and warm against hers, and she liked the weight of him bearing down on her. Suddenly, his grip on her wrists felt secure in a sublime way.

He flinched in surprise at the sound she made and swiftly leaned back. With his sharp brows furrowed and his lips flattened, a mingle of confusion and surprise was evident in his narrowed features.

"Shit," he grated out, his voice strained. "I don't know what came over me."

The vines loosened and began to recede, except for one. Zylah immediately turned her gaze down to what was resting against her stomach, and reddish pink instantly lifted into her orbs. She couldn't completely tell if he was hard since his pants were baggy and loose, but if Fayren's books were any indication, she had a feeling she was right.

Her pants quickened just in reaction to the *idea.*

"Sorry," Jabez grumbled, as he lifted off her with his gaze averted. "I've just been without my magic for so long that I got excited. It's a very cathartic feeling to have it back."

Before he could fully get to his feet, Zylah tackled him and reversed their positions. She straddled his waist and pinned his forearms to the ground. She received a dark glare, but she was too giddy and shocked by the hardness pressed against her backside and tail to care.

"Zylah..." he warned, his eyes narrowing further.

Her sight flickered with purple, while her conflicted heart softened and raced for an entirely different reason. She licked across the top of her bony snout in interest as she peered down at him.

"You're hard?" Although her question was meant to be a statement, she was too uncertain to truly make it a fact.

As if he hadn't expected her to say that, his glare disappeared, and another emotion took its place. His eyes widened in what could only be horror or mortification, while the tips of his ears bowed backwards.

She squealed when he managed to kick his leg to the side, fold it over her thigh, and roll them over.

"No," he bit out, as he rose up to get out from between her thighs.

Zylah hooked her legs around his waist to stop him from getting away. Purple permanently lifted into her sight when she ground against his erection.

"I think you are," Zylah rasped around panted breaths.

Despite how much he'd freaked her out earlier, Zylah couldn't help being overjoyed. In some way, even before she knew what she wanted, she'd been hoping for any indication that he wanted more from her. She wanted his desire, his arousal, and only knew what that meant after Fayren's.

Her chest panged when his nose scrunched up and he let out the strangest deep noise from his lips at the motion of her hips. She did it again, and he shoved his right hand against her pubic bone and pushed down to prevent her from doing it a third time as a harsh exhale fell from him.

"Stop," he grated out, unable to fight against her strong legs. "Release me *now*, Zylah."

"Why?" she whined, gripping at his back so her claws could trap him.

"Because I'm not myself right now," he stated in a quiet tone, his head tilting to look down at the way they were pressed. "Release me on your own, or I will simply teleport away."

Yes. Now that she'd seen him do that multiple times, she knew he could easily leave her trappings. But the nagging that he hadn't done it already made her braver than usual.

"But I want your arousal," Zylah answered back in a small voice. In just a matter of seconds, she was thrumming with desire. She felt it between her thighs, in her blood, in each of her shallow pants. "I want it."

She wanted touch, and she didn't care how. She wanted it from him. She'd been trying to get closer to him, just without knowing how until the previous night. The moment she knew what it was, what she needed, thoughts of exploring all the different ways to touch she'd been shown had run through her mind.

It'd made her ache in Fayren's hut to an unfathomable degree.

But after what happened today, she'd thought it was entirely one-sided. She'd been trying to swallow that knowledge while wondering if it was possible to change it.

Yet, what she wanted was currently pressing against her, and she was overjoyed by the possibility that she may not be feeling this on her own. Because of that, she couldn't... *wouldn't* let him go – not of her own volition.

Not if it meant she could possibly cling until that barrier was broken – one she had no idea how to combat.

"Zylah," he stated around a sigh. She knew that pacifying tone. It meant she was failing.

It instantly made her chest heavier, and she clutched at him harder. She whimpered and tightened her legs even more so she could fight his pressing hand and grind against him once more.

Despite his sharpened, fierce gaze, she lifted her skull just enough so she could part her maw and... *lick* over his lips. She shuddered at how they parted under her tongue's merest touch. *They're so soft.*

A quiet, unnerving growl rumbled out of him, just as his head darted forward, and a sharp gasp rent out of her when fangs lanced the tough skin of her neck. Her back bowed at the sharpness of them, while she flinched away from the cutting pain. He bit harder with each passing second, and his snarl vibrated her flesh – almost like he was trying to punish her!

She tried to pull away from it, but then her breath *hitched* when he ground between her thighs and pleasure instantly sparked. He let out a shaken, rumbling groan around his mouthful of her.

His hands shifted to the ground beside her, and she heard his claw-like nails ripping into the hardened earth. His next thrust had her melting beneath him from the way his body ground against hers, combined with his forceful bite. She wanted to think it was with fondness now, and that's how she decided to take it.

Especially since she couldn't see his face, yet he released another muffled groan against her.

A hand gripped her backside and lifted her just slightly, and he thrust his cock against her differently. Rather than the cloth-covered base rubbing her, she thought she may have felt the head shove against her swelling clit. Thankfully his pants weren't particularly rough, and she was wet enough to ensure the glide was easy.

Her claws dug a little, but she instantly released them when she smelt a hint of blood and quickly healed him. But the scent of it, of him... hearing his little grunts and feeling his warm body lying over hers, had her mind growing foggy.

Zylah panted heavily, lost in the wave of strange new sensations suddenly bombarding her. The bite of his fangs felt incredible, and she grew dizzier as she tried to grind back against him.

She wanted more. There was a pulsing deep within, radiating across her lower abdomen. Heat swelled between her thighs as wetness dripped from her. The more swollen she felt, the faster her breaths became until they were shallow and sharp. His scent was choking her, but she licked at the drool inside her maw in reaction to it.

Another moan slipped from her constricted throat, and the purple in her sight deepened.

*Please. Don't stop.* She angled her snout to caress the side of his head and pointed ear in appreciation.

# NINETEEN

Simmering just beneath his flesh, chaotic magic sparked all throughout Jabez's body. His muscles flooded with strength, with an energy that continued to build and weave through his long-deadened system. His mind was melting in euphoria, while his blood boiled with restrained aggression that finally needed an outlet.

Like his entire system was exposed to everything, every sensation bombarded him at once.

The smell of water, dirt, and tree roots had sharpened his mind, only for Zylah's jasmine-and-violet scent to overshadow them with dizzying sweetness. The coldness in the air gave way to the heat of her body, while her claws tickled down the sides of his back, only to elicit a sharp sting when they dug deeper. The sound of trickling water was replaced with high-pitched feminine hitches of breath, and quiet, needy whimpers – each one making his hardened cock pulse.

Even the taste of her blood was sweet, and the drips slipping down his throat flooded him with more strength, more aggression, more... stupidity. Suddenly he couldn't get closer, no matter how hard he shoved his erection against her, no matter how deep he sunk his fangs as he let loose a vicious, desirous growl.

He wanted more warmth, more touch, more scent and taste, his body and mind shifting into a singular focus.

And the longer he lay over her, the more fixated he became on her.

He didn't know when he'd shoved his hand under her dress, but he registered utter softness in his palm. He brushed his thumb over a hardened nipple, his hand kneading her small but firm breast, while his other hand already gripped her plump backside tightly. Fur tickled his fingers and palm, and the sensation was welcome.

Her breath brushing over his drooping ear had his body growing lax, despite how her noises made it twitch. Although his muscles continued to swell with desire, the cuteness in her sounds, her little breaths, and how she trembled with need softened his grip. Even his fangs released, and with blood-covered lips, he gently licked at the wound to see how she'd react.

She produced the sweetest little cry, her body shuddering beneath him, and feverish humour crinkled his dazed eyes.

He liked that she didn't seem to mind the harshness of his bite, and instead of pulling away from it, had eventually leaned into it. But his softer affection gave him a more exciting reaction.

Instead of biting her again, he scraped his sharp fangs down her chest. She gripped one of his horns, and her claws deliciously cut into his scalp, sending a twinge down his spine. He licked upwards with the points of his fangs following his trail, and she shivered in reaction.

Her claws were surprisingly gentle, and she caressed his skin like a woman with long nails. For a moment, he'd almost forgotten he had one of the most dangerous creatures in his arms. He didn't need to rein back his strength, didn't need to be considerate of buttery-soft skin.

That lack of restriction, funnily enough, tempered his desire to bite and claw. The fact that he could... *tease* with them instead, made him want to be gentler – just so he could trick her when he did cut deep and offer different sensations.

He couldn't remember the last time he'd had such freedom.

In the back of his mind, he knew he should be concerned about what he was doing with this female. He'd been holding back for a multitude of reasons, none of which had gone away simply because he was bombarded by energetic magic. They lingered, whispering in his ears, telling him to stop, yet... the deeper they *both* fell under this spell, the less he cared.

She smelt wonderful right then. Her pretty scent mixed with her strong arousal had him huffing for more, and they didn't have to be fully intimate for him to do so.

There remained a line that he couldn't cross, but surely a *little* pleasure shared between them wasn't too terrible. Or perhaps that was just his engorged cock and denied lust muddling his usually perceptive thoughts. The ache in his balls needed release, telling him everything about this right now was a grand fucking idea.

*I want to touch her.* What he truly wanted right then was to shove his cock into her, but touching was as far as his mind would allow. *I wonder what she's like when she comes.*

Just the idea had his cock jerking hard until he released a drop of precum. And seeing this sweet, innocent female all pent up had him grinding between her thighs harder.

She'd asked for this. Her scent was rich with deep arousal, and his conscience was satisfied she understood what it was she sought. Or rather, he allowed that to eliminate any misgivings he had regarding his actions, and he knew, without a doubt, that she wasn't going to stop him, nor did she want to.

Especially when she produced an adorable moan when he pulled the top of her dress down and brought her dark-grey nipple into his mouth. *Finally* giving into that damn urge, he grazed his tongue against it with a harsh lick.

Her head tipped back and to the side, and she cupped the end of her snout as if she wanted to hide her pants.

Lust-filled purple orbs glowed, but it was obvious they weren't looking upon him. Her shoulders flinched and her grip on his horn tightened when he sucked the little bud hard, and her trembling only worsened when he constantly lashed it with his tongue.

Since his body had slipped lower, he felt no reason to grind his cock against the air now that his waist was between her thighs. She refused to release her legs wrapped around him, even when he attempted to pry one off. Her strength was commendable, and no matter how hard he yanked, her locked ankles refused to relent.

Only when he raked his nails down over what he could

reach of the inside of her thigh did it let go so it could twitch, shudder, and kick. Her back bowed when he clawed his way back up to her knee, while he gave a harder suck at her breast.

Her reactions were sweet, but she was overly sensitive to each touch. It was a reminder that she was new to all this. *I must be slow.* He had no damn clue how she'd react, and her claws could gouge his skin far too dangerously.

*Thank fuck I can teleport if that happens.* He knew her desire wouldn't outweigh a strong scent of blood, and if this female turned vicious with blood-lust, then he had an easy escape.

Another idea came to him – one that had mischief curling his lips.

Tingles caressed his skin as he made his own scent stronger, hiding any traces of blood in the air. He tried not to make it too strong, as he'd been told it could be unsettling to those with a sensitive nose. *But I already know she is fond of the way I smell.*

Satisfied that he'd dealt with the potential danger, he lifted his hand so he could watch as he used magic to trim down the claws on his middle and ring fingers so they wouldn't score her. Unlike most Demons, Jabez was unable to retract them. He brushed his palm along her thigh with one destination in mind, and the fur covering her shoulders and chest waved like a prickle of goosebumps assaulted her as he neared her centre.

*Her fur is really soft,* he thought, pressing kisses across her exposed sternum bone before using his nose to nuzzle the rest of her dress down so he could get to her other breast. He latched onto her nipple just as his hand cupped between her thighs. Dripping wetness instantly saturated his fingers, and he was relieved to find that her pussy was where it usually was on a female.

Pussy lips and folds greeted his exploring fingers, as did a sensitive clit. Jabez kept his gaze on Zylah's skull to make sure he didn't do anything wrong. Given that she let out a cute whine and bucked against his fingers when he grazed the little bud, she had no complaints.

Despite being a Mavka, she essentially felt like any other woman, except for one minor detail. He noticed little nodules on the inside of her lips, and she shivered whenever he touched them directly – as if she liked the contact. He had no doubt she'd be purple like with female Demons, rather than a variation of pink or mauve.

Her skull tilted to look down at his face past her own snout as he released her nipple so he could draw the full length of his tongue over it. Her maw parted to let out a cute squeak when he pinched her clit between the lengths of his fingers.

"How's that?" he asked, trying to stir her into giving him responses since he couldn't gauge the expressions of a bony face. He rolled his fingers from side to side to tease her.

"It feels really nice," she whispered around airy, hot pants, her voice dripping with needy desire.

Just the sound of her voice, all raspy and broken, had him stifling a groan, and he playfully nipped the side of her breast without breaking skin. He licked the fur there as he made her legs and abdomen twitch with each foray, while removing his hand from her backside so he could better hold himself up.

"Can I go lower?" he asked, requiring her to voice that he was allowed to explore deeper.

Zylah whimpered in answer, while nodding her head. Once more, she cupped the end of her snout, and he wondered if she was doing it because she felt shy. If so, he found that rather fucking *cute*.

His fingers slipped through her slick, before the tips of them found the source. He slowly pushed in his middle finger and a little pool of inferno greeted him in a nice fit. She caved in beneath him, her hips dipping while her thighs spread in welcome of the intrusion.

*She feels like any other female.* Perhaps a little warmer, from what he could tell, but her channel was soft and textured.

Considering he was able to add his ring finger so quickly, and only then did she stretch for him, humour lit up in his gaze. "Did you touch yourself at Fayren's?" Why else would she have accepted two fingers so easily?

To his surprise, she shook her head.

She was snug, but he could tell she could accept more with little effort. Which was fine with Jabez. The size of his cock was impressive, and he would rather have an easy entrance than fight through intense tightness.

Except he had no intention of penetrating her with his cock.

At that reminder, he hooked his fingers to see if Zylah had a sweet spot he could reach. It only took a few thrusts for him to find it. She shook as she held onto his horn, gripped his opposing shoulder, and ground against his fingertips.

Anywhere her juices touched began to tingle his skin, but he put that down to the overly wet sensation and his heightened awareness.

When he dug at her G-spot hard, he paused when she arched her back and let out a shallow cry.

"D-don't stop!" she moaned, her pussy clenching around him.

In the next instant, something... *strange* happened within. Something wrapped around his fingers, clamping them together and trying to keep him still. His brows drew down in confusion as he began to pull his fingers out, but only made it about halfway before something tightened and yanked him back in!

"What the fuck?" he muttered under his breath, shifting to his knees so he could see.

As he'd thought, her pussy was a moderate purple, and everything was swollen and puffy – no longer appearing like a hidden slit. Just as he was about to pull his fingers from her, he saw what had gripped him.

Little tentacle-like tendrils held on firm, although it was difficult to count how many as they criss-crossed over both his fingers. They refused to relent, even when he pulled a little harder. Now that he figured out what they were, warmth and mirth crinkled his eyes, as he found the feature quite unique.

*I've seen stranger things,* he thought with humour, before shoving his fingers deep.

He attacked her G-spot with strength, thrusting his fingers as he wiggled them. Her hands released him so she could claw at the ground when her back arched, her maw parted, and a loud moan escaped her. Her hips followed his movements, trying to match his thrusting, before one of her feet came off the ground.

The little tendrils released their grips at different intervals, like they wanted to constantly re-position their hold when his movements almost made them slip off. He figured his fingers were too small and tapered to hold properly, and he wondered what they'd feel like wrapping around his cock.

The idea of them playing around the rim of his cock head and his ridges had a shudder rippling through him. He'd bet *that* would feel amazing.

His lips pulled into a grin, his eyes wild as he watched her body twist and gyrate while his fingers plunged. He could see the moment she was about to come by how she dipped her skull back and to the side to evade her antlers. By how her claws gouged at the solidified dirt until she managed to leave marks behind. By how her cute little toes curled and she spread her thighs even further.

The tendrils gripped hard, giving him little room to move, as her core clamped up so tight it was like she was trying to crush his fingers. Zylah let out a screaming cry when her inner walls spasmed and liquid heat squelched around his thrusts.

Trying to see if he could draw it out, he kept his fingers deep and wiggled them, while placing his thumb over her exposed clit to press and tease it as well. Her cry quivered, and she grabbed his right biceps in tension – incidentally clawing it a little in the process.

Only when everything loosened – both her core and those tendrils – did Jabez stop. He slipped his fingers from her slowly when she grew lax beneath him, and noticeable liquid dripped from his fingertips to the floor.

He eyed her panting form before bringing his gaze to his fingers. *How far do I want to go?* he wondered, but licked his lips at the wicked scent of her arousal and feminine slick in the air.

It was so thick and tantalising it was making his mouth flood with drool.

His cock pulsed, leaking precum at everything he'd just done, and just witnessed. His eyes crinkled in anguish, while his nose wrinkled when he let out a desperate groan. He licked her juices from his palm, before he shoved his Zylah-coated fingers into his mouth.

The sound that fell from him was more like a pathetic moan

as heaven touched his tongue, and lust blasted through him more fiercely than before. *I fucking knew she'd taste good.* And he wasn't the kind of man to waste an opportunity when it was deliciously splayed before him.

He shuffled his knees back, curled his arms around her thighs, and shoved his face against her pussy without warning. His vision grew clouded when he licked from her opening all the way to her saturated clit.

He was probably going too fast for her, but he just hadn't been able to deny himself a taste.

She let out a surprised gasp, and her thighs came up to cushion the sides of his head. Her skull tilted down to him, and he saw it from the corner of his eye as he licked sideways across her clit. He was very careful as he brought the sensitive bud into his mouth, hoping her stronger exterior meant he wouldn't harm her with his fangs.

His fangs were usually a beloved trait of his, considering they were a perfect tool for brutality, but they often got in the way of this. Females were sensitive, and although they were jagged fangs, he hoped they were blunt enough for her when usually they were too much.

He watched as he cautiously sucked, ready to release at any indication that it hurt.

She gave a full-body shudder, just as one of her feet slipped over his shoulder and caressed down his back. Her right hand shoved into his hair and gripped hard as she tugged the long strands with a tight fist. At the same time, her foot between his shoulder blades pulled up like she was trying to draw him closer with both.

"J-Jabez," she rasped as she ground her hips against his face.

Seeing she wanted more, and seemed to be enjoying this, his heart raced a little faster when he sucked harder. Her thighs squeezed as she produced a sweet moan and tried to pull him closer. He lashed her clit with his tongue repeatedly, and she twitched each time.

He noticed that, like his fingers, his mouth began to tingle. Oddly enough, his cock hardened even further, as if a compound or enzyme in her feminine slick had some kind of stimulant effect. Or, perhaps, even some kind of mild aphrodisiac – not enough to make him crazed, but absolutely making him want more of her. Suddenly he was ravenous, the desire to *feast* nibbling away at him.

*How can she taste this fucking good?* Even the way her little nodules tickled his lips felt amazing, and he drew his tongue up them constantly.

The longer he observed the acceptance of his encompassing lips, tongue, and fangs, the deeper he fell into his teasing. Closing his eyes, he savoured her moans, the taste of her, and the way her clit and folds felt against his mouth. He lay down so he could get a better angle and pressed his engorged cock against the ground.

He released her clit so he could lick at the pool of her entrance, groaning as he shoved his hips against the ground again. *I'm so hard.* The need for release hammered at him, and if he wasn't too busy holding her thighs in place, he may have shoved a hand into his trousers and begun stroking himself.

He slipped his lengthy tongue inside her, swirling it just enough to collect her taste. Even then, she didn't seem to mind his fangs pressing against her as he delved as deep as he could, and he was enamoured at finally being able to pleasure a female with his mouth. He pulled away just so he could playfully nip at one of her lips before he lashed his tongue across her clit as a reward.

He sucked on it again, stronger than before, and her back arched as she threw her thighs open. He released it so he could nuzzle his closed lips against it, before licking from the pool of her entrance back up to it. He circled it, then wiggled his tongue side to side, trying anything to get her to tip over the edge again. It felt good to let out a bit of his playful self he'd been keeping hidden from her.

When he gave her clit another flat lick, her fistful of his hair tightened once more, and she ground against his tongue. She yanked hard enough to delightfully sting his scalp.

*Fuck. That's naughty.* His mind practically groaned out the thought when it felt like she was trying to fuck his face herself. *You act all innocent, but just look at what you're doing to me.*

He stuck his tongue forward for her and stilled it, making

sure his jaw was unhinged completely so her messy thrusts didn't catch his fangs. Then he worked with her movements, using firm pressure and going in the opposite direction so each lash would be stronger.

He peeked open his eyes to look up at her. Her fur was puffed, her snout tilted towards him as if she was watching him between her thighs. Her maw had parted on hitching breaths.

The moment she realised their gazes were locked, she whimpered. She trembled constantly, and that only deepened when her muscles visibly locked up. The moment she started to orgasm, Jabez did nothing but let her thrust her pussy against his mouth in the way she needed to ensure it was more blissful for her.

Her orbs turned black, and she threw her head to the side as she let out a cute cry. Her shoulders turned inwards, while her thighs clamped around his head in a crushing hold.

Only when she softened did Jabez take his reward. He dipped lower and shoved his tongue inside her to drink her orgasm, feeling the last of her core's shudders and quivers before he pulled away. He licked at his lips, her slick clinging to his cheeks and chin, as he raised himself up to kneel.

Panting deeply, finally able to take proper breaths, he stared down at her pussy with his hands on her thighs.

His eyes crinkled as his balls gave an uncomfortable throb.

Right now, what he wanted more than anything was to shove into her until their hips were flush. If she could handle his hands and mouth, then she'd be able to handle a completely wild and feral Jabez pounding into her. And he knew he'd be wild after experiencing all this, especially with the taste of her lingering in his mouth.

To finally let go of his strength...

*I can't.* He couldn't do that. He couldn't cross that line with her, not when he was still harbouring the secrets he did. He'd give anything to throw his conscience to the wind, but he knew it'd weigh too heavily in the future.

But he needed to fucking come, and the wet spot on his pants was a good indication that he'd be fast and sensitive.

He loosened the tie at his waistband, then grabbed her thigh and pulled her closer. She chittered in surprise before letting out a gasp when he shoved his lips around her left breast. He tongued her nipple as he slipped his hand into his pants, grasped his cock, and stroked it.

The backs of his knuckles brushed against her abdomen through the material, and he stifled his groan when the ring of his fingers squeezed over the rim of his girth.

She obviously felt it, since she turned her skull down to him and asked, "Jabez?"

"I'm very horny right now," he grated with a husky voice, as his lips purposefully brushed over her saliva-coated nipple. "I'm going to jerk off."

Hopefully she wouldn't mind him playing with her tits while he did. It was exciting him and would absolutely ensure he reached his own release much faster. He couldn't help grazing the little bud with one of his fangs in appreciation, which made her twitch and let out a rasp.

*Shit,* he thought, as he stroked faster. *I really like that she enjoys my fangs.*

"But I want to see you," she whispered, lifting up slightly to get her elbows beneath her.

"You want to watch me?" he asked, pulling away to lean on a straightened arm above her.

He wasn't actually against that, considering they'd just done much worse. *I probably shouldn't encourage her, though.*

She licked across her snout, her skull twisting like she wanted a better view of his groin. With her purple orbs clearly upon him, she reached out to slip her claws into the waistband of his pants.

He *almost* chuckled. *For a female new to all this, she's rather bold.*

Giddiness thrummed through Zylah as she tugged on his pants and he didn't stop her. Short white hair came into view before the base of his shaft was revealed. She felt the need to go slow in case he spooked, and she licked the inside of her mouth when she'd brought the fabric most of the way down.

Although his hand covered part of him, ridges on both sides

were visible. She twisted her head in surprise, since they hadn't been there before when she'd seen him soft. Then, finally, his cock came free. Jabez pulled his hand away so he could shuffle the waistline of his pants lower until he revealed his hair-dusted ball sac, as if he found that more comfortable.

He gripped his length once more, his fingertips having at least an inch of space between them like he couldn't completely encompass it.

"Oh wow," Zylah rasped, her gaze fixated as she noted the exposed mauve head. "It's not little anymore."

A singular snort of laughter came from him. "It's not nice to call a man's cock small, even when it's soft."

"Oh." She chittered nervously. "Sorry, I didn't mean–"

Her words died when he brought the ring of his fingers up until his thumb flicked over the wet rim of the head. "It's fine," he grated lowly, before a small pant came from him.

Any self-consciousness dissipated as she watched Jabez stroke himself, his fingers waving as he ran over the ridges.

*It's so much bigger than before.* It looked hard, thick, and long enough that she'd require two hands to fully cover it from head to base – and her hands were rather big.

The head was also exposed, when before it'd been sheltered. A pearly white bead formed at the slitted hole on the tip, and Zylah shivered at the naughty hint of salt in the air. None of the books she'd read detailed males having an arousal scent, but it was hard to miss now that his cock was free.

Still throbbing with need and curious about it, about him, she reached out without thinking. She wrapped her hand around the head and thumbed that bead of liquid.

He released a groan as his shaft thickened momentarily in her grasp. "I guess you don't want to just watch," he rasped out, letting go as if he didn't mind her taking over.

Which had not been her intention! Zylah didn't know what to do, and momentarily panicked as she tried to mimic his stroking. She found it awkward, so she shifted her palm a little to hold it similarly to how he had.

"Fuck!" he choked out as a shudder racked him. "Careful of your claws. Don't tickle it."

He said this, yet another heavy drop of precum spilled from

the tip of his cock.

"Also," he started, before pulling her hand to the side to expose the top of his shaft. Then, a line of saliva spilled from his lips and onto it, before he let her hand go. "It'll be easier and feel better if it's wet."

"I'm wet," Zylah stated, wondering why he hadn't just collected the liquid dripping from her.

"That's true."

Zylah squeaked when two fingers shoved inside her. Her knees tried to close, but his body between her thighs prevented her from doing so. She moaned when he wriggled them around in her juices, only for him to remove them and slap his now drenched fingers over his cock.

"Better?" he stated with a pant.

Zylah nodded and attempted to stroke him with a shaking hand. She hadn't realised having her own slick on his cock while she touched it would be so erotic, and wondered if that's why he hadn't done it in the first place.

"Tighter, Zylah," he demanded softly. "You don't have to be so gentle."

As much as she felt like she was fumbling through this, she was thankful for his direction. She could wield a lot of strength and was worried about hurting him. She squeezed until the hard muscle pushed back.

A groan rasped past his lips as he jerked forward into her hold, and she took that as a good sign. Especially when his slightly wet hand came forward and cupped her left breast.

She hadn't expected him to touch her while she stroked him, and she finally looked away in awe from his cock to his face. He leaned over her on a straightened arm, and Zylah instantly melted under his expression.

Although his gaze was locked to her chest, she'd never seen it look so... soft before. His features were relaxed, his lips parted to release quiet pants. His eyes no longer held the cold, callous, or indifferent iciness in them, but looked heated and dazed. His long eyelashes dipped as he blinked lazily.

Half of his long white hair had fallen to rest down his bare chest, while loops of it curled beneath his pointed left ear. She watched as his naked pectoral muscles clenched and rippled whenever she ran her fingers over the head of his cock and the ridges going down the side of him.

As much as she wanted to observe how his bulging abdomen muscles twitched to her movements, she couldn't stray away from his mesmerising face. She soaked in the way his features creased – especially his nose – as she touched him, and she watched with rapt attention as his soft lips parted to moan lightly.

Her breath was nearly stolen when his eyes flickered up to her orbs, and she wondered if he could feel her gaze upon him.

*He looks beautiful like this.*

The lustfulness in his eyes made their red irises almost appear like fire. Having them so strongly on her, knowing it was because of her, had her pussy walls fluttering.

Her arousal was still strong, her clit pounding for more attention. Each pinch or thumb pad brushing against her nipple only deepened her need.

"Inside?" she rasped, surprised to find her voice so shaky and croaked.

She wanted his cock in her. His fingers felt so good, especially when he'd stretched her a little. She imagined it would feel even better if something much, much bigger was inside her.

His lips closed and tightened, while his eyes crinkled as if in anguish. A muffled, yet loud groan came from him, and his cock pulsed in her palm, seeming to harden even more.

He shook his head. "No. Just this."

"But..." She paused when she didn't know how to convince him.

"We can only do this," he stated, while bringing his hand away from her breast.

Panic shot through her when she thought he was taking his touch away, but it quickly settled when he caressed his hand down her side.

"Is this better?" Two fingers slipped into the folds around her clit, then he rubbed back up to graze it with the tips of them.

Zylah moaned as her trembling thighs spread in welcome but shook her head. "Deeper," she pleaded.

A cry ripped from her when he shoved his fingers inside her and thrust them deep. Her toes curled, and her grip on him strengthened as she stroked faster.

"*Nhnn.*" He quaked above her as he picked up speed. "You can be a rather needy thing, can't you?"

Unable to speak, Zylah just nodded as her hips tilted back and forth, while she attempted to maintain the momentum of her own hand. She tried to keep her gaze on his handsome face as he looked down to watch what they were doing to each other, but her sight darkened into such a deep purple it was threatening to turn black.

His hips began to thrust into her hold, his huffs quickening and growing even more shallow.

Her entire body radiated with bliss as she momentarily switched her focus to his fingers moving within her. She felt so hot, swollen, and wet within, and the sound of it rang in her ears. Her chest constantly bucked upwards, her breasts wanting more attention as her nipples tightened in the cool air.

"J-Jabez," she whimpered when her pussy spasmed and grew tingly. She felt herself trying to latch onto his fingers, her inner walls clamping rhythmically and growing hotter with each thrust.

As if he could sense what was about to happen, he hooked his fingertips and dug deep. Her maw parted when she let loose a sharp cry just as she came, while her muscles clenched and trembled.

He didn't stop, even when she stopped stroking him, unable to do anything but ride the wave of her orgasm. Her feet arched, her knees coming up, and she squirmed beneath him.

*I want more...* She wanted something bigger, deeper. She wanted to feel him holding her as she came, her heart aching for him tenfold and making her orbs waver in need of him.

This felt amazing, but there seemed to be something missing, and all her mind could grasp was that it was missing more of him.

The moment her body went lax, he spread her slick over his cock and gripped her loose hand. He tightened it himself and made her stroke him as he thrust into their combined hold.

She was too relaxed to truly help. Her clit pounded in

satisfaction, and a pleasurable pang radiated in her chest before bolting down her body as she took in his features.

His eyes had sharpened, aggressive and yet needy, while his lips had pulled back to reveal his fangs.

He quaked as he grated, "I'm about to come."

His jagged fangs parted as his jaw dropped, just as he gave a full-body shudder, all his muscles dancing when they leapt and contorted. A loud, deep, and haunting groan came from him, as pearly white liquid burst from the tip of his cock in a heavy rope of seed.

She gasped when it landed across her sternum, then the second release shot onto her right breast. As he came over her body, Jabez placed his other hand against the ground to grind into their combined fists. His hips continued to jerk, and his groan morphed into a subtle rumble the longer it went on.

*Oh wow! So much is coming out!* It smelt salty and mingled with his earthy scent.

After the last rope came from him, he let out quick, shallow huffs above her. His eyes and lips closed momentarily as he gave a last muffled groan and a lock of his hair fell across his brow. His head dipped forward, and Zylah removed her hand when his cock softened in her grasp.

For a few seconds, all she could sense was his warmth, his pretty scent, and his racing heartbeat pounding loudly while he released short breaths. All the places he'd touched throbbed in awareness of him; her hard nipples, her swollen clit, and her pussy all thrummed for more.

She wanted to watch what happened now, wondering if it would go small again. Already she could see the stiffened ridges fading, as if they were only visible when it was fully erect. She thought his cock was kind of cute flopping down, since it had been a long and thick jutting rod between his hips when they first pulled it out.

Still thrumming with want, Zylah watched as more of his hair slipped forward. Her heart squeezed as she recalled clutching at it with his face between her thighs, or how she'd grasped one of his black horns. Considering touch between them had been very limited before this, she was surprised by how much he'd allowed.

He'd never let her touch his silky hair before.

She reached up to caress his cheek and push a few strands back to see his cruelly handsome face.

Jabez lifted his head, and his eyes still appeared soft and languid. However, the longer he looked upon her face, the more a shadow crept over his expression. His brows drew together, and her chest tightened in reaction as she slid her hand away.

He almost appeared anguished... or regretful. Especially with how his cheeks crinkled around his eyes.

Hoping she was misreading him, Zylah lifted her head up and licked the corner of his lips deliberately and slowly. "More?" she pleaded around little pants.

His lips parted in surprise, and his expression gentled before his mouth twisted for another reason. Humour lit up his face, and he shook his head.

"No. This is enough for now," he answered, finally lifting to kneel between her legs. He pushed his shaft back inside his pants, and she wanted to pout that he was hiding it away again.

He grabbed the bottom of her dress to tug it up, and she lifted her hips to give him access. Although disappointed he'd rejected the idea of continuing, she couldn't help being confused about why he was stripping her.

"Why are you taking this off?" she asked, as she lifted her arms for him willingly.

"Because I came all over it," he stated with a quiet chuckle. "If we don't clean it before it dries, it'll stain."

He moved to kneel beside her and slipped his arms behind her back and knees. Zylah let out a surprised squeak when he lifted her into a cradle as he stood, then walked her towards the pool in the middle of this underground pocket of earth.

Even though he took her to something that could drown her, she had full trust in him and didn't feel the need to question what he was doing. He wouldn't hurt her.

He carefully placed her backside on the ground with her knees together and to one side. Then he dropped into the water and began rubbing the material of her grey dress together to clean it. He did the same to his pants without removing them.

He offered her his side the entire time. His lips had lost their usual hard press, but his brows were furrowed once more. He glanced at her from the corner of his eye, then he averted his gaze with his ears drooping further than ever before.

She had no idea what any of that meant.

He appeared relaxed and sated, but as usual, his hidden thoughts remained guarded, even upon his face. She wished she could decipher them, and that he was easier to read.

Purple still lingered in her sight, but she scratched at the fur around her neck when shyness crept around her heart. She had questions after what just transpired between them.

Would they be able to do this again? She wanted it more than anything, especially with the way a fluffy feeling had sprouted in her chest. She liked the physical contact, and she was still in awe he could touch in so many different ways.

His lips drew her attention, and she shivered at the memory of his sharp fangs scraping against her. She doubted she'd be able to look at his face the same way now, especially when recalling the image of his head between her thighs instantly had her body pulsing. She squished them together.

*I wanted his dick inside me, but he said no. Why?* She didn't understand what the issue was. *But he touched me.* The yearning she'd felt before had now grown claws, and they tore into her stomach with need *and* with uncertainty.

After what he said in the forest, it was like he'd been planning on letting another male gain her attention. Like... he didn't care for her.

"Does..." Zylah started, before having to stifle the urge to chitter in nervousness. Part of her wanted to cover her exposed and tingling chest, but she also didn't find her nudity that much of an issue. It was only because he'd touched her breasts with his hands and mouth that she was suddenly bashful about them. "Does this mean you like me?"

He paused what he was doing, and staring down at her garment with both hands, he fisted it tighter. He never looked at her as he said, "I'm attracted to you, yes."

Hope swelled behind her sternum, as did tenderness and a mess of other emotions. She tilted her head at him, as bright yellow flickered in her sight.

"I'm surprised you answered that."

"Kind of hard to hide it now," he answered with a dull chuckle, before turning to her.

She wished humour was present in his handsome features as he laughed, but it was missing. He waded towards where she was, and once more, she noted he was avoiding meeting her orbs.

Her tone was coy as she tried to soften her next question. "Why were you hiding it?"

He cupped handfuls of water to her chest, and the coldness of it shocked her. It didn't take long for her to realise that he was washing away the seed that had collected on her chest. He seemed to be extra attentive to anywhere his release clung to her fur, lightly scratching to clean it.

She liked that he was caring for her in this way when she'd never considered this issue. Now that he was doing it, she knew her fur being unclean would have bothered her in the future, especially if it grew clumpy.

*He is very considerate.*

"There is much you still don't know about me," Jabez finally answered after a short bout of silence. "There are secrets I keep that I know I must share with you. Any affection you hold towards me could subside at learning them, and I thought it best to refrain from any intimacy."

"Oh," Zylah muttered, her orbs sinking back to their normal teal. She fidgeted under the weight of his words as uncertainty clutched her stomach and knotted it. "So they are not pleasant?"

His lips hardened into a flat line before gentling. "No."

He threw her dress over his shoulder and hopped out of the water. She noticed it steaming, as if he was using some kind of magic to dry it like he had done to his pants earlier. Just as she went to get up on her own, he held his hand out to her and she flinched in surprise. She gingerly took it.

"I'm not the kind of person who shares my thoughts easily," Jabez said as he helped Zylah to her feet. "I'm also very calculating when it comes to what I disclose, and when. My intention has always been to speak with you on such matters, but it was difficult in the beginning."

Her orbs shifted to a reddish pink. "Because I wouldn't

have understood what you were saying?"

His lips quirked at that. "Yes. Now, lift your arms."

Zylah did as she was told, and he helped her redress. The material was dry, warm, and felt silkier than before – like it always did when it was cleaned.

"Why not tell me now?"

She wished she hadn't pushed him with her question when his gaze immediately darkened.

"I ask that you wait. There is a beginning and an end, and I must wade through where to start." He brushed off his pants, which he'd also dried. "A lot of my sense of security has returned now that I have my power back. I will be more at ease."

"You did say much would change between us if you got your magic back," Zylah conceded with a forced laugh.

She didn't know how to truly respond. She didn't like that he was openly admitting to hiding dark things from her. Now she worried what they could be, while she thought about all she'd learned of him so far.

As if he could read her mind, he cocked a brow. Then the strangest grin curled his lips until it flashed his fangs, and a mischievous light glinted in his eyes.

"Perhaps I want to show you other things about me in order to soften what I do reveal about my past."

Attempting to play with him, her tone was light and humour filled. "Wouldn't that be considered manipulation?"

"Absolutely it would be," he answered without a hint of guilt. "But that's what getting to know someone means. If you share all the bad first, you scare people off."

"But I don't have any bad qualities," she answered without thinking. Her orbs deepened in their embarrassed hue, and she brushed the fur around her neck bashfully. "At least, I don't think I do."

"None that I've found so far," he replied, surprising her.

Her head reared back, and she chittered under the compliment. She absolutely hadn't expected him to *agree* with her, at least not openly.

Her knees knocked inwards, her heart leaping with affection while her tender pussy pulsated. Both were such strange things to feel at the same time, new and exciting.

"So, Zylah. How would you like to walk through Spiral Haven?"

The question was so sudden and shocking, it made her momentarily cease dwelling on what just transpired between them.

"Really?" she asked, her voice turning higher pitched in joy.

He lifted a hand to shrug while walking over to their bags and his shirt, so he could slip it over his muscled body. "I can already tell you're curious, and there's no harm in us doing so now."

Zylah's feet couldn't move fast enough when he picked up his cloak and threw it around his shoulders. She sprinted to her bag, her feet bouncing with giddiness as she slung it across her torso.

*I can't believe I get to see the village!*

# TWENTY

Zylah's legs wobbled when she and Jabez materialised outside the tunnel's entrance they'd crawled through earlier. Dizziness swam, and she reached out to grasp at nothing when it felt like her head was spinning and she was about to fall.

A strong hand wrapped around her forearm to steady her.

"I forgot teleporting can be disorientating for others at first," Jabez muttered, as her vision began to clear. "Hopefully you get used to it, since this will be our mode of transport in the future."

Zylah nodded, before stepping to the side and rushing forward with her tail wiggling behind her. Each twitch had her still hot, swollen insides quivering, but she liked the sore sting of it. She liked the constant reminder.

"Where are you going?"

"To the village!" she exclaimed, heading towards one of the entrances around the massive tree base.

"Not without a glamour you're not." When she turned to give him a puzzled head tilt, he turned towards the closest trunk, placed his hands on his hips, and looked up. "We're also not going that way."

"What do you mean?" she asked as she came back to him. "How else would we get inside?"

He pointed to the lowest branch, which was at least forty feet away, if not more. "I wonder how high you can jump."

She cupped her hands over her stomach as her orbs lightened in their teal colour in worry, threatening to turn white. "I am... I don't think I'm good at climbing."

"Don't know unless you try."

Zylah stood close to the tree's base and looked up. *Maybe I can make it?* Then again, she didn't have much faith that she could actually jump that high. If she managed to grip it with her claws, the bark should allow her to stay attached to it.

Deciding it was just better to face her newfound fear of heights, Zylah lowered into a crouch until her backside touched her heels. Then she jumped.

She knew immediately that she'd fallen short by at least ten feet and tried not to scream as she headed back towards the ground. With her arms waving, she accidentally tipped her body backwards, and her sight darkened in preparation for landing on her arse.

Instead, she landed in a set of arms with an *oomph.*

The laughter that burst from him was bright and warm, and vibrated against her torso as if it came from his very chest.

"I didn't actually think you'd try. There was no way either of us would make that," he exclaimed around chuckles. "Fucking hell, Zylah. I guess my humour *can* be a little dry."

Before her orbs could flare an embarrassed hue, dizziness assaulted her when the world went dark and then brightened. This time, her stomach fluttered with a queasiness she'd never experienced before, and she went lax in his arms as she tried to breathe through it.

Strange lights in the distance twinkled in her spinning vision, as did a warm and comforting orange glow.

"Like I said, teleportation is easier," he explained. "Are you okay to stand?"

She shook her head and closed her sight so she could escape it. He placed her down on solid, rough ground with her legs dangling over the edge of something. Thankfully, when she shot her hand out to stop herself from falling forward, she found more hardness.

She opened her sight once more when she heard his clothing rustling as he sat next to her. With one of his feet flat against the gigantic tree branch they were seated upon, the other one dangled over the edge like both of hers. He folded one arm over his bent knee and leaned back on the other.

"Magnificent, isn't it?" he asked, nodding his chin to what lay before them.

Now that the dizziness had settled, she turned her gaze forward. Her gasp was loud, and she straightened her posture so she could get a better look.

"Oh, wow," she rasped, eyeing all the buildings and different colours.

Most of the houses or establishments had either clay tile or straw roofing. Most of the structures were made of stone, more clay, or wood, and everything was lit up by hundreds of lanterns, which was where the comforting orange glow was coming from. Many of the buildings were two levels, some even perhaps three, and they were all closely cluttered together.

She could tell there were levels to the village, since stairs allowed people to climb down towards the centre with ease.

"I don't know why, but I thought it'd be darker," she commented, noticing hundreds, if not thousands, of Demons walking on dirt or stone paths. Every few feet, lanterns situated at the top of wooden poles, with colourful flags swaying underneath them, lit the way for all.

"Because it's a village for Demons?"

Her orbs shifted to reddish pink. "Well... yes."

"We seek the light as much as everything else. No one wants to live in the dark, and since we can't enjoy the sunlight, we do what we can."

She nodded as if she understood, then drifted her gaze upwards. She took in the long pieces of wide cloth that hung from the very top where the twisting tree canopy came together. Green leaves rustled from the lightest wind, creating a *shaa* sound. A few came loose to dance around the purple, red, blue, and yellow cloths that were attached to the lowest branches on every tree surrounding the circular village.

It took her a while to notice, but strange noises could be heard even from a distance. They didn't overshadow all the chattering, but they did manage to soften it. They were odd, something she'd never heard before, causing her head to twitch this way and that as if it would help her understand them.

"What is that sound in the background?" she asked, intently scanning her orbs over the busy village in search of its many sources.

"Music," he told her. "There is entertainment to be found all over. Many play drums, pipes, or guitars from their homes, or others will follow behind a performer. Ribbon and fire dances are common, and it livens up the place between all the merchants and stalls."

"Why would they do all this?"

This... wasn't what she expected at all. Then again, she had nothing else to go off besides her one adventure through a human town at night. She truly never expected it to appear so... happy, warm, or inviting.

"Demons who are near completion seek out company like any intelligent species. Spiral Haven gives all a chance to share their hobbies and interests in a place where they can be appreciated. Knowledge can be used as a way to trade for other things, such as clothing, food, and tools."

"Can we go down there?" she asked with hope in her tone, turning her skull to him in a silent plea. "I'd love to see it all properly."

"We'll go down in a minute. I thought it would be nicer for you to see what it's like from above." He faced her slightly so they could connect gazes. "It means you can gauge what it's like before dealing with all the people. It gets rather crowded, and I didn't want you lost or confused while you initially took it all in."

Even from way up here, she found it startling; she was new to all this.

Bright yellow lifted into her orbs, and she made sure she shone it at him, so he knew how much she appreciated that. *He is so kind to me.* He could have been inconsiderate and thrown her into a difficult situation without care, but he wisely hadn't.

It was just another reason why she liked him so much.

Leaning back to get comfortable while crossing her ankles, she soaked it all in as her gaze drifted every which way. She even followed a particularly tall Demon with large bat-like wings as they made their way through the crowd.

In the middle of the village stood some kind of statue, and

she thought it may have been a man. Since they were seated behind it, she couldn't see its features well, but he did look rather glorious with his clawed hand raised in a powerful stance. He had long hair and horns like Jabez, but she couldn't make out anything else – she figured these features were common in Demons.

Surrounding it was a path for pedestrians, with carts on the outside that had people lining up for whatever wares were being sold.

"I'm surprised they managed to make their own scent glamour," Jabez stated quietly. "Since I lost my ability to use magic, the permanent glamour I placed over the whole area would have disappeared."

She tilted her head at him. "You had a scent cloak on the village? Why?"

"They sell meat," he answered, pointing to where she could see the statue. "It can be unpleasant for those who haven't managed to control their urges against the scent of fear and blood. It also allows a haven for females, as it masks any heat pheromones. That cloak assists with many issues and allows everyone to walk freely without worry."

*I didn't think of that.* Her heart warmed that it was a safe place for females, and for those dealing with blood-lust. If she had scented blood, she may have already tried to climb down and hurt people.

"This place has always given me a sense of pride," he muttered, his voice soft and filled with satisfaction. "When I was discussing problems with the more highly evolved Demons, they informed me that they wanted a place they could congregate. A place like the Elven city, or the human towns. They wanted to feel like people, rather than like beasts."

Zylah turned her skull to him once more, and fondness swelled within her, hot and heavy.

He really did look more at ease now than before he'd reobtained his magic, and his gaze was filled with compassion. His lips had a small curl to them, but it was enough to round his cheeks and lightly crinkle the outer corners of his eyes. Long, loose white hair fluttered around his chiselled brown face in the light breeze, while his ears were pointed up but didn't appear alert.

He wasn't looking at her. Rather, his deep red eyes were fixated on the village of Demons, and they squinted with pleasure at different things.

Her heart quivered in her chest, as bright pink lifted into her orbs at seeing his handsome features so gentled. The unknown emotions that came with this strange, new colour were so bubbly and tender, awe radiated within her and kept her quiet as she listened.

"It took me months to grow the trees," he continued, his eyes scanning them in the distance. "I mapped out the space between each one, ensuring there would be plenty of room, and then planted the seeds. I spent most of my days in the lake that used to be in the middle, trying to grow them."

He let out a small chuckle, as if he was looking back at that time fondly. Her toes curled in delight at the dulcet sound.

"I would get so frustrated when it wasn't working. I read a book on growth magic when I was younger, and the instructions were simple. Just obtain a mana stone, place the seed, and then concentrate. I failed repeatedly until I realised I was expending too much of the little mana I had trying to grow them all at once. I had to sit at the base of each one and grow them individually, and *then* network them once they'd grown deep roots. The lake dried up as they took the nutrients from it."

Zylah couldn't imagine how much time and effort it must have taken to do all that. *He must always work hard.* She knew it to be true by how he taught her constantly and trained his body to keep it strong.

"Where we were earlier was the bottom of that lake. I placed a protection dome down so the stone had a place to rest while still feeding them magic. We filled it with dirt and boulders as best as we could, but that's why the village dips in at the middle." He drew a circle in the air to show where he meant, then his smile brightened as he looked up. "Every year, there was a celebration where I'd go down there and check the stone, feed it some of my own mana, and I'd make the trees bloom with red flowers. They were unnatural, so they quickly died by the end of the day, but the Demons here liked the entertainment.”

“You obviously care very deeply for this place,” Zylah stated, her orbs brightening in their pink hue.

She didn’t know what the colour meant, and she didn’t care. It made her stomach flutter while her chest felt all fluffy and tingly. She *adored* the way it kind of hurt.

She wished she hadn’t said anything because his face grew clouded and the cheer in it waned. He lowered his bent leg so it would dangle as well and rested his forearms on his thighs with his hands between them.

“This is one of the few things I’ve done that I haven’t regretted.” Then, as if to mask the sorrow she’d witnessed playing across his features, he drew a line in the air towards the village. “I actually helped construct lots of the buildings you see further in. There weren’t many of us at the time, so it took everyone pitching in to help to get this place established. I think I should have made it bigger, since they started to run out of space a few decades ago. I just hadn’t expected we’d all still be here.”

“What do you mean? Were you planning to leave?”

He turned to meet her gaze, his lips parted to say something. Instead, his eyes snapped open wide, and he darted closer to get a better look at her skull. Zylah startled and leaned back in surprise when his nose was barely an inch from her own.

“I don’t think I’ve ever seen a Mavka’s orbs turn pink before,” he said as he twisted his head, and a fang-filled grin curled his lips. “I wonder what this colour means. I thought I knew all of them.”

Zylah didn’t know why she felt the need to turn away and cover the side of her skull with her hand to hide it from him.

“I don’t know what it means either,” she grumbled, fidgeting shyly at the colour being commented on – which was odd, as she was usually fine with that.

“That’s okay,” he answered with a small shrug. “We can figure it out together. Perhaps it has to do with you being further from Weldir in blood, since I’ve also never seen teal until I met you.”

Zylah just nodded, unsure of how to respond.

As if he could sense she no longer wanted to speak about the colour of her orbs, he gestured towards the village with his chin. "So, are you ready to go down now?"

She looked out over the crowd of Demons below. "Yes."

"I'll need to place a glamour over both of us, though, as I'm unsure how they'll react to a Mavka. I also don't want to be noticed."

Twisting to face her, he bent one leg on top of the branch they were seated upon while the other remained hanging off the edge. He was slow to reach out to her skull, like he was unsure if she'd be comfortable with the touch, and she quickened the pace by leaning forward.

Zylah trusted him with all her heart, and she had absolutely no qualms about him touching her. Actually, she was hoping anything and everything they did now would allow them to become intimate like what they did within the mana stone's pocket of earth.

Since he was wearing his shirt and cloak, she couldn't tell if any of his symbols lit up upon his body. She felt warmth buzzing around her skull like fluttering moths, and she giggled at the way it tickled. Her toes splayed and then clenched, and she squirmed a little.

"What kind of glamour are you giving me?" she asked, when the fluttering descended over her body.

"Nothing too substantial," he answered, his brows furrowing as he concentrated. "I'm changing your face to look more like a deer's with fur to match your antlers, since having them on a rabbit is a little strange and may draw attention to you. I'm also hiding your skeletal bones, and shifting your fur to look more like the night sky reflecting off water, as with most Demons. I'm also giving you eyes, since your orbs would be a dead giveaway."

"Would that not make me look like a..." She had to think for a moment to remember what he called them. "Lesser Demon?"

"One's appearance doesn't always match their humanity level. If a Demon consumes many kinds of animals, especially the same type, and just as many humans, the physical transformation can be delayed." He shrugged as he pulled his hands away, and the fluttering settled to only a tiny tingle. "There are actually quite a number of Demons that prefer to keep their beastly appearance for ease of life. Fayren, for example, was keen on keeping some of her fox nature because it makes her swifter. Some prefer to even keep their wings and tails. It really depends on the Demon, but being at that level of humanity means they can consciously make that decision."

As usual, Zylah appreciated that he was always so willing to explain such things to her – and often with great detail. She just wished he was more forthcoming about himself.

*Hopefully that will change.* He did say he'd eventually reveal it all to her, and she held onto that.

She didn't think anything he told her would make her have a change of heart. The pleasurable feeling in her chest from earlier hadn't gone unnoticed, especially as it continued to linger, and she knew it had a deep meaning. She didn't think her affections for him would wane easily, and it was because of the way he treated her.

Even now, his touch and words remained gentle. He'd always been kind to her, regardless of the fact that she was bigger, stronger, and faster than him. He didn't treat her like a beastly Mavka, but like a being worth being soft to.

"My turn," he stated, just as his features began to change.

His long hair morphed to black, while the red in his eyes brightened to mimic other Demons. Although his face shape didn't change, most of the brown in his skin darkened to a glossy, void black and covered from his right cheek to up and over his left temple, leaving only his mouth, nose and jaw the same. He did the same to his fingertips, while changing his nails to proper sharp, shiny black claws.

Her heart stuttered a little when she noticed two of his nails had been trimmed from touching her earlier, and the fact he now hid them did little to settle her. It was hard to forget that, considering her pussy still felt swollen from his enthusiastic ministrations.

Next, his black horns began to take on a dark-taupe colour, and the tips morphed to point at the ground rather than the sky. Two boorish tusks appeared to push his lower lip forward before they grew to the edges of his nose.

The changes were startling, and she turned her gaze away since his face was now strange. She also noticed that his scent had changed, which added to her uncertainty.

She scratched at the fur around her neck.

"There are many people down there," she started with an anxious note in her tone. "If I can't recognise your face or scent, how will I find you if we get separated?"

He waved his hands at her, gesturing for her to bring her skull forward once more. She did as she was instructed, and he covered her orbs with his palms.

"Since you don't have eyes, per se, I don't know if this will work, but there's no harm in trying."

More warmth radiated over her skull, although this time localised to her eye holes before slipping down her snout. Before he'd even removed his hands, she could once more take in his proper scent – although it felt layered with the unnatural one he'd given himself.

When his palms slipped away, his face was normal again. Small dots of perspiration lined his forehead, as if he found this expenditure of magic tiresome.

"Did it work?"

Zylah nodded. "It did. Thank you."

"Perfect," he said, before he lifted his arms above his head and arched his back to stretch. He tilted his head both ways to crack his neck before relaxing. "I'm going to leave you here for a few minutes on your own."

"What?" she exclaimed, turning her sight down to the long fall below her. The ground slipped further away, and her stomach tightened in nausea while her lungs seized. "Why?!"

"Because Spiral Haven has some of the best meat sticks and I'm fucking starving. If we want to have a good time, we need items for trade. Since it's still nighttime, I can go to that village near our cave and steal a bunch of shit. Demons are fond of human coin, but they do prefer useful items, and I know just the place to pilfer."

Her claws stabbed into her perch. "What if I fall off?"

"Don't do that – it'll hurt," he answered with a playful hint. "Just be a good girl and sit still for a few moments. I won't be long."

Before she could argue with him more about it, his grin was wicked and *mean* as he disappeared in a split second.

Zylah was left by herself.

*Okay. I can do this.* She tried to focus on the wide array of pedestrians below, and how excited she was to be among them soon.

# TWENTY-ONE

Once more steadying a wobbly Zylah with a grip on her forearm, Jabez waited for her to settle after they teleported from the tree branch to the ground. Since he could see past all the glamours he'd placed on them both, he waited until her white orbs morphed back to their alluring teal, then let her go so she could stand on her own.

He'd made sure they materialised in a spot where there were no people, as he was almost certain he was the only one with the ability.

It was a rare one, which had taken years to perfect.

*I'm still thankful I discovered the secret room in that ruined mountain library.* In Nyl'theria, many books and scrolls had been lost due to the Demon scourge and the Elvish fleeing, which had left treasures of knowledge behind for Jabez to find.

The Demons destroyed most of what lay within the main area of the library, except for a hidden section that held special scrolls of magic. Among other things, there was information on teleportation, portal magic, and the ability to regenerate — although that last one he discovered on his own through necessity.

Most of this knowledge had been deemed forbidden due to how dangerous it could be. He'd suffered many of the aftereffects from wrongly executing the different abilities and had nearly lost his life many times.

He couldn't teleport across realms, although he was sure if he held greater mana, he may have been able to. He'd originally learned how to do it so he could perfect singular portal magic. Unfortunately, portal magic was far more difficult, unless one were to create chaos portals.

He had managed to perfect that ability to a certain degree with the help of some exceedingly rare gilded ore.

He'd been hoping to create his own portal to Nyl'theria for the Demons to travel through, but the distance was too far, and just one portal alone could severely deplete his magic. In reality, the furthest Jabez could have created a portal was a few thousand kilometres – which mostly limited him to within the Veil.

*That magic is lost to me now.*

After the battle between himself, those pesky humans, and the Witch Owl, the necklace he'd smelted of gilded ore had been destroyed when he consumed its power to save his own life. A small cost to pay, considering he'd been holding up the weight of his own castle as it threatened to crush him.

Not that it'd mattered in the end.

*I can go back to that mine, but I don't think I'd risk it again.*

Gilded ore was considered sacred and mining it got you cursed. Then again, touching the very essence of the Gilded Maiden's tears – the head deity of the Elysian Elves – was considered taboo. He hadn't given a shit; she was no goddess of his and he refused to respect her rules when it meant more power for himself.

Still, although he deemed that endeavour a failure, his ability to teleport now was second nature to him. It was a useful tool in his arsenal and had made him appear godlike in the eyes of many worshipping Demons.

As much as it humoured him to see Zylah's knees turn inwards, he understood what she was experiencing. It was disorientating. He'd help her through it until her body adjusted to the sudden hurtling that brought on motion sickness.

*I have to be careful about how much magic I expend right now.* Teleporting so frequently and casting not only two physical glamours, two scent glamours, and giving her the ability to sense through them, already drained his newly re-invigorated magic heavily.

The mana stone he'd consumed only sparked his magic

back to life and gave him a little to immediately expend. It'd take time, days even, to be at his optimal strength and capacity.

*I probably shouldn't have altered my body so heavily.*

Although most of his glamour was visual, he did give himself one physical change; he tucked his balls and dick away behind a false seam. The likelihood of getting into a death brawl in Spiral Haven was exceptionally low, but Jabez liked to be prepared for anything.

Demons were rather callous when it came to battles, and they fought without honour. If they could tell he had something dangling between his legs, they'd waste no time trying to grab his nutsack with a clawed fist and squeeze until he screamed.

A quake of repulsion ripped through him in memory of the one time he'd actually been dealt such pain. Thankfully he'd managed to break their arm before they could rip his balls off, but it was now a fear he refused to repeat.

Thus, he constantly shielded all his dangly bits behind a seam like most Demons. Being punched there was preferable over a gory removal, although that could still make his eyes water in agony.

When he was alone with Zylah again, and wasn't surrounded by potential danger, he'd release them to their natural state. Doing so for the past two months had been pleasant, and it reminded him how much his precious jewels preferred the freedom.

*Ah, the things I have done to protect myself.* Another was hiding his Elvish markings by morphing them into the black streaks he'd displayed for most of his life, giving him more of a Demon appearance.

Once Zylah was able to stand on her own, she was quick to move, as if she wanted to throw herself into the chaos of the village. Her excitement was contagious, despite the fact that he'd walked these streets countless times.

He tried to see it through her eyes, especially when she let out a cute rasp at the twinkling lights moving here and there.

Now that they were on the ground, the last remaining fireflies swarmed as they tried to escape before dawn. Something about this place brought those insects here, and he often wondered if it was the nectar mead that many establishments sold.

Hanging between the browns, creams, and clay orange of the many buildings, lanterns helped to illuminate the splashes of colour. Red was the most common, but Demons enjoyed the luxuries of different colours. They tried to make Spiral Haven as bright and beautiful as possible, and they all involved themselves in that task.

The music was much louder now, as was the chattering and laughter coming from the throngs of people.

Her head twisted and jerked, facing one way and the other as she tried to pick up on strings of conversation. He thought the sudden loud influx of noise would bother or overwhelm her, but her excited panting and her bright-yellow orbs gave away that she was overjoyed.

*She's very different to the rest of her kind.*

She was tackling this head-on, when he knew other Mavka would have immediately been on high alert and aggressive. She even ran straight into a street without caution, and immediately bumped into a group of Demons who were distracted by a heated conversation.

They offered no apology, even when she stepped back in surprise and knocked into Jabez. He pushed against her lower back in order to stop her from tripping, and she turned to him with reddish-pink orbs.

"Oh wow. It really is busy!" she stated from their empty pathway, her head constantly scanning the crowds.

Many different Demons passed them as they made their way lower into the village, each of them on their own mission. Some looked nearly human with varying skin tones, while others had a mottled, patchy appearance that mixed in with their void-like absences of flesh. Then, of course, there were many more that completely lacked human flesh and still had more animalistic features.

"Careful," he warned when it looked as though she was about to throw herself into the street again. He grabbed her wrist to halt her. "It'll annoy people if you constantly barge into them. You have to be self-aware when in busy crowds."

She nodded as if she understood, but he had a funny feeling she wasn't truly listening.

"I've never seen so many people," she whispered with a coarse voice, before turning her head up to the closest rooftop.

A scrawny male with wings played some kind of flute. She pointed right at him and giggled when the male waved at her between notes. She was taller than everyone else, as was Jabez, making them easy to spot.

Most human-eating Demons didn't gain great feats of height, but he'd met Elf-eating ones that were nearly as tall as himself. Jabez had, and likely would, tower over everyone who wasn't a Mavka.

She waved back before facing Jabez with her feet stamping in joy, and he chuckled at her for it.

Part of him wanted to tell her to calm down, so she didn't draw too much attention to herself, but he also didn't want to take away her fun.

*This is the first time she's been in a village like this.* She likely wouldn't get to experience this again unless he brought her back here, or he achieved his goal and overtook the Elven city.

He also reminded himself that she'd been in isolation for all her life, and likely had oodles of energy to expend. He could imagine what that was like – feeling different and finally getting to experience being 'normal.'

When he visited here, he often wore a glamour just to hide his identity and mingle as someone other than himself. His presence as Jabez, the king of Demons, meant people treated him differently.

Which often robbed him of normality.

He'd been robbed of that from the moment he was born.

Which is why a small smile curled his lips as he watched her bounce on her little bunny feet. *It's nice to see her experience this so joyfully.* Even his chest radiated with warmth, although he wished he could have experienced such exhilaration alongside her.

At least he could do so vicariously through her.

Seeing she was getting impatient when she grabbed his forearm and tried to tug him into the street, he rolled his eyes playfully and let her lead him. Her touch was not unwelcome, even when she held his wrist and dragged him through the bulk of the crowd heading towards the centre of the village. They wanted to get to the markets before everything shut near dawn, which was when most of the stalls would close for their owners to grab a few hours' sleep.

Getting bumped into didn't bother him, but they each gained a wary eye as they passed people. He had to remind himself that he looked much different, and she appeared as a normal Demon.

Zylah pointed at everything that grasped her attention, which incidentally had her forearm shooting over the tops of heads. Many ducked, and a few wandered away from the potential of being smacked in the face with an irritated grumble or grunt.

He smiled at that. Even if she upset a few, Jabez was certain he'd be able to deescalate any situation should it come to that.

Perhaps because her feet moved so fast, it took a while for her to finally let out a yelp and stumble backwards. She hopped on one foot before tentatively placing it back on the ground.

She shuffled them to the side of the street. "Someone stepped on me."

The laughter that burst out of him was great and loud. "Zylah, I'm not sure if you noticed, but you've been stepping on everyone we've passed."

Multiple people had staggered because of her, and they hadn't even been on the street for five minutes.

"Sorry," she said to some random passer-by, who frowned and shook their head in confusion at receiving an apology.

He covered his face when the urge to laugh struck him again. *Fuck me. What am I supposed to do with this female?* He'd never seen her appear so bubbly, and he found it rather adorable.

She chittered nervously, and he lowered his hand to find her shoulders had turned inwards self-consciously at his snicker. He thought he'd hidden it well.

"It's fine. They'll get over it. A moment forgotten in the many others they'll have." When that didn't seem to appease her, he cocked a brow as he tried to hide his humour. "How about I lead?"

He should have been doing that in the first place.

He waited for a nice pocket of space to open up before he took them back into the crowd. This time, they were able to walk side by side with ease, and he made sure they remained at the same pace as everyone else.

"They really can't see us," she stated with awe.

He placed his forefinger over his lips. "Not too loud with comments like that." His gaze drifted over those around them, and thankfully no one had noticed. "It's also best that you refrain from saying my name."

He really didn't need someone realising who he was.

"Okay. I'll do better with that than last time."

He nodded to show his approval before he deviated off the main path to one that was a little less crowded.

*I don't want to take her to the centre of the town.*

They had no reason to go to the meat market, and he wanted to avoid looking upon the ridiculous statue they'd made of him. He really hated that thing, and how Demons sometimes knelt and prayed to it like he was some kind of deity or saviour. He was neither, obviously.

But people of all species needed a faith to cling to, and he'd allowed the Demons to hold onto his promises. It kept them compliant.

They emerged onto one of the widest pathways designated for popular food stalls. Demons were already lining up for certain carts, all of which contained some kind of meat. Each store specialised in a different way to cook or serve it.

Whatever scent cloak they were using to mask the food was efficient, ensuring all those nearby who couldn't control their bloodthirst weren't impacted. Unlike his cloaking spell that allowed the waft of herbs, spices, and oils to float through the air while hiding the smell of meat, he noticed theirs cloaked everything.

It was a sad realisation, as it took away an important aspect of walking through a food market, but it was something that couldn't be changed without his interference. Surely in the future they would eventually figure out how to mimic what he'd been able to do, but for now, this was sufficient to allow for harmony within Spiral Haven.

He slowed their pace to more of a meander to allow Zylah freedom to take it all in. Despite certain meats not being to his liking, he allowed her to be curious. She could likely read the signs crudely written on wooden plaques, although some were faded and needed repainting.

Some offered small spiced chicken pancakes, while others sold steamed baked potatoes sprinkled with pork. One of the most popular stalls was that of a folded omelette mixed with flecks of human meat, and another of fried fish on a stick.

What Jabez sought was simple, and his mouth watered the moment he found it. The stall was busy, as it always was due to its tasty contents.

They waited in line, and when it was their turn, he didn't hold back.

"Three beef skewers and one chicken," he told the male Demon attendant behind the counter working a coal grill.

Ansel, who bore a slashing claw scar across his entire tanned face, nodded, held his palm outwards, and flapped his fingers. A person of few words, he was asking what Jabez's offer of trade was.

He placed a single piece of square human coin, pressed with a corn cob design to show which town it came from, into the man's hand. Ansel picked it up and inspected it before curling his scarred lips back with disdain.

The burly Demon wiped the sweat away from his brow with his thick, hairy forearm, smudging charcoal up to his blond hair, then wiped his palm on his stained white apron. He threw four skewers onto his coal grill next to the many others already cooking, then slapped wooden tokens down on the counter. Three of them indicated beef, while the fourth represented chicken. Then he nodded his head for Jabez to move to the side.

A knowing smile curled Jabez's lips as he took the tokens.

*Had I come here with my usual glamour, he may have been more welcoming.* The one Jabez currently wore was new, ensuring he wouldn't have someone pull him into a conversation and push Zylah to the side by accident. To Ansel, he was just another nobody; a fresh face among the thousands who came here.

"Why did he look unhappy with your payment?" Zylah asked as she huddled between him and the stall's corner.

"He prefers spices," Jabez muttered quietly, watching as Ansel cooked. His stomach grumbled at the idea of proper food after fucking *months* of eating raw meat, fruit, and vegetables. "It's always best to trade with what they are interested in. Food market stalls prefer anything that helps them continue cooking, whereas craftsmen prefer certain stones and crystals."

"But he took it anyway? Was that a human coin?" she asked, causing him to cock his brow in surprise that she knew that. "I read about them in one of my books. Money, they call it?"

"They'll take what they can get and will later trade those items with others for what they need. Jewellers will always take some form of coin because they can melt them down or make charms out of them."

"Can I try paying for something next time?" she asked, her skull twitching side to side in bashfulness.

"Sure. Next time I'll make sure it's the appropriate trade."

She nodded, her orbs flaring bright yellow in joy, before darkening into curiosity – the colour they had been since they'd begun adventuring through the village. Zylah constantly watched everyone passing by, occasionally rudely staring at those with distinct features.

He couldn't tell if she was more curious about those who looked more human, or those with obvious snouts. Someone with a piggish nose and tusks snorted laughter, gaining her focus until they looked upon her like they felt her stare. She didn't pull away from them, and almost rotated her head a hundred and eighty degrees as she walked past them.

A loud grunt called his attention. Jabez pulled away from his leaning post to place the tokens down on the counter while taking the offered skewers.

His mouth watered further at them in both his hands, and he immediately devoured one of the beef skewers drizzled in some kind of peppery sauce. He threw the wooden stick into the bin next to the stall – something Ansel had set up to help with waste management.

Zylah watched him intently as he chewed the last piece, then he held the single skewer in his left hand out to her.

"Want one?" he offered.

She tilted her head, then shook it. "No. I don't want to go into a rage."

Jabez rolled his eyes and waved it in the air at her again. "You won't. Since the smell of it is hidden, and it isn't raw, it'll do little more than make you a bit hungrier."

"Then why would I want to eat it?"

"Because it's fucking delicious?" When she still didn't take it, he sighed. "Just trust me. I wouldn't tell you to try it if I wasn't certain of your reaction."

She tentatively took it, allowing him freedom to steal the chicken skewer from his other hand and begin devouring it. She was hesitant to take a bite, as if she thought it was poisoned, and grew annoyed when sauce dribbled onto her fingers.

Since she didn't often open her mouth, it allowed him to watch how her maw parted. The large holes in her rabbit jawbone split apart alongside the black jagged teeth that filled in those gaps, but her ability to chew was stilted by the fact that she didn't have cheeks to contain her food. He wondered if he should, at some point, explain to her why she had such a function.

*Her kind look like little blobs as younglings.* They remained featureless, black, and almost gooey in nature until they ate their first creature. But he'd learned something peculiar about them as adults by fearlessly poking around inside of Merikh's mouth in curiosity.

Their featureless baby heads fitted inside their adult skulls, helping to fill in the gaps and crevices so their drool didn't leak and their tongues didn't dry out. It also kept their jaws together by sinew and tendons, and filled in their empty eye sockets, so what lay deeper within their craniums remained hidden.

Their skulls were merely exterior.

Her rabbit teeth and black jagged Mavka fangs parted in surprise as she sniffed the first chunk of meat, and she threw it across her tongue to fully taste it. As he thought they would, her orbs turned red, but she hummed in enjoyment. She was quick to swallow and consume the rest, although her fur puffed a little in aversion when she ate them too quickly.

"It tastes amazing, but it hurts my stomach after a little while," she stated, throwing her stick away when he did.

"That's the only problem for your kind. You may like how it tastes, but it doesn't curb your hunger, and if it isn't fresh meat, it doesn't sit well."

"If you knew that, why did you let me eat it?"

Answering around a cheek full of food, he said, "Didn't it feel nice to experience something everyone else can?" He pointed his last half-eaten beef skewer at another person, who was scoffing their food down like their life depended on it. "Experiencing sensations is the joy of life. Food is a big one for most, and the better it tastes, the more enjoyable it is."

She cupped the end of her snout in deep thought, lingering on what he said, before nodding. "Thank you. I guess it was nice, and I've never done that before. I didn't even think to try."

*I know, which is why I'm allowing this outing.*

He was in high spirits today, even with how horribly it'd started. His gaze lifted up towards the twisting canopy above, trying to muster up the regret he'd felt earlier. A small amount came, but not enough to squash his elevated mood.

When he'd woken up at Fayren's that morning, sour from a shitty sleep, he'd resigned himself to cut off any form of attraction he held for Zylah. It was safer for her and safer for his peace of mind.

*I can't believe I didn't even last a full day.*

In the underground pocket of earth, the chaotic energy sparking beneath his skin had caused him to falter with very little effort from her. His magic had stimulated his senses. He'd been foolishly overwhelmed from his body heating up with life, and the sensation of power thrumming through him pestered other parts of him.

He still didn't know what had overcome him when he'd threaded vines over her limbs, but her scent of jasmine and violets had fuelled the flames within him. Even the warmth of her waist between his thighs had tingled his groin, and her panting had been exciting.

Months of no magic and weeks of his emotions swirling into a whirlwind of disarray had warped his damn brain. That, and constantly ignoring his desire for this female, broke his resolve a lot faster than he could say he was proud of.

Then she'd licked him, kissed him in her own way, and his heart had pounded with feral need. He may have resisted if he hadn't bitten her, but the moment he sank his fangs into her and she accepted them, his brain had feverishly melted.

*I gave in so easily.* He'd like to think he wouldn't do so again, but he was self-aware enough to know the truth. *I like her.* He was attracted to her, regardless of the fact that he didn't fucking know *why.*

The moment she turned around as if she wanted to move on, his gaze drifted down to her arse.

His nose wrinkled as a quiet groan hummed behind his lips. *I should have touched her fucking tail.* He'd been wanting to for ages, and he'd had the perfect opportunity and he'd squandered it.

He wanted to know if it was as soft as it looked, if it was sensitive. Did she like it being touched, or would it wiggle in his palm in aversion? Was her spine sensitive right above it like most with tails?

As much as he wanted to touch it, he considered it as inappropriate as just grabbing her breast, arse, or between her thighs at random. And he wasn't so pathetic to 'slyly' attempt to do so in his own perverted curiosity. He'd either find out next time, which he would try to resist, or not at all.

It was probably a good thing he didn't know, as it would only make him naughtier. The urge to twirl his forefinger around the tip of that fluffy tuft to tease her was nigh overwhelming.

At this rate, he doubted he'd last until the end of tomorrow either. *I'm still fucking horny.* Whatever enzyme was present in her arousal fluids continued to tingle his lips and fingers, and having it in his system from eating her out was keeping him high with need.

Her little moans and soft pants had also been sweet in his ears, and watching her bashful reactions to his ministrations still frolicked in his mind. She also seemed to be a needy creature for someone who was new to sexual intimacy, which only made him wonder what she'd be like if she had experience. What would she be like if she truly learned how to tease sensually? What about if she took control in a way that gave his hands freedom to caress as they pleased?

Her fur was so damn soft it'd tickled his face and palms earlier. What would it look and feel like to experience her tail brushing over his abdomen as he shoved his cock into her from behind? Jabez mildly shuddered at the imagery, while his shaft jerked behind his false seam.

Yes, still very horny, and after what they'd done, his mind had more to add to that perverted fantasy.

However, looking upon her tail, and the bottom of her plump, fur-covered butt did make him frown. *Shit. I forgot her dress doesn't fully cover her.*

He glanced at those passing by, making sure no one was leering at her. Skilfully holding his last skewer, he managed to untie his cloak one-handed and throw it over her shoulders to shield her. He didn't like how his ears heated in embarrassment when his motives for doing so weren't entirely selfless – there was the smallest possessive need to hide those features from other males... like an *idiot.*

She pulled it so it sat better, while tilting her head in question.

"I think it's time we acquire you proper clothing." Something that wasn't crudely made by him.

He removed the last two pieces of meat from his stick so he could toss it into the bin. Sauce leaked onto his fingers as he ate and led the way to a suitable garment store a few streets over.

From the corner of his eye, he noticed her orbs flicker purple for just a second as he was licking sauce from his thumb and middle finger.

The sane part of him told him he shouldn't do what his mind suggested, while the more devious side of him was as perverted as always. Then again, what was a little mild teasing when he'd had his head shoved between those furry thighs of hers not even two hours ago?

He extended his decently long tongue and purposefully

wrapped it around his thumb, then drew the digit into his mouth to suck it. He made sure to hold her gaze, and her orbs flickered a brighter purple. She chittered before looking away.

A laugh rumbled in his chest as he brought his middle finger in next, although he didn't do anything perverted with it since she'd looked away. Her shy reaction had been cute, and it only made him want to tease her further.

*Mavka make it too easy to mess with them.*

Their colour-changing orbs were like a book to him, and unfortunately for her, he was blatantly aware of what her mind wrote.

*This is fun.* He couldn't remember the last time he'd freely enjoyed himself like this in a female's company.

It helped that he'd recently come, finally expelling much of his need. He was sexually sated for now, with a gut full of tasty food, and he had an alluring person fuelling him with high spirits.

Nights like this were non-existent in his life, and he'd try to savour it without regret.

He was uplifted despite the tiredness that began to weigh on him. With his weaker than normal mana waning from the creation of their scent masks and glamours, and his excessive use of teleporting, as well as the lack of proper sleep in nearly a week, everything was waning his strength.

Jabez ignored his exhaustion for now, for her sake. He could rest later.

*There's much more I can show her here.* And, for the first time in a long while, he was actually looking forward to it.

Zylah wasn't vain, she wasn't self-centred, nor was she high-handed. He'd never courted a female like that, someone who didn't exude confidence, and he was surprised to find he liked it.

*I think taking her shopping will be nice.*

It hadn't originally been in his plans for tonight, but he had a feeling she'd be charming and appreciative.

# TWENTY-TWO

Zylah looked up at a painted wooden sign nailed above a door frame. "Goldie's Garments," it read in big white words.

She hesitated to enter until Jabez placed his hand on the small of her back and gently pushed her forward.

From the scent coming from the azure door, there was at least one female Demon inside. Walking through a street of them was one thing, but her past experiences told her she wasn't wonderful at making conversation. She doubted her books that detailed such stores would actually be beneficial.

A bell chimed above as they both ducked beneath the tiny door frame, informing the attendant of their entrance. Zylah startled at the unfamiliar noise and spun to inspect it, tapping at the golden bell with a claw so it would make the noise again.

Her head twitched when the female said something in greeting, but she didn't understand the language whatsoever.

She turned to a Demon behind a large wooden counter who looked completely like a human except for her red eyes and the sand-coloured ram-like horns that curled behind her ears. Her blonde hair pulled back into a neat bun fully revealed her lightly tanned complexion. She was obviously beautiful with her small lips, sharp features, and darker blonde brows.

Zylah brought her gaze to the back of Jabez, who was deeper within the establishment, when he responded in the same unfamiliar language.

They spoke among themselves momentarily, and she was able to understand two words: *English* and *Nyl'theria.*

The Demon pursed her lips, then turned and curled them up in Zylah's direction as if she wanted to appear inviting. Zylah clasped her hands near her chest as nervousness skittered beneath the surface of her flesh.

"My apologies. It's rare to find Demons of your heights who don't know Elysian. My name is Madame Goldie, but you can just call me Goldie."

"This is Zylah," Jabez stated, while taking off the cloak he'd placed around her shoulders, as if to fully reveal her, before clipping it back around his own throat. "She's the only one you need to worry about. I'm just the trade pouch tonight."

Goldie laughed so brightly her eyes filled with mirth. "We like males like you; ones that understand their place in my store."

"What does she mean?" Zylah whispered to him.

He glanced at her. "There is no male clothing here."

"Unless you, sir, wish to buy something for yourself. If so, I have no objections, and I have much that will fit your frame."

A small chuckle fell from him as he waved his hand dismissively near his temple. "No, that will be fine. Just attend to Zylah, and I'll sit in the waiting area."

He stepped to the side and sunk into a long lounge that could have fit three of him side by side. The brown leather cushions squeaked as he made himself comfortable, throwing his arms across the backrest while he placed his right ankle on top of the opposing knee.

He looked all self-important in his cream tunic, mauve pants with a front flap, and his cloak spread out across the chair. Some of his long hair had settled against his wide chest, and with his ears upright and his black horns catching the light, he appeared overconfident and relaxed.

Having no idea what to do, Zylah chittered with both their gazes on her. Her shoulders turned inwards, and she distracted herself by looking around.

The direct area she stood in was open and square. With the door behind her, and the seat to her right, clothing hung from horizontal poles against every available wall. To the left had more space and garments, and a long supporting wall cut the area off.

Above, and offering plenty of distance from her antlers, hung a simple iron chandelier full of candles. It provided plenty of light and ensured the store was bright and welcoming.

There was room to go further into the establishment, and the counter Goldie was situated behind partially blocked it off. Two sets of white drapes hung to the ground, both open, with booths behind them.

Goldie stood from some kind of stool and came out from behind the counter. Her long red dress with a side split danced across the wooden floors while a set of tall, strappy black shoes clicked on each step. Zylah noted that the dress was formfitting and was so tight it allowed her large breasts to pool into the low neckline as if they were moments from spilling out.

"My breasts are not that big," Zylah commented, pointing at her bosom. "I don't think such an outfit will suit me."

The female gave a sultry laugh while shaking her head as if Zylah had said something strange. Now that she was closer, she noted that the little Demon barely came to her chest height even with her tall shoes. Yet, she suddenly felt too big and imposing, and Zylah backed up a step and cast a set of reddish-pink orbs at Jabez to ask for assistance.

His expression was blank, and he remained where he was seated.

"Everyone can pull off this outfit, no matter their body shape." She tentatively reached out to Zylah's side and gently nudged her to the left, where all the garments were hanging. "But don't worry. If it's not something you'd like to wear, I offer many styles. Do you know what you'd prefer? Your current outfit is a bit... how do I put this kindly? Crude? Do you want something this short again, or something longer?"

Too many questions were thrown at her, and she didn't like the mean comment regarding the dress Jabez had made for her. She looked over her shoulder to see if he was upset, but he looked the same: completely unhelpful.

"No. I don't know what I want."

"Hmm. Alright, big boy, are you willing to be a good puppy and sit there for us, no matter how long this takes?" she asked, slightly raising her voice.

"Depends on if it will take until dawn," Jabez answered nonchalantly. "There are other places I want to take her."

Goldie looked at Zylah from the corner of her eye and drifted her gaze down to her feet before coming back up to her face. Zylah was not surprised she wasn't put off by her skull like Fayren was at first, due to the glamour hiding her, but it still felt strange to have it looked upon.

"No, it won't take that long," Goldie eventually responded, before going through articles of clothing, pulling hangers apart to get a better look at each one. "Alright, Zylah, your height will be a bit of a challenge, since I don't get many people in this tall, but I think I have three outfits we can start with to get a better idea of what you'd like."

Like she'd done this hundreds of times, Goldie pulled pieces of clothing from their poles. Moving quickly as she searched, she threw them over her shoulder one by one while taking wide steps to avoid dozens of others. It was like she knew roughly where they were located within her mind.

"Could you please follow me to the change room, Zylah?" Goldie gave the smallest bow, and her tall shoes clicked as she walked away.

Zylah rushed to follow, wishing she didn't feel so out of place. Goldie gestured for her to stand inside one of the booths before hanging up two of the garments on a hook to the left and then placing a set on the right one.

"Get changed, then come out and show us," she said, offering another welcoming smile as she closed the white drape.

Zylah's breaths sounded loud in the confined space as she reached down to pull off her light-grey dress. She halted as she took in the garments before her, unsure which one to start with; there were too many choices. She would have preferred to have been given one at a time.

*I don't... like this.* This wasn't fun, and her knees knocked together when she was unclothed.

When she took too long, Goldie called out to her, and her fur puffed in worry. She quickly turned and grabbed some kind of long, frilly white tunic and shoved it on.

Since she'd seen Jabez button his tunic many times, she tried to copy what she could remember. She fumbled with the buttons down the front, and not even sheathing her claws seemed to help.

*Shit,* she muttered, having learned this was an appropriate word for moments such as this. *Shit! I don't know how to do this!*

Giving up, she yanked on the brown skirt, and was thankful there was only one large button which was easy to thread through the hole. With her hands now shaking, wondering if she was taking too long, she attempted to do up the stupid tunic.

"Zylah?" Goldie's voice called. "Do you need some assistance, doll?"

"I... um." The embarrassed hue in her sight brightened. "Yes."

She almost shrieked when Goldie opened the drape and entered the tight space with her.

"First time with buttons?" she asked, her tone lacking any condescension or judgement. She shone her red eyes up at Zylah, and they came across as kind and understanding. "Don't be nervous. Many people who come here are new to them. I'm happy to assist, and you can watch what I'm doing to learn."

She said this, yet she was so swift that her hand movements were almost a blur. Zylah did observe the way she pushed them through the holes and used her fingertips to wedge them a certain way. Once they were done up to almost her neck, Goldie undid the button of the nearly floor-length skirt so she could tuck the white tunic into it. Then she yanked it up to Zylah's waist, and put the button through a different hole she hadn't seen to make it snug.

She opened the drape and gestured for Zylah to exit before spinning her to some kind of reflection. She was more interested in what the odd device was, considering she'd never seen it before, and wondered how it was standing out in the open.

"Here, let me adjust the mirror for you," Goldie said, as she tilted it back slightly to allow Zylah to see herself in full.

"What do you think?"

She shrugged and turned to Jabez; she would make him help her pick something since this was his big stupid idea. His face was already in her direction, and his features cringed to the point his lips pulled to the side and partially revealed his fangs.

"Do you like it?"

Zylah patted the skirt before itching at her covered arms. Immediately upon realising something was lying over her fur, she began to scratch at herself. "It's itchy and long."

"Thank fuck for that," he rasped. "You look like a peasant farmer."

"Okay, nothing that covers the arms," Goldie said, before reaching into the changeroom to take the longer dress away that had sleeves. She quickly returned with a similar one that lacked them.

Before Zylah knew it, she was shoved back inside the horrible changeroom again. After watching Goldie before, she was able to undo the buttons herself and take off the clothing. A hand shoved in through a gap in the booth as Goldie told her to give her hangers and clothing to put away.

Zylah grabbed the long black dress that was just put there and was thankful it lacked buttons. She was easily able to slip it over her head and thread her arms through, although she had to squeeze it over her wide backside. She hated the way it pushed her tail down until it was lying flat along her rump, rather than going up her lower back.

She opened the drape herself.

"That one's much better," Jabez commented, as if he could feel her growing glare of frustration.

With just a few words, he managed to soothe her.

However, she only took two steps forward in her normal long strides before the constricting skirt made her fumble. Jabez rose to help, just as Goldie held her arms out to catch her before she completely tripped over.

Zylah chittered as her sight turned blue and began to waver at the bottoms. She let out a whine. "I don't want to do this anymore."

"Okay, no long, constricting skirts," Goldie offered with a

sympathetic smile. "How about you try the last one on? It's similar to the one you wore in, although it has a little more coverage on the legs."

Her whines didn't settle when she was helped back inside the booth. She attempted to take the dress off and almost ripped it trying to get it back over her thick backside. She gazed at the last garment in disdain, wanting to tear it to shreds and don her light-grey one.

Still, she gave the long one to Goldie's extended hand and put the shorter one on.

Dark green, and somewhat form fitting around her chest, this dress was cut low, but in a way the collar of fur around her neck filled it in completely. Its skirt was actually rather flowy and came midway down her thighs. It lacked any major design and was plain except for some black cross stitches along every seam.

She felt more comfortable, since it was similar to the one Jabez made her, just longer and looser around her legs.

"Oh wow, that looks wonderful on you," Goldie complimented, her hands quietly clapping in front of her, but Zylah didn't trust her.

Zylah turned to the mirror, and twisted one way and the other to see what it looked like. Maybe Goldie wasn't lying, as she did rather like it. She spun to Jabez with her arms open at her sides.

"I like it," he offered, giving her a small smile. "It suits you, and it looks like you're comfortable."

*I liked Goldie's compliment better,* Zylah grumbled, before turning to adjust her pushed-down tail. It looked like a lump on her backside.

"I don't like the way it pushes on my tail," she muttered, worried about disappointing them.

"That's fine. This was just a trial dress," Goldie said, walking over to her counter to grab some kind of flat string lying on top of it. There were numbers on it, and Zylah tried to work out what it was when she brought it over. "If you don't mind lifting the back, I can measure your tail and find one that has a suitable hole for it. Do you like this colour, or would you prefer a different one? I have forest green, navy, crimson, black, and white."

"It can't be white," Jabez stated. "That'll stain too easily. I also think black would fade into her fur too much."

Zylah couldn't have been more thankful for his input. "What is navy?"

"It's a dark blue," Goldie answered as she lifted the back of the skirt, which Zylah held for her.

She liked that it would be similar in colour to her orbs, and she didn't want to be hidden in the forest if she wore green. Red also seemed too flamboyant, especially on Goldie, although she wasn't entirely opposed to it.

"Can I try the navy one?"

"Mhm. Of course." Goldie pulled away while holding a certain measurement and went to the hanging clothes to go through them.

She came back with a dark-blue one and Zylah quickly ducked behind the curtain to change into it. She managed to find the tail slit herself, and it was much more comfortable having it poking out. *It reminds me of Fayren's skirt.* No wonder she had clothing that allowed her red fox tail to swing freely.

The moment she stepped out of the change room, both gazes were fixed on her.

"You were right, navy suits you better," Jabez commented, nodding in approval.

"This is actually one of my favourite dresses I've made," Goldie said, eying Zylah from head to toe. "If you spin, it'll show you why."

Zylah did as she was instructed and was pleasantly surprised when the skirt fanned out wide. *Oooh, pretty!* Her orbs finally morphed into something other than embarrassment, and bright yellow shone in her sight. A small giggle fell from her, as she was excited about the function and how surprisingly flowy it was. She spun the other way, watching it twist before it fanned out again.

*I like this one.* Perhaps even more than the one he made.

She looked over her shoulder and wiggled her tail to make it vibrate, happy with the freedom and the way it looked. She turned to Jabez to ask if she could get this one, only to immediately pause.

His features had lost their aloof softness and instead had a dark, hardened edge to them. His eyes zeroed in on where she'd just wiggled her tail and backside since her side had been turned to him. His jaw was clenched, cheek muscles twitching as his gaze slowly moved up her body.

Palming his face and turning it away, he muttered so lowly she barely heard him, "Fuck, that was cute." He waved his other hand in the air. "That one. We'll get her that one."

Zylah didn't know if it was his heated expression, his words, or the way his ears drooped, but one or all three caused flutters low in her belly. She'd been uncomfortable during this entire process until now, and she scratched at the fluffy fur of her neck when she realised something so simple stimulated her desire.

*He likes it.* The dress, the way she spun, her tail wiggling... *her.*

If picking an outfit gave him that kind of reaction, she was far more inclined to do it again. She drifted her sight to Goldie's much more sensual outfit. If she hadn't stumbled, would he have found her as alluring in it as the little Demon was?

Goldie let out a small feminine chuckle at their exchange before gently holding Zylah's wrist to spin her towards her. She patted down her sides to push the dress down and make it sit better.

"Do you want to wear it out, or do you want to change into your other garment?"

"Can I wear this?" Zylah asked, her voice thick.

"That was the point," Jabez grated out with strain.

Goldie entered the booth and collected Zylah's grey dress with a rather rude pinch of her fingers. She also picked up her satchel and gave both to her.

"If it were me, I'd incinerate the old one, but perhaps you can wear it as a nightgown." Then she dipped her head towards Jabez. "Unless you're planning to buy a second dress. I have plenty more, and I am having a ball with you two."

Zylah grumbled at the incineration comment, quickly tucking her beloved gift from him into her bag before the

Demon could take it away.

"Ask her," Jabez stated behind his hand. "The trade I'm offering is worth at least three of your best quality garments."

Goldie's features brightened, and her sultry eyes lit up with joy and *greed.* "Well, Zylah? Do you want to look at others?"

"Can I have this, but in the crimson?" Zylah asked, wanting Jabez to get some of his trade's worth but refusing to put herself back inside that horrible booth. She would refuse a third if they tried to make her pick one.

"Of course."

As Goldie went to fetch another dress, Zylah walked over to Jabez. His ears shot up at her approach, but he only lowered his hand from his face when she poked him in the shoulder.

"Can I trade for it?" She wanted to have a play at partaking in a transaction.

His lips were tight as he opened his satchel. What he obtained was small, and she tilted her head at it when he placed it in her outreaching palm. She'd seen this once before, but in black.

*This doesn't look like it would be worth much.*

Still, she shrugged and took it to the counter, since Goldie was standing behind it with an expectant look.

"What have you got for me?" Goldie asked, and Zylah held her hand out with her palm facing up. The Demon's red eyes widened, and she snatched it so fast her movements were a blur. "Holy shit! How did you get this?! It's barely even used. Do you know how many dresses I can make with this, how many colours I can dye it?"

Zylah hadn't expected her to be so excited over a white roll of sewing thread. It wasn't even particularly large.

Though, seeing the difference between a Demon selling wares receiving a lacklustre trade in comparison to a worthwhile one was remarkable. Would that meat-stick-selling merchant have been giddy had he received what he would've preferred?

"You little puppy!" Goldie exclaimed across the counter while tilting to the side to look at Jabez. "This isn't worth three, it's worth five. You made a poor trade this day, giving me this for only two dresses."

One side of his mouth twitched in obvious humour, as he finally stood and approached. He pulled Zylah's new crimson dress across the counter and tucked it into her satchel for her.

"I think you're forgetting the cost of her enjoyment in receiving your garments," he commented, flicking his gaze to Zylah before looking away. "You have been a welcoming attendant and made this much easier for her. Your reputation in customer service precedes you."

"Oh, hush," Goldie said, flapping one of her hands forward. "Everyone deserves to feel sublime and comfortable. I'm only here to dress canvases of beauty."

He chuckled at that, while Zylah took the compliment even if it wasn't meant for her.

"Ready to leave?" he asked her, and she nodded.

He put his hand on the small of her back again to lead her, and her feet were slow to move when she noticed how *low* his hand placement was. If he went any further down, he would have put his hand over her upward-pointing tail tuft.

Actually, she thought his pinkie may have touched the very tip of it.

He pulled the door open for her, the bell above ringing as he did, and ushered her forward. Zylah stepped onto the empty pathway, and he veered them to the right.

"Where are we going now?" she asked, anxiously looking around at the different signage.

She hoped it wasn't anything that would be as awkward as Goldie's Garments. But, now that she'd experienced such a setting, she may be more at ease with the next one.

"To a shoemaker," he answered, his eyes never leaving their path like he knew exactly where he was going.

"Why?" She dipped her gaze towards his bare feet. "You don't wear them."

"It's not for me. The Elvish don't wear shoes, since we're capable of using magic through our feet. We must touch the ground in order to do that."

"But I don't need them," she argued. "I'm comfortable how I am."

"You're not making it easy to splurge on," he answered with a mildly annoyed sigh. "Even if we walk out empty-handed, the experience is all that matters. It'll also hurt less if someone steps on your toes."

Zylah silently grumbled, but allowed him to lead the way without any more complaints. She did have a question, though.

"Why did Goldie call you puppy? What is that?" she asked, looking down at her new dress. Satisfaction radiated within her heart and mind as she watched the way it danced around her thighs. "She also called me doll. What is a doll?"

"A puppy is a baby dog, think like a wolf, and a doll is usually a pretty toy in the shape of a woman. The nicknames are meant to be engaging, and it was Goldie sweetening you up so you would enjoy yourself. Since I didn't give her my name, she used puppy as a way to refer to me – another way to sweeten the transaction in hopes we would give her a preferable trade. She's always been like that. She's very cunning when it comes to making her customers feel wonderful upon leaving her establishment."

"Oh," Zylah rasped, her head falling at the crushing realisation that hit her. "So she was only nice to me to get a good trade?"

He slowed their pace when he must have heard the dejected tone in her voice.

"No. I can tell she genuinely liked you by the end."

She raised her head and turned it to him. "Why do you think that?"

His eyes narrowed in a way that almost appeared annoyed. "Because I've seen what it looks like when she doesn't like the person she is tending to." He glanced at her from the corner of his eyes before rolling them at the dark yellow that lifted into her orbs. "I'm assuming you want me to elaborate?"

Zylah nodded. "Yes, please."

"Despite her youthful appearance, Goldie is almost as old as I am. She didn't travel to this realm with me, but she was part of the first few swarms that came from Nyl'theria and she was quick to develop while she was here. She doesn't look it, but she is an exceptionally skilled and ruthless hunter. Her interest in clothing was one of the reasons she had the most persistent voice in me creating this village. She actually hated hunting, and she refused to do any form of farming. Simply looking at her, you can tell she's the kind of person who prefers to live luxuriously."

"What does this have to do with her not liking the person she is tending to?"

His cheeks crinkled into a cringe, then he smoothed his expression. "I'm explaining that. As you know, I've been on Earth for hundreds of years, and there have been just as many Demons who have as well." His lips tightened as he turned his face to her while they walked, and he sighed in irritation. "If I wish to bring a female to go shopping for clothing, Goldie's is where I always take them. She is the best in the village, not just in the quality of her clothing, but also in her professionalism."

"You have taken other females there?"

Zylah didn't know how she felt about that. A rather detestable feeling clung to her sternum, but she tried to shed it, as she didn't understand why she was having such a reaction. Or why it made her orbs flicker a colour she'd never seen before: bright green.

Thankfully he didn't see the change, and they morphed back to her normal teal before he turned his gaze to her again.

"Goldie and I have a good, although minimal, friendship. To your face, she is all smiles, but if she doesn't like her customer, and there is no one else in the store to see, she will sneer behind your back. Her dislike of someone never changes how she treats a person, so everyone adores her no matter how she feels towards them. Difficult customers annoy her."

"But I was difficult," Zylah stated with her heart dropping. "I didn't know what I wanted."

"That doesn't bother her. She would've had fun watching you try on every outfit in her store, ensuring you left happy." He halted them to run his fingers through his long hair, exasperated by something. The fact he was able to retain eye contact with her let her know she wasn't the source. "The last person I took there, we frequented the shop whenever the whim struck her. One thing Goldie hates is someone criticising the clothing she makes. If the person asks for alterations outside of hemming, ensuring an item is form fitting, or adding a tail slit, it upsets her. She is an artist by trade, and having someone poke and prod at her designs – her art – is wounding for her."

"Oh. Did this female do that a lot?"

Zylah didn't understand that. Sure, she hadn't liked everything for different reasons, but she didn't blame the design for it. She thought everything had been nice, just not on her.

"Constantly," he said, and although he didn't roll his eyes, she heard it in his tone. "Rarely anything was good enough, and it didn't take Goldie nor I long to realise it was simply because of *what* made it. She was a very prejudiced person, and anyone outside of her species she considered beneath her."

She tilted her head. "I don't understand. Demons feel this way about each other?"

He released a small humourless chuckle. "Well, yes. We can be pricks to each other, but she wasn't a Demon. She was a human."

Zylah reared her head back in surprise. "I thought you didn't like humans."

"I don't, not particularly. It's a complicated topic, one I will be reluctant to share more details regarding." Instead of offering his usual indifferent or chilly expression, he gave her a small smile before his eyes brightened with mild humour – it came across pacifying, more than anything. "Goldie liked you because you were so unsure. She doesn't mind helping those who are a little self-conscious, and prides herself on making them walk out feeling beautiful. That was her intention with you, and I knew it when she refused to leave her spot next to the changeroom so she could assist you immediately. It's a small gesture most wouldn't notice if they didn't know her, but it meant she was trying her hardest to be attentive to your needs."

*I didn't realise it was so obvious that I was self-conscious,* she thought with a sulk. But his words did ease her, and her chest felt warmer than it did before, to the point her orbs shifted to bright yellow. *She liked me.*

And Jabez had shared something new about himself, even though it was small and mildly uncomfortable. She didn't know if it had any relevance to anything, but it was nice to learn something new.

*I didn't realise I would like Demons this much.* All she'd known them to be were hurtful creatures with sharp fangs and claws. But both Fayren and Goldie had not only been kind to her, but were helpful and welcoming.

*I hope the next one I meet is just as nice.*

He wasn't.

The moment they entered the shoemaker's store, he appeared surly. He was much older, with long eyebrow hairs threatening to curl into his eyes. Only part of his skin had morphed to a deep tan, while the majority of it remained the void-like gloss of most Demons. A set of tusks were slotted next to his upturned nose, and his red eyes were constantly narrowed in a small glare.

He did look rather neat in some kind of black suit with a white button-up tunic, his brown leather boots shining in the dim candlelight. Even his brown hair peppered with grey was slicked back with some kind of liquid that made it shine.

"Good evening," he greeted, but in a grated tone that informed her he didn't think it was particularly good. "What do you want?"

He stood up from a small chair in the corner, situated where he could look out the low window. Shoes were lined up on racks, in all varying kinds of shapes and colours.

"I'm guessing a set of heels would annoy the shit out of you," Jabez said, ignoring the male Demon, and he gestured for Zylah to sit on one of the two available seats.

She eyed the other people within the store – a pair of males who spoke in low tones as they tried on different boots. The attendant silently picked up after them when they left boots here and there without care.

"That was what Goldie was wearing?" Zylah asked, bringing her gaze away from the other customers when one darted their face towards her for staring. "No. I think I'd fall."

"Alright, something small. I don't think you'd like boots either, if I'm being honest." He turned to the slow-moving attendant, who immediately looked bothered at his approach. "Where's your foot measuring tool? We can start after we figure out what size she is."

"A possessive one, aye? You know part of my job is to help little maidens put their shoes on." The attendant gave a surly chuckle. "I'm not going to whisk off with your female if I touch her foot."

"Old man, I'd be surprised if you could *see* her foot."

"They look hard to miss," he answered, while walking to the counter to reach underneath it. "Here, lad. Do it yourself. Saves me the trouble of getting down on one knee with my bad back."

He slapped a wooden slab in Jabez's hand. Jabez swiftly turned to come back over to Zylah, and the distressed wooden floor creaked under each of his footsteps. He knelt down for her, picked up her foot, and placed it on the board that had multiple squiggly lines – she figured they were the shoe sizes.

He left to go speak with the attendant once more, who, again, was slow to move around the store as he showed Jabez what he had available in her size.

She listened in and watched them with her knees pressed together. Although he was doing everything for her, she actually found this experience a little easier since the focus wasn't completely on her. It allowed her a moment to relax and get her bearings, and mull over everything she'd witnessed so far.

"Have you heard the Genverous brothers are at it again?" one of the customers said to his companion, their voices quiet, but her sensitive hearing picked it up with ease.

"Great. Do they never learn?" the other responded.

Zylah's gaze slowly moved back to them as she focused on their conversation.

The first one who spoke wore a cloak, which hid most of his features except for a boorish snout. His features were mostly void-like, making it difficult to see within the shadow of his hood. The second male had black hair, his skin a light brown, and he sported a big set of antlers that looked heavy. He appeared further in completion except his bare hands still retained the black, glossy sheen of most Demons she'd encountered before the village.

"Yes, well, with our king dead, they believe they are best suited to take over," the boorish one stated.

"Didn't he cut out Kaan's tongue for speaking out against his rule?" the antlered one asked.

"Yeah, but Zyier is speaking on their behalf, and we all know he's the brawn and not the brains. He fumbles every announcement like a fool."

"Kaan was only marginally better." The antlered one shook his head as he shoved his strange, half-hoofed foot into a boot. "Neither seems to comprehend we just don't want a replacement. Our king may be dead, but most of the laws and rules he put in place still stand. We don't want change."

"They're likely only being so loud since there are little repercussions now that he isn't around to punish them for the big idiots they are." The boorish one removed a boot and dumped it on the ground next to him while obtaining a different kind. "It is concerning how much disarray has befallen us since his death. He may have been a tyrant, but he sure as shit knew how to keep people in line."

"Hmm. I wouldn't call him a tyrant. He always had a reason for killing or punishing, and he did go out of his way to make our lives easier."

The boorish one scoffed at that. "Soft-hearted wimp. It's only because he sided with you in that argument that you're so beholden to him."

"He made them give back my chickens! If I don't have eggs, I have nothing to trade!"

"Learn to hunt, like the rest of us. Or pick up a craft. Don't be lazy and make animals do your work for you." The boorish one pulled back his hood slightly, revealing messy brown hair. "You, guy with the tusks. What do you think of our old king?"

He tipped his head to look at Jabez standing in the aisle near him, who was waiting for the attendant to rise after pulling open a drawer filled with shoes.

"I have no interest in trivial matters," Jabez answered, waving his free hand dismissively.

"Ugh." The Demon's snout created thick creases in his cheeks when he grimaced. "What a limp-cocked answer."

"I would like to remind you that we have a female in our presence," Jabez warned, his tone darkening multiple depths in anger.

The boorish one glanced at Zylah and narrowed his eyes. Uncomfortable with multiple stares now on her, including the attendant's, Zylah turned her limbs inwards, wishing it made her invisible.

"Sorry, lass. I'll watch me language." The male twisted to look at the attendant. "What about you, geezer? Got anything to add?"

After giving Jabez a set of shoes, the attendant groaned and held his back as he tried to get up from the ground. He turned to pull out one last box and obtained something that looked like an open-ended leather cylinder with lots of strapping attached to it.

"I have little to add. The Genverous brothers are always up to no good, and they'd ruin this place if we let them." He shuffled his feet as he made his way back to his counter and sagged into the seat next to it with a huff of relief. "I didn't mind how ruthless our king was. Now, lesser Demons feel like they can run through the inner rings without his army keeping us safe, and we have fewer volunteers guarding each entrance of Spiral Haven. With order comes sacrifices, and his promise of returning us to the Elven world is now non-existent. The loss we have faced in his death means all our hopes died with him. We shouldn't be speaking such ill of him."

Displeased by his answer, the other customers grew quiet. The air in the shop immediately thickened with disgruntled tension.

Zylah was thankful no one asked her opinion on the matter, as hers wasn't pleasant and she knew she couldn't share it. *He told others how to kill my kind – shared our weakness, our secret.* She found it hard to shed how much she disliked him, regardless of how nicely they spoke of him. *They even called him a tyrant, who kills and punishes cruelly.*

It didn't matter that they also stated he was protective and helpful. Perhaps her feelings were biased, but she was relieved he wasn't around anymore if he was so hateful of Mavka and wanted them all dead.

Jabez returned to her, his expression unbothered, as if no one had spoken at all. He placed one knee on the ground in front of her, while he rested on the sole of his opposing foot for stability. He put down two pairs of small, flat shoes and the strange strapping *things*.

His touch was careful and gentle as he lifted her left foot to slip a black shoe onto it. It almost fit perfectly, except that it had a lot of wiggle room at the back around her narrow heel.

"How does that feel?"

"I don't like it," she answered, splaying her toes and finding the constriction uncomfortable.

"I had a feeling you'd say that, which is why I asked for this."

He slipped the thick, wide leather cone just past the pad behind her clawed toes, while pushing an attached cushioned tongue against the underside of her foot. He then began to wrap the arch of her foot, ensuring it was tight but not painful.

He kept his gaze set on his task as if he found it important.

Zylah watched him intently, wishing she had the confidence to push his hair away from his eyes so she could see more of him. She leaned forward a little to better observe what he was doing, which brought their faces closer. She stole a few quick sniffs of his scent, and his ears twitched as if he heard them. He looked up and cocked a brow, making her straighten her back and put space between them at being caught.

*I can't help it. I like the way he smells.* She wished she knew *what* he smelt like, other than him giving off an earthy aroma.

She also liked that he was the one assisting her, rather than the cranky attendant.

When he was done, she wiggled her free toes and inspected the apparatus he'd put on her. The strapping started just behind the pad of her foot and stopped right before the heel.

"What is the point to this? It barely covers anything."

"Better foot support, and it stops rocks and sticks from stabbing into the sensitive arch of your foot. The open toe and heel design is better suited for those who are more active or have feet that don't sit well inside an enclosed shoe."

She placed her foot down and pressed it multiple times, finding it comfortable. It did feel odd to have something fixed to her, but she figured she'd get used to it, like how she'd gotten used to wearing her dress.

"So how about it?" Jabez asked, crossing his arm over his stomach while placing an elbow onto his bent knee. "Did I make a mistake in bringing you here?"

She lifted her skull up and away from him. "Okay. Maybe it isn't so bad."

"Cheeky." He obtained the second piece of leather so he could wrap her other foot as well. "I'm glad you like it. Many start off with these and eventually switch to shoes or boots after they are used to wearing something. I was worried my efforts would be for nothing, especially since the shoemaker over there walks as slow as a snail."

"I heard that," the attendant grumbled, folding his arms with a huff.

"You're lucky your store is the best one in the village," Jabez answered as he stood and walked over to him. "I don't remember you being this aged the last time I saw you."

"The fact I don't remember your face shows how little of an impact you make. Hurry up and trade so I can shoo you out of my store."

Zylah didn't see what Jabez gave him, but he didn't look entirely pleased. Yet, as they were leaving, Zylah peeked over her shoulder to see he had a small smile.

He gave her a wink when he noticed her looking at him.

Okay, so maybe the surly old shopkeeper wasn't too bad.

# TWENTY-THREE

Although tiredness truly began to weigh on Jabez, he decided one last adventure through Spiral Haven was warranted.

He noted the spring in Zylah's steps as they threw themselves back into the throng of people. His gaze drifted down to the specialised strappings on her feet, and he was pleased that she seemed to be adapting to them already. They were dark brown and highlighted her little bunny toes more than before.

*It really should help cushion her feet.* Unfortunately, it did little to protect her toes from being squashed under hard-soled boots, which she hissed about. She never complained, now understanding this was just a normal part of being in a crowd.

*She's very adaptable.* Had she been another Mavka, she would have been overwhelmed by their visit so far. It was hard not to be proud of her, especially as he considered it a respectable quality in another.

They stuck with the flow of people heading deeper within the village. There were far fewer than before, as most were likely heading home to tuck themselves into their beds or nests.

They had about an hour before shops would start closing, and he was taking them the long way to their final destination.

A small, knowing smile curled his lips. *I think she'll be rather fond of the last place.* Humour tickled his chest at her awkwardness in both Goldie's Garments and Baret's Leather Shoes.

Baret had always been a grump. With the help of his parents passing on evolved genes, he was a human-eating Demon who had quickly reached completion in his younger years. He liked working with leather and hated greeting customers – he just wanted people to buy his shit to continue funding his hobby, without them annoying him. Alas, he couldn't have the best of both worlds, but he could often be found working at the back of his shop when one entered.

The conversation within his store hadn't been one of interest to Jabez, but he made sure to note Zylah's reaction to it. He cared little about what people thought of him as king, but it was a dark cloud that hung above his head when it came to her.

Knowing she likely hated him as the unnamed king of Demons, but was fond of him as just Jabez, brought on a wave of problems. Ones he didn't foresee going away easily. It was a reminder that the intimacy between them within the pocket of earth beneath this village shouldn't have happened.

*There's little I can do to change it now,* he thought, as they came to a string of carts selling wares.

Since there were fewer people around, it allowed Zylah to peruse what was being offered for trade at her own leisure.

She bypassed those selling fabrics, paints, games, weapons, and even knick-knacks. She also seemed to have little interest in those offering crafting supplies, such as beading, charms, and embroidery equipment.

She stopped at a cart selling herbs for various things – some for teas, others as spices for cooking. The cart next to it appeared to be run by a companion, who had contents that would be best for incense and essential oils.

Zylah smelt everything that was new to her, and both attendants were helpful in naming items and explaining their properties. If they had calming or sleeping qualities, they were quick to add in charming notes about them.

By the end, she held two specific plants to her nose hole: bergamot and sandalwood. He raised a brow when her snout repeatedly moved in his direction, like she was shyly glancing at him, but she quickly turned away when her orbs shifted to a reddish pink.

Before he could linger on it, his gaze lifted towards the canopy of leaves when he heard the lightest shaa. *It's raining.* He was rather fond of the way the rain hit the leaves above the village, and he almost closed his eyes in contentment.

It sounded gentle, like the droplets were light. The music of them was calming as they reverberated off the lush green foliage.

The canopy would only allow singular drops through here and there, and it wasn't a reason to close up shop and run. Most of the water would follow along the twisting branches and head towards the tree trunks. The multiple levels of branches helped direct that flow, and only the luckiest of drops would reach the lowest set of leaves and trickle against the ground.

It may grow muddy beneath their feet, but it would take a long while, or a much heavier downpour.

Once she was done trying to inhale the pieces of bergamot and sandalwood into her snout, sniffing wildly as she did, they moved on.

He almost chuckled when she halted at the first jewellery store. *I guess females are the same, no matter their species.* Then again, he thought what may have caught her gaze was the way the silver, gold, and gems glittered in the strategically placed firelight.

He considered these pieces of low quality. If she wanted nicer accessories, there were permanent stalls within the village that had jewellery that'd been crafted by those who were more skilled.

She eventually moved on until a better jewellery store caught her attention. *Human jewellery.* Obviously those pieces were stolen from corpses that had been eaten, or maybe they were hunted and their parts brought back to the Veil for meat – which was a feat all on its own.

Getting fresh, sellable meat of any creature to the inner ring of the Veil was difficult. Due to the low availability and the challenge of getting it here safely, anything pertaining to meat was expensive.

The shopkeeper, a male who was scarred but mostly humanoid, tried his hardest to snag a sale from her. His tanned hands picked up different pieces to show her, letting each one sparkle against his fingertips before he reached for something else. He complimented the colour of her fake void-like fur and told her which ones would best suit her features.

Jabez leaned against the corner post of the rickety store and raised both his brows at them interacting. *He's good, I'll give him that.* Zylah had been quieter and less confident at the beginning of their exchange, and only grew flustered under the weight of being told a certain necklace would look pretty on her.

Jabez knew that was a lie, considering it instantly sunk into the thick collar of her fur around her neck and almost disappeared. But he had no intention of ruining her fun.

*At least none of it seems to be cursed.* He would have been displeased had any of the pieces spooked her due to being an anchor for a human Ghost. Not all Demons could see them, but he had a feeling all Mavka were able to.

*They are a part of life and death.* This he knew, and not only had Merikh told Jabez of his ability to see them, but Zylah had pointed one or two out this night.

Jabez's brows narrowed. *The Witch Owl has been here recently.* There would be far many more had she not been.

Despite how much the Witch Owl pestered and annoyed him, stopping her from this task would have brought on more problems than it was worth. Allowing her here promoted synergy within the village, and peace for those wandering it.

Jabez did wonder what would happen to the souls attached to the anchors if they were to be swallowed by a Mavka. This thought wasn't a new one, especially when he'd always wondered what happened to the clothing, armour, and accessories worn by humans they'd eaten. If they didn't produce waste, then where did it all go?

*Perhaps it deteriorates in their non-existent but existent stomachs.* He hummed in thought, knowing vividly how the inside of one of her kind worked. It was honestly a mess, nothing truly solid except for their hearts, lungs, and muscles. He'd found no liver, no kidneys, no digestive tract – it was like it all just turned into goop.

Zylah picked up different pieces of jewellery in interest, lifting them to the lantern light nearby to better see how they gleamed. She seemed fascinated by gems the most. Her tail wiggled in delight at certain ones, especially if they were large.

*Goldie did wonderfully.* Zylah looked comfortable in her new outfit, and it was far more flattering than what he'd made. The moderate navy was a nice, subtle contrast to her natural fur tones, and he did like the way the skirt swayed around her thighs.

It also covered that round, kneadable backside of hers, and that's what he considered most important. More for his sanity than really from preventing others from leering at her – his cloak had been a good shield for that.

Though, he actually found it more titillating to watch the back of her skirt *bounce* like it might gift him a naughty peek. Did any male not feel hope that they just might get one? It was like a game to his eyes, seeing if he could catch a rare moment.

The outfit also accentuated her sensual hourglass curves, such as her small chest, her tucked-in waist, wide hips, and those kneadable, glorious thighs of hers. *I do like her thighs a lot.* They helped to support her thick backside, which also looked fun to play with and was currently what his hungry eyes hoped for a peak of.

He slid his gaze up when she attempted to slip on a ring, only for it to stop right before the second knuckle. She lifted her head and hand in his direction and wiggled her forefinger.

"I don't think any of these will fit me," she stated with a small laugh, unbothered by such a notion.

Jabez opened his mouth to respond, but was silenced quickly.

"Well, your hands are rather large," the shopkeeper said with a chuckle. "Perhaps a bracelet?"

The shopkeeper waved his hand towards the bracelets available, and Jabez knew anything that was feminine wouldn't fit her. Human females tended to have dainty, breakable wrists. If anything, only the thick, braided silver chain obviously once belonging to a male would fit.

Figuring what Jabez had, she shook her head and lost interest in the stall. She waited for him to push off from his leaning post once more.

"There is so much here I don't understand," Zylah said

quietly, coming just that little bit closer to him. "I noticed there are tools to make certain items, but I don't know what."

"That's fine. If you come back here one day, you can ask and figure out if perhaps a craft is to your liking."

"Can we really do that?" she asked, her orbs morphing to a bright yellow with all this hope in her voice.

"Sure," he lied, averting his gaze to the side.

How quickly she tried to involve him in her future wasn't comforting. *I can't wait much longer to tell her the truth.* Perhaps that's why he had allowed them to come here.

The things she experienced tonight would be critical for her future. Like a cloth soaking up water, Zylah drew in knowledge like it was second nature. What he'd taught her here was invaluable in developing social skills for situations outside of those she could trust – like him.

*If she comes here on her own, she'd have no issue communicating to storekeepers.* She wouldn't be startled by the crowd, the people, the place. They were surely allowing Mavka to return in his absence, as they'd never truly been put off by them – although wisely wary.

Hell, with Jabez gone and no longer placing a glamour on her, she may even make a friend. He'd been aware of a few who had come to know Faunus, the feline-skulled Mavka, well – which, unfortunately for him, made him an easy target for Jabez.

He paused when a particular store had something that caught his eye, which he would have missed had he been continuing to focus on her. He turned towards the counter and spared a glance at the bird-like features of the female seller.

She watched him like a hawk as he picked up a silver piece, whereas he slipped his gaze to assess the width of Zylah's waist. *Getting this would be invaluable for her.* But, fuck, was it awkward. He'd have to explain its use to her, without raising her hopes of what it meant.

He put down the long silver chain and picked up the longest one made of gold. It looked like it'd fit.

His lips thinned at what he was about to do, but it was imperative that he actually checked it. The moment he shoved detection mana into it, his gut twisted and sweat rose on the back of his neck.

The detection showed that the enchantment was strong, and he eyed the attendant. She raised a feathered brow at him before her red eyes narrowed into a glare.

"It's rude to check a person's enchantments," she stated coldly, her tone revealing she was a moment away from pecking him with her pale-pink beak.

"I'm merely checking its quality before I buy it," he answered dully.

She folded her thin arms. "Well? Is my magic suitable for you?"

*I could do better.* But yes, it was good enough quality.

He reached into his bag, shoved his fingers past the drawstring of a coin pouch he'd stolen, and acquired three gold coins. "As a token of apology, I'll give you extra."

The moment he placed them on the table, she snatched them up and gave him her shoulder. "Appreciated. No take backs."

He nodded and shoved the chain into his bag. Zylah tilted her head when he approached.

"What was that?" she asked, looking down at his satchel.

"I'll explain what it is and give it to you later." He looked up to mentally map where they were in the village before veering them to the right. "For now, let's head to our last destination."

As much as he could tell she wanted to walk the last street block of markets, that additional expenditure of magic rotated a ball of nausea in his stomach.

*I need to shed the glamours soon.* Actually, to give himself breathing room, he removed the physical one containing his genitalia in order to preserve what little mana he safely had left to expend.

*I should have let myself heal first.* The well of his magic was currently lacking in volume. A wiser choice would have been to sit with it for a day or two before he started spending it.

It was also making him unwell. He only had a little while longer before the second signs of ookmanik sickness truly came on. The first signs were sweating and nausea.

Thankfully, there were deeper signs, and he was conscious of them.

But his reason for going against his better judgement looked as though she was about to break into a skip beside him. *It's the least I can do.* And he likely wouldn't have brought them back here had they left straight away.

Even when he took her down darkened streets, she never lost her enthusiasm for where they were going. He'd already informed her he had a surprise for her, one which, without a doubt, she'd adore.

The moment he saw the sign down a tucked away, almost hidden street, a grin threatened to lift into his mouth. She hadn't noticed it yet, and he hoped she didn't at all.

They approached a heavy wooden door with a single step, and she tipped her skull back to look up at the big sign above.

"Black Cat's Bookstore," she read out with a thoughtful hum, then a gasp ripped out of her. "Wait! Does this place have books inside it?"

His eyes crinkled as a chuckle flittered past his lips. "The sign gives away the surprise."

Visibly vibrating with excitement, she almost pushed him out of the way when she bolted to get inside. He winced when the door swung open and bashed against the outer wall from her carelessly tossing it like it weighed nothing. The bell above chimed and smacked against its metal holder, and after ducking beneath the small doorway, he reached up to settle it so it didn't break.

Rows upon rows of books were brightly lit up by glass lanterns, all of which were bolted to the walls so they couldn't accidentally be knocked over. Each section was separated into genres, from books pertaining to the history of humans and those written by Demons, to those of fiction of great tales, adventures, and romances. There were multiple academic sections for geography, geology, and psychology, as well as those for cooking, baking, crochet, and even paper folding.

Many more were labelled with painted plaques.

Zylah was quick to go to the first free-floating section and pull out a book to see what it was about. The plaque above stated it was an autobiography.

"Hello, welcome to my bookstore," the male attendant greeted warmly, disregarding the book he'd been reading and hopping down from a stool behind the counter.

The black feline ears poking up from the top of his head twitched in glee as he approached. His face was entirely cat-like, to the point that he had a feline, upward-pointing nose and muzzle. His body appeared humanoid except for his digitigrade legs, but it was hard to tell due to his long suit trousers and enclosed black boots. A nice black suit jacket sat over a lighter grey shirt.

Although it may have been difficult for most to see, Jabez could tell the void-like aspect of his Demon flesh had actually changed to appear like normal black fur. It was almost similar to Zylah's, except it lacked the glossy shine of blue like hers.

*If he'd continued to eat humans properly, he could have transitioned into a more humanoid form by now.* Instead, he was one of the few who stunted the change by relying mainly on animal meat once he'd developed proper intelligence and humanity, making him appear more beastly.

*Still fucking short as ever, though,* Jabez thought warmly, seeing he still came to his waist height.

"My name is Rook, and I'll be happy to assist you however you need," he continued, flashing them a fang-filled smile.

With her hands on her thighs, Zylah leaned down a little, so they were at a better head height – not realising this was rude.

"I'm Zylah." She lifted back up so she could look across the top of the floating shelves. "You have so many books here. I don't even know where to start."

His red, feline eyes filled with easy tenderness, overjoyed to meet someone who obviously liked the same hobby as him.

"Well? What interests you?" Then, as if he didn't wish to leave anyone without a greeting, Rook leaned around her to look at him. "And what about you, sir? Do you also need assistance today?"

Jabez answered him with a grunt and waved his hand. Figuring they'd be here until the bookstore closed, he sat next to the door where there was an empty spot that didn't contain books and wrapped himself up in his cloak to contain the sickly chill starting to rush through him. He propped the hood over his head to shield his face and hide from the light.

Seeing as Jabez had no care for the conversation, the two of them began to go through what may interest her. Jabez watched her intently, ensuring if she needed his help, he'd be able to jump in.

She immediately forgot about his presence, her focus solely on Rook and the hundreds of books around her. "I wish I could read them all."

If Jabez had been able to speak without detection, he may have joined in on their fun. Especially since Rook ran around his store like a maniac, wanting to show Zylah everything – and most of all, his favourites. His long tail curled here and there when he obtained a book, its erratic movements an indicator of his glee.

But Jabez couldn't talk, as the feline Demon was exceptionally perceptive. Those big ears had heard his voice time and time again in this quiet bookshop from before he'd began hiding his face behind glamours, and he would immediately be suspicious of it.

*I can't properly glamour around him.* Rook was aware that Jabez wore different faces, as he remembered all those who came to his store – he never forgot a person. Because of that, Rook was always able to figure out who he was by the sound of his voice, even if he couldn't see past the magic.

So, for now, he was merely a quiet spectator.

*I must admit. I'm enjoying myself, though.*

Zylah was even more animated than when they first entered the village. Not once since they'd entered the store had her orbs stopped shining the brightest yellow he'd ever seen from her. They even flickered with bright pink, and he truly did wonder what it meant now that he was seeing it again.

*Adoration?* That seemed like it fit.

Whatever it was, he found himself letting down his guard while he peacefully watched her. She even plopped that cute tail of hers against the ground with a pile of books next to her so she could go through them. Rook joined her on the wooden floor, opening the contents of one book to show the best part while she skimmed through another.

Jabez couldn't tell if the second pile she was making was a rejection stack or an 'I wish to take this home' stack. They had more than enough room in their satchels for her to buy multiple novels. So, whatever amount she settled on, he would try to procure for her. He had plenty of trade left, and Rook took almost everything with contentment.

The trade he found best was the joy of a fellow bookworm leaving his store pleased. He had a room in the back where he sometimes kept certain pieces to remind him of favoured customers.

With the door to the back room slightly ajar, Jabez noted an amethyst crystal reflecting the low light. Next to it was a tiny wooden figurine. Neither meant anything to him, but he found that sentimental quality about the feline Demon endearing.

He had a feeling with the way Rook was attending to Zylah, he'd keep a part of their trade to remember her fondly.

His eyelids drooped, the stationary position and the safety within this hidden-away store allowing the fog of exhaustion to crest over his brow. No one would come here.

*Hopefully she doesn't want to take the whole store.*

After being in the store for quite some time, Zylah flicked through some kind of horror novel, finding it lacked any scary qualities. It spoke of monsters, and it was hard to be frightened of something she could easily rip apart with her claws.

She carefully placed it on her discard pile when Rook leaned over to show her the inside of a mystery novel.

"The writing for this one is unique. You don't know who the murderer is until the end, and I can tell you now, you'll never guess who it is!" he exclaimed with exhilaration, his feline ears darting back as he laughed.

She took his offering and skimmed through it briefly. "I don't think this interests me," she answered, hoping the apology in her tone sounded sincere. "I am... new to reading. I like books about adventures to strange places I've never heard about. I don't understand society well, so I don't like things with complicated interactions with others."

*Although, that may change after tonight.* Witnessing what she had in this village filled in the missing pieces she'd lacked when reading anything pertaining to cities or towns.

"I have plenty of fiction books," Rook said, his puffy cat mouth curling into a fanged smile. "Depends on the adventures you're after. There are fabled tales of dragons, wars, the chosen one off to defeat the evil sorcerer. Or there are romances about people falling in love."

Zylah cocked her head at that. "I've never read a book about love."

Although Fayren's books had very briefly and confusingly detailed it, she still didn't fully understand this concept.

Rook's eyes lit up like she'd just presented him with the finest piece of treasure.

"If this is new to you, then I may have just the books for you!" He sprung up to stand, and hastily disappeared behind a shelf like his tail was on fire.

She peered through one of the craft books she'd picked earlier, flicking the pages with her clawed thumb to get a brief understanding of what it contained. Although it interested her, much of it required tools she lacked. She put it to the side, but would remember it in case she ever obtained those tools.

She picked a book about herbs next, but her shoulders lifted sheepishly due to the reason she'd taken it.

*Jabez smells like bergamot and sandalwood,* she thought, flicking through the pages in hopes of finding more about those plants.

The store selling herbs had revealed this to her, and she'd liked the way they smelt so much she'd considered eating them just to taste his scent. She'd been overjoyed to learn their names, and she hadn't been able to contain the way her heart had nearly wept at the time.

Remembering someone was missing from beside her, she looked to the left to find Jabez. She felt bad that she'd completely disregarded him from the moment she entered the bookstore.

Like they had been the entire night, she expected to find his eyes upon her and for their gazes to meet. They didn't. She dipped lower on a bent arm to see past his hood, noting his eyelids were shut and his mouth was slightly parted.

His knees had been propped up earlier. Now, they both fell to the right as if his body had gone lax.

*He fell asleep?* she wondered.

She regarded him more closely, and his skin did look rather ashen. The dark smudges under his eyes had grown from when they'd first entered Spiral Haven. As they were walking through the village, she'd noticed the occasional dots of perspiration, but she'd assumed that was normal for his magic use.

Perhaps it wasn't.

Had she missed his deteriorating wellbeing over the course of the night due to her awe? If so, she felt rather guilty about that, and her orbs shifted to bright orange as the emotion sat queasily in her gut.

*Should I let him rest, or wake him so we may leave?* Did he know he'd been falling asleep, or was it an accident? He was such a cautious male that she didn't think he'd leave himself vulnerable in a place he considered unsafe.

It had taken her weeks to be able to approach him from behind, and even longer to get near him while he slept without waking him. She bet if she got in his direct vicinity while they were in this place, he'd spook and wake in an instant.

*I should leave him.* She was enjoying herself, and she was here to protect him while he rested. Some sleep may do him some good.

She absolutely wasn't thinking that just so she could be surrounded by books for longer.

Zylah continued to flick through the herb book's pages. She grumbled when it had nothing on bergamot and only had a small passage on sandalwood.

In the distance, a chime rang from somewhere deeper within the village, its high-pitched sound soft and quiet. She lifted her gaze to the front window just above Jabez's head.

"What is that?" she asked, her head twisting and cocking as she tried to make it out.

"Have you never been in Spiral Haven when dawn comes?" Rook asked, returning with three books in his arms. He sat down next to her, although a little closer than before.

"No," she answered, eyeing the thickly bound novels he'd brought. "This is my first time here."

"I figured as much, all things considered as of late," Rook answered cryptically, sounding somehow forlorn. "It's to let everyone know that dawn has finished rising and it's time to leave. They have about an hour to cross the meadow before they're unable to."

"Oh." She looked down at the novels around her, most of which she hadn't managed to get through yet. "Does that mean we should leave?"

His eyes softened, and a gentle smile lifted into his feline features. "No. You are welcome to stay a little longer. I don't mind keeping my store open later for you. It just depends on if you plan to leave the village before the sunlight fills the surrounding meadow like everyone else."

Zylah wasn't affected by the sun, and Jabez had his cloak to protect him. *Jabez can just teleport us away anyway.*

"We will be fine. Thank you," she said with tenderness pooling in her chest.

He gave a small chuckle as he looked down to obtain one of the books he brought over. He shook his head as he said, "Well, it's not often I have a Mavka in my store."

*No. I guess that would be strange,* she thought, while laughing in return. Then what he said truly sank in.

Her head reared back, and she cupped the side of her skull with her orbs flaring white in worry.

"The glamour..."

"It fell quite some time ago," he stated quietly, with his head bowed and his ears flattening. "I considered telling you, but you were just so interested in our conversation and my books that I didn't know when to interrupt you."

Zylah glanced over to Jabez, thankful that his hood was shielding his features. She didn't know what to do. Should they leave immediately upon someone seeing what she was, and potentially recognising him?

"I'm sorry if that's an issue," Rook continued, lifting a green bound book in her direction. "You're not the first Mavka I've had in my store, and I'm hoping you will not be the last."

Zylah brought her gaze back to him and fidgeted nervously.

"You are not against Mavka?"

His eyes crinkled at that. "No. Admittedly, I was nervous at first, but he showed me your kind can be just like us." His expression deepened into one of kindness and warmth. "I also very much liked the human he brought here. They returned one last time before our late king forbade their entry."

Her sight flickered with blue. "He forbade Mavka from entering? Why?"

"I'm not entirely sure," he answered.

*Just more proof of how little the king of Demons thinks of us.* Zylah would love to return here. She looked around at all the shelves, and the hope and adoration she felt in her surroundings left a lightness within her mind. *I can pick my own stories to read.*

There was so much to learn here. She imagined she could spend days, even weeks, just curled up in a corner and reading each one. To forbid her kind from entering Spiral Haven, and therefore this place, felt wrong.

*And Goldie...* She'd left her clothing store feeling wonderful. Even though the little Demon hadn't been able to tell Zylah was a Mavka, she'd still made her feel beautiful. *I don't think it would have mattered if she did know.* Something about the female said that she would have tried to better match Zylah's attire had she known she bore a skull.

"Thank you," Zylah said as she took the book and hugged it to her chest. "I appreciate your acceptance more than you can ever know."

"Oh, I think I do. When I first met Reia, I was delighted to meet my first human. I was worried she would be repelled by my company." Then he gave another small chuckle as he said, "Although she was obviously very wary of me, she befriended me on her own terms. She dragged her Mavka back here to greet me, and I spoke with her at length. I've learned much about humans from her. She's my... *friend.*"

"Why was a human travelling with a Mavka?"

Zylah realised she was being greedy by staying without a glamour, knowing Jabez would be against it, but she just couldn't find the will to end the conversation. Not only did she not want to be rude towards Rook's kindness, but she was curious. About Rook, about these people he spoke fondly of.

"Reia is Orpheus' bride," he answered. "He's a funny fellow. He was much more cautious of me than she was. I really do hope they are okay. I haven't seen them for quite a long time, but there are whispers throughout the village that they are still alive and together."

"What kind of skull did he have?"

"A wolf one, with Impala antelope horns."

*I have not met this one.* Then again, she'd only met the raven-skulled Mavka with short pointy horns briefly enough to forget most of his features, and her father, the fox-skulled, antlered one.

*At least I now know Orpheus' name,* she thought warmly.

As nervous as she was about the prospect, she eventually wanted to meet all the others. *Uncles* Jabez had told her they were, which meant they were *family.* She'd read how much those blood ties could matter, despite not truly feeling any emotional depth regarding the concept.

The more she understood about the world, the more she wanted to reach out to anyone who could possibly be welcoming. At the time, she'd disregarded her parents as strangers, but she'd love to meet them again and come to better know them.

She looked upon Jabez, who was still asleep. *He is a barrier.* But maybe one she could help break. Surely what he'd done could be forgiven, especially as she'd forgiven him easily for it.

*I can do it.* She would be stubbornly determined, and if they refused to accept him, then they would lose her. He mattered more to her than strange relatives she didn't know.

"You're very different to Orpheus," Rook said, his gaze flicking down to the book in her arms. "I don't think he can read well, and you're much more friendly. Hopefully Reia has helped him come out of his shell."

Zylah giggled at that, and finally opened the pages to skim over its contents. She already knew this book was one she'd like to take, since Rook had been the one to give it to her; she was obtaining all kinds of gifts from people today. She was also curious about what a romance novel was, and hopefully it would shed light on that question.

"I would like to come back," Zylah said, finally voicing her inner thoughts. "I've deeply enjoyed my time here in Spiral Haven, and everyone has been so nice even though they didn't know what I am. I've experienced so much I never even dreamed could exist. I'd like to do that as myself."

"Much has happened in the last few months," Rook said, flicking through the pages of another book to show her. "We're mostly happy with the laws placed upon us, as many of them keep us safe. But there's a large group of us who would like to remove the ban on Mavka and their brides. My mate has already stated she is willing to travel to the outer ring to inform them of their ability to return if it's allowed."

Zylah knew what a mate was, as Fayren had explained it to her. It was when two Demons, sometimes more, formed a lasting companionship because they 'loved' each other. Although, some did form that bond due to other reasons.

"What is a bride?" Zylah asked, tilting her head. "I've never heard this term before."

His forehead and lip whiskers twitched as his brows drew together. "How can you not know about this?"

Zylah scratched at the side of her snout bashfully. "Truthfully, I haven't spent much time with my own kind."

"Well, I think a bride is like a mate for Demons, but a partner that a Mavka chooses. It's what Orpheus called Reia." He flashed her an apologetic grin. "Sorry. I don't know much about this myself. All I know is that your kind is very protective of them."

"I see." *A bride?* She wished she had more information about this.

Once more, she brought her gaze to Jabez. She bet he knew. *Could he become my bride?* Oddly enough, just the thought of him becoming her partner brought on a fluffy warmth in her chest, and her orbs morphed to bright pink.

She covered an eye socket when she turned back around, and Rook's expression widened. He shoved his face right into hers, and his wet, twitching nose almost touched her bony snout as he inspected her orbs. It reminded her of Jabez's earlier excitement over the colour.

"You Mavka are so strange with your colour-changing orbs. I've always wanted to know what they mean."

"I can't help it," she grumbled back, her shoulders turning inwards self-consciously.

"Don't be nervous about something natural to your kind! Be yourself with me, I don't mind."

The tension that had been clinging to her muscles eased, and they once more became engrossed in the books surrounding her. Rook brought her more until there was a noticeable mess surrounding them, occasionally putting away the ones he could tell she didn't want.

Then an idea popped into her head! With a gasp, she dug through her satchel and grabbed her favourite book – the one of three humans going on an adventure and winning many battles along the way.

"Have you read this book?" Zylah asked, holding it out to him.

Rook took it and thumbed the embossed title on the front of the leatherbound book. "No. I don't have this one."

She propped up the first romance book he'd given her. "I've already read it twice. Would you like to trade?"

"Really?" he exclaimed, his eyes brightening as he gifted her with a large, fanged smile. "It is so hard to acquire new books! I would love to trade book for book."

His feline tail curled in obvious delight, and he immediately opened it so he could get a feel for the pages. "This is the best trade. Thank you." Then he waved to the other books on the ground. "But you can continue to look. I will take anything, so if there are more you would like, please do consider them."

A certain giddiness made her chest ache, and she safely tucked the book away so she could go through the many others. Already the urge to flick it open and begin reading nagged at her conscience, much like Rook, who was already lost in the words of the one she'd given him.

Her orbs flared bright yellow. *I traded on my own!*

Zylah continued to look, setting aside two she could already tell she would enjoy. She didn't know how much time passed, mere minutes or hours, but her happiness never waned.

That was until a female Demon stormed into the store from a back area. She looked similar to Rook in that she was feline in nature and had black fur, but a patch of light-brown skin had formed across a humanoid appearing cheek, chin, and jaw. Like him, she also wore some kind of suit, but it was a dark green and more feminine in design.

With her furry, pointed ears back in irritation, she placed her hands on her hips with her legs parted wide. "You," she hissed with her eyes narrowing at Rook.

"Eliora," Rook muttered quietly, his ears flattening. "I can explain."

The lightest scent of *fear* cascaded from him. Not enough to stir true hunger, but enough to make Zylah's gut twist and her orbs flare red.

"Explain nothing!" Eliora stated, while throwing her hands up. "You're supposed to close at dawn."

He quickly stood and gestured towards Zylah. "But I have customers."

"Then tell them to lea–" her words cut short when she finally looked upon Zylah. She stepped back with a gasp. "It's a Mavka."

"Yes, see? This is important," he said, walking over to her.

Her lips turned inwards as she thought deeply, while Zylah rose to stand. Eliora's hands fell from her hips when her irritation waned.

"I'm sorry," Zylah said, putting space between them. "I didn't mean for him to be in trouble."

"That's not your fault," Eliora grumbled, before cutting Rook a mean glare. "You should know better. You always find an excuse to hole up with your books."

"You do know me, my dear," he answered with a chuckle.

He continued to laugh even when she yanked on his ear in annoyance. Zylah could tell Eliora was upset, but there was affection in her tugs. Standing side by side, Eliora was much taller than Rook, but their relationship was playful and friendly.

"I'm really sorry, but I must ask that you leave," Eliora said. "It's bedtime and I'd like my mate back."

"That's fine," Zylah said, turning to wake Jabez.

He was already rising, likely awoken by the sudden commotion. Steadying himself against the wall for support, his movements were slow and lethargic.

"Shit. I can't believe I fell asleep," he muttered, rubbing his face before adjusting his hood so he could see properly. His drowsy gaze found Zylah when she neared. "Have you had fun to your heart's content?" he whispered, keeping his voice low.

"Wait," Zylah rasped, reaching for his hood.

It was too late. He'd pushed it off before she could stop him, and she inwardly cringed.

"Oh *shit*," Eliora grated out under her breath. "It's King Jabez."

Jabez froze, then his eyes darted up to them. "What did you just say?" he stated, before he looked at his hands in disbelief. "Shit. Did my mana run so low that the glamour gave out?"

Then his disorientated, softened gaze instantly hardened, before it slowly lifted to the pair of Demons behind her once more. There was a dangerous glint to it, one that even had Zylah's fur puffing.

"Y-your highness," Rook stuttered out, retreating to Eliora's side to grab her wrist. "You're alive? Had I known it was you, I would have better attended to you."

*King...? Your highness?* A horrible realisation began to settle over her entire being like a heavy, cold blanket, and Zylah stumbled back and *away* from him. *No. Don't tell me he's...*

"How could you not know he was here?!" Eliora quietly hissed at Rook, who instantly shot back his ears even further.

"He was hidden, and their glamours made it hard to scent them properly."

Jabez's eyes flicked towards Zylah, who continued to put space between them, and the chill she saw in his glare was frosty and harsh.

"You should have woken me," he growled out.

Before Zylah could say anything, he disappeared in an instant. She spun around when both Eliora and Rook let out a sharp gasp, and found he'd materialised behind them with both their small necks in his grasp. He didn't appear to be strangling them, but his nails were threatening with the way they dug into their jugulars.

"Vow that you will never speak of my return, or this will be your last day."

"Jabez!" Zylah shouted, reaching an arm forward.

His snarl was vicious as he chomped his fangs in warning in her direction. With them bared, his nose wrinkled, and his eyes slitted in utter fury, she worried getting too close would only mean harm to her new friend and his mate.

"Vow it!" he roared, tightening his grip. "The only reason I offer is because of our entangled pasts."

"Of course! We would never betray you," Rook stated, while Eliora, with a narrowed glare, nodded and said, "I vow it."

Zylah couldn't believe how easily he'd threatened their lives! A trickle of betrayal ran down her nape, and her orbs didn't know if they wanted to flicker blue in sorrow, or red in anger.

How was she supposed to accept that the person she cared for so deeply not only lied to her, but had been the one to cruelly share how to destroy her kind? *He* was the one who hated Mavka, and yet he'd been by her side, had helped her, been kind to her... *touched* her.

Her hands shook as she clutched at her chest right above her heart that felt so tight it made it hard to *breathe*. Betrayal crept down her spine like an icy trickle of water, making her shiver as her orbs wavered in sorrowful pain.

"You are the only ones who know," Jabez said in a low, deep tone. "Be mindful of that."

Then he was gone, and her fur instantly puffed in fear and aversion when the air shifted behind her. She didn't make it a step before a firm hand gripped her forearm.

"We need to talk."

The room disappeared, throwing Zylah into a whirlwind of darkness she screamed into when they teleported.

# TWENTY-FOUR

The moment Zylah materialised into a dimly lit cave, she ripped her arm from him. She stumbled as she tried to get her bearings, her mind swimming while the sound of the rain pelted too loudly in her throbbing ears.

A black blur darted past her, and she gasped and tripped while trying to move away when a vicious hiss resonated. Cowering in the corner, a Demon swiped its claws.

She managed to catch Jabez appearing out of thin air next to it before they both disappeared. In the seconds they were gone, Zylah placed her hand against the wall for support to catch her breath and steady her accelerated heart rate.

She was getting used to the sudden teleporting, the waves of dizziness dispersing faster than before.

*I can't believe he lied to me...*

The betrayal that seeped into her chest was nasty and sickening. The onslaught of sadness and anger binding together into one agonising emotion was the cruellest kind of wound.

Just as her sight stopped spinning, Jabez reappeared next to her. She turned to him, her orbs flaring red as she let out a confused roar of anguish.

He did nothing. He didn't even flinch or bother to look afraid. That only infuriated her more. She hated that he had such a powerful ability to evade her by teleporting — it made him cocky and arrogant!

*"You!"* she snarled, her anger deepening her voice an

octave, like when she was in her monstrous form. *"You are the king of Demons!"*

"This wasn't how I wanted you to find out," he answered dully, as if he felt no regret. He rolled his shoulders back, folded his arms, and straightened his head superiorly.

*"You lied to me!"* she shouted, only for her lungs to wheeze at how much knowing that *hurt*.

"Actually, I didn't. I never lied to you."

Her fur puffed, and she stamped a foot forward while she swiped her arm through the air, wishing she had the strength in her heart to slash at him with her claws. He was making her *want* to be violent when she usually didn't feel that way at all.

*"You never told me,"* she snapped.

"Exactly," he stated, cocking a brow. "An untold secret isn't a lie. It's merely the absence of truth."

Her sight shifted to blue, sadness winning against her anger as it pooled behind her sternum like burning molten fire. She couldn't believe he was defending his actions. *Does he not care about how I feel?* He was smart – he should have known how distressing this would be to discover.

Instead of trying to soothe her, he was being cold and callous. She hated that she *wanted* him to be sympathetic, to look apologetic, to give her warmth and tenderness like their time in Spiral Haven.

Was how he treated her a falsehood just to make her compliant? It only made her wonder what he really wanted from her, why he'd done all this, why he'd been... *kind* to her. What did he want... if he hated Mavka enough to want to eradicate them? Why befriend her or help her?

*Was it all a trick?*

"You spoke of yourself as if you were someone else," she stated with a whimper, the bottom of her orbs breaking like glass. Ethereal tears floated around her eye sockets, obscuring part of her vision as she gripped at her chest right where her heart felt like it was bleeding. "You deceived me."

"Yes," he admitted, his expression empty. She'd never known how cold crimson could look until it was reflected in his eyes. More than ever, it sent a chill through her. "It's the most cunning form of manipulation."

"Why?" she whimpered, her claws cutting deeper into her flesh.

"Because you couldn't speak properly at first, and then you lacked the comprehension skills to *understand* what the fuck I was saying until recently."

"I know that!" Zylah shouted, her tears floating faster and disappearing into glitters. "But I have been able to understand everything for weeks."

"And we began to speak about it. As I told you, I would eventually explain all this to you, and I preferred to do it *my* way. Not forced upon me by a pair of Demons in a dusty bookstore."

"It's not my fault you fell asleep and dropped your glamours!"

"I never said it was," he replied, his brow furrowing. "Before I could speak to you about this, you went into your heat cycle and I was forced to take you to Fayren. I prioritised what I thought was most important for you."

"How was that more important?" she asked, shaking her head in disbelief. "I would have preferred to know the truth first."

"Because if you came to hate me for what I told you, you had knowledge that would protect you in the future."

Zylah didn't know how to respond to that. It sounded like he *foresaw* Zylah's reaction, and correctly summarised that she would feel a mingle of betrayal, hurt, and anger. She wanted to believe he'd chosen the events of the past few days purposefully to protect her, but she just didn't know how to swallow this.

The tightness of his folded arms loosened a little, and he let out a small sigh. He ran his fingers through his long hair, brushing it back from where some had fallen over his features.

"Zylah, I have lived an exceptionally long time. The pain that lack of knowledge could have caused is far more brutal than me withholding the truth from you for a few more days."

It didn't feel that way. Currently it felt like her insides were being gouged into ribbons, just like her flesh had been torn apart by Demon claws. Because of *him*, because of his stupid kingly decree to have Mavka hunted by Demons, because of his personal aggression against *her* kind.

"You were the one who shared our secret," Zylah said with a curt whine rattling her chest. "You were the one who wanted us destroyed. Because of you, they... *hurt* me."

"I know."

"Why?!" she screamed. "I have never hurt anyone purposefully! I tried to *heal* creatures I found, hoping they would stay with me. I never attacked Demons unless provoked. I stayed away. I... I even *healed* you! Why do you hate us so much that you want us destroyed?"

"I don't hate Mavka," he answered quietly, averting his gaze to the entrance of the cave.

Rain was collecting at the entryway, and she realised then that this was *their* cave. He'd brought her... home.

"Then why?" she rasped, her voice cracking from her anguish.

He covered his face in what could only be exasperation before palming it downwards.

"Because my age doesn't prevent me from being an idiot?" he said, lifting his palm away with a noticeable scoff. "For a hundred and eighty-seven years, that human woman I told you of was my companion, and *she* hated Mavka. The wolf-skulled one in particular. In her own right, she had every reason to, despite her own shortcomings. She wanted revenge, and I sought to give her that."

"What did he do that was so bad?" Zylah asked, lifting her hands in exasperation. She just couldn't see anything being worth death for the entirety of her kind.

"What they did to each other is exactly why I took you to Fayren's. I wanted to prevent that from happening to you." When she shook her head to signal she didn't understand, as she couldn't fathom how intimacy could be wrong, he gave her a sigh. "It's complicated. It's nearly two hundred years to unpack, and much of it regretful on my part."

"Then try?"

"I don't fucking know how!" he roared, unfolding his arms to swipe through the air like she had. She startled at the loudness of his yell, the bass of it, and the fact he'd gone from emotionally empty to distressed within a heartbeat. "My best friend was a fucking Mavka! That's why I know so much about your damn kind. I watched him grow intelligent, helped him do so, just as I did for you. I've never hated your kind, but I *did* care for my human companion enough to not care about anyone other than Merikh. Orpheus meant nothing to me; he would just be another death among the *thousands* I'd already caused. Human, Demon, Mavka, it didn't matter to me so long as those under my protection were content."

"But what about the rest of us? Those who had nothing to do with Orpheus. You wanted us *all* dead by sharing our secret."

"Because I was angry, Zylah!" he shouted, his nose crinkling in rage. "Orpheus' little bride *killed* Katerina, and I was angry, I was mourning, and I only know how to destroy what displeases me. I also needed to hurt Weldir long enough to lower his ward so that my people could leave this wretched fucking realm! That required me killing your kind in order to weaken him. Any time I tried to fuck with his ward, he would awaken and near kill me."

Her enclosed fists loosened. "So this is about the vendetta you have against the Elves?"

The moment those words left her, she realised she should have figured it out sooner. *He said he lived in a castle.* She should have put it all together. Only *kings* lived in castles, only those in a position of power built and governed villages like Spiral Haven.

*I'm so dumb,* she thought, tears rapidly floating from her once more. *How did I not see it?*

"It's always been about my vendetta," he answered coldly. "Everything I have done has been in the pursuit of my own revenge and survival. Every needless death, every bit of torture, every deception I have woven, was cleverly designed to bring me to Nyl'theria to destroy the Elvish. That has *always* been my goal."

Zylah covered her orbs when she wished the tears would stop. She didn't want him to see them or her pain, when he was the cause of both.

"Couldn't you have found another way?"

"I did," he stated, causing her to lower her hands. "And it

was too late by the time I discovered it. I'd already learned that breaking your skulls was the answer to killing your kind, after centuries of trying to find out how, and I gave my decree immediately upon gaining that knowledge. Once I let go of my anger surrounding Katerina's death and finally breaking free of her hatred fuelling my own, I figured out the answer. But, like I said, it was too late. Decrees and bounties take *time* to spread through the Veil, and even longer to undo them. If you were attacked within the last five months before my 'death,' then I'd already removed my order and it mattered naught. I even told my army to leave your kind alone completely."

"You undid it?" she asked, hope flaring in her chest.

"Yes, but what did it matter? The path I took to discover how to kill your kind means everything I did was unnecessary. I wasted *years* on a pointless vendetta for another person, and ruined my own." His right hand fisted as he threw his head to the side with his features twisted into what she thought, *hoped* even, was shame. "I allowed it to go on for too long."

"So you made a mistake?" she asked, creeping a foot forward as she dipped her head to the side he'd turned his own.

*Please say it.* She wanted him to admit to it, to apologise for it. She wanted him to regret it, because if he did... she may be able to forgive him. She wanted that more than anything.

Zylah... *adored* him. She didn't wish to lose that if it was over something that brought him shame. People made mistakes. Of course, not as horrible as this, but she also didn't *care* for anyone outside of them.

Well, perhaps she now cared for the few kind Demons she'd met recently, but that was only because she'd come to know them. Fayren, Rook... both these people had known her as herself, and they hadn't shunned her. Instead, they welcomed her warmly and gave her a sense of self she didn't know she lacked.

One without him. A sense of independence. She was capable of befriending others on her own.

She didn't need him anymore, but she... *longed* for him. Could that be enough? She wanted it to be. These feelings of betrayal hurt, but so did the idea of losing him.

The past few months were hard to let go of, even if this

startling revelation was painful. He'd done much for her, more than anyone else had. She also didn't want to be *alone* again.

"Of course I made a mistake," he answered, shrugging one of his shoulders. "It's the nature of those with intelligence, no matter what species. But the cost of certain mistakes is irredeemable, and I'm aware of that. I lost my friend many times over because of my fuck ups, and I doubt this conversation will end any other way but the same. I've always known that, which is why I sought to give you all the knowledge I could before then."

Once more, hope fluttered in her chest.

"Did you help me to make up for it?" she asked, her tears ebbing until her orbs turned solid once more – despite the bottoms of them continuing to waver.

From the corner of his eye, his gaze slid to hers. Hardness befell his features as he said, "Partly. You did save me from death, and I felt indebted to you for that."

She hated that he used the word *partly*, and a soft growl came from her. "You're *still* hiding things."

"Of course I am," he said with a cruel chuckle. "The further you dig, the more you'll find how much of a despicable person I am. The question is: how much do you want our time together to weigh on you painfully?"

His response made her gut tighten with worry. She chittered nervously and scratched at her collar of fur in thought. But she knew her answer.

"I want to know everything."

"You really want to know?" It sounded like a warning and a threat all rolled into one.

Her shoulders turned inwards as anxious uncertainty made her want to hide. "Yes."

Once more, his expression grew dark and unfeeling. And Zylah saw it for what it was: a wall. Not for her, but for himself. It was his way of hiding from his own emotions, to the point he suppressed them under callousness and emptiness.

"My main goal was to manipulate you enough that you felt indebted to me and disregarded your own wellbeing. And if you sought my companionship so deeply, you'd want to follow me anywhere, which meant becoming a tool I could wield in

Nyl'theria. You would protect me as I made myself a champion with the Elvish Demons, convincing them to join my war and take over the Elven city. To essentially be my living shield and sword in a realm ruled very differently to this one, and one in which I am a nobody and my power is unknown. Once they saw your loyalty after you'd spilled your own blood for my sake, and the undying strength I wielded through you, then witnessed the overwhelming strength of my magic, they would bow to my whims until they gave me what I want. *That* is initially what kept me to your side."

Of its own accord, her jaw fell in disbelief. Her sight deepened in its saddened hue, and she turned her skull away as a painful whine ripped up her throat.

"Quite horrible, isn't it?" he said coldly, and she looked away even further until she couldn't see him at all.

Zylah hugged her midsection, wishing the answer she'd sought wasn't so despicable. She whimpered uncontrollably when it felt like her heart was about to give out.

"That is the kind of person I am. Everything I do is enveloped in cruelty and selfish gain. I take what I want with very little care for others, so long as I complete my goal."

"So *everything* was, essentially, a lie." She was determined to hold back her tears this time, even if she sniffled and whimpered.

"In the beginning, yes," he confirmed, and it felt like a claw strike right to her being.

"Everything you've done for me... taking me through Spiral Haven, to Fayren's, what happened after you got back your magic... all of it was to trick me into feeling more for you so you could make me some kind of tool? You even used my enjoyment of books against me."

"No. None of that was intentional," he said, his tone surprisingly gentle.

Confused, Zylah covered her bony face when she couldn't hold back her tears. "What does that even *mean*?"

"You are missing the parts where I said *initially* and *in the beginning*," he answered. "My intentions changed quickly when I could see you didn't want to cause harm to others. The feelings I wanted to manipulate were platonic. I've never been the kind of person to manipulate a female's *affection* for my own gain. It becomes entangled with anguish too quickly. It's also easier to manipulate someone when I feel nothing in return."

"Then why did you do everything?!" she shouted, her orbs, and therefore her tears, flaring into crimson. "You are being needlessly confusing!"

"I'm answering your questions, that is all. Zylah, I began teaching you for two reasons: one was entirely selfish, and the other was as a way to make up for what I've done. If I could save one Mavka from my own actions, and ensure they live a better life, a part of me hoped that would assuage my own guilt, which, once again, was inherently selfish. I gave up both of those weeks ago."

"Explain it to me in a way that is easier to understand, because right now, you are making me *hate* you."

Exasperated, Zylah lifted her skull and looked at him from the corner of her sight. As if he didn't realise she was now looking upon him, she noticed his brows were narrowed, while his eyes were crinkled in what could only be sympathy.

Something became startlingly apparent.

"You are doing it on purpose. You *want* me to hate you."

The expression was once more hidden by his *false* indifference. "Hate is a much easier sorrow to bear. It kills one's affection for someone swiftly and far less painfully."

"It doesn't feel any less painful!" she shrieked, her right hand curling into a fist. She wasn't sure why, maybe to finally fucking hit him!

"This conversation will end only one way," he said, tilting his head. "After today, I doubt you will want to be near me. The least I can do is share the worst about me to make that easier for you."

"I want the truth!" she roared, baring her claws when she wanted to slash out at him and gouge out her heart at the same time. "All of it!"

Her ribcage felt so tight around her anxiety-filled lungs, squeezing against them from the inside. It was as if her entire torso was being strangled tighter and tighter until something would break or die within her. Every breath that escaped her was so sharp with pain, she was almost wheezing.

"The truth comes with consequences. Concealing them is what is best for you."

"I don't *care* what's best for me. *I* am the one who gets to decide that. You don't get to have a say!"

His features dropped into a small glare. "I do when it involves me."

Zylah scoffed. "Coward. You are hiding for yourself. After this conversation, even *I* can see that." What else was that but cowardness?

"You're wrong," he snapped back with a small growl.

Oh! She probed a sore spot. She guessed he didn't like being called a coward, or at least someone *seeing* past his false exterior.

A small, spiteful laugh left her. "Am I? Because it doesn't seem that way."

Mimicking him from earlier and wanting to appear indifferent, Zylah folded her arms and lifted her head superiorly.

Honestly, she was one last push from telling him to just... leave. The only things stopping her were that there was more he was hiding, and she could tell that's what he wanted. He was still here for a reason; he would have disappeared otherwise.

It felt as if Jabez was just waiting for Zylah to give up and push him away permanently. Like if he truly killed enough of her affection, she'd no longer want to be near him.

She wanted to be wrong, but the ache in her heart told her otherwise.

"I just... want to know what was real and what was a lie," Zylah eventually stated with sorrow. "I feel like I at least deserve that."

Zylah gasped and unfolded her arms when the stone ground *cracked* beneath his right foot, just as a charge of magic sparked in the air. When she brought her sight back up to his face, all she saw were screwed-up features and his ears darted back in rage. Eyes narrowed into a deep glare, his lips curled back to bare his fangs in a deep and vicious snarl.

Even his arms shook with anger, his fingers curled like he

wanted to stiffen them for a debilitating claw strike.

Fayren did inform her, in front of him no less, that he had a horrible temper. He also admitted to it. After how badly he'd upset her, she refused to feel shame in using that knowledge against him to get what she wanted.

She wanted him angry, and therefore irrational.

Zylah let out a bitter laugh, her head lowering while she curled her left hand into a fist. "What is worse than what you have told me? You already admitted to wanting to destroy my kind, to wanting to use me like I'm nothing but a... a bloodthirsty *monster*. I thought at least *you,* of all creatures, would not think that way about me."

The charge in the air became more chaotic, to the point her fur lifted in alert, warning her of imminent danger.

"You said you didn't lie–"

"I already told you I didn't," he snarled, his eyes sharpening.

"But all you have done is lie. In your actions, your kindness, in everything you've done for me, it was all just to manipulate me. Nothing was genuine!"

"Zylah," he warned.

"You're either a coward who cannot admit the truth, or you think so little of me that you believe I cannot handle it!"

The ground cracked a little more before he stomped his foot forward in anger.

"I wouldn't have shoved my head between a female's thighs for manipulation, but because I wanted to know what she fucking tasted like! *That* shows how little you know of me."

Goosebumps erupted across her flesh in a sudden wave at his unexpected admission, causing her fur to puff with the most confusing and alarming arousal.

Trying not to let her heart stutter, she shouted, "Because you refused to tell me anything!"

"Because I care about you, you silly female! Why do you think I stayed by your side when I realised obtaining your help was fucking pointless? I knew it when I told you 'the king of Demons' shared how to kill your kind, and yet I didn't know how to admit the truth to you because I didn't want to. And I have been questioning every action I have taken since then."

"That was weeks ago," Zylah stated, shaking her head.

"Exactly. But a part of me didn't want to leave, and yet I knew the moment I told you the truth, that would be the end. Fuck's sake, Zylah. Do you think I would just take anyone through Spiral Haven for fun? I only did it because I wanted to bring you joy, when it gained me nothing. I risked my own discovery to do so, knowing my magic use was making me sick. I didn't *faint* simply because I was tired."

"You didn't have to do that for me," she tried to shout, only for it to come out softer than she intended as guilt weighed on her.

She hadn't known it was making him *sick*.

"No, but I did it because I wanted to." He covered his face just as the sparks of magic in the air began to dissipate. "I don't know why I feel this way about you. In all regards, it makes little sense. What I've done to your kind should have been enough of a barrier for me, yet I find you attractive all the same. Like I said, entangling affection into manipulation is idiotic, especially when it comes to *my own.* Yet, no matter how much I told myself I should reveal everything to you and leave, I found you alluring to the point I just *couldn't.*"

*He finds me alluring?* Zylah thought, her head rearing back in surprise. Her stomach betrayed her by fluttering in joy.

"You want the ugly truth so bad? Fine." He lowered his hand so his gaze bore into hers unwaveringly. "How I feel changes nothing. It doesn't fix what I've done, or how I've wronged you and the rest of your kind. It doesn't matter that I find your beauty otherworldly, or that I think your personality is charming. Or that every time I look at that cute little tail of yours, it drives me fucking insane to the point I want nothing more than to shove my cock in you until I hear you scream."

Despite the horrible emotions swirling in her chest, her sight flickered purple against her will. *That* was not what she had been expecting him to say, and her pussy immediately clenched in reaction, the image compelling and wild.

Noting the flicker of desire in her orbs, his eyes crinkled in... anguish? She wished she could properly decipher it.

"And whatever it is you feel for me is irrelevant. I'm a very broken man who is incapable of feeling anything truly deep. I've lived my life purposely guaranteeing no one can get close to me. Asking for anything more is a foolproof path to disaster."

Zylah cupped her hands to her chest to fidget with them. "But maybe I can..."

"Do what? Change me? Fix me? I've worn my flaws as a shield from the moment I left Nyl'theria. It is what has kept me alive, and no one has managed to change me in over three hundred years."

"But maybe I could be different," Zylah whispered, gripping her left biceps.

"You *are* different," he admitted, making hope flare in her chest.

If what he said was true... then the past few weeks, the only ones that truly mattered, were genuine, and her feelings didn't need to change. She wanted to hold onto him, to the way she felt about him. It touched her to know he wanted her, desired her, found her beautiful, alluring, and cute. He'd never said remotely anything like that to her before, and it instantly made tenderness spread throughout her chest.

She thought those things about him too.

Sure, he'd lied to her by withholding the truth, but he'd admitted to not wanting to because of his own *affection*. He'd wanted to... *be* with her, even if it was hidden behind deceit to simply prolong their time together.

He'd even once said he would share all this with her eventually, but he wanted her to like him more first.

She'd thought little of it at the time, figuring he was just being playful because she'd assumed nothing he told her could truly be that bad. It was all horrible, and had he kept quiet about how much he desired her, she may have truly come to hate him.

But she could see he regretted his past actions, that they did hold weight to him. He'd even tried to undo them. *He really has been trying to protect me.* From himself, the world, from everything that could potentially be a danger.

She now understood why he'd been refraining from being intimate with her, or being affectionate with her when it was obvious she wanted more. He knew she'd feel betrayed by learning all this and hadn't wanted to deepen that.

Even if he'd done many cruel things, he'd never purposefully done them to her. He didn't even know her before two months ago. Sure, he *had* been intending to manipulate her, but if he was being honest and he truly had disregarded that weeks ago, then... she knew she could forgive him.

Her reasons for keeping him hadn't been fuelled by innocence. She wanted someone intelligent to teach her, but even before that she'd wanted someone, *anyone*, to ease her loneliness. She hadn't cared if it was a fox, a human, or him. Just something.

And she'd killed many creatures in her attempts at that. If the raven-skulled Mavka hadn't taken that redheaded human from her, she likely would have killed her too. But she had disregarded the danger she presented to the little female in the hopes a human could ease her loneliness.

That was considered selfish, wasn't it?

"You knew telling me this would stop me from hating you," she eventually stated, figuring that out on her own.

"Which makes the wound that much harder to bear when I leave."

Zylah swallowed thickly. "B-but I don't want you to leave."

His lids lowered in obvious annoyance. "Come now. You can't say you want me to stay after everything I just told you."

"Why not?"

His head cocked like he hadn't expected her response. "Because it would be foolish. I just told you I'm incapable of giving you anything of value, that I have caused immense pain to your kind, and I have deceived you. This will irrevocably destroy your trust in me. You will question everything I do and say from here on out."

"But if you promise to be honest from now on, then I could," she rebutted, tilting her head. "I understand enough about my own feelings to know what I want and know what I can forgive."

Perhaps it was naïve of her, but she did think if she showered him with affection, he'd truly return it. He'd already admitted to feeling *something* for her. Could that be enough?

Zylah didn't know the depths of what she wanted, but maybe they could discover that together.

She still had questions, like what a bride was for a Mavka. She didn't even know what that was, and she'd instantly felt a pull towards him upon just learning of a possible deeper connection. She longed to know what it meant, and why her orbs flared pink when she'd looked at him when they were sitting on that tree branch in Spiral Haven.

His brows narrowed deeply and his ears drooped. He frowned, like he couldn't understand her, to the point he even shook his head.

"I always knew you were hiding things," Zylah admitted, bringing her hands down to fiddle with the bottom of her skirt in nervousness. "No, I didn't know they would be anything like this, but I was hoping you'd come to care for me enough to share everything about yourself. I already knew some of it would be dark and nasty, and I did prepare myself a little."

His lips pulled tight in disbelief, and he waved a hand through the air. "You have no idea what you're talking about. I've seen people try to mend broken trust time and time again, and it always fails."

Zylah hated how he immediately dismissed her. He was purposefully trying to kill her feelings for him, and she was beginning to wish that was possible. Perhaps she shouldn't have pushed for the whole truth, since she really was finding it difficult to accept him leaving when she knew he felt something for her.

She didn't even care how small that something was, which made her feel unbelievably pathetic.

The bottoms of her orbs wavered, but she tried to stop herself from crying again. A small whine ripped from her, just as the inevitable happened and floating droplets obscured parts of her vision once more.

"Why am I not good enough for you to *try*?" He said he cared, but he wasn't willing to try, and that felt worse than anything else.

"Because I'm a monster!" Jabez roared, his fingers curled to bare his sharp, near claw-like nails as he threw one of his arms to the side. "What I have done is not forgivable! From the moment I stepped into this godsforsaken realm, I have been nothing but a darkness upon it. I have killed in leagues, tortured, bullied, and done everything in my power to get my way. I made sure anything that didn't worship me feared me instead, and what retaliated against me died without remorse."

He stomped closer, and the rage she saw was entirely directed inwards. It was nothing like before when he'd charged the air with chaotic magic. Instead, she thought she may be witnessing anguish, regret, and... self-loathing.

"You know *nothing* of what I have done, or what I am truly capable of. I would kill my friends so long as it benefited me. I tortured one of your kind, Zylah. You are holding on to tenderness for a monster who brutalised someone who had done nothing to warrant it. I plucked him from the inner ring, and I shoved him in fire, drowned him, buried him, cut off his head. I cut him open while he was conscious because your kind is *indestructible,* but I wanted fucking answers. I did anything and everything I could to see how to kill your kind because I'm fucking *evil.*"

"I don't even know who that is!" she shouted back, trying not to flinch or grimace at the horrible things he was saying. "You want me to feel pity for someone I don't know because you think it'll make me hate you!"

"It *should* make you hate me. I know you Mavka can be driven by your emotions, that your familial ties mean little to you unless you develop a deeper bond, but this stubbornness is foolish!"

"What difference does it make to me? You already admitted to torturing people. So long as you stop–"

"When have I ever stated I would stop? I told you, I'm incapable of change. Nothing you do or say will stop me from going to Nyl'theria and trying to take over that world. I will not waste the last twenty-one years of my life by giving up now. What I will have to do there is instil fear, as they are brutal Demons who will refuse to follow someone like me."

"Someone like you?"

"I am part Elf, Zylah! My scent gives off that I am different. If they don't fear me, they'll hunt me until they have consumed me. They war among themselves to further their own completion, consuming each other as there is nothing else left to *feed* on. And the only way to instil fear is to hurt everything that tries to touch me until they worry for their own demise. My hands are coated in blood, and I am willing to shed more."

"Then I will go with you!" Zylah blurted out.

"You can't mean that," he grated out, his head flinching back as his face twisted with confusion, like he couldn't fathom why she was being so stubborn. "You have no desire to hurt others. Taking that journey with me will only bring you pain."

"I know... and I don't care," Zylah whispered, before hugging her midsection again. "Isn't that what you wanted? For me to go with you so you could finally destroy the Elvish?"

"Yes, but..." His words died when his eyes crinkled in an emotion she couldn't read.

He didn't finish what he was saying.

She wasn't sure if that was because he didn't know what he wanted to say, or if he was withholding something important. She knew pushing further would get her nowhere.

"I'm offering to help you, to give you what you want."

"Why?" he asked, his voice breaking.

"Because I want you to stay with me."

He let out a sigh, his expression falling into something that appeared numb. He covered his face and shook it. "I think you need time alone to think about the weight of that offer, and what it truly means. I won't accept the emotionally driven words of a person who's obviously in distress."

How dare he! Zylah knew what she was saying!

She snapped her jaws at him in warning, stamped her foot until it made a dull thump, and produced a growl with her sight flaring red. "If you leave, I will be angry."

His lips twitched in annoyance as he rolled his eyes. "You're already fucking angry." He ran his fingers through his hair, a sign that he was deeply frustrated. "You've already proven how little your anger matters to your own sense of morals. You're being irrational."

"If you leave now, maybe I will not want you to come back then!"

She instantly knew she'd said the wrong thing when he grimaced.

But she wanted to resolve this. She wanted answers and to feel better – she could only do that with him here. She didn't want to be on her own, not when it felt like part of her heart had been ripped out of her chest cavity.

She wanted *him* to make her feel better.

"Another lesson to teach you, Zylah. You should watch your words, as they can have lasting effects."

Before she could even try to take them back, he was gone.

With nothing but the sound of rain and his lingering scent to help her through this, Zylah covered her face as a whine rattled her chest. She crouched down to make herself feel smaller, to shelter the pain that lingered in her abdomen and made her sniffle and heave.

*What am I supposed to do?*

She no longer knew how to feel.

# TWENTY-FIVE

With his cloak hood hiding him further under the cover of night, Jabez sat on a tall pile of pointless rubble. The last time he'd been here, he knew part of his castle had still been standing.

Likely due to the weather and the foundations already being weakened, the last section had come down in the past two months.

In front of him was a crumbling wall barely tall enough to come to hip height. Much of what surrounded him was broken or cracked boulders, or sections of carved stone that refused to topple. Behind him was nothing but a flat mound of jagged rubble.

Where he sat was once his throne room – the place where his rule had ended.

Perhaps another would be upset by the state of the mess, but Jabez was unbothered. He had other things on his mind.

He didn't like that once he immediately left Zylah's presence, the only place he could think to go was Fayren's. The little fox Demon had fretted upon finding him nearly passed out in front of her cottage, but his exhaustion and mana-depletion sickness had finally taken its toll on his body.

She'd annoyingly cooed and mothered him as she dragged his weak body to her bed, and then he passed out immediately. Fayren had attempted to help with the fever racking his body by dabbing a cold compress against his forehead. She'd stopped when she realised it only woke him whenever she approached, and he'd grabbed her wrist to prevent her from touching him.

She left him be, seeing that he didn't want nor need her help, and she was only disturbing him from finally achieving rest.

For weeks he'd been suffering from a lack of sleep. *More like years.* His mind had never truly felt at ease – always alert for danger, always whirling with dark and unwelcome thoughts.

As much as the ookmanik had ensured he suffered, he'd managed to gain at least twelve hours of rest – which was more than he could say for most of his life on Earth.

He'd hidden all this from Zylah, of course. He wasn't one to admit to his weaknesses, especially not in front of someone clearly upset. It was partly the reason he'd left. If he'd continued to stay and argue with her, he likely would have collapsed.

He also did truly believe she needed time to *think.*

*I didn't expect her to offer to come to Nyl'theria on my behalf,* he thought as he picked up a small chipped stone and inspected it. He realised he should have, but he'd just been foolishly *hoping* she wouldn't.

He'd considered her offer idiotic, not that he would say that to her bony face. *Her emotions were just high. She had no idea what she was saying.* Not the weight of it, nor the repercussions.

She'd forgiven him far too easily, and he found that to be rather absurd. *She cares for me a lot more than I thought.* As honoured as he felt about that, the issue remained that it was making her foolish. No one's heart should be this set on a person to the point they'd completely disregard the horrible things someone had done in the past.

*But that's what Mavka are like.* Once they had their heart on something or someone, they were hard to dissuade. They didn't think nor act like a human and were emotional creatures.

Now that he'd slept, finally recuperating enough mana that expending it shouldn't lead to any more problems, he sighed at his behaviour. He tossed the stone aside in annoyance at himself.

*I should have just kept my fucking mouth shut.* It would have been much easier had he not stupidly blurted out his own fucked-up, confused, and insane feelings. Feelings he had no idea how to dissect and assess. None of it made sense, yet they were obviously present, and he had no idea if they ran deeper than merely surface level.

They could be nothing but infatuation and curiosity. Maybe even loneliness eased by the contentment he found near her. They could even be more than just simple desire – but one thing he did know for certain, lust did not make him act like an explosive *idiot*.

Sure, it could blindside him like anyone who was obsessed with another, but it shouldn't make him act irrationally. It shouldn't make him stand in a cave and shout at a crying female pouring her heart out to him, just because seeing her damn tears wounded him.

With his elbow stabbing into his folded knee, he shoved his fingers into his clenched eyes in frustration at himself. *What is wrong with me?*

His thoughts were unravelling more than usual, chaotic and intrusive in the worst way possible. Where was his hyperfixation for his revenge? Why was he sitting on a pile of rubbish instead of heading through the portal hidden away by a garden just on the other side of the wall in front of him?

The answer was simple: it was because he didn't want to, and the reason lay over a thousand kilometres away in a fucking cave. Probably crying, wondering if he actually did not intend to return because of her foolish jab at him.

Perhaps she didn't want him to.

That would make things much easier for him. A clean cut was always easier to mend, rather than the mess he'd torn between them.

*I know I don't love her.* Love was just not an emotion he was capable of. He was too ruined inside, too broken. He'd removed his tender heart when he'd been a mere boy and made sure to never transplant another one within him. What sat in his chest was an empty hole no one could fill.

Not the female Demons he'd attempted to court, all of whom failed to gain his full affection. Not Katerina, who he thought may have been a good fit for him, as she'd been toxic in all the ways he was – manipulative, cunning, broken.

Unfortunately, they were also traits he disliked in himself.

*But I would be an idiot to ignore that Zylah loves me.* At least, to some degree. Enough to shed her own morals and join him in his war like a lovesick woman chasing after a careless man.

He doubted he'd ever be able to return such affection. He didn't believe someone had to love themselves first to be loved, but the person just needed to seek it in some form. Jabez definitely lacked the first part of that sentiment, and he didn't give a flying fuck about the second part.

He wanted nothing from anyone, unless it was to fuel his own bloodthirst.

Those had been his thoughts for the past three centuries, so why did he feel himself wavering now? For a fucking Mavka, no less.

She should hate him. In retrospect, she should have attempted to kill him for what he admitted. He was an atrocious person, and he'd leaned on that his entire adult life. If he admitted to that, then anything he did was born from something wrong and evil within him. He'd used that as a way to shed any guilt, putting it up to being a cruel, unfeeling, self-orientated person.

A person couldn't hate themselves for something they were knowingly doing. They also didn't have to like themselves, either.

Instead, he'd tried to mould himself into an idea. An idea didn't have to have a heart, morals, or compassion. An idea was not a real person. He could feel desire and affection, although it was never deeper than surface level, so the emptiness within him mattered naught.

He could look in the mirror that way. Actually, he made sure doing so allowed him to fixate on the Elvish parts of him in order to fuel himself as an idea. To hate that part of himself, and to think of the Demon in him as a priceless tool to be used.

His magic was simply both sides of himself managing to bleed together to make him into some powerful being that consumed more, and more, until he could be unstoppable. A god in the lowest mortal sense.

It'd worked up until recently.

So why was the empty hole in his chest trying to grow a heart he didn't want and had never needed?

*I'll only bring her pain.* In her one-sided deep affections, in the fact that he would likely always prioritise his vendetta over her, and how he was absolutely willing to die for it. Of course he tried to avoid his own death, but that was simply so his plans could come to fruition.

So his idea didn't die alongside him.

*I should just leave–* Before he could finish his thought, he sensed the air around him shift.

In all rights, what he felt shouldn't be perceivable, but he'd long realised when Weldir's black mist was being disturbed. And, since his disappearance, this area had become darker due to that demigod's intangible reach.

Only one creature could do such a thing.

*So, that Mavka and his bride told the others I'm still alive.* Then again, he'd foreseen that. It'd only been a few days since he and Zylah had met them, after all, and he was certain they were trying to figure out some kind of scheme to intervene. Her *parents* wouldn't like that she was spending time with him.

Unless, of course, Weldir sensed him hanging out in his foreboding mist. *That's a possibility.*

Jabez picked up another stone and rolled it in his palm as he coldly stated, "You would be wise to remain incorporeal."

Weldir's mist shifted as a figure – so transparent she'd lost all colour and had turned white as a Ghost – floated to his left. With her toes hovering barely an inch from the ground, she slid through the air like one might across ice and moved in front of him.

For someone he hated, it was impossible to ignore that she was a pretty thing. When she wasn't incorporeal and almost invisible, her brown skin was near flawless – not reflecting the hundreds of years she'd lived. If he had to guess, Weldir must have found her when she was in her early twenties, and she hadn't aged a day since then.

Her hardened personality matched her sharp but feminine

features – which he'd once found contradictory when she'd been a softer being. Her brows were arched, her cheeks high, and her jaw strong. Her nose was rounded and sat above a set of full, plump lips.

Her loose corkscrew curls were often messy from travelling through the Veil, but her dark-brown hair had always appeared glossy, even when it was littered with leaves or twigs.

Her curved and busty figure was hidden underneath her white cloak of feathers, but he vaguely remembered it from before she'd obtained this covering. It used to be black, like a raven's dowl, but she'd opted for a more owl-like quality after a few decades. Her outfit over the many years had changed often, evolving to what it was today: a white dress that left her legs bare from the knees down.

She used to wear boots and flats, but he figured she'd given up on those. They wouldn't last through her years, and she probably discovered being barefooted made her more nimble.

Jabez ignored her ghostly appearance as he looked down at what lay in his palm. He tossed it nonchalantly, as if to prove her presence here meant little to him.

"What do you want?" Jabez asked.

"To see you be miserable," the Witch Owl stated, before hopping up onto the stone wall in front of him as if it was a seat. She crossed her ankles and swung her legs, her bare feet going through the solid wall and disappearing before reappearing as they flung forward.

Jabez rolled his eyes and let his head fall to the side. "Misery you won't find." He gestured to the rubble beneath him, and made his tone exaggerated and flamboyant for his next words. "I'm merely scheming the best way to rebuild my castle and rise from the ashes of my death like a phoenix."

He lifted his gaze up to her face, just in time to see her smug appearance fall and dread wash over it. Her loose curls floated around her face and hung there as she lowered her gaze in anger, peering at him through long, dark eyelashes.

"You just don't give up, do you, Elf?"

He stifled the urge to sneer at what she'd called him, despising the word. Especially as it was intended to be an insult.

"No. I'm incapable of giving up." He cocked a brow at her, feigning smugness. "Why did you think it would be different this time?"

Her full lips pouted in ire. "I thought your near death would awaken you from your stupidity."

"So long as I live, while the Elysians hold their impenetrable city, I will always be steadfast in destroying it. That has never changed in the many years we've fought."

"Then why are you sitting on the evidence of your ruin like a pathetic man, rather than trying to rebuild it as swiftly as possible like last time?" She cocked her brow this time, and her lips curled knowingly.

"I'm searching for something vital first."

Yeah, the answer as to why he felt something for Zylah, to the point he had this strange, radiating ache in his chest right now. Maybe why his cock kept jerking at the smallest thing she did, or why he was so damn drawn to her in the first place.

Where did all his cunning callousness go? She'd offered him exactly what he wanted, and he was finding excuses *not* to take her up on it.

And rather than discarding her because he knew bringing her to Nyl'theria was a foolish decision on his part, he was fucking finding excuses to not do that either.

It should have been easy. Had any other female presented her manipulative ultimatum of him staying to give her what she wanted, or to leave and never come back if he did what he wanted, he would have smugly left in a heartbeat.

He *may* have inferred it with his last words, but they'd been hollow. Well, not at the time due to his anger, but after much reflection, he realised they'd held not an ounce of weight. Instead, they only added to the chaos of his thoughts and questions as to why he was still fucking *here* in this godsforsaken, shitty realm.

But he really did adore needling the Witch Owl, and he let a malicious grin fill his face.

"Coming to pester me like this will only fuel my hatred and push me to rebuild faster." With the stone clasped firmly in his grip, he lifted his forefinger to tap at his lips in smug thought. "Now you've revealed that you know how to trap me, and I doubt you have a second stone to blast me with. You have no secrets, nothing left to fight with, and, Lindiwe, we *both* know how much of a cunning bastard I am. My Demons will only see my return as further proof that I'm all-powerful, and those who didn't follow me will surely do so now. You've handed me the perfect opportunity to come back stronger than ever, with more influence. What will you and your offspring do when my demands hold even more weight?"

He gave her his best charming smile at the end, especially as he could see her delight waning with each word. Her humour-filled lips uncurled, and her brows slowly furrowed until they pathetically made her eyes appear beseeching.

"Can't you just leave us alone?" she rasped, her distant voice cracking with emotion. "We want nothing to do with this."

"You have Weldir to thank for your situation. Had he joined me like I offered, everything would have been different."

"But he does not hate the Elves like you do!" She threw her arms out to the side in frustration.

"We were cut from the same cloth. Both created by the Elvish trying to intervene with the Demons, both of us scorned and locked away, both then freed only to be trapped in a world we can't escape."

"Just because you experienced the same doesn't mean he has to feel the same way you do." She sighed, and let her arms fall into her lap in defeat. "He wants to protect, and you want to destroy. Can't you just find another way and leave us be?"

Jabez rolled his eyes and then brought his arm back to toss the stone in his hand at her. It sailed through the air, went through her intangible body, and clunked against the ground on the other side of the wall.

"Quit your whining," he bit at her lightly. "I have no intention of harming your little Mavka anymore. I gave that up a while ago."

"You had them hunted!"

"And I removed that order months ago too." When her lips parted in disbelief, he shook his head. "Demons like to hunt. They jump on bounties and spread word swiftly. They are less inclined to share the removal of a decree so enthusiastically.

You attempted to destroy someone who no longer had the desire to harm you."

"You had my son killed," she stated, hurt further bowing her eyes.

"And how many sons, daughters, fathers, and mothers have your precious sons killed?"

He cocked a brow at her superiorly and her lips tightened.

She couldn't deny it; she was a hypocrite in her own right. She allowed them to be brought into the world, knowing they would be violent and unsympathetic towards the hundreds they'd eaten – families destroyed or broken apart. It didn't matter if they were humans or Demons. She never stopped them from killing, and he wondered if she'd shed her guilt about it in the same way he had.

She wanted him to feel sympathy when her hands were just as unclean as his were.

But Jabez knew how much her children meant to her, and he *was* in a giving mood. Surprising, since he was feeling rather sour after his argument with Zylah – or maybe that was why he was inclined to pity her this night.

Jabez picked up a new stone to play with to appear indifferent. "What was his name?"

He noted her brows drew together in confusion at his question. "Aleron," she answered quietly.

"I apologise for Aleron's death, then," he said nonchalantly. "Like I said, I'd already removed my decree by then."

Actually, he'd done it before the day he'd asked Merikh to join his side once more and come with him to Nyl'theria. He'd already been formulating his next plans, and they'd involved him – someone he trusted, someone he had faith wouldn't fail him. When his old friend didn't turn up at the castle like he'd expected him to, Jabez had then begun figuring out other options.

One in particular required no Mavka's aid nor death, but it was dangerous. Possible, although it could take years to give him what he wanted.

Years he no longer wanted to wait. He was getting older, which tamped down his rage in withered tiredness.

"Is that supposed to make me feel better?" Lindiwe asked

in exasperation, shaking her head at him.

"No. It matters naught. It changes nothing and doesn't bring him back." He inspected his new rock, finding it rougher than the others – likely a piece of broken clay that kept the stones of his castle together. "But it's an apology all the same. Through my false death, that decree has been abolished, and your terrifying children are free to walk Austrális and eat everything they stumble upon. *That* should at least bring you peace."

Once more, she looked as though she didn't know what to make of him. Then again, it was rare for Jabez to apologise, and he only did so for her benefit rather than his own.

What would his regret do to aid her, other than make him appear like a pitiful man seeking sympathy for his own stupidity?

"I guess knowing you will leave us be does bring me peace," she admitted after a small silence of her weighing his words. Then her lips curled as she looked off to the side. "And Weldir brought Aleron back anyway."

Jabez paused and tilted his head as he lifted his gaze to her properly. "He is a god of the afterlife. That shouldn't be possible." When her lips curled further, tenderness and joy filling her expression, his features twisted into a cringe of disgust. He threw his hands up. "Great. He's figured out how to return the dead. What's next? He'll obtain a physical form and finally be free?"

That would irritate Jabez to no end.

He wanted Weldir to suffer as much as he did, especially for getting in his way for the last three centuries. If it hadn't been for that demigod and his damn ward blocking his Demon army from leaving Earth... Jabez's plans would have come to fruition decades, if not centuries, ago.

He didn't trust the way Lindiwe's expression creased in humour as she shifted to fix it on him. He didn't like that his exasperated question... could be the truth. She didn't deny or confirm it.

*Fuck,* he thought, tossing the stone to the side. *Something has changed.*

Much had changed in only a short period of time, and none

of it was in his favour. The past three years were evidence of that, from his own demise, to Katerina's death, to the other Mavka constantly obtaining new brides... to Zylah.

The world was shifting. His time here was ending.

Part of him was relieved about that, as much as it brought on a new page of darkness.

"Where is Zylah?" she asked.

*She didn't call her... what was it again? Fyodor?* So, she truly had spoken to Zylah's parents.

"I'm surprised you don't know," he answered, lifting a shoulder to shrug. "Don't you watch all your children? I'm betting Weldir watched us walk through his mist."

Even now, Jabez had the inkling there was a set of creepy eyes tingling the back of his neck. Hopefully his worry over Weldir's physical form was nothing but paranoia, and he didn't come to smite Jabez while he sat here, unaware of the potential danger.

Or, perhaps, he knew Jabez was ready for anything and everything. He had his magic back; nothing could stop him from creating a protective force or teleporting the moment he sensed another presence.

He'd be gone before they even had time to blink.

"Zylah is not his direct descendant. He can't feel her like he feels our children, and I didn't know where her burrow was because the moment I left her to help another of my children, our inability to scry for her meant we lost her."

Just further proof that she was different from the rest of her kind. She was even out of Weldir's gaze, and he hadn't thought about what that would have meant for him up until now. It was a relief to know their privacy hadn't been violated.

"It also didn't help that she was taken from sight by the whims of an unpredictable man when he *did* find her."

Ah, so they had at least watched *some* of their time together in the Veil since they'd likely disturbed his mist. He doubted Weldir had been able to observe in the underground pocket beneath the village, as the stone itself had an additional spell on it to stop those from seeing that area. That spell was tied to the mana stone, ensuring it didn't need Jabez's help to fuel it – he'd always been worried about someone trying to steal it.

They'd likely watched them at Fayren's and within Spiral Haven. A smile threatened to curl his lips when he thought that may have been confusing for them.

Watching him care for Zylah, spending time with her like a male courting a female... yes, that would be very confusing.

They likely didn't intervene or show themselves earlier with her by his side.

Jabez waved his hand through the air dismissively. "She's somewhere safe."

Lindiwe's lips flattened disapprovingly. "Whatever it is you're planning with her, I ask that you stop. She is my grandchild, after all. I want to see her safe as well."

Not liking being told what to do, Jabez chuckled, his eyes crinkling with mischief.

Then he lifted his right hand to show her his uneven nails, brought the two he'd had within Zylah's pussy to his mouth, and sucked on them. At her horror, he brought them out with a wet pop and gave her his trimmed middle finger.

She visibly shuddered, and he found that utterly satisfying.

"I do what I want," he answered with a large grin. "Haven't you learned that trying to tell me otherwise just makes me want to do *exactly* the thing you don't approve of?"

"You're disgustingly vile."

"I'm an opportunist," Jabez answered with a shrug. "Such are the woes of an uptight prude like yourself."

If she wanted to see the worst in him, then so be it. He had no interest in correcting her, especially as he refused to let her know any truth pertaining to his inner thoughts. Her opinion mattered little to him.

His humour didn't fade as he asked, "How is Merikh these days?"

She stiffened and then appeared guilty as she looked off to the side. "He's fine. Happy, I hope."

Happy. Jabez could live with that.

"Has he found a bride?" he asked nonchalantly, pretending not to care.

"I... believe so."

*A bride, then.* So that's why Merikh didn't come to his side. *I can live with that too.*

After all, even if that bull-horned, bear-skulled Mavka hated Jabez, he still considered him a friend. His only true one. At least one of them deserved some happiness after their shitty, lonely lives.

When Lindiwe said nothing, and Jabez offered only silence, he thought she'd finally disappear. She got what she wanted: answers and peace.

Instead, she remained, haunting him as she'd always done. She'd always liked lingering in his castle, following him as a pestering, untouchable force. The only way to battle that was to taunt her in return, and he'd completely lost the will for it.

He'd lost the will for much these days.

"Why are you still here?" Jabez asked, annoyed that she was choosing to remain when their conversation was obviously done.

She offered him a small smile. "To watch you be miserable."

He sneered at her for that. "Misery you won't find," he repeated.

"I still hate you."

"Feeling is mutual."

Jabez then ignored her completely, while making sure she didn't move from her little perch. He didn't trust she wouldn't try to end him while he receded once more into his thoughts. He could see Lindiwe attempting to mete out justice for all he'd done to her and her kin.

For now, he would allow this amicable truce; this wasn't the first time they'd done this. Two enemies conversing, who had done so for centuries.

In the time they spent in each other's uncomfortable, silent presence this night, only one truth came to him. Digging through the rubble of his past allowed him to clear away just one lingering thought.

A stupid one on his part, he knew, but one that had twisted into an irritating ache in the back of his mind.

He lifted his gaze towards the clouded sky, thankful the rain had disappeared but annoyed he couldn't see the stars and their mystical glittering.

*I want to see Zylah one last time.* And to say a proper

goodbye. Not just for her sake, to give her closure, but also... for his own.

Funny that, as his non-existent heart *squeezed* painfully at the thought of doing so.

*Fuck, I'm pathetic.*

# TWENTY-SIX

After wrestling with his thoughts, those that told him to stay away and those that fought against that notion, Jabez gave in.

The purple of dawn already dimly lit the cave, but nowhere near began to enter it. It would be hours before the thick forest allowed the true strength of the morning to touch the world.

He immediately winced upon entering their cave.

Zylah had managed to dig out their bedding, her books, and everything that they had tucked away in a hidden nook before they left for the Veil. She'd rolled out *both* their bedding in hopes that he'd return.

She sat in the middle of hers. With her lithe arms cuddling her legs and her skull buried against the nook of her knees, blue ethereal drops floated around her head. Every time they splattered against her antlers, they broke apart into tiny fragments, only to disappear in fading sparkles.

Those tears of hers were becoming a sore spot for him, and his chest panged in guilt at being the cause of them. He hadn't liked seeing them the previous morning either – another reason why he'd foolishly snapped.

This wasn't the clean cut he'd been trying to give her.

She didn't scent his arrival, but she did flinch when he approached to sit next to her so they could have a *calm* conversation. She gasped in surprise and lifted her skull. Just as he was crossing his legs to sit, his arse almost made it to the ground when she broke from her self-cuddle and flung herself at him.

"Jabez!" she exclaimed, her voice cracked and laden with sorrow.

He grunted when her entire body impacted against his own and her protruding sternum bashed his forehead. He steadied his hand behind himself to stop from falling, just as she wrapped all her limbs around him into an inescapable clutch.

Her arms crossed behind the back of his head and horns, her claws digging into his shoulder blades as her legs wrapped around his waist. She nuzzled the side of her snout against his hair and a horn.

"I worried you weren't going to come back," she cried, her entire body quaking around his as she sniffled and heaved.

He attempted to speak, but fighting through a face full of fur and sternum bone made it difficult. She squeezed his head so hard he worried she would crack it in her arms. He hissed when her claws stabbed so deeply into his back that the sharp tips of them had penetrated through his cloak and shirt, and he arched his spine to escape the intensity of them.

Trying to push her away gently via her sides only made her hold tighter. Her clawed bunny toes scraped against the rocky ground when she tried to use them to get closer.

"I'm sorry. Please do not leave again." She gave a curt whine as she nuzzled against his hair harder, threatening to wear a bald spot into his scalp. "It's okay. I forgive you. Just... *please*."

He considered teleporting out of this strangling hold.

She wasn't giving him the opportunity to speak, and Jabez didn't want his return to be misleading. He had no intention of staying, as she so sweetly begged of him, and he knew that was best for her.

Whatever she wanted from him was doomed to fail, and she'd be the one left hurt the most. The sooner he left, the easier she'd be able to mend.

Or not, if Orpheus was anything to gauge a Mavka's heartbreak by.

He knew it was best to put space between them, but he found it hard as he soaked her in. Her little whimpers were painful even for him, and her trembling only worsened with each passing second.

A part of him wanted to offer the comfort this deeply distraught female sought.

So, instead of prying them apart through force or magic, a small, defeated sigh fluttered from his lips. He bowed his head and wrapped his arms around Zylah's narrow midsection to hug her tightly. He even lifted her enough that her legs slipped beside him a little, so she was close to kneeling instead.

He let her feel his strength and warmth as he felt hers. He tried to let it soothe her, and whatever strange aches that panged within him as well. Once she was calmer, no matter how long that took, they could speak.

He was patient, and he was in absolutely no rush. No, quite the opposite in fact.

It took her a long while to stop trembling, and even longer to cease near crushing him to death. *It's lucky I'm not a human.* He either would have popped or suffocated in her fur.

Fur he found himself burying his face against as he took in her lovely jasmine-and-violet scent. It was even stronger up close and coming right off her skin, yet its subtle gentleness was as mollifying as it had always been.

It managed to soothe him, and his eyes closed under the drowsing power it had over him. Her strong heartbeat radiated against his forehead and thumped in his ears. He focused on it, and the tension he'd been holding in his entire being unwound itself.

Perhaps this cuddle was something he needed as well, and just never knew it. Then again, he'd never had a female cling to him with a nice set of tits cushioning either side of his head. He thought this may have been the most tender moment he'd ever shared with another, and the way it made him feel ensured it was even harder to let go.

He shifted his arms until his hands held her hips so he could draw her closer.

Although she was heavy despite her lithe form, she was really warm and soft. Her body had just enough muscle to be firm but forgiving in his hold.

Zylah eased a little more, and her whimpers ebbed. She gave him just enough room to breathe properly, but he didn't move, rather content where he was. Actually, the tenderness of this had his mind melting in the strangest of ways, and he no longer knew if it was her or him refusing to let go.

Every twitch of muscle, every breath from her, was read by his body touching hers. Her fur tickled his brows, cheeks, and lips, but it was so silky he didn't mind. Not even his squished nose against her sternum bothered him, although his dipped head did help in that regard.

For a moment, he wondered what it'd feel like to sleep next to someone like this. He'd had many restless, listless mornings, his mind refusing to be at peace over the many years he'd suffered.

Even now, he should be alert in her hold. He was in a very vulnerable position, with a creature who meant death everywhere she went. She could shove her claws through his back and into his heart without him ever seeing it coming.

He'd be dead within seconds.

He'd deserve it too.

He'd never let anyone trap him this way before.

Yet, it felt remarkably... *safe*. Like he could close his eyes and bask in her womanly curves, her scent, her warmth.

His brain was going numb to the point his damn ears were drooping. He felt no fear, no worry, and not a single fibre of him was alert. Instead he had to stifle the urge to nuzzle deeper into her chest in contentment.

That was until she sniffed around the right side of his head, and his fucking ear sprung up when her breath cascaded over it. It sent a shock throughout his entire body to the point even his groin tightened. The longer she did it, the more a tremor ran down his spine, causing his nape to prickle in goosebumps.

"You smell like Fayren," she croaked, her voice languid and sultry from crying. That same tone could easily be mistaken for someone who had cried out in lust rather than sadness, and it made his eardrums tingle.

Her orbs deepened in their teal colour, like a mixture of possessiveness and sorrow struck her at learning he'd been in another's company.

"I visited her," he muttered, not letting go since she hadn't.

Twice he'd visited that pesky fox Demon while he'd been parted from Zylah: firstly to rest, then after his conversation with Lindiwe. He'd been hoping she'd talk him *out* of coming to Zylah, and instead she further convinced him to return.

He'd said goodbye to her, explained that he likely wouldn't be returning and why. She'd hugged him tearfully while he offered the little old lady a sympathetic head pat. Then she'd asked where Zylah was and berated him about her absence, somehow knowing it was his fault.

He left before she'd finished nagging him...

And pouted in the forest like a dickhead.

He'd never taken the easy path, and him being here now was further proof of that.

She continued to sniff around his head, and it was only after her next words that he understood she wasn't seeking to find where else Fayren's scent clung to him. No, she was searching for his, wanting to be enveloped in it – if her attempt to bury beneath his hair was any indication.

"I missed you," she whispered, brushing her snout against him. "Please don't leave me again."

His closed eyes clenched tightly as a groan of dismay nearly crawled up his throat. They opened, just so he could stare at nothing.

*I shouldn't have said anything,* he thought with deep regret.

Had he done what he'd been attempting, and wisely stuck to making her hate him on his exit, this wouldn't be happening. He wouldn't have returned, and she wouldn't be saying something so sweet.

She'd never had the confidence to cling to him like this before, and it was all because he'd given her something she'd lacked. The opening to be more tender with him in the knowledge that he'd likely accept it. Like he'd said in the underground pocket of earth where he'd collected the mana stone – why hide it anymore?

Without ever knowing it, she'd been chipping away at his hard exterior. His defence against her had been growing more pliable with every minute he spent with her, bending and shifting over the past few weeks.

Had he not blurted out his attraction to her like an idiot, he could have leaned on that secrecy. He could have feigned disinterest, like he had been. He could pretend to do so now, but she was smart and would likely see right through him.

Those mesmerising teal orbs of hers were surprisingly insightful.

Worse still, the fact that she'd been on the forefront of his mind the entire time he was gone meant only one thing: he'd missed her too.

Fuck, he had *not* wanted to come to that realisation right now.

He wished she would let go, as if she hadn't been waiting eons to embrace him. *I came here for a reason.* But his mouth was apparently glued shut against his protest.

He did loosen his arms and let them droop a little, hoping that doing so would eventually make her let go.

Something tickled the back of his wrist. Jabez frowned since he hadn't been expecting anything. He flipped his hand over and shoved his hand through whatever it was in curiosity. His fingertips dived through wispy fur, just as something thin, hard, and long butted up against the webbing between his middle and ring fingers.

Zylah stiffened in surprise as his eyes opened wide and his cock jerked *hard* in realisation. A palpable groan fell from him and his mind rasped, *Holy shit. Her tail feels like a fucking cloud.*

It was so damn soft that its wispy ends tickled his entire palm as he brushed through it. The pad of his thumb stroked up the hard length of her tail bone before flicking the very tip.

Zylah let out a strangled gasp, and what he was doing struck him. He was fondling her tail like a pervert until his cock had become fully erect and throbbed within his trousers. In his defence, he hadn't *meant* to do it, but he'd been thrilled to finally touch it, knowing it felt as fluffy as it looked.

"Fuck, sorry," he grated out, ripping his hand away as his face, ears, and neck heated in embarrassment – and arousal. Thankfully she wouldn't see the way both emotions crinkled his features with him pressed against her chest.

"It's okay," she stated quietly. "You don't have to stop."

She even wiggled her hips and dipped them back in search of his hand, and he almost lost his mind.

*I shouldn't,* he told himself. Desire was already boiling in his blood and racing through his cock, and continuing to touch her tail would only make him want to touch other places.

At least he had fed his curiosity so it wouldn't linger in the back of his mind.

Jabez let out a small sigh and loosened his arms even more. He should just do what he came here to do. He'd be better off getting it over with, and he prepared himself for a painful argument.

"Zylah, I can't sta–" A choked gasp rent out of him when she grabbed the ends of his hair and tugged his head back with it. Pain lanced up his overextended throat as she suddenly forced him to look up at her.

One moment his lips were parted, and the next, a tongue was shoved between them. He'd never had someone successfully dominate him like this before, and shock had him pausing as her tongue swiped over the top of his. She gave a moan as she cupped the side of his head to keep herself to him.

That little sound she made and the feel of her tongue twisting and catching on his fangs was enough to make his body pulsate. If it had been anyone else, he may have bitten her tongue to prove a point. Instead, a hungry growl slipped from him.

How fast he gave in was utterly pitiful, but the cold pang in his chest had eroded away from her wiles so swiftly that he was left reeling. He wasn't really willing to catch himself.

She gasped when he sucked on her tongue hard, and she retracted it in surprise, while fighting the power of his suction to get away.

"How do you like it when someone does it back to you?" He shoved his head forward and licked across her front teeth, black jagged Mavka fangs, and then her jaw.

She gifted him another little moan and turned her skull to the side like she wanted to escape him. "You licked me!"

He had no idea why she was so surprised about that.

Maybe it was simply his need to win everything like a competitive bastard, but he wanted to see her squirm after yanking on his fucking hair. He shoved his hand beneath the skirt of her navy dress and drew his sharp nails down her spine until he reached her tail.

A squeak mingling with a sharp hitch of breath tore out of her, and she shoved her hips against his waist just as the fluffy tuft wiggled like crazy. Which instantly had him groaning as he grasped it, just as the scent of her sudden and deep arousal flittered around his senses.

He drew his nails down her spine again, although slower, and her reaction was even more intense. *She's sensitive here, like I knew she would be,* he thought, as he tickled his fingertips just above her hips.

While her body trembled and arched in reaction to his touch, she sat down properly. Her kneadable thighs pillowed the top of his own when her round arse landed in his lap like she'd lost the strength in her legs. With his cock nestled between her cheeks, he felt each of her wiggles against it.

He knew then that he was an actual idiot, and a very greedy man, but he was really fucking horny now, and unbearably *weak* to her. He also realised he didn't actually want to leave her, because in the depths of his messed-up, twisted being, he godsdamned liked her for unknown reasons.

What he did know was she felt warm and sensual in his arms, she felt *safe*, and she smelt pretty. Her otherworldly beauty kept tantalising him, so different to this human world in the same way he was. And her personality was sweet, gentle, and charming in all of its unwitting wiles.

Instead of pulling away like he *should,* he leaned forward, panting deeply, and kissed the corner of her jaw. When she shivered and turned her head away from him, he kissed over the collar of her neck fur before nipping hard enough through it for her to feel it.

Just as he reached up with his free hand to grasp the back of her dress and pull it down, he paused before he made a foolish mistake. *Fuck. Don't,* he told himself. He buried his forehead against the crook of her neck as he cringed at himself, at what he was doing, what he was *about* to do.

He wasn't a good person; he knew this. Them sharing pleasure was only going to make everything harder – for her, for himself. Especially with whatever emotions were being tangled between them.

He didn't care about how it impacted him negatively, but it

was unfair on her. He'd been bearing the weight of guilt and regret his whole life, no matter how painful it was. She'd done nothing to deserve him gifting that to her.

Yet every time he managed to wrestle his lust back in check, she somehow unravelled him.

"Why do you keep stopping?" she rasped, her voice laden with arousal, the air clogging and thick with the scent of it.

She was gentle this time, and wisely used his horn to dip his head back so they could meet each other's gaze. His nose wrinkled in a silent groan at her purple orbs, only for it to grow loud when she licked across his closed lips.

She pushed her backside down against the length of his cock. "Please don't stop."

Where did she get all this fucking confidence from? If she'd just acted like a trembling, uncertain maiden, he would have easily won against her. He didn't need her to be ardent and libidinous – not if he wanted to stay sane.

"Because you can't take it back," he answered, before he slipped his tongue against hers when she went to lick him again. "And I can't promise you anything."

Because right now, he had no fucking idea what he was doing. Not even when he pulled the back of her dress down, the thick straps sliding down her biceps and revealing her breasts, did he know why he couldn't seem to stop.

When he lifted her so he could softly bite the side of her perky breast, she moaned at his fangs, and he liked it. He slipped her firm nipple into his mouth and sucked hard until her needy gasp tingled his ears. Each time she reacted exactly how he wanted, all trembly and raspy, he found himself sinking deeper into this.

*She's so sensitive. So easy to tease.*

He pulled her dress down until she freed her arms from it. Then he reached down to grip her arse in a tight, kneading hold, while making sure her tail sat between his fingers so he could touch it. He kept her up, taking most of her weight so he could generously lavish her nipple with his tongue without her escaping.

His other hand unbuttoned his cloak so it would fall off, and he only removed his mouth from her long enough to remove his satchel.

A strangled rasp tore from him when her claws tickled his lower back as she grabbed the bottom of his tunic and yanked it up. Tension shot through him as he read her want and intentions; they were anchoring his own. He lifted them both off the ground so he could throw her back against the bedding. She took his tunic with her, and he parted from her long enough to help remove it before bringing his mouth down to her right breast so he could suck it hard.

"Jabez," she moaned when he shoved his hand under her skirt and cupped her pussy, his middle and ring fingers grazing down the sides of her clit.

*She's so wet,* he thought with a groan.

Her arms trembled with need as she crossed them over his bare back, her soft palms brushing his heated skin. The tips of her claws tickled him wherever her hands roamed, only ramping up his desire into a feverish degree.

Bringing as much of her breast inside his mouth as he could, he bit the mound of it while his tongue swirled her nipple. At the same time, he petted her clit in circles, and her spine arched in reaction to both as she let out a sharp cry.

Then he shoved both his trimmed and prepared fingers deep inside her. Her thighs parted as she bucked in welcome to them, her pussy instantly clenching. Her little tendrils wrapped around his fingers as he thrust them, and he felt how wet she was inside, how needy and swollen she was for him.

His cock pulsated so strongly he knew precum had leaked from the tip. *I want to fuck her.* His body was literally begging for it at this point. She'd be so warm and welcoming, and he wondered how her tentacles would feel around him.

Just as he hooked his fingers to find her G-spot, she pushed off the ground to sit up. He let her tit go before he actually hurt her, and she almost head-butted him when she grabbed his wrist to stop him.

"Wait," she pleaded. "I don't want this."

*What the fuck?* She was the one who had driven them here, despite his constant hesitancy.

Before he could pull away, heeding to her confusing rejection amicably, she removed her hand from his wrist and grasped the head of his cock. Considering he'd probably been tenting his damn trousers since the first moment he touched her tail, he wasn't surprised she found it so easily.

His nose scrunched and a deep pant fell from him when she gave it a tentative squeeze.

"I want this," she said, as she lifted her snout to his neck and licked it.

Goosebumps rose on his flushed skin where her tongue had touched, and she left behind a sweet trail of saliva which she breathed over.

"I need to prepare you," he said, thrusting his fingers once more, splitting them to stretch her and get her ready. "This is your first..." His words trailed off.

Shit, it was her first time having sex, and she'd chosen *him*, of all fucking people.

That shouldn't have excited him as much as it did. His entire body throbbed with lust at the idea, but it also left him with a deep sense of doubt.

With a distressed huff, Jabez slipped his fingers from her. He placed both his hands on the bedding on either side of her waist.

"Are you sure about this, Zylah?" he asked quietly, because he needed to hear it. He needed *her* to hear herself say it and leave no doubt between them in this moment.

His lust-filled brain couldn't think of anything *but* her, and consequences were sifting through his head like water moving through a damn sieve. The last taut string of his self-control was about to reach its peak tension, and it'd break and fray until he was done pounding into her.

His fingers gouged into the bedding below her. *I want her so badly,* he thought with an agonised wince. *Say no.*

"Yes. I'm sure," she whispered, licking across her snout while staring at his groin.

Just like that, the string snapped and his muscles swelled.

"Then come here," he bit out with a growl.

He grabbed one tie of his trousers, yanked the bow apart, and let the material fall to his knees. With his cock jutting between them, throbbing and hard to the point the ridges on both sides had flared, he grasped her inner thigh. The skirt of her dress met the top half bundled around her waist, and completely moved up out of the way when he yanked her across the bedding.

He tilted his hips so the head of his cock could slip through her bright-purple folds, and she instantly spread slick over the underside of him. With his body nestled between her bent legs, and his hands on either side of her, he thrust forward so her clit could get a feel of his cock.

Her little bud grazed the frenulum right behind his head, while her lips kept him nestled between them with warm pressure. *Shit, that feels nice.* She twitched each time he rubbed over the bundle of nerves.

Wherever her arousal clung to his shaft, it tingled, and he noticed through his sharpening breaths that he was growing harder in reaction. Precum leaked from him, and each time he produced more, his brain grew foggier. If just a meagre touch could ignite his body so fiercely, he could only imagine what it'd be like when he was fully enveloped by her.

She released sweet little pants as she watched, her hands reaching up to hold his broad shoulders. "Please," she begged, lifting her hips to greet him.

Unable to resist any longer, Jabez gripped the base and held his cock still as he drew his pelvis back and nestled the tip against her entrance. His hair tickled his neck and shoulders when it fell forward to hang between them, deepening his shudder as heat and wetness greeted his sensitive head.

Her pussy easily accepted him, and he found himself sinking into her with little resistance.

"Oh, *fuck,*" he blurted out, his lips parting as a deep groan fell from him. "So warm."

He was barely halfway inside, and she already felt like hot heaven. She was so soft around him, yet snug enough to feel like a cuddle. He went slow for her sake, but each inch further, each ridge popping and sinking deeper, had him wanting to thrust in hard to be given salvation quicker.

As he pulled back to collect her slick, her tendrils slipped around him, trying to figure out how to grasp something as big as his cock. He pushed back in, while making sure to watch for any kind of indication that he was hurting her.

He felt nothing that would be hard to push through, and she never tensed up. She seemed to lack a hymen, and he couldn't be more relieved.

Instead, she accepted him to the point she dug her heels into his arse to get him to hurry up. It was naughty of her and threatened to incite him to go feral.

He flicked his hips forward, shoving hard until his hair-dusted groin pressed against her and he sheathed himself fully. She arched with a moan at the suddenness, only for it to end on a shudder when he then ground his cock inside. He repositioned his arms to better hold himself up above her and waited for her to adjust to him.

He didn't think she needed to, considering he hadn't fully reached the end of her. He didn't mind, not when she was squeezing him from all sides and her tendrils were still swirling to clasp him fully.

"I'm inside you," he informed her around pants, while grinding harder so she could feel he was seated deep and her folds were pressing against him.

She gasped and shuddered at his words, only to tighten up.

Jabez's eyes flung open, and his knees almost buckled inwards when her insides slammed down around him. His back arched as a strangled moan pushed past his lips.

*Holy shit.* His eyes closed in bliss when he ground into her and resistance met the tip of his cock. *Did she just... fit around me?* He pushed forward a second time and pressed against her cervix now – not hard. He was just lightly grazing it.

Her body had changed to accommodate his impressive size.

He gripped the bedding roughly and jerked inside her *hard*.

*Shit. She feels amazing.*

Looking at where they were joined, Jabez lowered his eyelids in bliss as he pulled back halfway, only to thrust forward. Her hands slipped to hold him just above his elbows, and he began a slow, tentative rhythm as he let himself be lost in her.

He watched his drenched cock slipping in and out while her heat and tightness cuddled him. His ears twitched each time she let out cute moans, gave soft and shallow pants, or at the slap of their bodies meeting each other.

Her fur brushed his legs as he thrust between them, while her feet constantly slipped against his backside. Her jasmine-and-violet aroma was saturated with her arousal, making him want to deepen it until it had him salivating.

His heartbeat pounded in his chest, hard, chaotic, and fast.

The past few weeks had been chaos to his mind, and days of need had only twisted him further. To finally give in... and *finally* give them what they'd both been unknowingly seeking radiated a strange ache behind his sternum.

It felt wonderful inside her. The fact that she'd adjusted to fit around him meant she felt perfect – soft, warm, tight – and her tendrils only aided to make sure each of his glides had him near rolling his eyes. One had even wrapped behind the rim of his head, pulling on it every time he slipped back.

And whatever aphrodisiac enzymes were in her wetness meant his entire groin had lit up. He didn't know if it was because of that, or simply because he was just so fucking excited to be inside her, but his cock was unbearably hard. It throbbed so deeply that it kept sending tremors through his abdomen muscles until the veins around his groin thickened and were visible.

Her knees shifted to cup his sides as her hands slipped away from his arms to hold his lower back. Her head bowed forward until the top of her bony snout was pressed against his chest. Now that she was closer, he could feel how much she was trembling.

Her moans turned into soft, sharp cries as her inner walls tightened and softened in intervals. Sensing she wanted him closer, he dipped his head forward so he could deeply huff right next to her head, letting her hear intimately how feverish he sounded, and so she would catch any quiet, unbidden groans he produced. His cheek and the side of his lips brushed over her skull, while his breaths fanned across her temple, and Zylah shuddered wildly against him.

Her breathing hitched and ceased when her pussy clamped tight around him. Her limbs tried to lock around him as well, and his arms almost caved in weakness when her body started to milk his cock. She wetly spasmed as she came, and a pitiful groan tore from him when her internal tendrils felt like they were trying to squeeze him in a vice grip.

*There we go,* he thought as he quickened the pace to get her to spiral deeper. She tightened up even further and her claws dug into his back. His head shot back as he thrust through it, his balls clenching in reaction.

When she settled, he shoved harder just as she tilted her hips up for him.

*"Oh!"* she rasped, before bringing her knees higher until she was cuddling around his ribs. It tilted her pelvis even more, and her thighs spread when she realised she had changed the angle of them greeting to better suit her.

Her back arched, and she tossed her head from side to side as her moans grew louder. Zylah bucked, trying to get her hips to meet his harder, and a small, desirous growl vibrated through his gritted fangs.

Only for it to die when she produced little whines instead, her snout turning one way and then the other. He managed to catch her purple orbs and noticed the bottoms of them were wavering. Jabez slowed, then stopped when a little droplet floated from one of them.

Although his heart felt like it'd moved and was now racing in his engorged dick, he cupped the side of her head to get her to face him.

Heat continued to flood his veins, his brain muddy with need, and if he didn't keep thrusting, he thought he'd fucking erupt in rage. Yet he fucking paused anyway.

"Why are you crying?" he asked, wondering if he'd done something wrong. Not that he knew what. She'd come for him, and her orbs were lust-filled.

His nose bunched with desperation as he thought, *Shit, I don't want to stop.* His cock was *tingling,* and he wanted to come so badly he'd do it in his fist if he had to, but he wanted to reach that end with her.

He was only going soft and slow for her.

His body quaked with hidden restraint. He was trying his hardest to be *good,* when he wanted to fuck hard, fast, and deep until he threatened to split her in two – while confidently knowing he'd never be able to do that to her. To go feral like the Demon he was, while biting, clawing, and tossing her around.

Her strength and indestructible nature called for him to be ruthless instead of gentle. Yet it was *her* gentle and sweet personality that made him want to twist her up until she was a naughty, wanton little female pleading for a cock.

Trembling, she clutched low on her abdomen and her insides squirmed around him blissfully until his vision blurred.

"You feel so good inside me," she whispered with a sharp whine. "I don't know what to do. I want more." She wiggled her hips against him, forcing him in and out of her, and made a shudder rack her own body. "Please don't stop, Jabez."

The quake that struck him, causing his muscles to clench and spasm – from his chest and shoulders to his abdomen and lower back – wound his lust up tighter than he could remember. His vision darkened just as a vicious growl rumbled from him.

Jabez dived forward until both of them crashed against the bedding. Leaning on his right elbow, he hooked the left one behind her knee and drew it up to her chest. With his chest thrusting up against hers, her pussy tilted just right to take his sudden hard plunges, Jabez shoved his face against the side of her jaw.

"Fuck that was cute, Zylah," he grated out with his voice huskier than ever. He fucked into her harder, slamming his hips against hers so he penetrated deep. "If you want to cry about how fucking good it feels, then cry as much as you like."

With his arm supporting her leg to ensure she was spread wide for the taking, he cupped her arse to keep her in position for him. He licked and sucked the corner of her jaw, making sure each of his pants petted right next to her ear hole.

Louder than before, whiny moans broke from her as she wrapped her arms under his and dug her claws into his shoulder blades.

"Jabez," she cried, unable to do little more than hold him and moan.

He tried to go faster without losing the power of his thrusts. Because soft and slow were no longer in his capacity. He needed to take this female like the Demon he was. Like a man who was broken by lust and finally able to slake it on the creature who could take it. Strange, tender emotions were running rampant in his chest, and each time she clamped up around him, the deeper they ached.

Pain lanced his flesh, but it made a growl rip from him and his cock plunge faster. He was panting so rapidly he thought his lungs would give out, while his heart beat so violently it threatened to punch through his ribcage.

And then she came *hard*, and the moan wrung from him was unbearably pathetic. She squeezed him so tight that if it wasn't for her tendrils and his strength, her lovely pussy may have pushed him out. *Oh fuckkk.* Her claws tore across his arching back as she screamed, and his eyes rolled up in violent bliss.

He managed to catch her purple ethereal tears turn bright red.

Letting go of her leg, he shoved his hand over her nose hole, shielding her from the intensity of his blood scent in the air. His magic swirled around them as he produced a thick, scent-cloaking aroma without slowing his thrusts and was able to push back her blood-lust in time.

Zylah didn't have time to register that she'd ripped his skin apart. Not when he grabbed both her hands and pushed them down above her head, threaded the fingers of one hand between all of hers, and pumped his cock rapidly into her. Her cute bunny feet bounced against his lower back and arse as he steadied himself with one arm.

But what she'd done had forcibly pushed him closer to his own release, like the violence made him a maniac. His own blood tickled him. His huffs kept clogging in his chest, his groans loud each time his balls clamped up with his pending release. Her cries were killing him, and she accepted everything he was giving her like such a good girl.

Her tendrils softened each time she came, just caressing his cock, but clung hard whenever she was close. And they did so right as he was about to pull out before he exploded.

"I need you to let go," Jabez pleaded. He yanked his hips back only to be tugged forward against his will, and each thrust forced from him had his eyes crinkling as euphoria began to climb up his cock. "Fuck, Zylah. Let go!"

Her ankles crossed over his backside, and her tendrils gripped harder. They'd slipped between the grooves of his ridges, but it was the one behind his cockhead that refused to relent. Each time he tugged on it, he grew thicker as seed climbed up his shaft.

*Shit!* It was too late.

He plunged forward, and his hips jerked wildly as his eyes rolled back and he roared out his release within her. Bliss captured him, and it only deepened when his grind through it sent her over the edge as well.

His orgasm was accompanied by heat, wetness, and sweet pulses from her. His entire brain went numb as pleasure clutched him all the way down to his essence. His balls clenched so hard they threatened to retreat inside him, and a shudder racked up his spine each time.

When the last rope of semen shot from him, she softened around him. Yet he kept thrusting, unable to stop when it felt like coming didn't *ease* him. He should have lost his erection, and instead he was still hard as stone, still tingling from her arousal.

He groaned at his heightened sensitivity. *Why am I not going soft?* Why was need still clinging to his chest like a creature latched on with its claws? *Fuck. I don't want to stop.*

And Zylah kept moaning and undulating her hips for more, twisting him up further. His balls still felt full, like he hadn't completely emptied them after that mind-scrambling release.

*I'm going insane*, he thought with his eyes crinkling in anguish, before he wrenched himself from her. He kicked his pants off from where they'd fallen to his ankles, completely freeing himself.

"Wait! Don't stop," she cried, then squealed when he grabbed her legs and rolled her over.

Jabez grabbed her waist, lifted her arse up until she was on her knees and chest, and slammed his cock back inside her. She let out a gasp, then a shivering moan as he began to thrust hard and fast. His hips punished her for causing him to feel this way, for screwing with his mind and body, making him undeniably broken in that moment.

Worse still, when he felt something soft and fluffy

constantly brushing up his stomach, his eyes crinkled even further. He let go of one side of her waist and drew his nails down her spine to the base of her tail. She let out a sharp rasp, her back arching downwards deeply, as the adorable appendage wiggled against him.

Her insides clamped and spasmed frantically around him, and he knew he was fucking doomed.

He raked his nails along her again, but in the opposite direction, so he could grab her waist once more, and he gained the same reaction. This time, his head tipped back as he quickened the pace of his thrusts.

*Fuck me, she feels amazing.*

No one should feel this good. No female should have this kind of power over him. No pussy should have him panting until he thought he'd happily cease breathing, so long as this was the last thing he experienced.

When she tried to lean up on straightened arms and rock to help him, Jabez kicked her knees further apart. He shoved his hips hard enough that her arms gave out and she slid forwards across the bedding.

He didn't need her help; she'd already ramped up his lust. He just needed her to keep being a good girl and scream for him as she took his cock.

When she tried again, Jabez changed their position to where her body was stretched forward, her legs tilted heavily and her hips barely off the ground. Then, just to make sure, he grabbed one of her dainty antlers, snatched her head back and forced her into a deep and unbreakable bend as he leaned back.

Her adorable purple floating tears never ceased, and they only came from her faster as she climaxed for him repeatedly. Her parted maw ensured she was loud, and each of her whines and cries echoed inside their cave. Zylah clawed at the bedding, Jabez watching every little thing she did in a haze.

Her erect tail kept drawing his eye, and he found this position just made it even more erotic for him. He'd wanted to fuck her like this so many times, and now that he was doing it... it was even better than his perverted fantasies.

When she lost the strength in her body and jerked them both forward by dropping her hips to the ground, Jabez laid over her.

He shoved his arms underneath her, with one hand crossed under her chest so he could knead a perky breast, wrapping his fingers around it in a way that let him thrum her nipple. The other pushed her hips up so she could still receive him, and he cupped her pussy. When her hips rose up on their own at his touch, and her knees tried to close despite him being in the way, he messily played with her soaking clit to tease her.

Sensitive from orgasming, she twitched each time he petted her breast and clit just right as his cock moved within her.

But the aggression in him was fading the longer he held her in his arms, and he found his body softening so he could just cuddle her. The force of his thrusts gentled and instead he kept them quick as he nuzzled his face into the fur around her neck.

*Nhnn. She smells so sweet.* Now that her floral aroma was so close to him, free from the scent of her arousal, it lulled his mind to the point his eyes fluttered as they closed. Her fur was soft, and it caressed his arms, his chest, his legs, and especially his abdomen, where her fluffy tail was squished between them.

He didn't know how long he lay over her, hugging her as he pumped into her with lustful abandon. His chest ached more and more with each second until it felt as painful as his shredded back.

Yet both aches were wholesome, were giving and sweet.

He parted his fangs and lightly bit into her shoulder, his features twitching as prickling goosebumps raced up his spine. He didn't even try to pull away this time, his body too weak. Jabez gave a soft moan when his balls drew up, and the first mind-numbing rope of cum burst from his pulsating cock. His thrusts turned into rocking shudders as he let her perfect pussy nurse him through his orgasm.

All the muscles in his body leapt, and his legs shook until the strength in them gave out.

When he was done, his sigh of relief was palpable as he felt himself finally softening. Her pussy clung to him hard, as if trying to stop it, but he was completely drained and spent. Euphoric satisfaction sung through him, and he could barely keep his eyes open despite his efforts.

His heart was beating too fast and thumped pressure in his

temples. His head had exploded with heat, making sweat trickle down his forehead and back, and aftershocks had him twitching until his whole body jerked.

Zylah wiggled beneath him, her hips shoving up at him. "Why did you stop?"

The laugh that burst out of him shook them both. "Because I came twice, Zylah," he told her, his voice cracked and deeper than normal.

She tilted her head so she could look at him over her shoulder. "So?" She wiggled her hips again. "I came many times."

Despite being rather content where he was, Jabez leaned up and gently slipped his cock from her.

"Men aren't supposed to come multiple times in a row." By the ever-night, he didn't even take a break. *That* wasn't supposed to happen.

*I may be a Demon, but I'm also an Elf.* And he absolutely didn't have the strength or stamina of a Mavka.

He offered her one last groan, his nose wrinkling on one side as he watched a small amount of his seed leak from her stretched opening. *Fuck,* he cursed while biting his bottom lip with a singular fang. *That's kind of hot.* Especially when it dripped down to her clit and a droplet fell against the bedding.

A second later, his eyes flung open wide, dread clinging to his spine.

"Oh shit," he grated out, before twisting side to side so he could search for his satchel.

*Fuck, I came inside her!* He had no idea the repercussions of that. Considering humans and Mavka were apparently producing offspring, he worried what that'd mean for them. Sure, he was different – he was a hybrid – but he absolutely refused to take that chance.

When he found the strap of his bag hidden underneath his cloak, he grabbed it and dragged it closer. *Thank the ever-night I had the foresight to think ahead.* Not that he'd thought he'd need it for *himself.*

"Jabez?" Zylah asked in a small and uncertain voice, attempting to turn to her side and sit up. He was still between her legs, so she struggled to untangle herself from him.

With single-minded focus, he dug into his satchel and fumbled for the golden chain he'd bought from Spiral Haven. Once he had it in his fist, he showed it to her.

"I would like for you to wear this," he stated, fully removing her dress bundled at her waist so he could wrap the simple golden chain around her more easily. He clicked the clasp together, and it glimmered briefly with yellow magic. "It has a contraceptive enchantment."

She looked down and brushed her clawed fingers over it. "I read about this in one of Fayren's books."

As much as he would have preferred to get her consent first, it was *his* semen involved. Males had no contraceptive options, and this was the only one available for Demons.

"I ask that you don't remove it," he said, meeting her gaze firmly. "Only you will be able to break it, so this will protect you."

He didn't like her thoughtful silence, nor the way she lightly tugged on it with her thumb.

"Okay," she eventually said, and he sighed with relief. Then her little tail swayed as she lifted her head to him. "Can we keep going now?"

*That's what she's concerned about?* Once more, a laugh fell from him, although quieter than before. *She's worse than any female I've ever come across.* Usually it was Jabez who wanted more, his stamina strong when he at least had a chance to *breathe* first.

Two releases in a row had nearly felled him.

He needed a short break, then they could fuck more.

"Unfortunately no." He sat next to her just as she gave a sulky harrumph. Shoving his arm around her chest, he tackled her to the bedding, making her squeal in surprise. "But we can cuddle. Me and my dick are tired."

For pity's sake, the sun was up now, and it was barely dawn when he'd come back here!

He wound his arms around her and pulled her until she was shoved up against his body. Reaching back, he dragged her blanket over him, since his back was protectively towards the cave entrance, and then he grabbed his own to cover her. Finally he retrieved her pillow and tilted it so they could share while her head was pressed against his chest.

Zylah squirmed against him, her arousal scent refusing to relent. But she did soften when she pressed the side of her skull against his sternum as if she was listening to his heart. She eventually slipped her arm over his side and pressed her knee between his, snuggling closer.

Avoiding his wounds as much as possible, he rolled to his back slightly when he noticed she wanted more, and she laid her head on his chest. Once she settled into a comfortable spot, she let out an endearing huff of contentment.

"See? Isn't this nice?" he asked, only to receive an annoyed, although half-hearted, grumble.

All went quiet except for their shallow pants, and his post-nut clarity surfaced through the haze of his thoughts.

Jabez looked up at the ceiling.

*We... probably shouldn't have done this.*

As much as he knew they needed to talk, the least he could do was offer to hold her in sleep rather than ruining this for her. He also needed to *think*, because he wasn't sure what he wanted anymore.

Sex hadn't made his chest feel any lighter. He was thrumming with satisfaction, but the worries that pestered hadn't faded. Nothing had been resolved.

But he didn't regret this. Far from it.

Rather... it felt like something had grown to irritate the hole where his heart should be. He kind of liked the feeling, and his flaccid dick pulsed in agreement.

A small smile curled the corners of his lips when she dabbed her tongue against his chest, right as her orbs turned black and she nuzzled it instead. With her lying on his arm, he held her waist and gripped her other thin wrist to stop her from tickling his damn side with her claws.

*I can think about it later.*

The problems he faced, his goals, what he wanted and didn't want to do, they could wait. He was tired, he was content, and he had a pampered female in his arms. Whether he deserved a moment of ease or not, he was giving it to himself anyway.

Especially as she didn't seem to regret it either.

He peeked down at the top of her skull and suddenly disliked how far she was from him. *Come here, you,* he thought, as he grabbed her arse and drew her even closer until she was almost on top of him. The crown of her head butted against the underside of his jaw while one of her antlers nestled against his neck and behind his ear. Her snout ran over the top of his chest, and he winced when she almost kneed his nuts.

Then he let her warmth, her softness, her scent lull his eyes closed. *She feels nice in my arms.* He brushed his fingertips up her furry side in appreciation, and allowed his mind, for the first time in a very long time, to shut the hell up.

The last thing he did before he let sleep overcome him was place a protective barrier against the entrance.

# TWENTY-SEVEN

As much as Jabez would have liked to continue lying down with his sleeping companion, he eventually abandoned their cuddle. The gashes in his back constantly throbbed, as did his mind. His movements pulled across his taut skin when he quietly slipped on his pants and tied them.

Then, facing Zylah, he rested against the wall with only his horns and upper back keeping him upright.

His mind remained dozy – groggy even. Despite the concerns looming over his head like a cloud of rain, he couldn't remember the last time he'd slept that well.

Perhaps it had been the nestle of her body up against his own as the satisfaction still simmered beneath the surface of his skin. Maybe it was because it just felt nice to hold someone while he slept, rather than strategically annoying the shit out of his companion, so they didn't know he was making them leave through manipulation.

Jabez always slept alone for his own peace of mind.

It's funny how that had stopped being an issue with Zylah quite some time ago. *One of the most dangerous creatures in the world, and I slept like a babe today.*

His gaze drifted to the late-morning sun peeking into their cave, and he reached his hand out to touch it. Since he used his magic to cover his skin in a barrier that could handle its intensity, there was no burning sensation like usual.

*If only I'd been able to protect myself then.* Had that barrier assisted him in his fight against Lindiwe and her three little humans, he wouldn't have needed saving. He wouldn't have almost died.

He wouldn't be here, with Zylah, with conflicting thoughts and feelings. For many reasons, he wished that battle had never happened.

*I'd probably be gone by now.* He'd already schemed his next plan and had just finished scouting Nyl'theria to come up with the best strategy. He had multiple options – some suicidal, some not.

*To rain down terror, or be... political.* Political was never his strong suit. He liked things going his way, and he liked things working in his favour. He was argumentative, arrogant, and stubborn – an unbending force. He would rather head-butt the person he was arguing with than listen.

The political option would be slow, which, in his mind, meant pointless. He wanted what he wanted, and he wanted it *now.* He'd been saying that for over three hundred years, after all.

*Had I left before facing that battle...* His gaze slipped to a sleeping Zylah. *None of this would have happened.*

He would have continued forward, blissfully unaware of her existence. No worrisome thoughts, no concerns about his faltering emotions. He would've been empty inside, and part of him preferred that.

He hated this wavering; it'd never happened to him before.

He also hated himself for knowing the absolute truth. He still planned to leave this realm because he could never choose her over his vengeance.

He'd have to give up... *everything.* And everything was the one thing that had kept him alive and fighting all his life. To lose that would be like losing his sense of self. It was who he was, and all he'd ever known. He'd have to reshape himself completely, and doing that in this realm was abhorrent to him.

He hated the Elvish, not Nyl'theria. He missed home, and he'd missed it his whole damn life. He missed the heat, the plant life, and the lifestyle. He was tired of being resilient, of being strong. He wanted support, comfort, and to be among people that wouldn't scorn him nor try to hurt him.

He was *tired* of freezing his ass off in a world of humans

who rejected him, and it was only the monsters in the shadows who accepted him – while wanting a piece of him for dinner.

*The humans are cruel.* They would never welcome Demons into their fold, not even non-violent and fully complete ones.

He'd experienced firsthand what that was like, the callousness humans were capable of, and he refused them just as much as he refused the Elysians.

So where did that leave him? Not here, obviously. But what did that mean for Zylah? He kept wishing for clarity on that, but Jabez was entirely torn. He wanted her to come with him for all the right reasons, but he wanted her to stay where it was safe for all the right reasons too.

Sure, she had Demons and humans to contend with here, but it was nothing like the violence within the forests of Nyl'theria. *There are some Demons bigger than me there.* And he usually towered over everything except a Mavka.

In the Elven world, even Mavka would end up being prey, depending on the kind of swarm chasing them.

*Shit,* he thought, shoving his fingers into his clenched eyes. *It would have been easier if I'd never met her.*

Why did she have to be this damn way? She had no right to be so cute or sweet. And after this morning, he knew her to be naughty, sensual, and could wind him up into a madman. A conflicting mixture that was apparently just the right blend to confuse the hell out of him.

That bundle of adorable chaos stirred, breaking him from his thoughts when she suddenly sat up. She immediately searched for him with white orbs, and her tense shoulders softened at seeing him still here.

He'd been hoping for more time to piece together his mind. A few minutes was barely enough to digest anything – let alone their intimacy that had him questioning much.

At the reminder, his dick jerked, ready to go again after the rest he'd gotten. It didn't help that the blanket fell to her hips, revealing her naked chest and the contraceptive chain around her waist.

"Morning," he greeted, forcing a mild smile.

She turned her head away as she scratched at the side of her neck. "I don't know why, but I worried you left without saying anything," she muttered, her orbs shifting to a reddish pink.

So, part of her was instinctively aware or intuitive enough to know something was wrong.

"I wouldn't do that," he lied.

He absolutely *would* do that, just apparently not to her.

Then, to his absolute destruction, she shifted to her hands and knees... and *crawled* to him. Naked. Her tail and small breasts were easily viewable, and the evidence of their prior intimacy clung to her scent.

Jabez stifled his cringing groan, his cock jerking once more, and hid his heating face behind his hand. Apparently his body was still hungry for her, and she wasn't making it any easier for him.

She paused at his reaction right as she was above his straightened legs and sat back on her feet. "Did I do something wrong?"

He drew his palm down his face, as humour lit his distressed gaze. "I just had a female I'm attracted to crawl to me naked on her hands and knees. How did you think I was going to react?"

She lifted her arms to look down at her body, as if she didn't see the issue at first. It apparently registered, because she fucking flicked the head of his hardening cock. He flinched and bit out a growl as he grabbed her and brought her closer so she couldn't so easily touch it again.

*I think I need tighter pants.* The loose material constantly gave him away like a horny virgin ready to get his first lay.

"Why is that a bad thing?" she asked, tilting her head as she settled on his lap, his dick precariously nestling between her cheeks.

And just like that, his earlier whirling thoughts dissipated under the power of her unwitting wiles.

It made him want to be playful with her.

Jabez had yet to be truly that way with her. He knew how to fight sensuality with sensuality, and *that* he could effortlessly win against her.

She'd quickly learn he could be rather devious and cheeky. If she was this way already, he could only imagine how much he'd screw himself over by teasing her when she'd likely turn it around on him and get him riled up. He'd always been a fan of those kinds of games.

Jabez grabbed the end of her snout and wiggled her skull side to side in his big fist. "I should have known this skull type of yours would end up meaning you're a menace. I'm assuming you've never heard the term 'fuck like rabbits,' but it shouldn't be too hard to guess its meaning."

She produced this little giggle that instantly knotted his chest and stomach.

"Does that mean we can do it again?" Her orbs flickered with bright yellow, and he *swore* the base of her tail wagged in excitement... right on his cock.

*I'm doomed.*

He avoided her gaze by looking down, and a set of tits came into view, both nicely tipped with dark-grey nipples. The urge to touch them pestered him, his tongue licking against the roof of his mouth at the idea of tasting them again, but he managed to restrain himself – barely.

He sighed, realising the view wasn't helping, and looked back up. "You're worse than any female I've ever met. How can you be this obsessed with sex already?"

She'd had one proper feel of cock and apparently it was on the forefront of her mind. The fact she wasn't even hiding it didn't correspond with the shyness she'd once held, nor the fact that she'd only done it once. Well, technically *twice*.

Zylah scratched at the side of her bony snout bashfully. "Because I like it. It feels good."

"We need to talk," he redirected with strain, wincing because stating it hurt *him*.

Her orbs flickered with blue this time, but they quickly settled to teal. "Can't we talk later?" She shook her backside against him. "I want more."

Now that they'd broken down the physical barrier between them, and she knew he desired her, Jabez wondered if she was purposefully trying to utilise it against him. Did all this confidence truly come from her own desire, or her reluctance to let him go? Perhaps she thought the more they shared their bodies, the less likely he'd say what he came here to explain.

It was a good plan. Had he been a weaker creature, he may

have faltered already. The talk of being intimate with her again had ensured his blood was throbbing against her, and his mind was getting fuzzy in its clarity.

Grappling to get control of the situation before he couldn't think of anything but being buried inside that hot, perfect, tight pussy of hers, he searched for an out. Something to put between them, or rather, to bolster his self-control.

"Why don't you show me what you look like in the other dress you got? The red one," he asked, hoping that clothing her would ease his thoughts. It surely would stop his greedy gaze from drifting down to her breasts again... like it did now.

"Why? I'll just want it off again." Cheeky little minx.

She went to wrap her arms around his neck, but a hiss of pain whistled past his bared fangs as his back arched in surprise. She flung her hands away, only to pull his shoulder forward to look over it.

"I... you... you're *hurt*!" she cried. "Did I do this?!"

Just as he was about to chuckle, the pain inconsequential to him, coolness radiated around his wounds. A curt snarl burst from him as he gripped both her wrists and shoved them into the air near her head.

It was too late. The sting of her claw marks faded, and his irritation only deepened when he tossed away her arms.

"You shouldn't take away a man's trophies, Zylah," he rumbled with a glare. This time, he pulled her shoulder forward so he could see the wounds she'd taken from him. "Now you're pointlessly hurt, when I'd been planning to heal myself."

He'd just needed blood or meat – he could utilise either. He was also hungry, so it would have killed two requirements.

He *may* have been considering healing them only to a point. He usually ridded himself of noticeable scars, but he'd been fond of the idea of having the signs he'd pleasured a female well on his back. Her, especially. A little gift for him to remember.

"But I hurt you," she whined, her orbs shifting to blue as she looked down at her sharp claws. "I don't even know when I did it."

He drifted his gaze to them and thumbed the needle-tipped

point of one. "It would be wise for you to sheath your claws when you're being intimate." Then, thinking better of it, because *he* liked them scoring him, he added, "Or you can file them back, like this."

Like he'd done to his own nails, he managed to singe away the sharpest part of her claws until they were blunter. She'd still be able to rend flesh with them, but it'd require much more force. If the male did her right, he shouldn't have a problem gaining his own little trophies... just not so deep.

"I'm sorry," she grumbled.

"I bite, you scratch. It's fine," he stated, offering her a pacifying grin.

She chittered, the sound light and sweet as she avoided his eyes. "But I don't mind your fangs."

Jabez didn't know whether to sigh at how she wouldn't let this go, or instantly nip her in want because she liked his fangs. No one liked his fangs. They weren't short like human teeth, and they were pointed and sharp. He lacked long canines that usually helped to stop the rest of one's fangs from sinking into someone unless a lot of pressure was given.

Instead, Jabez had a mean bite and needed very little pressure to pierce with them.

One reaction did eventually win out, and he leaned forward to close the space between them. He let his lips and the points of his fangs scrape up the length of her jaw, and her responding shiver delighted him. His hands moved of their own accord, steadying her by gripping both her arse cheeks, and once he felt them, he squeezed.

He stifled a groan at the growing scent of her arousal and resisted the urge to sink his fangs into her neck or shoulder.

"Get your dress, Zylah," he pleaded, removing his shaking hands from her before he did actually lose it.

She let out a cute little growl before shuffling back and away. "Fine. I will find it."

Obviously sexually frustrated and annoyed with him, she started throwing their messy bedding around as she searched for her bag.

His eyes crinkled in anguish when she did it on her fucking hands and knees! She dipped her torso, pushing her hips up right in his direction, and he caught a glimpse of her purple slit, pretty folds, and the entrance of her pussy.

His cock pulsated *hard,* the wrestle with his desire failed him, and he folded. A pant fell from him, and he *knew* all his precious blood was draining away from his brain and into his groin. He'd be useless in formulating a proper thought, and hopeless at fighting her if she argued with him.

Jabez dived forward. Grabbing her ankle, he yanked it to make her crumble and tackled her, pinning her down from above.

"Fine, you win," he rasped against the back of her neck. Then he sunk his fangs into it while sliding his two trimmed fingers into her hot cunt from behind.

She instantly moaned and lifted her hips in welcome, and he shuddered at the wetness that greeted his delving fingers.

*Screw it. Another day isn't going to change anything.* Or perhaps a few.

It wasn't like Nyl'theria or the Elven city were going anywhere, and he really hadn't gotten his fill of her yet.

Buzzing with satisfaction that she had gotten her way, Zylah threaded her right leg between both of Jabez's when he rolled away from her after he came. She slipped her arm across his heaving abdomen and plonked the underside of her jaw on top of his chest to trap him down.

She liked how his heat and heartbeat radiated through the underside of her skull, and that his bergamot-and-sandalwood scent was right on the tip of her nose. She snorted a huff of contentment as she soaked in his naked body against hers.

At the sound, he tipped his head forward to look at her before his eyelids fluttered and his eyes rolled back. A last tremor came from him, and his nose wrinkled like he may have hidden a groan.

"You are going to be the death of me," he croaked, his dulcet voice groggy and sinfully deep.

"Why?" she asked, squirming to get closer. Zylah still wanted more, but it was he who had been the one to stop.

*I thought males were meant to have good stamina.* Well, that's what Fayren had warned her about when it came to Demons, not that Zylah understood why.

"Because there's something in your arousal that keeps me hard even after I come, and then it makes me even more sensitive the second... third time." He tilted his head to the side and fetched the pillow to shove it under his head for support. It also dipped his head forward, so he was able to look down at her. "It's actually really fucking worrisome. That's how you make someone's heart give out."

"You say *fuck* a lot," Zylah commented, her purple orbs shifting to dark yellow.

"Is that a problem?" he countered, lifting a brow at her.

She shrugged. "You've never explained what it means."

She knew a little about it from the past day, since it could be used in relation to the act of sex, but she hadn't understood why he stated it in this context.

"Fuck has many meanings, from being frustrated, to angry, to sex. Same with the words: cunt, shit, damn. They're curse words, usually used to be derogatory and offensive." His relaxed features shifted into a malicious grin. "Which is exactly why I like them."

She accepted his explanation and let silence fall over them. Zylah just gazed at him, liking that his red eyes were upon her and completely lacked any of their usual iciness or indifference. Elation simmered inside to see them shining so softly and warmly in her direction.

She released his torso so she could slide her hand up to his face. She sheathed her claws and touched his lips that had petted the side of her skull with what she thought were panted kisses. She brushed her fingers up the side of his high cheekbone, then up to his temple, before coming down to trace the path of his strong jaw.

"You are very pretty," she whispered, brushing her thumb over his right brow, letting the short white hair tickle her.

His lips curled as his eyes crinkled in humour. "Only on the outside."

She caressed one of his black tapered horns before sifting her fingers through his thick, long hair. "I don't think so."

"That's because you don't know me well enough," he rebutted. "Most would say I'm ugly on the inside, and I've never had an issue with that."

"Well... you've never been ugly towards me." When his expression darkened, and he opened his mouth as if to refute her, Zylah slapped her hand over it. "You have never truly been mean to me directly. That's all I care about. You have been kind, and I have seen that."

His lips shut and flattened, but his expression didn't soften.

She didn't mind. Not when he let her brush down the curve of his nose with the side of her fingertip. Considering not even a month ago he appeared to hate being touched or having her near in any form, she was happy he'd let down his guard with her. He even let her cup his pointed ear so she could massage up the arch of it.

A shiver racked her spine when he trailed his fingertips along it like he wanted to pet her in return. Fondness ached behind her sternum at how he didn't seem to mind caressing her fur, especially since he lacked any.

"You seem to like being on top of me."

"Sorry." Zylah leaned up to take away her weight. "Am I heavy?"

He wrapped his hand around the back of her skull and shoved it back down. "It wasn't a complaint."

Bright yellow lifted into her sight as she nuzzled into him. She shifted slightly, so more of her was on top of him, like she wanted to from the very beginning.

She wondered if he'd only commented on their position to distract her. If so, she wouldn't let him get away with that.

"Will you tell me more about you, then?" she asked, hope filling her voice as she settled her hand on his chest.

"There is nothing pleasant for me to tell you." His gaze hardened, and he looked down at her hand placement. "If you are seeking a happy conversation, this isn't how to start one."

"It doesn't have to be happy, or important. Anything will do." When his brows furrowed at her, she squeezed closer. "What about when you first came to Earth?"

"Ah, yes. Let's start at the very worst, shall we?" he stated with a sigh while rolling his eyes. "I told you, Zylah, nothing is pleasant. Any memories I have that may have once been fond are shrouded by later events that made them unpleasant. People I've known who have died, left, or I fought with. Anyone remaining... those moments are merely empty events that hold no value, and I would consider them as pointless as talking about the weather. Anything else is merely time spent being social, as that is normal for any intelligent being."

Disheartened to the point a pang blossomed behind her sternum, Zylah slipped her head to the side with a deep huff. Her orbs shifted to blue as sadness made a chill seep into her chest.

"Are you seriously pouting?" he asked incredulously, his jaw falling. Zylah let out another huff and turned her snout away more. "Ugh, *fine.* But I did warn you."

Pleased she'd gotten her way, her tail swayed as she brought her gaze back to him.

"I had only just turned seventeen when I came to this realm," he started, lifting his eyes to the ceiling as if he found it easier to talk to it. "After I spent so many years locked away, I admit my mind wasn't well. I brought all those who were trapped with me to Earth, and we all struggled to adjust. It was cold – I think either winter or early spring – and I had to rely on my fellow Demons to help me through it. I didn't know how to start a fire, how to hunt, how to fight. I only knew my instincts, and even then... I'd been locked away for so long that my instincts often failed me. I was young, ignorant, and my body was weak from disuse."

Jabez absentmindedly traced his fingertips up and down her back, like he couldn't help touching her. Perhaps he was just trying to distract himself.

Zylah tried not to arch into it, despite adoring the attention.

"The events of the first year are a little... messy. I don't remember much of it. I have a scar across the back of my head from where some humans managed to club me with something, but I have no memory as to how I even got into a situation to be struck. It's only been recently that those memories have begun to resurface, and I'm realising I may have accidentally entangled what happened afterwards with my treatment from the Elysians."

"Do you know why they are resurfacing?" Zylah asked, curious if there was a reason that ignited it.

His lips tightened as his brows furrowed in deep thought. "I visited Merikh recently, and there was a familiar scent clinging to him. It reminded me of my childhood, and I think it's triggered them."

"Merikh is the bear-skulled Mavka, correct?"

"Yes. That's correct." One side of his mouth lifted as a chuckle fell from him. "Fuck, he's gotten so big. I bet he would be an absolute beast to spar with now. With that much weight on him, it'd be impossible to take him down, and I'm sure he knows how to wield it. I think it suits him well. Unfortunately, his quills stop him from looking like a cuddly teddy bear, but I do wish I'd needled him with that, as I'm sure he would've taken it as an insult."

He said he didn't have anything pleasant, but Zylah found his humour and obvious fondness for this Merikh warm and tender. Was this the... *friend* he'd spoken of?

That warmth swiftly died, and his gaze turned distant, as if he could see past the ceiling.

"I learned quickly that humans are horrible little cretins when given the chance. They're a superstitious bunch. They think a rabbit's foot is lucky and will wear it on their person. I also believe they thought us to be pure Elves, and they wanted us to grant them wishes and gift them luck. Of course, being Demons who couldn't understand their language, we did nothing more than hiss and snap our fangs at them. They caged us in silver, which they believed weakened us from the myths I've read. It doesn't. But being strung up off the ground, incapable of using my earth magic, and being starved for days left me weak. They took us out one by one to harvest body parts and be cruel. No one managed to escape their own cages in time to stop the humans from siphoning my blood or cutting off my left ear as a charm. But the Demons did manage to save me. However, my blood scent is rather potent to them, as it has an Elvish tang to it that makes them rabid. So my allies then tried to eat me, even after promising they never would, but I don't particularly blame them for that. They couldn't help it."

Zylah swallowed thickly. She wished her orbs didn't reflect

a sorrowful hue for him, especially when he looked down at her and his eyes bowed, but he patted the back of her skull.

"See? I told you; it's unpleasant. There's no need to feel sympathy for me, Zylah. I've come to accept all this, and I feel nothing regarding it."

"But that's horrible."

Jabez shrugged. "I can't change the past – not what has happened to me or what I've done. All those who harmed us died that day, and I managed to learn how to transplant body parts to myself, so I've always considered it beneficial."

"Trans... plant?" Zylah asked, tilting her head. She'd never heard that word before.

"When you're in pain and scared, you do stupid things. Once everyone calmed down and finished eating the humans, I was found trying to stick my own ear back to my head." Despite the horribleness of what he just said, a boisterous chuckle came from him. "There is magic that is considered taboo, and I just wanted my own damn ear back so much that I managed to figure out how to heal it back onto myself."

"That's not funny," Zylah grumbled.

"Maybe not, but I do find it rather pathetic of me." Humour still lingered in his expression as he looked down at her. "If I wasn't so distressed, I wouldn't have figured out I can also use *other* people's body parts to heal myself. Without that knowledge, I would be nothing but an earless, limbless torso rolling around on the ground. I would have perished a long time ago."

"That sounds disgusting." Zylah stuck her tongue out with a bleh.

She also couldn't imagine doing such a thing, or the pain of having one's ear removed – especially as she didn't have fleshy lobes. But... she did know what it felt like to have her limbs missing, and she would never tell him that she had partially gone through that when she'd healed him.

The urge to caress his ear pestered her, and she wished she could soothe it now to make up for what happened back then.

"It really is. But you do what you can to survive. It takes a while for the attached limb to grow to my body size and match my skin colour, and about the same amount of time for me to fully use it. It also takes a lot of magic, so it left me ill from the ookmanik until I grew my mana capacity."

Wanting to get away from this particular part of the conversation, Zylah asked, "What did you mean that you confused what the humans did to you with the treatment from the Elysians?"

Once more, he lifted his gaze to the ceiling. His tone was detached, as if he was talking about nothing important or of consequence. Zylah found it rather courageous that he could speak on these matters with such emptiness, whereas she likely would have grown teary.

She also found it really saddening. She wondered if cutting himself away from his past like this was the only way he could cope with it.

"My childhood still isn't clear to me. I think the humans fractured my skull and impaired my memory when they hit me. I kind of remember my mother because she was always there whenever I was receiving treatment, and my stepfather assisted since he was a doctor. They often took blood from me, but I think... they also gave me much because I was unwell as a child. They fed a carnivore a vegetarian diet without realising it, and it was killing me. Those blood transfusions are likely the only thing that saved me, but seeing blood in a tube and then once again with the humans who were greedily taking it from me, I think I combined it all to be the Elysians. They locked me in a prison, and my damaged mind saw them also placing me in cages. I always remembered humans cutting off my ear and the fight that ensued afterwards, but I thought that was simply the result of a battle. Like I said, after visiting Merikh, only recently have those memories split apart and become clearer."

"If that's true, does that mean your hatred of the Elysians lessened?" If he misinterpreted what happened through injury...

"No," he stated with a dark growl. "They may not have been the ones to torture me, but if they hadn't locked me away like I was nothing but a beast, I wouldn't have fled to Earth. Had they treated me better, done more to understand me, I wouldn't have been subjected to everything I have suffered here. I never would have left my home, and I may have been able to live peacefully. All of that was stolen from me as a child."

Unsure of how to respond, Zylah fidgeted through her unease by scratching her foreclaw over his chest.

"I will admit... my prison wasn't as terrible as it could have been. They did *try* to make it comfortable, but it was a cage all the same. They gave me books to study, as if they thought one day I would be able to leave it. They gave me toys, puzzles, and anything a child could need to distract themselves. That didn't stop me from going insane, bashing my head against the wall in my tiny world, but it did help. It's just unfortunate I was so starved of the nutrients I needed that anytime someone attempted to speak to me for too long, the smell of their blood, their meat, the sound of their heart beating in their chest, would send me into a hunger-filled rage. I was starving, and with the transfusions I needed, it always ended in me being bound to a bed as I fought to get free to eat whoever was trying to help me. It prolonged my stay, despite them trying to rehabilitate me for the outside world."

"Couldn't you just tell them you needed to eat meat?" Zylah asked, unsure as to why he hadn't shared that answer. He'd made sure she was aware of his need for meat, and she'd barely been coherent enough to understand him.

"I didn't know," he answered. "The Elysians are entirely vegetarian for physical and spiritual reasons. Me being part Elf meant it just never registered to them because it's not their way of life. They did the same thing to the fully evolved Demons who asked for salvation, who all tried to live their way of life and ended up turning on them without meaning to. The hunger doesn't *feel* like hunger. My stomach didn't grumble, it just felt nauseous. I ate the fruit and vegetables they gave me, and those foods filled my stomach up without providing the nutrients I truly needed. I couldn't ask for something I didn't understand. I just wanted the stomach pain to end, but no one knew the answer, and they didn't wish to cut me open to see if there was something wrong with my organs."

"What did they do to those Demons?" Her orbs darkened in their blue hue, worried for the answer.

"They were imprisoned with me. It was foolish of the Elves, and the books they gave me to study were what eventually led to our escape. The ability to use earth magic through stone is not common, but I think my hybrid blend has gifted me with additional mana strength. I managed to learn how to do it with nothing else to keep me distracted; all I had was time to practise. Someone offered me their blood as a component to help strengthen it, rather than weakening myself, and I managed to destroy part of our underground prison. The bars of our cells were strong enough against us, but not from part of the ceiling collapsing. I used that same magic to create the canyon of the Veil."

With a gasp ripping from her, Zylah sat up. "*You* made the canyon?"

"When will you accept that I am a very powerful being?" he asked, a laugh at her expense bursting from him. "The humans think we arrived only three hundred years ago, because that's when the canyon was formed. I was here years before that. More Demons were crossing over from the portal stone I'd stolen to escape Nyl'theria, and we needed a place that was shaded and dark. It helped that the centre of Austrális was nothing but brittle desert, and there were already many canyons. I just expanded them with what I'd learned from escaping my prison, and used the mana stones I obtained from Nyl'theria to aid the spell. It helped that I managed to teach that magic to the Demons who came here with me. I didn't do it on my own, although I did grow most of the forest. I was a man who had a lot of anger and needed an outlet, so I found one."

"When did you grow Spiral Haven then?"

"About a hundred years after that."

With Zylah still sitting up in disbelief, she watched as his gaze drifted down to her bare chest, and then it darkened. His pupils expanded, and his jaw muscles flared as if he clenched his teeth. He sat up so he could curl an arm around her shoulders and drag her back down.

"Lie down."

With a harrumph, Zylah conceded. It wasn't hard to, since she was thrilled to be able to soak up more of his warmth, scent, and deep voice.

"What else can you tell me?" Zylah asked, her tail swaying. She didn't care if it was all horrible and saddened, she just liked discovering more about him.

"I'm almost thirty-eight and feel fucking old." When she licked her mouth in agitation, his response obviously not good enough, he groaned and threw his arms wide against the ground. "I don't know what else you want to know. I only like to read because it makes me smarter. I hate hunting; I find it boring because I'm so good at it. I once liked travelling this realm because it has its own beauty that is unique in comparison to Nyl'theria, but I've seen it all now. Why don't you tell me something about you?"

"But I don't have anything to tell you. I don't remember much from before you made me eat all those humans. You know everything about me."

His eyes squinted at her, his white upper and lower lashes touching before settling back open. He sighed as he said, "I should have expected that answer."

*Hmm. What else can I ask him then?* It appeared he needed direction. *I don't want to ask about any females.* Just the idea had her sight wanting to shift to bright green from a nasty emotion nipping at her chest. *I think if I ask about Merikh, it will upset him.* If he thought so fondly about him, then Zylah imagined what happened between them would only aggrieve him because his friend was no longer in his life.

She did have something she wanted to know, but she was uneasy about asking. *But if he tells me everything... then he will see how much I care about him.* How willing she was to forgive and forget whatever he'd done in the past.

"Is there anything pertaining to Mavka you haven't told me?"

Her sight shifted to a reddish pink when he gave her a suspicious glare. He said nothing for a short while, and she thought he wouldn't answer.

He threw his head back against the pillow. "I guess the only thing missing would be that I and my human companion emotionally tortured one of your kind over the course of a hundred and eighty years." He lifted a single finger, as if telling her to wait. "But, in my defence, he was the source of much of his own suffering."

She tilted her head on his chest. "What do you mean?"

"Orpheus, the wolf-skulled Mavka, would seek a human offering every ten years. My companion didn't like this. I don't know if it was just because she hated him or if she was jealous – she was weirdly sensitive about the whole thing. We only stole six out of however many there were. He killed and ate many of them on his own, or they foolishly ran away into the Veil like idiots."

"You stole his human companions?"

"Yes." He shrugged, then looked in disinterest at the ceiling. "I've already explained, in part, why she hated him, but we *did* leave him alone the rest of the time. I couldn't enter his protective salt circle when he was there, as all my threatening energy towards him would prevent me from doing so. Since he rarely left it, choosing to wallow in his own self-pity, he was essentially untouchable."

"What... did you do to those humans?" Zylah asked, swallowing thickly.

"She told them she wanted to save them and would take them home."

Why did Zylah get this terrible, foreboding chill down her spine? "What did she really want?"

"She didn't care. She passed them on to me and would just watch my viewing rings to see how Orpheus fared in their absence." He cupped his mouth and turned his head to the side. "I had no interest in eating them since the idea of eating something that can speak to me, beg and plead, actually leaves me with a sour taste. But they were food for my army to further reach their completion. I saw it as no different to what I did to help you. Human life is meaningless to me."

"It's meaningful to me," Zylah grumbled, turning her skull away with red flickering in her sight.

A singular laugh hummed behind his closed lips. "I think it's cute when you pout like that."

And just like that, her annoyance faded and her sight shifted to reddish pink in bashful embarrassment.

"I don't think I'm cute," she muttered, hiding her orbs with a hand when the colour deepened. She liked that he kept calling her that.

"Why not? You want to convince me I'm capable of kindness, yet you won't allow yourself something so simple."

"I don't know." Zylah shrugged. "I have a skull, and I'm aware this is unusual. I am big, and I am scary. I've always known that."

She actually thought many would find her skull ugly, especially since many creatures, humans and Demons, screamed at it.

Two warm and calloused hands cupped the sides of her jaw, and he forced her head forward. She lowered her hands to look at him.

"You are beautiful how you are. Unlike me, you are pretty on the inside and the outside." Then he let her head go and it plonked back onto his chest.

Strange flutters quivered her belly, and she covered her face with her arms to fully hide it. She didn't like how deftly his words made her chest squeeze in tenderness. How she felt about him conflicted with how she viewed what he'd done, and she wondered if it was wrong of her to harbour such affection for someone like him.

He wasn't good; she could see that. She also *still* didn't care, so long as he never directed all the malice he was capable of on her. She wasn't innocent, she'd killed many creatures, and she didn't even remember their faces.

She wanted to think he would change after he got what he wanted, and that he would stop this needless killing and bloodshed when he'd ended his war. She thought if that was possible, she'd be truly happy.

"What happened to your female companion?" Zylah asked, wanting to get away from the heart-stuttering conversation revolving around herself.

"Orpheus' bride ran a sword through her chest," he answered quietly.

Zylah gasped and removed her arms to unblock her sight, only to notice his features looked... calm. He didn't go inwards and feign indifference.

"We had it coming," he continued, his eyes flicking side to

side as he bounced between her orbs. "Everything has a consequence, and if I hadn't been so selfish in only learning how to heal myself, I could have saved her. But that's what happens when you deal in death, you receive it back. I was angry at first, but I eventually realised it was a consequence of our actions, and any hurt was deserved. It was hypocritical of me, considering everything I've done in the name of my war."

"You really are strange. You know you've done terrible things, you've accepted it and wear the weight of them, and yet..."

"I keep doing them?" He raised a questioning brow at her, and Zylah nodded. "Everything I do, no matter if it's a mistake or not, is a step towards my goal. I shed how I feel, the good and the bad, and move forward. It's how I've survived. I've been desensitised to it all after so long."

*I don't think I want to learn anything more about his past right now.* This was enough. It was a clear image to explain his past. She could piece the rest together in her mind from what she'd heard about humans, the Elvish, and then witnessed in Spiral Haven. He hated everything, even his own kinds, but forced himself to be accepted by the Demons.

And those Demons, too, had hurt him, tried to eat him. Even after he'd done so much for them by making the Veil and Spiral Haven.

He left carnage in his wake because everything wanted to see him suffer in some way, whether it was purposeful or an accident. No wonder he had no pleasant stories to share.

But Zylah did have one last question, and it had nothing to do with him. He'd even reminded her of it by speaking of Orpheus.

Zylah let her orbs shift to dark yellow in curiosity. "What is a bride? Rook spoke about this as well."

His eyes widened, and the ball at his throat bobbed as he swallowed hard.

"Shit," he grated, covering his face as his ears tipped back. "I think this is enough talking for now."

"Oh no you don't!" Zylah exclaimed, sitting up so she could snatch his hand from his face. "I want to know about this. He said it's like a mate, but for Mavka."

His eyes crinkled as he sat up as well. He steadied his seated position by leaning back on straightened arms. "Yes, but if I tell you, I can already foresee you wanting to do it."

"Please?" she tried to sweetly beg.

"It will only upset you once I explain it to you and you try to ask me for it."

She scratched at the side of her snout to appear coy. "I promise I won't?"

His handsome features twisted up. "Zylah..." he warned.

She shuffled her way into his lap, since that usually seemed to make him more receptive to her, and forced a whine to rattle from her chest. "If it's something important about Mavka, don't I deserve to know it?"

"Absolutely, but I'm trying really fucking hard not to hurt your feelings."

Zylah shoved his shoulders until he was forced to lie against the ground, then gave him a half-hearted growl. Something tapped against the apex of her thighs, instantly quieting her in surprise.

"We could fuck instead?" he offered, looking down between them with his tongue dabbing at the seam of his lips. "I kind of like you on top of me like this, all growly and controlling."

She didn't like how arousal instantly heated her, and she reluctantly shook her head. As much as she wanted more, if he was evading this so much, then it was obviously important. It bothered him to tell her, and she wanted to know why.

When she didn't falter, his face stiffened and turned cold. "I can easily teleport out of this position."

"B-but you won't," she lied, unsure if that was true. When he cocked a brow at her incredulously, she chittered nervously. "You said you didn't want to hurt my feelings. It will upset me if you do."

His nose bunched up before he let out a deep groan. "Damnit, Zylah."

She squealed when he rolled forward, easily battling her to sit up. Being careful of her own claw mark wounds on her back from healing him earlier, he wrapped an arm around her waist and shoved his head against her chest. An annoyed sigh fluttered out of him, making her fur wave around his face.

"A bride is the Mavka equivalent of a Demon's mate. However, and I'm just guessing here, it is probably monogamous, it is likely permanent, and it appears to turn their companions into Phantoms." His words muffled against her chest as Jabez spoke. With his head bowed, she could see nothing else but the top of his long white hair and dark horns. "Mavka can, essentially, live forever so long as your skulls aren't destroyed. Since the Witch Owl has lived hundreds of years, I'm guessing that same quality has been passed down to whoever they choose to bond with. It's... forever."

"Oh," Zylah rasped, her stomach knotting instantly.

He was right, and she kind of wished she didn't know this now. Because as soon as he said it was forever, she immediately knew she wanted it to be him. She'd like to be tied to him permanently, but he'd already insinuated his answer to that would be a rejection.

Her sight swallowed up to a deep blue, just as the bottoms of her orbs wavered.

"I've... seen it. I watched Orpheus' bride offer her soul and him eat it. I wasn't even surprised when I watched it happen, or that a soul was involved. It was just an answer to a question I never knew I had."

"Okay," she replied quietly, letting her arms fall to the side. She managed to stifle any whimpers and held back the bottoms of her orbs from shattering.

Jabez tilted his head back and butted his chin against her chest. Noticing the wavering in her orbs, his eyes bowed. "Zylah, I can't–"

"I don't want to talk about this anymore right now," Zylah admitted. Feeling rather hollow, she didn't want to hear the rest. She didn't want to hear that he couldn't or wouldn't, nor whatever lame reason as to why.

She also refused to let him continue, in case he tried to say there was something... wrong with her, or that he wanted to *leave* her again. He'd come back when she'd truly feared he wouldn't, but she constantly had this nagging sense that he was trying to make it temporary.

She didn't want to believe that. She wanted his continued

presence to mean that he felt deeply for her, and maybe... just maybe, the longer he stayed, the more he'd want her.

He nodded before his arm loosened. "Do you want me to let you go?"

Zylah shook her head. She liked being held, even if she was upset.

Perhaps it really was silly of her, but she wanted to believe she could change his mind. All he saw were flaws in himself, but she wanted the parts he couldn't seem to see.

She didn't care if it was wrong, if others thought less of her, so long as she got to see this... *caring* side. He understood she was upset, and he seemed to think well enough about her to know she'd figured out why he was so hesitant to tell her. She appreciated that, just as much as she felt the hidden compassion he had for her by simply holding her comfortingly.

She longed to believe it all had a deeper meaning, and that she wasn't being silly.

*I want to embrace all of him.* The good, the bad, the happy, and the sad. She'd longed to hold his body, but now... *I want his soul to embrace.*

To hold it, keep it safe, maybe even nurture it.

"Do you want to go outside?" he asked, appearing to grapple for a way to make her feel better. "There are many places I can take you in an instant that you've likely never seen. The beach, the north, the top of the highest mountain in Austrális."

Zylah shook her head again. She didn't know what she wanted right then.

*My chest hurts.*

# TWENTY-EIGHT

Jabez's right ear twitched at the shuffling and movement he heard behind him. With his eyes closed, his face lifted towards the sky, and seated in a cross-legged position with his back facing the entryway, he listened to Zylah.

He'd not long ago awoken after another deep and restful sleep and had managed to teleport from her limbs without disturbing her. She'd struggled to fall asleep, and it had taken effort on his part.

*I wonder if she's still upset.*

He'd tried his hardest to make it up to her, since he knew he was the source of her disquiet. However, she hadn't wanted to go anywhere, she'd been less enthused about talking, and she hadn't even wanted to read. Instead of hunting like he'd planned, he'd teleported to the human cornfield village to raid one of their butchers and returned to find her even more distressed than before he'd left.

She'd been awfully clingy.

That wasn't something he was usually inclined to enjoy. He generally lacked anything warm and fuzzy within him, so he found clinginess abhorrent and frustrating. He didn't like the clutching, as if they thought they could possess him and take his non-existent heart for themselves. He'd liked his bed-companions as distant as he was, to be there for the sex, maybe some playful teasing, and then to get up when they knew they were overstaying their welcome.

Katerina had been a little different, as she'd been his

companion for a long time. In some aspects, she'd become his sole confidant, but he never shared anything important pertaining to his feelings. Just his plans and goals. She'd sip wine and offer pointless human ideas and sentiments while trying to fuel her hatred through him. Then she'd try to redirect his thoughts to the destruction of Mavka, and therefore, Orpheus.

The idea of falling asleep next to her left him paranoid that she was lying to him as well and would eventually stab him in the heart while he was unaware.

So absorbed in herself, she never even noticed him growing more and more distant with each year – especially towards the end.

But with Zylah...

His lips twitched to curl in humour at himself.

The more she'd clung to him, the tighter he'd tried to make her latch. Her body was sensitive all over, and even just running his fingertips through the fur of her back had her trembling for more. She was exceptionally receptive to any kind of touch. Whether it be his palms running over her, or his fangs scraping against her, his tongue, his lips, even his long hair, she reacted to it.

By the time he had his cock inside her, he realised he was trying to consume her *tenderly.* He never fucked with tenderness. Sure, he could be entirely focused on someone else's pleasure, rather than just his own, but Zylah's clinging had him trying to get closer, deeper, or hold her as tight as possible.

What he found distressing about it was that the damn hole in his chest felt like it was growing something. Each of her soft sounds, her claws trying to dig, all of it ached behind his sternum as he gave long and slow thrusts.

Everything seemed to be different with her, and Jabez was finding it hard to digest that. *I still don't know what it is about her...*

"I'm surprised to find you sitting in the sun," Zylah's voice drifted to him as she approached.

He opened his eyes and turned his face from the beckoning light to watch her take a seat beside him. She seemed most comfortable with her bunny feet out in front, her legs straight, and her back curled forward.

"I like the warmth," he answered, noting she'd finally chosen to don the red dress he bought her. Most Demons, including himself, had an affinity to red due to their eye colour. "Now that I have my magic back, I can protect myself from burning, but I still feel its heat."

He wore nothing but his mauve pants, choosing to soak in the rays without a shirt. He may be a creature of the shadows, but this was a small pleasure he'd gifted himself once he'd learned the spell. It piggybacked off the one that shielded him from the cold, and both were the only reasons he could truly stand this realm.

Zylah's orbs turned black as she lifted her face to the sun like he'd been, letting it cascade over her. It made the bones of her skull appear even whiter, and the shadow of her dainty antlers longer and more menacing.

*She's pretty in the light.* It even made her fur shine.

"This is nice," she commented, eventually opening her orbs to reveal bright yellow. "I've always wanted to sit in the sun with you."

"I would have sat in it with my cloak on had you asked."

"Really?" she blurted, her voice high with joy as she turned her face to him. Her little tail tuft swayed lightly. "I wish I had known that."

He offered her a small smile to reconfirm what he'd said.

They sat in comfortable silence as they stared into the descending hill of forest before them. Only half the trees had their leaves, but they would surely begin to grow back once winter ended. He imagined that was now less than a month away, and he almost couldn't believe it'd been that long.

A small breeze wrapped around them, light and airy, fresh and filled with dew.

This moment with her was surprisingly serene. The quiet, soaking up the world, the sun, even the wind, while knowing she was by his side, was tranquil. He'd never been this at ease before.

The only way to have made it better would have been to bring her into his arms so he could share it in a more intimate way.

He checked on Zylah when she fidgeted, the quiet sound of her claws clicking together making his ears prick. Her teal orbs were bluer than normal, and he figured she was still dwelling on their conversation from the previous day.

Unfortunately, her pushing for those answers meant the conversation he'd been evading steadily approached. He could prolong this. He could ignore it for another day or two just to have more of her, to figure out what was happening within him, but what was the point?

His goal would never change, and that had been firm this entire time. Not even the confusing feelings he had for her were wavering his need for vengeance, only how he wished to enact it.

He *wanted* to be a waking hell, so that he could obtain the Eden he'd been seeking all along. A real, tangible piece of heaven that was built on the decimation of an entire species until he was the last one left.

"Zylah," he called gently, lifting his hand so the back of his knuckles could brush against her bony cheek. A cold pang lanced his chest as he softly stated, "I can't stay here for much longer."

The bottoms of her blue orbs instantly wavered. He wished that cold pang didn't grow wider across his torso or make his stomach tighten.

"Why not?" she asked, her voice cracking as she fisted the skirt of her dress.

He tried to make his tone as gentle and regretful as he could. He wanted her to understand that his goal meant something to him, and that this decision was hard for him as well. "I need to go to Nyl'theria and finish what I set out to do. It was never my intention to make Earth my home. It was always temporary."

"T-then I will go with you."

He opened his mouth to refute her, but closed it and turned his head forward. His gaze dropped to look down at his hands on his lap.

*So, her answer hasn't changed.* He didn't think it had, but it was still hard to accept. After the last two days, he'd likely further solidified her feelings for him, but he didn't know what he wanted anymore.

"You shouldn't," he finally answered.

"Why not?!" she cried, bringing her feet back so she could bend her knees and hug them. With her feet overlapping each other, she buried her skull against her knees just as floating tears sparkled in the sunlight. "You said that's what you wanted. To use me in your war against the Elvish."

But that was the issue: he knew, with absolute certainty, he no longer wanted that.

Yes, that would be the best advantage for him. Having the strength and speed of a Mavka at his side would make it much easier for him to dominate against the Demons there.

The reason he was so reluctant to accept her offer was actually remarkably simple.

"I don't want to see you hurt," he admitted, having finally come to understand the problem.

She wasn't just some strange Mavka to him anymore. He... cared about her – in ways he didn't want, and yet couldn't seem to resist drowning in.

If the last two days were any indication, he wanted to entangle his body with hers constantly. Not because he was simply a male who was horny and happy to bed anything that came sniffing his way, but because he liked her.

She was all sweetness. Her personality was soft against the sharpness of his own, her kindness soothing against the malice within him. She was the parallel symmetry to everything that was wrong with him. Others may have been concerned she bore a skull for a face and was covered in fur from neck to toe, but he found her beauty enchanting because of it. She was smart, her conversations engaging and holding his attentive interest.

She'd been turned into someone remarkable, and he liked how he'd never been able to shape her personality to his whims. Instead, she remained steadfast in her own self, and slowly opened up into a creature who had been driving him insane with the opposite of what he thought he'd want in a mate – if he ever chose one.

He thought he'd want someone bitchy and catty so they

could be strong against his crude arrogance. Someone sexual and overconfident, so he could dominate them for fun.

Instead, Zylah was cute and gentle, making him want to pamper her rather than needle her. She was sensual in a way that was bashful and shy, which only made him hunger to make her naughty and wicked. She was confident where it mattered, but easy to emotionally control, and *that* had him wanting to heed to her rather than have her bend to him.

He found her comforting, her scent and voice having the power to lull him. He'd never been able to find that in another – not even within himself.

She was the opposite of what he thought he'd consider attractive in another, and it kept throwing him off. Unpredictable, yet easy to read.

This is what he'd discovered in the past few days, and it only ensured he was more conflicted than ever.

With her skull buried against her knees, and refusing to unfurl herself, she asked, "But shouldn't I be the one who gets to choose if I get hurt or not?"

"You're asking to join me in a war, Zylah," he stated with a solemn sigh, lifting his gaze to the forest to stare at it. "You're asking me to watch you be hurt for something that is entirely my fault."

"And what about you? What if you get hurt, or... or *die*?" she croaked, her arms tightening around her legs.

"That is the price I'd pay for something I started."

"But I'd never know... and I wouldn't be there to *heal* you."

"I have looked after myself my whole life," he stated, as if she'd forgotten all he'd told her. He was capable of protecting himself to some degree and could heal himself. "This is my last chance, and if I don't succeed this time..."

Well, Jabez wasn't sure if he *wanted* to survive. He doubted he'd be able to live with the crushing defeat and regret. All he'd done... all the horrible, shitty, vile things... they'd be meaningless. He'd forgiven himself simply because there was no other way to move forward if he didn't, so long as he still reached for the reason he did it all.

If that was gone, then he'd just done a bunch of fucked-up shit for no reason. Even if he'd failed miserably many times in the past, they had all been stepping stones in some way – a tactic that failed but ensured he made better moves in the future.

"Can't you find another way?" Zylah pleaded, as a haunting whine ripped from her.

He crinkled his eyes in anguish, finding the sound unbearably painful, like it'd scraped against his very essence.

*But I don't want to be the reason she's hurt.* Physically... or emotionally.

Once he went to Nyl'theria and began his plans, he had a feeling he'd harden. He'd be on alert constantly, paranoid about those all around him. He'd be curt with her in front of Demons he didn't trust, having to feign a lack of interest in her simply so they couldn't use her against him. He thought she had the intelligence to understand that, so behind closed curtains he could dole affection on her freely, but she'd be a vulnerability for him.

A very, very difficult one to exploit, considering her attributes, but one nonetheless.

But he didn't want his callousness or his actions to hurt her heart, which he thought may be a much easier way to pierce her. He'd be distracted, unable to give her the attention she sought, simply because he wanted to infiltrate the Elven city.

How was that fair?

The darkness in him wanted both: her *and* his goal. But at the same time, he wanted to be selfless for once. To protect her, even if it meant cutting himself out of her life.

He could ask her to wait so they could revisit *them* in the future and see what possibility could truly work between them. He was currently infatuated with her to the point she was halting him from moving forward. If there was a chance that he could develop more for her, he wasn't against trying.

But he could be asking her to wait a long time for something that may never happen. He could die and never return. Presenting that future to her seemed crueller than anything; it could be a year, or a hundred, before he obtained what he wanted.

In that time, he didn't know what he was capable of, nor who he may turn into. He may not want to come back once he was done.

She could find another and become besotted with them instead. And if he didn't return, she may even be set on waiting for someone who never came. She could miss out on other opportunities, other potential companions who may be better suited and weren't full of ugliness on the inside.

Yet it was that same ugliness that wanted to be greedy and selfishly keep her by his side, no matter the consequences.

So Jabez was stuck in this limbo of needing to decide if he'd let her come with him because she had managed to gnaw her way into his essence, or leave her behind so he didn't destroy her. She may not even want him by the end if he killed her affection for him through his own arrogant stupidity.

She may continue to love him regardless.

There were so many unpredictable paths.

*But there is one way...* Just one where he felt he could have both.

Sure, there would be times that were hard, but they wouldn't be smothered in bloodshed until the very end. Not like if he were to attempt domination by instilling fear and violence to get his way – which, of course, was the most dangerous option, and the fastest.

The slow political route. The one he'd sneered at since he'd learned of it because he was impatient to end this.

His lips tightened in resistance as he wrestled with the urge to tell her. *What if I'm wrong, though?* What if the political route was the worst one he could take?

He could lean on the violent option as an alternative if it failed, but what would become of them then? She'd be more attached – he could be as well – and he'd be fucking stuck in this same conundrum again, but it'd be even more painful in the future.

*Fuck. I hate this.*

This constant wavering, this back and forth between his wants and desires, was crushing his ability to see clearly. Everything looked too murky.

If he only had himself to worry about, he had no qualms about running horns first into danger. He wasn't afraid of death; he just stubbornly refused it.

Another much higher pitched and distressed whine ripped from her. She dug her claws into her thighs until he thought she might draw blood, and he was thankful he'd blunted them for her, otherwise she may have. Her trembling worsened with every second he said nothing.

More than ever, he longed to bring her into a comforting hold. He couldn't; he needed the absence of her right now.

Yet her tears and whimpers were ripping into his chest, and the coldness in him was beginning to burn in ways he'd never experienced before, like frostbite eating away at him.

"There is a small group of Demons, maybe a hundred or so, who have taken over the ruins of an Elven village," Jabez reluctantly stated, giving in to her, to himself, as his shoulders drooped in defeat. "It was the last foothold of resistance, other than Lezekos City, and it already had walls to protect them. It's why they lasted so long."

"Why are you talking about this? I don't care about the history of the Elvish right now!" she shouted, shaking her head.

He winced and rested his elbow on his knee so he could palm his face.

"Because I've already spoken to the leader there. They are fully completed Demons who sought refuge and wanted to rebuild in the forest, away from those who would seek to eat them. They are peaceful people who no longer want to be in danger." He ran his hand up his face and caressed a horn in frustration. "But their village would be a perfect place for me to initially set up my base because they are tame. I wouldn't need to worry so much about them turning on me, and I can slowly recruit my army there. It'd be slow to spread word, as the Demons are untrusting of each other, but the potential to invade the city and find actual Elves to eat to further develop, rather than consuming each other, will be hard for many to resist."

"What is the point in telling me all this if you don't want me to join you?" she cried, lifting her face to shine orbs so dark the blue of them was threatening to turn black.

Now that she was no longer pressing against her knees, he saw just how fast her tears were trickling from her. They collided with each other to form big, hovering blobs, and took even longer than usual to fade.

"I'm trying to explain that there *is* another option," he stated, resisting the urge to bellow or roar at her.

His heart was beating hard and fast, and he was trying his best to keep everything in so he could be *calm*. Yet inside, he was anything but fucking calm.

He was going against his better judgement and the right thing for her, simply because *he* didn't want to leave this realm without her. And it wasn't *easy*. He felt like he was doing the wrong thing, and the guilt of that was twisting into him like a damn knife.

He wanted her. He didn't know why, and this was something he'd never faced before. He was treading new territory, when he'd always been an unmoving, unbending, unfeeling force.

"There is an option that is safer," Jabez continued, averting his gaze from her because he just *couldn't* look at her right then. "One in which you could come with me."

"Really?" she asked, her voice thick from her sadness, yet her tone so full of hope it was bruising.

"I wouldn't need to instil fear, but rather a collective ambition that aligns with my own. If my estimations are correct, I can recruit an army that would be a five-to-one ratio against the Elvish. I wouldn't need to fight to enforce that rule, and my ability to teleport is unique – without me, this plan fails. I could make sure they understand that killing me would ensure failure, because if I alone get access into Lezekos, I can teleport to the mana stone that powers the dome that protects the city. Then I can destroy it, leaving the shield vulnerable."

It would take a long time. Slowly building such an army would mean he would have to prove his prowess with his magic time and time again. He'd be placing himself in danger, but it was nothing like needing to spar with those who thought him weak.

Using his ability to teleport as leverage was the only way to ensure his safety. Kill him, then they'd be back to fighting with each other for completion. What he'd be offering was a real source of food, one which they hungered for deeply.

Unless they discovered his secret... then he'd be *fucked.*

"What I'm trying to say..." he continued, a defeated and harsh expire falling from him, "is that it would be safer for you, so long as you agreed not to interfere. You would have to promise that you'd stay out of the way and just observe. You would never fight, never protect me, and just have faith that I can do this on my own, even if someone attacks me. If I gain enough loyalty, I should have others who would be willing to ensure my safety in order to protect the grand plan."

Jabez was usually a good judge of character. He'd figure out those who were loyal enough to act as bodyguards, just like he had here. Before it was destroyed, those in his castle, even some lesser Demons, had believed in him so much they were willing to die for him.

"But if you were hurt..." she rasped, and Jabez brought his face back to her just in time to watch her clasp her hands to her stomach.

"You would do nothing," he stated firmly, holding her gaze so she would see the unwavering resolve in him. "I don't want you to heal me and bear my wounds for me, leaving yourself in pain. I can do that myself. If you even try to fight for my sake, or heal me, I will bring you right back to Earth and leave you here."

A whimper escaped her, and she looked down at her lap. "But I'm strong enough to–"

"Zylah," he warned, his voice deep as he narrowed a glare at her. "That is the only way I'll agree to this. The only reason I would want you to enter into any fight is to protect yourself, to ensure your *own* safety. Should it come to that, I'll try to take over for your sake and you will retreat to the side and let me handle it. If you fall into a rage, I can teleport you to places where I can calm you down without anyone being in the way of your destruction."

"Why don't you want me to fight? I just don't understand." Then she softly added, "I want to... help you."

"Because I care about you! Isn't that *obvious*?!" he shouted, running his hands through his hair before throwing them forward. "It's why I'm still here. It's why I haven't left already. It's why I don't wish to see you in pain that would be entirely my fault! I won't ask someone I care about to fight in my stead, to be a fucking tool for massacre while I stand back like a sadistic prick and watch."

"But you're asking me to watch *you* be hurt!" She yanked her arm to the side, gesturing at nothing but the forest. "You said you wanted Merikh to do this. He's a Mavka, so why would it be any different?"

"Because he *enjoys* killing. He likes to rampage, he likes to fight, and he finds delight in destroying everything until he is the victor. He would threaten anything that looks at him funny to purposely taunt them into attacking him because he is a ruthless, hateful being who gets off on it and would *laugh* once he's done ripping them apart."

He also had protective quills covering him, meaning the potential of injury was much less likely. He'd also make fun of Jabez for needing assistance, rather than coddle him in worry.

Zylah flinched in understanding and dipped her head. "Oh."

"Yeah," he said plainly. "You, on the other hand, don't like to hurt, and would likely feel guilty over anyone you harmed. I can see you trying to peacefully avoid a fight and leaving yourself open to attack. He's experienced in battle, whereas you're not. He would revel in the fight with me, and then we would have spoken about it with glee around a damn campfire. You and he are not the same."

Zylah chittered, a sign she didn't know what to say. She continued to shake, continued to whimper quietly, but at least her tears had finally ebbed.

"It will take a long time," he admitted, softening his tone. "And I can't promise anything more than what we currently have until I've finally taken over the city."

"But you said... but if you become a Phantom, that would mean you can't die."

*I'm not willing to tie myself to someone when I'm uncertain of my future.* He also wouldn't do it just to ensure he was unkillable and could, over the course of forever, entertain this goal.

He was tired of his life as it currently was. If he couldn't achieve his goal in his long lifespan, and it withered away into nothing but an unobtainable dream... then he doubted he'd ever be at peace. He'd give up, and a person who had completely lost their sense of self never lived the rest of their days well.

He'd likely grow depressed with nothing driving him forward. He could see himself checking out of reality, because he'd have nothing positive to reflect on. No happiness, no fond memories, nothing that would fuel him.

Tying himself to someone who would end up being a witness to his mental decay wasn't a wound he wished to give. Especially as they'd always question why they were never enough to save him from himself. He wouldn't trap someone without giving them the opportunity to have an out when he was so riddled with uncertainty.

That would be too cruel, even for him.

It was either this or nothing.

If he did achieve it, then he'd allow himself to bask in it. He could focus on other things while knowing everything he'd done had a reason.

He'd have his Eden, his peace, the life he'd always wanted. A home that was permanent, colourful, and filled with pleasantries in a magnificent city that was his to play in. The idea of sharing that with her... it warmed his chest and left him even more hopeful than he thought possible.

Especially as the Demons would welcome her, unlike the humans or Elves. She wouldn't be an outcast – they were less likely to scorn someone just for the way they looked. She'd have a home where she was accepted, and after how she'd acted towards Fayren and those in Spiral Haven, he thought that might bring her joy.

She could become a librarian like the bookworm she was or a doctor like the healer she wanted to be, or something else entirely if she so chose it. She could feel like a real person, and not some bloodthirsty monster that was feared by all.

*That* was a future he'd like to present to her.

He'd like to witness it.

His goal had grown to be much bigger than himself, now involving her and her happiness. Who would she become when she had free rein to just simply be herself, with people to immerse herself in and teach her other interesting things?

She must have taken his silence as a rejection, because her shoulders dropped in defeat. "Okay," she conceded, before subtly shifting her skull in his direction. "But this means I can come with you?"

"Yes," he said, hating the way guilt nipped at him.

"Then I will do as you ask of me."

He lifted his face to the sky, realising the sun had faded over the mountain and they were left in the shade. *So, that's it then.* This was the path he was taking: the safer, political path... that allowed her to stay by his side.

Doubt and worry riddled beneath the surface, but it was something. He peeked at her, hoping he wasn't making the wrong decision by agreeing to bring her – and just persisting with her in general.

Yet, as he looked upon Zylah, he had to fight the urge to fucking smile in triumph. He was getting both the things he currently wanted.

He reached towards her until he'd grasped the side of her waist furthest from him. Then he forcibly dragged her closer until she was between his thighs with her back to his chest. He curled his legs around her backside while wrapping his arms around her midsection to hold her.

*Oh, the naughty things I'm going to do to this female,* he thought with humour, scraping his fangs down her shoulder blade just so she would shiver.

*I also can't wait to show her Nyl'theria.*

It was a beautiful realm in the daytime, and even more mesmerising at night. He could imagine her awe and curiosity as he showed it to her.

His eyes gleamed in delight. *I bet she'll be cute.*

"I like you in this dress," he offered, wanting to defuse the tension between them now that a decision had *finally* been made. He plonked his chin on her shoulder. "Red suits you."

She let out an annoyed huff, but he noticed her orbs flicker with reddish pink in embarrassment in his periphery.

Zylah better be ready for him, because she'd just given him the opening to do whatever he wanted with her. And if that was to compliment her until she squirmed, and give her affection, then so be it.

A devious, quiet chuckle rumbled from his chest as he lightly bit the muscle of her shoulder in fondness.

# TWENTY-NINE

Zylah looked down as her left foot was lifted, and she had to grip one of Jabez's horns for balance. He slipped the shoe strapping over her toes before wrapping the rest up. He did the same to the other foot, and she had to stop herself from kicking him when his fingers accidentally tickled her sole.

Despite him doing something nice for her, since she was sure she could do this on her own, his expression was firm and hard in comparison to how they'd woken up.

By the dark smudges underneath the inner corners of his eyes, she didn't think he'd slept much.

She'd woken up snuggling him as his nails lightly brushed through the fur of her neck. When she'd peeked up at him without moving, he'd been staring off into nothingness, appearing to think deeply.

He always thought deeply.

What went on behind those eyes of his was a mystery, and after the last few days, she knew it was more complicated than she could ever fathom. The more she learned of him, his past, the hidden parts of his personality, the less she seemed to understand.

Yet, when he noticed she was awake, he'd given her a small smile and let her lie there for as long as she wanted. With her pointed snout buried against the side of his bare chest, she'd soaked up his warmth, his bergamot-and-sandalwood scent, the strength in his muscles, and the softness of his brown skin.

When he was lying down, he was more docile. He always let her touch his handsome face when the longing struck her.

A short time after they'd woken, he left to hunt. Then he took them to the small lake to wash.

They were leaving Earth.

As thrilled as she was about being able to go with him, Zylah was nervous. She had no idea what was in this other distant realm, and the hardness in his features told her he was wary. The fact he felt this way, and was taking them there, just made her wonder what they'd be coming up against.

He lacked his cloak, and from their earlier discussion, she knew he intended to leave without it. He didn't want to wear something that was grabbable, choosing to take only a bag of food.

Jabez stood and offered his hand out to her. "Are you ready?"

She nodded and tentatively placed her palm in his.

They teleported instantly, and Zylah was thrown into brightness. Still early in the afternoon, the sun shone over the big open area he'd taken them to in the Veil.

More adjusted to his teleporting now, Zylah easily steadied her queasy stomach and wobbling legs to look around. His hand fell away as he stepped to the side, but she didn't immediately follow.

*I remember this place.* Although those memories were now blurry in her mind, the rubble they were next to was unmistakable. *This is where I found him.*

Had it already been nearly two and a half months since then? It felt like longer.

Her orbs shifted to blue at the memory of how she'd found him. It'd mattered little to her then, but looking back on it made her heart squeeze.

Parts of his face and torso had been marred with the evidence of healing burns, which is why there was now a baldness around his right ear like a curve. One arm had been missing, as well as a leg from the knee down.

There had been no blood, but that was likely because he'd

managed to rid himself of it. He'd healed himself just enough to stop her from turning on him in a hunger-filled rage and the fact that she could have eaten him... her stomach knotted.

She'd never have known about his existence. He would have just been another thing she'd eaten, and all these warm and tender emotions wouldn't exist. She also wouldn't be intelligent, nor have learned the things she'd come to discover. She never would have met Fayren, Goldie, or Rook, and learned that Demons weren't all terrible.

How vastly different things could have been was startling and harrowing to realise.

"Zylah," Jabez called.

She lifted her skull in his direction to find him standing next to a wall of shrubbery. She quickly shoved her despondent thoughts to the side and ran over to him.

Before she was even upon him and could apologise, he stated, "Don't linger on it. Many things could have happened."

She chittered at that, her shoulders turning inwards at how he somehow read her mind. Then again, the colour of her orbs likely gave her away, and she nipped at herself for it. *I wonder if there is a way for me to suppress my orb colours.*

She would like to not be so easily read.

He took her into an opening in the wall of shrubs that stood taller than even her. She believed they were hedges, and she noted those closest to where his castle once stood were bowed, bent, and missing their leaves.

The further in they went, the more shade crawled over them, as the rest of the hedges were healthier – just a little worn from some kind of wind explosion. Many of the shrubs appeared to be forming new leaves.

Within minutes, a glow up ahead stole her attention.

Yellow and cloudy, a ring of magic stood in the middle of some kind of large iron-caged dome. A giant hole had been ripped open from the inside, as if someone or something had forced their way out.

Her fur lifted the closer they got to what she assumed was the portal, and the middle of it looked like murky water. It wasn't completely opaque, though, and she could see a blurry image of the iron cage and hedges on the other side.

"There's no door," Zylah commented, trying unsuccessfully to find some kind of way in or out of the dome.

"No." He dipped his head to the side to look at her. "I purposefully made it without one."

"How is anyone supposed to get in or out?" she asked, leaping into action when he strolled to the side where the gaping hole was.

"That's the point; they couldn't without my intervention." He indicated to where they were going. "The cage was strengthened by my magic. The Demons who passed through found no issue getting out on their own once the magical reinforcement was gone. That's why there's a hole now."

The dark yellow of curiosity lifted into her sight. "Why would you make it that way?"

"I assessed every Demon who crossed the portal," he stated while carefully stepping over and around bent metal. "If they were a lesser Demon, I teleported them to the outer ring so they couldn't instigate violence against those who live peacefully in the inner ring. To those who were near completion and intelligent, I offered guidance, explaining the way of life here, and told them about Spiral Haven. It meant everyone could be placed where they needed to be."

Her tail wiggled lightly at that. *He took on this task just to ensure the safety of those nearby.*

He'd tried to make her think him evil and callous, but this was evidence that he did have goodness in him. Perhaps only for his fellow Demons, but he cared enough to take up a duty that likely would have been bothersome and annoying.

He ensured he didn't allow total chaos under his protective watch and then even took the time to *help* those who needed it.

When he must have noticed her reaction, his eyes flicking in the direction of her tail, a small chuckle rumbled from him.

"I think you're misinterpreting my actions, Zylah. I did it to keep those who would seek to eat me far away from myself."

*Liar*, she thought, her tail swaying faster.

Maybe that had been his intention in some way, but she didn't think that was truly his sole reason.

He rolled his eyes as if he could read her thoughts. "It also stopped people from attempting to dig for the mana stone that powers the portal, since it's buried right beneath it."

"Do you mind if I ask why you chose to come to Earth?" She was curious if he'd chosen this realm because it had humans in it.

"I just took the first stone I could find, and it led here. The fact I could even activate it was a miracle, and a total fluke." He pushed his hand out in her direction to halt her. "Now... give me a moment. I'll check to make sure the other side is clear, and then I'll bring you through."

He walked through the portal without another word. The centre of it dipped around him before giving way with a ripple like someone had thrown a rock into water.

Seconds later, half his body dipped back through, and he waved for her to come. "Alright. Let's see if I was right that you'll be able to access it."

He retreated to give her space, disappearing once more.

Zylah didn't know what she expected. She thought it would be like teleporting – darkness giving way to a disorientating new environment, while her mind was wrung like a damp cloth.

Instead, all she felt was coldness as it crept along her body, goosebumps making her fur puff. There was no disorientation, no queasiness. It was like she'd merely stepped through a threshold and into a new world shrouded by the dark of night.

The very first things Zylah noticed were how much warmer it was, and the gigantic moon that lit up the sky.

Pale bluish white, it appeared to have green streaks of gas roaming across it – although that could've just been the moon's surface. Two rings made up of what she thought might be dust and rocks circled it in a cross pattern, and they sparkled in a reflection of the moon's light.

Earth's moon appeared tiny in comparison, barely the size of a human coin Jabez had shown her. This moon was so large she could barely see the night unless she looked way up. *Thousands* of stars glittered in the distance, some flickering red, others green, as celestial dust flittered all throughout.

At least the rest looked black, just like on Earth.

"Pretty, isn't it?" Jabez stated softly, drawing her gaze to find he was looking at it as well. "I'm guessing you think it's a moon?"

Zylah chittered at that and scratched at the side of her neck awkwardly. *Well, yeah.* It looks like one, just massive.

"It's actually a planet." The mischievous smile on his face told her everything she needed to know; he was going to tease her the entire time they were here. "It's called Otholla."

Zylah looked around them, noticing how the portal was surrounded by trees on one side, and a vast meadow on the other. In the distance, she heard the rush of a strong stream, but couldn't see it over the rolling hills.

Stillness surrounded them and only the very tips of the tall dark-teal grass moved in the whisper of a breeze.

Her gaze drifted up to the very tops of the tallest trees she'd ever seen. The bark itself appeared to be white, as if bleached, but the leaves were a gentle light pink or purple. They barely rustled, but she did note how large each leaf seemed to be.

It helped there was a fallen one nearby, and she tilted her head when she thought she could have laid on top of it and her toes would likely not stick out past it.

Jabez took a single step, and she shuffled back when the ground lit up momentarily. She looked down at her own feet, and each time she moved or settled her weight differently, the grass remained dark, but the dirt beneath it seemed to ooze with a bluish colour.

He must have noticed the way she lifted a foot just to step it down in a different spot, because he said, "There's mana in almost everything around you. It's in the dirt, reacting to the pressure of your steps, in the water, so it makes it glow when it's moving or disturbed, and in many of the plants that absorb it."

"I like how it looks," Zylah said, her sight shifting to a bright yellow. "I wish Earth glowed like this."

It would make the world less foreboding and sinister at night.

Although the pink leaf on the ground was dark, she noticed the softest, barely visible glow on the stems of each one connected to the branches above. It was like a canopy of dull light, not sharing any with the ground but enough that she could see the twists of branches or tree trunks in contrast.

"We won't be able to walk to where we're going, as it's a little far to the ruined village, and doing so would be undeniably *stupid.* I also won't be able to teleport us right into the middle, as that'll likely spook the inhabitants. I'll take us somewhere close by. There may be a lot of dematerialising and materialising involved. If you start to feel unwell, let me know."

"Okay," Zylah stated with a nod, agreeing just to follow whatever he thought was best.

He placed his palm on her forearm, and they teleported to a new environment once more. This one was in the very centre of the forest, and somehow, the trees appeared to be even taller and more daunting. Or perhaps that was just because she was now standing right underneath one.

The bases were around the same thickness as those in Spiral Haven, and she thought they could be close in height, if not a little taller. She noticed the bark of the trees surrounding them was a brownish red, and the leaves glowed a faint blue on their stems.

The area was fully cast in shadows, and not even Otholla, the planet she'd mistaken for a moon, could be seen through the thick canopy above. She didn't know why, but she had this overwhelming sense that everything around her was ancient.

Even before Jabez removed his hand from her forearm, new, interesting, and strange scents flittered around her.

When her gaze dropped from the scenery above, it landed on glowing mushrooms. Those on the ground had a white glow to them, and she noticed they looked like fish tailfins, although round rather than forked. The blue ones clinging to trees looked gooey, and she watched a droplet fall from one to splatter against the ground.

"Be careful about touching any mushrooms that appear red," Jabez told her just as she reached out to touch at the goo coming from a tree one. "Red polleshrooms and their spores can be quite nasty if they get into your bloodstream."

"What about these ones?" Zylah asked, tilting her head at the blue ones that looked entirely like some kind of semi-transparent jelly.

He muffled a soft chuckle behind his closed lips. "Those are harmless." He came to her side while rolling up his sleeves and reached out to take two in his hands, each the size of one of his palms. He squished them in his fists with a wet squelch. "The Elysians used them in the past for dances."

Then, as if to demonstrate, he smeared the goop all over his hands until they both glowed brightly with a translucent whitish blue. He lifted one to her nose hole, and she sniffed it to find it had a sweetness underneath its bitter musk.

"Watch."

The slime on his skin began to change colour, just as she felt subtle pulses of magic coming from his fingertips. Then the mushroom residue exploded off him like fire made of glowing red before twinkling into nothingness, leaving his skin clean once more.

"Why did the Elysians do this?" she asked, touching the side of her forefinger pad against the last remaining mushroom to take some of its goop. She smeared it over her fingers to play with its slippery consistency.

"It really depended on the dance. Some were just for entertainment, and others were on the day of a bonding ceremony. They even danced at funerals, utilising their magic in a profound way to celebrate anything, even if it was something such as death." Any warmth that had been in his gaze slowly died, and he looked off to the side as he said, "I'll be honest, I don't have any recollection of these dances in my childhood – I only read about them. I don't know if doing them is common anymore, as I was never invited to any such gatherings, or if it's due to the inability to get them – or anything – from outside the city's walls. The city has underground greenhouses, though, so I'm sure they somehow kept such an important tradition alive."

As she watched his features fall into his usual indifferent mask, a coldness dripped into her chest.

*That's... really sad.* He didn't know something so simple due to not having gone to any events, as if he was an outcast.

"We should start moving," he said, changing the subject of the conversation as he walked in a certain direction through the overgrown foliage. "The village is only a few minutes' walk from here. I didn't want to bring us too close in case we stumbled into a group of scouts."

When Zylah drew level with him, he looked at her from the corner of his eye.

"Be mindful that the Demons in Nyl'theria are wary of all. They have been warring among themselves for a long time, so they often see everyone new as a threat or potential food."

"How do you know that?" Zylah asked, looking around at all the different kinds of plants.

Most had a teal or pink tinge to them and appeared to consist of large leaves that made up the entirety of the plant, rather than small leafy shrubs. Nothing here appeared to be small except for the mushrooms they saw, and even they had been the size of one of her palms.

"I came to Nyl'theria often. I returned at least once a year so I could remain informed, as well as scout for potential ways to get through the city's defences, on the chance they had started to weaken. I've watched this world fall deeper and deeper into despair over the last few centuries, but it was already in full chaos before I was born. The Demons were here long before they arrived on Earth, and there are no Elysians left outside the city's protective dome."

"Do you know how long it's been?" she asked, hoping to keep him talking while he was so willing to share.

He didn't often talk of himself, and he was actually a very quiet person, so hearing him speak felt like a blessing and a reward. She didn't care if it was over something as unimportant as this foreign world and its past, not when she could hear the silky bass of his masculine voice, or watch his expression change as he spoke about it.

She could tell, in some way, he adored this place. Despite how his ears twitched constantly in alertness, there was less tension in his shoulders, as if he found the environment more comfortable to be in.

She never expected the deep laugh that came from him next.

"It's really hard to explain it, as the time differences are vast." His lips curled then, and he turned his face to her. "Zylah, to this world, I have only been gone twenty-one years. The Demons have been here for over a hundred Nyl'therian years, which equates to over a millennium and a half on Earth, if not two millennia. I doubt there are any elders left who witnessed the beginning, but their offspring were born into a world of fleeing and tragedy. How long ago it was that those who were unable to reach the city died is unknown to the Elysians, and to me."

"You have lived a long time, I know that," Zylah commented, lifting her gaze when something different began to glow up ahead. It was easy to see with the darkness, since the only light came from the muted shine above, their footsteps they left behind, and the mushrooms she saw. "Does the passage of time feel different when you're here?"

She hadn't noticed anything different, but she thought that could be because of what she was used to. Then again, she'd never watched time tick like she'd read about from things such as clocks or watches, so it didn't feel tangible or truly understandable in her mind.

"If I'm being honest, it'll feel more natural for me. Life speeds past on Earth. The sun always rose when I was never ready for it to, and it went down in the blink of an eye. Here, it all moves slower, but it matches the speed of my age, my growth, my sleep. It will be a long time before the three suns rise here, not that it matters due to the density of the forest."

Was that why he was so desperate to return here? To return to a place that felt more familiar, rather than racing past in a way he couldn't seem to grasp?

Would it feel the same for her being here now? Would everything appear to be moving too slowly, or would Zylah be able to adapt?

*Isn't my grandparent a demigod of this world?* she thought, and paused her steps when the bright glow from earlier came into view. *Does that mean I could adapt to it?*

She'd like to think that was possible, rather than it be burdensome like Earth had been for him.

Zylah sniffed at the pretty aroma coming off the petals of a bright-red flower that had a glowing fuzzy yellow stem sticking out from it. The colours reminded her of a sunrise or a sunset as it cast its muted light across the horizon. Black dew clung to its five petals, and she tentatively reached out to grasp something so big she'd need to hold it in both her hands.

*This smells really nice.* She tried to figure out its scents from those of Earth, like that would make it easier to wrap her mind around its strangeness.

Just before she made contact with it, Jabez grabbed both her hands with his own and roughly shoved them down.

"You shouldn't touch that," he stated, before pulling her back by her hands to put some distance between her and it.

Reddish pink lifted into her sight, reflecting her embarrassment at attempting to touch something unknown in a foreign and unusual world.

"Is it poisonous?" she asked, wondering how something that smelt so nice it had her practically drooling could be harmful.

"No, it's not poisonous." She turned her gaze to him when she noticed the mirth in his tone, to find his eyes were crinkled with humour and the corners of his lips had curled. "It's called a draflium flower."

"Why can't I touch it then?" White flashed in her sight at

another possibility. "Wait... would it have tried to eat me?"

She'd heard about carnivorous plants in one of her herbology books. She tilted her head at it; it didn't look very nasty though, since she probably could have ripped it to shreds had it tried to capture her.

A chuckle rumbled from him as he shook his head. "More like you'd probably try to eat *me*."

That's even worse!

At the nervous chitter she gave, his laughter only grew deeper.

"The black dew on it is a strong aphrodisiac. It's so potent that just brushing up against it will cause intense arousal, and ingesting it will affect you twice as much."

*"Oh,"* she rasped, the embarrassed hue in her sight brightening. Yes, that would have been bad, although the thought did have her insides warming against her will.

"It completely lowers one's inhibitions, and in a place like this forest, that's a terrible idea. A Demon could come, and I doubt you would care if you were under the effects of its dew."

She was surprised no Demons had come already.

"Sorry," she grumbled, pulling her hands away from his hold of them. "I probably shouldn't be touching anything."

"It's fine, Zylah. You're welcome to be curious – just ask first." He leaned closer to sniff it before drawing away. "Luckily its scent is harmless, although inviting. It smells like orange and cinnamon."

"It does smell good," she stated, her tail wiggling at his reassurance. *Not as nice as him, though.*

"Here, come." He grabbed her hand and began to pull her along. "I know there's a meadow not too far from here, and it's closer to the village. Everything there is relatively harmless, so you're welcome to investigate to your heart's content."

She looked down at their entwined hands as she was dragged through the forest, not used to him doing this. It made her heart squeeze in joy. The fact that he was the one to instigate it, even if it was something as innocent as pulling her along so she couldn't touch anything else, had her clasping his hand tightly in return.

His ears twitched in reaction, but he didn't comment on her grip. She was thankful he didn't try to make it awkward by teasing her.

"Shouldn't we be heading to the village, though?" Zylah asked, unsure as to why he was deviating from their path.

"I have waited three hundred Earth years to get what I want, so taking a few minutes longer to show you something nice won't do me any harm." Then he finally glanced at her as he said, "This is the first time you are seeing Nyl'theria. It is prettiest at night, and your awe of it may wane the longer we are here."

When he turned back around to see where he was going, bright yellow lifted into her sight as she looked at the back of his long hair and black tapered horns. *Really? He would do that for me?* Her tail tuft wiggled a little at the realisation he wanted to do something special for her, despite how much his goal meant to him.

It didn't take them long to reach the spot Jabez wanted to show her, especially as this was all part of his design.

In reality, they weren't actually as close to the village as he'd let on. He'd originally planned to take them within proximity of it straight away, but when he observed her curious gaze at Otholla and the trees, his urgency had waned.

He'd almost forgotten what it was like to first see the Nyl'theria wilds. It'd been many years before he'd gained the courage to come back after abandoning it, and he'd never seen the realm outside Lezekos City's impressive walls.

As pretty as the Elven city was, it held barely a fraction of the beauty of this world. As a young adult, he'd been mesmerised upon seeing it, learning it, and investigating every new thing he came upon after returning for the first time.

In the same way, he'd been curious about everything on Earth. However, unlike that mostly colourless world,

Nyl'theria had much more to offer.

Wanting to experience that awe and amazement, but vicariously through *her*... well, that wasn't quite something he was willing to miss out on. He was sure they'd have plenty of chances for her to learn about this world in the future, but there was nothing quite like being thrust into it blindly.

He'd purposefully let her have small peeks by taking her through the forest, where she could slowly adjust to the glowing flora. Draflium flowers had once been picked to near extinction, but the removal of the Elysians allowed them to flourish again in certain areas.

He couldn't resist the potential of teasing her about them. He knew she'd likely try to touch that bloom.

In the future, he'd explain that the plants shone at night in order to rid themselves of the excess energy that came from the heat and light from the three suns. Without expending it, the world would have burned up and turned into some kind of desert realm, since it would be considered a hot and constant summer climate.

Even many of the fauna glowed due to eating the flora, although most of the animals besides small critters and insects had been eaten to extinction by the Demons.

What he was about to show her was something that only happened at night, and it would be much more enthralling if she provoked it.

The area he brought her to opened up into a tree-lined clearing, through which there was a gap that led to a much larger meadow beyond. It was far too open for his comfort, so he thought this smaller and more private environment would be safer, and *intimate*.

Otholla shone brightly down on the clearing, and dewdrops sparkled with reflections of its white light swirling with muted green.

As he thought, the first things that drew her attention were the shrubs just on the outskirts of the mostly unassuming, long teal grass. He released her hand so she could walk over to the closest ones, then propped his back against the trunk of a tree, folding his arms as he watched her.

Nervous about getting too close to anything now, Zylah crouched down and hugged her midsection to inspect what was before her.

Purple monstera-like leaves acted as supports for long tendrils that were about a foot in length. Glowing bright yellow all throughout, with little balls of green in their tubes, they waved any time there was the tiniest wind. From memory, he knew them to be mostly scentless, but she did lean forward a little to sniff at them.

"Touch one," Jabez told her with a sly smile curling his lips. "Everything in this meadow is safe."

The biggest danger was that a Demon would likely come upon them at any moment. He would be more annoyed that it'd ruin their fun than actually be a problem they needed to worry about.

She glanced at him, her snout moving ever so slightly in his direction, and he quickly hid his growing humour. She tentatively reached out to greet a thick tendril.

The moment she touched one, that particular glowing strand dimmed as it swirled to latch onto her clawed index finger. She gasped, quickly yanked her hand away, and it easily let her go to curl downwards, hiding as if it'd grown shy.

"It moved!" she squealed, before reaching out to let another one latch on to her.

The glowing green seed pods inside it quickly leaked from its tip, using her as a way to spread itself throughout the forest. She made it let go to inspect the two seeds upon her fingers, and the stickiness surrounding them ensured it was hard for her to pry them off. It would've eventually dried on its own, and when it did, the seeds would've dropped from her in hopes of sprouting roots into the ground.

Her orbs changed from the dark yellow of curiosity into the brightness of joy, then she leapt to her feet and rushed to a different shrub. He was glad she skirted the long stalks of grass, rather than walking through them, and she didn't seem to notice what happened when she accidentally disturbed them.

She didn't need to crouch this time as she touched orange moss clinging to the reddish bark of a tree. It reacted to her touch, likely hugging her fingertips, but was mostly lacklustre in movement and changes in its glow.

Many of the trees in Nyl'theria had orange moss growing from them, but it only specifically grew from those with reddish bark and blue leaves. The sap from those trees was spicy in scent and taste, and was a perfect nutrient for that variety of bryophyte.

Dull-green moss grew from those with bleached trunks and purple or pink leaves, but the moss itself appeared like tiny clovers. This section of forest didn't have those trees, but most of the world was covered in them, as they were the stronger species.

The smile that had been pestering Jabez earlier grew as she turned her attention to the ground between them.

Between the stalks of grass were glowing orange bulb flowers. Even now, he could scent their citrusy aroma.

She stepped into the thigh-high grass and gasped loudly when a flurry of red glowing circles lifted up around her. Unintelligible whispers emerged from the red orbs that moved as if they were alive – which they were.

Her head twitched and cocked as she paused, listening to them. Once she stopped moving, the annoyed tiny creatures turned blue as they found new stalks to land on before ceasing their glow in their new resting spots.

All the quiet chattering died, and she lifted her skull to him, tilting it in question.

His smile grew. "The best translation for their name would be whispering wisps. They're insects that turn red if you disturb them but glow blue when they fly. When they are at rest, you wouldn't know they are there." A few were still finding a place to settle around her, occasionally lifting off from the stalks that waved around her thighs from the light wind. "Many believed they held secrets of the past and would share them if you listened closely."

He doubted that was true. Their wings just made a sound that was inconceivable even to his and Zylah's sensitive hearing, and it was simply their minds trying to make sense of it.

Zylah took a step forward, and they lifted off once more, glowing red and whispering as they fled.

She giggled as she sprinted forward, her hands out to her sides so she could brush against the tips of the grass to disturb even more. A wave of tiny glowing red orbs sprung from everywhere she went before those furthest from her settled to blue as they looked for a new spot to rest. A spot they wouldn't receive, as she changed direction and agitated them once more by going back through them.

His eyes crinkled with fondness as he watched her playfully run through them, his chest swelling as his gaze moved with her. The whispers grew louder, but her bubbly giggle was far brighter.

*I knew she'd like them,* he thought, as he covered the lower half of his face to hide the grin forming and the way his cheeks heated at her show.

He hadn't known how she'd react, but he didn't imagine she would have done this. He thought she may have tried to grab at them like he'd first done to inspect them in his palm.

This was much more endearing.

The swell in his chest deepened to an almost painful ache when she went to the very middle of this small section of meadow and spun. The skirt of her crimson dress flared out, just as the wisps were forced to cyclone around her due to the pressure of the wind gust she was causing.

She halted just to clamp her hands to her chest and drift her skull up to watch them spin around her, and her orbs flared into a bright pink as they did.

"Fuck. That's too cute," he muttered to himself, resisting the urge to cover his entire face to hide from the sight of her.

She dashed through the wisps to go to one of the orange bulbs, and she leaned forward to sniff at it, her little tail tuft wiggling as she did. The moment she gently touched the underside of one, it opened up to spray citrus-scented pollen into the air. She stepped back in surprise despite the fact that she'd already opened up many of the flowers by running through the grass.

Standing tall, she turned to him slightly. "Thank you, Jabez. This is really pretty."

"You're–" His words cut short when her orbs flashed white and her skull darted in the opposite direction.

Any festiveness and amusement instantly left him as he darted his ears up to listen. He heard nothing, and the strong citrus aroma in the air made it difficult to smell anyone approaching.

But he trusted her instincts and senses, as they were sharper than his own.

"Zylah," he whispered, gaining her gaze as he waved his fingers for her to come to him. "Slowly."

Directing her skull to where she heard movement, she slowly crept towards him. When she was almost to him, her fur puffed with alertness, and a subtle rustling of shrubbery reached his ears. It was quiet, as if those approaching were being careful of their steps.

Zylah growled beside him, just as three Demons cautiously stepped out of the tree line.

Jabez didn't remove himself from his leaning spot, but he did slip his arm across her back to pull her to him. When he gripped the side of her hip and backside, she squeaked, and her hands flew up to her chest like she hadn't expected his intimate hand placement.

All three Demons looked close to completion, each with varying brown skin tones and the minute Elven-grey undertone. Their Elven hue was useless, as he couldn't sense any of the clary or sage scents of magic coming from them.

Each of them, like him, had red eyes and a different variation of horns. They all wore scraps of poorly made and revealing clothing.

Although he was annoyed they'd interrupted him and Zylah, he held not an ounce of worry. All three looked pleased, likely happy to find a food source that wasn't each other.

"What have we found here?" the one on the right asked, his lips curling back to reveal humanoid teeth with a set of large canine fangs. "Looks like a couple of idiots playing. Are you searching for the town?"

Before they could come closer or say anything more, Jabez chuckled. He lifted his free hand to wiggle his fingers at them in a cheeky wave.

"Bye bye."

# THIRTY

Without warning, Zylah was teleported into a new environment. The suddenness of it made her gasp and shunt forward, but Jabez's grip on her kept her securely on her feet.

Her fur remained puffed and agitated as she looked around before soothing once she sensed there was no danger anymore. She'd been expecting a battle, and she'd been rather nervous considering the size of the three Demons who had approached them.

All of them had been almost as tall as Jabez was.

"You okay?" Jabez asked, turning his face until it was barely an inch from her snout.

Her shoulders curved inwards in his grasp, and she was unsure as to why nervousness skittered beneath her flesh at his nearness. She'd been far closer to him in the recent past. After the wonderful experience she just had, which had been robbed from her, her emotions were all over the place.

She nodded, and he gingerly let her go.

"You looked like you were having fun," he said with a small smile curling his lips, as if the ending was irrelevant to his thoughts.

At the reminder that he'd watched her dart through the grass, her sight shifted to a reddish pink. She couldn't imagine what she looked like doing something that silly, but the desire had been so compelling she'd been unable to stop herself.

"That Demon spoke in a different language," Zylah

commented, trying to get away from the conversation of her behaviour. "You spoke it to Goldie when we first entered her shop as well."

His expression fell, and his brows narrowed in thought. Then he cupped his chin, subtly covering part of his lips as he drifted his gaze away. His ears twitched and flicked the way they often did when he was thoughtful.

"Hmm. I just realised you won't be able to understand a single word that's being said around you. I should have considered this."

"Oh." Uncertainty tightened her gut. She remembered how hard it was to communicate when she was first learning how to speak, and having to restart that again was daunting.

His lips flattened at the way she shifted her weight. "Don't worry. I'll teach you how to speak and read it. You're a fast learner, so I don't doubt you'll pick it up in no time."

"What is it?"

"Nyl'kira."

Zylah tilted her head at the word, finding that it sounded similar to Nyl'theria. "Nyl'kira?"

"I guess the English word for it would be Elvish, although that's grossly inaccurate. I'll figure out if there's some kind of translation spell we can use. The Elysians used to portal to other worlds, so it wouldn't be surprising if they found a means to communicate with their inhabitants." The right side of his mouth lifted as he said with mischief in his tone, "Although, if we speak English, it means we can talk freely."

Jabez then stepped to the side, and Zylah immediately followed. They only needed to pass one tree before a white sheen appeared a fair way ahead, flickering through the gaps in the trees.

Her fur lifted when she heard movement, and she accidentally bumped into him.

"I doubt there's actually any scouts," Jabez told her as he led her towards that sheen. "Any sound you hear is likely coming from within the village, and if something does approach suddenly, I'll just teleport us away."

Reassured, she managed to soothe some of the stress that had unsettled her flesh. Her hand constantly brushed against the back of his, but he didn't seem to mind her nearness as they trudged through odd plants and the occasional glowing flora. Most of it consisted of orange moss, glowing mushrooms, or various flowers she hadn't seen before.

Sensing they were close to their destination, Zylah resisted the urge to inspect anything new to her. However, her gaze lingered on the plants that were particularly strange.

As they approached the village, the colliding scents of a decent population of Demons flittered over the wind. The white sheen eventually revealed itself as some kind of transparent dome, and it encompassed a large, partially ruined village.

It was hard to see what it truly looked like behind a makeshift wall of reddish bark. It didn't look as though the wall was there for protection, but there to shield the outside and inside from viewing each other.

They approached a narrow gap where people could come and go if they were to lower the dome.

"Jabez," Zylah called, grabbing his forearm when she noticed a Demon watching them through the gap. "What do I do?"

He hadn't told her how she should behave or if she needed to be careful. Now that they were here, she couldn't stop the way unease twisted inside her.

"You don't need to do anything," he answered, shifting slightly so they could face each other. She refused to let go of him, and she was thankful he didn't stop her. "Like I said, I've spoken to their leader before. Once I explain why I'm here, and where we're from, he'll likely take us to somewhere more private so we can discuss it."

"A-and a glamour?" He hadn't told her if he'd put one on her like in Spiral Haven.

His features softened as he looked upon her skull. "There's no point in hiding what you are. Since we plan to be here long term, I'd rather they understand and accept you, as opposed to hiding what you are. We're Demons, Zylah. We're used to all of us looking different and strange even to each other, so the fact you have a skull will mean little to them. They will adjust, and I'm hoping you'll feel welcomed in this realm."

Her grip on him tightened as a lightness wrapped around her heart. She thought he'd hide her skull, or make her look different at first, but the fact that he had no intention of doing so made her really... *happy.*

She didn't mind if people looked at her funny, so long as she was able to be seen for who and what she was, and eventually be accepted. She'd wanted the same thing in Spiral Haven too. Zylah wanted to be herself. She wanted to know that it was actually okay to be a Mavka, that her skull wasn't ugly, and that she could be considered a person rather than a monster.

"The only spell I'm using, which I have been since we came here, is a scent cloak for myself," he continued, moving his gaze to the small crowd of Demons now at the narrow opening. "If they know I'm an Elf, they'll be unsure of my presence, and it could lead to danger."

Zylah nodded and loosened her grip before letting go. To her surprise, he placed his palm over her lower back to gently push her forward, and kept it there as if to let the warm pressure of his palm soothe her.

Only when they were at the narrow opening did he drop it so he could step closer.

The Demons on the other side gawked at her, except the one who began to talk to Jabez in Nyl'kira.

He looked just like Jabez, except his horns were pointing straight up from his head. He had pointed ears, sharp fangs, red eyes, and even white hair, which was short and spikey around his head.

They all wore some kind of strange material. Although dirt-smeared, it reflected the light from Otholla like it was silky.

Their pants were similar to Jabez's in that they were loose, but their shirts appeared to cross over the front of their torsos with long material flowing down their backs. She wondered if those capes were used as shields from the sun, or *suns*, as he'd mentioned once or twice.

Some of the males didn't wear shirts, and many of the females were scantily dressed, most opting for skirts or dresses, while a few had chosen pants.

Half were barefoot, just like him, while others wore some kind of shoe that lacked a sole. All of them had pointed ears, some longer or shorter than others, and their horns were all varied. Most of them had brown skin, although quite a few had patches of that void-like glistening Demon flesh.

They were also tall. Not as tall as Zylah, and Jabez seemed to tower over most, but there were a few who matched him, as if his height was natural here.

*They smell a little different.* Their scents were spicier than most of those on Earth, and they completely lacked any pungent, unpleasant odour that came from lesser Demons.

After a brief discussion between Jabez and the one who initiated their conversation, they all stepped back to make room.

"I noticed the word *dakura* spoken a few times," Zylah whispered softly, hoping not to be heard clearly.

"It's the Nyl'kira word for our kind," Jabez responded in a hushed tone.

Okay, at least she could start learning the language one word at a time. She put that one away, noting it was important to remember. *I think it'll be a lot easier to learn Nyl'kira, since he can tell me the English equivalent.*

A triangular gap opened up in the dome just large enough for them to fit their bodies through one by one. Jabez led the way, and she ducked ever so slightly when it was obvious her short antlers weren't going to let her through freely. She tried to remain as non-aggressive as possible when she straightened up on the other side.

Other than the handful of people who had come to watch them while maintaining a safe distance, the first thing she noticed was the inside of the village. Much of it appeared to be made of stone, and what once looked like houses or buildings lay broken or as rubble. Hide cloth had been strung up intermittently to act as shade, while giant leaves and branches had been installed as roofing.

Everything appeared broken down in some way, as if a battle had ensued here, or time had weathered it through disuse. She could tell there were attempts at making it liveable, most of it still in progress. She imagined it would be difficult to collect stone or ore if this world was even more overrun with Demons than Earth.

The smell of smoke was empty of meat, but all of it had essences of pleasant-smelling herbs – as if none of the fires were for warmth or food.

*I was expecting this place to look... nicer.* She'd been hoping it would remind her of Spiral Haven, not some war-torn village like in one of her books.

After another quick conversation in Nyl'kira between Jabez and the male who let them inside, they were led deeper within the village.

An ominous sense of foreboding crept up her spine the further they went as more nearly completed Demons came to stare at them. Heads popped out around leaf or stick doors, while others brazenly came closer to circle them as a growing crowd.

Her fur puffed in alertness, despite many of them appearing to smile warmly around tusks and fangs. She put the negative feeling aside, assuming it was just the adrenaline of being in a foreign world surrounded by fierce-looking Demons.

Many of them bore scars. Some here or there were missing an eye, ear, or even a horn, and their worn clothing was dirty or in tatters. Those close by looked nearly completed, although she did notice those further away were less so, with more void-like flesh glistening rather than brown.

At first glance, she thought those who were further from completion were hiding, but she figured it was just due to nervousness. Most were already peering at her with either a cautious or curious gaze, and she didn't want to do anything but follow Jabez in case she did something wrong.

As they passed a building, a male inside was pulling silky strands from the inside of a leaf, but he halted to watch them. The deeper they went, the more she saw people in the middle of tasks, most of which she wasn't familiar with.

They all abandoned their duties to stand and follow, creating a crowd behind them she found uncomfortable.

When someone came just a little too close to her, Zylah chittered and accidentally knocked into Jabez. He glanced at her, but offered no comfort or caring gaze before he lifted his eyes to the side.

In the corner of her sight, she noticed someone duck from view, and Jabez's brows narrowed. His ears twitched constantly, yet he wore a dull expression as he drifted his gaze around the area.

*He's hiding behind one of those false masks again.*

Zylah chose to focus on him, as she found that easier. She greedily sucked in his scent of bergamot and sandalwood to soothe her chest on each compression of her lungs, while her sight narrowed in on his features.

She wanted to hold his hand or arm, but she had a feeling he knew that since he gently, although purposefully, pulled away each time.

Then his steps began to slow. He spoke loudly – and in her opinion rather sternly – to the person in front of them. The Demon gave a deep laugh, turned his head to glance at them over his shoulder, then said something that was meant to put them at ease.

It worked. Despite the fact that she didn't understand a word of it, his tone appeared sincere and his expression was welcoming and kind.

Jabez answered him with a smile in return until the Demon faced forward once more. Jabez's expression instantly fell, and his head tilted forward ever so slightly so he could look around more subtly.

"Something is wrong," he muttered, his ears flicking in opposite directions. "Last time I came here, I wasn't crowded like this."

"Could it be because of me?" she whispered back, nervousness now clinging to every fibre of her being.

She looked around and found even more eyes upon her. There were so many faces that she couldn't even begin to describe all their startling differences.

*Perhaps he should have glamoured my skull after all.* It was obviously putting him on high alert, and she really didn't like how many people had surrounded them.

Jabez's features twitched, like he wanted to answer her, but his lips flattened in silence instead. She didn't know if that was due to thought, or because he wanted to minimise how much they spoke in English before meeting with the Demon leader. Yet his glare only deepened when the person in front of them took them to the very middle of the village.

Some kind of wide and spacious village square opened up, and Zylah's sight landed on the broken statue of a woman erected on a triangular pedestal. Half of her curvy body remained, while the top half lay on the ground. She had small ethereal wings that were partially shattered, while a motherly smile didn't match the golden tears that had been painted on her face.

A plaque at the bottom bore runic symbols made up of circles, triangles, and slashes that appeared to represent different letters or even words. She couldn't read what it said, but it was likely the name of the carved woman.

Jabez halted, and it wasn't hard to know why.

Before the statue stood a male who had his arms folded and a grand smile on his face. He bore no shirt, showing off the strength in his bulky arms, chest, and stomach, while his loose pink pants hid his legs all the way to his feet. Once more, she noted the odd, soleless footwear.

His hair was white, wavy, and cut into some kind of short mohawk that had been brushed back. A set of sandy horns curled around the front of his temples before going back to jut up behind his head. Multiple golden and silver adornments were attached to them, as well as bands around his wrists, biceps, and neck.

The fur on her nape puffed up in a wave when she sensed someone directly behind them. Zylah spun while stepping to the side but found no one there.

The spot behind them was empty, yet she... *swore* she could smell someone had been there just a second ago.

*I must be nervous.*

That was it. Her senses were going wild, her nose, her ears, her sight, and even her instincts – all of them had been screaming at her from the moment she entered the village.

They'd done the same thing when she'd first entered the crowd of pedestrians in Spiral Haven, although it'd been less ominous and threatening.

*I didn't realise knowing so many could see my skull would be this... frightening.* She could *feel* their judgement, their gazes. It made her fur itch in ways she'd never experienced before.

She realised then that Jabez and the male covered in metal jewellery were speaking, and had been the entire time she'd been turned around. He'd also stepped forward with his hands out as if to gesture or shrug, putting even more space between them since she'd stepped back.

Her gaze fell on the dozens of Demons who were covered in void-like, glistening flesh, and she found it difficult to swallow the lump in her throat. They skulked closer, making her want to retreat while the desire to growl pestered her, but she stifled it. No one appeared to look threatening, but they were strangers, and their approaching proximity had her growing more alert.

Her feet froze when her sight connected with someone who had such strange, inhuman features, she couldn't even begin to decipher them – some kind of animal she'd never seen before. She swore multiple little horns on his forehead even faintly... *glowed.*

*I thought he said these people were close to completion.* Or at least that they'd appear fully human – or Elvish.

Jabez's voice came out as a low rumble. Zylah sensed the hostility in it despite it being minor, as if he was trying to hide it. She knew him. Knew when he sounded displeased and untrusting.

Zylah spun to the male in the middle, who had a superior aura to him.

Disorientated, she couldn't seem to get her bearings, and she wished, more than ever, that she could understand what they were saying. Especially as the male's gaze was narrowed into a deep glare.

Jabez stepped back. He shoved an arm out to her, reaching for her, but only grasping air, since she was too far away. "Zylah, come–"

Before he could finish, he spun on the spot and shoved his hand up in front of him like a blade... into nothingness. An *euk* sounded, just as the clogging scent of Demon blood penetrated the air and began to drip down his fingers.

A body flickered into view, their arm raised with some kind of club in it, before they turned completely solid. Their throat materialised in Jabez's hand and then the rest of them came into view.

*I wasn't wrong,* she thought. Someone really had been behind them, but they'd just been invisible! *I didn't know that was possible.*

He quickly removed his hand from their throat, purple blood gushing as he did, and they dropped to the ground. The club thunked and rolled, but Jabez skilfully evaded stepping on it as he turned to Zylah.

"We need to leave. Now!" he roared, just as the crowd of Demons closed in on them.

Their expressions changed, most grinning as if they'd been caught in some kind of trap.

Just as Zylah took a single step towards him so they could touch and he could teleport them away, something snagged around her ankle and yanked. She fell forward, just missing his swiping grasp, and the underside of her skull bashed against the ground as she was pulled back.

She clawed at the ground to get purchase, and Jabez roared when some kind of rope was flung around his forearm. He pulled, sending the Demon on the other side forward with a scream.

That was the last thing Zylah saw before she was covered in a swarm of bodies.

Her orbs turned white as her heart clamoured in her chest, sprinting hard and fast. Fear shot through her, harsher than she'd ever felt, and only seemed to deepen the further across the ground they pulled her.

None of them appeared to want to intentionally hurt her, all grasps designed to hold her arms and legs down. Yet the more she struggled, able to rise to her knees despite their attempts, the harder everyone tried to squash her. When they realised she was stronger than she appeared, more Demons attempted to lie on top of her, as rope was used to bind her ankles together.

Something smacked against the back of her skull, but it merely bounced off, followed by a blunt, radiating pain.

The bottoms of her orbs broke into glittery white tears. *Why did I have to step away?* Why didn't she just stay glued to his side, rather than investigate behind them with worry? If she'd just stayed put and trusted Jabez, they would have been less than an inch from each other.

He would have reached her. She would have grabbed him before he even felt the need to.

She hadn't expected everything to spiral so fast, or for these Demons to be so swift, strong, or cunning.

She could hear Jabez's snarls and the answering calls of many others, but the sounds were muted, and she saw nothing through the swarm. Her fear for him grew, causing her breaths to come out as frightened whines.

Zylah fought back, her sharp claws slicing through torsos and rendering multiple Demons dead within seconds. She kicked her strong legs, shunting bodies back with surprised yells, as she twisted to get free before they could bind her fully. She tried to claw her way out, using all her strength and might to fight them off – and was succeeding. She was able to get her knees underneath her, then to her elbows to push off.

But the moment she'd turned violent, and the smell of their

fear tangled around her, was when *they* became violent.

An agonised squeal left her when something sharp lanced through the middle of her shoulder blades – as if they'd been going for her heart. She fell to her stomach at the shock of some weapon cutting right through her body.

Red flared in her sight, just as blood-lust ripped into her stomach like a set of claws. Hot rage burst into her veins, causing her muscles to swell and her fur to lift in aggression.

Jabez's face came into view, his knees resting on two different shoulders as he dug his way through the flailing bodies to get to her. His claw-like nails stabbed into the sides of faces and necks as he pried heads apart.

His face was fierce, nose bunched in fury and lips curled back as he bared his fangs, his red eyes never wavering from her. She'd never seen him look so menacing before, or so like a Demon – his snarl beastly. Uncaring about his own wellbeing, he fought to get to her, and his steadfast gaze promised he would.

Only a few seemed to notice him, but it was too late. He made enough space to reach a hand down to her.

Zylah tried to keep her Mavka instincts at bay against the pain and fear, even as she squealed when someone bit into the back of her calf. She felt the muscle tearing as they took a chunk from her, but she continued to reach up.

Relief swept through her like a blissful gust when their palms touched, just as a loud *thunk* came from above.

Instead of teleporting them to safety, Jabez's eyes rolled back and his grip on her loosened. He went languid, his body dropping forward as though he was unconscious.

A droplet of *red* dripped against her nose hole, and the smell of blood was saturated in bergamot, sandalwood, and copper. *His* blood. It sent hunger through her within an instant when it slipped inside the hole of her snout, shielding any other scent from her.

Suddenly the pain became irrelevant, not with the starving grumble in her gut that roared for a taste of him. To eat and consume the source that was even more delicious than any human or Demon she'd ever smelt. To get her claws into her prey until she was able to lick at the ground for the last few drops that remained once she was finished eating him whole.

Rage took hold, and her prey was dragged away right as it did.

Uncontrolled and no longer truly present, Zylah lunged.

# THIRTY-ONE

A jerk to his legs stirred Jabez awake, just as another yank slowly hoisted his body off the ground until only his elbows rested upon the dirt. Another brought him to his wrists before he was yanked to dangle higher, then higher still. Upside down, with his ankles caught in some kind of binding, all the blood rushed to his head as he tried to regain consciousness.

His eyelids refused to open, too lethargic against whatever they'd done to put him under.

A throbbing in the back of his head told him one thing for certain: they'd struck him hard, and right in the same spot as when he'd been a teenager. With the strength of an Elf-eating Demon wielding whatever barbaric tool they'd utilised, it wasn't surprising he'd passed out.

Lucky bastards. If they'd hit anywhere else, his strong skull may have stayed intact. Unfortunately, by the pain he was in, the fuzzy disorientation he felt, and the familiar sensation rippling along his head, he knew they'd cracked his skull. They'd given him a rather good concussion.

He'd not managed to heal that injury well as a teenager, and had to let it do so naturally.

His head felt like it was filled with cotton that was slowly being saturated with liquid. Being upside down, the trickle of blood that had begun to slow started up once more, and when he did crack open his eyes, he noticed a large chunk of his hair had turned bright red.

Remaining upside down caused his face and head to heat from excess blood. His heartbeat quickened to try to orientate itself for a natural flow, which only intensified the thumping in his brain and blurred his sight further.

In the muted background, as if he was below the surface of the water, the distressed roars of a creature reached his clogged ears. It sounded both afraid and enraged, and many voices responded to it in kind. A scream burst through the buzz muting his hearing before it quickly died.

*Zylah?* he thought, and his features twitched. *Fuck. My head feels like it's on fire.*

How he'd gotten into this position wasn't a mystery, but he sure as hell was angry at himself for it. Had he monitored her position better, she may not have been just out of reach when chaos ensued. He could have prevented all this.

Then again, he'd had an inkling that something was wrong halfway through the village.

There had been far more void-like flesh than he remembered, but he thought perhaps these people had allowed new faces to join. No one had looked similar. It was only when they greeted the leader that he *knew* something had happened since his last visit here.

The male Demon, Lueka, had been much younger than the previous leader, Szala. That had already raised his hackles, but the older leader had been well into his years, an elder who had been alive much longer than Jabez. It wasn't *that* unusual that he may have died, especially as he'd relied on a cane to keep his weak body up.

But speaking with Lueka had only deepened Jabez's mistrust, especially as he'd seen a scheming glint in the Demon's red eyes. Lueka had acted too cocky, too arrogant, too much like himself when he'd been king of the Demons on Earth.

To see his own reflection in another meant trusting him was unwise, and the closer the crowd came, the further Jabez wanted to distance himself from them. Not a single face had been familiar, and those he'd met here before had not come to greet him amicably.

It was too suspicious, even before they'd done anything malicious.

Then he'd detected magic right behind him. Although his foe had been invisible, he'd sensed them there – enough to land a killing blow before he could even be touched. The Demon had likely eaten many creatures that had camouflaging abilities.

If one person had the ability, he didn't doubt more did.

It's likely another had come along and bashed him over the back of the skull just as he reached Zylah.

If she hadn't been swarmed, he could have teleported to her with ease. But with so many bodies on top of her that he couldn't even see her, doing so would've had him materialising within someone – which would have instantly killed him and the other person.

Every ability came with a weakness, and that was a risky one for his teleportation. So, he'd materialised above the swarm and landed on top of the middle of it, shoving them aside to get to her.

All this did little to change what happened, but it meant his memory was intact. He needed to think so he could figure out the best way out of this, and he kept as still as possible while waiting for the rope to twist enough so he could see.

A horrible squeal had his ears pricking, and something dark clung to his heart when he knew the source. As he managed to orientate his mind, the buzz in his ears softened so he could properly hear the sharp, agonised whines and whimpers of a clearly distressed Mavka.

*Zylah,* he thought with a wince, trying to find her. There were too many Demons circling him now, blocking his slitted view of his surroundings.

He took note of his wounds and only registered the one across his fractured skull.

Someone grabbed his face and squeezed his cheeks just as he picked up on the string of conversation.

"He smells like an Elf, but he has Demon features," a male

stated, informing Jabez that his damn scent cloak had broken when he passed out. He forced Jabez's lips apart to expose his sharp teeth to all. "See? He has horns and fangs, but I've never seen a Demon bleed *red* before."

"He could be a hybrid," Lueka's deep voice boomed from the exact spot he'd originally been standing in, like he'd been a spectator to the fight Jabez had joined. "I wouldn't be surprised if those Elysians began creating a way to infiltrate our numbers and kill us from the inside."

Jabez considered two reasons as to why they hadn't immediately begun eating him. One, they usually did this to those who got caught in their trap – probably to share the pieces of him with all. Or, secondly, they wanted to question him now that his hybrid blood had been revealed.

The fact that he'd fallen for a trap at all was infuriating, but the last time he'd come here, which wasn't long ago, it was peaceful. It meant they'd only taken over recently. This ruined village made it difficult to decipher that it'd been recently attacked.

"He's strong and fast," Lueka continued, lifting a hand to cup his jaw and hide his short goatee. "That ability of his to disappear and reappear in another spot may be useful to us."

Zylah's scream overshadowed the conversation, and the pounding in his chest doubled at the pained sound. His gut twisted, and clarity flared in his hazy vision.

He found her, and the heat of rage simmered beneath his flesh at what he saw. Tied down by multiple enchanted trappings, many spears lanced her as she tried with all her might to get free. There was no red in her orbs, as it'd snuffed to white in what he thought was pure fear or agony, or perhaps both.

"You promised us food!" a bystander yelled at Lueka. "We haven't eaten in two days."

"We don't give a fuck about his abilities. Our hunters haven't returned, and many of us are starving."

"Feed us like you promised! If he's part Elf, then his meat will help us evolve more than eating our own kind. We can't mess up this opportunity. What if he escapes?"

Jabez picked up on the string of arguing, but his gaze never strayed from Zylah. *Let her go,* he pleaded, just as she let out a roar and managed to lunge forward in her bindings when another spear was shoved through her back.

She didn't make it far. The Demons holding onto the rope dragged her down and slid her back across the ground. They were too strong as a collective for even her.

"Shut that thing up!" Lueka bellowed, turning to her and the fuss she was creating. "How hard is it to kill one creature?!"

"We're trying!" one of them yelled in return, just as he lost his grip against her fierce tugging. "It's strong, and we've pierced it in the heart multiple times. It won't give up."

Because she'd never give up. Because in order to protect itself at all costs, her body would compensate for any injury to ensure she kept fighting or could flee.

His eyes bowed at the state of her fur covered in purple blood, and the way she fought while crying out.

"Break open its fucking head then. I'd like to see it move with its brains splattered."

Something cold and painful lanced his chest to the point his heart clenched up. At first, he thought it was a weapon. Yet there was no burn, no slice, and no blood, and he realised it had come from within him in reaction to their words.

The threat to her bit into his mind, and his lungs seized on a pant. Despite the languidness of his useless body, he felt a tremor rolling through him, of sickness, of revulsion, of strength.

Jabez teleported, intending to go straight to her side. Instead he fell against the ground face first, like he'd melted from the bindings, and the thud of his head hitting the hard dirt blasted agony through his mind. Trying to get to his shaking hands and knees to pick his sorry body up off the ground, he attempted to teleport to her once more, only to flicker in place.

*Shit. I can't teleport properly.* His cognitive abilities with his magic were disrupted due to his injury.

He managed to get to his feet, only to stumble to the side once he was standing. He staggered, half his body trying to crumple as he fought against the languidness and dizzy vision swarming him.

At least being upright stopped his skull from feeling like it'd implode.

"Let her go," Jabez demanded quietly with a wheeze, stepping towards her with a hand out.

"He got out of the bindings!" someone shouted with a gasp.

"How?! He should be unconscious!" another yelled.

"Shut up and get him!" Lueka bellowed.

Someone dived for Jabez. He dodged while thoughtlessly teleporting and slammed into a person on the other side of the statue. He knocked them over, and the impact of their collision thankfully stopped him from falling.

"Fuck," he bit out, since he'd been intending to go to Zylah.

He shook his head, feeling inebriated as he tripped forward. He held the side of his throbbing head, his left eye aching as if there was too much pressure behind it. Each step felt like hell, radiating up his bones to pierce behind his eyes.

But at Zylah's next scream, sharpness rushed into his senses, and the anger within him exploded.

The reason he hadn't wanted her to come to this realm with him... the reason he'd tried to go the political route as an alternative... was to avoid this. Her pain, having to hear it, see it, *scent* it.

The taste of her blood and fear in the air was nothing but fucking sour.

How dare they make him witness this!

"Let her go!" Jabez roared, giving up on his ability to teleport at the moment until he managed to heal himself enough to regain full control.

If he couldn't use his magic, then he'd use his entire body!

He ran and lunged for the first Demon he could find like an animal. With his feet against their broad chest, a rabid snarl erupted for him as he bit into the side of their neck and ripped their throat out. Blood gushed across his face as he swallowed to steal their essence.

He felt the warmth of a rune right next to his heart lighting up. What he'd stolen wouldn't do much in terms of healing, but it should help him to start gaining back proper clarity. Right now, he was relying on adrenaline and fury to fuel him, but he was aware his impulsive attacks would only hinder him.

He hissed as he jumped off the Demon crumbling to its knees to evade the swipe of claws coming from his left. He stepped on the back of his attacker's head, and his weight shoved them headfirst towards the ground. At the last second, he extended his legs to quicken their fall, and the satisfying crush of their skull splattering rang in his ears.

Just as a launched spear was about to connect with his chest, Jabez dodged, extending his left leg and placing his hands on the ground to balance himself.

Just as multiple Demons dived for him, Jabez ran forward and then slid on his side to go between their legs. They swiped as he passed them, but he quickly spun and used his right leg to trip the closest one before they could get their claws into him.

Closing in on Zylah and those still struggling to keep her down, he tackled a Demon to get his fangs into their throat. Their claws rent down his back as he drank from them with quick suctions, and the rune next to his heart turned hot.

The fog at the edges of his vision cleared as he let go, although excruciating pain remained.

Jabez refused to hide his blood scent by cloaking it, instead focusing all his mana on his own healing and his magic strength. Black markings around his ankles lit up green as he sensed for any roots hidden beneath the dirt. The resistance of flora chattered to him through vibrations, and his mana whispered back until the ground cracked open and they shot out.

Reddish roots covered in dirt entangled themselves around Demons who dared to come near him. The bindings were easily broken, as he didn't focus them on temporarily paralysing any individual, instead slowing down his enemies as a whole.

It gave him freedom to stalk his way closer to Zylah, his mind never straying from his singular task of rescuing her.

A snarl so beastly it ripped at his chest to the point of pain burst from him as a Demon raised some kind of club above her pretty skull. He teleported and materialised next to them while in a horizontal position in the air, and he kicked them so hard they flew above their companions holding her down.

He landed above another one holding onto the rope simmering with some kind of enchantment – likely to stop it from breaking, rather than interfering with magic use. He should be able to get them free from here as soon as he was able to touch her.

A few dived on top of her to shield her from his touch, to prevent him from getting near her. And he knew without a doubt they understood he wouldn't be leaving without her. He had no intention of abandoning this female, no matter what they did.

And they were right.

Running on pure instinct, he dug his nails into the face of the one he'd landed on top of and tore it open. They gave a satisfying scream, letting their piece of rope go to cover their face. He dived for another, tackling them to the ground to get them to let her go.

Someone grabbed the long length of his hair and yanked him backwards, and as he was dragged, he looked up to find it was Lueka. A grin curled Jabez's lips, and he teleported. The male came with him, Jabez's hair a bond to his mana manifestation. They didn't go far, literally just a foot to the left, but he got what he wanted.

Dizzy, Lueka stumbled and released him, giving Jabez the freedom to twist to his front, get to his feet, and lunge forward. He tackled the big Demon to the ground, flipped over him, and then grabbed his horns. Jabez stepped back, teleporting as he did to evade those coming near them, and landed right next to the broken statue of the Gilded Maiden, where it was mostly empty of enemies.

*They underestimated me.* What he was capable of, the kind of person he was. How ruthless he could be, and how little life mattered to him.

He'd been fighting against Demons his whole life! He trained his body relentlessly, refusing to be the scrawny boy he'd been when he first escaped his prison cell. He was *fast*, he was agile, and he knew how to fucking *kill*.

Not giving Lueka a chance to get his bearings or fight with the strength his large body obviously wielded, Jabez gripped his long horns firmly and twisted. The vertebrae in Lueka's neck popped as he snapped his neck, then just to make sure, he gave an additional twist until the Demon's face was pointing in the wrong direction. The tight muscles in his throat snapped his face forward when Jabez let go.

A few of the Demons paused their approach, baulking at how quickly he killed their leader. He stepped on Lueka's body to walk to the other side of him.

*Should have let us go when they had the chance.*

But the Demons were savage, and his Elven scent in the air was fuelling them. The death of their leader was meaningless, and they dived for Jabez just to get a taste of him.

He jumped before they could reach him and then teleported to Zylah's side while he was in the air.

He grabbed the back of a Demon's pale hair, someone obviously lacking any magical capabilities, and threw them off her. He did the same to another, and another, kicking away those that tried to get ahold of him.

He winced when someone from behind managed to get their fangs into his right forearm, but he pulled it forward with all his strength and let them take a large chunk of his flesh.

Jabez roared as he shoved his foot down and just his toes managed to skim the ground. *Get the fuck away from her!*

Roots sprang from the dirt and wrapped around all those surrounding Zylah. His roar grew louder as he shoved a large wave of his mana into the dirt so he could use them like limbs, and they picked up the Demons who instantly shrieked in surprise. Dozens of enemies were sent flying as the roots dipped back and flung them away, scattering in all directions and crashing into many others.

But Zylah was freed.

Just as he went to touch her, she lunged for him. He managed to dodge her dangerous maw, but her claws swiped across his face. Spittle sprayed from his mouth when she succeeded in tearing his lips, nose, and right eye apart. The point of a claw sliced through his cheek like butter and even dug around a single back fang to pull it out.

*Fuck!* Jabez hissed at the agony splitting apart his face, but didn't allow himself a moment to adjust to it.

Blinded in one eye, he teleported behind her and grabbed her calf. It was severely wounded, her blood instantly smearing against his palm, and he gave a strong wince when she yelped, hating that he was causing her more pain.

He didn't know why he looked up now that he had her, but he thought it may be due to the multiple gasps he heard.

The one who had bitten his arm had red blood dripping from their mouth. A cold chill crept through him, just as all the void-like flesh upon their skin receded to gift them with the Elysian brown of this world. Others had noticed their strange behaviour and the change.

Jabez had to make a choice.

Kill everyone here in order to preserve his life and goal, despite how that could bring further danger to Zylah, or flee to save her from more pain.

Zylah ripped her leg from his loosened grasp, and turned to him with an ominous, rage-induced growl. Yet her orbs were pale red, her fear strong against her Mavka rage. She dived for him, and Jabez made his decision upon seeing the colour.

He darted forward, greeting her head-on to avoid her claws and maw, and met her tackle with his own. He flung himself downwards to shoulder her waist as she leapt above him. The moment their bodies impacted against each other, he closed his eyes to picture where he wanted to take them.

They disappeared, but a deep, disheartening sense of failure came over him in the split second of darkness.

Had Jabez been alone... had this deep tug in his heart driving him to her not been present, things would have ended differently.

*What a fucking waste.*

# THIRTY-TWO

The moment Jabez materialised within the underground section of a ruined library, he flung the feral Mavka off him.

Zylah slid along the ground, her body flailing across rubble and old tomes before crashing into a stone statue of some kind of bird. It broke apart under the impact of her hitting its base and knocking it over.

He cringed when she gave a terrible whine in response, but he'd done what he needed; he put space between him and the immediate danger she presented.

He had no ability to restrain her. The ground beneath was a thick layer of polished, cut stone, and there was no earth here for him to wield. Nothing grew here, and the area surrounding it was a mountain of rock and ore.

The only thing shedding light was a reflection that caught Otholla's brightness from the surface and somehow directed it to the ceiling. Streaks of a material unknown created a checkered, glowing dome above that dimly lit up the area just enough for him to see. He imagined that light was nothing but ornamental in the past, and they would have used torches or mana stones to light the room up in other ways.

Zylah leapt to all fours and immediately bolted for him.

*Sorry, bunny, but I'm not prey for you,* he thought, as he teleported to relative safety.

He materialised to a support column holding up the ceiling and stood on the ledge that once had a statue situated on it. It'd long fallen, likely due to some kind of earthquake or perhaps the rumble of when the gods tried to help the world and failed miserably.

Zylah jumped and dug her claws into the side of the column to climb up to him. She slid down, unable to get any purchase with her back feet being from a creature that wasn't adept at climbing. She tried continuously, snarling and snapping her maw, and he knew she wouldn't settle until his thick blood scent was gone.

Staring down at her, he was surprised to find she'd managed to retain her satchel, although his was lost – likely when he'd been hung upside down.

Jabez winced as the agony in his back, face, and arm flared in the cool air. He covered the blinded side of his face and hissed. *She gouged my fucking eye out.*

His mouth had been torn open to his cheek, and the top of his nose was sliced open, rendering him incapable of smelling anything but coppery blood. The back of his head continued to throb, and he cursed the suns that the Demons had managed to hit him in the one fucking spot that drove him unconscious.

*What are the chances?* Low, but he thought the gods were just screwing with him at this point. It felt like they'd been doing that since the moment he was born.

He shook his head when he realised he was focusing on the wrong things. He peeked down at Zylah, who refused to give up despite her injuries. She limped constantly, only to steady her footing before each useless jump.

He was like a piece of meat dangling above a mindless, starving beast.

*I need to heal.* He needed blood and a body to steal from.

Jabez teleported back to the village to find they'd already begun feasting on their fallen comrades.

It gave Jabez the perfect opportunity to sneak up behind one who was close to completion and tear his claw-like nails across the front of their throat. They gave a choking *uek*, alerting the others, but he materialised to his spot above Zylah with the dying Demon in tow before they could do little more than turn to him.

Ignoring her frothing snarls, her roars and whimpers, and the way rocks rolled underneath her hands and paws, Jabez sat down on the ledge.

Noticing it was a male Demon, he didn't care to take in any more of his lifeless features. He would have eaten Jabez given the opportunity, which elevated any guilt he felt over what he was about to do.

Jabez bit into the side of his neck and drained every last drop of blood he had to fuel his own strength. Then, being careful not to mess it up, he used his index nail to carve around his face so he could skin it. As disgusting as he found it, he placed the Demon's face over his own and closed his remaining eye as he concentrated.

He had to hold back his scream of pain when the edges of his wounds burned as the mask of skin melted around his own and bonded. His toes curled as his muscles leapt in repulsion, but he resisted the urge to kick his legs. Agony radiated as he used another's face to fix his own countenance seamlessly, and his hands shook to keep it pressed to him until it was done.

It would only take an hour or so for the wounds to truly settle and for such a topical injury to revert to his own skin colour perfectly.

Jabez then carefully dug his thumbnail around the man's eye and stole that, too, so he could replace the one Zylah had taken from him. It burned, as doing this kind of transplant always did, and it wasn't for the faint of heart nor those weak to suffering.

Heaving and needing a small break to *breathe*, Jabez rested back against the column while holding tightly to his victim. The eye he'd transplanted remained sightless, and likely would for a few hours, but he'd know if it had taken when he began to see cloudiness from it. If so, it would clear. If not, he would need to obtain another.

*How many times in my life have I done this now?* Countless. The number of times he'd needed to heal such wounds was far too many, and his swiftness in dealing with them proved just how normalised it was for him. *None of this should be normal.*

He shouldn't have needed to live his life like this.

No one should.

But the world had been consistently unkind to him, and he'd found a way to fight back against the universe trying to snuff out his existence.

Once his shaking managed to calm, and he'd grown used to the new additions to himself, he bit into the man's arm, took a chunk, and then spat it out into his palm. He placed it over his own bite wound and groaned as pain forked up his arm.

He only had one wound left, and to be honest, he wasn't looking forward to it. He'd liked having Zylah's claws marring his back from pleasure, but knowing these came from a violent battle left him only with throbs.

He turned the dead male Demon over, ripped open his tunic, and skinned his back. Once he was done, he carelessly kicked the corpse off the edge, and it landed against the ground with a wet splat.

Zylah dived for the corpse of the significantly evolved Demon and immediately began eating him. Jabez doubted he could have gotten Zylah to eat another person willingly, so at least something good had come from this. *This will only add to her humanity, and it will make her stronger.*

Listening to her eat her meat, Jabez removed his own shirt. He placed the Demon's back skin over his open wounds while bent forward to ensure it fully laid over him, then concentrated on his healing mana.

Once more, the excess skin melted around his own, but he didn't have the tools nor the means to take only what he needed. Then he focused on removing his blood from his direct vicinity by sizzling it until it dried and disappeared. He didn't need to touch it, as it was his own essence, but there was little he could do with the smears of it on the ground behind Zylah. He wasn't close enough.

With all his wounds tended to as best as he could, Jabez rested back against the column supporting the ceiling. He let a scent cloak roll off his flesh like an invisible cloud that would slowly fill up the area.

*That should calm her down soon.*

Tiredness squinted and drooped his eyelids, but the fracture in his skull was taking longer to heal than he would like, despite his ingestion of fresh blood. There was nothing else he could do to fix it except for a bone transplant, but filling or fixing broken bones was not an agony he thought he could handle right now.

He'd rather just let his healing magic slowly fix it, and likely leave him with another raised scar on the back of his head. He was fine with that, as his hair would hide it and he really didn't care about something as vain as his appearance right now. Not that he'd truly cared about that in the first place.

Transplanting body parts was just a much faster way to heal.

With an enraged Mavka below him, Jabez lifted his face to the cracked stone ceiling. Shards of crystals reflecting the glowing dome glittered to create some kind of heavenly sky, but they were too broken and chipped to make out what the true image was. Everything here was covered in the grimy smears of time slowly rotting it all away.

*Damnit. I came here too late.*

Had he gone to the village sooner, he could have prevented the death of those who had been peacefully occupying it. He knew they hunted other Demons in a desperate bid to stave off starvation, but they did so sparingly. They'd been peaceful people who had tried to welcome Jabez – an unknown man – with open arms.

Those who had taken over... they were obviously a violent tribe who now used the knowledge of the village as a trap. A trap he'd fucking walked Zylah into.

*I only visited four months ago.* In that time, much had changed. He was annoyed he'd missed out on this opportunity.

Worse still, his secret was likely out. Word would spread, and Jabez and Zylah would be hunted until the Demons here got their claws in him. *All that damn planning has gone to waste.* He could still try to achieve his goal, but it would be far more dangerous than he'd been hoping for.

He'd constantly have to watch his own back, and he'd given away his weakness this day.

He covered his face in annoyance. *The moment she was in danger, I acted like an idiot.* But something sharp had been twisting his chest at her distress. Allowing her to be in pain or afraid while he *calmly* eased the situation just hadn't been at the forefront of his mind.

His usual self would have...

He would have ignored her cries to get what he wanted. Lueka must have been a ruthless male to become a leader of such a barbaric group of Demons – cunning, too, since he likely set up the trap.

*He would have been the perfect person to work with.*

Had Jabez been given the opportunity to speak with Lueka, he would have explained why he was there. He would have done it while he was upside down and hanging from whatever they'd tied him to, his arms folded arrogantly, with a snide grin marring his face. Given that he'd seen himself in Lueka, he figured the large male would have jumped at the opportunity to get his claws in the Elysians. They probably would have made a formidable team, and Jabez could have used Lueka's people to spread the word to other tribes and factions.

The perfect opportunity had been presented to him, and it could have quickened the pace in comparison to working with Szala, the elder leader from before.

Unlike those who had occupied the village beforehand, he needed youth, and he needed those who were instinctually violent. He needed people who were hungry to feed and would be ravenous for red Elven blood.

*If it hadn't been for Zylah...*

Had he just been fucking alone, this night could have been the start of a rebellion against the Elven city. His goal could have been in his grasp, and he would have fed off the glee of it for ages. He would have had a small army already, and just needed to grow it.

*I fucked up.* His fucking *feelings* had gotten in the way!

*This is why I don't care for anybody.* This was why he kept everyone at arm's length, refusing to allow anyone to seep beneath his skin and ruin him.

Had it been anyone else, no matter who they were – Fayren, Katerina, fucking Goldie – he would have carelessly thrown them to the Demons as a sacrifice to get what he wanted. What was one more death of a companion if it meant success?

*How could I let this happen? Why?*

She was supposed to be able to take care of herself, so why the *fuck* had she needed saving?! She was more formidable than him!

He'd brought Zylah because he hadn't foreseen this happening, and he'd let his heart and dick get in the way of everything. This had never happened to him before, not this blatantly, and that knowledge was hard to swallow.

And yet, if he had to do it over again, Jabez knew... he knew, with every fibre of his being... he'd *still* choose Zylah in that moment. Even if he knew the outcome, her pain had just been too great against the will of his selfishness.

Somehow, she had become something greater to him. She'd burrowed into his chest, and he didn't know how to stomach that either.

As much as he resented this outcome, he couldn't find it in himself to regret it. It wasn't her fault, and the decision had rested squarely on his shoulders. It'd been risky to begin with – he just hadn't expected this turn of events. Then again, anything involving Zylah was unpredictable.

So what now?

*I'll have to face the Demons once more.* This time with the knowledge that they likely knew his damning secret. He could bear that.

What he didn't know if he could bear... *I will have to take her back to Earth.* He'd have to leave her behind if he wanted to move forward with this.

She was a liability.

She had become a glaring vulnerability for him.

He'd be incapable of thinking clearly should she be in such

danger again. His enemies could try to use her as a way to control him.

When Lueka had told them to break her skull, without even knowing that was the one way to destroy her, something cold had spread outwards from his sternum. Although he hadn't registered it then, it had been intense fear, all for her sake.

He hadn't felt fear like that since he was a young adult fighting for his life. It reminded him of the day the humans had cut off his ear and had been moments from bleeding him dry just for the possibility he held magic in his blood.

Irrational terror. The kind of horror that could warp one's thoughts.

Just as it had this night.

*I can't... choose her.* He didn't know how to do that. He didn't know how to get what he wanted and keep her. *I can't watch her be in pain because of me.*

Just witnessing it once was enough to make his eyes crinkle and bow with anguish. He'd fucking grown a heart when he'd never wanted one!

But the idea of letting her go left him feeling hollow inside for some stupid reason. The emptiness in his chest that he'd been carrying his whole damn life *ached* at the prospect, and it was worse than when he'd killed his heart as a child.

When he'd been rotting away in his prison cell, he'd painfully gouged out the soft, calm, and submissive child he'd been. The boy who wanted to be nothing but a scholar in the hopes that gaining knowledge and becoming a valued part of society would make them see him differently. Would stop them from looking at him like he was an *eyesore*, something to disdain and fear.

But it'd never mattered.

*I should have walked away weeks ago.* Before it was too late. Before she could sink her pretty, glossy claws into him.

Jabez smacked the back of his head against the column in outrage, only to groan at the way he hurt himself like a moron. He cupped the back of his head, feeling his own drying blood caking his long hair as his knees knocked inwards from the pain.

*Idiot.* He wasn't used to calling himself one.

But his feelings were, truly, making him stupid. And like a festering, infected wound, he should cut them away before they could kill him. That would be the wisest choice.

So why couldn't he seem to do it?

Like before on Earth, where he'd been going back and forth, weighing all his options in their shared cave, he had no idea how to move forward without losing her.

*I don't know what to do,* he thought, his chest swelling with pain he didn't understand. Whatever affection he had for her was *paralysing* him, and he didn't know how to fix it.

With his thoughts wildly spiralling into a pit of despair, he didn't know how long he waited for Zylah to settle. When her growls receded and were replaced with whimpers, he peeked over the edge of his seat so he could look down at her.

Limping and refusing to settle her right foot on the ground, she stumbled. Her arms caved in, and she fell to the side and released a horrible yelp when she landed on her wounds, the broken bits of rock on the ground likely inflicting more pain.

Jabez's stomach gave a horrible twist, and he teleported to her. Crouching beside her, he gently brushed his fingers into the fur around her neck.

*"Jabez,"* she whimpered, weakly reaching an arm out to wrap around his hips and tug him closer.

He sat and let her curl herself around his body. He helped her to lift her head onto his crossed legs, and she whimpered as she used the last of her strength to get her knees behind his backside. She trembled, her entire body shaking and refusing to settle even with him there.

*"It hurts."*

"I know it does," he stated softly, stroking her neck where it was uninjured in an attempt to soothe her.

Now that she'd laid her front on top of him a little more, he inspected the multiple puncture wounds between her shoulder blades. There were at least a dozen of them, each of them still bleeding; her constant moving had likely reopened them.

Her right leg had been bitten into multiple times, clearly from someone trying to eat her on the sly while covering it up as their attempt to stop her from fighting back. There were gashes all over her back, sides, and thighs from them grabbing her and pulling her back so she couldn't escape. The front of her throat didn't appear to be fairing any better, as if they'd attempted to slit it open to stop her from moving.

All their attempts had done nothing to stop her, and only ensured she'd suffered and continued to do so.

He hated the way her body shuddered deeply on each breath that ended in a curt whine, and that her legs kicked in aversion to it every time. He hated that she held him so loosely, as if she didn't have the strength to cling to him like usual.

He *despised* that the female who had stolen a piece of him as she giggled through whispering wisps now lay covered in her own blood, which oozed to puddle beneath her.

*Fuck. It's all my fault,* he thought, covering his face as shame prickled the back of his neck.

"I'm so sorry, Zylah," he rasped out, hoping she could hear the utter sincerity in his voice.

*"Are you... hurt?"* she whispered, reaching up to touch the back of his knuckles.

"Don't you dare," he warned, lowering his palm just enough so she could feel the weight of his harsh glare. "My wounds are healing."

She gave the most pathetic chitter, her white orbs flickering with reddish pink at being caught. Thankfully she didn't try to take his wounds, and he lowered his hand so he could gently stroke his fingertips over her snout.

"Just sleep, Zylah." Her orbs were dim, threatening to turn black, and he knew she must be exhausted. "We're safe now, and I'll watch over you."

As if all she needed was to feel secure and be in his arms, her head went limp and her orbs darkened into black. Her form began to shift into her more humanoid version, and her red dress lifted to the surface to immediately be soaked in purple pungent blood.

He removed her bag so it wouldn't press on any of her wounds and hurt her further.

It took a long while for her bleeding to finally stop, but the hissing of her strained and shallow breaths never ceased. They only grew softer in sleep, and he wished he had the ability to induce a coma until a day had passed and she healed on her own.

In essence, he could do that by removing her skull from her body and letting it reset within a day, but the idea of doing so sickened him. Although it would spare her from this pain, he completely lacked the desire to be callous or cruel towards her with his own claws.

Watching over her as he stroked her with trembling hands only made him feel worse with every damn slow minute that passed.

He bent forward until his forehead rested against her bony brow. *Fuck. My damn chest hurts so much.* It kept tugging, kept twisting, and he knew it wouldn't stop for a long time – long after she healed.

The guilt of this was killing him, and he held her as he let his eyes wander to the right to look at where they were.

This hidden, ruined library had given him many spells. The knowledge here withered away with every year and turned to dust. Much of it had already been eaten away by time or crumbled in his very hands at just the merest disturbance.

To his left was a door that had the image of a three bronze suns on it. It was slightly ajar from when he first discovered this place. Going through the secret passageway led to the main part of the library that had been decimated by Demons, and many of the books were gone. He imagined the scholars had likely fled with countless books in their arms, trying to preserve as much knowledge as they could.

*What if I can find a healing spell?* He let his gaze drift to the tomes and other reading material that had lasted through the test of time. Stone shelves were filled with rotting pages, but there had to be *something* he could do to aid Zylah.

He knew it was unneeded, as she would heal within a day,

but if he could just do something as minor as take away the worst of her pain, then he wanted to. He wanted to help this female any way he could, to try to make up for all his fault in this.

As much as he didn't wish to cease comforting Zylah, Jabez gingerly moved her skull from his lap. He teleported to the platform above and grabbed his shirt, folding it as he materialised back to her. He knelt beside her head and cushioned it while letting her have his scent if she needed it.

Then he turned to what remained of the library and began his search.

# THIRTY-THREE

*Damnit!* Jabez's mind roared, and the urge to throw the rotten book he held across the room was nigh overwhelming. *There's nothing here!*

Nothing left he could use.

This part of the library, this hidden away section, held collections of past histories that mattered naught. They held pointless secrets, taboo spells, and ancient words not even he could read. There was nothing here on healing, and the only thing he'd managed to learn was how to put her to sleep and wake her up once he did.

A plethora of books were scattered across the ground while empty, dust-covered shelves surrounded him. Jabez had flicked through everything that didn't crumble apart under his touch, and not a single scroll or page was useful for what he *needed* right now.

After he'd fully healed until not even a scar marred his face, back, or arm, he'd gone outside of this secret room and to the library above. Searching that area was impossible. There was a tribe of winged Demons who had made the sheltered library their home. He wouldn't have been able to fight them off while searching for the scraps of books that remained, no matter how hard he tried.

They'd been quick to instigate a fight, many of them hungry, many of them having children they wished to feed. They'd had no interest in speaking with him; he was an outsider, a wingless one at that.

They saw him as an easy target, without knowing just how *wrong* they were about that.

It meant he couldn't search that level, although it was likely most of the knowledge up there had been destroyed by weather, time, and Demons ruffling through its decaying mess.

He carelessly dropped the last book he had access to, hearing it thump against the ground as he covered his face with both hands. *I'm going fucking insane.* He'd been searching for hours, hope sparking when he thought he may have found something to help heal her, only for it to wither away when he made it to the last page.

His eyes landed on Zylah, who lay peacefully asleep under the spell he placed over her. Her whines had ceased, her mind too far receded to register anything. He could have screamed, or the world could have been struck with an earthquake, and neither would have woken her.

A growl bubbled from him as his hands clenched into tight fists. *Why isn't she healing?!*

When it'd felt like time had just been moving far, far too slowly, he'd teleported to the peak of this mountain. Otholla, although still bright, had moved from the northern horizon to the south.

Although Nyl'theria had quadruple the number of days and they were each three to four times longer than those of Earth, he could feel the stretch of time. If his estimations were correct, and the many hours he'd spent mindlessly reading garbage indicated anything, an Earth day had surely passed. No, he was absolutely *certain* of it.

So, why did this female continue to lie there, wounded?

Giving up on his useless search, he walked over to Zylah and sat next to her. He hoisted her torso onto his lap, and the tremors in his hands were worse than they'd ever been as he patted an uninjured section of her side.

"Why aren't you healing, Zylah?" he asked her limp body, hating that he'd forced her silence just to spare her pain.

The sickly twists in his gut had transformed into pure

anxiety. Every beat of his heart felt like it was pushing barbed venom into his veins, while sand seemed to clog up his lungs.

"Fuck. Just heal for me," he whispered, burying the side of his face against her neck.

He took in her jasmine-and-violet scent, despising that it was saturated in the metallic tang of blood. He shivered against the coolness in her body that shouldn't be present.

She should be warm and full of life. She should be chittering and giggling, with her orbs flaring reddish pink in embarrassment at his damn teasing. Her tail should wiggle in joy that they were in a library, constantly drawing his eye to it until his face heated in want, rather than her lying limp like this.

The cute bookworm would have *loved* this fucking place, and instead she was too injured to enjoy it.

*Is it Nyl'theria?* Did bringing her here stop her natural abilities? *Did the Demons discover some kind of poison that stops someone from regenerating?*

No, that answer seemed too unlikely.

*Shit. What do I do?*

He nuzzled her soft fur with his nose and lips before sliding his head forward until he was able to glare at nothing. Tiredness made his vision blur and his mind was grainy, but he tried to think of a solution. If he couldn't heal her, then who the hell could?

He groaned as he buried his face against her once more, wishing the answer would come to him as the hook of regret sunk deeper into his heart.

*Had I just thought to learn healing magic that benefited others, I could have done this myself.* Years of self-centredness were currently coming around to bite him in the arse with sharp, mean fangs.

*Those fucking Elysians have healing magic that can aid her.* He sneered in disgust, doubting it would matter that she was different to them. Their spells would likely work alongside her natural regenerative abilities.

His damn stepfather had been a doctor; he bet that fucker

would have been able to do it. Hell, his mother would have just *loved* to poke and prod this female like a scientific experiment until she made Zylah better.

He thought this, his disgust and disdain stronger than ever, and yet... the hook in his chest let up a bit as he thought of them. Of his parents, the people who abandoned him, the damn hospital he'd sat in for much of his childhood.

"Don't," he pleaded to Zylah, clenching his eyes shut as his grip on her tightened. "Please. Don't make me do it."

His body quaked as he resisted his thoughts, his heart pounding in quick succession. His mind refused to find a different solution when there was one present before him – because he doubted any other could trump it.

He grasped onto a more pathetic route instead. *Maybe if I take her back through the portal, she'll heal,* he thought, standing as he lifted her into a safe cradle in his arms.

His arms shook at the dense weight of her, his body tired after not sleeping for so long and wasting so much mana.

He teleported back to the specific portal that would take him back to Austrális, rather than one of the many others that would have taken him to other Earth countries, and immediately walked through it. What he'd been hoping for didn't happen. Zylah didn't regenerate, not even when the sunlight touched her. The dawn of a new day proved he'd been right – a full Earth day had passed.

Jabez let out a hiss through his fangs, having forgotten to ward his body against the sun. His skin tingled like it was moments from burning, and he reactivated the spell to protect himself.

For a few minutes, he waited as he stared down at her.

"Heal, Zylah," he pleaded, his brows narrowing at her limp form when she didn't.

He really had been hoping that bringing her back would instigate it, but he was left with only crumbling defeat. Why did he always fail? Why did this feel like the worst failure yet?

His lips pulled back and he stared at her, baring his fangs as a growl bubbled up his throat. Hostility and hate squinted his eyes into a glare, and the strength of it was near crushing for his soul.

*Fuck! Fine! You win!* He couldn't take this anymore, and the uncertainty of *her* future was killing him.

Clutching Zylah protectively, he stepped backwards through the portal and knelt down once they were shrouded in the darkness of Nyl'theria. He placed his hand against the side of her temple, and a new ring marking – with a dash above and below it – on the first knuckle of his middle finger glowed white.

She flinched, then her body curled inwards as she let out a sharp whine. The sound of it gouged at his chest worse than ever.

"Zylah," he called, propping her up so she would sit.

She answered him with a weak moan before her orbs opened to a pale blue. They highlighted her pain and sadness.

"Where are we?" She shifted slightly and turned her head. Then a loud, distinct whimper burst from her when she noticed the portal. "No! Please! I don't want to go back without you."

Despite her injuries and how much they had to hurt, she frantically gripped onto his biceps, clinging to him until the sharp points of her claws latched deep. He winced but gave no other reaction.

"Hey, it's fine," he reassured, wishing his stomach didn't twist unbearably further. "We're not going through the portal. I already did to check something."

"Promise?" she croaked, refusing to let him go as the bottoms of her orbs wavered.

The fact she could be made to cry so easily didn't bode well for Jabez. He usually laughed in people's tearful faces, finding the manipulation of them sickening, but he found Zylah's glowing, ethereal, floating droplets difficult to stomach for entirely selfless reasons.

He didn't like being the cause of them.

"Promise," he answered thickly, because he didn't think she'd like what he planned to do either. While crouching, he stepped back a little to give her room. "Can you stand on your own?"

The moment she even tried to get her feet under her to stand, she yelped. He settled her back down to the ground and hooked his arms under her legs and around her back. He lifted her off the ground once more and took her heavy weight.

"Don't worry. I'll just carry you."

A light gust of balmy wind wrapped around him, yet it didn't feel nice – not with how he was feeling right then. More than anything, he wished for an escape from what he was about to do, but he didn't know of any other way besides Lindiwe.

And he refused to go to someone like her for help, no matter that she was likely the best choice. *She's probably healed her other children. But if I take Zylah back to Earth...* He'd have to leave her there permanently.

And Earth wasn't any safer than Nyl'theria. It was just as full of Demons, and even horrible humans who would hunt Zylah because of *what* she was, rather than giving her a chance.

*I just want to put her somewhere untouchable.* A place where this sweet female would never be in pain again, with or without him.

When she was secure in his hold, and she'd wrapped her arms around his neck for support, Jabez took in her pretty white rabbit skull. His gaze flicked up to her dainty antlers and how they each had only one small fork three quarters of the way up. But he shied away from the way he could feel her gaze on him, and how hollow it made him feel inside.

Just as he was about to teleport to the biggest blight in his mind, Zylah gingerly touched the side of his jaw.

"Why does your expression look like that?" The blue in her orbs deepened and swallowed up some of the white.

He knew what she meant. She wanted to know why his features had gone cold and indifferent, his mask firmly in place in order to spearhead himself through his next tasks.

Quietly, and without looking down at her in his arms, his gaze instead fixed on the invisible road before him, he answered, "I'm taking you to the Elven city."

She jerked in his arms. "What, why?"

"Because you're not healing, Zylah, and I don't know why. I took you back to Earth and nothing happened." Trying to be steadfast in this, he refused to meet her orbs. "I don't know what's going on, but I can't see any other way."

She chittered nervously, lowering her hand to rest against her chest. "But you hate the Elves."

His head lowered as his ears drooped. "I know."

*But right now... my worry for you is stronger than my hatred.*

He knew he could wait on Earth and see if she healed the next day, but that was just another day of pain. What if it didn't work anyway? What if this ended up becoming her permanent state the longer he waited?

He hated unknowns and unpredictability for this reason. He wanted to fix her injured state, and he wanted it *now*.

Without speaking another word, his hands tightened on her. Jabez teleported them to one of the two gates belonging to Lezekos City.

Cream stone walls ran around the city, acting as a blockade against sound and sight for the peace of mind of those just on the other side. It was also the final defence if the translucent bubble dome with a rainbow shimmer popped.

All his life, he'd seen these walls as nothing more than a taunt, a barricade to what he wanted most in this world. Now, they just appeared daunting, and he worried they would be a barrier to the safety and nurturing that could be provided within.

*How many times have I looked at this gate?* Jabez thought with pain as he stared at the tree of resilience's knotted design.

The bleached-white tree was a symbol of hope for the Elysians. It stood taller than any other tree in this realm and towered over the entire city. With its pink-and-purple leaves, its branches reached out for kilometres, blanketing the city in shade to protect those below it from the heat and radiation of the three suns throughout the day.

Otholla could just be seen cresting over the forest far to the right, but it would've been beautiful had it been directly behind the tree. It would have made the leaves glow brighter than they already did, and would have stopped it from looking like a shadowy creature ominously reaching for all and blocking the night sky.

The people here had literally taken a piece of its bark for the gate's double doors and dribbled gold, silver, and bronze into carved grooves to make a glistening tree design with its roots encompassing a seed. The Nyl'kira written around the top border of the door stated, "The tree of resilience will shelter all."

The first time he'd read those words, he'd laughed and thought it was bold of them to assume they'd rely on such petty, hypocritical words. Now, with Zylah in his arms... he for once hoped them to be true.

A sense of doubt trickled down his spine. *What if they don't let me into the city?* He needed to explain who and what she was, her strengths, and where her weaknesses lay without revealing how to destroy her – not that these people would even dare harm a living creature.

The last time he'd been inside, he'd instigated bloodshed and fear. He'd murdered anyone who'd gotten in his way, blinded by hunger and the potential to feed properly for the first time in his life. Since then, he'd sworn vengeance and death to these people, and he'd told them.

He still wanted that.

Yet Jabez stepped closer than he'd ever dared to before.

"Do you mind knocking for me?" he asked with a strained voice, having to fight the clog of emotion behind the ball in his throat. "My hands are currently full."

Zylah's shoulders turned inwards, and she tipped her skull to him slightly. "You don't have to do this. I'm fine. I'm sure I will heal eventually."

*I'm not willing to take that chance.* It'd already been too long, and... *This city is the safest place I can take her to in any realm.*

Here, she'd never have to worry about Demons hunting or

attacking her again. She wouldn't have to watch her back in case human Demonslayers were hiding in the snow or brush.

Zylah would be safe and sheltered behind an impenetrable fortress not even *he* could infiltrate without trickery.

*I know they've been accepting Demons into their fold.* He was sure they'd figured out that they required meat and began compensating for it. He knew they'd been trying to rectify the mistakes of their past by doing the right thing in the present. *Surely... they'd accept a Mavka seeking refuge.*

So long as they covered her snout with a material soaked in a scent-cloaking spell, Zylah would be harmless. All they'd need to worry about was her anger, which was almost non-existent.

She was sweet and perfect, and she deserved to be in a place where she could be protected.

"Knock, Zylah," Jabez urged, bringing her a bit closer.

She tentatively raised her hand and tapped her knuckles against the door. No matter that she'd done so lightly, a small rainbow bubble formed around them as a protective dome. The main barrier never disappeared, refusing to allow them inside just yet.

The short hairs on the nape of his neck and forearms lifted in aversion, and regret simmered beneath the surface of his skin. He felt trapped within their Elven magic, when he'd spent his whole life fleeing from how that had made him feel as a child.

Within seconds, the rich metal ores on the gate sprung to life. Unknotting their interlocking patterns, they receded like water being sucked backwards through the grooves, and flooded the mechanism that allowed the gate to open on its own. Then the double doors creaked and groaned as they swung inwards.

Two soldiers stood on the other side of the threshold, waiting for the doors to open fully. They both held Elvish rankae glaives that looked like cutlass blades attached to their metal poles. At the base of each blade was a ribbon that highlighted their ranking within the army. Considering they were stationed here at night, it was no wonder both of theirs were red, revealing them to be high-ranking individuals.

Swirling, knotted patterns had been etched into the seams of their armour. Although they were similar, each groove told a story of who they were, what family they came from, and any remarkable achievements they'd carried out.

Although their white armour shone like metal, it was actually made of silk that came from the very leaves of the tree in the middle of the city. They didn't need to pluck them, as the leaves fell naturally, and the Elysians were watchful to make sure they didn't land upon anyone. The silk itself was stronger than any ore that could be mined.

It allowed them flexibility, while remaining durable and strong.

The only visible parts of the soldiers were their faces and the undersides of their hands. Like all Elysians, their skin was one of the various shades of brown, but he did note that the one on the right had red eyes, as if he were a Demon. It was hard to tell with their winged helmets on.

Jabez stared at them, and they him. When it went on for too long, especially when they shared an uncertain crinkle of their brows, his eyes narrowed.

"Well?" he asked in Nyl'kira. "Are you just going to stand there or are you going to do something?"

"You have brought a Duskwalker, Demon," the Elven one on the left stated.

Jabez's head reared back. Firstly, because he'd called him a Demon as if he didn't know who he was, and secondly... *How do they know what she is?*

"If you don't mind, you will need to stay there while we speak with the head of security. He will likely come and investigate this himself."

"Since you know Nyl'kira, we won't have to obtain a translator to speak on your behalf," the Demon soldier stated.

Jabez opened his mouth to grill them with questions, but he wisely shut it. *Just get her through the gate.* It was a relief that his actual face was entirely unknown, as he hadn't thought to glamour himself.

"Sure. We'll wait here," Jabez bit through clenched fangs. "But I urge you to be quick. She's injured and I seek to take her for healing."

"The Duskwalker is hurt?" the Demon asked, before stepping back with a nod. "Understood. We'll ensure this is dealt with in a timely matter."

They both left, sprinting as they did, and he appreciated they didn't intend to dawdle like a pair of fuckwits.

"Do you mind if I put you down?" Jabez asked in English. He lowered to his knees, refusing to let her rest any weight on her injured leg. "We have to wait here while they speak to the head of security."

As much as he would have liked to hold her, she was heavy, and resting his arms and legs for a short while would do him some good. There was no point in wasting energy when he didn't need to.

Zylah nodded and released her arms from around his neck. He carefully settled her on the ground and sat next to her so he wasn't hovering over her.

He looked past the open gate and down the long, tall, and wide hallway through the stone walls that led deeper within the city. Just beyond it lay houses or establishments, none fearing their proximity to the walls that had protected them for so long.

Other than when he'd left this city, he'd never been to the outskirts of it. He didn't know if much had changed. He didn't care to inspect it, so he brought his stare back to Zylah, who was trying to stifle her soft sounds of discomfort.

"Are you okay?" He checked on the wound on her leg to see it hadn't changed at all since she obtained it.

She lifted her snout towards the opening. "This place smells nice."

He allowed her to redirect the conversation. "It does."

It smelt like... *home*. Like the forest, like flowers and herbs. The aroma of vegetarian food cooking flittered to them and made the wind smell lively and inviting, as did the scent of the pollen that came from the central tree.

A crack of loneliness struck his chest, and he turned his back on the city to face her fully. Right now, he just needed her gaze to keep him focused while he let his mind wander.

*How do they know what she is?* As far as he was aware, no Elysians had crossed over to Earth, let alone Austrális. *Is there a Mavka I don't know of here?*

If so, that would be beneficial for her case. If they allowed one here, then surely they'd allow another. Despondent hope pulled at the edges of his mind.

*This is a good thing. She'll have another of her kind to lean on.* They even had translators, meaning someone could teach her Nyl'kira or speak on her behalf as she adjusted to the city and its way of life.

*So why do I feel so hollow about this decision?*

"Jabez..." Zylah called, reaching up to cup the side of his face. "Why do you look so... sad?"

*Because I plan to leave you here.*

With the intention of coming back when he was ready to destroy these walls. Then he could obtain her once more, unless she fell in love with these people, and then she'd only hate him for it.

*Shit. What kind of decision is that?* It felt like the wrong one entirely, but the only other option was for them to leave together, or for *him* to... stay.

He didn't want to stay. He didn't want to live among these people. He didn't want to face those who had turned their backs on him just for being born, and then drove him to madness within the lonely darkness of an underground prison.

"I'm just tired," he lied, unsure of how to broach this subject with her while she was still hurt. He didn't want her trying to scamper away in rejection of his leaving before she was healed. "I haven't slept since we left Earth."

"You never rest," she grumbled, sheathing a claw to poke him in the cheek.

He gave a small, half-hearted chuckle. "Are you seriously pouting right now?"

She darted her skull away. "No."

His chuckle brightened at that. *Cute, my fluffy bunny. Cute.*

They sat in silence facing each other, and Jabez lifted her left hand with his right, and let their fingers touch. His thumb played with the side of one of her glossy black claws as he simmered in the bubbles of pain and sorrow surrounding his essence.

Thankfully the wait wasn't agonisingly long.

Feet shuffled behind him, and his ears twitched at their calm approach. He scooped Zylah into his arms and stood to greet them.

The moment he saw the face of the Elysian man approaching, Jabez's head tipped to the side and a low groan exploded from him. *Fuck me. You're joking. This idiot is the one who became the head of security?*

Great! Fantastic! Jabez was *screwed.*

At Mericato's narrowing glare, Jabez's ears shot back in hatred as he returned it. He'd never forget that name, nor this man's face, even though the last time he'd seen it, they'd both been eleven and now it sported a short beard.

Dressed in the formal attire of a councilmember, Mericato wore a blue tunic that had the tree of resilience stitched into it with silver thread. A pair of light-grey pants flowed around his legs and danced above the soleless shoes covering the tops of his feet. His companion wore a similar outfit, although his tunic was green, and he was much thinner than Mericato's muscular frame.

They stopped barely a few feet from the dome's edge.

Then, to Jabez's surprise, Mericato began to sign with his hands, silently speaking to the person in green. Jabez realised then that he was a translator. After a small exchange, his translator's eyes widened in disbelief and his shoulders stiffened midway through as he read his gestures.

"You have quite the nerve to come here after all this time, Jabeziryth Kneis," the translator stated, keeping his tone smooth to hide his shock.

The revulsion that struck Jabez's gut at hearing his full

name made drool collect in his mouth in preparation to vomit. Worse still, this bastard had tacked on his mother's maiden name to drive the knife deeper, likely knowing Jabez hated it.

The two guards from earlier parted their lips at his name on a silent gasp and shuffled nervously behind them.

"If we could skip the hostility, I believe all are given a chance at rebirth when they enter the city," Jabez stated with a flippant tone of arrogance. "All past crimes and transgressions against the Elysian people are voided, and a new life is offered."

A muscle in Mericato's jaw ticked, and Jabez had to hold back a smirk. *I bet your customs haven't changed.* It's what they offered to Demons when he'd been a child, and he was more than happy to use it against them. Mericato ran his fingers through his brow-length white hair, before darting his eyes to the side to think.

Once more, he began to sign.

"That is only upon first entry. This, technically, would be a re-entry."

"Listen, you—" Jabez's word cut off when he'd been about to spew a tangent of insults. He willed himself to remain calm, his arms tightening around the most important thing to him at the moment, then he let out a pacifying sigh. "Look. The *Duskwalker* is injured. She seeks refuge. *She* has never harmed a single Elysian her entire life. Surely that counts for something. Let her be healed and offer her sanctuary."

Mericato's brows furrowed. "You want us to take only her?"

Jabez's lips flattened before he released them. "Yes. I have no intention of remaining."

"We can't do that. We can't allow her into our city."

His jaw fell, just as fury heated the back of his neck. "What the fuck do you mean you can't take her? Isn't that the point of the script on the fucking door? If someone seeks sanctuary, you will give them a chance to speak to the council and be properly evaluated!"

Mericato tsked with his features twisting into a cringe. He

went to gesture with his hands, but Jabez wasn't done.

"Are you seriously going to turn away an injured female in need? I understand not letting *me* through these gates, but she's done nothing to warrant such disrespect or hatred."

"It has nothing to do with what she is. I can allow you entry, but not her."

Jabez stepped back when his right knee almost caved in at the revelation he was hit with. "You would take *me,* but not *her?*"

That didn't make any sense! Not when Jabez had threatened their destruction! It was the last thing he'd ever said to them, and he had no doubt that if Mericato knew about Mavka, then they must know what he'd been up to all these years. That he'd tried to build an army to decimate this entire shitty city.

"I'm sorry," the translator said on his behalf, and his tone was remarkably sincere. "But we are already aware of the dangers of an unbonded Duskwalker. She will be too volatile. There are too many people here that have a fear scent or may accidentally bleed. We can't allow such a risk for a creature that is able to easily destroy dozens of people in the span of minutes. Not even our soldiers are able to properly defend against a Duskwalker, and we know trying to will only enrage her more. We also don't wish to harm her for something she can't control."

Taken aback, Jabez was rendered silent.

*They don't just know about the existence of Mavka, but they deeply understand them.*

"Who is it?" Jabez asked. "What Duskwalker resides here? Who gave you such information?"

Mericato shared a distrustful look with his translator. "Who they are is irrelevant. We won't give you the name of one of our people in order to preserve their privacy."

The bitter, spiteful laugh that exploded from Jabez was *nasty.* His eyes crinkled in hateful fury as his voice darkened when he growled, "I should rip your fucking throat out again."

Mericato's pointed ears drooped, and he looked away with

a pained expression as he covered the scar across his neck. There was a hint of regret in his eyes, but Jabez cared little for it. He didn't care if Mericato wore that scar as a badge for what he'd done to Jabez, or as penance for how he'd treated him and how he'd been part of his demise.

He deserved it.

"So, you're telling me you won't let this *Duskwalker* into your stupid city because she's unbonded?"

"Yes."

*By the cursed light! Damnit...*

Jabez swiped his foot against the ground, and warmth swelled through the sole of it and up his ankle. As the hexagon symbols over the arches of his feet connected to swirling patterns around his ankles and glowed green with mana, a blockade of grass formed around him and Zylah. A shield from sight and sound filled the entire Elven bubble dome surrounding them.

Then he knelt while placing Zylah down in front of him and rested his hands on the ground. All of a sudden, it felt like his lungs were being strangled from the inside, like someone had filled them with water, and he struggled to breathe. He was fucking *drowning*, and he had no means to reach the surface for air.

He huffed above her, trying to come to grips with a decision he had to make.

It choked him so tightly, he feared his throat was moments from closing, while his heart raced from the deep anxiety that clutched him. He released a scent cloak to stop Zylah from turning on him, just as Mericato stated she would if left with her insatiable and uncontrollable hunger.

"Jabez? What's going on?" Zylah asked, and he lifted his widened gaze to her.

*It's either my goal or her,* he thought, letting his eyes flick over her rabbit skull, her white orbs of worry, her dainty antlers. *It's either me or her.* His gaze dropped to her blood-stained dress, and how it did little to hide the deep, flaring punctures and gashes between her breasts and arms, and had ridden up to reveal those on her thighs. Her mangled right calf had been visible the entire time.

*Her safety... or my vengeance.*

His feelings of tenderness he'd only known for a few short weeks, or the weight of his hatred he'd been holding up for years.

At his silence, she chittered and fidgeted by clamping her hands on her lap. "Are they not letting us inside?"

He shook his head, unable to respond.

"Then we can go back to Earth."

To Earth. To the place he didn't want to return to ever again. He was done with that realm, and he didn't think he could bear to face it ever again without good reason – and he couldn't think of a single one. He'd hated every minute of being there since he arrived, and it never felt right.

He'd never be happy there. He'd done too much to it, he'd been too violent and cruel to want to live in the mess of his failures. He just couldn't do it.

*I don't want to leave her there either.* Unprotected, with swarms of lesser Demons that hunted everything indiscriminately, with Demonslayers, and even with her own kind, should they grow enraged at each other. He knew she could protect herself, but should she *have* to? She didn't want to harm anything, didn't want to fight.

She'd just be hurt again and again. Demons and humans alike would try everything in their might to destroy her. Every creature there was *vile* in some form.

He once thought he could stomach taking her back there, but the more he lingered on it, the less he wanted to. He'd brought her to this wretched city's gates because he wanted her somewhere safe, even if it was without his predatory gaze protectively watching her back. A place where she could flourish without fear or worry.

There was nowhere else he could take her to guarantee that peacefulness.

Yet they wouldn't let her in.

*Fuck. Why does my chest hurt so much?!* He wished it

would stop! It felt like it was on fire, like his damn heart was trying to incinerate him from the inside out.

With his arms shaking, his nails gouged into the dirt around her injured leg. He bowed his head.

"You..." The muscles in his jaw knotted when he clenched his fangs. "You said you wanted to bond with me. Is that still true?"

Her head reared back in surprise, and she squeezed her hands together as her orbs turned reddish pink. "Of course."

He waited for a sense of foreboding or complete aversion to crest over him. For something, anything, to stop what he was about to offer. Nothing happened, and somewhere inside him said this was the *right* choice.

But he wouldn't do this without being truthful.

"They won't let you into the city unless you are bonded," he informed her. "But... I'm choosing to do this because I want to. I want you to understand that."

If he didn't want to, if there was even a speck of doubt in him, he wouldn't be offering his soul to her. He wouldn't tie himself to someone he didn't want or hold a deep affection for.

He was making this choice because he cared for Zylah more than he – apparently – cared for himself.

But he wanted her to be informed in case, in the future, the truth of this moment came to light and it cast doubt into her mind. He'd rather rid them of the potential now to save her from mulling over it later and hurting herself. He couldn't start this on a half-truth, knowing she'd want complete transparency like she had argued with him for in the cave.

*So how do I do it?*

He looked down at his bare chest, expecting his soul to flow right out of him like it had when he'd witnessed Reia giving her soul to Orpheus.

Something did flicker at the surface, a bluish flame that appeared to break through water, like his skin was liquifying.

Okay, so maybe he wasn't truly certain, but his mind had yet to tell him this was the wrong decision. He dived his hand into the surface of his flesh, and it surprisingly sank right in without pain or resistance. When his hand met squishy heat, he pulled, and it came out easily.

When he let go, his soul floated between them.

His nose crinkled on one side as he thought, *Why is it... aqua?* Well, in reality, it was actually a mixture of blue and green, the two different flame colours spiralling all throughout his essence's form like they were incapable of combining. *That human's was orange, like normal fire.*

Could it be because of his Demon and Elvish halves?

He also expected that he'd feel cold without it, but he didn't.

It sat in a cross-legged position, its arms resting loosely on its lap, and it hunched forward as if it didn't have a care in the world. It was how he often sat when he was mulling over things. It looked exactly like him, from the bulk of his muscles all over his body, to his horns, ears, and even his current hairstyle. It even had two red slits that he figured were meant to be his eyes.

He was surprised to find it was animated and appeared aware as it looked at him and then over to Zylah's skull.

In the shade of the grass dome he'd created, it glowed brightly between them. He realised the centre of it actually appeared to flow like lava, while blue-and-green flames flickered around its form. Its long hair waved and sent off sputtering flames before they died.

He liked that it didn't appear fazed, like it'd been expecting this outcome. That it saw no issue being exposed and under her gaze.

All his earlier anxiety and worry faded the longer he stared at it, and he fell back to sit on his ankles when bizarre tenderness eroded any misgivings in him. *This is surprisingly... surreal.* A sense of awe came over him.

He brushed it with a forefinger curiously, and it raised a brow up at him, seemingly unbothered. It turned its head towards Zylah and then down to her reaching palms before it settled upon them willingly.

"Pretty," she rasped, bringing it closer.

Oddly enough, for the very first time, her stomach gave a loud rumble. He didn't know why that made him laugh, but he covered his mouth with the back of his forearm to hide it. Even more so when she licked across her snout before tipping her skull up to him.

"Are you sure I can have it?"

Jabez *swore* he heard dirt lightly shifting, as if her little tail was wiggling.

"Yeah, Zylah," he stated softly, his eyes crinkling in fondness as the warmth of it radiated freely in his chest. "It's all yours."

Her orbs flared bright pink, and she brought it closer to her chest to inspect it. She brushed the pads of her forefingers across the top of its head and horns, and it reached up to stop her as if it didn't like being petted – like him. Although, he had a funny feeling that if she actually tried to do it, he may welcome it so long as it didn't feel condescending or pitying.

"I have this urge to eat it," she grumbled, cradling underneath it protectively with both hands.

*Always so soft and gentle.*

"That's because you're supposed to." At least... that's what Orpheus had done.

"Really?" More dirt shifted behind her and she raised it higher towards her snout.

He watched her tip it into her mouth and swallow it whole.

Although he physically felt no different, something in his heart shifted.

*All my life, I didn't think I would ever have a mate.* He didn't even think he wanted one until now, but he'd chosen her, no matter the reasons or how it came to this – or what he had to give up.

In some ways, he was relieved. He'd struggled for a long time with the thought of being alone, of having no one truly close to his heart.

*I guess I just needed a bunny to skip its way to me.* He was satisfied that it was her.

She was beautiful, kind, and dangerous. Someone he didn't

*need* to protect, but someone he wanted to because they were benevolent. Someone he would try to take care of, and hoped she'd forgive him if he messed up because he had no idea how to be a giving person. He'd try for her, and hoped he learned how to through her.

Perhaps they could learn this together.

"My stomach feels warm," Zylah stated with a small giggle present in her voice. "I don't feel hunger anymore. It's nice."

He smiled lightly at her. "That's good."

It didn't take long for his soul to crest through the top of her bony head. Black goopy strings shot out from it to tangle around her antlers. His soul willingly lifted its chin so the dark threads could wrap around his throat like a collar with leads from both sides, before more wrapped around his biceps, thighs, and waist.

*I guess that settles it then.*

He let the woven-grass barrier surrounding them fall and glanced over his shoulder to greet Mericato's gaze.

"There," he stated sternly, narrowing his eyes on the man. "She's no longer an unbonded Duskwalker. May we now enter?"

"You understand what you have done, don't you?" Mericato's translator eventually stated on his behalf after he signed. Mericato's expression was bland, but it did hint at surprise and mild concern. His hazel eyes bounced between them, unsure about what he was witnessing. "You said you had no intention of staying."

Jabez scooped his new mate into his arms and lifted her into a safe cradle. "Minds change. You presented me with a challenge, and I chose the best way to overcome it."

He walked towards where the two barriers met, and waited for Mericato to live up to what he'd said before: he would allow Jabez inside, and her if she were bonded.

"You both will need to be bound if you wish to enter."

Jabez looked down at Zylah's skull. "If you think to take my wounded female from my arms, I won't allow it amicably. With her presence, you have a power over me. Once you have taken us to the hospital or healing area or whatever it's called now, I will allow you to bind us both, but *only* then. She is currently unable to walk without pain, and if you hold any regret for what you did in the past, you will allow this."

"You sure have grown cocky in the last twenty-one years."

Jabez merely raised a brow and waited for Mericato to inevitably lower the ward barring the entrance. Mericato nodded, indicating for the two soldiers behind him to act.

"Fine. I will allow you entry. Don't make me regret it."

*You probably will,* Jabez thought, as he tightened his grip on the only creature in both worlds who had done something no one else had managed.

She made him have a heart he wanted to give.

# THIRTY-FOUR

After they wiped down her entire body to clean it and inspect her injuries, Jabez watched as the Elysian healers removed the last of his female's wounds with nothing but yellow glowing hands. Their magic glittered and smelt of sage, but was light in its aroma.

When he first brought Zylah here, they'd shared their doubt in being able to aid her due to her extensive injuries. They'd stated she needed surgery first, but he made them try anyway. He was thankful it'd worked, and her natural regenerative abilities had aided the process, otherwise he may have started pulling on his horns in frustration that he'd brought her here for no reason.

Once her chest had closed, and she finally stopped releasing quiet sounds of discomfort that constantly tugged at him, the healers helped her to stand. She patted her right foot down multiple times, checking to make sure it didn't hurt under her own weight, and her orbs flared bright yellow. She lifted her skull to him.

They'd tried to make him leave the room while they healed her, and he'd told them that wasn't happening. He knew he was pushing too hard, but she was now his mate, and he wasn't letting her out of his sight until the council's approval was stated.

She was precious to him. He'd guard her no matter what they said or wanted from him.

Zylah towered over all of them, and he had a feeling she would be one of the tallest occupants of this city, hands down. Unless, of course, the other Mavka was taller.

He still wanted to know who it was, but Mericato wouldn't say shit about their identity until their trial was over and they were approved to stay in the city. Self-righteous ass.

"She's fully healed," Kusai, Mericato's translator, stated.

Jabez rolled back a little from where his shoulder leaned against the doorway to glare at them for disturbing his relief. With an annoyed sigh, he stepped to the side and crossed his arms behind his back with his forearms touching and parallel to each other.

"Seems you haven't forgotten how this works," the Kusai stated while a different guard – there was a small army of them in the hallway – placed the bindings on his arms.

They looped a belt around each elbow resting against each wrist to secure them together. There was a strap connecting them, so they had something to hold and direct him with.

"Hard to forget that," Jabez commented with a dark tone, grunting when the guard ensured it was so tight he could barely move his arms.

Then, just to make sure, he attempted to teleport and nothing happened. Re-enforced against strength and magic, his bonds now held him completely at their mercy. Or, rather, that was the belief, since they unwisely kept his legs free.

He had a mean kick, since he'd trained every part of his body to be a weapon.

"Zylah, they will bind you as well," Jabez informed her in English, as he turned to show her his back so she could see what they'd do. "It's just a precaution. They'll likely take us to the conference chamber now in order to discuss our admittance."

She nodded and turned while mimicking his arm position for them to bind her as well. Jabez stepped back from the room so she'd follow, and then he placed himself behind her by half a step so she was protected.

With a nod from Mericato, the guards surrounded them and

led them through the central tree's twisting pathways. Mericato remained behind them.

In his periphery, Zylah's head twisted one way and the other as she looked around over the heads of the guards to gawk at everything. Although he was a little taller than most, the Demon in him ensuring he was towering, he kept his head down. He wasn't fond of this walk of shame, and he'd done it many times in the past.

He had no desire to greet the gaze of the few who were awake and lingering through the night. The first sun was yet to rise, and with how dark it was through the windows, he doubted it would rise for quite a number of hours.

*It's barely been a full night here.* He knew they were well into a second day on Earth, and he was unused to the slow flow of time.

It meant their movements were unhurried, as if the Elysians had all the time in the world.

"You're lucky you arrived when you did. I was able to wrangle the other councilmembers from their sleep for you," Kusai stated under Mericato's directive. Jabez figured it was because the first meal was close to being served. "You should feel gracious that they were so willing to begin your trial straight away rather than making you wait."

Jabez's feet paused for a split second when the urge struck him to spin around and punt the man in the forehead with one of his horns. He managed to catch himself and continue walking, but fury simmered beneath the surface of his skin.

"Are you stating I should feel gratitude that you didn't lock me within the prison they kept me in for years?" he asked, his tone rumbling with hostility.

He glanced over his shoulder to sneer at the man, letting some of his fangs show his displeasure at the thought, and Mericato's gaze instantly fell away. He straightened his blue tunic before letting out a solemn expire.

"What happened when we were–"

"Save it," Jabez stated, snapping his face forward. "I don't give a shit about your feelings – if you hate me or feel regret.

It changes nothing. You were a coward then, and it appears you still are, since you can barely even look me in the eye."

"You're forgetting who I am in this city now. It would be best not to aggravate me when I'm attempting to be sincere. Your admittance must be approved by an overwhelming vote by the council, and you'd be wise to filter your words."

Jabez bunched his fists, thankful his arms were bound, or he may have captured the man's scarred throat in his palm and crushed it. He glanced at Zylah, who was unaware of the negative conversation as she inspected every new thing in their environment with adorable curiosity.

The reminder of her presence soothed his anger, and he released his clenched fists. *He's right. I can't let my hatred of these people get to me.* He would need to remain calm, collected, and *quiet* most of all, when he wanted to spew threats and insults.

*If I say one wrong thing, they may not allow her into the city.* They were now a pair, incapable of being separated through her Mavka bond. If he was rejected, then so was she.

As they climbed higher through the white wooden hallways of the central tree, his features twisted in tormented misery. *I can't believe it came to this.* And when they reached a set of doors that looked similar to the city's gates, a horrible, soul-crushing nostalgia twisted in his stomach.

How many times had he seen these doors? How many times had he gone through them, hoping to be freed from his cell permanently – only to be denied? That was until his mind had broken and he'd turned rabid, barely able to be taken from his prison cell without a muzzle due to being a high bite risk.

His memory of those times was fuzzy, and perhaps for good reason. He didn't wish to remember himself in such a pathetic way. Starving without feeling hunger, frothing at the mouth to swallow down just a drop of blood to sate himself.

The ore in the double doors turned molten as it sucked away from the tree of resilience's design, and they slowly swung open.

Inside, the roof glowed with different planets that reflected the suns and Otholla's cycle around the realm. Since it was nighttime, Otholla's mana stone was the brightest to highlight its strength currently in the sky.

The conference chamber was a pyramid in shape, the walls reaching the centre point in the ceiling where the lights were. Behind them, shutters of gold metal sheets could be moved to allow sunlight to filter through glass. In the middle of those lights, a purple flag hung down with three emblems stitched in silver thread: the synedrus council's emblem, the Elysian people's universal symbol, and, finally, the city's marking at the bottom.

Like everywhere within the central tree, the walls were white from its bark. Gold ore filled in the spaces between trunk notches and branches.

Two guards led both him and Zylah to a recess in the middle that allowed all eighteen councilmembers in front of them to view them freely. A guard told him to kneel on the obsidian floor, even though he'd already begun doing so, and Zylah chittered nervously as she copied him.

"It's okay, Zylah. This is normal," he reassured, watching Mericato take an empty seat to the right.

The guards attached ropes from their bindings to hooks in the ground behind them to stop them from moving too far. They were truly worried Jabez would attempt to hurt the councilmembers if they were doing such a thing.

The translator and the two guards both left the room, keeping it strictly confidential to just the defendants and the council.

In front of them were three curved sections of solid-gold tables that had elegant silver branching designs in them. Each table could hold six people, and they could be pushed together to create a perfect, enclosing circle. Currently, they were spread out.

He began to roam his gaze across the many faces, but instantly paused when he met a pair of red eyes. His brows furrowed deeply before he quickly scanned those currently boring their gazes into him and noted there were *multiple* sets of red eyes.

"Since when have Demons been councilmembers?" Jabez asked, cutting through the cold silence with a twisted lip of disbelief.

"Much has changed since you were last here, Jabeziryth Kneis," an aged voice stated from just behind him.

His back straightened from its familiarity, and he glanced over his shoulder to meet the green eyes of an old and withered man. His blurred features cleared in Jabez's memories of decades ago, as he recalled the man named Zerik. Jabez's nose scrunched in disgust, and he licked the inside of his mouth in agitation.

"You're still a councilmember, despite looking like you belong in a crypt, so I wouldn't say *that* much has changed," he stated darkly, spinning his head forward to ignore him.

"There is a term for Demons who have been accepted into our society. They are called Delysians," an elderly woman's voice rung out to his right. "Please ensure you respect them by calling them by their proper titles."

He turned his head in her direction and narrowed his brows when another face in his memories became clear. *Laele too?* Well, shit. This didn't look good for him.

Although, when he did drag his gaze across the councilmembers he could see, only Zerik, Laele, and Mericato's faces were familiar. That softened his shoulders, especially since a few looked young and may not properly remember the chaos he brought on his final day within the city.

He figured it was now part of their history lessons, and he would just *adore* seeing how they twisted it. Had they painted him as some awful villain who deserved what they'd done to him, or had they been truthful about their own wrongdoings? He'd always hated how the past was written by those who held power, and they always wrote it in a biased manner.

"Would you mind telling us the name of your companion so we may speak of her properly and not have to reference her as Duskwalker for the duration of the trial?" a gentle voice asked, and he darted his gaze to almost directly in front of him.

His brows twitched with his subtle frown as he took in the way she didn't look at them, but rather over them, as if she stared at nothingness.

*Is she... blind?* he thought, as he took in the white starburst pupils that were encased in brown irises. Her white curly tresses were styled in cornrows from the front to the crown of her head, while the rest remained loose around her head and shoulders.

Removing his eyes from the woman he didn't know the name of, he tipped his head towards his female. His voice softened as he said, "Her name is Zylah."

Zylah's skull darted to him, and she tilted it in question.

"They asked for your name," he told her, before he cringed inwards in realisation. "I'm sorry, but I think it's best if we don't waste time by me translating everything. You will likely hear your name often, and I will explain the result of the trial once we're done."

His ear twitched when the woman who asked for Zylah's name began translating for *him*, so the other councilmembers were informed of what he said in English.

He lifted his face to her with his brows furrowing deeply, wondering how she understood English, an Earth language. *Perhaps she's a linguist?* He wouldn't be surprised if there were those who had sought to learn the many languages the Elysians were aware of.

There went any chance of him being able to have a private conversation with Zylah within this room.

"Okay," Zylah said, before turning her snout forward to inspect those before them. "I trust you."

Once more, the woman translated on their behalf.

Each of the councilmembers went around the room introducing their names, and Jabez tried to remember each one. None of them sounded familiar, and he was unsure if that was due to the loss of his childhood memories through trauma, or just because he didn't know them.

He only remembered Mericato's name because his face had been one of the few he'd wanted to gouge into every day he'd been locked away.

"I'm worried a few members of the council will be incapable of having an unbiased opinion in this trial," Cleth stated, and Jabez noted that their features didn't lean towards masculine or feminine, but a near perfect blend of both.

Their hair was long on one side, while the other half was shaved. Their hazel eyes peered down at Jabez with distrust, and their small lips nibbled with worry.

"Whether we are biased or not, we all must be present in order to cast our votes," Silveria translated on Mericato's behalf.

The woman was lithe but short, from what he could tell. Her ears were also stout in comparison to most and were easily hidden behind the soft waves of her chin-length hair.

Someone in the room scoffed disapprovingly and Jabez darted his gaze to the scrawny man named Ulric. The top of his hair was fluffy and roughly gelled back, while the shorter sides flowed into a short beard and moustache. His green eyes were shrewdly judgemental, and when he opened his big mouth, his grainy voice instantly scraped against Jabez's ire.

"The fact that you brought him into the city at all shows you are incapable of being indifferent due to what has happened in the past. You are the head of our security, yet you brought inside a man who has sworn our demise from the day he escaped."

"He deserves a chance, like all Demons, to be reborn into the city," Silveria translated once more. "It's no different. How many Elysians have the Delysian councilmembers in this very room eaten in order to be here?"

Ulric slammed his forearm against the gold-and-silver counter before him. "It's different! They sought peace, but we're aware of what he has been up to on Earth! He has spent decades trying to build an army, and he suddenly shows up at our gates, seeking sanctuary? This stinks of trickery, and you are being a *fool*."

"Why are you here?" Silveria herself asked Jabez, her soft voice hinting at concerned interest. She leaned forward across the table with her hands folded.

Mericato placed his hand on some kind of device or mana stone on the table, and a glittering orange ring lit up around Jabez and Zylah. He grunted when the sensation of a spell layered over his body.

"A truth spell?" Jabez stated with an indignant chuckle. "I have no desire to lie. I truly don't care enough about what any of you think of my actions to hide them."

"It is merely a precaution," Laele's elderly voice rang out, "to weed out any distrust in your words so we can make a clear decision. That's all."

His features dulled, but he willingly accepted it as he leaned back on his ankles. There was no strain in his tone, proving just how little he felt the need to hide the truth.

"I wouldn't be here if it weren't for Zylah," Jabez admitted freely. "Not even a few hours ago, I attempted to instigate an alliance within Nyl'theria in order to build an army on this side of my portal."

"See?!" Ulric roared, throwing a hand in Jabez's direction. "He's not here for peace. Such an admittance is enough to throw him from our city."

"You're welcome to do so," Jabez answered, darting a chilling gaze at the thin man. "But the next time you'll see me, it will be as I raze this place to the *fucking* ground."

Ulric flinched, as did many others. The one named Raewyn cringed and lowered her head as if in defeat, while Laele's hand closed into a fist on the table. Mericato slapped his hand over his face and shook his head in disbelief.

"The hate I hold for you people hasn't changed," Jabez continued, drifting his gaze across those before him so they could be pricked by his thorny stare. "There isn't a part of me that doesn't want to tear into each of your throats, including the *Delysians* that sit here by your side. But, as I said, Zylah is the reason I'm here. Since Elysians are no strangers to seeing magic and essence, I'm sure you can see the soul floating between her antlers. It shows that I have accepted her unbreakable Duskwalker bond. She is, in all ways, my mate, and I seek to protect my female – even if it is from myself and my own need for revenge."

"And what of her?" Cleth asked, tilting their face to her. "We have no idea of her intentions, or if you are using her as a ruse to infiltrate our city and destroy it from the inside."

"Are you stupid?" Jabez sneered, darting his head back in annoyance before he looked down at the magic circle around him. "What's the point of a truth spell if you are going to disregard the honesty that comes from me?"

They opened their mouth, only to wisely shut it.

"I'm unsure if anyone informed you of Zylah's state upon our arrival, but she was severely injured and her body would not mend itself. I solely sought to bring her here to have you heal her, and then I planned to abandon her in this city, where she could be safe from harm. Due to your apparent rule of refusing unbonded Duskwalkers within the city, I made a decision. Now I kneel before you, asking that she receive the sanctuary you offer, despite how it goes against everything I have wished for over these past years."

"But it means we must also accept you, and you've admitted that your intentions are still unpure," Laele stated. "We haven't forgotten what has happened in the past, and it has weighed on us every day since you left. We have been afraid of your return."

"You have two options before you," Jabez said calmly, his lids lowering in indifference as he spoke. "Accept her, and therefore me, and my threat that has lingered over this city disappears. Or... cast out the female I'm trying to protect and witness my return, which will be in violent bloodshed."

"How do we know you will not change your mind in the future?" Raewyn asked, her voice meek and shy, like someone who spoke as if they'd done so out of turn.

"I won't," Jabez answered, before letting out a sigh. "Do you think I wanted to come here? This decision wasn't easy for me, and yet... I made it. I have chosen her over myself, and I will live by that. Now *you* must make a choice, and I have informed you of the weight of each option. Choose wisely, or you may come to regret it. The Demons outside these walls are vicious and they're starving. It won't be hard to convince them to join me."

"The future you present is unpredictable," Ulric stated with a dark tone of distrust. "I think many of us would be willing to risk your threat, considering you've been incapable of enacting your pointless vendetta for the past twenty-one years."

Ulric's lips then curled in a smug grin. It was meant to be sharp, as if his expression was another attempt to cut through Jabez's threat.

The deep laugh that broke from Jabez was sardonic and full of malice. "I have spent the last twenty-one years on Earth chasing a dead lead. Now I'm here in this realm, and I've discovered the inner sanctum of Tck'ith, and much of it remained legible."

The moment he spoke of the mountain library he'd taken Zylah to, many faces turned ashen in worry.

"You have no idea of my capabilities, my strengths, and the dark secrets I discovered there. I wasn't able to bring an army through my portal due to Weldir's interference, but there is one here just waiting for a martyr. I'll happily focus them all on one goal."

"And you would willingly endanger your mate to accomplish this?" an individual stated behind him, speaking for the first time. He already couldn't remember their name, and he didn't care.

"If that's the only option you present me with, then what other choice do I have? The safest place across both realms is Lezekos City, and I don't care if it's occupied by Elysians or Demons, so long as it one day shelters her. Oh, and I should probably inform you that she has now rendered me incapable of dying." A grin curled back his lips and revealed his sharp fangs, while mirth crinkled his eyes. "I can try over, and over, and *over* again until the end of time."

All their expressions drooped in understanding, and many shared wary glances with each other.

"But the ability to turn incorporeal means you'll be incapable of being captured should you turn on us within the city," Raewyn stated with a touch more confidence. "And Zylah is a Duskwalker. If we threaten you, she will turn on us. She will always pick your side, no matter how wrong or right it is. As much as I don't want to admit it... you both are a variable we can't predict. If your hatred remains this strong, we won't be able to trust you. If you weaken our defences without us knowing, we put our people at risk because of your inability to let go of the past. I... *we* want to trust you, but you aren't making it easy for us to do so. We are at risk, no matter if we turn you away or accept you. The fear will never subside. We will always be wary and watchful of you."

"Then make up for what you have done to me," Jabez stated. "I'm offering you an opportunity to *subside* my anger and make amends, but that can only be done within the city. Treat my mate well, and my heart may change."

"Is that even possible?" Zerik asked, his aged voice shaken. "You have offered us no way to guarantee our future, yet the past is solidified in the incidental cruelty we have done to you while your present is cast in bloodshed."

"Then you shouldn't have done it in the first place," Jabez bit, shooting a glare at the elderly man. "You forget I was there when you all cast your votes to continuously detain me, and your voice was always the loudest, Zerik."

"We are sorry for what we have done, and we have been regretful since the day you left," Zerik answered, his wrinkles deepening as he frowned with obvious chagrin. "We have learned much of our faults and mistakes–"

"I don't care!" Jabez roared, the flames of his patience beginning to give out. "I have no desire to speak about the past when I'm trying to change my own future. Stop this useless circling and make your decision. There is nothing else to discuss."

A white dome shot over Jabez and Zylah, and all sounds muted beyond it. All he could hear was himself and her. His heart pounded in rage; these foolish councilmembers were unlikely to make the wisest choice he'd presented. But there had been no lie in his intentions, and if they allowed them into the city, then Jabez truly had no desire to endanger it in the future.

He'd come here for Zylah, and he was sure there were other ways he could help the Demons beyond the walls, even if it was peacefully. The only person who would be at a loss was him. They didn't seem to comprehend what he was giving up, all because they were afraid of a future he already foresaw not happening if they just *kept her safe.*

The tenderness in his heart had grown tenfold when he'd given Zylah his soul. Not because of the action itself, but what it meant she had become to him. These idiotic Elysians obviously lacked the understanding of what it meant for a Demon to choose a mate, but in doing so, his essence urged him to protect at all costs.

And the longer he sat in the bond, the more he felt it tearing him up inside. He was growing narrowminded; his thoughts were foolishly beginning to circle around her to make her his centre. This was enough in his mind and heart to tell him their union was unwavering.

*I'm trying...* he thought with a wince.

He had nothing else to offer them but his threat. And considering the truth spell, there had been no way for him to hide how he felt about these people. All he had was this ultimatum.

*Whoever informed them of what I was doing on Earth...* Jabez would love to get his hands on them. *I bet it was that fucking Mavka they have here.*

Whoever they were, they'd given these people too much information that was working against him. They likely knew of all his cruelty, all the things he'd done to build a *pointless* army.

*What else can I offer them to allow us to stay?*

Before his mind could sift through options, the soundproofing dome around them disappeared.

"The council is too undecided," Laele stated loudly. "We

need time to discuss this properly."

"That's fine," Jabez answered calmly, relieved they hadn't been rejected straight away. "We are willing to be patient."

It would also allow him time to think about other potentials he could offer to help sway the council. He could be cunning, so he was sure there was something that may interest them if he thought deeply enough.

*I could tell them of my secret...* He flinched in surprise at his own thoughts before he shook his head. *No. I won't give them what they sought all those years ago.*

"For now, we'll have to detain you both, as it may be a lengthy conversation," Zerik stated, and Jabez's ears pricked at the hint of *unease* in his quietened voice.

"Detain?" he asked, lifting his head with his eyes widening. He squinted a singular eye with suspicion. "You mean in the underground prison?"

"Unfortunately, yes."

"No." Jabez lifted his head back superiorly and let his features grow lax to hide his emotions. "I refuse."

"It's only temporary. It shouldn't be longer than a few hours, but it means you both will have the freedom to move around rather than kneel before us while you wait."

"I refuse," he repeated, just as the choke of terror clasped around his throat. He glanced at Zylah and gritted his fangs until his jaw muscles bunched. "I would rather we sit here."

"This is non-negotiable," Ulric stated coldly, his eyes narrowing. "This is how it's done. If you want us to accept you, then you will need to follow our rules and laws. Refusal is not an option, otherwise we will take you outside the walls if you prove to us that you can't obey."

His ears drooped as a sickening, cold, and heart-racing emotion clambered around in his chest. He jerked his head down in an attempt to hide the anguish in his features as he grated, "You will not place me in that prison, nor her."

In that darkness.

In the place he'd suffered for years, feeling himself slowly losing his mind, thinking the world had abandoned him. He did not want to face the prison cells and how those walls could quickly close in on one's mind. He also didn't want Zylah to have an intimate understanding of what his past had been like. She didn't belong in such a place when she'd never done anything wrong.

She didn't deserve such terribleness.

Memories Jabez had crushed in the miserable pit of his mind until they were nothing but fragments began to resurface. They rose as easily as a dust fluttered into the air from a single harsh gust of wind, or a strong hand stroke against an undisturbed surface. No matter how much he tried to squash them with his will, they flickered in the back of his mind and darted in front of his rapidly blinking eyelids. He tried to disperse them, but the threat of having to go back there, knowing what lay within that darkness, quickly ate away at his mind.

Things best left forgotten came back to him: images, scents, the feel of rock and dirt abrading his soft skin when he didn't lie on his bed. All the while, he'd been unable to feel the life of flora against his feet, his fingertips. How the interim between his own crazed yells had been so quiet that he could hear himself breathing, and his anxious heart pounding loudly in his ears.

How he'd picked at his own skin in boredom, in frustration, or he'd clawed at himself when it felt like the walls were closing in on him. The way the cold, lonely rock around him allowed his own pitiful sobs to echo in his ears as he rocked back and forth, wondering how or why the world had abandoned him. His nails had been filed down to nubs from him scratching at the walls, desperate to escape, while his fingertips bled every time he gripped the sharp edges of stone to pull pieces away, as if the outside was just beyond.

He'd never forget how he lay on his bed, feeling drool drip from the corner of his lips while he was caught in a mindless, dissociative haze just to escape the hell of his confinement. How it sometimes had been the only way to elevate the chaotic, whirling thoughts that refused to shut up.

He hated the pitiful memories of him eating pages of his books as a means to quell the ache in his being that thirsted for blood, trying anything to quench it. Or how he'd dug or bashed at the ground with a rock like a barbarian just to hear something other than his own internal organs moving and shifting in the constant quiet.

The days, weeks, months, *years* of the emotional anguish of wishing he'd never been born. How he'd hated the Demon side of himself because it was the reason he'd been locked away. How he'd tried to yank his own horns from his forehead so they'd be gone, or when he'd ripped his fangs from his mouth so he could grow normal teeth – only for them to grow back stronger than before. Looking at his own reflection had haunted him because the eyes of a Demon looked back at him, crazed and greedy for malice, as if it wanted to consume the Elvish part of him.

The self-hatred, the loathing, the longing to disappear. Yet he'd wanted to *live* just so he could one day be accepted, and tried so, *so* hard to not let his blood-lust get to him whenever someone visited him.

Only to fail.

The sound of their blood rushing in their veins or the scent of their flesh-covered meat turned him into a mindless animal frothing for food. They were forced to muzzle him and strap him down just so they could give him blood infusions and save him from dying from a sickness they couldn't diagnose.

He remembered every time they opened the door to his lonely cell – to feed him, offer him toys, books, puzzles, trying everything in their might to keep him sane – he broke a little more each time it closed.

For *so long*, Jabez had buried the trauma of those years.

"We understand this may be hard for you," Laele said gently, as if to soften the delivery of her words. "But–"

He didn't even realise he was keeling over in fear until he heard Zylah gently call his name out. But he couldn't stop the way he panted in distress, nor the bile rising in the back of his throat, or how his entire body was quaking.

He was fucking *afraid*, and he hadn't felt that way in such a long time.

How dare they ask this of him! How dare they even *bring up* that prison cell, as if they thought he'd walk to it willingly with his tail between his legs.

How dare they threaten *her* with it! To let her taste just a *drop* of the suffering he'd gone through.

The rage that boiled inside him had been simmering for years, and it finally bubbled past what he could contain. The fact that he'd managed to keep a hot lid on it just proved how much he'd longed to fucking *forget*.

"You will not put my mate in that fucking prison!" Jabez roared, rushing to his feet and balancing his legs into an offensive position. Every fibre of his muscles swelled to leap into battle, ready to protect and destroy at the same time. "I'll rip out your throats before I let you!"

"Jabez," someone warned, and he didn't care who.

He blindly ran forward. "I was just a *boy*!" he bellowed, reaching the end of the tether of rope connecting him to the hook in the ground. He fought it, his feet digging in to go forward, to run at them, to enact the violence he'd been waiting *forever* to gift them. "I was only eleven years old! You left me in that prison for *five years* to rot, when everything I did wasn't my fault!"

Some idiot named Kalmen, a young man who hadn't been there, who likely hadn't even been *born* yet, decided to take the mantle up to speak about the past. "You killed a fellow classmate, a teacher, and tried to kill Mericato, now rendering him incapable of speaking without pain. And let us not forget how you and the Demons who escaped with you murdered multiple people on your way out."

Kalmen's most basic retelling of history only infuriated Jabez further.

"Because of you Elysians! I was defending myself against people who were *hurting* me, and yet I was the only one locked away! No one stopped them from ripping my fangs out to watch how fast they grew back, or from trying to shave off my horns to see if they would regenerate too! I was mocked, ridiculed, and laughed at every minute of my life, and yet you expected *benevolence* from me?"

All his pulling at the tether did nothing. Sweating from fear and exertion, he fell to his knees as his foot came out from underneath him, and his forehead hit the ground.

"And you all did nothing!" Jabez roared, clenching his eyes when he felt liquid rising in them. "You all looked at me like I was a monster from the moment I was born. You let *her* bring me into this world because life is apparently sacred, knowing what she'd done, and yet you scorned every breath I took. You shunned me from society as much as possible, worried I would turn on you when you *drove* me to do so!"

With his face pressed against the cold obsidian floor, he opened his eyes to find multiple droplets on the ground. The warmth of wet tears cooled, only to be rewarmed by more.

He didn't know when he'd started crying, but he choked back his quiet sob to hide it. He was thankful his long hair had thrown forward from his fall, as it stopped them from seeing his pitiful face.

"You all pretended not to see it. You pretended that you were doing the right thing to alleviate your own guilt, and when I finally lost it, it was an excuse to get rid of me. To hide me away like I was a shameful creature to be forgotten, and then I was blamed for becoming what you turned me into."

A shudder racked his entire body, and he closed his eyes once more when he couldn't stand the sight of his own tears splattering against the ground. He took in a deep breath, trying to calm himself, and yet his stomach was just so knotted and sick it came out broken and harsh. His voice softened as the weight of what he was saying came down on him.

"How could you do that to a child? For all the things I have done, I have never been cruel to the young, to the truly innocent, no matter what they were. I sat in that prison wishing you would just put me out of my misery and kill me. Would show a scrap of decency and end me, so I no longer had to suffer. Yet every year, you did nothing but *hope* I would change, without doing anything to *help me.*"

At the silence that greeted him, he bit out a growl that quickly died. He couldn't muster up the anger he wanted when all he felt was pain. His damaged inner child gripped at the bars of a cage inside him, finally yelling what he'd never gotten the chance to voice as a boy.

This was never how he wanted to greet his traumatic past. He wanted to do so cackling as he stood on a mountain of Elysian corpses, not pitifully on his knees, with fucking *tears* coming from him. His shoulders drooped in shame, and he turned his head to the side so he could take a breath that wasn't brushing against the ground and fanning his own face.

"You only saw what you wanted to. I tried to be a good pet. I tried to get better. I ate what you gave me, and played with your toys and puzzles. But nothing will stop me from being what I am," he said quietly, wishing his chest didn't ache the way it did. "You have no idea what it was like being in that cell for years. It's inhumane to lock a creature away for so long, but you cared little for my wellbeing under the guise of protecting thousands. Yet you sit there, telling me you're sorry and that I should swallow your demand because it's *how it's done*? Where is the benevolence you believe yourselves to have? Where is your supposed compassion? From the moment I was born, I have seen nothing but your wickedness."

He heard a loud sniffle before a deep sob followed, and he cringed at the sympathy he could almost taste in the air.

When he lifted his head, he peeked through the long lengths of his hair to see who the fuck had the gall to *cry* for him after what they'd done to him. He was surprised to find many eyes were filled with tears, but it was the sightless woman with starburst pupils who was weeping loudly. She'd even covered her face, as if to hide and muffle it.

He grimaced in disgust at her. Why would she cry so deeply for someone she didn't know? He hated such softheartedness.

He looked away from her and purposefully met the ashen expression of Mericato, uncomfortable regret in his gaze.

"I don't care for your regret, your apologies, or excuses. I don't care that we were all just silly children, doing foolish things, because actions have *weight* as adults. I have done horrid things in the name of getting back at you Elysians, but at least *I* can admit to them. Find another way to detain us or throw us from this city like you all will decide to do. I refuse to be subjugated for one more minute in that prison, as I already wasted countless in it."

Then he lowered his gaze to his knees when he sat back.

*Zylah is healed.* Other than that, he regretted bringing them here and trying to move forward when they obviously hadn't changed.

They didn't understand just how deeply that'd scarred him inside; he was the only witness to it in the recesses of his mind. They had no idea how leaving this realm had further twisted him from all the cruelty he'd suffered at the hands of humans and Demons because he had nowhere *safe* to be.

From the day he'd defended himself in a savage, uncontrolled rage, the safety of this place had become nothing but a cage. A cage he'd been striving to return to, where only he held the key to the lock so he would always know freedom.

All his pain, all his suffering, all the horrible things he'd done... it was their fault. They'd taken a quiet, meek, and shy boy and twisted him into a hateful being. They made him into a monster, and he allowed that to be what he saw in his own reflection.

*I don't want to be here.* And they didn't want him here either.

He could already foresee they wouldn't reach a consensus.

Worse still, he could feel himself crumbling from the inside, the flames of his vengeance sputtering out. Because even if he hated the thought of staying... he would if they accepted Zylah into their fold.

A cold sorrow radiated behind Zylah's sternum as they were led through the bleached-white wooden hallways of the Elven tree. Every time she peeked beside her at Jabez, it ached and deepened.

*Something happened,* she thought, her orbs growing darker in their blue hue.

The way he'd shouted and thrown himself forward, only to crumble to his knees, immediately set her heart into a panic. There was little she'd been able to do as she fought against her bindings to go to him. His voice had croaked, his body trembling as he'd spoken, and each word seemed to ring with unbearable torment.

He was always so confident and had a big personality.

To see him in such a state had been undeniably saddening. She'd thought it was just pure rage that they weren't giving him what he wanted, but it hadn't taken long for her to realise the truth.

Despite her inability to understand his words, it was clear he'd been speaking from a place of pain.

*I wish I knew what was said.* She hadn't liked not comprehending anything, but she'd trusted Jabez and remained quiet. However, what he'd shouted was obviously important to him, and the current listless stare of his faraway gaze was haunting.

He looked exhausted – more so than usual.

His eyes slipped to her skull, and Zylah faced forward to evade them. A chill crept down her spine despite the warmth she felt in the air.

They were taken to a wooden white door that had a long, wide yellow sash nailed to it. She couldn't read the symbols or words on it, but nervousness struck her at seeing it. *Where are they taking us?*

She'd been expecting Jabez to explain it to her, but he'd been wordless from the moment they were taken away from the conference chamber.

One of the guards opened the door for them since they were still bound, and a spacious room was revealed on the other side. Her fur lifted when she felt some kind of magic brushing over her flesh as she passed through the threshold.

The guard closest to Zylah touched her wrists, making her flinch, before the bindings around her arms loosened and fell away. Zylah stumbled forward to get away from them, and the aches in her biceps from being tied behind her back subsided. She rubbed at her forearms as she turned to watch them release Jabez as well.

When his arms were freed, however, he turned and offered them his wrists. They placed thick golden bands around them that shimmered with pink when they closed, obviously imbued with some kind of enchantment.

When Zylah offered her own wrists, Jabez placed his hand on her arm and shook his head. "No. Only me."

"Why?" she asked, watching as the guards stepped out of the room and closed the door behind them. There was the distinct *shluck* of some kind of lock being engaged, and the walls of the room glittered with blue before fading.

"It stops me from being able to use my magic," he answered quietly, his voice lacking in emotion. "It was the only way they'd agree to bringing us here."

Once more, she asked, "Why?"

Now that they were facing each other, she noticed dried tracks of salty-smelling liquid down his dust-smudged face. There were so many that on one side it just looked like a thick, blobby streak. His features appeared ashen and lacklustre, and she'd never seen them this way before.

His eyes flicked to her skull before darting away.

"Because every spell that lacks a mana stone has a code, and they can be broken. It's to ensure that I don't bring down the barrier keeping us locked in here."

*Is that what that blue glittering was?* she thought, looking at the wall around the door frame.

She tilted her head, considering his explanation. "But can't I do that?"

"No. It takes a very skilled magic user and years of practice." He rubbed at the bands covering his wrists. "They're wary because I was able to break down the one in my prison cell which, considering it was powered by a mana stone, was deemed impossible until me." Then his expression pinched as he muttered, "Give a child five years with the same puzzle, and he'll figure out a solution."

Zylah cupped her hands in front of her chest as her limbs knocked inwards. "What is going on?" she asked nervously, since the way he was acting only deepened her anxieties.

He stepped around her and waved an arm to indicate the room. "We'll be staying here until the council decides whether or not we're permitted to stay."

Zylah finally took it in.

The room was semi-circular, with a bed resting up against the only straight wall. All the walls were made up of twisting white branches, bronze ore, and glass. More of the tree lay beneath their feet, as well as some kind of thin yellow carpet that sat underneath the bed and led down to a seating area with two lounges and a stout oval table made of bronze.

The ceiling had a strange glowing light in the middle, but it was dim. She wondered if there was a way to brighten it before she brought her gaze to the forking branches of tree and glass to her right.

There appeared to be a room further in, since there was an arched door on the opposite side of the room.

Where they were wasn't big, but it was definitely larger

than their shared cave.

"Will we be living here permanently if we are allowed to stay?" she asked, somewhat liking its design.

Unlike Fayren's home, the seats looked big enough for her to sit in. The bed was huge in comparison to hers as well. Zylah thought she and Jabez could both lie on it with ease, rather than her being forced to curl up into a ball just to rest.

"No. This room is only temporary, but Zylah..." At the way his tone became strained, she turned to find his expression had twisted up. "The chances of them approving us are exceptionally low."

Any hope or excitement regarding the room rushed out of her in an instant. She cupped her hands once more to fidget with them, and her orbs retreated back to the blue hue from earlier.

"Then why are we still here?" she asked, unsure as to why he wouldn't make them leave if he felt that way.

His eyes flicked to her before narrowing at the room. "Because it gives me time to assess our other options while we are somewhere safe." His right hand curled into a fist, and he lifted his face towards the wall of glass. "It also allows us to rest, and I believe the door over there leads to some kind of personal bathing facility."

Zylah came closer and tipped her head to the side so she could meet his avoidant gaze. "Can you tell me what happened? I want to know why you suddenly..."

When his expression scrunched, her words fell short.

"My past is an issue," he admitted, greeting her orbs head-on. Then he lifted his hands and cupped the sides of her bony cheeks. "Unlike you, they're unwilling to forgive it. I'm sorry, Zylah, but my inability to shed my hatred of these people is what got in the way, and now I have tied myself to you, so even if they would have accepted you, we're unable to be separated."

Zylah placed her hands over his to hold them. "I don't mind where we are, so long as we are together."

As if that was the wrong thing to say, he stepped back while taking away his touch. He grasped the end of his hair to inspect the red, bloodied clump of it before he wiped at his face to remove some of the dust and his own dried blood.

"I need to wash. I can only imagine what I look like," he stated, heading to the door on the other side of the room. "Sit. I won't be long... unless I can't figure out how to power it or *can't* because of the bracers."

Then he left Zylah on her own.

Since there was little else in the space, Zylah walked over to the bed and sat on the edge of it. Not expecting such softness, she squeaked when her backside nestled right in, and she bounced on it in mild curiosity. Just as she was getting comfortable and lifted her gaze to the wall of glass, she heard the faintest sound of rain coming from the room Jabez had disappeared into.

As much as she wanted to know what it was and inspect it, she thought it best to leave him alone. She fidgeted with her hands as she thought, *He's... different.*

She didn't know what to make of his behaviour; he'd shied away from her repeatedly and refused to meet her gaze with confidence, like he usually would. She also had this niggling feeling that if she were to ask him about why he'd crumbled to the ground, he would avoid telling her the full truth of it.

*He's always been complicated.*

Despite her worry and unease, her heart skipped a little when she remembered receiving the gift of his soul. She could *feel* it floating between her antlers due to the mild heat there, and the desire to reach up and touch it nagged at her. When the urge became too strong, she hesitantly lifted her hand to where it rested, unsure if this was allowed.

Warmth greeted her, and she brushed her thumb over the little flame when nothing inside her told her what she was doing was wrong. She even gained the courage to clasp her hand around it and pull until she was able to take it.

White snuffed out the colour of her sight, and she reared her head back when she noted that it'd changed. She knew when he'd given it to her it'd swirled with blue-and-green flames, but the head of Jabez's soul had turned black and appeared like cracked stone.

It still rested in the same cross-legged position, but she thought its shoulders slumped more than before, as if it was tired. Red slits blinked constantly, but they were slow and languid even when they appeared to look up at her skull.

Zylah went to brush the back of her forefinger claw underneath its jaw, but the sound of rain cut off. She quickly placed her hand between her antlers and was thankful when his soul stayed there.

She didn't know why she felt nervous about him seeing her play with it, but she had to hide her chitter and stop her shoulders from turning inwards self-consciously when he emerged.

*His hair isn't wet.* Nor was his body. *Maybe they have a drying spell, like the one he can do?* It looked as though he'd washed his pants as well.

"There's no bath, but they have a shower. I'll show you what that is if need be," he stated, looking at her before glancing over his shoulder. "I know they cleaned you at the hospital, but did you want to wash?"

"No," Zylah answered while shaking her head. "I'm okay."

As curious as she was, she didn't want to be alone any longer when she was in an unfamiliar environment and so concerned about his wellbeing. He did look a little brighter after washing, but she thought that may just be because he was clean and no longer caked in grime.

Accepting her answer, he came and sat beside her on the bed. His weight made her bounce momentarily before everything settled, but he didn't seem to notice as he clasped his hands between his open knees. It took him a while to settle his gaze somewhere. When he did, he looked out the glass in front of them.

She did as well.

They were unable to see Otholla, so she guessed it was behind them. She couldn't see the forest either. Instead, a vast amount of dark, inky water reflected the sparkly stars.

"Is that an ocean?" Zylah asked, having never seen one before.

"Ocean, or a very large lake, depending on your opinion, since it's completely surrounded by land. It's also fresh water, and not salty."

Silence fell over them, and Zylah picked at the silky bedding as she reached for something else they could speak of. There were so many questions she didn't know where to start, and she didn't know what was safe to talk about right now. She could tell something was wrong with him, as he seemed to have lost his usual spark, but she didn't know how to broach the subject so she could help.

She felt a little... lost, and out of depth with the situation.

They were also sitting on a big comfy bed together. Since she'd slept recently, she wasn't all that tired yet, but she did know of other things they could do on it. They were also alone, and despite everything and the uncertainty of their future, she wanted to appreciate him for giving her his soul.

She wanted to cuddle, she wanted to touch, she just wanted to feel... close to him. Would now be an inappropriate time for that?

*What do I call him?* she wondered, scratching at the side of her snout. *Do I call him my bride or a mate like his kind?* Bride sounded funny; any time she'd read about a wedding in her books, it was usually a female's title. *Groom? Husband? I'm so confused.*

Zylah peeked at him from the edge of her sight, but it was impossible to gauge his emotions with his expression so empty. It didn't help that his hair wasn't neatly brushed back to sit between his horns like usual and was shielding his face from all sides in a throw of messy strands.

"Jabez?" Zylah called, reaching out to brush his long fringe back and tuck it behind his pointed ear – that didn't even flick when she accidentally caressed it.

Without taking his gaze from the world outside, he answered, "Yes, Zylah?"

"What is wrong?"

His face dipped down to his clasped hands, and she noticed the way they clenched together tightly. For a little while, he said nothing, and she worried he wouldn't answer.

His voice was quiet, soft, and lacking in emotion as he said, "I don't know how to answer that question right now." Then he lifted his gaze forward once more. "I'm just... thinking."

"Aren't you tired? You haven't slept since we came here."

"I can sleep later – when I've figured out a solution that I find fitting."

Her heart sunk a little at that, and her sight shifted to blue as she lowered her head. It sprung back up when an idea sparked in her mind. "Can I hold you then?"

He lifted his arm to create space for her. "Of course. You don't need to ask."

Zylah considered tucking herself into the nook he created, but chose to slip to the ground and place herself between his knees. He looked down at her just as she wrapped her arms around his waist and rested the underside of her snout against one of his thighs. His arms softly came down around her shoulders, his fingers diving into the fur across her back, and she wanted to purr at how quickly he accepted her embrace.

Their cuddle was loose, but Zylah's orbs turned dark as she took in the feel of him and the fact that he was holding her in return. He even began scratching her soothingly, and she wiggled forward just to get that little bit closer.

*He smells so nice,* she thought with a contented hum, resisting the urge to nuzzle her snout against his side. Since his scent was now clean, she soaked in the aromas of earth, of flowers and wood, and her mind eased.

Zylah really didn't care where they were, whether they were in this city, back on Earth, or fighting against Demons in Nyl'theria. She just wanted to be near him. So long as he let her hold him like this, she knew she'd be content anywhere.

Next time they faced a situation like the nasty village of Demons, she'd be more prepared. She wouldn't leave his side, and she wouldn't hesitate again to defend herself. She'd listen to her instincts when they were nagging at her that something was amiss.

She'd do better to ensure she didn't worry him again. Admittedly, she was a little concerned that she hadn't been able to regenerate, but she was sure they would find a solution. The Elvish people had healed her, so maybe they could learn together how to aid each other in the future. She didn't mind being hurt, so long as they both survived in the end.

She wondered if those thoughts were currently what weighed on his mind. She knew voicing that she wasn't concerned about possible future injuries would do little good and would likely result in a disagreement.

Her arms tightened around him as she sheepishly thought, *But he can't leave me again.* He was hers, and Zylah wouldn't give up this bond even if there was a way.

His soul was hers to embrace, as were his heart, his mind, his body, and his past. She'd do so openly until the end of time.

Just as her tail began to sway in adoration, the tuft puffed out when the strangest chill touched her bony forehead just below where his soul was and slipped down her spine. She looked up, finding that Jabez hadn't moved from gazing outside and that he appeared the same as before.

Yet the warmth of his soul had dimmed heavily.

Her ears rang at the loud, distinct, and noticeable *crack* she heard. It sounded like glass and rock breaking in half at the same time. She ignored it at first, until she heard another, and another, and the warmth of his soul disappeared completely.

At the same time, a strange cold ache struck her.

Panic swelled in her muscles, and she shot her hand up to his soul to take it from her antlers and check on it.

A high-pitched, sharp whine escaped her when she saw that his entire soul had completely lost its colourful flames and had crumbled like fragile rock. Rather than sitting upright, it'd fallen to the side, and no longer hovered above her palm but rather lay on it. It was cold, no heat to be found, and pieces of it seemed to be missing.

At the whine that left her, Jabez groaned and dug his nails into her back lightly. "Please don't make that sound right now," he grated out, his voice hoarse and laden with emotion. "I can't take it."

As much as Zylah tried to be quiet, her distress only grew when more pieces of his soul broke off and withered into nothingness. It started at its hands, feet, and face, before more and more slowly chipped away until there was nothing but a torso.

Zylah leaned back when her heart clenched so hard it felt like it was about to burst. *Why is it disappearing?!* She fretted, her hands shaking as she watched it with no idea how to stop it. Then its torso caved in and cracked open, revealing a tiny flame of blue and green that floated out of its chest.

It hovered there, nothing else remaining but the tiniest sputtering flame.

It floated away, trying to go back to between her antlers, but she grabbed it and stopped it. She stared at it once more.

"Jabez?" she asked, lifting her skull to his face.

His body flickered and vibrated between solid and transparent, as if it wanted to turn ghostly, but the golden bands around his wrists shimmered bright pink. She wondered if they were stopping whatever was happening to his physical body.

Seeing that his soul was no longer changing, but was at least still alive in some form, she returned it, then rose up on her knees and grabbed his cheeks in both her palms. She forced him to look away from outside, but his eyes refused to leave it until she turned his head so far to the left that he had no other option.

His gaze landed on her, and she found it just looked... *hollow.*

*I don't know how to help.*

She didn't even know what she was fighting against.

# THIRTY-SIX

Zylah dived forward, wrapped her arms around Jabez's neck, and clung to him. She trembled as she held him, wishing she knew what to say or do in this moment. Something was wrong with him – he obviously wasn't okay – and more than ever, she wished she knew what had been said within the conference chamber.

The only solace was that he slipped his arms around her midsection to hug her, but she could *feel* the distance between them. Even with their torsos tightly meshing together, it was like he was slipping miles away.

"What's wrong?" she whispered, as she dug her claws into his shoulders. "Please tell me what is going on."

"Sorry, Zylah. My mind isn't well, and I can't think clearly," he answered, his arms loosening. She hated how deadened his voice sounded.

Unsure of what else to do, she drew her tongue up his jaw and then his cheek, licking to show him that she was there, that she cared, and that he didn't have to do this alone. She wished he'd seek whatever he needed from her, rather than retreating into his head. She understood that he'd been this way for a long time, alone and unable to trust anyone else but himself, but it was hard for Zylah to know what *she* could do to bring him out of it.

*When I was upset, he distracted me from my sadness.* But her sadness had revolved around him, and being intimate with him had helped to ease her loneliness and fears.

"Is it my fault?" Zylah asked, her voice rising an octave.

His body reared back, forcing her to let go when he stared at her with his brows furrowing.

"Not at all," he answered, and she didn't know whether to believe him or not.

She let out a whine and leaned forward to lick across his lips, kissing him the only way she knew how. When he didn't respond other than flinching, Zylah did it repeatedly, feeling his closed lips move under the power of her tongue.

He let out a small sigh. "Zy–"

She cut off whatever he was about to say by shoving her tongue into his mouth.

One of his hands shot up to grip the back of her neck, and his fingertips dug in like he was trying to pull her away without hurting her. She held the sides of his head so he couldn't distance himself with force and brought her tongue back before thrusting it forward to lick across his.

She didn't even care that his fangs were sharp, not when desperation bolstered her.

The longer she did it, the more his grip on her nape softened. His tongue greeted hers subtly, almost shyly, then he let out a small groan and palmed the back of her neck to bring her closer. Zylah lifted herself until she was able to slide her knees around his hips and sit on his lap, closing the distance between them and ensuring he couldn't get away.

He made her squeak when he sucked on her tongue and his sharp fangs scraped against the underside and top of it. She ground into him in reaction, causing him to jerk and let go, and she retracted her tongue with a pant.

Just as she went to go back in for more, he shifted his face to the side and buried it against her shoulder.

"More," she demanded, shoving at his chest until he fell backwards against the bedding. She leaned down and licked across his lips, trying to get him to open up again so she could get another taste of him.

"You're being awfully clingy right now," he stated around

warm pants. Just the sound of his breaths, the life in his tone, had her heart beating faster.

*Because you're scaring me,* she thought, giving up on his mouth to lick at the side of his neck in hopes he'd shudder for her. *Because I don't know what else to do but this.* To distract him from the thoughts he wouldn't share, to try to make him think of something else for a little while.

So it didn't feel like she was... *losing* him.

His head turned to the side as if to give her more room, but his hips didn't greet hers when she tried to grind on him and stir his body.

"I don't think I'm going to get hard right now," he admitted quietly with his brows furrowing.

Refusing to let that dishearten her, Zylah licked up his pointed ear and whispered, "Can't I try?"

"The council could make their decision at any moment."

"Then... we'd better be quick."

Quick wasn't really in her nature, if she were being honest. Having sex just once or twice didn't seem to be enough for her body, but she wasn't doing this for her own pleasure. Right now, she was solely focused on him, hoping touch would make him feel better like it had for her in the past.

She was thankful he didn't try to stop her when she lowered her head to dab her tongue against his chest. He didn't even halt her hand when she slid her palm down his muscled torso while lifting her hips. His gaze was steady on her skull as he let her cup his cock with sheathed claws.

*It's soft.* She didn't know why she was surprised considering what he'd said, nor why she was a little hurt by it. *I do not know how to be arousing.* She'd never tried to be sensual and instigate sex before. *Maybe I'm no good at this.*

Zylah leaned back and straddled his waist so she could look down at him and figure out another way to be enticing. Not realising she was right at the edge of the bed, her knees slipped off. A loud, surprised squeak burst from her as she fell to the ground and landed on her backside.

Embarrassment clamoured around her chest as she moved

to sit down properly between his spread ankles. Her orbs wavered with brimming tears because that was the opposite of the arousing she was going for.

A small, short laugh had her head lifting just as Jabez moved to sit up. He placed a hand on top of her head.

"That was cute," he muttered, his eyes lightly crinkled with warmth as he looked down at her.

Okay, cute was good. She could handle that.

"Can I keep going?" she asked, shuffling closer as she placed her hands on his parted thighs.

His lips grimaced and pulled to the sides. "Are you sure this is what *you* want right now?"

She reached for the ties of his pants. "Yes."

Just as she managed to unknot his pants, he grabbed her hands to stop her. "If you're going to do this, take your dress off. I can't stand the sight of it anymore."

Zylah tilted her head to look down at the skirt of it resting over her thighs. The red colour of her dress was stained in so many patches of her own dried blood that most of it had changed to purple.

*He can be really odd.* He didn't seem to care for his own injuries or the fact that he'd had his own blood smeared all over his body earlier. Didn't he also kill countless people in the past? The idea that he found blood uncomfortable was strange – especially since she'd seen him drink from a person's jugular multiple times.

*Is it because it reminds him of my injuries?* But they were healed now, so what did it matter?

Wanting to please him, Zylah grasped the hem of her skirt and lifted the dress over her head to remove it. When she went to drop it beside her, he grabbed it and let it fall out of sight next to the bed.

Before she could do anything else, he palmed the flat part of her chest. "Most of your bones have sunk beneath your skin," he commented, brushing his thumb down her sternum.

Zylah felt the tickle of fur shifting rather than his finger pad brushing over bone. Tilting her skull, she assessed her naked body.

He was right. Her sternum bone had completely disappeared, and only her bottom two ribs remained. She also hadn't noticed before, but most of her hand bones had been covered except for a few of her knuckles.

"Is that a good thing?" Zylah asked, lifting her sight up to him.

"You look softer. Healthier." Then, one corner of his lips twitched upwards momentarily as he cupped underneath her left breast. "And these look bigger."

His red eyes were warmer than they'd been since they arrived in this room, and he didn't seem to notice a few strands of his hair slipping from behind his ear as he gazed down at her chest. He ran his thumb across her dark-grey nipple, and it hardened under his touch as she twitched at the tickling sensation.

Zylah reached forward and pushed the front flap of his pants to the side. The remaining material fell between his thighs before slipping over them to fully reveal his groin. Although his cock was still soft, it did look a little longer and thicker than when she'd grabbed it earlier.

He leaned back to give her freedom to touch, and Zylah slipped her hand around him. She ignored his observant gaze as she stroked him, and although he jerked against her palm, he didn't harden immediately like she'd been hoping he would.

It was actually remarkably awkward to pump her hand around him while he was flaccid. Her fist was too big in comparison to the size of him when he was small like this, and she worried if she squeezed any tighter, she'd crush it.

*I don't think I'm doing this well,* she thought with nervousness skittering down her spine. She wondered if her hand just didn't feel nice like this.

"Sorry, it might take me a bit," he stated softly, as if he could sense her self-conscious unease. "Do you want me to take over?"

She shook her head and let out a quiet, although frustrated, huff. "No. I want to do it."

He grew a little in her palm, and she lifted her snout to him in surprise. At her dark-yellow orbs, he gave her a small, half-hearted smile. "I like it when you pout."

Grumbling at that, she rattled her head side to side as she looked back down, since her strokes were a little easier. Her tongue came out to slip across the top of her snout.

"Can I lick it?"

"I thought you were going to, since you're already down there."

Her sight flickered with a reddish pink in embarrassment, as she hadn't known her placement indicated that. She only came up with the idea now. Zylah shuffled a little closer, relieved he was letting her play with him however she wanted.

It seemed like he wanted it, since he hadn't tried to stop any of this like she knew he could, but his body just wasn't in tune with him. At least he was getting bigger, which made her feel as though she wasn't actually failing at this.

Tilting his cock to the side, Zylah ran her tongue from the base to the sheltered tip to leave behind a trail of saliva. She liked that he thickened even more and let out a quiet pant, and that one of his hands came to rest against her nape, just below the base of her skull.

Unsure of what else to do, as she'd need to part her jaw wide to get him inside her mouth, Zylah just licked up and across the length of him. He was smooth under her wet tongue, his skin velvety and warm. In certain spots, she could feel little thumps of his heartbeat, and she grew fixated on where else she could sense those pulses.

Then she slipped her tongue one way and accidentally wrapped around him a little. When he gave a quiet grunt, as if he liked the feeling, she stuck her tongue out as far as it could go and twirled it around him until she wrapped it twice. She pulled upwards so it would stroke him, then tried to do the same thing while going downwards.

But even after she did it multiple times, he still hadn't grown fully hard, and she didn't think this was working as much as she wanted it to.

"I'm... not good at this." Zylah pulled away to stroke him instead, and her saliva coating him made it easier. She tried to hide the dismay in her voice as she said, "I don't think my mouth is right for this, and I don't have lips like a human."

"It'd feel better if I was harder," he admitted, before rubbing up the back of her skull. "But it did feel nice. It reminded me of your tendrils, although a rather big one."

Zylah paused at what he said and tilted her head. "Tendrils?"

His brows twitched and drew inwards. "Yeah. You don't know that you have little tentacle-like tendrils inside you?"

"I do?!" she exclaimed with a gasp, letting him go to look down at her pelvis.

Her ear holes tingled when he let out a light chuckle. "Have you never felt inside your own pussy?"

"Well... no. Not really," she grumbled, slipping her hand down to touch at her slit in curiosity.

Her clit instantly greeted her like it had in the past, and wetness coated her fingertips. This was as far as she'd ever explored before.

*I have tendrils inside me?* None of Fayren's books detailed such a thing.

Wanting to understand what he meant, Zylah ran her middle finger down her slit until she found the hole of her opening. She sunk the digit inside until her palm was nestled against her... and waited.

She felt nothing but warm inner walls. Her insides did spasm around her finger, and she hooked the pad of it forward to search for any indication of what he meant. It was hard to feel around with just one finger, so she slipped a second inside, and shivered as she stretched herself.

Something brushed against her fingertips, and she hooked them forward to chase it, only to moan softly when she pressed against somewhere tender. Her thighs parted, and she rested her palm against her clit, following the tingle of pleasure she felt within. Zylah pushed deeper. Her pussy clenched, and she gasped when multiple little limbs wrapped around her fingers.

The dark yellow in her orbs quickly bled to purple as she thrust just to feel the tendrils better, and deep arousal bounded its way into her. Her calm breaths turned shallow as she pumped, her insides clinging tighter as she hooked her fingers like he'd done to her in the past. She accidentally brushed against that tender spot harder than before – the one that had her vision darkening with need and her pussy growing wetter within an instant.

She licked across her snout as her interest in the tendrils faded. Instead, she pumped because it felt amazing, and the desire to come hungrily ate at her like it usually did. A loud, strangled moan came from her, and she looked up at Jabez's face to pant at him when she thought he responded with his own.

Lips parted on shallow huffs, he watched her with rapt attention, his eyes much more heated than before she'd gone exploring.

Her pants turned shallow, and she jerked against her own fingers at the pleasure. Her toes curled when his eyes bounced from between her thighs, to her breasts, then her skull, and dropped back down. His pricked-up ears twitched when she released a sharp breath.

Realising what she was doing in front of him, reddish pink blasted into her sight. Zylah chittered self-consciously and pulled her fingers away.

"S-sorry," she whispered, lifting her hand now saturated with her arousal and having no idea what to do with it.

"The hell you apologising for?" he grated out, his eyes darting to her wet fingers. "And why'd you stop?"

"Because I was supposed to be touching..." *You,* she finished in her mind, which was promptly distracted when she noticed what was now between them. "Oh. You're hard..."

His cock now jutted from his hips, full and engorged to the point the mauve head had come out. Even the ridges on the sides of it were now pressing against the inside of his flesh, and she knew they only did that when he was fully erect. It pulsated along with his loud heartbeat.

"I just watched you masturbating in front of me for the first time," he rasped, stroking up his cock. "Of course I'm hard."

The blushing hue in her orbs flickered in and out, fighting with the purple of her desire. "Do you want me to keep going then?" she asked, giddy that he liked watching her so much.

If she'd known that from the beginning, she would have started with that!

"Fuck yeah, I do."

Purple won out, and Zylah slipped her hand down to pet her clit, making herself twitch. She touched it curiously, pressing on it hard and swirling her fingers, until her clenching pussy had her chasing to push her fingers back inside herself. Re-stretching herself felt wonderful, and she liked that she knew exactly where to slide them now. Shuffling so she was seated on her ankles and propped up higher off the ground to give herself room, she thrust them like before.

She watched his eyes drift down to her moving hand, just as his own began a steady stroking rhythm around his cock.

*I didn't realise I was so warm inside,* she thought around heated pants as she pumped, feeling the way her pussy was formed. Her tendrils greeted her again, and they were smooth in comparison to her snug, textured walls.

She pressed deep and wiggled her fingers forward like he'd done for her in the past, and a loud, hitching moan broke free. Her thighs spread, and she pumped her fingers faster as her insides squirmed. She grasped the top of his thigh to balance herself when her hips moved on their own, bucking forward and back as she sought that tumbling bliss.

Her gaze landed on his cock and the drop of pearly white liquid that had bubbled at the tip. Her maw parted on deep pants before she licked across her snout in interest. She slowly drew her hand closer, sliding it across his thigh with the need to touch it.

"I want this inside me," she whispered, knowing it was much bigger and longer than her fingers. It would feel better and touch sensitive places everywhere all at once.

And it would make her feel closer to him. She had this wonderful desire to be filled to the brim.

"You can have it when you finish fucking yourself and come," he muttered softly, making her fur puff at his erotic words.

His hand fell away when she wrapped her own around him, but she was unable to stroke it as she ground on her fingers with a moan. She thrust faster and dug harder against her most sensitive spot, and her vision nearly blackened when she felt herself clamping up momentarily.

Once her sight cleared, she noticed the white bubble of precum had slipped down the head, and Zylah leaned forward to lick across the tip of his cock before it could fall. She wanted to know what his seed tasted like, but she hadn't expected it to be salty and sweet at the same time. The moment it touched her tastebuds, her tongue shot forward to wrap around his cock as she let out a greedy moan, hoping to collect more.

She had no idea what she was doing anymore as ravishing need blasted through her fiercely. She licked at him, shivering every time she got another taste of seed, and *fucked* herself harder, faster, until she was releasing moan after moan. She bounced on her hand, trying anything to fall into bliss, finding it difficult when her tendrils clasped tightly.

Her tongue adored the bumps of his ridges slipping across it, and she looked up into his riveted gaze as he produced a body-tingling, husky growl in response to her.

Then her inner walls swelled hard, and she let him go as her skull limply fell to his lap when she started climaxing. She had to hold back her claws from extending as she thrust out her hand and gripped his thigh, and her fingertips dug into him hard when she let out a loud cry. Her pussy pulsated as wetness squelched within her, and she shuddered each time she prodded the spot that made her orgasm more powerful.

Before her body could go fully lax, she was yanked from her knees and thrown against the bed. Her back arched off it when Jabez nestled between her thighs, enclosed one of her nipples with his lips, and thrust his cock against her clit.

He sucked her nipple hard enough to sting it, causing her to cry out and push at his head. The moment her hand came near him, he let her breast go to lick her slick from her fingers. He brought them into his mouth to suck all the liquid from them and she'd never realised her fingers could be so sensitive until that very moment.

"Did you have fun doing that? Next time, I'd like to watch with your pussy on display for me." Jabez leaned back onto his knees to rise above her and push her thighs apart. Exposing her, his nose scrunched, and he let out a groan at what he saw. "Fuck. I need inside you. *Now.*"

Still panting wildly, Zylah looked down when he grabbed the base of his cock to position it. Since he hadn't been expecting it, when she shoved his chest with all her strength, he fell to the side and landed on his back. She climbed on top of him, settled the slit of her pussy on his shaft, and pinned his shoulders down.

"I want to do it." To let him know she was being stern, she extended her claws free so she could stab his flesh with them.

He leaned his head up and managed to lick against the underside of her chin. Then his lips brushed the bone of it as he muttered, "Why? I can go a lot faster."

"Because you're always on top," she said, grinding her clit against him and spreading her wetness.

*And because I want to take care of you.* Yes, she was very excited right now, but she'd started this for him. Zylah wanted to show how much she cared about him. She wanted to be close to him and make him feel pleasure.

She hadn't done well with her hands and mouth, and she wanted a chance to do so with her body after failing so miserably.

When the tension in his shoulders softened, she took that as him submitting. She lifted her hips and gripped the base of his shaft to nestle the head against her entrance, and just the blunt pressure of his cock felt wonderful.

She dropped her hips all the way in one go, and she realised she should have done it slowly when the stretch was harsh and she let out a choke. Each of his ridges had felt like bubbles going in, spreading her repeatedly as she speared him inside. Her pussy immediately clenched around him, and she placed her hands on his broad, muscular chest to steady herself when her knees knocked inwards at the intense girth.

*Nhnn. Why does he always feel so big?*

Jabez's hands slapped her arse as he grabbed it in a rough knead. He shoved her down as his hips shot up and forced himself even deeper, ripping a gasp from her. He groaned, grinding into her, and his head tipped back to expose the thick, popping veins in his neck.

"Fuck, you're so wet," he growled out with his nose wrinkled hard. Another deep groan fell from him as he shuddered and looked down at where they were joined. "And you're really tight after coming."

"Jabez," she rasped when his hips dropped down, only to slam back up, making pleasure strike profoundly.

"Shit, Zylah. Move or I'm going to roll you over and fuck you as hard as I can."

His pectoral muscles twitched, and his hands grasped her arse so tight it was almost bruising. She could sense the restraint in his body, like aggression was skittering beneath the surface.

His fingers pushed her hips until they slid forward, only for his palms to push her hips back. Following the way he guided her, Zylah slowly began to move, and her panting breaths sharpened at the feel of his cock moving.

*He's inside me,* she thought, adoring the way he slipped in and out. He was hard and long, stretching her and touching everywhere she needed. His ridges waved delightfully against her entrance every time one popped in or out.

"You feel so good inside me," she whispered, snapping her hips back and forth in earnest to go faster.

Her hands massaged his strong chest with unashamed, rough grabs. She used her arms to go up and down at the same time, wanting to feel herself come down on him harder.

Both his hands caressed up her body, slowly touching her

hips, then her sides, and her spine arched when his nails scratched into her back. He cupped both her breasts, and she hadn't realised they felt so heavy and starved for attention until he clamped her nipples between his thumbs and index fingers. There was a pleasurable pinch every time he kneaded her breasts and his fingers clasped her nipples tightly, but that only made her go faster.

Her vision grew dizzier, her body hotter, and her maw parted on sharp, shallow pants. She didn't care if she was crushing his hips every time she shunted back hard to feed his cock in her all the way to the base, wanting to feel it push up against the end of her. Her head tilted back and her toes curled when it felt just right.

There was a painful bite each time he slammed his hips up as she seated herself deep, but for some reason, it only made her ache further. It only made her want to pump her pussy around him with more vigour until he tore her in half.

She could feel how wet she was, the slides growing more and more slippery each time his balls touched her backside.

Then her claws dug into his chest as a loud cry escaped her, and she moved her hips as fast as she could when her orgasm crashed over her. Her pussy swelled, nestling his girth within her until all she could feel was the head shoving against exactly where she needed for her pulsing release to be even stronger.

Her purple orbs wavered as her climax tightened her chest with tenderness. Now that she knew about them, she could perceive her tendrils clasping onto him tightly so he couldn't get away while she used his cock thoroughly, keeping him within her until she was done.

She didn't get a moment to breathe when her body finally stopped milking him.

With a deep growl, Jabez grabbed one of her antlers, yanked on it until her arms caved in, and wrapped his free arm around her torso to lock her chest to his. Then his hips thrust so fast from below she could do little more than squeak and fight against seizing breaths.

His fangs lanced deep into the muscle of her shoulder as he bit down hard, and Jabez snarled against her flesh as he pumped furiously. Shivers racked her body, and her orbs broke as intense pleasure made tears float from her.

She couldn't even muster up a scream when he forced another orgasm to grip her. Lungs ceasing, she clutched the bedding beneath them to hold onto something, anything, for dear life as her body felt like it was about to obliterate.

Her heartbeat raced so fast she feared it was threatening to burst, but she didn't care as her head lolled in the bliss weakening her. *So good. It feels so good.* Her claws tore into the mattress, ripping it to shreds, the pleasure bordering on pain as she orgasmed.

He unlatched his bite to release a deep, haunting groan. He gripped her arse to keep it from shunting away as he fucked into her as fast as he could from below.

"That's right," he grated against her neck. "Come all over my cock, Zylah. Fuck, you're squeezing me so tight."

Her insides trembled at his heavy voice right next to her ear, and her ethereal tears floated from her in heavier drops.

Even when her body grew lax, he didn't stop the speed of his thrusts, as if he wanted to send her hurtling into another climax. Needing to escape the intensity of it, Zylah fought against his strength so she could take over again.

She managed to push off, and he finally ceased pumping, although his hips continued to grind into her lightly as if he couldn't stop them from jerking.

But she'd liked the way he'd been able to pull so far out, so she leaned back until she was fully seated on him. She bounced up and down with her strong legs, rather than moving back and forth, and she instantly wanted to melt.

*"Nhnn,"* she moaned when she slammed down hard.

She placed her clawed fingertips on his thick, muscled abdomen for balance in case she accidentally fell. Her slick was everywhere, coating her thighs and his entire pelvis, making her a little self-conscious about the wet slapping and squelching noises coming from where they were joined.

His hands gripped her knees, like he didn't want to get in the way of what she was doing but wanted to hold her. His jaw flexed as his nose scrunched momentarily.

"I should have known you'd be so good at bouncing on me," he rumbled, his eyes riveted to where he was constantly disappearing inside of her, and his bottom lip slipped between two fangs like he was biting on it. One of his thumbs delicately slid underneath the gold chain around her waist. "Good bunny, keep bouncing your pussy around me until I come inside it."

Zylah shuddered in reaction to his unbidden words, finding them naughtier than she probably should. Then she observed his expression properly for the first time, and lustful tenderness pooled in her gut.

With his lips parted on quick huffs, he licked across his sharp fangs when it must have felt just right. His nose and cheek on one side crinkled tightly whenever he produced an excited, lustful groan or grunt. His eyes appeared deliriously heated, and they rolled back slightly before he fought to refocus and keep watching her bounce on him.

Whenever her pussy spasmed and squeezed him, his features would twist up and he'd bite one side of his bottom lip again just as he pulsated inside her. She noticed a small amount of blood forming around his fangs, but he didn't seem to care that he was hurting himself.

He looked really pretty right then, his red eyes watching her with greed and hunger. Zylah took in his black tapered horns and long white hair resting against the bed. His strong, masculine features looked so twisted with need that she just wanted to eat him up.

Considering how fast she was bouncing on him, her pussy was trying to do exactly that.

Her gaze drifted down to watch how his pectoral muscles and biceps flexed and twitched constantly. *He has a vein there,* she thought, when she noticed a thick vein in the vee of his groin, and she instantly longed to lick the swollen, throbbing line.

She adored how big his body was, how strong and broad it

was in comparison to her. She wanted to worship his muscles with her hands, to knead them and lick them, but she refused to change what she was doing.

Especially when his eyes darkened in pleasurable anguish and he moaned, "*Zylah.*"

His fangs clamped shut, and he gritted them until his jaw muscles popped and knotted, just as his eyes rolled back fully. He shut them, his long white eyelashes fluttering and twitching, and his head shot back. The thick veins in his neck popped as his back arched, his fangs and lips parting wide as a quiet roar shook out of him.

His palms slipped from her knees, up her thighs, and over her hips to grasp her backside firmly. He tried to shove her down and keep her there as his hips lifted and squashed their pelvises together.

Zylah fought him, moving her hips up and down on him to chase the orgasm that was so close she was already beginning to spasm around him. Liquid heat burst inside her, and she could feel his cock thickening repeatedly.

Zylah knew he was in the middle of coming within her, and her hip movements were torturing him, but she couldn't stop. Instead, her sight vanished as her pussy squeezed and quivered, crushing him, her orgasm cresting over her as her mind repeated, *He's coming. He's coming inside me.*

Knowing she was the one to make him do so was what sent her over the edge, and she let out a shallow cry as her body shivered above him. She refused to stop bouncing until it was over for her, even when she could tell he was finished. She was too wrapped up in her own pleasure, at the spine-trembling thought of his seed inside her, and how her orgasm gripped her hard and refused to let go.

She felt slicker inside, stickier – and hotter and tighter because of it.

He produced little groans, his hips jerking like her bucking was causing groin-deep aftershocks to assault him.

He was still so hard that when her own orgasm ended, she didn't cease. She wanted more, didn't want this feeling to end

– just like always.

*Mine. He's mine.* All of this was hers – she had his soul to prove it – and her heart wanted to burst at the knowledge.

"Shit. Stop, Zylah," he pleaded, darting up to sit and wrap his arms around her and forcibly hold her down. He even pinned her arms to her sides, stopping her from separating them when she tried.

She let out a whimper, and he slapped a hand down on her arse to shove her hips forward and tuck them together so she couldn't even subtly move them.

"I just came, and my head is swimming," he told her, grazing his fangs against the side of her breast. "If we go again straight away, I think I'll actually pass the fuck out this time."

"But you're still hard," she whined. She yanked on her arm, wishing he'd let her go.

"I shouldn't be. Whatever component is in your arousal tingles and keeps me erect. It also makes me cum really hard."

He held her tightly as he panted against her. After trying to no avail to keep moving her hips, she gave up. Only then did he loosen his arms so she could free her own, and Zylah gave a sulky whimper.

"Don't be like that," he whispered gently.

He lifted her slightly and made room so he could cross his legs before settling her back down on his cock until he was seated deep. He slid his head forward until his forehead was buried against the short fur covering her sternum.

"Let's just stay like this. I'd like to hold you for a little while."

Zylah grumbled, and the urge to smack the top of his head struck her, but it quickly died when he nuzzled his face between her breasts. His arms also repositioned so he was holding her midsection in a tight cuddle, and she could almost feel the contentment radiating from him.

She gave in and slipped her arms around his head to hug him back, and her breasts pressed into the sides of his face more firmly.

Her voice was soft, although croaked, as she whispered,

"You do like holding me like this."

She liked it too. She found it lovely.

"Yeah, I know." She heard a grumbling pout in his voice and wished she could see it. He nuzzled harder, taking in a deep breath as if he was drawing in her scent, and his body grew even more lax than before. "If you promise not to think differently of me, I'll tell you why."

"Differently?" she asked, unsure of what he meant. "Like... badly?"

A sigh caressed her chest. "Never mind."

"No. I want to know," she pleaded, and immediately panicked when he shook his head. "You cannot say something like that and not tell me!"

"The moment I said it, I wanted to take it back. I'm actually not proud of it."

"Please, Jabez?" she whispered, hoping softening her voice would be more convincing. When that didn't work, she gripped the end of one of his horns and tugged to make him look up at her.

He gave her a half-hearted glare, his eyes hardening, only for them to gentle an instant later.

"Fine," he grumbled, shoving his head forward against her as if to hide it. He was silent for a moment, his muscles tense with restraint, before he let out a growl that ended in a defeated expire. "It makes me feel... safe. I've never truly felt that way."

*I make him feel safe?* Despite how saddening she found his admission, she couldn't help the way fluffy lightness sprouted in her heart. Her purple orbs shifted to bright pink, and her arms squeezed him in adoration.

Her tail swayed behind her, and he stroked his fingers through it – incidentally causing her insides to flutter wildly around him, and they both let out a raspy breath.

"I think it's due to how I can feel and hear your heartbeat," he mumbled against her, and she wondered if he was continuing due to her giddy reaction. "You also feel nice to hold, and I can take in your scent coming directly off of you. I've never allowed another to hold me like this. I've never trusted anyone else because it leaves my back vulnerable and I can't see."

Her orbs brightened in their pink hue, and her chest ached with such a wonderful tenderness that her orbs threatened to waver. She didn't mean to whine, but her affection for him became so powerful in that moment that it bordered on pain.

That was until he slapped one of her cheeks when he went to hold her arse and purposefully ground her pussy around his cock. "It also feels remarkably more intimate with me inside you like this. I like you cock-warming me."

Seeing as he'd likely said that as a way to escape the conversation, Zylah didn't reply. Instead, she hugged his head tighter, causing her breasts to squeeze the sides of his face, and nuzzled the side of her snout against the top of his head.

"You can cuddle me this way any time you like," she said, basking in this sweet moment that *he* instigated.

# THIRTY-SEVEN

Lying on his side with a sleeping female in his arms, Jabez reluctantly moved his face away from between her breasts to glare at the oncoming light.

Dawn was finally breaking across the horizon, casting an eye-piercing beam of sunlight into the room. The sky itself turned aqua as the first sun of Nyl'theria, the green one named Pire, mixed with the lightening blue sky. The sky would change colour depending on the season and by which sun, or suns, were closest.

He lifted his hand to touch the refracting ray on the wall above their heads, only to wince and pull away. *They lock away my magic behind an enchantment, but put me in a room that's likely to kill me if I don't cover myself.*

Then again, they'd warned him of this only possible alternative to the prison cells, and he'd agreed. There had been nowhere else to put them, and the council only allowed this so long as he submitted and let them put these golden bracers on his wrists.

He noticed the way they shimmered as they nullified his magic when he tried to cast a sun barrier against his skin. The mana flow tingled, but nothing happened.

*The fact they haven't learned how to do this kind of spell surprises me.* They had Demons in their midst, yet they weren't protecting them fully.

Then again, it wasn't hard to stay in the shade, so long as

the person wasn't an idiot.

He let his arm fall and curled it around Zylah, pulling her soft body closer so he could rest his tired eyes. *I still haven't slept.* Something had been weighing on him since their arrival in the city. It had grown heavier in the many following hours, but his mind refused to quieten to let him sleep.

A curse that had been strangling him his entire life.

Had he not been injured and expended such energy in order to heal himself, it may not feel so pressing. Still, closing his eyes for a little while and holding her had relieved some of the pressure behind his aching, squinting eyelids. He could only imagine how bruised the inner corners of the flesh beneath his eyes appeared.

As much as he would have liked to fuck her relentlessly in the confines of this room, unsure when they'd have the freedom to do so safely again, he hadn't been able to muster the strength for a second round, let alone more. He was just too tired, and his heart had been throbbing in his chest. He'd managed to convince her to let them cuddle while lying down, and he removed his cock from her to stop her trying to wiggle on it.

After he caressed her back, feeling how few protruding vertebrae she had, she'd quickly fallen asleep. It gave him time to think and reflect without her noticing him retreating into his mind.

As resistant as he'd been about being intimate, at the time truly doubting he'd be able to get his dick up, he was thankful Zylah had pushed for it.

Jabez knew the distraction had been needed. He'd been able to sense his mind slipping into unfiltered chaos. He'd been losing his sense of self, unable to stop reflecting on his life, his past, his mistakes, and how it'd all led to this place where he felt so damn lost. He'd been reeling from the moment he walked through those hallowed gates of false promises.

He'd been sinking into the muck of depression.

Every time he'd shaken his thoughts and tried to refocus them back on figuring out a solution and mapping out the course of their next actions, where they would go or what they would do, they kept going back to his behaviour within the conference chamber. He could only imagine how pathetic he'd appeared, slumped over on his knees with his arms bound behind his back, *crying* like a damn child.

He hadn't cried since the day he left Nyl'theria at seventeen, and he hated that he'd been harbouring such torment, only to release it in front of those particular people. They were his enemies and were the cause of his suffering to begin with.

He couldn't believe just the possibility of being returned to the place he'd been locked away had so easily broken him under the weight of his fear. He'd once vowed that he'd never feel that way again.

That being said, he also vowed he'd never return here without an army.

He'd also been battling with the way he tried to think of a solution that meant they could remain here, just so Zylah's safety was guaranteed. He didn't care for his own wellbeing – he was used to being amidst destruction and violence – but he didn't want that for her.

Yet he'd foolishly tied her to him, and he'd felt like a horrible anchor for her because of it. It was his fault that they'd be turned away, and she'd suffer as a result.

And after experiencing her in agonising pain, he knew he couldn't bear it again. The anxiety, the grief, the regret, and the self-loathing had been too much for him to swallow. It'd been too thick and hard for him to gnaw his fangs through without shattering them.

That was even before she became his mate.

For a moment, he'd regretted giving her his soul because it meant *she* was stuck with *him*. Not quite the self-loathing realisation he'd wanted to come to right after committing to her.

So, he'd been giving up. His vengeance and need for retribution had been slipping through the cracks of his fingers, and it brought on a sense of loss. He could feel himself withering away on the inside, no longer knowing who he was supposed to be or what he was supposed to do without his goal driving him forward.

Jabez did not know himself outside of his idealistic goal.

His eyes cracked open so he could lazily stare at Zylah's fur-covered sternum. *She'll never understand what she did for me.*

He'd needed her to wake him from his stupor before it was too late. He'd needed her to be her sweet, cute, and arousing self, completely ignorant and unaware of how broken he'd been inside. Her actions may have been the opposite of what most would consider appropriate for someone suffering within the depths of their misery, but it'd been perfect for him.

He didn't know how to talk about his innermost thoughts, especially with her, as he didn't wish to burden her with them. Giving him a sympathetic hug would have done little more than offer him warmth as he dwelled in those same thoughts, and it may have actually worsened them. He imagined coddling him like a child would've only reminded him of the motherly affection he'd been torn from. After that, the only thing he'd had to embrace him all his life was the cold, numbing darkness.

No, he'd needed lust.

Using his body was the only way he knew how to communicate with another, whether it be sexually or violently.

She'd also stopped him from fucking into her with feral aggression as he tried to pound his anger and frustration into someone who didn't deserve it. He could only imagine the shame that would have crested over him afterwards had he been the one in control and let his agony lead their intimacy. Instead, she'd taken him her way, forcing him beneath her and being *mostly* in control.

Her beginning attempts had been clumsy, but he'd found them arousing all the same. She'd made him laugh when he doubted anyone else could have, and watching her fumble had been winsome. It reminded him of all the parts he liked about her gentle but curious personality, and how he could easily grow fascinated by the way she figured things out on her own.

And watching her explore herself for the first time... even now, a desirous shudder rippled down his spine.

All this had allowed him to settle gently into their intimacy, while his thoughts and lingering pain dissolved until all he could think about and feel was her. Until his heart realigned as she became the focal point of his feelings and reminded him of *why* he'd been so desperate to bring them here. Not for himself, but for her.

She also showed him that he now had a mate he could lean on. Someone who twisted him up inside in so many different ways that the unpredictability and mayhem of them often left him raw. Someone who was soft where he was jagged, sweet where he was nasty, and sensual when he was indifferent.

Someone who, from this day forward, could be his task.

He had nothing else to hold onto. If he couldn't bear to throw her into the violence of his vendetta, then she would need to be what drove him forward without it. He would have to find his happiness within her, as he knew there was nothing else that was going to give it to him.

At least... not in this wretched city.

Without knowing it, Zylah had become his centre.

He was surprised by how much that didn't bother him. In the past, the thought of a female being the cause and result of all his next choices had been abhorrent to him. He hadn't wanted anyone to fill the void in his chest because it meant letting go of who he was.

This female, his own personal bunny, was just cute enough that he didn't mind.

It meant he now had to make choices he was uncertain about, but he was starting to accept them. Enough so that he gingerly sat up without disturbing her and shifted off the bed so he could stand.

Grimacing in disdain at her blood-soaked dress, he searched quietly for his pants. He yanked them up his legs and tied them around his waist while trying his hardest to avoid the beam of sunlight cutting across the room.

He should have known she'd sense that he abandoned her, since she groaned and shifted on the bed. *I should've covered us with the blanket.* Regardless, when her orbs flickered open to teal, informing him that she was awake, he knelt behind her and placed an arm on either side of her torso.

Jabez leaned down to her and brushed his lips against her bony jaw. "Go back to sleep, Zylah. I'll return shortly."

She turned a little and cupped the side of his face. "Where are you going?"

"To speak with the councilmembers." He kissed her cheek, her brow, and then the side of her snout. "Don't worry. I won't be long, and everything will be fine, I promise. Stay here. Rest."

Then he pushed off and walked to the exit, grumbling when she went to sit up despite what he'd said. He knocked on the door, and the guard on the other side cracked it open so they could speak. Jabez wondered if he heard their moans earlier, but decided he didn't give a shit either way.

"Take me to the conference chamber," Jabez *gently* demanded.

"They're still discussing—"

"I'm aware," he cut in. "However, I have new information I wish to share that may sway their decision."

Showing he held no ill intention, Jabez turned and folded his arms behind his back in offering. It didn't take long for the guard to make his decision. He stepped into the doorway to remove the golden cuffs from Jabez's wrists, then replaced them with the proper prisoner bindings, which dampened both his strength and his magical capabilities.

"Jabez, why are you leaving without me?" Zylah asked while sitting up on the bed and kicking her legs to the side like she was about to get up.

He looked away when her orbs shifted to blue, although was thankful the door would be shielding her nudity from the guard's view.

"There's no need for you to come. You won't understand anything, and I'd rather you sleep more."

When he offered the best reassuring smile he could muster, she settled back onto the bed with a nervous chitter.

Jabez then turned and exited the room. There were multiple soldiers lining the hall, and he figured they'd increased their security here in case he managed to escape. The guard who bound his arms spoke to a fellow soldier further down the hallway, explaining what Jabez wanted, and they exchanged him so the original man could return to his post by the door.

The soldier was a *Delysian* female this time, who was quick to hold the strap between his clasped elbows and wrists to ensure he couldn't run away easily. Her companion fell in line in front of him, and they led him through the central-tree palace together.

A few more soldiers along the way noticed and joined them, creating a thin barrier between him and the many people who were now awake due to the first sun's rising. They helped him avoid the sunlight peeking through misshapen branch windows, but he figured that was the Delysian soldier just trying to protect herself as much as him.

Civilians stared as they passed them, likely curious about who he was and why he was being led through the hallways. He doubted any of them knew of his arrival, especially since they lacked fear in their gazes or scents.

Most were Elysians in well-tailored, flowing outfits, each of them wearing different colours and styles. Many of the males were either topless or wearing intricate singlets that crossed over their torsos and tied at their waists. Some women were fully covered except for their arms due to the heat, while others wore what could only be considered loose strapping to hide their breasts and privates.

With perpetual summer being a constant, the need for heavy clothing or the desire to cover up was low. There was a reason the Elysians had used magic to grow this tree to its daunting size: they required shade or they'd all incinerate over time from the heat.

It didn't take his entourage long to enter the hallway of the conference chamber, and he could already see the large double doors at the other end.

When they were only a few metres from the entrance, the door suddenly opened for them. His brows furrowed in concern. He'd essentially given no notice, so they should have remained shut until the guards around him notified those inside of his desire to speak with them.

When a tall, daunting being stepped through the doorway, he realised it'd been unintentional and a mere coincidence.

His feet immediately halted, incidentally causing the female Delysian soldier to smack into him and make him stumble forward. His upper lip twisted in shock, as his jaw fell until it threatened to unhinge and fucking fall off.

"Merikh?" he grated out, barely believing that his old friend stood before him.

The large Mavka appeared unfazed as he stomped across the obsidian floor towards him, although his naturally red orbs did brighten menacingly in apparent anger at seeing him.

Standing two inches taller than Jabez's own six-foot-nine height, the bear-skulled, bull-horned Mavka looked exactly how he had only a few Earth months ago. Well, his rounded, muscular gut did, as did the short black fur covering him.

However, he now wore a pair of black pants that had been tied around his knees. It left his calves free for white, armoured guards to be strapped over them protectively, ensuring he didn't hurt others with his echidna quills. More intricate, segmented guards covered his bare forearms, with a large one strapped underneath the silky red singlet covering his torso. The singlet bore a silver strip where it crossed over his chest to be tied at his side.

His bull tail flicked back and forth, and the tuft of fur on the end of it curled.

Before Jabez could even begin questioning Merikh with how he came to be here in the Elven city, realisation dawned.

"It was you!" he growled out, snapping his fangs at him. "You're the one who's been feeding them information about Earth, you jerk of a Mavka."

The burly male burst out in a joyful chuckle, stopped barely a metre from him, and folded his arms. "Absolutely."

"Do you have any idea what you've fucking done?"

Anger clutched his gut, and he stomped down the hallway, alerting his guards, who suddenly chased after him.

Whatever he'd told the synedrus council meant they knew all about Jabez's escapades and actions. That information had been vital in ensuring the councilmembers were swayed to likely *not* let them stay in the city. Had they been uninformed, they wouldn't be aware of his callous bloodshed and the depths of his hatred!

Sure, he figured Merikh didn't know Jabez would try to enter Lezekos while it wasn't in flames, but *still*.

It also meant that these people were aware of Merikh's kind and had made it impossible for him to enter with an injured Zylah without bonding to her. He still didn't regret it, but he would have liked to make that choice when he wasn't under duress. By the cursed light, he would've liked to have the option to be lame and make it *romantic*.

"I don't really give a shit, if I'm being honest," Merikh chuckled back.

His fangs vibrated as he produced a deep growl, knowing the big fucker was only full of mirth because he wasn't the one tied in restraints. Considering the bear-skulled Mavka was usually bull-headed and had a temper that was meaner and more violent than Jabez's own, had their roles been reversed, Merikh would have tried to eat him by now.

And had Jabez not been restrained, he likely wouldn't be so overconfident.

"So this is where you ran off to?" Jabez asked, shaking his head in disbelief. "How'd you even *get* here?"

"I had a pretty fairy help me escape without your help," Merikh answered, tilting his head in a way that could only be condescending. "My bride is something you hate the most. I found that rather humorous when I thought about it. I also think you'd be disgusted to discover just *who* I've been shoving my cock into each day here – repeatedly, may I add."

Jabez's eyes flicked up to the bright-blue flaming soul

between his tall bull horns. Other than the fact it had long, coily hair and pointed ears, nothing else about it was recognisable.

He shook his head, his lips twisting in disgust – regardless of who it was – before they softened. His brows narrowed.

"I don't understand. You were my fucking friend. Why would you feed them information *knowing* how much I hated them?"

Any humour in Merikh's voice died, and his orbs deepened to crimson as he bit out a snarl. "I haven't been your friend for a *long* time, Jabez. You made sure of it."

He scoffed at that, especially as he doubted that was true. He knew this Mavka more than anyone else. After their last interaction on Earth, Jabez knew if it hadn't been for the potential of a bride and a new life, Merikh would have returned to his side. Likely with a few conditions, but the temptation to rekindle their friendship had been easily recognisable in his body language.

Sure, Jabez *probably* shouldn't have threatened his siblings, but he also knew Merikh didn't give a damn about them – only that they were safe. Jabez had been attempting, in his own way, to show he had no intention of going after them anymore. He also hadn't wanted to give away anything about his emotions, nor his regrets, unsure if he'd actually been able to trust his past companion due to old wounds.

Obviously done with the conversation, Merikh stepped to the side to go around him. Jabez glared at him, and it only deepened when the Mavka slowed to place his hand on his shoulder.

"I want you to know," Merikh started quietly, his tone dark and deep as he leaned his head down to Jabez's level, "I advocated for your *removal* from the city."

Merikh purposefully sunk his razor-sharp claws into the bare flesh around his shoulder until they cut through muscle, and then he shoved Jabez forward. *Bastard!* He hissed through gritted fangs as warm blood quickly rose to the surface. Of course Merikh had to inflict a wound on him like the violent asshole he was.

"I'm trying to protect one of your kind by bringing her into the city," Jabez told him, surprised Merikh would go out of his way to ensure another of his kind was in danger.

"Heard you bonded with a Mavka – a female, no less. You can bet I was surprised to learn that." Without turning to look at Jabez, he shrugged with one hand. "It's her fault for being an idiot for choosing you as a bride. You reap what you sow, Jabez. You have no one else to blame but yourself."

"I'll remember this," Jabez warned.

A malicious grin curled his lips when Merikh waved goodbye with the back of his hand. *If they allow us into the city, one of the first things I'll do is knee you in the seam.* And considering what he planned to reveal in that chamber, the chances of them staying were much more likely.

*He's forgotten how cunning I can be.* He shouldn't have taunted Jabez so much. *You reap what you sow, Merikh.*

He spun around, and incidentally spooked the soldiers who'd been gawking at them. They didn't know any of the English they'd spoken. He nodded and walked towards the doors, then waited for them to announce him.

Jabez chuckled quietly to himself when the doors creaked open. *I must admit, arguing with him did give me the energy I was lacking.* His confidence had renewed, as did his normal vitality. Nothing could stoke his inner flames quicker than anger.

When he entered the conference chamber, he noted the unease in all the faces of the councilmembers. Considering he was walking in right after they interrogated Merikh, he doubted they were feeling trustful or inclined to give him what he wanted.

But the tides of a mental battle could swiftly change, and he knew he'd be victorious this time.

Jabez quickly took his place on the lower platform in a kneeling position, then waited for the guard to tether him to the ground and leave. Surprisingly, they didn't this time, but that may be because he'd shown he *could* be compliant. Once the doors shut and it was just him and the council, he lifted his head, offered them all a dull gaze, and waited for them to start the meeting.

"We have not yet made our decision, Jabeziryth," Ulric quickly spat out while leaning against his golden table. "And after what we've just heard, we'll absolutely need adequate time to discuss the concerning matters pertaining to your time on Earth."

"What you heard from Merikh will be completely irrelevant," Jabez answered, saturating his voice with conviction. "My past is violent, and the things I've done unforgivable, disgusting, and deplorable." He had to stifle the urge to grin in satisfaction, simply because toying with them was actually rather *fun*. "You *will* overlook them after this conversation."

Ulric laughed, leaned back in his chair, and stroked his short beard. "That's doubtful. Nothing you say will sway those of us who are against your admittance, and I'm sure those who were unsure now lean towards your removal."

"Why have you returned?" asked Teyen, a female Delysian who had been utterly silent last time.

He dipped his head to the right to take in the small, clay-red horns that shot forward from her forehead. Her canine fangs were large, but the rest of her teeth were flat like most Elvish, yet she lacked the white hair of their kind. Her brown bob swayed around her chin as she glanced at the other members.

"This city has stood for over a century," Jabez started, bringing his gaze forward so he could look upon the random councilmember directly in front of him. He'd already forgotten their name. "Before I was locked away, I overheard my mother and stepfather speak of the dwindling power supply. The mana stones are running out of energy, and no matter how much of our own energy we pour into them, if they are unable to hold mana anymore, there is nothing we can do."

"We didn't ask for a history lesson, nor do we need someone like you to inform us of what we already know regarding the state of the city *we* govern," Ulric retorted loudly, then scoffed.

Jabez's lips curled knowingly. "How is the mana stone that protects the city?" He tilted his head just as the man's features fell. "How many years does it have left? You don't know, do you? But I'm guessing it's beginning to dim."

"What of it?" Cleth stated, leaning their arms upon the table while clasping their hands. "If you're here to find out about our defences, then we'll need to ask you to leave."

"I can get you a new mana stone. The right kind, and a large one that can power the protective dome for just as long, if not longer."

"How do you suppose you'll do that?" Ulric sneered, before waving his hand to the right and almost smacking his seating partner in the face. "There are scores of Demons out there, and the mines are full of nests."

Jabez's eyes crinkled in humour. "I thought you spoke to Merikh," he stated, realising the bull-horned Mavka actually made this much easier and likely more convincing. "I'm sure he told you of my ability to teleport. I can go anywhere whenever I want."

"That is a forbidden spell," Laele muttered, her aged tone hinting at deep concern.

"Yes, but only because of the danger it presents to its user," he answered, tilting his face in her direction. "Most die due to materialising inside a tree, the ground, or even another person. I've perfected it over the years to the point I'm now able to take two people with me safely, and I've already been inside multiple mines within Nyl'theria. I can teleport in and out in very little time, unscathed. With someone able to watch my back, mining a stone the size you require would be easy with my increased strength and speed in comparison to a normal Elysian."

"Are you saying you're willing to face such danger just to ensure your approval to stay in the city?" Raewyn, the sobbing woman from earlier, asked.

His gaze flicked to her, and he hardened his tone. "Yes,

that's one of the things I am offering."

"And you expect us to *trust* that you won't attempt to make contact and scheme with those outside these walls? We'd be fools to allow such a thing," Ulric argued. "I can already foresee you attempting to build your army right beneath our noses."

"By the holy maiden, *you* are fucking obnoxious," Jabez blurted out with a cringe of disgust, using *their* form of a godly curse. "Has anyone told you to shut your mouth?" He looked at the other councilmembers with a confused shake of his head. "Does he usually prattle on and argue about everything like an ill-tempered child?"

Oddly enough, Raewyn was the one to choke out a singular laugh before covering her lips with a fist and masking it with a cough. Mericato, on the other hand, held his throat to stop himself from laughing, before keeling forward with a hiss when pain must have struck his scarred throat.

Ulric shoved up from his table to stand and slammed his hands down on it. "How dare you! I am a respected–"

"A wise man listens before he speaks," Jabez stated over the top of him. "As I said, this is merely *one* of the things I'm offering. I've already explained that my mate is the reason I wish to enter this horrid city, and I will do what is necessary to ensure her safety. I'm even willing to let my justified anger go. At least *I* am attempting to make amends."

He was even willing to be subservient if need be. He had nothing else to lose, and his pride would never falter no matter what he did for them, so long as they treated his tantalising mate well.

Seething, Ulric sat his arse down and folded his arms. "Get on with it then."

"You are behaving much more calmly now," Zerik commented.

Jabez smiled to no one at that. "You'll be surprised how a little rest and a quick fuck can soothe me."

The old man choked in surprise, while a few others gasped.

Considering the man was cupping his scarred throat once

more, Jabez could tell Mericato was attempting to stop himself from laughing again. He signed when his coughing eased, and this time Cleth translated on his behalf.

"At least he's honest."

"I've been nothing but honest since I arrived in this city," Jabez stated, looking down at the ground to find that they'd forgotten to power the truth-speaking spell.

*They trust me more than they did last time.* It likely wasn't much, but enough to not use the spell or tether him to the ground. That should work in his favour.

"My second offer is that I will give you the answer my mother sought all those years ago."

His voice echoed in the chamber as complete silence descended upon them. The weight of what he just said was heavy, not just for them, but for him as well. But if sharing his secret was the answer to his and Zylah's admittance, then so be it.

Raewyn was the one to break the silence. She stood with one of her hands pressed against the surface of her table for support. With her sightless eyes wide, she licked at her lips nervously.

"Are you... are you saying you found the way to aid the Demons in reaching full completion?"

"Yes," he answered, cocking a brow at the excitement in her tone. "However, I will only share this knowledge with three restrictions. Firstly, only the person who took over my mother's work will be allowed to know about it. I understand this may make the other councilmembers uncomfortable, but I ask that you have faith I have good reason. Due to the nature of it, I have kept this secret from the moment I discovered it and have not assisted any Demons in their completion. It's dangerous."

"You are asking that we are kept in the dark re–"

Raewyn cut Ulric a glare in his general direction to quieten him before leaning forward. "What are your other restrictions?"

"Only I will volunteer for the role. I refuse to allow others to be brought into this, and the fact that my mate has made me deathless ensures this won't have lasting effects." When no one disagreed with that notion, he let his gaze dull to indifference. "And, lastly, my mother must never know the answer."

Raewyn flattened her lips, obviously upset by his third restriction.

"Are you saying you want us to withhold from her the reason she brought you into this world?" Laele muttered quietly. "Even after everything she's done and lost, you would be so callous as to not answer her life's work?"

"The fact that my conception was nothing but a tool to further her science means I want her to die never knowing, while understanding that *we* have that answer. I want her to feel regret when she burns on her funeral pyre and greets her death feeling as empty as I have my entire life."

Raewyn's features twisted into dismay. Losing her enthusiasm, she sat back down in her chair slowly, with a forlorn expression on her face. Even her pointed ears drooped heavily.

"*If* we allow you to remain in the city, we can only fully adhere to two of those restrictions," Cleth stated, their eyes drifting to the upset woman. "Raewyn is the one who took over your mother's work, and as you can see, she is vision impaired. Her assistant will be required to be well informed in order to aid her."

*Ah, so that's why she was so excited.* Her reaction made much more sense now.

"So long as it remains confidential, I have no problem with her assistant knowing in order to help her," he answered.

"I must admit, what you've stated here this morning is rather convincing," Teyen commented with her hand cupping her chin. "No wonder you walked in so confidently."

"I'm not done. I ask that you hear me out fully before rejecting it." He shot Ulric a death glare, and the bearded man rolled his eyes before turning his face to the side with a childish sneer. "I'm unsure if you're aware of the devastation that is happening outside your walls, but the Demons have hunted most animals to extinction. They are starving and have resorted to eating each other, regardless of whether they have fully achieved completion or not."

"We are aware," Teyen stated, her red eyes narrowing on him.

"I scented animals within the city when I was brought through it, and I'm guessing the herds you tended when I was a child in order to preserve those creatures from extinction are now being used as food for the Delysians within the city."

There was no other explanation as to how the Demons here were able to live peacefully to the point that three of them sat in this very room as part of their governing system. After he left, the Elysians figured out they were starving the Demons of the nutrition they needed in order to survive.

"I ask that you consider building a second city within the forest in order to save those who seek peace."

In the corner of his eye, he watched as Ulric opened his stupid mouth. He promptly shut it when Jabez turned his face to him and raised a brow.

"If you do this, the Demons can begin to build a civilised society that has agriculture, food, and proper housing. It will lead to the decline of violence outside these walls. The potential to take back Nyl'theria through a means of peace will slowly allow Elysians to flourish. I'm sure Merikh spoke of the village of Demons, Spiral Haven, on Earth. I grew that place to do exactly that, and with the proper systems in place and adhered to with the help of soldiers and guards, it is entirely possible. Spiral Haven is already proof of that. Demons also have little issue with killing each other, and they can continue to feed and help those close to completion by eating lesser Demons until there are no wild ones left."

Jabez respectfully went quiet when Mericato began to sign with his hands. Oddly enough, after Jabez's last visit to this chamber, and with how the man had laughed at his brash honesty upon his return to it, his feelings of hatred towards him had... lessened.

"How are we to know the Demons won't try to build an army through this second city and attempt to destroy us?"

"You don't," Jabez stated truthfully. "But are you willing to give up the potential of peace and the possibility of building an alliance with them? This city can only last so long, and there were already housing issues when I was a child. I wasn't ignorant of that fact. It may take another hundred years for them to remove the less-developed Demons from the realm, but isn't the chance to one day be able to walk through the forests of Nyl'theria without fear worth it?"

"How would we do this?" Silveria's soft and angelic voice rang out.

"Currently, the village that took the last stance in Nyl'theria is occupied by a rather violent tribe of Demons. The protective dome podium still stands, and I can find a more adequate stone to power it like I can for Lezekos City. If we take over the village, we can slowly rebuild it and fill it with those who wish for a more peaceful way of life. Word will spread, and they will have to screen those wishing to enter like you already do here. Your truth spell will allow them to weed out those who are intending to enter under falsities, and I guarantee you, by doing this, the Demons will feel gratitude for your aid. You've already brought many into your city, and you understand that they seek a new, safer way of life. If you trust the Delysians you allow here, then there is no reason you can't trust the Demons outside these walls who *will* have good intentions."

As much as Jabez's goal had spearheaded him through life, the nagging desire to help his fellow Demons had always sat in the back of his mind. Just because he had to give up his vendetta, didn't mean he had to give up on the idea of helping them.

Although this would be a much more peaceful and political way to achieve that goal, he was hoping doing this could count towards his penance for all he'd done. He'd never seek forgiveness, but he surely could begin to make up for what he'd done in the past.

Rather than remaining a violent plague upon the world, he

could become a healing force instead. *Zylah is the reason I realised this.* She wanted to be good, and he was finding that naïve morality quite infectious.

"You make a very convincing argument," someone behind him stated, and he had a feeling it was one of the other Delysians within the councilmembers. "It's true there are other Demons who seek peace, and many of us Delysians have always wished they would shed their fear of the unknown and attempt to enter the city as we have. I've already been considering such an endeavour, but travelling through the forests has always been dangerous. Your ability to teleport lessens that danger, but having to place our trust in strangers is still concerning."

Jabez gave a hum, their concerns making him reflect on a possible solution.

"Actually, now that I think about it... if you intend to do this, I suggest lowering Weldir's ward to allow some of those who occupy Spiral Haven to relocate and ensure the start of the new village."

"We are unable to do that," Zerik stated loudly. "What Weldir does to protect us from the thousands of Demons who have gone through his many portals is one of the reasons we've survived the last twenty-one years. You are right, our protective dome is currently weak, and if more Demons come to attack us, it won't be long before it breaks."

Jabez sucked in a deep, calming breath before releasing it. *How little they know.*

"I'm not saying lower them all. I'm saying allow those occupying Spiral Haven to come through and then ask him to reinstate it. The laws and rules I placed on that village were cleverly crafted and have been tried and tested. *They* will also govern and teach the Demons not used to civilised society, which would quicken the process."

"We would have to trust Weldir would do that," Zerik argued. "We have no idea as to why he has continued to keep his wards in place, since he likely feels abandoned by his mother and the other remaining gods. We have no idea of his intentions. If he chooses to be a malevolent demigod, we may not survive him and his growing power."

Jabez chuckled and lifted his eyes to the ceiling. "Weldir has no desire for destruction," he informed them confidently. "If he did, we would have joined forces many years ago and already razed this city to the ground. He rejected the notion, and his mate has made it known he has no intention of harming you. You fear a demigod who seeks nothing but acceptance from the Gilded Maiden."

"You have spoken with him?" Cleth asked, their lips flattening and their brows narrowing at him.

Jabez lowered his gaze to them just in time to see their disgruntled expression.

"No, but his mate and I have spoken under temporary truces many times. He listens and speaks through her when he can."

Many of the councilmembers cast each other wary glances, as silence descended upon them. A few shuffled in their seats, and he allowed them time to digest everything he'd said while he knelt before them.

"You have given us much to think about," Silveria stated quietly. "You understand that it will take time for us to discuss all this?"

"I do. Considering you're allowing us to stay where we are, I see no issue with awaiting your answer, no matter how long it takes." Then he paused, wondering if he should speak his request before shrugging. There was no harm in trying – all they could do was reject it. "I do ask that you forgo the magic-dampening bracers in the meantime, unless you wish for all of this to be a pointless conversation because I've gone insane from burning alive multiple times."

He rolled his eyes as he thought, *I've almost done that one too many times than I can say I'm truly comfortable with.*

The Witch Owl had now, officially, set him alight twice. He'd also been stuck under Earth's sun with little escape except for sparse shade in the distance.

He didn't really wish to burn to a crisp in front of Zylah

either. She'd bring him back to life through her Mavka bond, only to watch him disintegrate again.

Not really how he'd like to spend his time waiting.

"You're a very different man than when you walked in here mere hours ago," Laele commented. "I'm sure many of us didn't expect such intellectual and well thought out plans from you."

He quirked his lips in humour, knowing he had Zylah to thank for that.

"Last time I was fuelled by my anger, and my emotions were unsettled because I carried Zylah within the city to be healed. I was given little time to calm before I was brought before you." His ears twitched, and he grinned towards the ground. "I'm actually a very cunning man, and I'm quite strategic when given time to assess. You should have already summarised that, considering I've lived so long *despite* everything I have done. There was a reason I was called King Jabez on Earth and managed to retain that title the entire time without being killed or usurped."

"Do you understand that we'll never accept you as a councilmember, so if you seek such power again, you'll never achieve it?"

A laugh burst from him. "I have absolutely no interest in governing the city. I never did. I've always wanted nothing more than to live in the home I'd been born into, without being looked at like I was a disgusting piece of vermin."

A few members grunted or lowered their gazes at his brash words, but he refused to withhold how he felt.

"If you have nothing else to share, we'll call the guards in to take you back to your room," someone from the left stated.

Jabez nodded and stood, showing them he was done.

He was quickly removed from the conference chamber, and he was glad to hear that they told the guards to remove the restriction of his magic use. The walk back through the hallways was much easier due to the weight lifted off his shoulders, and his feet moved fast to return to his mate.

The moment he was brought inside his room, Jabez zeroed

his eyes in on Zylah sitting on the bed, waiting for him. They removed the bindings from his arms, and he immediately cast a sun barrier to shield his body.

The door closed, and Jabez hastily crossed the spacious room when she went to stand. He tackled his female to the soft mattress before she could even get a step away from it, and she let out a surprised scream. She was still naked, warm from sitting in the sun, and smelt like hot jasmine and violets as he wrapped his strong arms around her narrow waist.

Nuzzling the fuck out of her, he squeezed her so tightly she gave a cute squeak.

"Did you fall back asleep?" he asked, burying his face against the crook of her neck when he turned them to their sides.

"No," she answered, hugging him in return. She rubbed the side of her snout against his hair and horns as if she missed him in the short time he was away. "I couldn't while you were gone."

"Then rest with me now." He dug his elbow into the bed and dragged them higher until they both had a pillow to lie on. "I think I'll finally be able to sleep."

"Is everything okay now?"

He shrugged. "No idea, but I've done all I can."

Seeming to accept his answer, she went quiet as she deepened their embrace, and Jabez's eyes closed. He soaked in the sound of her heartbeat, the feel of her soft body against his, and let her scent lull and soothe him like it always did.

Sleep swept him under in moments, and for once, it was tranquil.

# THIRTY-EIGHT

*He's been asleep for a long time,* Zylah thought, as she sat down on the edge of the bed and turned to the male laying on his side in the very middle.

She brushed the back of her knuckles up the side of his face before lifting them to the centre of his forehead to lightly caress his temple. Jabez's ear twitched when she tucked loose strands of hair behind its pointed length so she could better see him. She also gingerly untangled the strands wrapped around his segmented, tapered horn.

With a flat pillow under his head, one of his arms was beneath the pillow she'd been lying on earlier. The other was curled up in front of his chest from where she'd gently placed it earlier. She'd gotten up to look out the window and distract herself from this long wait.

The wait wasn't truly that long, but it'd been a few hours, and he usually didn't sleep like this. The fact she was also able to touch him without waking him was also strange.

*His eyelashes really are silvery.* In the sunlight currently showering over him, they looked like sparkling moth wings. She lightly stroked her claw over their soft lengths and his eye twitched.

*Such a pretty male.* She gazed at his handsome brown face, admiring the graceful arcs of his brows, his smooth, nearly flawless cheek, the straight line of his nose, and even the ball at his throat. She brushed the pad of her thumb over his parted full lips and accidentally revealed the sharp points of his fangs.

Zylah was happy to see him finally resting like this. She wondered if her touch didn't wake him because, somewhere deep within his sleeping conscience, he could sense it was her and trusted he was safe. She wanted to believe that was the reason as she trailed her knuckles down his pulsing, calm jugular.

Her hand didn't go any lower, but she let her sight fall to his broad chest and how his bulging pectoral muscles squished together as he lay on his side. Then her focus drifted to the sets of chiselled muscles bulging against his abdomen before she followed the trail of silvery hair that started a path from his navel to his groin.

The circles, triangles, stars, and bands of runic symbols all over his body caught her focus, and she hoped one day he would explain what spell each of them represented.

*My pretty bride,* she thought with a silent giggle, squeezing her torso with her arms in joy. She'd learn in the future what he actually wanted her to call him, but for now, she was going with that.

*He's like the prickly rose I held in Spiral Haven.*

As much as he'd witnessed her bloom into the being she was, watering her with knowledge and care along the way, she knew he was beginning to flourish as well. Sometimes his petals withered, as if autumn had come. Other times, he was frozen and hidden away like in winter, but she hoped the rain of her affections, like spring returning, helped bring him back to life and regrow.

He was also mesmerising and delicate in his own way. The aroma of bergamot suited him. Sturdy like a tree, but he was also like a flower which could bear thorns. He was mean and cruel, but that didn't have to detract from his beauty so long as she held him just right.

*He is my enchanting thorn.* Her mesmerising Elvish-and-Demon bride.

Just as Zylah stroked the back of his shoulder, Jabez's parted fangs snapped shut to let out a half-hearted growl. It quietened quickly as his hand reached out to clasp her thigh before slipping off, like his unconscious reach had been expecting to throw the weight of his arm over her entire body.

Worried that if she continued to touch him, she'd disturb him from the sleep he obviously needed, so she left him be.

She pulled his soul from between her antlers to look at it again, as she had many times since she'd woken. She stroked the back of her index finger under its jaw, pleased that its body had returned.

His soul sat exactly how it had before and looked exactly the same. The only difference was the spiral of its blue-and-green flames rotated in the opposite direction as if it'd... *changed* in the smallest way. Its horns were still green, its long ears and hair blue, and she realised all the physical parts of him were differently coloured.

Those that were obviously Demon were green, while those that were Elvish were blue. Everywhere else, like its arms, legs, torso, and even half of its face were split with the spiralling colours.

Eye-shaped sharp red looked up as it tilted its face to her. It never seemed to sleep or rest, since every time she handled his soul, it always sat in a cross-legged position. Occasionally its hands and arms would move in reaction to her touch, often grabbing at her fingers when she tried to stroke it, but it seemed to tilt its head back in welcome when she caressed under its jaw.

*I love his soul.* She adored staring at it, and she knew she'd greedily covet it and do so forever.

She placed it back between her antlers and glanced at Jabez. The urge to touch him again itched at her fingertips, so she turned away before she gave in.

*What else can I do then?* She'd already tried to press her skull against the glass to look at the city below, as well as the ocean in the distance.

The first sun had already risen, and a smaller blue one had also peeked over the horizon.

Her gaze slipped to the door at the back of the room. She

let her curious nature take her feet there, and she opened the space. It was small in comparison, and she had no idea what any of it was.

Almost square with rounded corners, the entire area was made of obsidian with smelted bronze ore keeping the stone in place.

There was some kind of seat with a hole in it to the left, but it looked wildly uncomfortable. There was also a counter with a shallow bowl fitted into it and some kind of silvery spout. The only other thing in the room was an empty space that had a much larger and wider spout that towered over even her height.

She sniffed at an unusual sweet scent and found multiple wooden containers had been placed on a shallow shelf next to the taller spout. Just below it, she noticed a small pulsating purple light.

*What is that?* She touched it inquisitively. As soon as her hand made contact with it, warm rain suddenly fell over her, and she squealed and slipped.

Her arms swung and flailed, and she grabbed some kind of pole that had a fold of fluffy material over it to steady herself. It broke under her weight, and Zylah fell to her backside as the water continued to sprinkle over her miserably slumped form.

With her orbs white and her fur completely drenched, she scrambled to touch the purple light again. *What is happening?!* Unsure how she'd managed to turn on rain *inside*, especially as she'd never had the power to do so before, she couldn't help panicking that she'd broken something.

Before she could even rise from her knees to her feet, they came out from under her again. She fell forward with a squeal to smack her chest and the underside of her jaw against the wall.

With one last attempt, her claws gouging into a sheet of obsidian to steady her shaking arm, she reached up. A chunk of black crystal broke off, but she did manage to get the rain to stop before she slipped forward again.

A hand snaked out to protect her forehead from bashing

against the wall. On her knees, Zylah gasped and darted her face to the side just as Jabez crouched down beside her.

His eyes glinted with mirth, as he flashed her a humour-filled – although groggy – smile. "Having fun?"

"No!" she exclaimed, wondering how pitiful she looked sitting on her backside with her legs bent to her sides, drenched from head to toe. Her orbs shifted to blue and the bottoms of them wavered. "I don't like this thing."

He caressed the top of her skull soothingly, then reached his hand out to her. "Showers can be slippery."

"Did I wake you?" she asked as she placed her palm in his and let him help her to her feet.

"Hard not to wake up with you screaming," he answered with a hint of laughter. "Are you okay? Did you hurt yourself?"

She threw her arms to the side, causing water to shoot off her fingers and splatter against the ground. "A little. Now I'm just wet."

"Here." He gestured for her to stand under the spout and he waved his hand over a different dreaded pulsating light she hadn't noticed before.

This one was red, and it glowed just as heat and air silently swirled around her. When it stopped on its own, he had to wave his hand in front of it to power it again since she was still partially wet due to her thick fur.

Just as she and the ground and walls dried, a knocking came from the entry door of the room.

He cocked a brow as he stepped back. "Are you going to fall over again if I answer that?"

Her sight shifted to a reddish pink, and she scratched at the nape of her neck. "No," she grumbled.

Nervous about being in the obsidian room alone when he teleported away, Zylah steadied her hand against the wall as she slowly and carefully escaped. He'd already answered the door and closed it by the time she stepped out of the small room and back onto the wooden floor of the blessed white tree.

In his hand, he held a red tray, and she noticed all the

different pieces of food on top of it.

"I was wondering when they'd try to feed us." Jabez walked to the bed and sat down near the headboard with one leg bent up and his other foot remaining against the ground. He picked up a square piece of pale-green *something* and sniffed it.

"I think they knocked earlier." She cupped her hands together nervously when he paused, popping whatever food it was into his mouth, and lifted his face to her with a frown. "I think that's what woke me, but I wasn't sure what it was. You, um, were very deep in sleep."

He scratched the side of his head as he chewed. "I'm not surprised. If it was about the council's decision, they would have been incessant." Then he shifted so he was sitting back against the pillows and wall. "Come sit with me."

Zylah walked over to the bed and sat next to him, only to gasp when he curled his left arm around her waist and dragged her between his outstretched legs. With her back resting against his bare chest, he kept his arm around her tightly, like a hug, and reached out with the other to slide the tray across the bed so it was closer.

"Here, eat," he told her, lifting a slice of something pink and veiny.

Zylah sniffed it before pulling her nose hole away. "Why? I no longer feel hunger after eating your soul."

The corners of his lips curled slightly. "Even if I have to feed you tiny bits of meat forever, I'd like to see these disappear." His left hand clasped hers and he brushed his thumb across her remaining protruding knucklebones. "It'll mean your body has reached its fully evolved state, and then you can decide if you want to be plumper or not."

"Do you not like me how I am?" she asked, as he wiggled the flap of meat at her.

"You're perfect as you are, but I'd prefer you to be what is considered healthy for a Mavka." When she refused to take the food, he shoved it into his own mouth and loudly chomped on it. "Those with lots of their skeletal bones still showing tend to look underweight and sickly in form. If you are happy with the way you are, that's fine, and if you wish to look as big as Merikh, I don't mind that either."

"I don't know how Merikh looks," Zylah said, as she watched him pick up an orange slice of something that smelt fruity.

"You will soon," he answered with his mouth full. "He's in the city and you'll likely meet. He's currently being a cunt, but I'm sure he'll seek you out in curiosity eventually. He won't be able to stand not knowing who you are or what you look like." He pointed a finger at her face. "Don't let him be a prick to you. He's an asshole at the best of times, and none of it is meaningless. He'll like it if you snap back at him, since he actually likes arguing."

Grumbling, Zylah wiggled her head. "I don't like arguing."

"Trust me, he'll make you want to bite his head off. He has a way of getting under your skin." Jabez picked up another slice of the strange meat and it flapped limply as he held it towards her. "Now, do you want to help me eat all this food?"

She glanced at it before greeting his red eyes. Although Zylah didn't mind how she looked, and appreciated that the choice to change it a little was entirely up to her, she leaned forward and took it.

Since she lacked cheeks, she bit off a little piece with her jagged Mavka fangs before swallowing it whole, and was pleased to find it didn't unsettle her stomach. She took each piece he offered, and he only ate the fruit so she could have the meat.

*I like this.* She liked sharing such a simple task with him while looking out the glass at the bright world. Basking in the intense sunlight together, the warmth fought against the tender ache inside her chest already trying to sear her. It was tranquil.

It made her feel closer to him, and like a normal being who needed to eat. She also adored that he was holding her tenderly as they did this, and she hoped they did this often in the future.

Her tail wiggled as she took the last piece, hoping if they were able to stay here in the city, this was what their future would be like.

Jabez grunted, then his hand shot down to cup between her thighs and shove her backside against his groin. "Be careful where you wag that thing."

"Did I hurt you?" She tilted her skull to the right to see him better.

"No," he answered as he wrapped his other arm around her and buried his face in the crook of her neck. "But you're going to make me hard if you do it right against my dick."

"Oh." She giggled when she felt it hardening against the underside of her tail pressed against him. She stretched her head to the side when he grazed his fangs against her neck. "I don't see a problem with that."

"Neither do I." His hand gripped her hip while the other came up to caress up her chest, his palm giving her breast a tentative squeeze. "But, considering they brought us food, I'm sure the council will make their decision soon. I'd rather not be interrupted."

He said this, yet he gave the corner of her jaw a messy kiss with his tongue darting out, before scraping his fangs against it like he wanted to nip her. Zylah shivered, and she did so repeatedly as he did it multiple times. His mouth made a slow path down the length of her jaw.

Everywhere his lips went, his warm, now fruity breath cascaded over it, causing her fur to puff from goosebumps trailing down her spine. She trembled and her pussy spasmed when he drew the points of his claw-like nails along her sternum and then down her abdomen.

"Jabez," she moaned as his mouth lowered to her neck and nipped at it multiple times. Each one was mild in pain, as her flesh was protected against his fangs due to her fur.

She'd never had him be so utterly affectionate like this before, and she felt herself melting under the power of it.

"You're so easy to arouse," he muttered against her, then lifted his head up to lick over the corner of her jaw. His fingers stopped before he could reach her swelling slit and instead drifted up the side of her abdomen to make her arch.

Within seconds, Zylah had turned into a panting, needy mess, her sight saturated in deep purple. She mewled at each touch, at each time his tongue lashed her or his lips caressed the bone of her face. She slowly turned her snout to him and tried to lick his tongue.

He sucked his own back inside his mouth before she could, and he gave a quiet, muffled chuckle behind his lips. When she tried to turn so she could force him to accept her kiss, he gripped one of her antlers and yanked her head to the side.

"I told you," he grated against her taut nape, nipping at it and causing a raspy pant to come from her. "The council will likely make their decision soon."

"Then why?" she whined, her pussy throbbing due to *his* ministrations. Why was he instigating this if he had no intention of continuing?

"Because, my bunny, I'm a very devious man." He kissed the side of her cheekbone. "And I've never been able to truly tease you like this before. You picked a mean mate for yourself."

A small growl bubbled its way up her throat, her tongue curling in horny agitation as her maw parted, and he chuckled at her for it. Then, he bit into the side of her neck hard and cupped her left breast with his free hand, forcing a haunted moan from her.

*Mean, huh?* She wondered how she could do it back to him to see how he liked it!

Just as she went to retaliate, a loud knock at the door caused her to jump and him to freeze. He pulled away as he said, "See? I told you."

She *whimpered* when he pushed her forward so he could get up from around her. As much as she knew the council was important, now she was just horny and frustrated.

As she was getting up, her orbs flared red at his back in annoyance when he opened the door and spoke to the person on the other side. They handed him a bundle of material, and he closed the door just as she'd picked up her stained dress.

"Absolutely not," he bit out, coming over to her as he held

out some kind of plain cream-coloured dress. "When they brought us food, I asked them to procure clothing that may fit you. It lacks a design, as that's cheaper, and I'll obtain you something nicer once they've given us their approval."

"You suddenly sound sure that they will," she commented when he handed it to her.

Lacking in sleeves, the dress had a small amount of cleavage and went all the way down to the bottom of her calves. It was rather loose on her lithe form when she slipped it over her body, but it also felt too short, considering its design looked as though it should come to the backs of her ankles.

She didn't expect his features to brighten with what could only be malicious humour. "Because they'll be unable to resist what I've offered."

Knowing him, and what she did of his past, Zylah could only imagine what that meant.

*I'm beginning to not trust that look.* It meant her enchanting thorn was – or had been – up to something naughty.

# THIRTY-NINE

As Jabez had foreseen, he was right, and he could tell from the moment they walked into the conference chamber.

The councilmembers watched them enter with softer and more inquisitive gazes, and their postures lacked the sticks-up-their-arses quality from before. Ulric had his arms folded like he was a petulant child who hadn't gotten his way, and his refusal to look upon Jabez was telling.

With Zylah kneeling at his side, he had to refrain from grinning like an overconfident bastard. He kept his back straight, leaned his head back superiorly, and let his eyes trail across the faces in front of him.

Silveria was the first to speak. Despite her gentle and angelic voice, she addressed them firmly. He had a feeling she was the one to deliver the news due to how soothing her voice was.

She looked down at a small pile of neatly stacked parchment in front of her. "We have decided to approve your stay within the city so long as you adhere to a few rules."

*I figured there would be restrictions placed upon us,* Jabez thought, as his grin finally filled his features. *So, here is where we'll be staying.*

More than ever, he was thankful for Zylah refocusing his thoughts when he'd been struggling to on his own. If it hadn't been for her, he wouldn't have had the clarity to speak of what likely helped them make this decision.

"Firstly, until we are fully confident that we can trust you, we will be assigning you a guard who will follow you wherever you go. Any form of evading them will be considered a violation, and you will only have a limited amount of strikes before we deem you incapable of following our rules. This means that you will be allowed the use of your magic within the city, and we believe that to be a fair compromise – unless you'd prefer it to be the other way around."

He'd expected them to restrict him in some way, but not that he'd have an option of choosing how they did so.

"I would prefer a guard," he answered, refusing to have his magic locked away. "Will Zylah have one as well?"

"Temporarily, yes. You're a pair, and we can't afford for you to distract us while she goes off to enact any potential plans." Silveria nodded and then looked down at the parchment once more. "Secondly, if you are found anywhere near the room that holds the mana stone to our protective dome, where our soldiers are housed and train, or anywhere near the walls of the city without permission, we will consider this a breach of security and you will immediately be thrown from the city. Considering your ability to teleport on a whim, we'll be increasing our watch in those areas, and those there will flee from you to inform us of your trespassing."

"That sounds justified to me," he easily conceded.

"Good. If you instigate any violence within the city, steal, or do anything that would be considered a crime, we will punish you how we punish everyone." She lifted her gaze from the parchment just to narrow it at him. "We will imprison you temporarily, and your mate will join you. If you commit manslaughter, whether incidentally or purposefully, you will be thrown from the city, but we will place our magic nullifying bracers on you as additional punishment for such callousness."

"Tsk." Jabez clicked the inside of his mouth while rolling his eyes. "That's rather cruel."

"We consider murder to be the vilest thing a person can do. Life is sacred, and you have already ended the lives of many upon your escape. Such a punishment would be deserved."

"Am I allowed to defend myself?"

"No one would dare–"

"You currently have a bull-headed Duskwalker in your midst," Jabez stated over the top of her with his eyelids lowering. "Merikh is no stranger to swinging his fists."

Silveria's expression inwardly cringed, and her eyes darted to the side. He wasn't able to grasp who she looked at quick enough before she looked back at him.

"*Should* you be attacked for any reason, you may defend yourself. However, we implore that you use your teleporting ability to evade such instances and ask that you report them for the record. Like I said, any death, even to a deathless creature, will not be tolerated, as it's preventable."

"Understood. Anything else?"

"Those are our restrictions, but we wish to discuss what you have offered, as well as make some requests." Silveria shuffled the top page of her parchment to the back so she could keep reading. "We will take you up on your offer of obtaining mana stones for us, and we will assign you a team that we would like for you to train with."

"I would like Merikh on that team," Jabez quickly cut in, making a few on the council frown in confusion.

"If this is a way to get back at him," Raewyn started, her voice ringing with concern, "then we ask that you let go of the hostility between you two. He has a justified reason to be angry with you."

"Hostility?" Jabez stated with his head rearing back before he shook it. "It has nothing to do with hostility. He's likely the strongest being within the city, including myself. His echidna quills make him the best at defence, his large size would be a formidable blockade against a swarm of Demons, and he is ruthless in battle. If I'm going to endanger myself, I would rather the best chances of success. Now that I'm aware he is the Duskwalker in the city, I'd rather he was the one watching my back. To be honest, assigning a team would be useless when all I would need is him. Everyone else would just get in our way."

Although what he said was true, he did have an ulterior motive for requesting Merikh.

Jabez didn't want some snivelling, weak, inexperienced soldier protecting him. He hated people who were overconfident when they were actually nothing but a bumbling babe. They'd been locked behind these walls their entire lives and had likely rarely left the city to face any *real* danger.

Jabez imagined he would end up needing to protect them instead, as many would freeze up and piss their pants if a Demon were to attack them in the wild. And should he fail to save their lives, he'd be blamed for it. They could accuse him of killing them, or that he didn't care enough to prevent their death.

He'd rather avoid such an argument in the future.

He could protect himself, and Merikh would just be additional muscle and his handler for these councilmembers.

"We would have to ask him if he would be willing to work with you," Raewyn stated quietly.

"He's not wrong, though," Cleth translated for Mericato, who had a faraway look in his green eyes. "I've seen Merikh spar with my soldiers, and he is completely untouchable. We were concerned for Jabez's safety while he risked serious injury to procure stones, but this could be an alternative to endangering him, and it would prevent the possible loss of my soldiers. They're both deathless."

When no one objected, a grin so large it revealed the full expanse of his fangs beamed from him. *Ha! You fucker. I'll force you to my side if need be, and if you give me shit like earlier, I'll make you eat your own tail.*

Hopefully over time, he could find out what Merikh had shoved up his non-existent asshole and get the big guy back on his side.

Because, if he were being honest, the likelihood of Jabez befriending anyone within the city was low. Considering he distrusted everyone, was disgusted by Elysians, and was probably hated within the city for his past actions, kindling any friendships was doubtful. He could tolerate Merikh, and hopefully they became what they had once been: companions.

It was something he could look forward to.

"Regarding your secret revolving around Demon completion, we'll have you speak with Raewyn tomorrow so we can begin that project immediately. We'll be keeping you close, so you will remain in the central tree for the time being, and we'll have our soldiers escort you both to your new home after this meeting. You may relocate after you've gained our trust and we no longer feel the need to keep guards on you."

*I don't care where we are so long as they don't disturb me often.* The central tree was usually the nicest place to live, so at least that was a benefit, but it meant he'd be at their every beck and call.

"Regarding the potential of building a Demon village, we'll discuss this at length with you in the near future. There are still a lot of concerns and unknowns, but we're fully open to the idea of helping those outside our walls and obtaining peace. Since you already have experience in establishing such a feat, we'll seek your advice regarding this. Consider that a token of our faith in you, as your involvement will be vital, but it also poses a risk we're aware of."

A sense of relief washed over him that they were open to the idea. At least *part* of his goal could be achieved.

"And what of those in Spiral Haven?"

Silveria's lips thinned momentarily. "If it's the best option, and we're able to make contact with Weldir to see if it's viable, we'll consider it. We'd like to remove the Demons from Earth if possible, and we'll reveal ourselves to the humans in order to take back their world once we have managed to save our own. We're aware that we have a lot to make up for there, as well as to the Anzúli who have aided us. If Spiral Haven is a start to making amends, then we'd like to go down that route." Then Silveria clasped her hands on the table before her, as if she was done reading her notes, and met his gaze. "We have two final requests of you. Firstly, Zerik was interested in the texts you found in Tck'ith. Can you elaborate on the state of the mountain library?"

Jabez's brow cocked, and he shifted his eyes to the man to his left. The elderly Elysian gave him a sheepish smile, his eyes hungry for knowledge and the ability to preserve it. Jabez figured he was still the head of the library here in Nyl'theria, even after all these years.

"The main area is completely decimated," he stated, making the man's smile fall. "However, the inner sanctum does have a few books that have survived. I will admit, my discovery of it has rapidly increased its deterioration, but I could obtain everything there easily since no Demons have ever found it."

"Whatever you are able to procure, even if it's just one book, I will be pleased with," Zerik offered. "Thank you."

"The last note on our agenda is the magic you have obtained," Silveria stated firmly. "Merikh has recounted all he knows of your abilities and the spells he's witnessed you use."

"Has he now?" Jabez said with a smile, despite clenching his jaw in vexation.

"We would like for you to teach us what you can, especially the spell that protects Demons from the sun. Merikh said not only can you shield just your body, but also an entire castle. Ensuring the safety and wellbeing of the Delysians within the city would be greatly appreciated."

"I will teach you everything that I'm willing," Jabez answered, lifting his chin defiantly. "Much of what I've learned would be considered taboo, cursed, or wrong – such as the ability to transplant body parts to myself in order to regenerate limbs. I also won't teach anyone how to teleport."

"Why not?" Ulric snapped out, bashing the side of his fist against his tabletop.

"It's always good to keep your most valuable attribute close to your chest," Jabez stated with a dull expression and his lids lowering in disinterest. "I like being powerful and needed. Makes me feel important."

He pushed his bottom lip forward to feign a pout and fluttered his eyes coyly.

When Ulric opened his mouth to be pissy, Silveria quickly spoke before him.

"Agreed. We already discussed the possibility of you rejecting such a request, so the fact that you are willing to teach us some things is better than we hoped for. Your sun barrier is what we are most interested in, although your ability to create stable portals with nothing but a wave of your hand is also high on our priority list."

"I don't think you will be pleased if I reveal the main requirement for such magic," Jabez answered, and sheepishly averted his gaze to the ceiling. "You may throw us from the city once you learn of it."

A few of the councilmembers shared wary looks due to his dark, humour-filled tone.

Silveria waved her hand towards Mericato, and the soundproofing dome from the first meeting enclosed them. They had a quick conversation in private amongst the council to discuss what he'd said. Once they were done, it disappeared.

"If you're willing to share it, we have agreed that we'll overlook it and our approval will still stand," Silveria stated.

"I have your vow on that?" Jabez asked, and she confirmed. "It requires the use of gilded ore."

Ulric stood so fast that his chair knocked back and crashed against the ground, then he bashed both his palms against the table. "That's sacrilege! No one is allowed to touch the Gilded Maiden's tears! To mine such ore is one of the few restrictions the deities have placed upon us."

"She is a goddesse who rules over Elysians, not Demons," Jabez told him, his grin widening.

"You are an Elf, whether you accept it or not!"

"And yet here I kneel, unscathed," Jabez rebuffed. "In order to control such chaotic magic, you need a power source strong enough to withstand it. I also used such ore to extend the life of a human well beyond her years, something considered impossible with a regular mana stone."

The ore itself was difficult to mine, and its metal was so soft that it dripped like tears when touched. The moment he touched it, his hands had started to decay and his veins had blackened like flaming ink had slipped inside his bloodstream. He'd torn his own forearm off to prevent it from infecting the rest of his body, and it'd taken him multiple attempts at finding a material that could withstand it. Solidifying it was also difficult, and Jabez had success using only a tiny amount mixed with other metals. Once combined with other ore and the aid of prolonged stabilising magic, it was usable.

At the ashen, sickened expressions in the chamber, he brought his head forward to meet Silveria's annoyed gaze. "You made a vow, or is the word of your people so hollow?"

"We can't allow this," Ulric bit. "He will curse us all for such actions. The Gilded Maiden will not look down on us favourably should we allow such wickedness into our city."

"Sit down," Cleth demanded at the man, before folding their arms and leaning back. "You did say you were cunning. You knew we would be outraged, yet you still dared to speak the truth while forcing us into a corner."

"Is there anything else?" Jabez asked, tilting his head condescendingly. "I tire of being in this stuffy chamber."

"No," Silveria said as she motioned to another councilmember. They promptly stood to walk towards the exit doors. "Upon entry into the city, we provide everyone with a home and their own personal pouch of coin. You are free to go, but remember what we spoke about here today, Jabeziryth, and remember, we will be watching you closely."

He stood just as the door to the conference chamber opened and two guards came to release him and Zylah.

"I have a final request," he stated as he rubbed at one of his wrists once he was freed.

"Speak it."

"Stop calling me Jabeziryth," he demanded, cutting her a glare from the side. "I haven't worn that name since I was a child, and not even my family spoke it. My name is Jabez."

When they agreed, a deep, overwhelming sense of triumph crashed over him. He'd won.

Walking side by side with Zylah, he caught her looking

down at her unbound wrists when they were exiting the chamber. "Are we staying?" she asked.

Placing his palm over her waist and pulling her closer with a smile curling his lips, he answered, "We are."

*I'll speak to them in the future about what she can do here.* He would also obtain books for her to study Nyl'kira so she could speak to everyone freely and integrate into this society.

He was curious to see what she'd make of herself.

# FORTY

*I'd been hoping to show Zylah more of the city before they called on me,* Jabez mused, as he was led through the central tree's hallways. *Then again, they did mention this yesterday.*

It was still rather early in the day, and the first sun barely crested over the horizon with an aqua hue. He was thankful their new home faced west and prevented the morning and afternoon suns' north-to-south arc from directly shining through their windows.

*The morning horizon kind of reminds me of her orb colour,* he randomly noted, liking this new facet of it he could appreciate.

Keeping his expression bored and dull, warmth filled his chest as he remembered her inspecting their house. It was larger than the one they'd been staying in and had a small kitchen should they wish to make a snack or tea – since it was common to eat communally. The bathroom consisted of a toilet, sink, and a shower, while a special bathtub large enough to fit them both comfortably had been built into the floor near the window of the main area.

A seating area consisting of two lounges and a small table was common among most households from memory, but there was also a small dining area for two people as well. With their bed situated against the wall, similar to their previous room, the foot of it was positioned towards the bathtub and wall of glass panes.

There was a spacious area free of any furniture that they could fill themselves, and he had no idea what they might put there. He appreciated that, as it meant their home could evolve freely. There was also a small private room that could be turned into a study should they choose it.

Their home was considered bigger than most, but that had been done on purpose to keep him complacent. Had the councilmembers tucked them into some tiny nook as a form of punishment, despite them being taller than everyone else in the city, he would have been annoyed.

*They wisely thought ahead.*

After the council meeting and then being shown their home, he sat Zylah down and finally explained everything that had happened since they entered the city, so she wasn't left out. She'd been concerned when he explained his behaviour in the first meeting within the conference chamber, but he figured she deserved to understand.

It also allowed him to share some of his childhood experiences, which he'd never explained to anyone else before. It'd been a hard conversation to have, but she was his female now, and keeping the truth of his past, where everything had started, was unfair.

He also... *wanted* to share it with her.

How he'd been treated as a child and all the way through to his late teenage years had been a heavy burden to bear. He was tired of carrying it on his own, and he wanted her to understand him in a way that no one else ever had, or ever would. It also let her know that his mind may not always be well, and that he may sometimes recede into the depths of his past while they were here.

When she'd attempted to coddle him, as he expected she would, he'd made the excuse to show her around the central tree. There were no shops inside, but there was still much to show her, and it took the rest of the day. He also wanted to familiarise himself with an environment he'd barely known as a young boy.

They sat in the communal eating area for dinner. He'd been

uncomfortable with the inquisitive stares, mainly because they were cast at her and not him. She hadn't seemed to care, too busy staring back at them in curiosity herself, which almost had him laughing.

His face and name would become known, and soon the citizens would grow wary of his presence. He was excited for that, and couldn't wait to see people cast their uneasy, frightened stares away from him.

Since the days were so long here, they'd had plenty of time to spend with each other in just a single one. There would be many more.

Which was why, when he was led through the halls, he wasn't *that* annoyed he'd been stolen from her. Zylah had wanted to come, but he thought it was best she remained behind.

*I will have to find things for her to do when I'm called away.* She'd already shown her dismay at the idea of being left behind when he did go outside the protections.

Where he was being led to was on a far outreaching branch of the central-tree palace, as if it had purposefully been designed to be out of the way. At the end of a long, empty hallway, a set of double doors came into view.

A woman, who was obviously an attendant for the councilmembers, rapped her knuckles against the door. Her hair was short, only coming to her chin, and she'd dyed the ends bright red. Many Elysians played with the white of their hair, dying it an array of colours to show their individuality.

"He may enter," Raewyn stated on the other side.

When Jabez had first laid eyes on the willowy woman and her soft, freckled features, he never would have guessed she was one of the head scientists. Considering she'd taken over his mother's work, he figured Raewyn had a good relationship with her. He intended to keep the woman at arm's length.

As he opened the door, two scents wafted through the crack.

One was gentle and sweet. He frowned when he found it familiar in his memories, but he struggled to place it. *Maybe I did know her as a child.* It'd been hard to pick it out in the conference room due to the other seventeen councilmembers.

The other scent had one side of his nose wrinkling in surprise. *Merikh?* Hard to mistake that citrusy, spiced, masculine aroma.

As soon as Jabez tried to enter, Merikh's broad, muscular chest came into view and was entirely in the way. Arms folded above his rounded gut and partially leaning against it, a growl rumbled from the Mavka as he tipped his bear skull down to him. His bull tail flicked to the side in irritation.

Since he had no issue getting into the Mavka's space, his chest grazed the back of Merikh's armoured forearms when he stepped forward and closed the door behind him.

He peeked up at Merikh, just as the burly *bitch* growled, "Behave."

"I am the epitome of tranquil and controlled," Jabez said with a shit-eating grin less than a foot from Merikh's. "You're the one who doesn't know how to keep himself from losing it. How's your mother? Does she know you're here?"

Speaking of the Witch Owl – who Merikh hated – was a terrible idea on Jabez's part. But he was incapable of not needling the brutish male, and after how things had ended during their last conversation, he did really want to get back at him.

He expected the roar that came from Merikh. What he hadn't foreseen was a massive fist slamming into the side of his face until his cheekbone *cracked.* Being shunted to the side with nothing but a singular, unexpected punch, Jabez crashed into a long counter. Glass jars filled with herbs, questionable liquid, and who else knew what, knocked over, rolled across the counter, and then smashed against the ground.

"Merikh!" Raewyn yelled at the top of her lungs. With her fingertips brushing the edge of the counter to orientate and guide herself within the room, she ran to the side. "I told you that if you couldn't keep your temper under control, then you weren't allowed to be here today!"

She spoke in English, probably due to Merikh still learning Nyl'kira. Jabez continued in the same language, so all understood.

Immediately discombobulated, Jabez used his elbows against the counter's top as he fought to get back to his feet. More jars shattered and broke. He wiggled his jaw to make sure Merikh hadn't fractured that as well.

"I'm not quite sure I deserved that," he muttered with a pout.

"You killed my brother, you pointy-eared fuck!" Merikh roared with his claws bared. He stomped towards Jabez, his heavy, bare, claw-toed feet slapping against the obsidian floor, and he was surprised the big bastard didn't crack it.

*Oh shit!* Jabez teleported before Merikh could even swipe at him and ended up on the opposite side of the enraged Mavka.

*I guess I did deserve it.* He hadn't known Merikh was *aware* of what had happened to his winged brother.

Merikh snarled as he turned with orbs so red, Jabez was surprised he hadn't fallen into a rage. "I should break every bone in your fucking body."

"Temper temper," Jabez taunted, stepping to the side before Merikh could swing. "If *you* can't behave, perhaps you should leave."

"And leave you alone with my bride?!"

*Figured as much.* Why else would Merikh be in this laboratory? The reminder of the woman had a callous glint lifting into his features.

Jabez teleported again. Raewyn gasped when he clasped her face from behind and pressed his chest against her back to keep her still. She stiffened in his hold, especially as the point of his right index fingernail stabbed into the thin, fragile skin right beneath her eye.

"Calm down, Merikh, or else," Jabez warned.

"You're a fucking coward!" Merikh snarled, refusing to move with his precious bride now in harm's way. The guards covering his forearms and calves were struggling to keep his quills down, and he appeared to be moments from shredding them apart.

"Cowardliness is just a word." Jabez brought his face right next to Raewyn's and gave the brute a glare. "A smart man will use any means to take back control of a situation, and we both know I'm no stranger to hurting someone's mate to get my way."

"You've been here a little over a day and you've already violated one of your restrictions," Raewyn sneered, her gentle voice hard and unbending.

"How so?" Jabez let a chuckle fill his tone. "So far I have harmed no one, and *threatening* someone has never been a violation of a crime. I was told to use my ability to teleport to evade a fight, even in self-defence." Then, right next to her ear, he stated, "You demanded I come here this morning, then kept him here, knowing he was angry with me. What did you think was going to happen?"

Although he preferred the terms playful and witty, he was sure Merikh told them he was an asshole or something. Of course Jabez would go out of his way to annoy his old friend, and Merikh should have foreseen this outcome.

"He refused to leave me unprotected. Can you blame him after everything you've done?"

"What about what he's done?" Jabez countered, raising a brow at Merikh when he dared to step closer. "He helped me raze towns, even an Anzúli one. He's eaten people, and killed countless humans and Demons. His hands are just as bloodied as mine."

"He didn't kill your brother," she muttered quietly, but her lips did flatten, unable to deny what he'd stated.

"I removed that command *months* before it happened," he informed them. "Sure, it's still my fault for issuing it, but I attempted to stop my destruction of Mavka. I wasn't pleased when they brought me the winged one's skull, and in fact, I punished them for it to ensure word spread faster that I'd undone it."

"You revoked your order?" Merikh asked, the red in his

orbs dimming.

"I did it before I last spoke to you on Earth. I realised destroying Weldir wasn't the way to get what I wanted and had already planned to abandon Earth with or without you." Then Jabez's brows drew together as something became startlingly apparent. "You don't know, do you?"

"Know what?" Merikh bit out.

"Weldir brought that Mavka back to life."

Merikh's orbs flooded with dark yellow as he stepped back on a shaky leg. "What?"

"I was surprised, too, when I heard of it," Jabez admitted, as he softened the stab of his sharp nails on Raewyn's pretty face. "But Lindiwe confirmed it." He shook his head as an annoyed chuckle came from him. "You fucking attacked me and tried to prevent us from entering the city when your brother still lives."

"He still *died*." Then he folded his arms across his chest with a scoff. "You deserved me hitting you for a lot of reasons."

Maybe that was true, and Jabez couldn't deny it. He had much to make up for regarding Merikh, but he was *willing* to try.

Now that things were calming, he slowly removed his hands from the scientist. She stumbled forward against the edge of the counter, and Merikh quickly rushed to her when it appeared like she'd fall.

But Jabez's temper was still high; he was annoyed, and he despised the way his fractured cheek throbbed. A bruise was rising and blood dripped from a rather nasty gash.

The fact that Merikh nearly had a hand in endangering Zylah, when Jabez had been trying everything to protect her, had anger burning in his muscles.

He teleported right in front of Merikh, and with the force of them approaching each other, he kneed the Mavka right in the groin. Merikh choked and then wheezed as he cupped right where his seam would be. The hit had been so hard that it sent the guy to his knees and the bottoms of his orbs wavered when they turned white.

"Control your fucking temper," Jabez warned, giving him a steely glare as he looked down. "Especially with your mate nearby."

Then again, Jabez knew he was being a hypocrite. Unashamedly, he often was.

"I should kill you," Merikh quietly growled up at him.

Jabez crouched down next to him, although wisely out of reach. "Can't kill something that doesn't die," he answered with a sickly sweet smile. "I'm a Phantom now, Merikh. Zylah has ensured I'm untouchable. The ability to teleport *and* turn into a Phantom? Could you imagine what violence I could have unleashed had they thrown me from the city? They were wise to approve us, otherwise the next time we met, it would have been me ripping into your mate just to *hurt* you for getting in the way."

Then Jabez placed his hand on Merikh's shoulder and teleported them both next to Raewyn's side. It got him out of the way so Jabez could put space between them after materialising next to the door, and it allowed the couple to be together after the mess Merikh had caused.

"You have no idea who she is, do you?" Merikh stated with a chuckle, slapping his hand on the counter next to Raewyn to support his attempt to rise.

Jabez looked at the pathetic way the Mavka had shakily gotten to his feet. He inwardly winced. *Perhaps I did knee him just a smidge too hard.* He bet rage was simmering beneath the surface of his agitated, flared muscles and fur.

"Should I?" Jabez asked, tilting his head.

"Merikh, don't," Raewyn whispered before nibbling at her bottom lip.

"I thought you were lying or just insane, but you actually don't remember," he said with a wheeze. "I never picked you for having memories missing in that stupid fucking head of yours."

*She's a councilmember, a scientist that took over my mother's work, and knows different languages like my stepfather.* It didn't take him much to figure it out. *Is her surname the same as...?*

The laugh that burst out of him almost had him keeling over. "Let me guess, she's my half-sister?"

The little girl whose face had only recently been haunting his dreams. He should have picked it, considering the familiar hair and scent, but she'd only been, what, seven when he'd been taken away permanently? How was he supposed to know what she'd look like at thirty-two?

*We don't even share the same last name.* Jabez had his mother's name, and he'd been the only one to use it even when she'd chosen her life partner in Doctor Daefaren. His stepfather refused to properly adopt him, a Demon spawn, or maybe no one had thought to do so yet. Regardless, the lack of action from his 'parents' had weighed heavily on his conscience.

"Why the fuck should I care?" Jabez countered, causing her sweet face to twist into hurt. "We were children when I last spoke to her, and much has changed. I let go of my family when I was rotting in my prison cell."

If she wanted some fateful, long-awaited hug from him, she was poorly mistaken. Jabez had no affection for her, nor anyone from his past.

"I visited you," Raewyn stated softly, turning her head to the side.

"And what good did that do you?" Jabez asked, folding his arms across his chest defensively. "I didn't want anyone watching me falling into madness, and reaching for you did nothing but deepen my hurt. You were free, I was not. You were an Elysian, and me a hybrid cursed by the very mother we share. I hated that you had everything I never did."

"That wasn't my fault!" Raewyn screamed while placing her hand over her heart. "I loved you! Looked up to you! You have no idea how much I missed you, worried for you, cared for you!"

"I was locked away inside darkness for so long I forgot your face," Jabez told her. "Missing you in return only made everything I lost hurt more."

She flinched, her ears twitching as if she misheard him, then slowly brought her head forward. "You... missed me?"

"You were the only thing that made me happy as a child," he admitted, his arms tightening as his gaze narrowed. "You were my only friend. I lost you, and everything, the same day. I had to let all that go in order to protect myself."

She nibbled on her bottom lip as tears flooded her eyes. She was strong-willed enough to stop them from falling, quickly blinking them away before they could spill over. He was thankful for that, as he didn't want to have to pretend he cared – and likely wouldn't have.

"I'm so sorry," she muttered as she raised her trembling hands to cover her lips.

"Can we get to the point as to why I'm here?" Jabez asked, wanting to get away from this uncomfortable conversation.

He was sure they would have many more in the future, but he wasn't open to rekindling any kind of relationship with his half-sister right now. He didn't know if he ever would be. Maybe Zylah could help him open his locked-up heart – she had a way of doing that – but now wasn't the right time.

He'd just been accepted into this horrid city, and his senses had been on high alert since entering it. At the moment, he wanted little more than to get to know his mate better and discover that bond far more intimately. His deep affection for Zylah was entirely new to him, and he was still learning who he was as a bonded male.

Just a few days ago, his goal had been everything, and his hatred the backbone of who he was.

He needed time to adjust to all these new changes.

Jabez appreciated knowing the truth, especially as he'd be having a lot of contact with her through her work and Merikh. Being uninformed over the course of weeks would have infuriated him and would have destroyed any trust in her he *may* have developed, despite that being unlikely.

Although her features scrunched with further hurt, she snapped her face forward and cleared her throat.

"Yes, maybe that's for the best," Raewyn muttered as she stepped back behind the main counter in the room and took a seat on a stool. She skilfully managed to harden her voice like a true councilmember and the head of a scientific department. "Merikh, go clean up the mess you made."

Grunting, the bull-horned Mavka deepened the naturally red colour of his orbs at Jabez before doing as he was instructed.

"Good little assistant," Jabez playfully sneered.

"Fuck off," Merikh snapped at him. "Next time, I'll kick you in the seam, unless you're letting it all swing again. If so, I might just rip your balls off."

A grin incidentally caused him to flash his fangs. *Fuck, I missed him.* That argumentative temper of his matched Jabez's own.

His humour died as he looked towards Raewyn, who had her left ear turned more to him. *She's very pretty – no wonder Merikh was enthralled by her. I imagine he likes taking care of her, since he's usually so destructive.*

He was even obediently sweeping up glass with a dustpan and broom, and Jabez doubted he could ever make Merikh do such a thing. She had a special hold on him.

*Whatever makes him happy.*

"Now that I know of our relationship, and how it means you likely have a close bond with our mother, I expect you to keep your word and not reveal to her what I'm about to disclose," Jabez stated clearly, and likely a touch too loudly, to make sure she heard him well.

"Yes, I vow it." Raewyn cupped her hands and placed them on the laboratory counter in front of her. "It will be hard, but I promise the information will not leave this room."

"Merikh?" Jabez asked.

"Yeah, yeah." Then, under his breath while he cleaned, he muttered, "Not that I can really talk to anyone properly yet."

Jabez nodded, satisfied with both their answers, and tapped a finger against his biceps to battle the restraint he held on his secret. His following silence made the noise of Merikh fixing the counter he'd shunted Jabez into louder than it needed to be.

"She was close," Jabez finally admitted, letting his mask of indifference neutralise his tone. "But Dr Kneis lacked one thing for getting the answer: callousness. I know she tested my blood repeatedly and it brought no answer. That's because she needed to *feed* it to a living Demon. I'm guessing the idea never crossed her mind, considering no one thought to feed me blood or meat."

Raewyn's lips parted on a quiet gasp. "Wait, are you saying...?"

"Yes. My blood, the blood of a hybrid, quickens the process of completion. I've tested it, and I've been able to prove my theory that if a lesser Demon were to eat me whole, they would reach full completion in one go, rather than needing to eat multiple people."

"You're joking," Raewyn muttered, running her hand over her braided fringe. "The answer was that simple?"

"You can imagine why I couldn't share that secret."

Had it become known that eating him could finish their evolution, Demons would have done anything within their means to trap him. Then they would have bled him, waited for him to regenerate, and repeated the process. That's if someone greedy didn't get their claws into him, mercifully killing him on the spot.

Merikh's comment was accompanied by the rain of glass shattering as it fell into a nearby bin. "I've eaten bites of you multiple times and it didn't do shit for me."

"I think my DNA balances out other Demons," Jabez said, ignoring him. "I'm the perfect blend because I was born naturally this way. I imagine it'd be the same for other hybrids."

"But that means there is little we can do to help them," Raewyn said as she turned her head down and ran her thumbs over the top of each other in forlorn thought. "If that is the only way, then there's nothing we can do."

"What are you talking about?" Jabez scoffed. "Didn't I

already state that I would be willing to help?"

"But it would mean we'd have to extract from you."

Jabez tilted his head when he could see the moral dilemma in her features. *Weakhearted.*

"Exactly. I won't allow any of the councilmembers to dissuade the others of your *tentative* approval. Since one of my conditions for sharing this was that it remains confidential, not assisting with this could be considered me going back on my word. The others will be too curious as to *why* it's not possible, so I'd rather avoid that and just do what needs to be done. Considering I'm deathless, bleeding me repeatedly would do little but make me feel a bit weak. Since there is no reason for me to fight, I see no issue with it unless I'm mining for mana stones. The healers here can help me, as they did for Zylah."

"Did you just say you needed a healer for a Mavka?" Merikh asked as he stomped his way to Raewyn's side. "Why didn't you just wait a day?"

Jabez's brows furrowed, and he loosened the fold of his arms. "I did. Her body wouldn't regenerate."

"Were you in Nyl'theria or Earth?"

"We were already here when we were attacked."

Merikh let out a warm laugh. "Did you wait a Nyl'theria day or the equivalent of an Earth day?"

"An Earth day." As soon as the words left his mouth, his eyes widened. "Are you kidding me?! If we'd waited a full Nyl'theria day..."

"Idiot," Merikh choked out with a laugh, before pointing at him. "You brought her here for that reason, didn't you? I bet you feel like a fuckwit now."

Jabez rumbled out a growl, his eyes narrowing into a glare. "How the fuck was I supposed to know her body would match this world's sun cycle?" He slapped a hand over his face and let his annoyed rumble die. "I guess that means she'll heal on her own now."

"And so will you," Raewyn interjected. "Although we are able to heal you, if that's how you'd prefer it."

"I'd rather not be touched by Elven magic, if I'm being

honest." The idea made him shudder with disgust. *Don't touch me, you horrible cretins.*

He'd only offered to be healed by them as an alternative – one he likely wouldn't have actually used.

"Thank you for speaking with me on this," Raewyn offered, as she tipped her head up towards Merikh beside her. "I'll consider our options, and once I begin formulating a plan, I'll call on you for your assistance. In the meantime, perhaps it would be wise to begin collecting from you as soon as possible in order to slowly build our resources to help as many as we can once we start." Raewyn cupped her chin in thought, and like she was sharing the inner workings of her mind, said, "If you're willing, I can run experiments to determine *what* it is in your blood that allows for their completion, and maybe we can develop a means of extending it so we don't need as much from you."

"Whatever makes it easier."

She nodded, keeping her hand on her chin. With her voice distant, as if she was already working out theories or whatever in her head, she said, "You may leave now."

Jabez turned and headed towards the doors. When he opened them, he drifted his face to the side and said, "I'm sure you'll ask Merikh sooner rather than later about mining mana stones if you want me to start on that promptly."

Before he could obtain an answer, he left to let his statement hang between them. The curious Mavka wouldn't be able to resist finding out what Jabez was insinuating, and he would no doubt force her to have the conversation even if she wasn't ready.

It also allowed him and Merikh to begin training together, which was best to start now, rather than delaying it, if they wanted mana stones soon.

On the other side of the door, he met the eyes of his Elysian guard. A smile curled his lips. *I guess our family is insane.* Considering both of them had chosen Mavka as their partners, perhaps it was in their blood that they'd be different.

Then again, Jabez had an excuse for openly accepting the

unusual. *But she did grow up with me.* He and Raewyn had a healthy bond before he was ripped from his family. He figured because he was different and she'd been exposed to that young, she was more accepting than most.

It was a pointless theory, but one he found humorous all the same.

He stepped towards the guard. "Take me to the library."

The man nodded and led the way, while Jabez silently followed. He was taken down the central tree until its base touched the ground, where a network of roots arched and twisted, allowing for plenty of rooms and public spaces.

At the hollow, open entrance was a semi-circular desk. Its purpose was to allow true civilians to make requests or ask for passes into the central tree. Jabez was led in the opposite direction, to the back of the tree's arching roots, where he followed his guard through a large doorway.

Inside, thousands of books were neatly placed on dust-free shelves on multiple levels with stairs. Many people were already inside the library, either searching for books or sitting down in comfortable areas to read freely. The place was quiet except for the occasional footsteps, a cough, and pages flipping.

To the right of the entrance, a long counter desk was situated in front of a shelf with nooks filled with scrolls of information pertaining to the library. Behind the desk, Zerik sat reading a book, wearing a pair of reading glasses.

The guard hung back as Jabez approached the counter, and Zerik paused to peer over his glasses. He flinched, shut his book without his bookmark, and shifted in his seat.

"Jabezir–" He cleared his throat nervously and removed his glasses. "I mean, Jabez. What brings you here?"

Zerik was unable to hide the way uncertainty filled his wrinkled face, nor how mild fear lifted into his scent. Considering that he was the one who had pushed so hard for a young Jabez to be imprisoned, the man likely worried about his potential retaliation.

"I would like to borrow all the books you have in English,

if you have any. It's an Earth language."

His bushy brows twitched; he was clearly not expecting that kind of request. The man nodded as if he understood, then his eyes flicked to the side like one might if they were about to turn. He was too nervous to do it, as if he didn't wish to expose his back.

"I-I should be able to locate them easily with one of my organisation scrolls. We only have a small number, though, and they aren't in the best condition."

"That's fine. Zylah is unable to read Nyl'kira. Anything would be helpful, so she has something to entertain herself with." Then he placed his hand on the counter and thrummed his fingers. "I would like books that'll be useful in teaching her Nyl'kira."

Seeing that Jabez had no intention of starting anything violent, or wasn't attempting to strum up the past in anger, Zerik's stiff shoulders softened. He gave Jabez a relieved, although forced, smile.

"Do you plan to be the one to teach her Nyl'kira? You can bet I was surprised by how well you've managed to remember it, even after all this time."

"Yes, I'll be teaching her. Do you also have anything on creating a translation spell that would help? I'd like for her to be able to read on her own, but also being able to speak with others while she's learning would be beneficial."

Zerik finally stood, and his long, flowing, sleeveless robes fluttered as he turned. He pulled scrolls from the organisation nooks, unfurling them to check their contents, then put them away when they weren't the ones he wanted.

"Translation requires the use of a mana stone. You haven't been informed yet, as we haven't even begun that endeavour, but you won't be permitted to keep any for yourself."

Jabez's jaw clenched before he muttered, "I figured as much."

At his tone, Zerik glanced at him from the corner of his eyes. Then he looked away sheepishly, with his very long ears drooping. "Give me a moment. I'll be right back."

He ducked around a partition to go behind the organisation shelves to a private room. He returned shortly, and impishly checked that Jabez's guard wasn't watching as he slid a small dark-brown pouch across the desk.

"What's this?" Jabez asked, taking it and opening its drawstrings.

"It doesn't have much power left, but it should work in the interim," he said, just as Jabez peeked inside. His ears perked up when he saw the faintest pulsating yellow glow of a mana stone. "It's from back in the day when we were forming bonds with those on the other sides of portals. I used it when I was a young lad."

Jabez lifted his head and cocked a brow at him. "I thought you said I wasn't allowed any mana stones."

Zerik's head dipped downwards as his shoulders lifted and his features turned shy. It was a startling difference to the overconfident man from years ago, who'd acted similarly to Ulric. Loud, obnoxious, rude. Considering he was likely in his late seventies, it shouldn't come as such a surprise that his personality had changed over the years.

"There is little harm in me giving this to you. It's almost at the end of its life. If you were to attempt to change its use, you'd destroy it in the process." He pulled another scroll from the shelf and placed it on the desk. "It's... very precious to me. It's the only personal stone I've kept, as all others have been confiscated for powering aspects of the city."

"If it's so precious to you, why give it to me?"

With his back turned to Jabez, Zerik's face tilted towards the ground. A loud, solemn sigh shook from the elder, causing his shoulders to droop heavily.

"It's my attempt at making amends for the past, and how much I had a hand in it. Many of the other councilmembers stepped down after you left, too shamed to remain in their seats. I stayed because I wanted to prevent it from happening ever again, as did Laele." After obtaining one last scroll and confirming it was the one he wanted, Zerik placed it on the desk next to the first he'd taken. "We really are sorry–"

"It will take more than this to fix the past," Jabez stated over the top of him, while placing it in his pocket.

Zerik's wrinkled features cringed, and his eyes hinted at regretful sorrow. "I know."

"If you truly wish to make amends, then I have a counteroffer," Jabez stated, once more thrumming his fingers on the desk. His eyes narrowed into distrustful slits. "I have little interest in whatever words, apologies, or actions anyone will attempt to rectify what has happened to me. However, Zylah has already shown to be a rather cute bookworm, and she enjoys learning. You giving me this stone means she can already start coming here. If you take her under your wing and help her any way you can, answer her questions about anything she needs further clarification on, and maybe one day let her work under you, it will appease me."

"The Duskwalker is interested in books?" Zerik asked, his expression lifting warmly. "I'm always willing to help those in need in my library. The stone only translates the written word, but if she shares it with me while she's here, we can communicate through paper until she understands Nyl'kira."

The corners of Jabez's lips quirked to smile, but he quickly hid it. "Then I'll let her know."

With a renewed spring in his step, Zerik moved to open one of the scrolls. "Let me find the books you requested. There may be quite a few, so if you wouldn't mind helping me carry them, these old bones would be grateful."

Jabez stepped back and waved his hand to the side, letting the man know to begin their search.

*This will make her happy.*

# FORTY-ONE

When Zylah entered her new home alone, she hadn't expected Jabez to already be inside it. *I thought he was mining stones.* She didn't know why, but she felt the need to hide the bag she was carrying behind her hips as her sight turned reddish pink.

*He has a gash on his forearm,* she thought with dismay, noticing claw marks and dried blood. The smell of it had been spicing the air, and she hated that it did – despite how delicious she found the aroma.

She made no comment on it; it would only bother him, and he'd refuse to let her heal him anyway.

"And just where have you been?" Jabez asked, his tone hinting at playfulness as he stood from one of the yellow lounges.

There was a suspicious, although curious, hint to his warm gaze as it slipped to her hips. Zylah's hands tightened on the bag she was hiding.

"One of the councilmembers took me for a walk while you were gone," she mumbled coyly, stepping to the side to enter deeper into their home.

His expression dulled in a way she knew meant he wasn't pleased. "Was it Raewyn?"

Her head jerked in surprise. "How did you know?"

"She's the only one who can speak English, and the only one I can think of who would try to form a bond with you," he answered, stalking closer with a predatory glint in his eyes.

"Did she tell you she is my half-sister?"

"Maybe." She chittered nervously, her sight deepening in her embarrassed hue at being caught. "Is that okay?"

"I expected that she'd try to speak with you while I was out mining with Merikh. I just didn't think she'd be so diligent to try the very first time. I can already tell she's going to be a nuisance."

"Why didn't you tell me she was your sister?"

Jabez shrugged. "I don't know her, and I've only spoken to her a handful of times now, but it's been about business."

She wasn't surprised that their interactions had been limited, since they'd only been in the city less than a week. Almost twice a day, Jabez had been called away to do *something* for the council. She usually remained behind due to him feeling bad she wouldn't understand anything that was said.

She tried not to be annoyed that they were apart and was just relieved it was always for short periods.

He'd already started teaching her Nyl'kira. It was something they did every day, but it wasn't an easy language to learn. She was also trying to learn to read and speak it at the same time, making the process even slower.

"Now..." Jabez started, before stepping to the side suddenly and going behind her. "Just what are you hiding?"

Zylah squealed and spun to evade him, giggling as he chased her around their home. "Raewyn took me to the markets."

"You went shopping? Without me?" He stopped and placed a hand over his chest. "That hurts, Zylah. If you wanted something, I would have liked to go with you again."

Zylah grumbled, knowing he probably wasn't upset at all, and wiggled her head. "I didn't know I'd want something."

"I guess it's only fair, since I procured something while you weren't with me as well." He gestured towards the lounges he'd been seated at. "I have a few things for you."

Her chest filled with tenderness and excitement. *He always gets me gifts.* At least once a day, he brought her something new.

Zylah followed him, her sight drifting over the new clothing he'd bought for himself while they'd been exploring the city beyond the central tree.

A dark-navy, metallic singlet covered his torso. The straps of it were wide and rested over the rounded joints of his shoulders, and always left his arms free for her to drool over. The neckline was a thick collar around his throat, and the front of it crossed over to his left hip, where it was tied. Light-purple harem pants were tied up around his knees, and the loose material fluttered around his legs.

He wore nothing else, and the gold bangles that had been around his left ankle and right biceps had been removed when he entered the city. He said something about starting over new, and he no longer wanted to wear those self-appointed achievements.

His hair had also changed since their arrival. In order to balance it, he'd gone out of his way to shave the other side around his ears. He often tied the top half of his hair into a loose bun in order to stop it from slipping in front of his eyes, and she liked that it meant his handsome face was always clear to see.

As soon as Zylah sat down, she bounced forward on the plush seat when she saw what lay on the table. "Is that my bag?" she asked, reaching for it.

"I convinced Merikh to let me go to the inner sanctum of the library to obtain it."

"Convinced or forced?" she muttered, before opening it, doubting he'd actually given Merikh a choice. Her sight immediately shifted to bright yellow as she kicked her feet. "My book from Rook is still here and so is my dress from Goldie!"

She opened the book and her heart nearly wept in joy. She thought she'd lost this forever, and she hadn't even managed to read it yet. It was one of her most prized possessions, and she hadn't really had any.

She looked up at him while hugging everything to her

chest. "Thank you, Jabez. I appreciate this very much."

Her gaze flicked to the stacks of books he'd obtained for her already, but she knew she had to return those. The few books in this bag were all hers to keep.

A small smile curled his lips. "I thought you might."

Then he dug into one of his pants pockets and pulled out a pouch. Considering the last one had held a translation mana stone, she was giddy to learn what was inside it. When he held his fist out, Zylah offered her palm so he could drop two bands onto it.

Both golden and thick, the bands were open as if they were designed to be fitted around something. On both, two little gems – one red and the other teal – dangled from them on a short chain.

Jabez sat down next to her and revealed two others that looked similar but were also different. In his hand, four golden bands with a long chain linking two together gleamed in the bright mana-stone-powered light above. On rings, a teal gem was connected to the bottom of a red one.

"What are they?" she asked, brushing them with her fingertips of her free hand.

He placed the ones he'd been holding on the table, stood, and took the ones from her palms.

"Demons have their own way of forming bonds with the mates they choose. Since most of us have horns, we tend to fit the bands to them, although those without them will pierce their ears instead," he answered, as he fitted them to the singular forks on each of her antlers. "Since Demons can be polyamorous, wearing one on only one horn informs everyone that the bond is open and allows others to join it, while wearing two means it's closed. It's how we silently communicate we're taken, and the level of it."

He took the ones he'd been holding and fit them to his own horns. One thick band was clasped and bent halfway down, while the second sat closer to the tapered points of his horns. The long chain connecting them allowed the joined gems to glitter and shift freely between the two bands. He applied one to his right horn, and then the left.

"I have no interest in anyone else, and I know Mavka are possessive creatures." His smile brightened at her pink orbs and the way the bottoms of them wavered. "Although that's not why I got them. I doubt the Elysians do this, so most of the population likely won't understand this custom. It's mainly because it makes me feel better, and like we have done this properly in *both* our customs."

Zylah leapt to her feet to wrap her arms around his shoulders and hug him tightly. He returned her embrace by enclosing her waist and burying his nose into the fur of her neck.

"Now, are you going to show me what you bought or leave me in suspense? I'm curious, since I never know what to expect with you."

She knew that was his way of evading any kind of conversation that was too heavy or emotional. She didn't mind that he avoided things like this when he was open in the ways that mattered.

"Wait here," she said, grabbing the thin bag she'd been given to carry her shopping.

Taking it to the empty private room so she could change her clothing, she removed the light-purple dress she'd been wearing and donned her new purchase. *I'm really glad I have my dress from Goldie's. They don't have anything like that here.* Most of the Elysian clothing was loose and flowy.

Zylah stepped out while patting down the skirt of the dress she'd bought today. She'd been thrilled that it fit, and the design allowed for her to tighten it to her body, rather than being loose around the waist and chest.

Jabez had moved and now sat on the edge of the bed. He liked sitting there, and she often found him lying back on the mattress like he wanted to be lazy. She noticed a coil of strange rope beside him.

His crimson eyes drifted down her body as she walked over and then came back up when she was right before him.

"I was drawn to the colour," Zylah admitted.

"It's similar to the colour of your orbs," he answered as he looked over the teal dress.

Then his hands came up to touch her bare hips and outer thighs, since the split in it nearly made it to the bottom of her ribcage.

A thick collar sat around her throat, but the ties at the back of it meant her plush fur didn't get in the way. There was a diamond-shaped chest window that allowed her to show cleavage, and the bottom point met her waist. At the same point, the sides of the dress opened up, while the back and front tapered before turning into triangular points that came to her knees.

She'd also been attracted to the etched, swirling black designs on it.

"It's very revealing," he commented, easily snaking his hands inside it from the sides to touch her back.

Uncertainty clasped her sternum. "Is that a bad thing?"

His lips quirked. "Not at all." Then he grabbed her hips and forcibly spun her around until her back was to him. Zylah gasped at a tearing sound. "That's better."

Her tail was freed by his nimble fingers, and she looked over her shoulder to inspect the new slit in the back of the dress for her tuft to poke through.

"Thank you. I was going to do that."

"Well, I already know you don't like your tail being covered or pushed down."

The tuft swayed softly as she turned around and lifted her arms. "Do you like it?"

She was hoping to find other designs similar to it, as she didn't like the long, flowy dresses these people wore.

Placing his hands on the backs of her thighs, he pulled her closer to nip at her exposed side. "Very much." Then he pressed his chin against her when he looked up. "I have one last thing to show you."

Zylah squealed when she was thrown against the bed suddenly. Before she'd managed to settle, he held the coil of rope that had been at his side and licked at the seam of his lips.

He pulled back as he wrapped both ends around his hands and snapped his arms to the sides until the rope was taut.

"I found it in the library. Since it's enchanted, you won't be able to break it."

"I don't understand," Zylah admitted, her sight shifting to dark yellow.

She wanted to shrink under the devious grin he produced. "Since you're strong and have a habit of clawing me, I'm going to bind your hands to the wall and have my wicked way with you."

When she chittered nervously, despite her pussy walls pulsating at what he insinuated, he leaned down. He pressed a kiss to the side of her snout with a hungry rumble vibrating from his throat – or maybe it was a mean chuckle, she wasn't quite sure.

"You'll have to take that dress off for me, though."

# FORTY-TWO

"I'm not sure about this anymore," Zylah said, as she pulled on the restraints around her wrists. She tugged them apart and the two inches of rope connecting them refused to budge.

Jabez's bare chest brushed the tip of her snout as he leaned over her. A subtle gasp left her when he yanked on what remained of the enchanted rope that had been threaded through a natural notch in the wall and stretched her arms above her head.

"You'll be fine," Jabez rebutted. "If you get too stressed, I've tied you in a way I can easily undo."

Although he didn't say it, she could hear in his gentled tone that he wanted her to trust him.

She tried not to be self-conscious of the fact that the only item of clothing between them was his thin pants. Laying here naked while he bound her in a way that left her defenceless was nerve-racking. Her heart had been racing since this started, and her knees knocked together.

Desire and anxiety warred with each other.

She dipped her head back as best she could, since her antlers got in the way, and inspected how he tied her. He'd coiled the rope around each wrist multiple times before attaching them together. Apparently doing so helped lower the chance of cutting off circulation in her hands, but it was snug.

She yanked on the rope to test it. The natural, although thick, loop in the smooth bark creaked under her strength. He placed his hand over her wrists to stop her.

"Try not to break the wall. *That* isn't enchanted against a Mavka's strength." Since he was straddling her waist, he leaned forward and stretched out until they were almost nose to nose, and his bergamot and sandalwood scent flittered in her senses. With his eyes staring into her orbs and his voice low, he asked, "Is it uncomfortable or too tight?"

The gems dangling from the chain of his left horn glittered in the disappearing sunlight and snagged her sight. She adored what the decoration meant, and that he wore something permanent, in the same way she held his soul between her antlers.

She wondered if he'd chosen the colours of the gems based on their orb and eye colour. If so, then she adored them even more.

Wanting to show she trusted him and the bindings were fine, she dabbed her tongue against the corner of his full lips. They twitched under her press and he leaned his head down.

"I guess we can begin then."

Her head tilted to the side in welcome when every time he pressed a kiss down the length of her bony jaw, his tongue rolled between his lips. Although she knew her face to be unusual, Zylah... *loved* that Jabez never shied away from being attentive to it, like it didn't matter that she was so different. Like... he found her beautiful, regardless of it.

And, as he bent down further to nip into the side of her neck, causing a shiver to break across her flesh, she melted under the power of his bites. In some ways, she felt spoiled by how affectionate his mouth had become with her in the past few days.

He shuffled down until he was able to get a knee between her thighs, and she let out a rasp when he gently bit into her shoulder. Her earlier hesitant anxiety began to thaw at each new pet of his mouth. Her heart raced for a new reason when his hands shifted down her naked sides, and his long, silky hair slipped across her fur.

As if he'd been able to sense her thoughts, he said, "I like that my fangs don't bother you." He lowered even more to lick her sternum before sinking them into the side of a breast, making her arch in want and her nipples harden. "They've always gotten in the way, but you enjoy them."

Then he enclosed his lips around her nipple, and his fangs scraped against her as he sucked on it. A shallow moan broke from her throat and she pushed her chest against his mouth, uncaring of the sharpness when he lashed the tip of the hardened bud. She wanted it deeper until he'd sucked the whole thing inside.

He palmed the inside of one bent leg, and her inner thigh twitched when he made a path deeper between them. Her sight flared with purple as heat swelled inside her pussy. Zylah started to pant when he softened his abusive mouth by kissing between her breasts to make a path to the other.

His eyes shot up to hers as he messily licked across that nipple and then circled his tongue around it repeatedly.

"Jabez," she moaned as she spread her knees for him when his hand stopped its path downwards.

His eyes crinkled in humour. "So easy," he muttered, before he gave a playful snarl, shoved his face against her breast, and sucked hard.

Zylah knew she was easily aroused, and she really didn't care. She adored this male, and the fact that he could be so naughty with her only set her alight. How was she able to resist him when he seemed to know her body better than she did?

He shoved his other knee between her thighs and forced them even further apart to fit between them. He kissed a path downwards, nipping at both her sensitive sides and causing goosebumps to puff her fur. He bit against the side of her navel, then lower down, before licking up over her hipbone, unbothered by the short, minimal fur there.

Although purple had blasted into her sight, she squeaked when he nipped at her pubic mound.

*Is he going to lick me again?* After the first time in the pocket of earth beneath Spiral Haven, he'd only done it one other time, and she was in love with the feeling. It always left her aching for more, like it was nothing but a naughty tease that had her insides quivering for attention.

Both his hands ran up her thighs to her knees as he backed away, and she produced a gruff noise of disappointment. He chuckled as he brought one of her knees closer and bit into her thigh right above it.

"Patience, bunny. I'll get there."

"Why do you call me that?" she asked, wanting to know what it meant. She couldn't recall when he started calling her bunny, but it always made her insides flutter.

"Well, firstly, because of your skull and that little tail of yours that makes my dick go nuts," he muttered as he manoeuvred her leg forward so he could nip into her calf muscle. She looked down to find his cock already hard and bulging against his pants, and she licked her snout in interest. "Mainly it's because you're a horny little thing and want to fuck like one. You're also cute, fluffy, and soft like a bunny." He bit into her ankle, causing her toes to twitch and clench in confusion at the pleasurable pain of it. "I'll be honest, I'm... not used to pet names, Zylah. I've never given one before. I can call you something else if you like: baby girl, sweetheart, darling. It's really up to you."

"N-no, I like it," she said, before letting out a squeak when he bit the side of her foot! "I-I keep calling you my enchanting thorn in my mind," she admitted weakly.

"Really? I don't mind if you call me that. I can be rather prickly." Then, as if he wanted to escape the conversation, or maybe just punish her, he pressed his thumb into each of the toe bean pads of her foot. "I wonder if you'll ever lose these? I hope not."

Zylah shivered at the tickling sensation and had to stop herself from kicking him by accident. When he kept doing it with a dangerous look in his eyes, Zylah inwardly cringed.

"Stop that."

"Why? It's not like you can stop me right now," he stated around an evil little chuckle. "Shouldn't have let me tie you up if you wanted a say."

When he tickled them purposefully for a split second, his grip on her foot tightened to the point that when she did accidentally kick, he held it firm and prevented it. She screamed in protest, only to moan when he stopped and bit into the side of her calf harder than before. With her nerves on fire from his tickling, her back arched at the sensitivity running through her muscles.

Her body unclenched itself and she produced moan after moan as he quickly lowered his head with bites. Before she knew it, his tongue dipped into the slit of her pussy and her sight closed to black as she spread her thighs in welcome. Her hips bucked into his face, and he produced a pleased growl when he licked up to her clit to swirl his tongue against it.

"Already so wet," he grated as he licked across her pussy, before going the other way. "I guess you like being tickled."

Zylah wanted to deny it, but she couldn't muster the strength under the power of his tongue. *That feels so nice.* He slid it against one of her outer lips, then the other, before flicking side to side against her clit. It was warm, wet, and his breath fanned over her constantly.

She wanted so badly to grip his hair or horns so she could shove him against her pussy harder. Her legs pushed against his hands so she could enclose them around his head, but he refused to let her move them even an inch.

Zylah released an upset gasp when he pulled away and turned her to her front.

"Sorry, but I'm not done teasing you yet," he said as he bit into her backside so hard blood instantly welled to the surface of her flesh. He pulled back, brushing a hand over his hair as he licked at his lips to taste her slick and blood. "We do have all afternoon and night, and I plan to make the most of it."

He ran his warm hands down her back, causing it to arch downwards when his nails scored her lightly.

*"Jabez,"* she weakly cried as she shoved her arse up and stretched in reaction.

Her tail wiggled right as he got down to her sensitive hips, and he ground his cock against the cleft of her cheeks so he could feel her tuft move against it. His hands drifted to her sides, only to pull back so his nails could score her again and make her tail tremor in reaction when he got close to it.

He leaned over her and bit into her shoulder while thrusting against her.

"Do you want my cock inside you, Zylah?" he rumbled next to her skull, his soft voice hoarse with arousal and his breaths making her knees shake. "Do you want me to stretch you with my cock until you feel nice and full? Do you want me to fuck you until I flood you with my cum, while your tight pussy comes over and over again around me?"

Nodding, she whimpered, "Please."

"Too bad."

A raspy moan broke from her when two fingers slammed into her from behind. Her hips rose even higher when the tips of them prodded right against her most blissful spot, and pleasure struck her within an instant. Her hands struggled against her bindings when he began to thrust his long fingers, each time prodding right at that exact spot like the angle was perfect for it. He even hooked his fingertips downwards to shove against it harder and her toes curled in reaction, her feet lifting.

Her vision blurred as she looked at the wall in a haze while panting wildly. Her breaths came out more strangled when lust and need bled into her veins like an inferno whirling into a dangerous gust. She tilted her head back as she moved back and forth, trying to work herself on his fingers as he played with her.

"Does that feel good?" His husky voice sent her shivering in reaction. "Your pussy is already twitching so much. Fucking hell, Zylah. How can you be this needy? I've barely started."

She didn't even need to respond, not when her pussy clamped around him as she was sent hurtling into an orgasm. Letting out a loud cry, she shifted her hips back and forth faster as liquid gushed inside her spasming core.

Her abdomen pulsed repeatedly, and her body sagged forward as she rode the waves of bliss. His fingertips hooked downwards every time he thrust in, causing her sight to throb in and out of darkness.

The moment her body went lax, she was tossed onto her back. He let out a snarl as he buried his head between her legs to lap his tongue against her entrance, stealing the taste of her climax from her with messy licks. He wasn't gentle with his fangs, but his moving tongue and lips distracted her from any stings as he ravished her with his mouth.

With a loud, aching moan, she could do little more than arch her back when he shoved his long tongue inside her before licking up to her clit to suck it. Her thighs parted even further when he shoved his fingers back inside her, and she hooked her feet over his shoulders to keep her to him. Using the rope around her wrists as leverage, Zylah bucked against his face, wishing, more than ever, that she could grab his horns or hair and fuck herself against it.

Sucking hard and constantly lashing her clit with his tongue, he pumped his fingers fast inside her. Within seconds, Zylah was sent hurdling into another orgasm and her knees closed around his head as her body tried to take over. She could feel her tendrils clasping his fingers, refusing to let go of them until she was done, and he fought against them to pump his hand hard and fast for her.

"Jabez..." she called as her back arched repeatedly, her entire body wanting to lift and float off the bed each time bliss struck her.

She leaned her head against her stretched biceps as she looked down at the top of his hair and horns, wishing she could *see* how he was wonderfully torturing her. Her pants were harsh, ripping from her lungs violently, and they didn't calm even when her body stopped clenching and milking his fingers.

"Don't stop," she pleaded over and over again, her voice growing hoarser and more croaked with each second. "It feels so good. I love your mouth on me. Your tongue, your lips, your fangs. *More.*"

She shuddered out a moan and tried to cross her ankles

across his back to stop him from escaping her. He produced a wet snarl against her pussy as he removed his fingers to lap at her wildly. He grabbed the back of her thighs to give himself room to dip his head up and down, to come at her folds any way he could.

Every time he struck her clit, a quiet whimper broke from her. When he knew she was getting close again, he slipped his tongue inside her as far as it could go. She *swore* she felt a tendril trying to clasp around the tip of it and keep it inside as he thrust it.

Just when she was about to come, he stopped. He managed to wrestle with her legs and win so he could pry them away and shove them apart. Then he pulled away all too soon to lean back, and panic flooded her.

"No! Don't stop, *please*."

She kicked while trying to fight against the bindings so she could shove his face back down.

"Sorry, Zylah, but I can't wait any longer," he stated around deep huffs.

With his nose, cheeks, and chin covered in her slick, Jabez licked at his lips as he looked down at his pants. He fumbled with the ties before just tearing at them, and his cock sprang forth. He was fully engorged, and even his ridges had flared more than usual, precum making the head glisten. He didn't bother to fully remove his pants, choosing to let them fall around his knees and stay there for now.

Jabez grabbed the back of her calves and slammed her shins against the mattress so her feet rested next to her antlers. The angle forced her back to curve and her arse to lift off the bed until her pussy was almost facing the ceiling.

"I was hoping I could hold off for a bit longer, but if I'm not balls deep inside you in the next few seconds, I'm going to go fucking crazy."

He slammed his cock to the hilt in one go, and the broad head and following ridges popped past her entrance and bubbled against her most sensitive spot on their way in. Zylah screamed out a moan at the sensation, and at the blunt girth and hardness that speared her. Her pussy immediately squeezed as liquid heat flooded within, her brain disintegrating from the pressure of his cock.

"Oh fuck," Jabez groaned, pumping his hips hard and fast without giving her a moment to adjust or calm. "You're coming already."

His hands tightened on her calves as he put more weight on them. With his eyes rolling, his expression pinched until his clenched fangs were bared and his head tipped back. He fucked into her wildly, and Zylah could do little more than take it with the way he held her down with her wrists bound.

She whimpered beneath him as she intimately felt his ridges within her swelling, snug walls. Her sight blackened as her orbs closed, when pleasure struck her like a bolt and ensured it continued on and on.

"That's right," he said around hot and feverish pants. "Come all night for me."

Zylah shivered when the last of her orgasm was wrung from her. Her tense muscles loosened, and her body going lax made her bounce each time he shunted against her. Everywhere they touched felt like her flesh was being branded by him, and she hoped his hands just above her ankles left permanent marks.

His hips slammed harder as he opened his eyes and looked down to where she was swallowing him. A deep, dark chuckle vibrated past his lips.

"I'm going to show you what it feels like when I ruin this pussy, and I'm not going to stop until you *beg* me to."

*Shit, my jaw is killing me,* Jabez thought with a complaining groan as he swirled his tongue around Zylah's clit. She twitched in reaction before her thighs shook as he hooked his fingers right against her G-spot.

His hand ached, too, and he'd needed to take breaks between his mouth and fingers over the course of the last hour.

Considering the passage of time in Nyl'theria, he knew it'd been *many* Earth hours since they'd started being intimate.

When he'd first fucked her, dusk had still been present. Night had long come, and their home was shrouded in darkness except for her glowing purple orbs and the dim light coming from both side tables powered by a mana stone he couldn't see.

He'd made sure to come over her rather than inside her pussy so that he could taste just her without his seed messing her. Since then, he'd managed to keep his dick to himself and solely focus on his horny little bunny.

Her pussy clamped around his fingers, and she let out a soft moan, but her orgasm was light and powerless. It ended on a whimper, and the heels of her feet shoved downwards against his back like she wanted him away.

That high-pitched sound was all he needed.

He slipped his fingers from the swollen wet heat of her pussy and finally removed his tongue from her, thankful they'd reached this point after so long.

Despite how tired he was, he still fisted the base of his throbbing cock and positioned the head against the hole of her cunt.

The tip was already wet and saturated with precum, and just the meagre touch of her pussy had his balls clenching. Even the sight of her golden contraception enhancement chain gleaming in the low light around her waist had a shudder assaulting his spine. Knowing he could come inside her and fill her to the brim with his semen without a shred of worry, since she'd never remove it without communicating with him, always turned him on further.

"Wait," she pleaded, looking down just as he started to mount her, only to throw her head back. *"Jabez..."*

He groaned in answer when he was seated deep and ground into her. As much as he knew she was done, he'd only fucked her once and his cock was *desperate* for release. He'd been a good boy, he'd been patient, he'd only taken her once and then gifted her climax after climax.

He may have been able to resist if it wasn't for the fact he'd been drinking down her orgasms. The aphrodisiac component in it meant he *needed* this. It'd been tingling his engorged cock from the moment he'd shoved into her, and it'd been flooding his blood stream with each lap of his tongue for *hours*. Every fibre of muscle in his body was now buzzing with lust.

He thrust into her overused, swollen pussy, and his eyelids flickered in bliss at how soft it was, how snug it'd become. When she gave a whimper, he lowered his body and held her tightly in order to comfort her. He went slow just for her sake, but he also knew he didn't need to pump into her like a feral beast.

He groaned against her neck when his cock pulsated *hard*.

*This isn't going to last long.* Even with just a few pumps, he'd been waiting so long, his hips grinding against the sheets with need, that he was already close.

One of his hands slid under her torso to cup the back of her neck, while the other kneaded her backside and lifted her hips to greet his own. When she gave another little whimper, his ears drooped as euphoria threatened to obliterate him.

"Sorry, Zylah. Just hold out a little longer for me," he begged, pushing into her until he reached her cervix to softly grind against it.

"I don't like this anymore," she whined, tugging on her bindings weakly. "I-I want to hold you."

Unable to stop thrusting, unable to stop moving like his life depended on it, he shuddered. He looked up at her wrists, and his dazed mind tried to think of a solution outside of letting this beautiful creature go. When she clamped up momentarily, a pitiful *moan* escaped past his panting lips.

Jabez teleported them in place and she slipped through the bindings.

"I-I like this," she whispered, as she wrapped her arms around his body so she could sweetly cling to him. "I like when our stomachs touch and I can feel you more deeply inside me."

*Fuck. Cute,* he thought, his eyes crinkling in anguish at her pure words. He laid over her so more of their torsos touched and meshed together, and it tilted the angle of their hips differently.

A sharp hitch came from her like his cock rubbed somewhere perfect, and her thighs spread for him. He shouldn't have let her be free. Now that her hands were clutching him, her claws *gouged* into his shoulder and side when her pussy wildly spasmed.

A flare of aggression cut through the languidness of his fatigue, and he fucked into her faster. Her claws ripped into his flesh, and he let out a roar, his fingers digging into her body to hold her still as his hips shoved into her harder.

He bit into the side of her neck, just as her pussy clenched around his cock, and he knew he was doomed. Zylah let out a whimpering moan as she milked him, producing just enough liquid slick to make his glides easier, faster, *hotter.* Her ankles tried to cross over his arse as he took her, and his fangs cut deeper and deeper until his eyes rolled back.

His balls drew up hard, clenching in his sac, and seed shot from him. He stopped thrusting and shoved his hips so hard she gasped.

"Oh *fuck*, Zylah," he moaned as he released his bite to *breathe* through his release.

His nose scrunched when tenderness clamoured inside his chest and seemingly made his orgasm more powerful, causing pleasure to ripple down his spine and spark all throughout his groin. He squeezed her to his torso, as his legs shook and his toes dug into the bed to push himself deeper. His muscles leapt each time semen burst from him, while his face twisted in agonised rapture.

Once he finally emptied his balls, he basked in the aftermath so he could feel her heartbeat thrumming around his cock and against him, and so she could sense his all around her. Their panted breaths tangled together, and the mixture of their scents had him pulsating one last time in an intense aftershock that fucking *pained* him.

He pressed a kiss to the side of her cheek before slowly slipping his cock from her, needing to escape her as much as give her relief.

Her arms fell to the bed, letting him go when she was too tired to do anything else but exist.

Overheating to the point sweat was slipping down his bleeding back and temple, Jabez climbed off the bed to head to the bathtub that was built into the floor. He crouched, waved his hand over the purple mana stone, and watched as temperature-controlled water rushed out from the side of the tub to rapidly fill it.

He turned and found Zylah lifeless on the bed, and a grin curled his lips. Wiggling his aching jaw and hand bones, he approached her.

Her orbs went white when she lifted her skull to him, and the gasp she produced was broken, hoarse, and filled with utter panic.

"You're still hard!" She turned to crawl off the bed, but her legs were limp and barely helped her. "No! I can't anymore!"

Jabez grabbed her ankle and pulled her across the sheets.

"And whose fault do you think that is?" he stated with a playful growl. "Now your pesky little enzymes can torture us both. I only came twice, Zylah. You usually *beg* for more, and I'm very inclined to give it right now."

She screamed and shoved her hands against his chest, but she was surprisingly weak as she fought him. He shoved her knees to the sides with his own, laid between them, and thrust his cock against her clit while burying his face against the side of her neck.

"Please, Jabez. I'm sorry," she whimpered, her body heaving against him with a sob. "I won't do it anymore."

His eyes crinkled in joy as laughter burst from him. "I'm joking, Zylah," he said, lifting his face so she could see his humour. "No more for tonight."

"You promise?" The heavy tone of distress in her voice hinted that she didn't believe him.

He rested his chin against her chest and smiled up at her. "How do you feel? Finally satisfied?"

She shuddered and nodded, and he pressed a kiss to her

sternum.

"Good, because fuck me, my whole body hurts."

He cupped his chin to push his aching jaw side to side, before doing the same to his neck until he heard a satisfying, relieving crack. Even the back of his damn tongue hurt, and he could tell the underside was inflamed from overworking it.

Her orbs flickered with orange. "I'm sorry."

"Don't be. I'm happy to do this every night, so long as my mate is having fun. It was bothering me that I wasn't able to fully satisfy you with just my cock, so I found a solution." He turned his head and grazed the side of her left breast with his fangs. "You're also so responsive to everything that I like touching and tasting you. I enjoyed every second of it."

"Really?" she asked, her voice light with hope as her orbs brightened into yellow.

"Really." He pulled back, stood, and then slipped his arms under her so he could carry her to the bath. "But I'm really sweaty and some heat will do us both good. I'm guessing you'll want to sleep soon."

They were both adjusting their sleeping patterns to Nyl'theria. Now that he was here, his body wanted to fall into its natural rhythm of sleeping away much of the night. Zylah, on the other hand, appeared to want to sleep equal to Earth's cycle, but she was trying to prolong it to keep up with him. In return, he cut his sleeps in half so they could rest together at night, and right after the second sun had almost fully risen.

By the time he carted Zylah to the tub, it was nearly full. He hissed out a breath through his fangs when he sat down with her on the seat available inside it, and water touched her claw marks marring his back. Thankfully he'd dulled her claws every morning in order to stop her from cutting too deep, which also prevented her from accidentally hurting others with them.

Settling in the water, Jabez waved his hand to stop it prematurely, so it didn't overfill. The temperature was perfect, making steam waft from the top of the water's surface, and the obsidian would keep it that way for quite some time.

With her resting across his spread thighs and her shoulder against his chest, he leaned into the backrest. He placed his arms across the back of it and looked outside at Otholla starting to peek its way into the glass from the left side.

"I really do like this view," he commented, eyeing the forest subtly glowing in the distance.

It felt like home, and it was what he always wanted – even if achieving it wasn't how he'd planned.

"I like it too," she offered as she slid an arm across his stomach to hold his side and keep herself steady.

She never floated in the water, and he preferred how heavily she sat in his lap rather than buoyantly bouncing away. Sitting in liquid heat, Jabez let his mind go quiet as he basked in the satisfaction of their sex, the bathtub and how it soothed them, and the view he'd always longed for.

Zylah lifted a hand and sheathed her claws to tap at the chain connected to the bands on his horns and make it sway. A subtle smile pestered his lips; he was pleased she liked them so much.

Organising them was one of the first things he'd done, and it'd drained almost all the funds the council had given him for entering the city. It was why he pushed for them to let him go mining for a mana stone today. Although it was a requisite of him being here, they were being fair and paying him for the work as well.

Every time he left the city or did anything for them, they were going to pay for his time.

Lezekos City was a trade city.

Food, housing, medicine, and basic furniture were all provided, but if they wanted nice clothing, quality adornments, or to add to their home, they needed to work for it or pick up a craft to trade with. Since they were new, it would take a long while for them to establish themselves. Doing work for the council would ensure he didn't have to learn a craft, meaning he and Zylah were free to do whatever they wished.

In essence, he could be lazy and dote on her whenever he wanted outside of when they requested his aid.

"Jabez," Zylah started, still playing with the gems dangling from his horn.

He tilted his head so he could face her. "Yes?"

Her teal orbs flickered with reddish pink and she nervously chittered. He frowned when her shoulders turned inwards shyly and she lowered her hand.

"Do you..." She squirmed and her orbs shifted entirely to her bashful or embarrassed hue. "Do you love me?"

His head twitched and reared back, not expecting the question; it sounded as though she'd been wanting to ask it for quite some time. He averted his gaze to outside, while his heart pounded harder in his chest, slamming deeply aching emotions into his veins.

"Yes, I love you," he answered quietly, and without hesitation.

She pushed against his chest to sit up with a shocked gasp. "Really?"

Not liking how surprised she sounded, he pulled her back down and the water rippled around them. "Of course I do."

*I gave up...* everything *for you.* What was that if it wasn't love?

Some men, immoral and cruel like him, might be willing to burn the world for someone they adored, but he'd already been trying to do that. Such a sacrifice was utterly meaningless with a past already filled with rampaging bloodshed. Giving her the world through domination was in line with his goal to raze this city, but entering peacefully? Not in a million years did he think he'd ever do such a thing.

He gave up his goal, his idea, his revenge, and even... his sense of self. He essentially tore himself to pieces until all that remained was his obsession, infatuation, and tenderness for her. Until all that remained of him were the parts that were connected to her, and he was unwilling to let her go or see her be harmed through his actions.

It was also what kept him subservient and obedient to the councilmembers.

*I hate being in this fucking city.* He hated doing what they wanted of him. He hated that he'd been pushed to offer his services in a way he found abhorrent. He hated that he'd shared his lifelong secret with another being, an Elf, no less.

Every fibre, every cell, every piece of his being, didn't want to be in the city. He despised their scents, their un-Demon-like features, their gazes, and hated the way they looked at Zylah with gross curiosity. Every time someone looked at her funny or was somewhat fearful, he wanted to walk right up to them and punt them in the face with one of his hard horns.

But he was tolerating it all, just for her.

He would continue to do so just so he could make her giggle like he had earlier when he chased her around their *home*, or fuck her until she begged him to stop. Just so he didn't have to see her covered in her own blood again as she whimpered in his arms from pain.

His heart had shifted, and he'd been born anew for her, although nothing would stop him from being an arrogant, self-assured prick.

Nothing would change the essence of who he was, and he was just lucky she seemed to like it, *mostly.*

He may not be perfect, but he would try for her. And his pride and masculinity weren't so fragile that he would be bothered by Zylah calling him her little bride, mate, enchanting thorn, or whatever she decided to settle on. He would just use it as a way to tease her by being overly dominant in those times to get a playful rise out of her.

He thought she might even like that.

A glittering drop floated into his periphery, and he glanced down to find her orbs were bright pink and shedding ethereal tears. She was looking off to the side with her hands clasped tightly, and a quiet whine ripped from her. He noticed then that her heart was beating excessively fast and her tail was shifting side to side against his outer thigh.

*That answers what the colour pink means.*

"Well?" he said with a light chuckle. "Are you going to leave me in suspense, or are you going to say it back?"

"I love you, Jabez," she whispered as she looked up at him.

"I think I have for a long while."

"I love you too," he repeated, just so she knew it was the truth.

He placed his index foreknuckle under her chin, lifted the underside of her bony jaw, and pressed a kiss to her incisors. She giggled underneath his lips as her pink tears floated faster and collided to create bigger drops.

He eyed them fondly, admiring her ethereal dark beauty while the aqua glow of his dual-coloured soul radiated above her. She owned the most secret parts of him, and he knew, in essence, that he owned hers as well – even if there wasn't proof of it floating above his head.

*I think you're the only creature in existence able to make me give up everything and fall in love instead.*

What a pathetically tender thought.

# A Duskwalker Family Reunion

Bonus Novella

Opal Reyne

# ONE



*One Nyl'theria month (three and a half Earth months) later*

Jabez's nose wrinkled as he bit back an unhidden groan through clenched fangs until a muscle in his jaw knotted. Watching Zylah bounce a sopping-wet pussy up and down his cock while facing away from him, he locked his heated gaze onto her fluffy tail as it brushed against his abdomen repeatedly.

He cut his nails down her furry back so when he got close to that little tuft of fur, it'd flutter. Along with it, her insides quivered around his cock, and his jaw fell.

*I love it when she does that.*

He brought his thumbs to either side of her slit and spread the lips of her purple pussy from behind so he could watch himself disappearing repeatedly into her snug heat. He licked across his lips as a shuddering pant fell from him.

When his seed started to rise, he held her hips and rammed into her from below at the same time. He slammed himself balls deep, making sure her cunt swallowed him whole.

The brightness of early morning darkened as his vision dimmed when his sac drew up tight, and he met her thrust for thrust. A tingle spread through his groin and ran up his sweat-coated spine. His stomach hollowed, his chest tightened when his breaths cut off, and his heart raced until it was a deafening roar in his ears.

Within seconds, he was spending inside her. Instead of trying to hold her down so he was as deep as possible, he let her playfully bounce on him. It ensured she utterly scrambled his mind as he lay there and just let her have her fun while he came. As he was finishing, her own orgasm had her claws digging into his shaking thighs, and she tipped her head back to let out a pretty cry.

*Fuck, she's going to kill me one day doing this.* He groaned as she squeezed his now sensitive cock tight.

Only when she was finished wringing herself around him did he grab her hips and hold her down so she'd stop. Which, of course, she didn't. She squirmed and twisted to keep going, releasing a whine of disquiet.

Slipping his cock from her, Jabez tackled her to the bed and her chest slammed against it. He held her down by straddling her arse, his shaft resting between her plump cheeks, and laid down over her. He pressed a kiss to the side of her neck.

"That's enough, Zylah," he told her, flicking his eyes up at the brightening sky.

"But I don't want to stop," she exclaimed, lifting her hips up to grind against him.

"Well, too bad." He nipped her neck as he ran his hands down her arms and held the backs of her hands. "You managed to convince me to have sex this morning when we were supposed to be getting ready. Merikh will get annoyed if we're late because we were fucking."

She turned her head to the side with a harrumph and then let out an annoyed snorting huff. *She's cute when she pouts.*

"I don't care how he feels," she grumbled.

He hopped off her and gave her plump backside a hard spank. "Atta girl."

Jabez quickly rolled off the bed and shoved his hand up to prepare himself in case a horny Zylah tackled him. She didn't, and he stood up straight as she climbed off the mattress. Then he turned and walked to the shower area while pulling free the half bun he had his hair in. He waved his hand in front of the temperature-controlled mana stone, and the shower came to life.

Before he entered the stall, he stepped back into the doorway to peek at Zylah, who was going through the hanging wardrobe situated against the wall near the bed.

"Are you coming?"

Her shoulders stiffened, her fur puffing along with the movement, and she turned her head away. "No. I don't like it in there."

"We don't have time for a bath." When she didn't immediately come, he held his hand out and beckoned her with it. "I'll make sure you don't fall again."

Zylah let out a sigh and waltzed her furry butt over to him. The moment she crossed the threshold into the wet area, her knees were unsteady, and she held onto his forearms. He closed her in under the water's spray by placing his hands against the obsidian wall on either side of her.

*She really hasn't gotten over that first time yet.* He tried not to laugh, as he knew that would only worsen how she felt.

Jabez tentatively removed his right hand from the wall so he could touch between her thighs and slip two fingers inside her. Not expecting it, she gasped and gripped his shoulders.

"I-I don't want to do it in the shower!"

"I'm not." Although... the idea of fucking her against the wall as warm water sprayed his back did make his still-erect cock jerk. "I'm cleaning you of my cum."

She let out an uncomfortable moan when he spread his fingers, but he was satisfied when sticky liquid dribbled from her.

"Why?"

"Because, trust me, it's probably better if I do."

Jabez normally didn't give a damn, but they were about to be around scent-orientated creatures who had very good senses of smell. They also hated him with a passion. He'd rather not make it more awkward for her, as she was the one who would be within sniffing distance while he stayed back and out of harm's way.

Once he was done, he helped her wash in their scentless

shampoo and then turned the water off. With a simple wave of his hand, the drying spell turned on, and the wobble in her knees eased.

She exited the room while he brushed his fangs, then he combed his hair and tied it back into a half bun again. He checked to make sure his face didn't need shaving, and he was satisfied to find it was barely prickly since he'd done it the previous day.

Just as he was leaving the wet area, he noticed her pull out her favourite outfit.

"I wanted to wear the teal dress," he said with a deadpan expression and tone.

Zylah's orbs flared bright yellow as she clutched the garment to her chest. She turned away from him to hide her giggle, trying not to encourage his mischief and how funny he found himself.

He donned a pair of black skintight pants and a long-sleeved shirt before cladding himself in his navy sleeveless tunic that had a tight, rigid collar. When he slipped his legs into his light-purple harem pants, he tied them around his knees so they didn't flap around his calves. He donned nothing else, but he pulled back the sleeves of the black shirt when the heat immediately started to make him sweat.

*It should be summer on Earth, but I'd rather not waste mana keeping myself warm.* He could already foresee how Merikh was about to abuse his magical abilities, and he didn't want to add to it.

Once they were dressed, they left their home. They only needed to reach the end of the hallway before the big Mavka and his bride could be seen waiting for them.

Dressed in a red sleeveless tunic almost identical to his own, Merikh wore black pants that tied around his knees. Like usual, he wore the armoured Elven guards to protect others from his dangerous quills.

Raewyn had chosen to don a pale-pink dress that was flowy, long, and would have been revealing if it wasn't for the black skintight pants and shirt she also wore. On her feet, she wore the decorative soleless shoes that most Elysians preferred, keeping the bottoms of her feet bare so she could freely use her magic.

A high-pitched giggle reached his ears as a small Delysian child let go of Raewyn's hand and bolted for him with a squeal. He watched the little girl approach and then quickly collected her into his arms.

"Well, good morning to you, too, Lehnenia," Jabez greeted in Nyl'kira, as he took in her features less than an inch from his nose. Her big red eyes, tipped with white lashes, bore into his own.

With horns running back over her head similar to his own, she gave him a fanged smile. Unlike him, the demonling had large canine fangs, and they were so big for her mouth that it pushed her shark-like ones forward in the middle to create a point. Loose, corkscrew curls bounced around her head and pointed ears as she gave him a wide-eyed greeting stare.

Like him and Raewyn, Lehnenia also wore a set of warm clothing underneath a pale-orange dress.

"Morning, Jabez," Lehnenia cooed, brushing her hands into the long lengths of his hair – that were free from his half bun – resting against his chest.

Considering they shared similar Demon and Elven features, she'd instantly become smitten with him. He wasn't usually a fan of children touching him, but he just *loved* pissing off her adoptive father. He was overplaying the 'nice uncle' act.

Jabez lifted his gaze away from the child so he could grin at Merikh. "At least someone is happy to see me."

The bull-horned Mavka folded his arms across his broad chest. "You're late," he said in Nyl'kira, since he'd been learning it for quite a few months here – he was mediocre at best.

Two silver bands were locked around Merikh's bull horns, each one with a thin chain of starburst charms dangling from it, and he noted a glint hiding behind Raewyn's voluminous hair.

A sly smirk twitched the right side of his mouth.

Merikh had seen Jabez and Zylah's matching pair of bonding charms and grown interested in the Demon custom. Especially as he'd noticed Delysian couples within the city wearing similar charms.

Jabez had a feeling Merikh probably wanted to visually mark his female like a possessive Mavka to keep others away from her. He liked that he'd given him the idea, and it was amusing how Merikh had tried to hide his awkwardness in asking for assistance regarding it.

He let Merikh decide his own charms, but he'd obviously borrowed the idea of representing their eye colours and used crystals and metal to symbolise his bride's rather mesmerising starburst pupils.

Raewyn patted Merikh's side until her hands found the cream satchel strapped across his torso. She dug into it with deeply furrowed white brows and spoke in English.

"Are you sure we have everything? Did you grab the snacks for her? You know she probably won't want to eat anything there, as it's new." She dug around a thick jacket, before gasping. "Where are her socks?!"

"They're in the front pocket," Merikh answered back, shutting the bag so the woman could stop fretting. "I've checked it multiple times, Raewyn. We have everything for her."

Jabez put the child down, who was reluctant to be let go. She went over to Merikh, rose her arms up to him with grabby hands, and demanded that her father pick her up. He easily complied, and Jabez was already aware he spoiled the demonling.

"Alright, are you ready?" Jabez asked, placing his arm around Zylah's waist. "I'll have to take you and Lehnenia first, and then Raewyn and Zylah."

Merikh scoffed. "Still can't take more than two people, huh?"

"Listen, you fuck. Do you know how damn dense your kind are?" Jabez argued, rolling his eyes like that should have been obvious. "You know I can only teleport what I can carry, and your furry arse is as heavy as a boulder the size of your torso."

"Can you please not swear in front of Lehnenia?" Raewyn bit out while folding her arms and narrowing her eyes in his general direction. She tapped her thin biceps in annoyance.

"It's not like she'll understand Engl–" He was cut off the moment the child repeated the word 'fuck' with a coy grin curling her lips.

Jabez chuckled as his eyes crinkled with humour. *Look at her go.*

He coughed and looked away when Merikh's orbs shone deeper in their reddish hue than normal. He almost began whistling like a deviant, but he knew that wouldn't bode well for him. *I'm not used to being around children,* he thought in his own defence. Filtering himself when he spoke had never been on his radar.

Much had changed in just a few short weeks of being here.

His relationship with Merikh had begun to shift to how it used to be, since the Mavka went everywhere with him when he left the city for the council. Training together, getting books for Zerik, and mining mana stones meant they were in each other's company almost daily and for an extensive period of time.

Merikh's anger towards him hadn't truly faded, but it had ebbed over time when he saw Jabez was... changing. Jabez would always be the same brash, cold, arrogant, and cheeky man when he wanted to be – as he'd always been – but his wants and desires had shifted entirely.

Jabez had also warmed up to his half-sister a little. He'd thought Raewyn to be a soft-hearted woman, but she could actually be rather stern and prickly when she wanted. She had a bubbly personality outside of the conference chamber and her laboratory, and she changed how she behaved upon walking out of those spaces.

However, he had quickly, and rather harshly, placed a boundary between them the first time she'd tried to bring up the idea of Jabez meeting with his mother and stepfather. He was in complete refusal of it, and he hoped he never crossed paths with them in the city.

The fact his stepfather still worked in the hospital left him ill with the idea of Zylah visiting it in curiosity. He told Raewyn if she went behind his back to introduce them, he'd cut emotional ties with her and his niece within an instant. He would also only communicate with her through Merikh, even within her own workspace, and he warned her of how cold and callous he could be once betrayed.

Her features had twisted, the idea of already losing the shaky bond he was allowing to form leaving her distressed, and she agreed. She'd even offered to help Zylah and him evade his parents to the best of her abilities.

He'd learned through such actions that Raewyn was exceptionally stubborn when she wanted to be, but willing to be passive when required. She was pushing for a bond with him and was doing everything in her power to make it possible, despite his original aversion to the idea.

He wondered if her stubbornness was how she'd won over Merikh.

Once everyone confirmed they were ready, Jabez released Zylah's waist and approached Merikh. He placed his hand on the surly Mavka's arm and teleported him and Lehnenia to the gate of the city. They left the safety of it while Jabez went back to grab their females.

Then he followed the same transport pattern as he took them to the portal to Austrális he'd created a long, long time ago.

*I still can't believe he forced me into this,* he thought, as he looked at the glowing yellow portal with utter disdain.

*To fucking Earth I go.*

# TWO

Once they all climbed out of the metal cage he'd installed around Earth's side of the portal, Jabez looked up at the brightening sky.

*Dawn is rising.* He was prepared to protect both himself and Lehnenia from the sun, but he'd rather conserve his energy until he really needed to. Teleporting six times within such a quick timeframe was fine. Doing so while carrying the weight of two Mavka had exerted him enough that his breath had turned shallow for a few seconds.

*This is only going to get worse as the day progresses.* He cut a glare at the back of Merikh's bear skull. *The bastard has no idea.* He probably also wouldn't care.

*He better be thankful I agreed to this.* It would alleviate Merikh's ire towards him, but he was also doing this to make Zylah happy. She'd been thrilled when he told her about taking a trip back to Earth temporarily.

The synedrus council had only approved a certain number of hours, but here on Earth, it equated to around two days. He figured Raewyn had used her seat to strong-arm the others, since Merikh had been the one to request this.

"I hate how cold it is here," Raewyn muttered quietly, blowing into her hands and rubbing them together.

Jabez lowered his gaze to the green hedges just beyond the portal's cage, most of which had their leaves now after being damaged by the sun bomb that had almost killed him nearly seven months ago.

*It's summer, from what I can tell.* The fact she was already cold after being here for a few minutes just proved how much Jabez's body had adapted after so many years of living on Earth. The night air did feel frigid to him, but it would feel lukewarm by the peak of the day. *She'd be freaking useless in the winter.*

Which is likely why this trip had been planned for sooner, rather than later.

Merikh looked down at the child shivering in his arms, and he pulled the jacket from his satchel to dress her in it. He handed Raewyn the set of socks they'd spoken about earlier, and the demonling screamed as they put them over her feet. They even gave her a set of gloves before they transferred her into Raewyn's arms.

Other than the socks, the gloves and jacket weren't common pieces of clothing within Lezekos City. Jabez figured Raewyn had gotten them tailor-made just for the excursion.

Now that he was free from the child, Merikh took a single step through the shrouding black mist with his muscles bunching in tension. He put a small amount of space between him and his precious family, who had sensitive ears, before roaring, "Weldir!"

Once done, he snorted out a huff through his nose hole.

"You called, little one?" a masculine voice stated from above, forcing them all to rotate to the cage behind them.

On top of it sat a figure shrouded in dark robes that hid all his features. Black mist wafted from underneath his hood and the seams of it, hiding him further, as if he didn't wish to be seen. From what Jabez could tell, he sat with his legs crossed and appeared to be peering down at them.

"So..." Merikh started, casting Jabez a glance before lifting his snout upwards. "It's true. You've obtained a physical form."

"What is it you need, Merikh?" Weldir asked, his hood tilting slightly to show he'd angled his face towards those behind him. Jabez could almost *feel* his creepy gaze on him.

"Where is the Witch Owl? She's usually the one who comes when I call you."

"You mean your mother?" he retorted disapprovingly, his tone stern. "She is resting. What do you need?"

As they spoke, Jabez took a step to the side to see if he could get a peek at the demigod's face. Even when he positioned himself in view of the open gap of Weldir's hood, black mist made it near impossible to see anything but a strange yellow glint. His skin looked shiny or glossy, but Jabez couldn't make out anything else in the impenetrable darkness.

"I'd rather not talk to you," Merikh grumbled, feeling the same way about his parents as Jabez did with his own. "But I guess you'll do. It's your power anyway. Show me where my brothers are."

Weldir didn't move a muscle as five seeing discs formed in front of them. Each oval disc had a mirrored surface with black sand glittering around its edges. The centres of them waved and rippled before each displayed a different image.

Jabez could produce such magic, so long as he had some form of the creature's essence to scry with, whether it be their fur, flesh, blood, or even bone. He wondered if Weldir needed such tools, or if he was able to sense where all his direct descendants were at all times.

Three of the discs produced locations that were familiar to Jabez, each one within the Veil he and his companions currently stood in the middle of. One was of Orpheus' log-cabin home and the salt circle surrounding it, another a sky view of a yellow dome with a house in the middle, and the third of a green dome with a similar log cabin to Orpheus'.

One of the remaining two was a known location to most, simply because of the heated springs near the base of the mountain. A pink protection dome sat over the top of a large section of it.

The last disc revealed a place he couldn't decipher due to it only being the edge of a very large orange protective dome. He squinted his eyes, as if that would be enough for him to gauge where it was, but there was nothing but a mountain wall and a cave entrance to be seen.

"An orange dome?" Merikh asked, tilting his bear skull as his orbs flared dark yellow. "What Mavka has orange orbs?"

"I would think you would know who they belong to," Weldir answered cryptically, with the mildest hint of humour in his tone.

"Unless Lindiwe has allowed her other younglings to form their skulls, the only Mavka I know to have orange orbs was... *Nathair*," Merikh said quietly, his voice at the end dripping with emotions Jabez knew all too well: pain and *regret*.

"Precisely," Weldir almost purred.

Jabez watched as the tip of Merikh's bull tail curled so tight around the tuft of fur at the end it looked like a ball. His orbs flickered with blue as his fisted hands repeatedly opened and closed.

"You mean... he's... *alive*?" Merikh asked, his voice raising an octave. "Where is he?"

"North." The image in the disc shifted to a town built into the side of a mountain. "Mated and happy."

Merikh turned from Weldir, giving the demigod his back, and his skull darted towards Jabez. He'd managed to stop his orb colour from permanently changing, likely to hide his emotions, but Jabez could hear how hard his heart pounded when he approached.

"Did you get all that?" Merikh grated.

Jabez nodded. "Yeah. Shouldn't be too hard."

"What are you planning, Merikh?" Weldir asked darkly. "You've brought your mate and someone we consider an enemy."

"You're no longer needed," Merikh bit at the demigod with a light snarl. "No doubt you'll watch regardless. Figure it out on your own, but stay the fuck away from me. Lindiwe too."

"I think it's best if we go to the fox-skulled Mavka's ward," Jabez stated, eyeing Weldir just to watch him disappear in a puff of black sand at his own child's hateful ire. He folded his arms and tapped his fingers against his right biceps. "They already know of me, and Zylah has met them."

"They are my parents, right?" Zylah asked, stepping closer to brush her fingertips against the inside of his forearm. She loosely held him in a way that indicated she was wary.

"Yes," he answered.

"I don't know the fox-skulled Mavka, though," Merikh rumbled in protest.

"No matter who we go to, things will go astray due to my presence. It's best we first face those who I've already spoken with and I know won't be on the immediate attack." Then he nodded towards Raewyn holding Lehnenia. "That one won't attack your bride and child, as he already has his own."

"Guess I can't argue with that," Merikh said as he took Lehnenia back from Raewyn. He turned to their females. "Don't get into too much trouble while we're gone. I'm trusting you, Zylah, to keep her safe."

"I think you're forgetting who you're talking to," Raewyn stated confidently, placing her hands on her hips and popping them to one side.

"Yes, yes. A pretty fairy who can protect herself with *grass*." Merikh rolled his head like one might roll their eyes in exasperation before he stepped over to Jabez to be teleported with his child. "You're as useful in defence as a fish is at walking on the ground."

Raewyn poked her tongue out at him, and Merikh's chuckle echoed all the way through Jabez teleporting them to the edge of Magnar's green ward. He watched to make sure they were able to enter it before leaving. He did the same for Raewyn and Zylah, clasping both their wrists before materialising them there as well.

When everyone stepped through the protective ward freely, Jabez eyed the height of its circumference. He then knocked a foreknuckle against it, expecting it to warble in reaction and not let him pass like in the past. His knuckle went right through it. He dipped his hand inside with his lips pursing in surprise, then stepped through.

*I wonder what's changed.* He'd never been able to enter a Mavka's ward before. Was it that he was now a Phantom and it'd been able to sense that, or was it due to his intention being non-violent?

He eyed Lehnenia and wondered how she'd managed to pass through despite being a full-blooded Demon. *Perhaps because she was being carried?*

As a group, they walked towards the large log-cabin home.

Just as Merikh placed a foot on the stairs of the porch, intending to knock on the front door painted green, it bashed against the wall when it was flung open. In the doorway, the fox-skulled, deer-antlered Mavka shone red orbs at them and blocked it so they couldn't enter freely. With neck feathers flared and a long, fluffy tail puffed out, aggression lined his entire body.

"Who are you?" Magnar bit out in English, his snout drifting over them all to show he was inspecting them. He produced a snarl, only for it to die as his orbs shifted to dark yellow. "Zylah?"

Zylah chittered and wrapped both her hands around Jabez's forearm to shield herself.

"Did you say Zylah?" Delora asked, groggy with sleep, as she peeked around Magnar's arm in a white nightgown. "Oh gods, Magnar! How did so many strangers get through your ward?!"

"A Mavka will always be able to enter another's ward, and I imagine that goes for their brides as well," Merikh answered, folding his arms across his chest to take his usual offensive stance. "I'm Merikh. I'm sure you've heard of me by now."

Frozen and unsure what to do, considering the mixture of people at his doorstep, Magnar did nothing more than stand in the doorway. Delora refused to leave his side, staying a step behind to glance around him, but her fingers did tentatively wrap around her Mavka's much larger hand. It was obvious when her gaze landed on Zylah that she wanted to greet her, but with so many strangers, she wisely remained where she was.

Her gaze narrowed into a glare in his direction, but he wanted to chuckle that both mother and daughter held their partners similarly to each other. He managed to hide his humour by dipping his gaze back to the fox Mavka's skull.

"What do you want?" Magnar tilted his head and almost smacked the end of his large antler rack into the door frame.

"Fuck, why is this so awkward?" Merikh bit under his breath, before snapping his fangs at Jabez. "I told you we should have gone to someone else. At least Faunus *knows* me."

He threw his free arm out to the side and shrugged. "Don't blame me. It's better we leave Zylah with people she knows. Just pull your bitch panties up and get on with it."

With an irritated huff, Merikh waved towards his family. "This is my bride, Raewyn. She's an Elysian from the Elven realm." Then he jostled the girl in his arms. "This is Lehnenia, our daughter."

Magnar's orbs darkened in their yellow hue, and his skull cocked to tilt again. "But she does not look like a Mavka youngling."

"She's a Demon we adopted from the city," he answered.

"Adopted?" he asked, tipping his snout to Delora for answers.

Her voice was quiet as she answered, "It means she was a child who lost her birth parents, an orphan, and they have taken her in as their own. She is not related to them."

"Look," Merikh stated with a sigh as he handed the child off to her mother. "I'm rounding up all you knuckleheads because my bride wishes to meet you all, and *apparently*, it would be good for me. Since Zylah is your kid, we figured it was best we left them with you while Jabez and I drag the others here."

"You... want to have a family reunion?" Delora asked with her voice high with surprise. "*Here?*"

"Where else?" Merikh asked, raising an arm and mirroring Jabez's earlier shrug, clearly uncaring that he was intruding on them. "Unless you'd like to do it in the Veil where Demons run rampant. Rather foolish, no?"

Delora's gaze slipped to Jabez again, then darted between him and Zylah. Her eyes froze and widened before her expression twisted into what could only be distress or anguish. Jabez let his eyes flick up to her antlers to look at the floating green-and-blue flame.

*She's probably only just realised Zylah has my soul.* She didn't look too pleased about that.

"Delora?" Magnar called, turning his head to her once more. "What should we do?"

"I... don't know," she mumbled. "I have no issue with people staying, so long as you all don't intend any harm. However, I do have a problem with *him* being here."

Merikh darted his skull to Jabez before rolling it away. "You're going to have to get over the past. He's here to stay, and without his help, this isn't possible." Then, with a rather mean chuckle, Merikh gestured towards him. "Say hello to your new son-in-law. Congratulations." He clapped while balancing the demonling on one inner elbow.

"If he can't stay, then I won't either," Zylah bit out confidently. "He is my *mate*, and that won't change."

Jabez noticed how she called him her mate rather than her bride. He'd told her either was fine, as his masculinity wasn't so fragile to be bothered being called a feminine term, but apparently, she still couldn't figure out what she felt most comfortable with. She kept changing it, and he was content to let her figure it out on her own.

The little human hid behind Magnar and produced an adorable roar of frustration against his furry back. She even stamped her feet childishly before ripping his arm back so she could propel herself forward by it with renewed confidence.

"Okay, fine!" She stepped out of their home and onto the porch, and her Mavka quickly followed to shadow her like a looming protector. "I'll be honest, we've been wanting to get everyone together again, but everyone is everywhere."

"If you're able to call the others close by and let them know, Jabez and I will go play fetch with the others further away. We are already aware of their locations," Merikh stated. "If they won't come willingly, I'll drag them here by their horns if I have to."

"Well, I know Ingram and Aleron are together with their brides, but no one will be happy to see him," Delora stated, while pointing at Jabez outright. "He has a lot to pay for."

"Oh, boo hoo," Jabez retorted with a sneer, rolling his eyes as he brushed a stray leaf that landed on his shoulder. "Everyone is alive and well, aren't they? Considering you blew me the fuck up to an inch of my life, I'd say you all dished out your share of justice."

"You ate me! You broke Faunus' skull! You tortured Orpheus for years and almost killed Reia! *And* you had Aleron killed!" Delora threw her hands to the sides. "Only the gods know what else you've done to the Duskwalkers that we haven't figured out yet."

"You did do a lot of nasty shit," Merikh agreed, leaning back to look at him past Raewyn. "Then again, how many times have I eaten a limb of yours? And how many times have I ripped a Mavka's skull from his neck? Even Raewyn here likes to go around kneeing Mavka in the seam."

"That's not fair!" Raewyn exclaimed. "You were scaring me, and I thought you were a human before you turned all 'big frightening monster' on me."

A laugh burst from Merikh. "What I'm saying is we all have committed our fair share of violence. Our bonds are eternal, and this fuckwit here has decided to have a change of heart. He's a part of the family, whether we like it or not."

"I'm starting to get bored," Jabez interjected with a sigh. "If you like, Zylah and I can leave so you can have a pity party all by yourself."

"N-no. It's fine," Delora quickly said, her tune changing as he thought it would. She reached out to his mate despite the distance between them. "I would like to talk to her again. The last time we went to your cave, you were both gone."

"So it's settled then?" Merikh asked. "We'll leave our females in your hands, and you'll bring the others close by?"

"I'm surprised you would trust us so willingly," Magnar commented while cupping the end of his snout. He tapped his foreclaw against the side of it as if he was musing *very* deeply.

*Don't hurt yourself there, bud,* Jabez thought, mildly worried that thinking so hard may have negative repercussions for the Mavka.

"I wouldn't if I had another option, but I'd rather not take a child into the wilds. So long as you keep your claws to yourself and keep them protected, all will be well." Merikh let out a warning snarl as he stomped his right foot forward. "However, if so much as a single hair is out of place on either of them, you will learn just *why* everyone in this godsforsaken family is so wary of me. I have no issue with ripping the heart out of your bride in anger and making you watch me eat it. Both Faunus and Orpheus know what it's like to cross me, and that one thing has always been unchanging. I. Always. *Win.*"

He wasn't wrong about that.

Even Jabez was stuck evading him in any sparring match they'd ever had. Although he could land a few good hits to the front of his torso, Merikh's echidna quills made him a formidable and unbeatable opponent. Not even Jabez's teleportation ability allowed him to get the upper hand.

"I will call for the others then," Magnar stated, before he tipped his head back and parted his fangs wide to let the full might of his roar come through.

Lehnenia squealed as she covered her ears but was seemingly unafraid.

Jabez hung back to give everyone space as Delora and Magnar descended the porch steps – and Zylah refused to let go of him. Merikh ushered Raewyn forward and allowed her to properly meet them.

The human's hands shook as she spoke with his half-sister, who was nearly a foot taller than her, but she managed to shove a false smile upon her face. Although quiet, meek, and shy with her greetings, Delora immediately came across as kind and welcoming, and rather quick to adjust to a situation thrown at her with no warning. She looked awkward and unsure as she greeted the demonling, who immediately shied away from the human and tucked her face into Raewyn's shoulder to hide.

"I don't want to stay here by myself," Zylah muttered,

refusing to let go of his arm. "I want to go with you both."

Jabez kept his voice low. "I imagine our next location isn't going to go over well," he admitted, foreseeing Merikh was likely to keep the emotionally hardest meeting for last. He turned to her fully and offered a reassuring smile. "I'm sure everyone will welcome you, so there's no need to worry."

Jabez also knew it would be best if she met them all without him by her side. He would be a hinderance to her, and he wanted her first meeting with her family to be pleasant. He'd rather they warm up to her first before having to swallow that she'd bonded with him.

Zylah already tended to feel awkward and out of place, but she had a radiant personality that people easily warmed up to. He was sure they would adore her as he did if she gave them the chance, but she could also be rather protective of him.

He just hoped they didn't say or do anything that made them irreparable in her mind, even if how they felt was justifiable. Just because she forgave him, didn't mean any of them had to – and they likely wouldn't, not unless he went out of his way to seek it.

That would require more time than the synederus council had allotted.

"You also have Raewyn," Jabez added, reminding Zylah of her new companion. "She'll help guide you, and I'm sure she'll be fine with you leaning on her if need be."

The woman really was a nuisance, and she tried any means to spend time with Zylah when Jabez was busy working for the council. He'd tried to prevent it at first, but decided it was healthy for Zylah to have an ally within the city – someone to spend time with, so she wasn't truly alone in an unfamiliar environment.

She was also helping to teach Zylah Nyl'kira while they spent time together. Both females liked each other, so he saw little harm in this. It's really what made him warm up to Raewyn in the first place.

"And," Jabez continued, darting his gaze to the side when he noticed Delora fidgeting and constantly glancing between

Merikh and his family, and them. He could tell she wanted to approach. "These are your parents. They *want* you to like them. I can tell Delora will go out of her way to make you feel comfortable."

The fact she was allowing Jabez to remain on her territory was already a testament to that.

"But they don't approve of you," Zylah grumbled with a pout in her voice as she averted her skull to the side.

"I know, but it's best you let everything play out freely and try not to judge them too harshly if they speak ill of me. Don't forget, I've done a lot wrong to these people, as Delora has already stated." He let an overconfident and arrogant grin fill his features. "Remember, Zylah, I really, *really* don't give a shit what any of these people think of me. I wouldn't have done what I did if such trivial things as words and little threats weighed on my conscience."

He'd spent every moment of his life filled with hate, and he had no qualms about receiving it in return.

Jabez stepped to the side and gingerly removed his arm from her hold so he could place his hand on the small of her back. He guided her towards an awaiting Delora so they could greet each other.

The little human's gaze abandoned Merikh and turned shy as they approached. She offered Zylah a sweet smile, her face turned up to both their daunting heights. *Humans are so small,* he noted, since she just came to his broad chest.

He subtly pressed his face into the fur of her neck to take in her soothing jasmine-and-violet scent and muttered, "I'll be back shortly."

Jabez then dropped his hand away, although he couldn't help twirling his forefinger into the tuft of her cute tail as he separated from Zylah. She gave a satisfying shiver while he was turning away so he could meet Merikh waiting for him.

Magnar spoke to Raewyn in abject curiosity, studying the child in her arms and their Elven features. Lehnenia was more inclined to interact with the Mavka, and he figured that was due to his skull reminding her of Merikh's.

Delora, a short human with tanned skin, dark hair, and round ears, probably appeared too alien to a Demon child brought up in Nyl'theria.

"Alright. I'm guessing the twins first?"

"I hate it when you do that," Merikh stated, while giving him a gruff nod.

A grin had him flashing his pointed fangs, knowing Merikh loathed when he assumed correctly, *repeatedly*. "Do what?"

"Don't give me that."

Merikh offered out his arm, and Jabez blatantly held his hand like a lover would with humour tickling his chest. Merikh gasped and immediately ripped his palm away in disgust. He raised his hand in a flattened manner, like one might when they were threatening to backhand someone.

"Do you *want* me to bash your skull in?"

Jabez threw his head back with a boisterous laugh. "I'd consider it foreplay."

The growl that burst from Merikh was feral, but it quickly died. His orbs flashed bright yellow in humour, and he hid his chuckle well behind a grunt.

They both glanced at their females one last time before dematerialising.

# THREE

A quiet chitter tickled Zylah's chest. She scratched the side of her neck awkwardly as she stared down at the little plump human who barely came to her chest height.

Delora looked up at her so expectantly, her brown eyes wide and glinting with emotion, and she had no idea what she was supposed to do or say.

Zylah took in the wavy dark hair that reached just below her shoulders, her tanned flawless features, and her full pink lips. The gown she wore over her busty figure was white and came to just below her knees, with frills around her neck and sleeveless shoulders. It didn't particularly look like an outfit for going outside, especially as she lacked shoes Zylah knew humans preferred to wear.

Although she'd met her before, and knew what she was to Zylah, it was still hard to digest that such a small thing was her mother. The fox-skulled Mavka she could understand, since they both wore a skull, antlers, and even a collar of a creature – hers being fur and his being feathers.

Zylah thought she may be a little under a foot and a half taller than her, which just made her wonder *how* she'd been birthed from this human.

"H-hi," Delora greeted, her croaked voice thick with emotion and trembling with nervousness. "How have you been?"

Why did the question feel so stiff? It didn't help that the

female's cheeks turned bright red, reminding Zylah of how her orbs would shift to embarrassment – something Jabez teased her about and called a Mavka blush.

"I've been okay," Zylah grumbled in return, scratching at her neck harder with the desire to leave this conversation already. Even her teal orbs shifted to reddish pink as she felt completely out of her depth.

Loneliness almost had her orbs flickering with blue, but she managed to stop them. *I wish he didn't have to leave.* She didn't want to do this by herself.

"W-we, um..." Delora licked at her lips and glanced to the side at Magnar. "We've returned to your cave a few times over the last few months, but you were never there. Magnar said your scents had faded, like you hadn't returned in a long time."

"We left to go to Nyl'theria," Zylah admitted.

Delora's high-arching brows narrowed as her head jerked to the side. "Nyl'theria?"

Zylah lowered her hand, surprised she didn't know. "Oh. It's the Elven realm."

Her complexion paled, her eyes twitched wider, and she fisted the skirt of her white dress. "T-the Elven realm?" she mumbled in a shaky voice. "Why?"

Zylah's first thought was to state the whole truth as to why they originally left, but she decided that may not be taken well. He'd wanted to enact his war, only for him to fail because she'd gotten hurt. Jabez didn't tell her this. Zylah figured it out on her own and thought it was sweet he'd done that for her because he *loved* her so much.

"Because we live there now," she answered instead, lifting her sight to Raewyn so she could find an out from the conversation.

She watched as Magnar waved his hand barely an inch from Raewyn's nose, as if checking she was truly sightless. She wondered if it was rude to do that, since it looked odd watching it from the outside, but she'd remembered doing exactly that the first time she met her. Perhaps it was a Mavka thing to be curious in such a way.

The tall Elven woman merely laughed, as if expecting it from him.

"Then how is it you walk around by yourself?" he asked her.

Placing Lehnenia on the ground to free up her hands, Raewyn unclipped an unassuming cylinder from the side of the satchel she'd taken from Merikh. The white cylinder had a brown loop on the end, and a tiny orange mana stone on its side. She placed her thumb over the stone for a few seconds, and a rod suitable for her height shot out from it. On the end, a small ball freely rotated for ease of movement across uneven surfaces.

The entire thing was made from the same nearly indestructible material the Elysians used as armour, which came from the silk thread of the central palace's leaves.

A strip of silver in the very middle stated the level of Raewyn's visual impairment, but the colour of it varied depending on the person.

Zylah had seen the female pull out her mobility cane quite a number of times, so she wasn't surprised. Magnar, on the other hand, gave a laugh of mild excitement as he touched it to explore what it was. Raewyn then showed him how she used it to see.

For some reason, seeing her *parent* react in the same ways she had was oddly soothing. Her heart swelled with tenderness at Raewyn's kindness in the face of it all; it was a quality she really adored about her. She looked so natural meeting new people, so open and welcoming despite that Magnar was something other to her.

*I want to be like that.*

Realising she'd looked away from Delora, and that she wasn't offering the same kindness she liked in Raewyn, Zylah brought her skull back to her. She flinched inwardly at the female's frowning and obviously disheartened expression.

"Why do you look so saddened?" Zylah asked, subtly tilting her head.

Delora gave her a shaky false smile, as if she wanted to

soften her next words despite how narrowed her brows were and how liquid had filled her eyes. "Because if you're in the Elven realm, it means we can't visit you."

"Why not?" Zylah asked. "The Elven city allows people to enter it, and they know of Mavka."

"Because we don't know how to get there. It's also in a realm we don't know, but we're certain is filled with Demons."

"I guess that's true," she grumbled, looking away as she scratched at her neck again. "Maybe Jabez can draw you a map from his portal or show you the way."

She didn't know why she was offering that, especially without his permission. Maybe it was because, in Zylah's heart, she knew he would do that for her if she asked. Not once had he ever rejected her requests, not that she had many, and he always tried to fulfil them as best he could.

"I... should go to Raewyn," Zylah commented, walking off without giving Delora a chance to say otherwise. "She doesn't know Earth well." But she knew enough, as she'd been here for quite some time with Merikh.

The half lie tasted sour, but Zylah just didn't know what else to say or do. She could have offered for her and Jabez to visit in the future, but she wasn't entirely sure she wanted that. Jabez may not be allowed to leave Lezekos City on a personal excursion like this again for quite some time.

She was also following Jabez's advice to lean on Raewyn, who may help her from feeling so out of place. She could follow her lead.

"Hello, Zylah," Magnar greeted, his deep, grainy voice warm and friendly when she reached them. "It has been a while since we saw you. I know Delora is very happy you have returned."

He tilted his fox skull in his bride's direction, and his orbs flared bright yellow. He lifted his arm to reach out to her as she came to his side so he could bring her into a side cuddle, and her face looked worn and paler than it had a moment ago.

Guilt immediately slipped down Zylah's spine, and her sight flickered with orange. Raewyn's full lips pursed and her brows knotted when she must have seen her orbs change colour – since the only thing she could see were the tendrils of magic.

"I was just showing Magnar my cane," Raewyn stated brightly, trying to distract from the current conversation for Zylah's sake. "Lehnenia's been chirping away as well. I think she's excited to meet more people who look like Merikh."

The little Demon gave a bright smile at the only word she understood. Then in Nyl'kira she said, "*Papa* Merikh! *Papa* Merikh!"

She pointed up at Magnar's skull as she chatted away incoherently, and Zylah was able to catch a few words that she'd already learned of the language: skull, fangs, and orbs.

Raewyn answered her with a laugh, and the conversation in Nyl'kira was immediately lost on her, Magnar, and Delora. The human held Magnar's hand tightly, while her lips were a thin line as she turned her forlorn gaze away from Zylah's skull.

"She's very cute," Delora stated after relaxing her expression. "I noticed her ears are like yours, but I'm surprised to see horns on an Elf. We have fairytales about Elves, but I guess they're wrong."

"That's because she's not an Elf," Zylah interjected matter-of-factly. "Lehnenia is a Demon."

"A Demon?" Delora asked, her features stiffening slightly.

"Yes, this youngling is a Demon," Magnar stated, tipping his snout towards Delora. "I'm sorry. I should have told you I scented that."

She gave a shaky, broken smile. "Okay. That's fine with us. I'm guessing it's different where you're from."

"Yeah, the Elven realm and our city are very different to Earth," Raewyn stated warmly, as if prepared for such a conversation. "So long as the Demon has reached full completion, they're welcomed into the city and are given a new title. My species are called Elysians, not Elves, although I know that's what humans call us. Any Demon who enters our city becomes a Delysian."

"So, you adopted her?" Delora asked.

"It's more like she adopted us." Raewyn gave a laugh and looked down at her. "Lehnenia was very smitten with Merikh when she first saw him. Since he doesn't want children of his own, at least not yet, I thought this was a good opportunity for us. Our relationship is still new, but bringing in a child that would accept him was a concern of mine. The fact that Lehnenia adored him straight away meant I knew we were making the right choice, even if the timing was wrong."

At the easy conversation, which Raewyn engaged in so confidently that it wrung out all the awkwardness, Delora also laughed. "Yeah. I bet that would have been difficult. I would've had the same concerns with a human child, although we'll probably have more of our own in the future."

"More?" Zylah asked with her head cocking.

Delora finally offered her a real and very tender smile. "Yeah. You'll have your own brothers or sisters in the future."

"Just not right now," Magnar grumbled with his naturally green orbs darkening in possessiveness. "I would like to keep my bride to myself for a little while longer."

Before anyone could say anything more, the rapid approach of heavy, galloping stomps and deep, snorting huffs stole all their attention.

To Zylah's left, a large creature with a wolf skull and Impala antelope horns emerged, his orbs blue and focused on them. He ran on all fours, his fluffy body partially humanoid while his legs looked wolven with big paws for feet. A pale human with long blonde hair held on tightly to his back while she was seated over his waist.

Like Delora, she wore a white dress, although her feet were covered in brown boots, and she had a sword scabbard strapped to her waist.

When he skidded to a halt, the female slid off him with her boots thudding against the ground. Gripping the hilt of her sword, she exclaimed, "Is everything okay?!"

Magnar raised his hands at the narrowed and hard gaze of the human. "There's nothing wrong," he stated quickly. "We just have some visitors who wanted everyone to gather.”

“Oh thank goodness,” the female said with a relieved sigh, her expression softening. “We thought something terrible happened since you called us so early in the morning.”

The new Mavka changed his form, going from monstrous to humanoid, and a pair of black pants rose to the surface of his flesh to shield him. Zylah glanced at Magnar, who was naked except for his fur covering him and his long fox tail shielding his backside.

“We’re glad to hear everything is fine,” the wolf-skulled Mavka stated, before he sniffed at the air. His orbs shifted to dark yellow in curiosity as he looked around Magnar to Raewyn, Lehnenia, and Zylah standing there. “I smell a Demon... and something unfamiliar.”

Delora approached the pale female, and Zylah couldn’t see her expression with her back turned to them. “This is Raewyn, Lehnenia, and... Zylah.” She turned and gestured towards them with her hand.

“Zylah?” the female stated with a gasp, her green eyes widening at her rabbit skull. “You mean *Fyodor* Zylah?”

Zylah’s shoulders turned inwards self-consciously; she wasn’t expecting to be known or for her presence to be so surprising. She stepped slightly in front of Raewyn and her youngling protectively when the unnamed couple came forward. She didn’t want any accidental harm to befall them – she also thought Merikh would be enraged at her if she allowed it or didn’t do everything in her might to prevent it.

“Hey, Zylah,” the female stated, a grin lifting into her sharp, although feminine, features. “I knew you when you were just a tiny little baby.”

Then, as if to show just how small she’d once been, she hovered her hands in front of her large breasts to create a ball that was barely half a foot in diameter.

Zylah gave a nervous chitter. “I’m sorry, but I don’t remember you.”

Her grin grew. “Oh, I already knew that. You Duskwalkers forget everything until you have enough humanity to form proper memories."

*Then why did she have to say anything about it?* Doing so only made her feel awkward and timid. She had no memory of being small, nor of this female, let alone the parents who had created her.

"I'm Reia, by the way," she greeted, before waving her hand at the wolf-skulled Mavka. "And this is Orpheus. We've been wanting to meet you again, especially since Delora told us she spoke to you a few months ago."

Zylah lifted her gaze away from the little human to the male Mavka only a few inches taller than her. *So, this is Orpheus.* Jabez hadn't spoken of Orpheus since before they bonded, but she remembered him speaking of the wolf-skulled Mavka.

She glanced down at the female beside him again. *And didn't Reia kill Jabez's companion?* Zylah didn't care that Reia had stabbed her in the chest; it wasn't done to her, or anyone she'd known. Actually, as *naughty* as she thought it was, she was thankful no one had been in her way when she'd met him. He was all hers and she liked it that way.

Rook also spoke highly of this Reia, and Zylah liked Rook very much. She wanted to trust him and his friendship with this blonde female – especially as he'd described her as being welcoming to him. That had to mean she had a good heart, right?

Orpheus held out his hand to her, and Zylah inspected it mistrustingly. She tilted her head, wondering what he was doing.

"You're supposed to shake it," Magnar said enthusiastically, reaching for Orpheus' hand to clasp his own in it. They gave a singular shake downwards. "Like this. It is a human greeting."

*I don't think I should greet him, though.* Zylah wondered how she could get out of it. Jabez wouldn't care, but she thought these people may be the most upset about her bond with him.

How was she supposed to proceed then? *Maybe... I can help them see him the way I do?*

"Go on, Zylah," Raewyn encouraged with a smile.

At their direction, and not wanting to appear rude, Zylah reached out and took his hand. His hold was gentle as he greeted her with it, both their palms almost fitting perfectly. *His hand is warm and rough.* Once they were done, she looked down at her palm, surprised by how much she liked doing the action.

She threw her hand out towards Reia, and the human's features brightened as she placed her tiny hand in hers. They shook, and Zylah attempted to be even gentler than Orpheus had been, considering how small she was. Just as Zylah touched her, some strange creature gave a squeak and shifted underneath the back of her dress.

If this was how she was supposed to greet people, she wondered why Delora and Magnar had never done so. Then again, all of their conversations and meetings had been saturated in a tense aura, much of it Zylah's fault.

It didn't help that Delora often looked just as frazzled as she felt, whereas Reia's confidence easily ate away at Zylah's nervousness. She found it easier to follow while she was still adjusting to meeting the others. It's why she appreciated Jabez so much.

He always led every interaction, and she was able to bounce off his energy and gauge how she should react. He was also kind enough to give her very direct openings so she could take control if she wanted to, and it was slowly building up her confidence.

He'd done it when she first met Merikh, and it was one of the reasons she liked the bear-skulled Mavka – no matter that his attitude could be rather sour.

Lehnenia spoke up at Raewyn while pointing at Orpheus' face, and Zylah figured she was commenting on his skull and features similar to how she did with Magnar. The interaction brought attention to them, and both Reia's brows lifted as she took them in.

She leaned closer to Delora while bringing her hand up to the side of her mouth. "Who are they?" she asked, when the question sounded more like, "*What* are they?"

"Raewyn is an Elysian Elf, and Lehnenia is her adoptive daughter. She's a Demon."

"Okaaay," she sang out low with a grimace. Her lips twisted as her brows narrowed. "I'm a little lost. Can you explain why they would be here?"

"I'm Merikh's bride," Raewyn said with a welcoming and unbothered smile.

"Ohhh!" Reia stated with her expression turning bright. "That makes total sense now."

"It's okay," Raewyn answered with a laugh. "I understand we're different to you humans, and our sudden appearance is strange."

"I'm kind of used to strange now, to be honest." Then, repeating exactly what she'd done before by raising her hand to the side of her mouth, she leaned towards Delora. "Who the fuck is Merikh, though?"

"He's the bear-skulled Mavka," Orpheus bit with rough darkness in his tone. He put his arm around Reia's back protectively and looked around. "I don't scent him. Where is he?"

"He's gone to get the others," Delora answered. "I think he wants to meet everyone, and it's why they're here today."

"I see," Orpheus said with a hum, cupping the end of his snout. "All Mavka and their brides in one place?"

Reia let out a groan as she gestured to herself. "And I'm in my nightgown? Seriously?" Her cheeks darkened with a small amount of pinkness. "I'll have to go change before anyone else turns up."

As if on cue, more people approached, but from the opposite side Reia and Orpheus had arrived. Zylah twisted to the right.

A feline skull with a golden crack in it came into view, his horns sandy and ram-like as they curled back over his skull before circling forward. Whereas Orpheus had fish fins going down his forearms, calves, and back, this Mavka had small spikes down the same places.

Like Reia had done, on his back rode a woman with long black hair and a fawny complexion. Unlike the two humans already there, she wore a pair of brown leather pants and a long tunic. A whip, dagger, and a sword were strapped to her waist, and she wore a pair of brown boots.

Her hair was loose, messy, and windblown when she jumped down from her Mavka. His orbs were yellow, but Zylah didn't think he was joyous or curious right then.

"Took you long enough," Reia commented loudly. "We all would have been dead."

"I was naked!" the woman yelled, stomping boorishly towards them. "It's stupid o'clock in the fucking morning. I had to get dressed." Her hard gaze immediately landed on Raewyn, Lehnenia, and Zylah before narrowing with suspicion. She placed her hand on the hilt of her sword. "Friend or foe?"

"Friend," Delora stated, and the newcomer's shoulders loosened.

She removed her hand from the hilt of her sword. "How friendly?"

"Raewyn, here" Delora started, and the Elf waved to show who she was speaking about, "is Merikh's bride."

She opened her mouth to continue, but a scoff came from the feline Mavka as he morphed into his more humanoid form. Naked, although very fluffy, he approached them.

"Merikh has a fucking bride? Since when?" he asked, annoyed, as if the very thought was ridiculous.

"I would say it's been around an Earth year," Raewyn answered in a sickly sweet tone.

"You must have your hands full then," he stated, coming to Orpheus' side while placing his hand on the hip of his female and dragging her with him. "That ill-tempered Mavka has a mean streak. No offense, but I'm surprised anyone would give him their soul."

"Admittedly, he has his moments." Raewyn's face followed where he went by the sound of his voice moving. "But he's actually rather sweet when you give him the chance.”

“I’ve had my insides ripped from me and my head decapitated one too many times to truly believe that.” Then, as if noticing her falling expression, he grunted and ran his hand over one of his horns. “Sorry. All of my interactions with him have been rather unpleasant, even when I’ve just tried to talk to him. It’s hard to shake that after so many years.”

“It’s okay,” she said with a cringing smile, then looked down at the youngling holding her hand. “This is Lehnenia, our daughter.”

“Smells like a Demon,” he commented, and Zylah noted his voice lacked any judgement. “She reminds me of those in the Demon Village. She’s reached full completion?” Reia and the shorter female gave a silent gasp at what he said, and he reared his head back in surprise. He looked at them all. “Come on, you all must know about that. Orpheus, you’ve been to the village a few times.”

“Since her parents achieved completion before she was born, Lehnenia is a fully developed Demon child, which is why she partially looks like an Elf,” Raewyn explained.

“I’m not surprised by the way she looks,” he said defensively as he folded his arms across his bulky chest. “Just that Merikh would take one in.”

“Very true. Well, if we’re introducing ourselves, I’m Faunus, and this is my bride, Mayumi.”

“It’s a pleasure to meet you all,” Mayumi said with a very small smile, like she was only putting it on for pleasantries. It fell, although her face didn’t appear vexed, just as if it was normal to be stoic.

Faunus gestured to a strange, blobby near-black creature that had been hidden inside his long fur covering his chest before pointing at a second one clinging to the crook of his neck. “This is sleepy, bitey, annnnd” – he looked over his shoulder, then down the front of his body, sticking his tongue out as he reached under his armpit for a third nestled against his back – “squealy.”

As if to highlight what he’d just called them, the little

creature let out a terribly high-pitched shriek as they were grabbed. They held on firmly to his fur but were easily removed, and he cupped the last one under his palm and nestled them to his abdomen.

"They're our children," Mayumi stated. She threw her body forward so her hair would flip, then wrangled the long strands into a high ponytail with a piece of ribbon.

"These are Mavka younglings?" Zylah asked, tilting her head as she stepped forward to inspect them just that little bit closer.

When they confirmed, she chittered as excited interest swelled her muscles. She'd always wanted to know what a Mavka youngling looked like, but she hadn't expected them to be so tiny. Although two were big enough that they'd fit in her palm nicely, the third was very small.

She peeked at Delora, and it now made sense as to how she may have carried her in her little human body.

"Do you want me to explain what they look like to you?" Zylah offered to Raewyn.

"Maybe later. Thank you," she answered with an appreciative smile. "But you should introduce yourself."

All excitement breezed out of her like a gust of wind, and she almost wanted to snap at the female for it.

"I'm Zylah," she muttered quietly.

"Your daughter?" Mayumi asked Delora, who nodded with eyes widening. Mayumi held the end of her chin as she folded an arm across her chest, before she gave a mild laugh. "Well, that explains why you called us here at butt fuck in the morning." She turned to Reia and pointed. "Ha! You didn't get changed first."

Reia's cheeks pinkened once more, and she threw her hands up. "It's not my fault! We thought they were in danger, so we left right after getting out of bed. I almost left Kevin behind since I was half asleep."

"Kevin?" Zylah asked, cocking her head quizzically.

"We have a baby as well," she answered, before pulling her nightgown to the side and reaching inside it.

Another little Mavka, similar in size to the small one in Faunus' arms, was revealed. They squeaked, their limbs waving around her palm, until she placed them against her chest. They clung to her dress, and buried an oval-shaped, mostly featureless face against her breast.

They were a lot easier to see against Reia's bosom since they contrasted against her white gown, and Zylah inspected them as best she could. Their flesh was such a dark grey that they almost appeared black, and they looked kind of... blobby. Then again, she'd never seen a baby anything before, so she didn't know what to compare them to.

They opened their mouth to yawn and revealed jagged fangs much like those that filled the gaps between Zylah's cheekbones and jaw.

"They were born in the spring," Orpheus said, with his orbs morphing bright yellow.

Mayumi placed her hands on her hips and turned to Zylah. "We're happy to see you're alive and well. You even have a soul!" She peeked around her to search for its owner. "Where are they?"

Zylah knew it was probably best she didn't say anything, but she also didn't want to hold back the truth. He was her mate, she wasn't ashamed of him at all, and she was prepared for negativity.

"Jabez has gone with Merikh to collect the others," Zylah stated confidently. "They will be back shortly."

By the ever-night, she hoped it was shortly! There were so many people here now, and she was growing overwhelmed. Thankfully they had no issue talking to each other naturally, which meant Zylah was able to insert herself as little as possible.

Mayumi's features hardened, and she lowered her head slightly with harshly tightened lips, whereas Reia's face did something similar but paled in worry at the same time. They silently shared a glance, before their gazes went to Delora, who instantly looked towards her feet and held Magnar's hand tighter.

The vibe in the air shifted so swiftly it was almost cold. Zylah felt her fur lifting in alarm in reaction to it.

"Delora told us you were with him when she last saw you. I was hoping that, since you're alone, you managed to get away from him," Reia said in a deep, dark tone.

"Are you saying you bonded with that vile fucker?" Faunus growled and stepped back from her while placing his arms around his younglings as best as he could. "Do you have any idea what he did to me?" He became overly protective against Zylah, as if he thought *she'd* harm them.

Orpheus was quick to place his arm around the front of Reia and draw her to his side, and both his and Faunus' orbs flared crimson.

Zylah placed her hands over her teal dress, right against her abdomen, when her insides twisted. The mood had darkened so quickly her heart clenched with a tender, painful ache. She stepped back, retreating into Raewyn's side.

She knew it'd be bad, but not *this* bad. Their reaction had been instantaneous, and the hostility coming from them was palpable.

"He isn't what you think," she said defensively.

"He cracked my skull," Faunus growled. "I know *exactly* who he is. Let alone what he's done to the rest of us."

"Guys, please stop," Delora pleaded, letting go of Magnar's hand to turn to them with her palms out.

"No, she has to learn what he's done," Reia said to her with her lips pulled back into a sneer. "We have no idea why he's bonded with her, what games he's up to. Have you considered this might just be another ploy or tactic to get to us?"

"He's asked us all to join his war, even me," Mayumi cut in, her hand falling to the hilt of her sword like she found it comforting and natural to hold it in tense situations. "What if he's using her? She can't leave him now, unless the spirit of the void knows how to break a Duskwalker's bond."

"If you could all just wait a moment," Raewyn said softly as she stepped forward.

"What if he hurts her?" Reia asked Delora as she waved in

Zylah's direction.

With her heart pounding in anxiety and anger, and her orbs threatening to flicker red in reaction to it, Zylah growled, "He wouldn't!"

"You don't know that," Reia said, turning to her with a shake of her head. Her eyes bowed beseechingly as she looked up at Zylah's rabbit skull. "We've seen what he can do, how cruel he can be. He uses people, and I wouldn't be surprised if he's trying to manipulate you as well."

"Has he even explained to you what he's done to us?" Orpheus asked with the undertone of a growl.

"Of course he has," Zylah bit out, her orbs flaring bright red.

"Truly?" Orpheus let out a dark chuckle that held not an ounce of humour. "He revealed how he and Katerina tortured me for years? How they almost killed Reia and took her away from me forever?"

"Yes, I know all that," Zylah admitted.

Reia's jaw dropped and her eyes widened. "And you *still* bonded with him?"

"He's changed."

"People don't change *that* much," Mayumi sneered. "Jabez's heart is rotten to its core. Whatever he's done to manipulate you will only hurt you, Zylah. I wouldn't be surprised if he hasn't already–"

"Shut up!" Zylah roared with her claws bared, and all the humans flinched. "I don't care! I don't care what he's done to you all! I only care about how he treats *me*."

They all wanted her to care about how they felt, but none of them were considering her feelings and how they could be hurting her with their words. And Zylah didn't *know* how to share her innermost thoughts now that she was upset.

More than ever, she wished Jabez was here to help soothe her when she felt like she was drowning.

Orpheus shoved his female behind him protectively with his orbs deepening in their crimson hue and a snarl coming from him. Faunus yanked the back of Mayumi's shirt to draw her closer to his body so she was a safe distance from Zylah. The female gave a surprised *euk* as the collar tightened around her chest momentarily.

"I know what he has done," she snapped out, her fur puffing all the way down her back until her tail tremored. "I know how he has hurt our kind, but he feels regret and guilt over it. You don't know him like I do, nor do you know what we have been through. Your past is not my own, and I don't *know* any of you."

Delora ran between them and placed her hands out on either side of her to act as a divider. "Everybody stop!" she screamed with her eyes clenched tightly shut. "She's right! We have no idea what has happened, nor is it our place."

"If you won't accept us, then we will leave today and go be by ourselves while the rest of you gather," Zylah warned sternly. "We only came because Merikh needed *his* help."

"Zylah," Raewyn softly called from the side.

With a snorting, enraged huff, she darted her skull to her with her orbs bright red, worried that Raewyn would try to convince her otherwise. With her hands balled into tight fists to the point her claws stabbed into the palms of them, she snapped, *"What?"*

"C-could you please help me find some shade? Lehnenia said the sun has risen."

*She wants shade?* She looked around, and the annoyed tension she directed upon the Elf diminished like a sharp and sudden gust of wind.

Zylah hadn't even noticed the dappled light peeking through the trees, although there was no direct sunlight to be seen. It was still too early morning for the sun to truly touch the Veil.

Despite being rather irritated, when Raewyn reached her hand out, Zylah immediately took it. She ignored the others as she guided the female to a spot beneath a tree that would shade them permanently.

She wished her fur would stop being puffed. Her breaths were hard and shallow, her heart hot and racing with aggression. All her muscles were locked, like her veins were filled with stone. She hated having her back to these people, but she also didn't want to look upon them right now.

She could hear Delora quickly muttering to the others, her voice high in distress. Zylah ignored her too.

*I want to leave,* she thought, looking up at the branches above them. *I don't want to stay here.*

She knew this wouldn't go well after how things had turned when she first met Delora and Magnar, but she just didn't think it would be this bad. After what she'd learned of Jabez's past, she *did* understand why they were so angry. She understood they were justified in that anger, but she just... couldn't handle the way they spoke of him.

He would never hurt her, and she knew he hadn't given her his soul to manipulate her. He... *loved* her, and she loved him dearly in return.

In fact, she adored him more than anything in the world, and she was happy with him in Nyl'theria. He'd been there for her through so much, but the others were too absorbed by their hatred to listen.

They didn't know him, didn't know how he cared for her, what he'd given up just to ensure she was safe. It made her heart hurt that they thought he'd be cruel to her when he was entirely the opposite. He could be distant at times, lost in his own thoughts with a miserable expression, but he showered Zylah with affection the rest of the time. He gave her gifts and tried to ensure she was happy by taking her for walks around the palace or even to the beach.

He was attentive and kind, and his mean playfulness had started to bring her out of her shell. He was a good mate, whether they wanted to believe it or not.

Look at what he was doing today.

Although Merikh had demanded that Jabez assist, she knew he had ulterior motives for agreeing. When he'd told her of Merikh's plan, he'd shared that he wanted her to meet everyone so she understood this family bond she was supposed to have. He'd even admitted that part of his reasoning was because it was something he'd lacked his entire life, and it had weighed on him.

He didn't want it to weigh on her as well, nor did he want to be the reason for getting in the way of it. He just admitted he wanted little part in it and was happy remaining as an unwanted outsider.

"Are you okay?" Raewyn whispered, her white brows knitted with deep concern.

Her starburst eyes sightlessly bowed and creased in sympathy up at her bony face, while her pointed ears had drooped back. With her hair framing her face in the added darkness, something became apparent. Zylah knew this female, who rarely ever leaned on anyone and preferred her independence, had only asked her for help in order to aid Zylah and bring her out of the unpleasant situation.

Frozen, unsure of what to do or how to make herself feel better, her orbs turned blue. The bottoms of them quickly wavered as she let out a small whine in answer.

"I know it's hard," Raewyn continued quietly, while offering a sad smile. "Hopefully they'll come around by the end of the day. After what Merikh told me of what he knows, there's a lot Jabez has to answer for. These people have been hurt very deeply, many of them facing death at his hands, and it's unfair of you to expect so much of them in a short period of time."

"But I don't want to hear it," Zylah said with a whimper.

"And I understand that. As his sister, it's hard to hear it as well, but what you said was right. They don't know who he is. Let it come naturally. Let them see what he is like now, and how he treats you."

"What if they never do?"

"Then what does it matter? Why should you care when you know the truth? He cares about you, that's all you need to remember, and I'm sure he feels nothing in regard to how they feel." She reached up slowly and placed a soothing hand on the side of Zylah's face, chasing the magical essence of her orb change like usual. "I know what Merikh is like. He's grumpy and short-tempered, but I love him all the same, no matter what anyone else says. You have to face that, too, but you also have to accept that they have every right to be angry at him."

Zylah wanted to pull on her antlers in frustration because she knew all that, yet it did nothing to stop the tears threatening to float from her.

"Zylah?" a soft voice meekly called.

The settling fur on her back instantly puffed once more, and she turned her head to the side to look at Delora through one orb. Clutching the skirt of her white gown, the female's brows were furrowed so tightly her forehead had pinched.

"I'm really sorry," Delora stated and nibbled at her lips. "So are they. They didn't mean to upset you, so please don't leave."

"We all have concerns," Magnar said at her back as he placed a hand on her curvy hip. "We just want the best for you."

Zylah considered facing away and ignoring them. It was only because Raewyn petted the side of her head soothingly that she gained the will to turn around fully.

She remained a safe distance from all of them.

"I understand he has hurt you all very deeply, and I *am* sorry that he has," Zylah stated loud enough so everyone could hear, since the others were collected a few feet behind them. "But Jabez has given up on his war. He even entered the city he sought to destroy just to *protect* me." Then she gripped her elbow and let her shoulders turn inwards. "Jabez wouldn't bond with me until he told me everything, and even then... he didn't want to because he was worried about how I would feel later. He thinks of himself as a monster for what he has done, but he had his reasons for doing it. I accepted all that because I love him, and because he is kind to me. I know it is difficult to hear, but we are bonded now, and even if I could undo it, I know I never would."

"We're not angry with you." Reia ran her fingers through her blonde hair, before scratching at the side of her head in obvious annoyance. "We just... we don't know if we can ever forgive him for what he's done."

"He doesn't want your forgiveness," Zylah stated with a saddened laugh, knowing that was the truth.

"You have to understand," Raewyn interjected from her side, "Jabez has been through a lot, and much of that is our fault. I'm sure understanding his past from before he even came to Earth would do little in assuaging your anger, but there is a reason as to why he was so set on destroying us, and why he would do anything to achieve it."

"Just because someone has trauma or whatever, doesn't excuse his behaviour," Mayumi stated from afar. "We also don't have to accept it."

Raewyn's lips tightened. "That's true."

"But..." Mayumi continued, letting out a sigh as she looked up at the feline Mavka's skull. "We will try our hardest to keep how we feel to ourselves."

"Just know that if he turns on us, it will not bode well," Faunus stated with a quiet growl.

"He won't," Zylah stated confidently.

"We don't want you to feel uncomfortable," Delora said as she looked at her beseechingly. "None of us hold anything negative towards you, and we've all been wanting to see you and meet you as you are now."

"Please don't let what's happened stop you from speaking with us," Reia added. "We really are sorry. We just... we weren't expecting it, and we weren't prepared."

"I don't want him near Kevin," Orpheus grumbled as he folded his arms and let out a huff through his nose hole.

"No, but I think we have to accept that for today," Reia said with a broken smile.

"At least you only have one to keep an eye on," Faunus stated, rolling his head to the side. "Bitey likes to run off now that they're bigger."

"Would you like to meet them properly?" Mayumi offered to Zylah, although she shot Delora a wary look. "Every Duskwalker we've met has been curious about seeing what they looked like when they were babies."

"Maybe I can show you around my home," Delora

interjected with a hopeful smile. "There will be a lot of us shortly, and we can talk and get to know each other better before everyone arrives."

"That'd allow me to go home and get changed," Reia stated as she looked down at her dress. "It won't take me long. We'll probably be around fifteen or so minutes if Orpheus runs really fast. I can bring some food over for lunch as well, and maybe some lemon for tea?"

"I'm fine how I am," Mayumi said, throwing her arms to the side. "I can talk to Raewyn outside so you can speak privately. I'm interested in learning about Elves and what your world is like."

Zylah's muscles eased at the change of energy and conversation, and the cold, aching twist in her chest unwound. Even her orbs reverted to their normal teal as she drifted her gaze over them all. It did appear like they really were *trying*, and that was all she could ask for.

They didn't have to like him. All they had to do was just quietly accept his presence for her sake. If they could do that, then Zylah could try her hardest as well.

"I do have one request, though," Reia stated with her lips pouting as she glanced up at the brightening sky with a devious look. "And it'll require the use of my sword, although I think he's fast enough to not get hurt."

"If you're thinking what I think you are, then I want in on it," Mayumi said with a mischievous grin curling her lips. "It'd be fun to play with Jabez a little, and it'll let us know if he truly is harmless."

Zylah rumbled out a half-hearted growl before it immediately died.

So long as it wouldn't hurt him, she knew anything they did or threatened would only make him chuckle. He'd likely taunt them. She'd seen him do this to the councilmembers on the odd occasion she went with him, and even if she didn't understand a word they said, she knew when his grin was mean and cheeky.

"If you tell me what it is, I'll consider it," Zylah stated with a sigh.

*If it makes them hate him less...*

And... he did say he didn't care what they did or thought of him.

# FOUR

"I think it might be best if I hang back for this one," Jabez stated, as he lifted a low-hanging branch to duck underneath its bushy leaves.

With Merikh to his left and walking directly next to the steaming pools of natural hot springs, Jabez was forced to evade the foliage and low branches to their right. There was a slightly sulphuric smell in the air, but it was light, as if there wasn't a lot of the mineral in the earth and water.

Not too far away, the large pink dome belonging to the bat-skulled Mavka glittered.

They had to walk to it, as he hadn't known exactly where to take them, just the general area itself since he'd been all over Austrális. Jabez's ability to teleport and the fact that he had a deep understanding of the geography was the reason Merikh was utilising him. Merikh hadn't even known these hot springs existed.

Then again, they were within the borders of the southlands and the wide, protective wall that cut off this part of the continent from the rest of it. It was an additional layer of defence which protected the many villages and towns inside it, and they had also erected individual fortifications. Traversing on this side of the wall was arduous and long, with many human towns to contend with.

Funnily enough, he'd been able to see the top of this very mountain from the much smaller one he and Zylah had set up as their cave. Their temporary home had been outside the southland's wall, though.

"Why should you hang back?" Merikh asked with a scoff. "Are you scared or something?"

Jabez rolled his eyes so hard his vision blurred momentarily afterwards. "Well, considering one of these Mavka did die because of me, and the other one's bride blew me up, I don't think it'll go over well that I'm with you."

He snorted a mild, condescending laugh. "Coward."

While brushing a leaf from the silky navy material covering his chest, wishing they'd all leave him be in this disgusting world, he stated, "I'm just saying it would be easier if you talk to them first. I actually like my outfit."

If he was going to be glared at all day, he could at least look pretty while enduring it. If he got into any brawls, they'd likely ruin his clothing and put him in a shitty mood.

"I'm actually curious to see what will happen." Merikh leaned to the side until their heads were aligned. "I wonder if they're still a pair of idiots sharing one brain. When I last saw Aleron, he was a Ghost and still rather low in humanity. I think his bride is the human who was accompanying him. Gideon, I believe his name to be."

"A gay Mavka?" Jabez asked, while cupping his jaw. He pulled his hand away to shrug with it, completely unbothered by this new information.

He was more concerned by how this bride would behave meeting the person who, inadvertently, killed his lover.

When they almost reached the dome, Merikh patted him on the back. "You're probably right. It would be best if you stay behind, but you're not going to do that. I want to see you get your arse kicked."

"You may be better at defence, but I'm better at evading," Jabez rebutted. "And attacking."

"Want to make a bet then?"

Jabez's ears twitched at the idea of a gamble. "I'm listening."

"If they leave even a scratch on you, you have to meet your

parents."

Jabez let out a low whistle. "That's a harsh bet."

He could hear the sly humour in Merikh's tone. "I guess you're not confident about it then."

*I bet Raewyn's been in his bony ear hole about it.* Merikh probably didn't care what Jabez did, and likely agreed with his sentiment of not wanting to meet them; he knew it would be a great loss for a bet.

Jabez cupped his jaw in thought as he tried to come up with an equal loss for Merikh. An idea lit in his mind, and he almost wanted to laugh at the ingeniousness of it. Especially as it was like killing two birds with one stone.

"If I win, you have to speak to Weldir about lowering his ward temporarily. The synedrus council are considering building a second city in Nyl'theria, and I want the Demons in Spiral Haven to inhabit the village."

A rolling growl bubbled from Merikh's maw, and his orbs flared bright red.

"Come now, Merikh. He brought your dear brother back to life. Time to let it all go."

Merikh spun and pointed a sharp claw at his face, showing his already limited patience was running out. He retracted his hand before snapping out, "Fine."

"Any restrictions?" Jabez asked, clasping his hands behind his back to appear aloof when they began walking again.

The chuckle Merikh produced was mean. "You're not allowed to teleport. It gives you too much of an upper hand."

A devious smile curled his lips. "Is that all?"

"That should be enough."

*Idiot,* Jabez thought with mirth, lifting his eyes to the brightening sky. "The sun is rising, so we better make this quick then. The bet is off if they don't attack, though, as I'm not going to provoke them into doing so just for a gamble."

Jabez didn't need these people to like him, but he did want them to tolerate him for Zylah's sake. Therefore, he had no intention of starting a needless fight.

"Sounds fair."

Just as they were about to enter the pink protective dome, a woman with bright-red hair stepped out of a cave with her arms lifted like she was stretching. Hiking up the skirt of her simple grey peasant dress, she stepped to the side with the intention of heading towards the forest, but froze when she noticed movement.

Her gasp was so loud it was almost a quiet scream, and she ran back inside the cave.

"It's the Demon King! Wake up!"

A kerfuffle could be heard as multiple bodies immediately went into motion, just as a handful of feathers fluttered out of the cave mouth.

"Oh wow. They didn't even notice you," Jabez commented as he folded his arms and waited for the inevitable.

From the corner of his eye, he noticed Merikh slyly sliding to the side to get out of harm's way. Then he just blatantly hightailed it out of there with his actual bull tail curling in delight. He stayed in sight, though, especially since he actually headed *towards* the cave entrance.

Just as he was taking a seat on the edge of a large rock like it was a chair, a roar sounded as a winged Mavka ran from the cave opening. He dived straight for Jabez, with his lizard twin brother scuttling with speed below him.

Although he had a very simple way to win this bet, something Merikh had overlooked, he merely ducked beneath the bat-skulled Mavka's claws. Then he jumped over the raven-skulled one, his legs going wide as he shoved against the top of his skull to go over him.

They both almost crashed against each other as they landed on the ground. Jabez turned just in time to watch the bat-skulled Mavka – he believed his name to be Aleron from his earlier conversation with Merikh – skid across the ground and narrowly stop himself from bashing into a tree.

He didn't know the raven-skulled one's name, but he was quick to dig his claws into the ground to get purchase and turn to him. He ran at Jabez with lightning speed, so he let magic cascade through his feet. Grass shot out from the ground and twisted around the raven's feet, causing him to trip as he easily ripped from weak trappings.

Aleron leapt into the air and circled above, readying himself for an opening. *He isn't attacking uncontrollably in a rage.* That at least proved he wasn't as unintelligent as Merikh had supposed.

Both their orbs were red, but they were still present, which made them much more calculating and harder to fight against.

Just as Jabez was backing up from the raven skull snapping his beak at him, the wind blew from behind in his direction. A familiar, feminine scent fluttered over him, far too close for comfort.

He peeked over his shoulder just in time to see the redheaded woman about to ram her sword into his back. He dodged to the side, rolling before sliding his leg out to retain his balance. He had to flip backwards when a small axe came down towards his head as the male human leapt off a rockpool's ledge towards him.

A snarl rumbled above him, just as another sounded on his left. The humans wisely stayed back as each of their Mavka dived for him simultaneously.

Jabez looked Merikh straight in his yellow orbs of joy and let humour crinkle his eyes. He turned incorporeal. Both Mavka bashed right into each other when they went through him, Aleron punting his own twin brother in the back with his skull and backward-spiralling goat horns.

"That's cheating!" Merikh roared as he got to his feet.

Jabez tilted his head back and laughed with his hands on his hips. "You only said no teleporting, you idiot. You forgot I'm a Phantom now."

*"Merikh?"* Aleron called in surprise, his voice distorted and grainy from being in his monstrous form, as he turned towards him.

The raven-skulled brother paused as well, as both humans turned to him stomping across the clearing.

"Yes, yes, hello you pair of boneheads," Merikh greeted, before getting in Jabez's face. "You win, but you're a sly fucking bastard."

"You," the male human sneered as he raised the blade of his axe towards Merikh. "I remember you from the Elven realm. You've teamed up with this asshole now, huh? Turned on your own family?"

Surprised the human man was speaking of him, Jabez looked around Merikh's wide body to be greeted by baleful green eyes. His long, flowing white hair curtained down one side of his tilted head. "I don't even know you."

"Yeah, well Emerie told me all about you," he said, as he stepped towards the redheaded woman. "You're the reason Aleron died."

With both Mavka on the other side of them, he and Merikh were surrounded. Merikh turned his skull around while keeping his torso facing Jabez.

"You should thank him then, considering that's the only reason you two met," Merikh stated, before he twisted his neck to look at the woman.

Her face was exactly how Jabez remembered it. With freckles on the right side of her light skin, and a mixture of white-and-pink burn scars covering the left side of it. He could see more freckles and scars going down the side of her neck and into her dress, as well as smudges of it on her biceps due to her sleeveless garment.

She narrowed blue eyes at him, and her glare was the same as the day she'd thrown that sun stone against the ground. Resentful but determined.

"You almost killed me, you know," Jabez stated, letting his features dull – he was still rather displeased about it. "Do you know how much pain I had to endure because of you?"

She lifted the tip of her sword to his face, and the polished iron glinted in the oncoming sunlight. "It's less than what you deserve."

*"What is going on, Merikh?"* Aleron asked in his monstrous form, as he flared his large, feathered wings. *"Why are you here with the Demon King?"*

Merikh placed an arm over Jabez's shoulders and leaned

almost the entirety of his heavy weight on him until he felt his knees trying to buckle. Then his bull-horned companion waved his hand in the air as if he was about to tell some grand story.

"Jabez, here, went and got himself bonded to a Mavka. He is now family."

"You're joking," the female human stated in utter disbelief. "What Duskwalker would bond with *him*?"

"I know if I try to describe her, I'd only piss you off," Merikh muttered to Jabez, since he'd probably spout something rude.

"Although her name is Zylah now, you probably know her as Fyodor," Jabez answered coldly. "The rabbit-skulled, antlered Mavka."

"Fyodor?" she rasped, before her eyes bowed in anguish. "Delora's daughter? That's just *cruel*."

Merikh *finally* removed his weight from Jabez, just so he could fold his arms. "Regardless, I'm demanding that everyone put their problems in the past."

"And who are you to tell us what to do?" the male human stated, twisting his axe at Merikh. "You were a prick in the Elven realm, and I'm not particularly inclined to trust you."

"Well, if you don't, I'll take it out on these two." Merikh hiked his thumb towards the twins beside them as he and Jabez both turned back-to-back to see everyone in their peripheries. "Currently we are collecting everyone and taking them to Magnar's ward. I have a bride who wishes to meet you all, and unfortunately, I needed Jabez's help to do that."

*"What if we don't want to go with you?"* the raven-skulled Mavka asked.

*"Ingram is right. Although we trust you, Merikh, the Demon King is not our friend."*

"I told you I should have stayed back," Jabez muttered, cocking a brow at the foolish Mavka. "You could have convinced them and *then* introduced me."

"I really do hate it when you do that," Merikh bit as he unfolded his arms and scratched at the side of his neck. He turned around to face his brothers. "Look, you two, I understand better than anyone that he deserves to have his entrails shredded to pieces, but what has happened cannot be undone. He is now a bride, and this day isn't complete if four of our family members are missing. Raewyn wishes to meet you both again."

*"Raewyn?"* Ingram asked with his head rearing back in surprise. *"The Elf with stars in her eyes?"*

*"Yes,"* Aleron confirmed for him as he sat back on his haunches to cup his bony bat chin. *"That's right. I met her again in the Elven realm. How is your little youngling, Lehnenia?"*

*"He has a youngling?"* Ingram asked, darting his beak in his twin's direction.

"She is here as well," Merikh stated.

"For what it's worth," Jabez started as he turned to face the twins fully, "I am sorry for what happened. I was angry when I made that order, and I rescinded it long before your skull was crushed, Aleron."

"Are you seriously seeking *forgiveness* after everything?" the female sneered.

"Actually no," Jabez stated as he glanced at her over his shoulder. "I don't give a shit if none of you forgive me, but it's an apology all the same. Isn't it better than me continuing my war with their kind until I managed to crush every single one of their skulls? You sought peace and to be left alone, and now you have it. Be grateful I had a change of heart *before* it came to further bloodshed. Had I not called off that order when I did, other Mavka may have perished."

Her lips flattened disapprovingly and her gaze narrowed further. She said nothing.

The male human lowered his axe and slammed the handle into a loop around his waist before brushing his black pants of non-existent dust. His brown boots gave a single squeak when he pressed off the ground to go to Aleron's side. Since the sleeves of his light-grey tunic were rolled up to his elbows, his strong forearms visibly flexed when he momentarily clenched his fists before releasing them.

"Look, I'll do whatever Aleron wants," he offered, brushing back the two-inch-long, caramel-coloured hair on top of his head before scratching at his stubble. His green eyes flicked to Jabez, then Merikh, then back to Aleron. "But what they're doing *does* sound harmless. They wouldn't take us to more Mavka if they intended anything bad, and I would like to meet the others again."

The female produced a scream behind her teeth and walked over to Ingram, just as the Mavka with short goat horns was rising to his feet. As if they'd shared the same thought, both Ingram and Aleron shifted into their more humanoid forms.

Both were naked, and Jabez almost wanted to throw his hands forward to gesture at their nudity. *See?* he thought, arguing with his past self. *These two are naked and I don't want to stick my dick in them.* So why had Zylah's nakedness eaten away at him so fiercely?

It was an answer he always knew he'd lack.

"What do you want to do?" she asked Ingram softly as she leaned into his side.

Aleron and Ingram turned their skulls towards each other and tilted their heads in opposite directions.

"I'm not giving you a choice," Merikh bit out firmly. "The only difference is how *difficult* you make this. Your brides might be harmed in the process by *me*."

Both twins growled and whipped their skulls towards Merikh.

"Fine."

"We will go."

*Finally,* Jabez thought, as Merikh explained what was about to happen. He cracked his neck one way and then the other before rounding his shoulders, preparing himself for how much this was about to exert his body.

*The teleportation of three heavy Mavka coming right up.*

# FIVE

With his lips flat and somewhat pursed, Jabez looked down at the pair of swords barely an inch from either side of his throat. A frown marred his features, but it was mainly out of surprise, as he'd *just* teleported the second twin and his bride, Gideon, into Magnar's ward.

To his right stood a very short woman with a light, fawny complexion and black hair tied into a high ponytail. Her brown eyes were furrowed into measured stoicism, and her sword didn't even tremble, like it was merely an extension of herself. He noted her *adorable* little hunter's outfit.

To his left, a pale woman with straight, blonde hair glared at him, her forest-green eyes filled with complete and utter loathing. Her pink upper lip was curled on one side, but unlike the other woman, her sword was unsteady. She wore a simple light-blue summery dress with a brown girdle and matching boots.

His ears perked up and a quiet chuckle rumbled from him as he tilted down towards the blonde. Right before her sword could pierce the flesh of his throat, he turned incorporeal, and the sharp blade went straight through his intangible, ghostly body.

"Hello, Reia," he greeted with a malicious, fang-filled grin. "I would say it's nice to see you, but the hatred in your eyes tells me you wish I would turn physical around this sword."

"You have some nerve showing your face here," Reia bit

out. "You should have known this would happen."

He twisted his head in an intentionally creepy fashion. "I wouldn't be here if I was given a choice." Then he stood and eyed the height-challenged woman to his right. "I remember you. Quite the swordswoman. You fought a group of Demonslayers rather gracefully."

"You're lucky we both held back at Delora and Zylah's request," the woman stated with an air of indifference. "Otherwise, we would have swung and cut off your head."

He lifted his red eyes towards the crimson orbs of Orpheus and Faunus, who both held Mavka younglings. Faunus held three, from what he could tell, whereas Orpheus had his hands cupped underneath a single one.

"Well, as fun as this is, I'm more afraid of Merikh than you two put together, and he is awaiting my return. We can resume in just a moment." With that, he stepped out of range of their swords, turned physical, and teleported back to Merikh.

Bright sunlight made him hiss, and he quickly placed his sun barrier spell over his body, but it did little to save his eyes from the way it reflected hot-white light off the pools of water.

"Took you long enough," Merikh stated with annoyance, before reaching his wrist out when Jabez approached. "Don't tell me you're getting tired. Is that sweat on your forehead?"

Jabez rubbed the back of his hand against his temple, surprised to find the Mavka was right and there was perspiration.

"Everyone wants a piece of me today," he stated with a tired sigh, already fed up with the threats.

"Orpheus and Faunus?"

"They looked murderous, but no. Their brides." He cocked his head at Merikh as he touched his arm. "Did you know they have younglings?"

Their conversation was seamless as Jabez teleported them both to Magnar's ward – but *away* from where the two humans had just tried to corner him.

"No, but I'm not surprised," Merikh said, before he headed straight for Raewyn and Lehnenia to check in on them.

Jabez skirted around the growing crowd of Mavka and their annoying brides to meet Zylah, who was already heading for him. He could feel multiple stares of orbs and eyes following him warily, but he mentally shrugged. He'd prepared himself for this.

"Are you okay?" Zylah cupped him underneath his jaw to lift his head back. With the way she tipped his head side to side and sniffed at the air, he knew she was checking to make sure he was uninjured.

"You're forgetting who I am," Jabez muttered, since the way she was holding his jaw kept him from talking properly. "I saw them coming from a mile away, but I think it's best if I let everyone get their anger out and face it head-on."

"I wish they wouldn't," Zylah grumbled with a small growl, before it came out as a sigh. "But I think you're right, and they *did* ask me if they could do it."

He cocked one of his brows. "And you let them?"

She chittered and her orbs flared orange. "You said you didn't care what they did."

He couldn't help the way his lips curled at his mate being naughty like this. "It's fine. I've faced much worse." They both naturally reached out a hand to each other so they could intertwine their fingers. She needed his touch as much as he needed the reminder of *why* he was putting up with all this bullshit. "How are they treating you?"

"Good," she admitted, her orbs shifting into a reddish pink. "They questioned me about you, and then tried to tell me about all the awful things you've done, as if I didn't already know."

His lips curled with tenderness at that. "I bet they were surprised when you didn't care."

She turned her head to the side with a huff, her way of pouting. "A little."

"Oi!" Merikh yelled across multiple heads, catching everyone's attention. "Get over here. Lehnenia needs protection from the sun."

His gaze drifted over the multiple people between himself and Merikh. *Well, I'm not walking through that.* As much as excessively using his magic was beginning to weigh on him because these Mavka were damn *heavy*, he dipped his head in their direction. Zylah nodded at his silent question, and he teleported her with him to Merikh's side.

Standing in the shade of a tree with Raewyn, Jabez balanced on the balls of his feet as he crouched down to the little demonling who held her mother's hand. He placed his palm on top of her white hair, and she giggled as he patted it while giving her a sun barrier.

"Alright, come here," he said in Nyl'kira so she understood, stepping back further into the sunlight while still crouched.

She shook her head and pressed herself against Raewyn's leg.

"It's alright, Lehnenia," he reassured, wiggling his hands in the sunlight. "See? I'm perfectly fine."

She fisted her light-orange dress with her other hand as tears brimmed in her eyes. "But I don't want to burn. It hurts."

"You won't. Remember, I'm all-powerful and magnificent." He gave her a wink, and her full lips pouted in cute distrust.

"It's okay, sweetie," Raewyn said, pulling their connected arms forward without actually forcing the demonling. "You won't get hurt."

She lifted her big, round red eyes up to the woman. "Promise?"

"Promise."

Lehnenia flicked her eyes down to Jabez's awaiting palms and tentatively reached out. She withdrew her hands the moment sunlight touched them, only to bring them right back when she wasn't burned by it. She stepped forward, braving the light, and giggled when it didn't hurt. She ran for him and held his biceps before looking up.

The moment she began to squint, he had to quickly cover her eyes. "Don't look directly into the sun. I can protect your skin from burning, but the light will mess with your eyes."

"Okie," she said, lowering her head.

Now that his task was completed, Jabez stood and faced Zylah, only to notice those behind her. He paused at the multiple people who had witnessed the interaction. He had no idea why his cheeks and ears heated in embarrassment, but he averted his gaze to the side when they all looked... *shocked* that he could be caring towards another.

Jabez was aware he was the most monstrous thing here, despite his handsome features. He'd long ago accepted that truth about himself.

*For fuck's sake. She's a child.* They were assuming the worst in him.

"You ready to collect the last piece?" Jabez asked Merikh, wanting away from these people.

The big, burly Mavka was quick to look away. "Yes."

*At least this one shouldn't know me.*

This wouldn't be a battle Jabez would have to face, but an emotional one Merikh would have to deal with on his own. Especially as Jabez doubted he'd lean on him for support.

*Whatever. I'll be there for him if he needs it.*

That's what a *friend* was supposed to do, right?

Although Zylah had allowed Reia and Mayumi to corner Jabez how they did, she felt entirely different after seeing it.

She grumbled as she moved closer to Raewyn, seeking to calm herself by being at the familiar female's side. She watched the four newcomers greet those they already knew, and they were all accepted into the fold without hesitation.

*Two of them look... familiar.*

At least, the little human's red hair looked familiar, and she did remember meeting the raven-skulled Mavka briefly. However, her memory of that time was really foggy, as it was before Jabez helped her gain so much humanity.

She eyed the only male human, who wore a large grin on his face as he patted Orpheus' back.

After leaving for a short while, both Reia and Orpheus had

returned wearing different clothing. Orpheus now wore a black button-up shirt with matching pants and boots, while Reia wore a light-blue dress with some kind of wide brown belt thing.

Even Delora had changed, and she wore a grey dress similar to Reia's, and had donned a pair of black flats on her feet. Magnar wore pants and a shirt, but the shoes he wore were similar to the ones Jabez had procured for her.

His five toes looked like hooves, and she bet they'd be uncomfortable in a pair of boots.

The only other Mavka to wear anything was Faunus, although he did so begrudgingly. He'd complained as he donned a pair of black pants that had been given to him by Magnar. They looked uncomfortable on him, since they stretched over his rump too tightly, while his long feline tail had been threaded through a slit in the back.

The new Mavka with large, feathered wings tilted back to look past the others with his bat-skull turned to them. His wings puffed and flared wide. On bird-like legs, he immediately ran over to them while holding the hand of the human male and unwittingly dragging him along.

"Raewyn!" he called, his orbs flaring bright yellow in joy.

As if her presence had only just been noticed properly, the raven-skulled, lizard-bodied Mavka jerked in their direction. He ran over as well, bumping into Magnar in the process like he couldn't get to them fast enough.

"We heard you were here," the raven-skulled one said when he was right in front of them.

"Aleron," Raewyn greeted warmly to the winged one, before turning in the other's general direction by following the sound of his voice. "And Ingram. It's so nice to meet you both again."

"Do you remember Gideon?" Aleron asked, pulling forward the human so he was in front of him. Zylah thought this must be his bride, since Aleron had a floating flame soul between his twisting goat horns.

Zylah noted his green eyes, his tanned, chiselled features,

and his orange-brown hair and how it was messily brushed back. This male also had muscles that flexed. Perhaps not as much as her own mate's, but he looked strong for such a little creature.

*His face has little hairs on it like Jabez gets after a few days without shaving.* The stubble wasn't very noticeable, but she always found the texture scratchy and nice against the bone of her snout. She wondered if his Mavka felt the same way.

"Of course I do," Raewyn answered. "It wasn't that long ago you both came to Lezekos City in order to gain permission to speak with the Gilded Maiden."

"You're still as tall as I remember," Gideon chuckled, smiling so brightly that a set of dimples dented his tanned cheeks. Then he crouched down to one knee and rested an arm across the padded leather covering it. "And this must be little Lehnenia."

The demonling's eyes widened as she pointed a claw at his face and bounced up and down while looking up at Raewyn. He placed his hand out, and Lehnenia rushed to touch his palm before slapping it a few times. She sucked in an overly animated gasp of wonder.

"That's right. Last time I was a Ghost," he stated with a chuckle.

"Raewyn, this is my bride, Emerie," Ingram said as he gestured at the female who calmly came to his side. "She has bright-orange hair and blue eyes. She looks like a butterfly."

Raewyn laughed at that. "I don't know what a butterfly is, Ingram."

He grunted, his head rearing back, then grumbled a moment later as he scratched at the scales of his neck awkwardly. The tip of his long, spiked tail curled with emotion against the ground.

Raewyn smiled as she said, "But it's nice to meet you, Emerie. Ingram and Aleron were so friendly towards me when I first met them. I bet they make you and Gideon both very happy."

"I've heard all about you," Emerie said with a warm smile,

while darting her blue eyes to Zylah. "And I guess we're meeting again properly for the first time, Zylah."

Her shoulders lifted, as if she wanted to recede into herself bashfully. "I'm really sorry, but I don't remember you well."

She drifted her sight over the webbed scarring on the left side of Emerie's face, and the freckles on the other side. She took in the colour of her eyes, her light complexion, and her toned muscles, trying her hardest to remember such features. She hated that they remained a blur, no matter how hard she stared.

"That's okay," Emerie said with an awkward, shaky laugh. "You kind of gave me and Ingram a fright last time, though."

Her sight flared bright orange, and she cupped her hands to her stomach. "I did?"

Emerie waved her hand up and down dismissively. "It's fine. It all worked out in the end." She drew her eyes down Zylah's body, looking over her and the teal Elven dress she wore. "I'm really glad you're doing well. Last time, you lacked a lot of humanity, so I never got the chance to speak to you."

"I'm Gideon, by the way. I'm Emerie's brother," he greeted, as he offered his hand out, and she was thankful she now understood this custom. Zylah went to clasp his hand. When she had a firm grip, his eyes glinted with humour as he said, "Please don't shake me headfirst into the ground. That's happened far too many times."

She did it softly, and his smile grew once more.

Ingram also shoved his palm out, although much more excitedly, and his grip was strong as he shook hands with Zylah.

"Me next!" Aleron called, his feathered wings flaring in excitement while his pink orbs changed to yellow to reflect that.

A laugh slipped from Zylah as she grew more comfortable with the greeting, and she did it with him as well. *These Mavka are nice.* But why did she get the sense that they... didn't have as much humanity as her?

They seemed rather giddy and loud, and lacked any

reservation with a stranger. Or maybe that was just how they were. She was curious about their pink and purple orb colours, though, since those emotions were startling ones she only felt with Jabez. It was actually remarkably uncomfortable to have such hues on her, despite being able to tell it was just their natural orb colours.

"Sooo," Emerie sung, her lips thinning as she placed her hands behind her back and rocked back and forth on her feet. "You bonded with Jabez, huh?"

"Yes?" Zylah answered in a low tone.

She threw her hands up defensively. "All good. Just curious and wanted to air it out. He and Merikh already told us, so I don't see any point in saying anything about it." Then she gave a cringing grin as she said, "You're not mad I blew him up... right?"

"That was you?!" Zylah exclaimed.

The woman gave an empty laugh as she threaded her fingers through the side of her long, wavy hair. "Yeah. I think it happened not long after we met, actually."

"Reia, Delora, Emerie, and the Witch Owl all went to his castle without us," Ingram stated with an annoyed grumble. "We were not pleased."

Emerie averted her gaze to the side coyly. "I'm surprised he survived, if I'm being honest."

"I saved him," Zylah admitted.

The female froze, and her eyes grew wide. "What?"

"I don't remember much, but I remember chasing a bright light and the pain of healing him after I took him to my burrow. It's how I met him."

The moment the words fell from Zylah, she wondered if she should be telling them this. She shrugged. It was the truth, and what had happened.

She remembered how her limbs had nibbled away bit by bit as she regrew his, how her fur had fallen out as blisters bubbled. The only thing that had pushed her forward through the agony was she could see her efforts fixing him – Zylah was learning she was rather stubborn. She'd been hoping he'd be thankful enough to stay and ease her loneliness.

Everything else had been forgotten, but she remembered those things.

"Oh," Emerie mumbled, her expression twisting into anguish before softening, and she lifted her face to Zylah with a strange smile. "I guess you met him because of us then." That smile turned mischievous and playful as she said, "You're welcome."

A small laugh came from Zylah, and her orbs shifted to bright yellow. *I like her.* She liked Gideon, too, since he'd managed to get Lehnenia's trust enough to pick her up and let her babble to him incoherently in another language.

"Hey, Zylah," Reia called, making her gaze slip over their shoulders.

"Yes?"

"Delora and I are going to prepare some food. Want to help us?" The female offered a smile as she walked over with her hands behind her back. "Delora's too shy to say what she actually wants, but I think she'd like some help picking out food from her garden."

Her sight darted to Delora to find she'd covered her face in embarrassment. Her ears were pink, and her shoulders were turned in self-consciously, much how Zylah's often did.

After the negative conversation that happened earlier, Reia and Mayumi had been trying to rectify it by being overly friendly with her. She didn't know if they were putting on an act to appease her, or if this was just the way they were. The fact they were trying did mean much, though, and she was thankful they were going out of their way for her.

And... Zylah also found it easier to forgive Reia due to the conversation she'd had with Rook about her and Orpheus. The fact that Reia was so accepting and kind to a Demon Zylah had come to care for, and Rook adored her in return, made her think Reia was a good person.

Zylah understood why they were angry, but their past wasn't her future. She hoped they could one day shed their pain and come to know Jabez as she did – especially as she thought they would actually get along, from what she'd seen of them in the last few hours.

Reia and Mayumi fed off each other, while both picked on their Mavka and everyone else freely. Although Zylah had been confused by it at first, she *did* occasionally have the urge to laugh when the males were annoyed. It reminded her of how Jabez liked to tease her, and she was glad she understood that.

It was also teaching Zylah she could do the same thing in return to him and it may not be taken as terribly as she thought. The males often huffed and grumbled while throwing their skulls around as if they were annoyed, but their tones afterwards held the mildest, fond chuckles as if they secretly enjoyed it.

The males also weren't as bad as they first came across.

Orpheus was a little prickly, but it reminded her of Merikh and Jabez. He was the wariest male of them all, and seemed to be the most protective of his bride and new youngling.

If he wasn't found at Delora's side, Magnar was often found at Orpheus', as if he sought his company the most.

Faunus, on the other hand, was loud and boisterous.

He laughed a lot and picked on his bride, who was quick to do so back. He even let Lehnenia hold his forearm as he lifted her off the ground. The little demonling had enjoyed that a lot, squealing as she kicked her feet and asked him to do it repeatedly.

After a while, Magnar had taken over with bright-yellow orbs and a quiet laugh. Even Orpheus let her have a go, but only after he handed Kevin to Reia – who had apparently been the one to give the youngling such a strange name.

Raewyn had been nervous at first about letting the other Mavka play with Lehnenia, but it was obvious she was just happy to know her daughter was having fun and being comfortable. Zylah also thought she may just appreciate that they were being so willing to accept her despite Lehnenia being a Demon, and they had all been very welcoming to Raewyn.

The more they brought Raewyn and Lehnenia into their

conversations – especially Mayumi, Reia, and Delora, who were trying the hardest – the more Zylah liked them. Their first meeting had been awkward, but their open acceptance of people who were becoming dear to her made her feel better.

"Go on," Raewyn whispered behind her, urging her forward. "Spend some time with Delora."

Zylah grumbled. "Okay. I will help."

"Really?" Delora rasped, her hands falling from her face to look up at Zylah approaching.

"I do not know what to do, though," Zylah admitted, her chest tightening with anxiety, but she pushed through it regardless.

Somehow, her conversation with Emerie had managed to make her feel more comfortable about interacting with everyone personally. The bold female almost killed Zylah's mate before she would've even got the chance to meet him, and yet Emerie didn't loudly cast out any negative feelings she may harbour.

Then again, she'd been prepared by meeting Jabez *before* meeting Zylah today. She wondered if that had made it easier for her to accept her bond with him.

"That's okay. I can show you," Delora offered.

"Alright, let's go," Reia said as she placed her hand on the small of both their backs.

The touch made Zylah flinch forward in surprise, and whether Reia noticed or not was unknown to her. She also lifted her arms, since the little female surprisingly had quite a lot of strength as she pushed them forward.

They made it about three steps when Reia paused and turned.

"What was that, Mayumi? You need me for something?"

Mayumi swung around with a frown on her face before her eyes flicked up to Zylah. She smiled in a strange way, then looked at Reia. "Oh. Yeah. Can you come with me for a moment?"

The interaction was odd.

Reia walked off towards Mayumi, and Zylah's head jerked,

realising she hadn't even heard the other woman call to her. Perhaps she just missed it, since she didn't see any other reason as to why Reia would leave like that. She didn't even give them notice.

Delora let out a cough, and Zylah turned her attention back to her... *mother*. Her cheeks were pink, and her brown eyes hinted at shyness. "So... the garden?"

She waved in the direction of the back of her home, and Zylah begrudgingly went that way. Just as they were passing the porch, Delora swiped up a basket sitting there that she'd brought out after changing. New people had arrived and interrupted whatever she'd been intending to do.

Delora had shown her around before, but their earlier conversation had been mostly quiet and awkward.

The shy woman had filled in as much of it as she could by telling Zylah of what she'd been like as a youngling, but she couldn't help feeling disconnected from it. She was still struggling to accept this bond, as she didn't remember living any of those memories with her. She also felt very little towards her, as if something was broken within her mind or heart and she couldn't figure out how to fix it.

She could almost... *taste* the human's sadness.

Although Delora was trying to hide it, she wasn't very successful. Her expressions often gave away that she was disheartened by Zylah's behaviour, no matter how much she tried to offer her broken smiles.

But, out of everyone, Zylah trusted her the most. She also found her the hardest to be around.

Her sight landed on the bright image that had been painted on the side of the house, depicting things she didn't understand despite already receiving answers. Apparently Zylah had clung to her chest as she finished painting it, or often played through the garden around her feet.

The unicorn, with a bright rainbow above it, stood majestically in the middle of a field, and there was a waterfall to the left of it. Zylah had never seen a horse, let alone this mythical creature, but at least the background was pretty and easy for her to understand.

They approached a tree just on the opposite side of the garden's fence.

"I think some apples would be a nice start," Delora said as she reached for one of the hanging red bulbs.

Her fingertips just lightly grazed its bumpy, uneven bottom. As she made to jump, Zylah easily grabbed the *apple* and handed it to her.

Delora gave her a tender smile. "Thank you."

"You're welcome," she responded, before obtaining a second.

She placed it in the human's palm, and the backs of her fingers brushed against the inside of it. The task may have been menial, but Zylah found herself enjoying it. It was better than standing there in uncomfortable silence with each other.

A sweet scent fluttered over her as she moved around the tree and picked fruit. Looking up as she reached for another, she hesitated to give it to Delora. To inspect it, Zylah caressed its hard red skin with the pad of her thumb and claw.

"This smells like you," Zylah muttered, refusing to look at her because she knew it would make her uneasy about admitting it. "You also smell cold, like peppermint or spearmint."

"Magnar says the same thing," Delora croaked in a trembling voice.

Zylah handed the fruit over. "It's... comforting. I like the way you smell."

*I like Magnar's scent too.* She didn't know what he smelt like, only that it was sweet, but also *felt* protective.

They hadn't been around each other much yet, but he always followed Delora like he was her shadow. He often scratched at the side of his bony fox snout, and he appeared just as unsure about Zylah as she was about him.

She kind of liked that, as it made him more relatable to her. Was he struggling to deal with this bond in the same way she was? He *did* appear more comfortable as he approached her to string up an awkward conversation, whereas Zylah was just being avoidant.

The tang of salt rose into the air, and her sight shifted from the apple Delora was holding to her face. The wet track of a lone tear going down her left cheek caught Zylah's attention, and others swirled unshed in her mother's brown eyes.

Zylah chittered nervously as her orbs shifted reddish pink in embarrassment. Just as she went to step back and retreat, unsure of how she'd upset her, Delora reached her hand out halfway.

Her lips trembled as she tried to curl them into a smile. "Can I... can I please hug you?"

Zylah's first instinct was to reject her, but something about her frowning, beseeching expression had her halting.

"Okay," she answered with a light nod.

Delora put the apple in her basket and placed it on the ground. Then she slowly, almost gingerly, came forward as if she didn't want to spook Zylah, who tried to ignore the way her fur puffed in aversion.

Yet, the moment the little human wrapped her arms around her narrow waist, warmth bled into her and soothed her fur. Delora was soft, her wide body moulding around the lithe hardness of her own, and her scent felt reassuring and protective.

Delora gave a sob when Zylah placed her arms across her back and held her in return. She did so properly, leaning into the embrace when tenderness swelled in her chest.

*This... feels nice.*

"I missed you so much," Delora said around tears. "We were so worried for you when you suddenly grew and wanted to leave, but we knew we had to let you go. Thank you for coming back, even if it's only for a little while."

Unsure of how to respond, Zylah said nothing.

She could tell in Delora's trembling form that she needed this more than anything. Zylah just held her mother tightly until *she* was ready to let go, even when it went on for too long.

Maybe she needed this too.

"Can I join in?" a masculine, deep voice asked from

behind.

Zylah spooked but didn't let Delora go as she lifted her head to Magnar. He was scratching at the side of his snout while it was pointed up and away, and his orbs were a bright reddish pink.

The fact he looked embarrassed, but had gained the courage to ask anyway, was one of the reasons she agreed. The other was because she enjoyed hugging Delora so much, she wondered if it would feel deeper if her *father* joined in.

There was only one way to test that.

Delora's sobs grew louder when he came up behind his bride and hugged her from behind, while his arms wrapped around Zylah's ribcage. His hold was loose, but tight enough to squeeze the little female between them. He gave a purr as he rubbed the top of Delora's dark hair with the side of his snout.

Zylah's sight blackened as a radiant ache swirled in her centre.

*I like this too.*

She liked the way they smelt together, and that their touch didn't feel foreign.

# SIX

*By the cursed light, that is the biggest creature I've ever seen,* Jabez thought, as he stared at the serpent Mavka who darted outside his cave entrance with fangs bared and a resounding hiss.

A set of back fins, that had to be at least three feet in height at their tallest point, had slapped together and fluttered alongside the warning sound he produced. His arm fins were also extended, and the soft frills going down his gigantically lengthy body even quivered.

Leaning on his arms, his tail waved behind him as he collected it outside of the cave opening like he wanted to make a protective wall to stop anything from entering or exiting his home. With his orbs bright red at them for entering his excessively large orange dome that shielded even the village nearby, Jabez could almost *taste* the hostility in the air.

Once he was done having a tantrum, and he must have realised they weren't foe, his fangs suddenly retracted into the roof of his mouth. His bony jaw snapped shut when he tilted his head.

The serpent Mavka looked between Jabez and Merikh, and his orbs went dark yellow as if in surprise or confusion.

"Holy shit, it's really him," Merikh muttered quietly to himself.

Merikh's own orbs shifted to dark yellow. His hands opened and closed nervously, or like he was subtly fidgeting to contain his emotions.

*I think we may have spooked him*, Jabez thought as he ran his gaze over a body that had to be over forty feet long. His torso was built and strong despite the number of extruding bones that remained present, as if all the people he'd eaten kept growing his body density without truly completing him.

That only begged the question... how much *bigger* would he get once he had his fill?

Jabez eyed the entrance to his home, wondering if his unusual Elvish-and-Demon scent mixing with Merikh's unknown one had confused and alerted him. The lingering scent of a female inside fluttered from within their home, and he figured the big guy had gone into ultra protective mode due to her.

Then again, the soul flame floating above his head was a dead giveaway that he was a bonded male.

"Nathair?" Merikh *croaked*, braving a step ever closer.

Nathair pushed his hands up off the ground to shove himself into what Jabez would consider a standing position for a snake and backed up slightly. The fact that he shied away instantly had Merikh halting and his orbs turning deep blue.

Nathair raised his hand to stop them, or to tell them to wait – Jabez wasn't sure – as he spun on his tail and practically dived within the cave. His entire body moved as one giant black wave.

Other than the shifting of his tail disturbing dirt and rocks, and the faintest sound of trickling water, there was a moment of utter silence.

"A Duskwalker is outside?" a soft, almost angelic voice rasped from within their home. "It's Merikh and a Demon?"

Jabez's brows twitched at the one-sided conversation, since Nathair didn't utter a single word.

"Are you sure it's safe?"

A loud huff was her answer.

Seconds later, Nathair exited the cave with a thin but busty female in tow. She was wearing a dark-blue garment that came just past her knees and had two side slits in the skirt of it. The sleeves were tight and ended above her elbows. Underneath the dress was a pair of flowy, pale-blue pants, and each step revealed a pair of black flat shoes.

Her ebony hair was woven into a set of braids that came down the sides of her neck, and the tips of them bounced just off her breasts.

Her light-brown, fawn-hued features were gentle, and she had one of the sweetest, heart-shaped faces he'd ever seen. Her eyes were a rich brown, but the moment she stepped into the sunlight, they almost appeared like molten hazel.

She offered them both a wary smile while holding a set of very tiny Mavka in her arms. Considering their size, he figured they were either very new, perhaps a few months old, or they'd never fed them to grow them.

Any aggression present in Nathair earlier had completely faded, and all his fins lay streamlined down his body rather than being exposed for intimidation. He looked aquatic despite how well he moved on land and into the sun, which caused a rainbow iridescence to shine off his body – similar to the raven-skulled Mavka's lizard scales.

"You holding up okay?" Jabez poked at Merikh.

The grunt he received was telling. No, he wasn't, and the spikey Mavka didn't want him to know that.

Unfortunately for him, Jabez was so close that his ears twitched at how hard and fast Merikh's heart was pounding.

Before anyone could speak, Nathair tilted to the woman, and she turned her gaze to his hands when they began to sign. She nodded, then brought her eyes back to them. The warmth in them battled with her uncertainty as she looked at Merikh before instantly shying away from Jabez.

Then again, he doubted she'd ever spoken to a Demon before. *At least she isn't trying to point a sword at my face.*

"Hello," she started. "My name is Linh and I'm Nathair's bride. Due to Nathair being nonspeaking, I will translate his sign language on his behalf, but he wanted me to let you know that he is very happy you're here, Merikh."

Nathair gestured once more, and Jabez picked up on one

sign that was very obvious. Considering he had a set of pointed ears, it wasn't hard to guess that he'd signed the word 'Elf.'

"He thought you were in the Elven realm," she continued.

"I was..." Merikh said quietly, his fingers twitching. "I can't believe you're here. That you're... *alive*."

A chuckle bubbled up the Mavka's throat, and he signed once more.

Linh changed the way she addressed them to better reflect that they were his direct words. "You have Weldir to thank for that," she translated, while watching Nathair's hands intently. "I haven't been alive for long. Around six months. As you can see, much has happened in that time."

"You found a bride so soon," Merikh grated, and his usually shitty attitude was apparently non-existent. "She seems very nice."

The woman's medium-brown, fawny features shuttered as her eyes darted to the side. Then a small, genuine smile grew.

"I can see you have a bride as well," she translated. "Is it this Demon male next to you?"

"What?" Merikh choked out, turning his face to Jabez with his orbs whitening. "Fuck no. This piece of shit wishes. My bride is a beautiful Elven female named Raewyn. This idiot's name is Jabez, and he's just helping me out for today."

Nathair's head cocked, and his yellow orbs darkened.

"Jabez? As in the Demon King?" As soon as she said those words, Linh took a half step back to put more distance between them. "Isn't he an enemy of our kind?"

Jabez folded his arms and rolled his eyes to the side. *Here we go.*

"That... is in the past," Merikh stated, before slapping Jabez in the back so hard he had to stop himself from staggering at the heaviness of it. He hissed through his fangs at the pain. "He is now the bride of a Mavka himself."

"So he is no longer hunting us?"

"No. He is now helping us."

"Then I will allow the past to be in the past," Nathair signed. "Just as I hope you and I can allow each other to let go of what has happened between us."

Jabez's ears drooped as a sense of... *relief* fell over him. He hadn't expected any form of acceptance or forgiveness, even from a creature he'd had no contact with. Hell, for most of this Mavka's return to life, he and Zylah had been in the Elven realm.

Merikh glanced at Jabez, just as surprised as he was.

An uncertain silence fell over them, as if their thoughts were so tentative and unsure that they didn't know how to continue this long-awaited conversation.

Merikh was the one who broke it by stepping forward. With orbs flaring bright orange in guilt, he asked, "Is this my fault?" he stated with a pained rasp. "Is what I did to you... the reason you can't talk?"

The serpent Mavka's hands flinched before curling into loose fists near his chest. "No. I did this to myself," he signed, his own orbs falling into a dark orange. "Please don't think you had any part in this. While I was in Tenebris, I ate souls when I shouldn't have, and they have rendered me incapable of speaking, among other things."

"He says this, but it isn't entirely true," Linh stated, her voice brightening as she spoke for herself. "I'm part Anzúli, and we believe my voice has magical properties. I'm able to sing and hum for him and it allows him to talk, but he just doesn't like doing it because it also allows his thoughts to be spoken aloud."

Nathair folded his arms and opened and closed his mouth as if he was mocking her by falsely talking. The female giggled as her eyes swirled with playful mischief.

"Fuck, man," Merikh grated, brushing a hand over the bone of his forehead. "I'm so fucking sorry. If I'd known crushing your skull would have... If we'd known what would happen..."

Nathair shoved his hand forward and shook it to silence Merikh. He signed once more, and somehow his orange orbs darkened even further.

"We couldn't have known. It could have been the other way around. I may have crushed your skull while we were playing, and our situation would have been reversed. I know you feel guilt for it, and I was once angry, but I've come to accept that it was an accident."

"But I took your life from you!" Merikh half yelled, throwing his arm to the side before baring his claws in front of his chest in frustration. "For almost three centuries, you were... *dead* because of me. How can you not be angry?"

"Tenebris isn't that bad. It was peaceful and there were no Demons. By the end, I didn't even want to return to life, but I only agreed to it so Weldir could make sure he could safely bring Aleron back to life." Then Nathair tipped his head down to Linh, his orbs instantly flaring bright pink, and the woman smiled at him in return. "I'm glad I did, and I'm thankful for the timing. I wouldn't have met Linh had you not killed me, and I am... *happy*."

Then he took the Mavka younglings from her arms and brought them closer. Linh followed, and she trusted his judgement so much that she didn't fret when Nathair pushed his younglings into Merikh's hesitant arms.

"Sorry, he's very proud of them," Linh said with her eyes crinkling and her voice filled with joy. "They were only born three months ago, and he likes to show them off to everyone."

"Are they twins?" Merikh asked as he fumbled to hold the younglings in his large palms and crossed forearms.

"Yeah, they're twins," Linh confirmed.

Jabez leaned forward to properly glance at them, and he took in their featureless, somewhat blobby forms. They were such a dark grey that they almost appeared matte black, and their bodies took on a baby-like form when they moved before sagging when they were stationary. Their faces were semi-pointed where their little nose holes were, but other than the small ear holes on the sides of their heads, there wasn't much else to them.

They had no eyes, nor any concave eye holes to hint at any. Their hands and feet were small, and their fingers and claws were so weak and malleable that they bent as they tried to get purchase.

One opened their mouth to reveal jagged lines as teeth, and a purple tongue curled as they silently yawned. They tried to crawl off of Merikh, both heading for their parents with deep sniffs to guide them.

Nathair took them and Jabez nearly had a fucking heart attack when the Mavka tried to shove them into his arms as well.

He lifted his hands up to avoid them. "I don't think that's a good idea."

It wasn't that he didn't like children, since the idea of having one with Zylah was not out of the question. He just wasn't confident with them being infants, no matter their species. They were soft, fragile, and he didn't want to mess up and accidentally hurt one and anger their parents.

Nathair's orbs reddened, and he let out a warning growl as he held his younglings out to Jabez. Not wanting to piss him off, simply because he was actually being *nice* to him, Jabez took them with an annoyed grumble.

They immediately hated being in his arms. He figured his lack of Mavka scent was sending them on high alert, and they both screeched in protest just as one blindly leapt out of his hold. The one remaining forced him to chase them until Nathair chuckled and took them back.

Thankful they were gone, he noted the heat they'd left all over his arms, while not leaving a single trace of scent behind.

*That was... weird.* Jabez scratched at the top half of his hair tied back into a bun. *I've never properly held a Mavka youngling before.* The fact that he'd been trusted to was even stranger.

Nathair gave them back to Linh so he could gesture with his hands. "Why are you here?"

"I'm rounding up the entire family," Merikh stated. "My bride wants to meet everyone properly."

A small chuckle rumbled from the serpent Mavka. "I'm surprised to hear that. I thought I would have to chase you into the Elven realm to see you again, since you have been such a nasty brother to the rest of our kind."

Merikh made a chomping sound when he clipped his fangs together, then let out an irritated huff through his nose hole. "I guess Weldir has been keeping you informed."

"You have been unfairly cruel to everyone since my death, Merikh. You shouldn't have taken it out on Lindiwe or Weldir. It wasn't their fault."

The burly Mavka folded his arms with a slight growl. "I beg to differ."

"You should have protected everyone as the eldest living Mavka," Nathair signed with his orbs shifting to deep blue. "You should have guided everyone, not turned your back on them."

"They wouldn't have listened!" Merikh yelled, throwing his arms up. "We're all a bunch of fucking idiots when we lack humanity. It's like talking to a damn boulder."

"At least a boulder doesn't try to strike you," Jabez muttered in his defence.

"Exactly! I tried to help, and then gave up when I saw it was useless. Everyone had to figure shit out on their own, just like I did." Then Merikh pointed a claw at Nathair's chest. "You were dead. You have no idea what it was like. I helped whenever possible and even fed information to Lindiwe, *despite* how much I hated looking at her. I did what I could."

A hissing snicker came from Nathair before he dived forward. Merikh immediately stiffened when the larger male wrapped his arms around his body and squeezed so hard that Merikh went to the tips of his toes.

It took him a moment to understand what was happening.

When he did, Merikh's orbs immediately shifted to bright yellow in happiness, and the bottoms of them wavered and shattered to produce ethereal tears. He slid his arms around his brother and returned his hug with his head angled to the side to make it even closer.

A small smile quirked at the sides of Jabez's lips as he watched them embrace each other. The moment was wholesome and tender, and his heart swelled knowing how much his friend needed this. Nathair tightened their embrace further by flicking the tip of his tail forward and wrapping it around Merikh's calves.

A raspy exhale came from the side, and Jabez's gaze slipped to the little human, whose eyes had brimmed with tears. They spilled over as she watched her mate with a smile, as if she, too, knew how much Nathair likely needed this as well.

Merikh stepped back when the embrace finally ended, but the floating drops around his face were slow to dissipate and stop.

"Will you be accompanying us on the journey?" Linh translated for Nathair. "I'll feel much better travelling such a long way with my bride and younglings if there are more of us. We were already planning to make such a journey, but we wanted to get used to our younglings and make sure the area was truly safe before leaving it."

"No," Merikh stated, his voice thick with emotion. He grunted to clear it before waving at Jabez. "This is where he comes in. He's going to teleport us to the Veil instantly."

Nathair nodded and turned to Linh to have a conversation that appeared more private.

"Yeah. That's okay," she answered before handing their younglings to him. "I'll let my father know we're leaving."

"Your father?" Merikh asked, tilting his head.

Her expression turned coy and sheepish. "Nathair is the official protector of these mountains. It's why his dome covers the village nearby. My father is the mayor of it." She lifted her face up to Nathair once more. "Can you get a bag ready while I'm gone? I won't be long."

He nodded, and she spun towards the village and ran off. Nathair put his hand out, telling them to wait, before slowly slithering into his home to collect what they needed.

"Don't you dare say anything," Merikh growled quietly, jerking his bear skull towards him.

*I won't.* As much as it was in Jabez's personality to be a cheeky bastard and pick on the male, he understood this was just too important for Merikh.

He intended to say nothing, as that's what Merikh would prefer. No sweet sentiments, no words of affirmation, nor did Jabez even think giving him a silent, comforting pat on the back would be helpful. Actually, he bet Merikh would hate it if he touched him right now.

Jabez had known for a very long time how much Nathair's death, and Merikh's hand in it, weighed on him. He'd always felt regret and guilt, and he'd freely shared that with Jabez during quiet and forlorn moments of trust. This wasn't his first time seeing Merikh cry over it, but it was the first time he'd seen the male shed tears of relief and joy.

He'd had a peek into a very private and heartfelt moment that he shouldn't have been a witness to.

He had no intention of ruining it for his friend.

# SEVEN

Once the little human returned, Jabez placed his hands on his sides and stared up at the daunting size of the serpent Mavka before him.

"I'm going to be honest with you..." Jabez stated with his brows narrowing. "I don't know if I'll be able to do this."

"What the hell are you talking about?" Merikh snapped at him from the side.

"I told you. I can only teleport what I can carry, and I'm guessing he's heavy." Jabez winced at that and glanced at his bear-skulled friend. "It might be beneficial to call for Weldir's aid. He may be able to produce a portal for him to slither through."

"You're doing it, and I won't take no for an answer."

He hid his grimace behind a childish pout, while his mind screamed in protest. He'd love to wring Merikh's thick neck right now. Just squeeze and squeeze until he snuffed the life out of him for being such a prick.

*If you didn't hate your daddy so much...* a small, half-hearted growl left him.

"Alright, fine," he conceded, before he waved Linh and Merikh closer. "It'll be wiser for me to take you and her first, since you're both lighter. It's also best that she carries the younglings."

Nathair quickly signed, his hands moving hastily. "I would prefer to go first, as there will be people and Mavka I'm not familiar with."

"That's not an option. There's a chance I may not be able to come back for her once I'm done with you. It's going to cost me a lot of mana to move you, and I will need to rest afterwards."

*It's good that we decided to meet him last.* He would have suggested it if he'd known how damn big he was.

Nathair let out a growl, but eventually nodded.

Jabez held his hands out, and both Merikh and Linh offered their forearms to him. He teleported them to Magnar's ward and then quickly ignored every stupid face that looked at him as he assessed the area.

He picked a location with lots of space and no trees to get in the way before he materialised back to Nathair.

The serpent Mavka went to offer his arm, but Jabez shook his head.

"I think it's best if I hold your middle. I don't want to rip an arm from you by accident."

He cracked his neck and rolled his shoulders to prepare himself, then stepped forward to essentially hug his waist. Jabez attempted to teleport, but they only flickered in place.

He took a breath, stepped his right foot back as if he was trying to drag something heavy while lifting something impossible, and tried again. A roar came from him as he put all his might into the spell, and it only grew louder when they merely flickered in place, their bodies vibrating. Within seconds, his muscled gut clenched until his stomach twisted, and sweat broke across the surface of his skin.

Blood rushed to his head as it boiled in exertion, and his fingertips dug into the male's sides as he tried to keep a good hold on him.

*Come on!* he thought with a feral snarl, and their flickering became incessant as he pulled. He clenched his bared fangs, closed his eyes, and pain exploded in his muscles as he managed to shift the Mavka barely an inch to the side.

They teleported.

The moment they landed within Magnar's ward, his hold

on the magic and his strength suddenly let go. Bile rose to his throat as his vision grew dark, and Jabez immediately crashed to the ground and slid across the dirt.

*Fuck.* His eyes watered when it felt like his nerve endings had been set alight, while lava replaced the marrow of his bones. He heaved as he clawed at the ground to get to shaking knees, his arms so weak that they felt like nothing but limp rags.

"Jabez!" Zylah called, and he heard gasps as if she'd pushed people out of the way to rush to his side.

*Fuck, it hurts so much,* he thought, as he struggled to get to his knees, his body constantly collapsing.

There was so much pressure in his head that he thought his thumping skull was moments from exploding, and he heaved again as sickness rolled in his gut. His heart was moments from bursting, his lungs caving in, and the nastiest stitch he'd ever felt assaulted both his sides.

An unfamiliar set of large palms went to grab his biceps and help him up, but he slapped Nathair away with the back of his hand. "Don't touch me," he wheezed, his gaze narrowing into a glare at the grass.

He sensed Zylah kneeling next to his pathetically crawling form, and he snarled at her too.

"Don't," he bit, darting his murky vision to her.

He didn't want to be pitied, nor did he want any help from anyone. He just needed a moment, that's all.

After a few shuddering breaths, his eyesight cleared a little and his lungs stopped trying to come up his throat. With an arm crossed over his nauseous gut, he managed to get to his feet.

The joints in his knees immediately protested, as if the heat within him had disintegrated the cartilage. The lava in his bone marrow felt like it was drying him out, and he limped by himself towards a low-cut tree stump.

From the corner of his eye, he noticed everyone watching him. He cast a foul grimace at their gawking faces, hating that they were seeing such weakness in him, and that they were *shocked* he'd allowed himself to be in pain for *them.*

As soon as he sat his arse down on the tree stump, his entire body slumped forward. Both Zylah and Merikh came to his side.

"Are you okay?" she asked, lifting her hand up like she wanted to cup his cheek in worry when she knelt between his thighs.

"That bad, huh?" Merikh stated.

Lacking his normal humour, Jabez snapped his fangs at him. "I told you he was too fucking heavy!" he roared. "I felt my body trying to split in two, you ungrateful prick."

"You still managed to do it," Merikh offered.

Jabez sighed as he tried to catch his breath, still his overworked heart, and calm himself. "Teleporting has its dangers. Going beyond your boundaries *usually* has lasting effects."

Merikh chuckled. "We're lucky you're undeniably strong then, and that you're deathless."

Jabez opened and closed his mouth mockingly. "Compliments do nothing to soothe my anger." Then he nodded his head towards the people staring at them. "Fuck off and go be with your family. My work here is done. Leave me be."

Merikh placed a palm on his shoulder, and Jabez just did not have the energy right then to swat it away. "I *am* grateful, Jabez."

He removed his hand and then walked off, leaving Jabez and Zylah alone.

"You look really sick," Zylah murmured with a nervous chitter. He groaned at the warmth of her hand touching his forehead, wishing it was colder, yet he still leaned into it. "You're sweating a lot."

"I'm fine, Zylah," he reassured with a cracked voice. "It'll go away. I just need to rest. You should go be with your family."

"I want to stay here." She wrapped her arms around his waist. "I missed you."

Lacking the strength to argue with his pretty and alluring mate, Jabez groaned and let his head fall forward until his forehead rested against hers. He took in her jasmine-and-violet scent, and just felt her against him as he held his aching stomach.

His eyes drifted closed, but he snapped them open moments later when he heard movement to his left. With his forehead still pressed against Zylah's bony one, he tilted his head to look at who approached.

"Thank you," Linh said, with Nathair at her side.

His first desire was to tell them to piss off and take their sympathetic gazes with them, especially as the Mavka's usually orange orbs were darker in guilt. Instead, he sighed and brought his face forward against Zylah's skull.

"You're welcome. I don't think I'll be able to take you back, though," he admitted. "Someone will have to ask the Witch Owl or the spirit of the void to do it."

"If need be, we'll travel back on our own. I already let my father know we might be gone for some time."

Jabez nodded and sagged with relief when his gut finally stopped throbbing. He leaned back, so he didn't look so pathetic, and sucked in cool air to battle the heat still clamouring beneath his skin.

They left to meet the other Mavka and brides.

He gazed at Zylah, who tipped her snout up to him, and asked, "How's your family?"

She scratched at the side of her neck as she averted her skull to the left, where no one was standing. "They are nice. They've all been very welcoming." Then she shifted nervously. "Delora has been hovering. I don't know how to speak with her when I can tell she wants more from me, but I guess I do like her."

"Just be open to it. She's your mother. I'm sure she cares for you very deeply."

"How do you care for someone you don't know? I hugged her and felt strange inside."

His lips curled into a small smile. "Humans are different to us, but even Demons have familial bonds. You left when you obtained your antlers, leaving everything behind and forgetting. It's not her fault your kind are designed that way."

Her orbs morphed into a reddish pink. "But even the fox-skulled Mavka follows. It feels odd having a male I don't know chase me around."

A laugh burst out of him, causing his eyes to crinkle hard at her. "Then stop running. He just wants to get to know his daughter."

"But you don't want to meet your parents!" Zylah *quietly* exclaimed.

Humour flooded his gaze. "That's different. Mine have wronged me, yours haven't."

She let out a snorted huff as she turned her head with her arms folding. She was pouting, and it instantly made his heart swell with tenderness.

"I don't understand why you care so much," she grumbled. "I'd rather stay here with you."

"Because we won't be able to come back often, Zylah." He lifted his face towards the large family that had gathered and was already creating a ruckus with lively conversations. "And I doubt an opportunity like this will come again without intervention. Drink it in while you can."

"Will you come with me? I would rather you by my side."

As much as he wanted to, Jabez shook his head. "It's best if I stay away. I agreed that I would help Merikh, but I knew I would be ostracised once everyone was together, and rightly so. Go, enjoy yourself. Get to know those who want to meet you." Then he gestured his chin towards Nathair. "That serpent Mavka and his bride are nice."

Zylah let out a solemn sigh, reluctantly nodded, and stood. As if she'd needed the guidance and was happy to follow his directive, she immediately walked to Linh and Nathair. She awkwardly introduced herself, and the little human was quick to smile at her.

For a time, he watched Zylah while picking up on different strings of chatter.

Since the humans had already swarmed around the newest

bride's arrival, and how it was apparently their first time greeting her, they quickly fell into a conversation about how they all met their Duskwalker. Even Gideon had joined them, since he'd been with all the males, and he immediately commented on how big of a fucker Nathair was.

Nathair and Linh juggled having separate conversations with family members, since she translated for him in addition to participating in other conversations. The serpent Mavka finally shooed her off, so he could be a silent participant of conversation, and his bride was dragged away by the others.

He noticed Zylah appeared uncertain over which group to join. She hesitated between the male Mavka who were of her kind, and the females like her.

She eventually folded when she was called by Emerie, and she wandered to the left to join them in the sunlight provided by a gap in the trees. He wondered how she and the redhead were getting along now that they'd been introduced properly, since he knew they'd met before when Zylah lacked humanity.

Ingram and Aleron walked behind Nathair to look at his tail in blatant curiosity of his size. Aleron flared his wings to reveal their true lengths, and Jabez guessed they were about twenty-two feet long, if not longer. Orpheus asked about Merikh's white armour-like guards, and he removed one to flex his forearm and make his dangerous echidna spines flare.

*I wonder if they're all having a pissing contest or just want to show off their differences.* He knew it was the latter when most of the Mavka dared to prick the tips of their fingers on the tips of Merikh's quills in curiosity.

"I don't have any cool features like this," Ingram stated with a fold of his arms and a pout in his voice.

"Neither do I," Magnar said, scratching at his feathers.

"Although... I am the only one with a pretty beak and defensive tail," Ingram added in.

"Well, that's what makes each of us unique," Orpheus commented as he rolled up his shirt sleeves to expose his forearm fins. "I think Nathair and I were both fed fish while we were young."

Nathair brought his arm next to Orpheus' and flared his fin purposefully. Orpheus did the same, although his were much smaller in comparison. Then Orpheus untucked his shirt to pull up the back of it and show the height of the fish fin embedded around his vertebrae. Nathair flared the set that ran down either side of his own spine. They touched each other to create one massive dorsal fin along his back before ending at what appeared to be a humanoid rump that turned into a snake tail.

Most of their orbs flared between their natural colour or dark yellow in curiosity as they inspected their kin.

*I'm surprised by how calm they all seem to be.* Very rarely did their orbs flare dark green in possessiveness, or red in anger.

Jabez's gaze then landed on the humans and Zylah, who had all taken a seat on some kind of blanket that had been laid out in the dappled light.

Lehnenia was seated in Raewyn's lap in bright sunshine, with Zylah next to her, likely for comfort. Of course Delora had taken a seat next to her, with Reia at her side. Faunus' female had chosen to lie on her side with her elbow bent and hand under her cheek to support her head, while Emerie leaned her side against Gideon, who had his legs out and kept letting out boisterous laughs. Linh sat alone with her feet tucked to the left, but a warm smile constantly shone from her as she listened intently to everyone's story after just sharing her own.

Multiple Mavka younglings either slept on laps or crawled around the group.

He could gauge which younglings belonged to who.

Linh kept hers close on her lap, whereas a very small one clung to the chest of Reia's blue dress. One sat in Mayumi's lap, while the other two belonging to her wrestled with each other on the blanket in the middle of the brides or crawled all over everyone.

He often noticed a set of eyes or orbs looking over at him, as if they wanted to check he remained where he was. Each time, the human either looked wary, or the Mavka flared red orbs at him.

Zylah did the same thing, although for an entirely different reason. Despite her being immersed in listening to them and responding when she could, her rabbit skull would often lift and search for him throughout the day. She was always checking on him, always wanting to see that he was still there and perfectly fine.

He felt for her whenever her orbs shifted blue in his direction, and he occasionally offered her a little hidden wave with his fingers to let her know he saw her too.

After a while, Gideon rose to go be with the other males and join in on their conversation. Delora also left, going inside briefly and returning with two plates of assorted fruit, vegetables, and bite-sized pastries.

Lehnenia refused to eat any of it, but she was being surprisingly obedient as she quietly ate what Raewyn pulled from her bag for her. Delora walked around the seated group to offer food, and Jabez brought his gaze back to all the Mavka.

Now *they* were all speaking about how they met their brides.

As if sensing she was needed by some kind of tell, Linh stood to go to Nathair's side so she could assist him. She also rubbed his back when he let out a shudder that puffed all his scales like he was growing agitated. He often held the side of his skull as if in pain, and his orbs would flare stark white.

Jabez overheard why.

"Nathair is suffering from voices," Linh explained with a beseeching cringe for them to understand. "He's getting used to being around others, but lots of conversation tends to make the voices within his mind louder." She turned to him and looked up as she asked, "Do you need to take a break? We can go somewhere and I can hum for you for a little while."

He signed something while subtly shaking his head.

Since Jabez had been listening in, movement from the side caught his attention. His expression dulled as he saw who was, surprisingly, approaching him.

"I don't know if you only eat meat, but are you hungry?" Delora asked as she held out her offering of what remained of the fruit and vegetables.

He eyed it cautiously before lifting his gaze to her face. When he didn't respond for a long while, her expression turned solemn, and she began to draw the plate away. He realised he'd upset her, but he was rather suspicious as to *why* she was even offering to begin with.

She hated him, so he thought she'd rather see him starve.

"I eat like a human," he stated, gingerly lifting his hand out when his stomach cramped in hunger. All his earlier mana use told him food would do him some good. "Fruit, vegetables, meat."

She placed the plate in his palm to allow him to keep what remained. He brought a leg up to fold it across the stump he sat upon and set the dish down in his lap to free his hands. Since he figured she wanted to see him eat her offering, he picked up a slice of red apple and popped it into his mouth as she watched.

He expected her to walk away, but she remained as she fisted the skirt of her brown dress. Her eyes bowed as her lips twisted, obviously wanting to say something despite her hesitancy.

He quietly let her gain the courage.

"I wanted to thank you for today," she eventually stated. "Although we have justified reasons for being angry with you, we all *do* appreciate what you've done to bring us all together."

"Don't thank me. Thank him," Jabez said as he nodded towards Merikh. "If it wasn't for Merikh, none of you would've needed to see me again. I guess that means you can also all blame him as well."

"But we know without your magic, this would've been a lot harder," she said, fisting her dress tighter. She was trying her hardest to remain calm and composed, despite whatever emotions were causing her heart to race so loudly that it sounded like a drum in his ears. "And you brought Zylah here."

"She needs to learn who you are." He looked up to find a number of people were staring once more, and he brought his gaze back to hers to avoid them. "I have no intention of getting in the way. When I can, I will bring her back here, so you may form a bond with her."

Admittedly, he thought it might be easier if they were alone with her parents and Zylah could lean on him. He could help direct the conversation. Right now, he was forced to be separated from her, and it meant she wasn't her most confident, cute self.

"When I first saw you with her, I thought you'd do everything to prevent her from knowing us, from... *learning* about who you really are."

He snorted out a scoff. "Zylah knows everything. I haven't kept anything from her relating to what I've done to you all."

"I know. She's told us everything in defence of you today."

A singular laugh came from him as he rolled his eyes. "I'm sure that went over well."

He could only imagine how much that annoyed Zylah.

"She cares for you very deeply."

He met this woman's brown eyes firmly, but kept his voice quiet as he stated, "I know."

He watched the moment her round face twisted up and her eyes flooded with tears. She wrung the skirt of her dress so hard he thought she was moments from tearing it. Her lips shook as she licked at them.

"Do you... do you love her?" she asked in a shaky, broken voice.

He opened his mouth to snap at her, since his feelings were none of her business. He also didn't like that she felt the need to fucking ask, as if what he'd done today, everything he'd given up, wasn't already proof of that.

Yet he promptly shut his lips as he took in her trembling form.

She was just a mother who was showing care for her daughter. He'd long forgotten what it felt like to receive that attentive kind of parental affection.

"Yeah, I love her," he said while looking away. "I wouldn't have given her my soul otherwise."

His ears drooped at having to admit that to her, his heart feeling a little too exposed than he could say he was comfortable with. His free hand curled into a fist, suddenly finding it hard to meet her teary gaze.

"That's all I care about," Delora stated with a trembling voice that also held a hint of relief. "All that matters to me is you treat her well and give her everything she deserves. I-I can... I'll forgive you for the past so long as you do that."

He glanced at her before looking down at the food she'd given him with a nod. She turned and walked away, and Magnar was quick to come to her side since he'd already been hovering.

His orbs flared red at Jabez, likely blaming him for her tears, before she mumbled, "It's okay. They're happy tears, Magnar. He didn't do anything wrong."

The Mavka's orbs then flared dark yellow as he looked at Jabez once more. Then he crossed an arm over her back to support her as he returned her to the other females, and even sat down with her between his thighs.

Jabez placed an elbow on his bent knee so he could rest his jaw in his palm. *I wasn't expecting her to do that,* he thought as he popped a strawberry in his mouth. *I guess she loves Zylah very dearly.*

She'd also solidified one thing today: he'd bring Zylah back here whenever she wanted, so long as the council approved it.

His ears twitched as Delora hinted at the conversation she just had with him to the puzzled humans, and his cheeks fucking heated in embarrassment. But a smile did nag at his lips, to the point he had to cover them, when it gave Zylah an opening to speak about him warmly. She explained how he often brought her gifts and went on lame long walks with her through Lezekos City.

Even though she was facing towards him with orbs bright pink, he could almost *sense* her tail swaying happily.

To his annoyance, a few of the males caught wind of the conversation, and they began to crowd around her and the humans.

It, apparently, gave Nathair an out, and he slithered away to sit back on his tail next to Jabez. He let out a very loud, tired sigh as Linh followed.

"Do you mind if we join you?" she asked, despite Nathair not really having given him a choice.

"Do what you want."

At his approval, Nathair collected the female holding their younglings into his arms and sat her on his tail. He wiggled down, sinking into the folds of his long body to get comfortable, and reclined back on himself.

"Is it alright if I hum?" Linh asked. "It quietens his mind."

"Go for it," Jabez answered as he popped a carrot stick into his mouth.

She hummed a very soft and quiet tune, and any stiffness in Nathair's coiled tail and body softened in relief. Jabez's ears pricked high at the lulling aspect of her voice, which was rather pretty.

He, too, found himself relaxing as he ate and watched everyone intently.

*I guess today hasn't been so bad.*

# EIGHT

Every so often, Jabez glanced up at the top of Magnar's home to the two beings seated upon the peak of its slanted roof. The Witch Owl watched over them all with the spirit of the void beside her shrouded in black sandy mist.

Not once had they attempted to mingle with their children and their grandchildren, nor did anyone try to speak to them in return. But they were there, as if they wanted to join the strange reunion distantly, much in the same way Jabez was being forced to. He'd observed them speaking to each other, but not even he was able to pick up on their hushed conversation.

Two little blobby babies crawled over them. The moment one went too far and began climbing down the slanted rooftop, they would float back to their mysterious father. The demigod barely twitched when he used his magic, as if he was able to search for and feel them without looking.

With them there, the entirety of the Mavka family, including every generation, was present.

"What's the Elven realm like?" Linh asked him, after some time of humming to Nathair.

Jabez mildly flinched, not expecting her to interrupt his thoughts. Actually, he'd assumed they would get up and leave once they were done.

Today was, oddly, full of surprises.

He eyed the Witch Owl and Weldir one last time before

looking down at Zylah between his knees. She'd come to rest her back against the stump he was seated upon, and he'd long ago begun raking his fingertips through the collar of fur around her neck to soothe her, content to have her near.

He didn't want to keep pushing her away when it was obvious she was growing tired and overwhelmed with everyone. So he'd silently given his approval when she sought to lean against one of his knees to rest. Since Linh had been humming, Zylah hadn't disturbed the quiet and instead basked in it with them.

Just as he opened his mouth to respond, Raewyn stated, "It's different to here. Earth is much colder, even in the summer."

He turned his face to the left to greet her as she walked with a tired Lehnenia rubbing at her eyes while holding her hand. With her mobility cane in one hand and the small hand of her daughter in the other, Raewyn stopped when the round ball knocked against his seat. She sat down with her legs straight, and the demonling was quick to lie down with her head in her lap.

"Yeah. I'd say our winters are warmer than this," Jabez added, lifting his gaze to Merikh who was fast approaching his bride.

"Move over," Merikh demanded, while shooing his hand at Jabez.

"Get your own seat. This one is mine."

"I don't see your name on it."

Zylah lazily slid her arm over Jabez's knee and growled at the male Mavka, who let out a grunt in return. He sat his ass down right next to Jabez's stump to lean his side against it. With one knee bent to make room for Raewyn, he slipped the other behind her for her to lean against and folded his arms as he made himself comfortable.

"It's called Nyl'theria," Jabez started, before he, Raewyn, and Merikh cobbled together a description of the world.

Raewyn answered questions pertaining to the Elysians and Delysians there, their governing system, and their way of life.

She and Merikh spoke mainly of the city, and Jabez was able to give insight into the forests and Demons there, since they were entirely unfamiliar with life outside the wall.

Even Raewyn asked him a few questions, as she and Jabez had never spoken about what he knew unless it was within the conference chamber.

It took Jabez quite some time to realise he was surrounded by people. He looked to his right at Nathair and Linh cuddling, then to his left to Merikh, Raewyn, and a sleeping Lehnenia, before dipping his gaze down to Zylah between his knees.

*I guess I'm not as unwanted as I presumed,* he thought, although it was glaringly obvious that this was as far as he'd be welcomed.

There was a very clear distinction between the group which currently sat with him comfortably, and the vast space between the many of those who refused to join them. He didn't blame Orpheus, Faunus, Magnar, Ingram, Aleron, and their brides for not wanting to be near him.

He'd done too much to them in particular, and their disdain towards him was justified. He appreciated the fact that they'd left him alone, permitting him to remain as a mostly silent spectator without causing any further arguments.

It was more than he'd hoped for.

He allowed a small smile to curl his lips as he spoke to those around him, and even allowed his own inquisitiveness to come to the forefront. He'd always been interested in what Weldir's realm was like. He now had someone here who had intimate knowledge of it and was willing to share it with him.

*I like Nathair,* he thought, as he lifted his eyes to the stars and crescent moon that had recently risen to shine above them. *He's calm.*

He liked calm, he liked quiet. Like Merikh, he was intelligent, and already the two Mavka had formed a deep bond while being here. They even allowed Jabez to join it by chatting with him in their combined presence, and the strangest sensation overcame him.

For the first time in his life, he was having a semi-normal

conversation.

He wasn't King Jabez, the tyrant Demons revered and feared. He wasn't the Demon King the Mavka all hated and tried to destroy. He wasn't Jabeziryth Kiez, the Demon-Elf hybrid child who was an outcast.

He was just... Jabez.

A friend to the bear-skulled Mavka to his left, the half-brother of the Elven woman before him, a new and friendly acquaintance to those to his right, and the mate of the female he loved between his thighs.

His smile grew as tenderness swelled behind his sternum, and he let out a genial laugh when Linh translated Nathair's next words.

"He called you a grumpypants," she said, since Merikh made a negative comment about Weldir and his realm.

"I call him grumpybear!" Raewyn exclaimed with a giggle.

"I call him a bull-headed fuck," Jabez added.

Merikh snapped his fangs at them all as his arms tightened in their fold, and a loud, bullish huff snorted from his nose hole. That was until the tension fled out of him and he let out a mild chuckle, his orbs flaring bright yellow as he said, "Fair enough. I can't help how I am."

Then Merikh wrapped his meaty hand around Raewyn's narrow side and forced her to lie against his chest. Lehnenia let out a disgruntled noise at the change, but remained asleep as Raewyn patted her hair and horns; the little girl was tired from so many new faces and experiences.

Jabez turned his face towards the others sitting in a circle some distance away.

Most of the brides had now curled up with their Mavka to speak to each other while resting in affectionate cuddles. No one was shy about doing so, as if it was normal to be so open. A few of them laughed, as if his negative presence had been accepted for long enough that he'd been forgotten.

Everything was peaceful, tranquil even.

He was glad this was how the day turned out. He was sure he'd see much more of these people in the long, unending, forever future they were all entwined to share.

He wondered how much of it would change as their children all grew and obtained their own brides. Now that he was no longer hunting them, this family was only going to grow, and many new skulls and faces would join it.

And maybe one day the animosity the others held towards him might fade. What would happen in another hundred years to allow for that healing?

With his arms around the shoulders of the female who had changed *everything* by embracing not only his rotten heart but also his literal soul, Jabez was looking forward to finding out.

Also by Opal Reyne

## DUSKWALKER BRIDES
A Soul to Keep
A Soul to Heal
A Soul to Touch
A Soul to Guide
A Soul to Revive
A Soul to Steal
A Soul to Protect
A Soul to Embrace
*(More titles coming soon)*

## WITCH BOUND
The WitchSlayer
The ShadowHunter
*(More titles coming soon)*

*Completed Series*

## A MM FAIRYTALE REIMAGINING
Chased by the Fairy

## A PIRATE ROMANCE DUOLOGY
Sea of Roses
Storms of Paine

## ~~THE ADEUS CHRONICLES~~
This series has been **unpublished** as of
20th of June 2022

Thank you so much for reading **A Soul to Embrace**, the
eighth book in the **Duskwalker Brides** series.
I hope you enjoyed reading this book. I know it was long,
especially with the side story attached, but I was worried that
if I didn't include it with the main story, readers would miss
it.
I found it really difficult to write this book, although I
enjoyed it!
For those who are sad that the series has ended… fear not!
The prequel will be coming in 2025.
You will see all your favourite Duskwalkers and their brides.
The timeline will start hundreds of years before A Soul to
Keep and will end just after A Soul to Embrace. You will
learn everything from start to finish, and any final lingering
questions will be answered.
Plus, who doesn't want to know how Lindiwe fucked the
spirit of the void? We must learn of the logistics of mating
with a cloud!

Now... for my final parting question.
Is this truly the end of the Duskwalker Brides series?
…
Nope! I plan to come back to the series in a few years once
I've written a few other series, written a few books for the
Witch Bound series, and taken a break from bone daddies.
I've been in this series for so long that I don't want to tire
myself out.
I also want to dive into what would happen if a Duskwalker
were to develop in Nyl'theria rather than Earth. Things will
start changing now with the peace Jabez can offer, which will
have a ripple effect within both worlds. I want to see what I
can make of Austrális, Nyl'theria, and other possible Elven
realms, but with a fresh perspective.

Please stick with me and consider reading my other books in
the meantime.
I have a fun trilogy planned for my mask and monster loving
peeps.

If you would like to keep up to date with all the novels I will be publishing in the future, please follow me on my social media platforms.

*Website:*
https://www.opalreyne.com
*Facebook Page:*
https://www.facebook.com/OpalReyne
*Facebook Group:*
https://www.facebook.com/groups/opals.nawty.book.realm
*Instagram:*
https://www.instagram.com/opalreyne
*Twitter:*
https://www.twitter.com/opalreyne
*Patreon:*
https://www.patreon.com/OpalReyne
*Discord:*
https://discord.gg/opalites
*TikTok:*
@OpalReyneAuthor